Women of Wonder

THE CLASSIC YEARS

Women of

Science Fiction by Women

A HARVEST ORIGINAL ★ HARCOURT BRACE & COMPANY

Wonder

THE CLASSIC YEARS

from the 1940s to the 1970s

Edited and with an introduction and notes by
PAMELA SARGENT

San Diego   New York   London

Library of Congress Cataloging-in-Publication Data
Women of wonder, the classic years: science fiction by women from the
1940s to the 1970s/edited and with an introduction and notes by
Pamela Sargent.—1st ed.
p.   cm.
"A Harvest original."
Includes bibliographical references.
ISBN 0-15-600031-8
1. Science fiction, American—Women authors.   2. Women—Social
life and customs—Fiction.   3. American fiction—20th century.
I. Sargent, Pamela.
PS648.S3W64   1995
813'.08762089287—dc20   94-42516

Text set in Primer
Designed by Kaelin Chappell
Printed in the United States of America
First edition
A B C D E

Permissions acknowledgments appear on pages 439–440, which constitute a continuation of the
copyright page.

Contents

Acknowledgments

I would like to thank the following people:

Richard Curtis, Joseph Elder, Anne Freedgood, David Garnett, Martin H. Greenberg, Virginia Kidd, John Radziewicz, Shirley Sargent, Ian Watson, and Janeen Webb.

I am also extremely grateful to my editors, Michael Kandel and Christa Malone, for their counsel and their patience.

Vonda N. McIntyre deserves thanks for helping to guide the first *Women of Wonder* anthology to its original publisher.

Special thanks are owed to Jack Dann for his brainstorming, and most especially to George Zebrowski, whose moral support, editorial advice, and library were invaluable.

I also owe much to the late Janet Kafka, who offered me the chance to edit my first anthology twenty years ago, and who was the kind of editor all writers hope to have.

Introduction

PAMELA SARGENT

Twenty years ago, my first anthology, *Women of Wonder,* was published. It was the first anthology of its kind: science fiction stories by women about women. For over two years, I tried to find a publisher for *Women of Wonder,* and the reactions of editors were instructive. A few editors thought the idea was wonderful but decided not to do the book anyway. Some editors found the idea absurd, a couple doubted whether I could find enough good stories to fill the book, and one editor didn't think there was a large enough audience for such an anthology.

But the audience was there, and so were the authors. By the middle '70s, the women's movement, however controversial in some quarters, was a growing force in American culture, and this affected science fiction as well. Not only were more women (and girls) reading science fiction, more women were writing in the genre. Ursula K. Le Guin, with the publication of her novel *The Left Hand of Darkness* (1969), which depicts a world that offers a different perspective on our gender roles, was becoming one of the most influential writers in the field. Joanna Russ was pushing at both literary and ideological boundaries in her short fiction and in her novel *The Female Man* (1975), while Kate Wilhelm was using science-fictional ideas to explore human relationships in *Where Late the Sweet Birds Sang* (1976) and *The Clewiston Test* (1976). Gifted new writers were producing science fiction, and now many of them were women, among them Vonda N. McIntyre, Octavia E. Butler, Elizabeth A. Lynn, C. J. Cherryh, Doris Piserchia, Marta Randall, and Tanith Lee. The name of James Tiptree, Jr., must be added to the list; when this writer of some of the most honored short fiction of the '70s was revealed to be a woman named Alice Sheldon, a lot of people had to reexamine their assumptions about the differences between men and women writers.

Science fiction was changing. *Women of Wonder* was soon followed by two more anthologies, *More Women of Wonder* (1976) and *The New Women of Wonder* (1978).

Since then, the impression has persisted that science fiction, once almost exclusively written by men for men, suddenly acquired a large percentage of influential women writers and a corresponding increase in female readers during the late '60s and early '70s. This isn't quite the case. Over the past twenty years, more of science fiction's most popular and influential writers have been women, but they are still outnumbered (some claim greatly outnumbered) by their male counterparts. More women are reading science fiction, yet there is some evidence that many of them aren't reading the kinds of books that have traditionally attracted male readers. But we should not lose sight of the fact that however outnumbered women science fiction writers have been, they have also been a part of the genre since its beginnings. As Joanna Russ wrote in *How to Suppress Women's Writing* (1983):

> When the memory of one's predecessors is buried, the assumption persists that there were none and each generation of women believes itself to be faced with the burden of doing everything for the first time. And if no one ever did it before . . . why do we think we can succeed now?[1]

As it happens, a case has been made that the first science fiction writer was a woman: Mary Shelley, the author of *Frankenstein,* published in 1818. So the British writer and critic Brian Aldiss claimed in *Billion Year Spree* (1973), his history of science fiction, and he repeats that claim, somewhat less emphatically, in that history's revised edition, *Trillion Year Spree* (1986, written with David Wingrove). Aldiss argues that in "combining social criticism with new scientific ideas, while conveying a picture of her own day, Mary Shelley anticipates the methods of H. G. Wells when writing his own scientific romances and of some of the authors who followed him."[2]

Whether or not *Frankenstein* is in fact the first science fiction novel, Mary Shelley definitely has a claim to being one of science fiction's earliest progenitors. After *Frankenstein*, she went on to write *The Last Man* (1826), a novel about a worldwide plague that destroys the entire human race. The post-holocaust story, showing what our world might be like after a nuclear war, environmental disaster, or other catastrophe, has since become a permanent fixture in science fiction. Inter-

[1] Joanna Russ, *How to Suppress Women's Writing* (Austin: University of Texas Press, 1983), 93.
[2] Brian Aldiss, *Billion Year Spree* (New York: Doubleday, 1973), 23.

estingly, these two novels lack important female characters, another pattern science fiction has often followed.

Shelley's place in the pantheon of science fiction writers seems secure, but other women, now largely forgotten, contributed to fantastic literature in the nineteenth century. Marie Corelli, Rhoda Broughton, Sara Coleridge, and Jane Loudon, among others, produced works bordering on science fiction, often influenced in mood and setting (as was Mary Shelley) by Gothic literature. Jessica Amanda Salmonson, in her anthology of feminist supernatural fiction, *What Did Miss Darrington See?*, points out that

> from the 1830s through the 1920s women were the dominant presence in British and U.S. magazines as poets, essayists, story writers, readers, and often enough as editors; hence, women dominated the fashions in literature. . . . Their supernatural stories amounted to a veritable school, yet almost no one in this century has commented on it.[3]

We can speculate about why most of this work has vanished or rarely been reprinted and also about why science fiction remained resolutely male during that same period. The two major nineteenth-century figures in science fiction, Jules Verne and H. G. Wells, paid little attention to female characters in their work. Verne's characters are nineteenth-century men essentially unchanged by their exciting adventures, strange new devices, or the discovery of other worlds. Wells was very much interested in the rights of women, but this concern is largely absent from his science fiction, although not from some of his utopian works.

The utopian tradition, in fact, seemed more congenial to women writers than the newer and still developing genre of science fiction. *Mizora* by Mary Bradley Lane, published in 1890, was an early all-female utopia. A far better utopian novel, still readable today, is Charlotte Perkins Gilman's *Herland* (1915), which depicts an altruistic all-female society. Sexuality, however, is absent from this utopia; it remained for later writers to deal sympathetically and openly with lesbianism, for example.

The most notable purely science-fictional work by a woman at this time was *The Heads of Cerberus* (1919), published by Gertrude Barrows Bennett under the pseudonym of Francis Stevens. The novel appeared as a serial in Street & Smith's *The Thrill Book;* it was later

[3] Jessica Amanda Salmonson, *What Did Miss Darrington See?* (New York: The Feminist Press of the City University of New York, 1989), x–xi.

reissued by Polaris Press in 1952 in a limited edition. *The Heads of Cerberus* may be the first work of science fiction to use the concept of alternative (or alternate) history, which assumes that there are parallel worlds that differ from ours as a result of different choices, circumstances, and historical developments. A story by the same author, "Friend Island," published in 1918, depicts a world in which women are regarded as the stronger sex.

C. L. Moore, who began publishing in the 1930s, was to make a greater impression on science fiction readers than any earlier female writer. (Some have assumed that Moore used initials in her by-line instead of her first name, Catherine, to conceal her sex. In fact, she was trying to keep the management of the bank where she worked from finding out that one of their employees was writing for pulp magazines.) In her tales of Northwest Smith, a rugged soldier of fortune who has adventures throughout the solar system, Moore proved able to write convincingly from a male point of view. But she also succeeded in publishing fantasy stories featuring a strong female character, Jirel of Joiry, in what editor and writer Lester del Rey called the "intensely male-oriented" magazines of the day. He has summed up the effect C. L. Moore had on the field with her first published story, "Shambleau" (1933), as follows:

> Here, for the first time in the field, we find mood, feeling, and color. Here is an alien who is truly *alien*—far different from the crude monsters and slightly-altered humans found in other stories. Here are rounded and developed characters. . . . And—certainly for the first time that I can remember in the field—the story presents the sexual drive of humanity in some of its complexity.[4]

Among Moore's finest efforts is the novella "No Woman Born" (1944), one of the earliest and best-known stories about cyborgs, people who are partly or mostly machines. Moore's cyborg is a woman, with the men around her fearing that she may be losing her humanity. Another novella, "Vintage Season" (1946), depicts a group of time travelers who arrive in a twentieth-century California town to witness, for amusement, the disaster they know is coming. Moore also collaborated with her husband, Henry Kuttner, and wrote for television, but she did little writing during the decade before her death in 1987. In spite of her relatively small body of science fiction, she remains one of the most important writers in the genre.

[4] Lester del Rey, "Forty Years of C. L. Moore," *The Best of C. L. Moore* (New York: Ballantine Books, 1974), 1–2.

Leigh Brackett began publishing science fiction in 1940. Along with Moore, she had no trouble winning devoted readers for her work in a predominantly male genre. Moore, however, had flouted one of the conventions of the field by centering several of her stories around strong female characters. Brackett's stories almost always feature male protagonists, among them her popular hero Eric John Stark, and are as "masculine" in tone as most of the adventure fiction of the time. Even so, she also put strong female characters in her fiction; if they tend to be subordinate to the men, they are still generally competent, intelligent, and able to stand up for themselves. "The Woman from Altair" (1951), included in this volume, is a Brackett story that, although told by a man, is centered around an alien woman who is definitely not the frail and delicate creature she first appears to be.

As a writer of screenplays, Brackett often worked with the director Howard Hawks, most notably on *The Big Sleep* (1946), in collaboration with William Faulkner, and on *Rio Bravo* (1959). Her most highly regarded science fiction novel, *The Long Tomorrow* (1955), is a realistic story of a pastoral community in a post-holocaust America. Brackett continued to write science fiction throughout her life and was at work on the screenplay for *The Empire Strikes Back* (1980) when she died.

A very different sort of writer, Wilmar H. Shiras, began publishing science fiction in 1948; her first story, "In Hiding," appeared in *Astounding*. In it, a schoolteacher discovers that a seemingly normal boy is, in fact, a genius, the mutant child of parents who were affected by an accident at an atomic energy plant. A sequel to this story, "Opening Doors" (1949), concerns another genetically altered child genius, a girl this time, who has adapted to life in a mental hospital. Shiras went on to write a novel about these children and others, *Children of the Atom* (1953). This sensitive book does not present the children as frightening threats but as interesting and concerned individuals and raises ethical questions about how they should lead their lives.

Judith Merril, who was to have a great influence on science fiction as both editor and writer, published her first story, "That Only a Mother," in 1948; it remains a moving tale of a world we might have had. In her novel *Shadow on the Hearth* (1950), she tells of a suburban homemaker who must look out for herself and her children in the wake of a nuclear attack. *Daughters of Earth* (1968) consists of three fine novellas about several generations of women on a colony world. From 1956 to 1970, Merril also edited fourteen annual anthologies of the year's best science fiction. By ranging far afield in selecting stories, publishing fiction by newer writers, and championing literary experimentation, she expanded the boundaries of the field, as she did in her own writing, by using a woman's perspective.

What Moore, Brackett, Shiras, and Merril—four very different writers—had in common was that they were seen as exceptions to the rule. However popular or well-regarded their work was, they did not change the widespread assumption that science fiction was essentially a masculine form. The genre was still seen by its editors, writers, and readers as fiction for men and boys. As a consequence, women and girls often believed that they would find nothing of interest in science fiction.

To be a woman writing science fiction, and to succeed, was to overcome great odds. Indeed, although Shiras, after *Children of the Atom,* continued to write stories, they were largely ignored; Moore drifted away from science fiction; Merril did more editing and less writing; and Brackett eventually concentrated more on screenwriting (where, as a woman scriptwriter of Westerns for Howard Hawks, she was also an exception to the rule). When assessing the work of these early writers, we should keep in mind that they were in a real sense pioneers, with few examples and female mentors to inspire and guide them.

During the 1950s, more science fiction written by women was published. Probably the most important women writers of this time were Katherine MacLean, Marion Zimmer Bradley, Margaret St. Clair, Zenna Henderson, and Andre Norton. The careers of these writers reveal some of the conditions under which women writing in the genre labored.

Katherine MacLean showed the ability to deal with technological and scientific themes in her stories, many of which were published in *Astounding* (later *Analog*), a magazine that has traditionally been, and remains, a bastion of "hard" or scientifically oriented science fiction. Her story "Contagion," published in 1950, presents an intriguing biological phenomenon on an alien planet but also underlines how much our feelings of personal identity can be tied to our appearance.

MacLean went on to win a Nebula Award, given annually for the best works of the year by the members of the Science Fiction and Fantasy Writers of America, for her 1971 novella "The Missing Man," yet many readers today are unfamiliar with her work. Part of the reason may be that she has written few novels. Unless a science fiction writer publishes a large number of novels, she is likely to remain relatively unknown, whatever her accomplishments in the shorter forms. (This seems to be even truer now than it once was. Among the rare exceptions to this rule are Damon Knight, Connie Willis, and Harlan Ellison.) The neglect of MacLean's work is especially unfortunate because she was one of the earliest women writers to concentrate on hard science fiction, most of which she wrote and published under her own obviously female name.

Marion Zimmer Bradley showed an early competence as a writer of science fiction adventure, but with her extremely popular Darkover series of stories and books, which she began writing in 1958, she was eventually exploring issues some might call "feminist." Bradley's own description of her motivation for writing in a largely male field is straightforward: "In my own experience, I was so bored by 'girls' books' that I read 'boys' adventure stories.' When the time came for me to start writing, I wrote the kind of thing I liked to read: adventure stories." She goes on to say:

> When I came into the field, nobody spoke of prejudice existing against women, except that it was expected that women would have to be about twice as good as men. . . . Most of us revelled in the thought that we'd made it against terrific odds, and took it as proof that we were at least twice as good as the men.[5]

Bradley's comments shed light on the situation in which she and other women writers found themselves and how some of them adapted to it. They accepted the strictures of the form in which they wrote and then wrote as well as they could within those limits. Interestingly, Bradley later went on to push beyond those limits in Darkover novels such as *The Shattered Chain* (1976), in which she depicts a society of Free Amazons who choose to live outside the restrictions that bind other women on their world; in non–science fiction novels such as *The Catch Trap* (1979), a homosexual love story set among circus performers; and in *The Mists of Avalon* (1982), an Arthurian fantasy told from the points of view of the female characters. Her story "Death Between the Stars" (1956), included here, is a tale of a woman whose encounter with an alien aboard a spaceship leads to an unexpected conclusion.

Margaret St. Clair became a prolific writer of stories under her own name and under the pseudonym of Idris Seabright. She also published novels and won praise for her sharp, elegant fantasies, yet she is one of the most neglected writers of science fiction. One reason may be

---

[5] Marion Zimmer Bradley, "One Woman's Experience in Science Fiction," *Women of Vision*, edited by Denise Du Pont (New York: St. Martin's Press, 1988), 86, 92–93.

that much of her work seemed to undermine the optimism characteristic of much science fiction; in her early work, as critic John Clute
put it, "a singularly claustrophobic pessimism could . . . be felt."[6] Her
characters, even when they have a sense of the universe's vast possibilities, often feel trapped, or they adapt to their situations in unexpected ways. St. Clair, one suspects, subtly made many readers
uncomfortable. Her gift for irony is evident in her story "Short in the
Chest" (1954).

Zenna Henderson, who also began writing in the '50s, was best
known for her series of stories about the People, benevolent humanlike
beings with psychic powers who have settled in an isolated area of the
American Southwest. These stories were eventually collected in two
volumes, *Pilgrimage* (1961) and *The People: No Different Flesh* (1966).
Her characters are often children and teachers; "The Anything Box"
(1956), included here, is an example. Henderson was an elementary-
school teacher by profession, and at one time taught interred Japanese-
American children during World War II. Her stories, especially those
about the People, were popular, yet she was often criticized because
of her subject matter. Teachers, children, and saintly aliens were acceptable topics in those days for a female writer, but writing about
them left her open to charges of sentimentality from certain critics.
One gets the feeling that, with some readers, Henderson couldn't win.

Andre Norton was publishing during the '30s but only began writing
science fiction in the '50s. Most of her work was written for younger
readers, and she was to become one of the most prolific and influential
writers in the genre. A few of her many novels are *Star Rangers* (1953),
Star Guard (1955), *Star Born* (1957), *The Beast Master* (1959), *The
Sioux Spaceman* (1960), and *Judgment on Janus* (1963). In several
novels she used Native Americans as protagonists, at a time when the
central characters in science fiction were usually white males. Writing
books for younger readers enabled Norton to accumulate a large audience over the years, but it also caused her to be neglected, until
fairly recently, by critics. She has said the following about her work:

> When I entered the field I was writing for boys, and since women
> were not welcomed, I chose a pen name which could be either
> masculine or feminine. This is not true today, of course. But I still
> find vestiges of disparagement—mainly, oddly enough, among other
> writers. Most of them, however, do accept one on an equal basis. I

[6] John Clute and Peter Nicholls, ed., *The Encyclopedia of Science Fiction* (New
York: St. Martin's Press, 1993), 1045.

find more prejudice against me as the writer of "young people's" stories now than against the fact that I am a woman.[7]

In 1983, Norton became the first woman writer of science fiction to be honored with a Grand Master Nebula Award, given for a lifetime's achievement.

The 1950s saw another development in science fiction that reflected the attitudes of the time. A fair amount of science fiction written by women centered on domestic affairs. Some of these stories featured homemaker heroines, who were often depicted as passive or addle-brained and who solved problems inadvertently, through ineptitude, or in the course of fulfilling their assigned roles in society. Often they, unlike the reader, would not really understand what was going on, even by the end of the story. These stories showed women as mothers whose children were generally a good deal more intelligent than they were; as consumers of goods, often in a future world where advertising and the free-enterprise system had run wild; or as wives trying to hold their families together after a nuclear holocaust or other disaster.

One notable example of this kind of story is Mildred Clingerman's "Minister without Portfolio" (1952). The central character is a kindly grandmother who meets some visiting aliens in a park. The old woman does not realize who or what they are, makes friends with them, and exchanges photographs with them. She is totally unaware that by being so friendly and nice she has convinced the aliens not to invade Earth. Although this story is well done and the main character believably portrayed, it follows a pattern of relying on the ignorance of its main female character to make its point.

It was also in the '50s that writers such as Carol Emshwiller, Kit Reed, Pauline Ashwell, and Kate Wilhelm were first published. Superficially, some of their early work may seem to fit into the "women's fiction" subgenre of science fiction that is centered on feminine concerns. But Kit Reed's "The Wait" (1958) gets at the horror underlying a seemingly normal community, and Pauline Ashwell's teenaged heroine in "Unwillingly to School" (1958) has no intention of settling down and doing what she is expected to do.

What can we conclude about women and science fiction during the '50s? Clearly, women were contributing to the genre. Some claim that certain editors were less sympathetic to their work because of their sex or asked them to put their female characters in more

[7] Paul Walker, "An Interview with Andre Norton," *Luna Monthly* 40 (September 1972), 4.

conventional roles; others assert just as vehemently that they experienced no prejudice at all. Katherine MacLean and Marion Zimmer Bradley accepted the strictures of the field and succeeded in their writing; Zenna Henderson and Mildred Clingerman centered their stories around traditionally female concerns; Margaret St. Clair and Kit Reed subverted the genre's assumptions. In other words, the writing and experiences of women in science fiction were diverse, and it is difficult to generalize about them.

Still, a not entirely mistaken impression persisted that women's science fiction centered around the hearth and home. Gifted writers, among them Judith Merril, Mildred Clingerman, and Rosel George Brown, wrote stories that resembled those that disparaging critics referred to as "wet-diaper" science fiction. Most science fiction writers also tended to use male and female characters who kept to the traditional social roles. For a literature that was by definition supposed to be open to new possibilities, science fiction remained sociologically conservative.

What were the male science fiction writers doing? For the most part, assuming that the mores of the future would not be notably different from those of the United States during the early and middle twentieth century. It's important to keep in mind that science fiction in the United States from the '20s to the '60s was largely a pulp magazine literature, written for readers who were looking for escape and entertainment and who presumably did not want certain presuppositions challenged, even as they speculated about the technical wonders that the future might hold.

But a few saw science fiction's inherent critical possibilities and went beyond the presuppositions. Stanley G. Weinbaum, who published stories in *Astounding* during the middle 1930s, wrote in "The Red Peri" (1935) of a female space pirate and in "The Adaptive Ultimate" (1935) of a woman who, after being injected with an experimental serum, acquires superhuman powers and strength. It may not be coincidental that Weinbaum was also a pioneer in his treatment of aliens; he depicted them as beings with their own ecosystems and their own often incomprehensible behavior. As Isaac Asimov put it:

> The pre-Weinbaum extra-terrestrial, whether humanoid or monstrous, served only to impinge upon the hero, to serve as a menace or a means of rescue, to be evil or good in strictly human terms—
> *never* to be something in itself, independent of mankind.

Weinbaum was the first, as far as I know, to create extra-terrestrials that had their *own* reasons for existing.[8]

Weinbaum's career was tragically short; after publishing for little more than a year, acquiring many devoted readers, and showing every sign that he would become a major figure in science fiction, he died at the age of thirty-three. We can wonder what effect he might have had on the genre had he lived longer. Perhaps because Weinbaum was able to create truly *alien* aliens who were not defined only by their relationship to humankind he was better able to develop unconventional female characters. As Ursula K. Le Guin writes:

> If you deny any affinity with another person or kind of person, if you declare it to be wholly different from yourself—as men have done to women, and class has done to class, and nation has done to nation—you may hate it, or deify it; but in either case you have denied its spiritual equality, and its human reality. You have made it into a thing, to which the only possible relationship is a power relationship.[9]

Sometimes, as in James Gunn's often-reprinted satirical story "The Misogynist" (1952), the women are quite literally aliens, beings from another world. One man in the story cites as evidence that women can find objects their husbands lose, that they furnish their houses with useless devices, that their thought processes seem alien, and even that they have cold and clammy feet at night in bed. This story cleverly transfers xenophobia toward aliens to women and becomes a *reductio ad absurdum* that both reflects and skewers its own culture.

The role-reversal or "woman dominant" tale was another way men handled female characters in the '50s. The writer would assume that women had somehow gained the upper hand and that men were limited to the roles women were traditionally assigned. Again, such stories often seem to be more reflections of the fears or prejudices of their times than serious extrapolations.

Some writers managed to write serious work using this theme. Philip Wylie's *The Disappearance* (1951) shows what might happen if both men and women suddenly found themselves in a world populated entirely by their own sex. In John Wyndham's "Consider Her Ways"

[8] Isaac Asimov, "The Second Nova," *The Best of Stanley G. Weinbaum* (New York: Ballantine Books, 1974), x.
[9] Ursula K. Le Guin, "American SF and the Other," *Science-fiction Studies* #7, 2:3 (November 1975), 208–9.

(1956), a twentieth-century woman finds herself in a future world where men are extinct. This future matriarchy is much like an insect society, as if the author is assuming that an all-female society would necessarily be static, but Wyndham does include some strong criticisms of the restrictions placed on women in our world. Few, though, went beyond envisioning matriarchies or separatist societies, as Theodore Sturgeon did brilliantly in *Venus Plus X* (1960), where our far-future descendants have each become both male and female.

It cannot be said that there were no memorable female characters in science fiction written by men before the '60s. Dr. Susan Calvin, an important character in Isaac Asimov's classic robot stories published during the 1940s in *Astounding*, is an intelligent and extremely rational expert on robots. Asimov is clearly sympathetic to Calvin, but she is also an individual who prefers robots to people and has never married. Married women in his other stories tend to follow more traditional roles.

Robert Heinlein, one of the most original and influential writers of science fiction, populated his books with female characters who were doctors, engineers, spaceship pilots, military personnel, and were skilled in higher mathematics. His women are capable of courageous deeds and intellectual activity, and this represents a notable advance over much earlier science fiction. Even so, they are usually subordinate to even stronger men, a situation they generally welcome. Capable as Heinlein's female characters are, and however involved they become in their outside pursuits or professions, their main goal in life often is to be wives and mothers, albeit in their own time and way.

This is a case of the author's culture spilling into his work and affecting his assumptions and characters. Heinlein, an individualist with a strong libertarian streak, made public statements in favor of women's rights, saying in a 1972 interview that he "would like to see some qualified women hit NASA under the Civil Rights Act of 1964. . . . How in God's name NASA could fail to notice that half the human race is female, I don't know."[10] If his women characters want to settle down with suitable men and raise families, it is because they value that role, not because they can't do anything else. Heinlein was often criticized for his depictions of women, but in our own time, with a backlash and many people waxing nostalgic over traditional roles, it's hard to call such characters unrealistic portrayals.

[10] Frank Robinson, "Conversation with Robert Heinlein," *Oui* 1:3 (December 1972), 112.

Often female characters were simply seen as irrelevant in certain kinds of science fiction. There was no need for the author to dwell on matters such as gender roles and the position of women in his imagined society if there were no women in the story at all. Some would argue that in the hard science story, one in which the scientific ideas or advanced technology is of central importance, there is no need to include women, or even to make the characters human. Perhaps what is actually being suggested here is that women are a distraction or that male characters are somehow more appropriate in an "idea" story. But in fact some writers, H. Beam Piper and Hal Clement among them, had no problem with female characters in their hard science stories and showed women whose most important characteristic was their intellect, as it was for male characters.

Some writers were able to look beyond their own time, however imperfectly and infrequently, and consider that the sociological future might not mirror the past. But for the most part, women characters in science fiction before the '6os were conspicuous chiefly for their absence.

The late '50s and the early '6os saw the entrance of more women into the field. Perhaps not coincidentally, science fiction writers and readers were at the same time reexamining the assumptions and even the literary style of the genre.

It is important to remember that science fiction has always been more than pulp adventure tales, hard science stories, and utopias. There is more diversity and variety in it than may be apparent to the casual reader, and as new subgenres developed, more women were drawn into the field. As I have already pointed out, a few had mastered the colorful adventure story, and even fewer the hard science story. Utopian fiction, often viewed as a separate form related to science fiction, attracted writers, women among them, who would never have considered themselves—and who often were not—science fiction writers. The growing interest during the '50s in stories centered around the social sciences, or in stories that used science-fictional themes and devices to satirize the author's own society, drew more women into the genre, even if many of them set their tales in the domestic sphere.

During the '6os, several science fiction writers—among them the British writers Michael Moorcock and J. G. Ballard and Americans Norman Spinrad, Harlan Ellison, Roger Zelazny, Thomas M. Disch, and Samuel R. Delany—experimented with both subject matter and style. For them, science fiction had become too predictable and hidebound, and was ripe for change. These writers and others, loosely grouped together under the somewhat misleading term "New Wave," rejected the elements of pulp fiction and often viewed technology and the future with pessimism.

Judith Merril was one of the anthologists who championed this new writing. The magazine *New Worlds* in England and Damon Knight's *Orbit* series of anthologies and Harlan Ellison's groundbreaking anthology *Dangerous Visions* (1967) in the U.S. contained stories in which writers aimed at a more literary and iconoclastic approach to the genre. In this atmosphere of change, women who wrote science fiction were likely to find a more receptive audience even if their stories violated some of the traditional canons.

Among those who first became known during the '60s, although a few had been published before then, were the British writers Hilary Bailey and Josephine Saxton, the Canadian Phyllis Gotlieb, and Americans Joanna Russ, Carol Emshwiller, Kate Wilhelm, Kit Reed, and Sonya Dorman (who now writes as Sonya Dorman Hess). Many of their stories, rather than dealing with the traditional "hardware" of science fiction, instead concentrated on the subjective by exploring the psychological effects different societies or perceptions might have on their characters. One notable example of such a work is *Memoirs of a Spacewoman* (1962) by the British writer Naomi Mitchison, an episodic novel centered around a woman exploring alien worlds and reflecting on her life.

Sonya Dorman Hess's "When I Was Miss Dow" (1966) is a notable example of a story that uses some traditional science-fictional elements—aliens, the settlement of another world—to give us a perspective on our own species. "The Food Farm" (1966) by Kit Reed is a horror story centered around mass communications, popular music, and food. In Pamela Zoline's "The Heat Death of the Universe" (1967), one of the most celebrated of the stories published in *New Worlds,* the entropic decline of the universe becomes a metaphor for the state of a woman's mind.

Anne McCaffrey also came to prominence during the '60s and was the first woman writer to win both the Hugo Award (given annually by members of the World Science Fiction Convention) and the Nebula Award. Although she is a more traditional science fiction writer than those just mentioned, female characters have always been prominent in her work. There is no doubt that McCaffrey, whose books eventually became best-sellers, attracted many new female readers to science fiction. Her most popular books are her Pern series, set on a world of telepathic dragons who are linked mentally to their human riders; the series includes the novels *Dragonflight* (1968), *Dragonquest* (1971), and *The White Dragon* (1978). "The Ship Who Sang" (1961) is characteristic of McCaffrey's work, imaginative in its science-fictional details and emotionally gripping.

Any doubts that women were capable of major achievements as science fiction writers were surely put to rest by the publication of Ursula K. Le Guin's *The Left Hand of Darkness* in 1969. With this novel, Le Guin established herself as one of the most important writers in the genre.

The Left Hand of Darkness is set on a planet called Winter, a world inhabited by the Gethenians, a humanlike race whose members are neuter except during kemmer, their monthly fertile season. At this time, each Gethenian becomes either male or female, with no control over which sex "he" will be. The social implications of such a physiology are profound:

> Consider: Anyone can turn his hand to anything. . . . The fact that everyone between seventeen and thirty-five or so is liable to be . . . "tied down to childbearing" implies that no one is quite so thoroughly "tied down" here as women, elsewhere, are likely to be. . . . Burden and privilege are shared out pretty equally; everybody has the same risk to run or choice to make. Therefore nobody here is quite so free as a free male anywhere else.
>
> Consider: There is no division of humanity into strong and weak halves, protective/protected, dominant/submissive, owner/chattel, active/passive. In fact the whole tendency to dualism that pervades human thinking may be found to be lessened, or changed, on Winter.
>
> The following must go into my finished Directives: When you meet a Gethenian you cannot and must not . . . cast him in the role of Man or Woman, while adopting toward him a corresponding role . . .
>
> One is respected and judged only as a human being. It is an appalling experience.[11]

Le Guin most assuredly did not find it appalling to be judged only as a writer rather than as a woman writing in a largely male field.

During the 1970s, women in science fiction were no longer isolated examples or exceptions to the rule. There were more of them than

---

[11] Ursula K. Le Guin, *The Left Hand of Darkness* (New York: Walker & Co., 1969), 68–69.

ever. Whatever residual prejudices or inadvertent patronizing individual writers encountered, there was a sense that an audience existed for their work and that publishers were more than willing to buy it. More women began to question the roles they played and the limitations on their lives, and science fiction, not surprisingly, reflected this development. Women, previously almost invisible within the genre, were soon providing science fiction with some of its best writers.

During the '70s, more women were coming to see themselves as a group, a class with certain common characteristics regardless of their individual circumstances. They might disagree—sometimes fiercely—about goals, means, and issues but could also aspire to a sense of sisterhood and solidarity, even if that hoped-for harmony was not always achieved.

Within the field of science fiction, women writers were also coming to consider themselves a group. This is not to say that they shared the same views, were equally doctrinaire in their feminism, or were similar in their writing. But there was a growing sense that science fiction was a form in which the issues raised by feminism could be explored, in which writers could look beyond their own culture and create imaginative new possibilities. This may be why an impression persists that women did not truly make their presence felt in science fiction until the '70s—even though women had been contributing to the genre all along.

Other kinds of literature can depict women imprisoned by attitudes toward them, women at odds with what is expected of them, or women making the best of their situation in past or present societies. Only science fiction—and in its own different way, fantasy—can show us women in entirely new and different surroundings. It can explore what we might become if and when the present restrictions on our lives vanish, or show us new problems that might arise. It can show us the remarkable woman as normal, where past literature has often shown her as the exception.

Joanna Russ is often credited with being the first science fiction writer to feature, in her Alyx stories of the middle and late '60s, a strong female character in the heroic sort of role usually reserved for men. (These stories were eventually collected in *The Adventures of Alyx*, published in 1983.) In fact, as I have mentioned, C. L. Moore had used such a character in her "Jirel of Joiry" stories in the '30s. But Russ is certainly the first contemporary writer of science fiction to be explicitly, even aggressively, feminist, and she was one of the first to deal openly with lesbianism. She won a Nebula in 1972 for her story about an all-female society, "When It Changed," in which women have learned to get along quite well without men, much to the dismay of the men who arrive on their planet. Her story "Nobody's Home" (1972), reprinted here, shows us a utopia in which problems still remain. Russ's powerful novel *The Female Man* (1975), in which four different versions of a particular woman live different lives in four parallel worlds, reflects the rage that some in the women's movement were feeling as they struggled to change deeply embedded attitudes.

Kate Wilhelm, another writer who came to prominence during the late '60s and early '70s, has important female characters in almost all her work. Superficially, she may seem a more conventional writer than either Le Guin or Russ; her work is rich in domestic detail and written in a smooth transparent prose. But by the end of her stories and novels, Wilhelm often undermines the reader's assumptions about her characters and their reality. Her characters, in their subtle ways, reflect the changing roles of men and women. Wilhelm's female scientist/researcher in *The Clewiston Test* (1976) has to struggle against both an oppressive husband and colleagues who grow to doubt her sanity. Wilhelm remains one of science fiction's strongest writers, especially in the shorter forms, and "The Funeral" (1972) depicts a harsh society that bears some resemblance to the dystopia shown in Margaret Atwood's 1986 novel *The Handmaid's Tale*.

Among the younger writers who made their mark in the '70s was Vonda N. McIntyre. Her first novel, *The Exile Waiting*, came out in 1975. With Susan Janice Anderson, she edited an anthology of feminist and humanist science fiction by both women and men, *Aurora: Beyond Equality*, in 1976. By then, she had already won a Nebula for "Of Mist, and Grass, and Sand," a novelette published in 1973 that became the basis for her award-winning novel *Dreamsnake* (1978). Both the novel and the novelette underline their tale of a healer with a feminist outlook; "traditional" roles for men and women are notably absent, even irrelevant to the story.

James Tiptree, Jr., was the pseudonym of a science fiction writer who was clearly sympathetic to feminist concerns. In Tiptree's novella "Houston, Houston, Do You Read?" (1976), three twentieth-century NASA male astronauts pass through a time warp and find themselves orbiting a future Earth populated entirely by women. During her career, Tiptree accomplished the difficult feat of winning critical praise both for sensitive characterizations of women and for being a strong male writer in the Hemingway mode. In 1977, she admitted publicly that she was in fact Alice Sheldon, a retired psychologist who had grown up in Africa and been an officer for the Central Intelligence Agency. Interestingly enough, she had never lied about her background when giving biographical information but had left it to others to assume that someone who had been in the army, traveled frequently to remote areas of Mexico, and enjoyed fishing, among other pursuits, had to be a man. Some of her work using what she termed "violently pro-woman ideas . . . that were simply not credible under a man's name"[12] was written under the by-line of Raccoona Sheldon. "The Women Men Don't See" (1973), included in this volume, is one of Tiptree's most admired stories.

There was every reason to be optimistic about the possibilities science fiction offered as a form during the 1970s. Elizabeth A. Lynn's first novel, A Different Light (1978), and Marta Randall's first, Islands (1976), showed them to be promising new talents. Chelsea Quinn Yarbro, later to become better known for her fantasy and horror novels, wrote several strong science fiction novels and stories during the '70s, among them "False Dawn" (1972). C. J. Cherryh, who published her first novel, Gate of Ivrel, in 1976, would become one of the most prolific science fiction writers, with much of her work featuring detailed depictions of alien races and cultures. Suzy McKee Charnas wrote of a culture in which women are no more than breeding stock in Walk to the End of the World (1974), then followed that novel with one in which women are dominant, Motherlines (1978). Tanith Lee treated gender roles playfully in such novels as The Birthgrave (1975). Doris Lessing, with The Memoirs of a Survivor (1975), Cecelia Holland in Floating Worlds (1976), and Marge Piercy, with Woman on the Edge of Time (1976), wrote science fiction novels after achieving renown for their other fiction. Other important science fiction by women outside the genre included Sally Miller Gearhart's The Wanderground (1978), Monique Wittig's Les Guérillères (1971), and Anna Kavan's Ice (1970). Octavia E. Butler, one of the few African-American writers of science fiction, and the only African-American woman writing science fiction for adults (Virginia Hamilton has written science fiction for younger readers), wrote three novels about telepathic people of different classes and races who bond together, then followed them with Kindred (1979), in which a twentieth-century African-American woman time-travels to a pre–Civil War southern United States in which blacks are slaves. Josephine Saxton continued to write her quirky

[12] Alice Sheldon, "A Woman Writing SF and Fantasy," Women of Vision, edited by Denise Du Pont (New York: St. Martin's, 1988), 51.

stories, of which "The Power of Time" (1971) is one of the best examples. Eleanor Arnason wrote of science fiction's tendency to pander to escapism in her story "The Warlord of Saturn's Moons" (1974), where she juxtaposes a woman writer living in a decaying world with the fictional character this writer has created.

Ursula Le Guin, having made her mark with *The Left Hand of Darkness*, published an equally ambitious novel in 1974, *The Dispossessed*, a utopian work that depicts an anarchistic society where no distinctions are drawn between the sexes; as a result, women and men are equally represented in every area of life. The political philosophy that resulted in this society is the creation of a woman, Odo; she is the central character in "The Day Before the Revolution" (1974), which appears in this volume.

In addition to my three *Women of Wonder* anthologies and Vonda McIntyre's and Susan Janice Anderson's *Aurora: Beyond Equality*, the '70s saw other feminist or woman-centered science-fictional publications. Some saw such efforts as patronizing tokenism or as reverse sexism, but in a genre replete with anthologies and magazines filled entirely with stories by men, such protests rang a bit hollow. *Analog,* under the editorship of Ben Bova, published an issue in which all the contributors were women. Anthologies of science fiction by women that came out at this time were Robert Silverberg's *The Crystal Ship* (1976), with novellas by Vonda N. McIntyre, Marta Randall, and Joan D. Vinge; Virginia Kidd's *Millennial Women* (1978), with a short novel by Ursula Le Guin and stories by several other writers; and Alice Laurance's *Cassandra Rising* (1978), a volume of new short stories by women. Among the other writers winning acclaim during this decade were Doris Piserchia, Lee Killough, Grania Davis, Phyllis Eisenstein, Suzette Haden Elgin, and Lisa Tuttle, who is represented here with "The Family Monkey" (1977), a story about an alien's effect on three generations of a Texas family.

Women in science fiction had become too numerous—and too successful—to be seen as isolated cases any longer. The concluding story in this volume, Joan D. Vinge's "View from a Height" (1978), is, fittingly, the tale of a woman whose physical limitations have cut her off from the world, yet who wins her own kind of triumph.

Stories published after 1978 are not included in this volume, partly because the third of the original *Women of Wonder* anthologies came out in early 1978, so this made a useful dividing line. There was space in this book only for writers whose work was reprinted in the earlier *Women of Wonder* anthologies, along with a few more writers who also contributed to science fiction during its classic period. In retrospect, 1978 can also be seen as the beginning of a period in which women science fiction writers were to have their greatest effect on the genre. A companion volume, *Women of Wonder, the Contemporary Years,* showcases more recent work.

Here I add a personal note. I published my first science fiction story in 1970 and was putting together the first *Women of Wonder* anthology at the time I was writing my earliest stories and my first novel. To read so many good stories by women, and such a wide variety of them, was heartening and inspiring; it put me in touch with a largely unknown tradition. At the same time, there was the definite feeling that science fiction was more receptive to women than it had ever been before. Whatever my difficulties and disappointments as a writer, and there have been many, feeling out of place as a woman in science fiction has never been one of them. I had too much company, for one thing; other women were enriching the field with their work. Knowing that they were there was encouraging.

Science fiction seemed open in a way that it hadn't been before, and this was at least partly because more women were writing it. This change affected the writing of men as well. Samuel R. Delany (always one of the most innovative science fiction writers), James H. Schmitz, Joe Haldeman, and John Varley were among the men writing about strong female characters in the roles of explorer, soldier, or scientist. Even writers who preferred to keep to customary social roles had to rationalize them rather than simply assume that they would inevitably persist.

More writers were coming to see that science fiction provides a unique opportunity to explore societies and characters that are not limited by our assumptions. In a world of rapidly changing technology, ethical questions raised by developments in biology and medicine and by increasingly sophisticated mass communication, serious science fiction may be better equipped than any other kind of literature to consider the dilemmas such changes present. By showing us worlds unlike our own, science fiction can help us to see our own world anew. At the core of both feminism and science fiction—at least what ideally should be at the core of both—is a questioning of why things are as they are and how they might be different. Science fiction, with more women writing it, had a chance to become what it had claimed to be all along—a literature that embraces new possibilities.

No Woman Born

C. L. MOORE

She had been the loveliest creature whose image ever moved along the airways. John Harris, who was once her manager, remembered doggedly how beautiful she had been as he rose in the silent elevator toward the room where Deirdre sat waiting for him.

Since the theater fire that had destroyed her a year ago, he had never been quite able to let himself remember her beauty clearly, except when some old poster, half in tatters, flaunted her face at him, or a maudlin memorial program flashed her image unexpectedly across the television screen. But now he had to remember.

The elevator came to a sighing stop and the door slid open. John Harris hesitated. He knew in his mind that he had to go on, but his reluctant muscles almost refused him. He was thinking helplessly, as he had not allowed himself to think until this moment, of the fabulous grace that had poured through her wonderful dancer's body, remembering her soft and husky voice with the little burr in it that had fascinated the audiences of the whole world.

There had never been anyone so beautiful.

In times before her, other actresses had been lovely and adulated, but never before Deirdre's day had the entire world been able to take one woman so wholly to its heart. So few outside the capitals had ever seen Bernhardt or the fabulous Jersey Lily. And the beauties of the movie screen had had to limit their audiences to those who could reach the theaters. But Deirdre's image had once moved glowingly across the television screens of every home in the civilized world. And in many outside the bounds of civilization. Her soft, husky songs had sounded in the depths of jungles, her lovely, languorous body had woven its patterns of rhythm in desert tents and polar huts. The whole world knew every smooth motion of her body and every cadence of her voice, and the way a subtle radiance had seemed to go on behind her features when she smiled.

And the whole world had mourned her when she died in the theater fire.

Harris could not quite think of her as other than dead, though he knew what sat waiting him in the room ahead. He kept remembering the old words James Stephens wrote long ago for another Deirdre, also lovely and beloved and unforgotten after two thousand years.

> The time comes when our hearts sink utterly,
> When we remember Deirdre and her tale,
> And that her lips are dust . . .
> There has been again no woman born
> Who was so beautiful; not one so beautiful
> Of all the women born—

That wasn't quite true, of course—there had been one. Or maybe, after all, this Deirdre who died only a year ago had not been beautiful in the sense of perfection. He thought the other one might not have been either, for there are always women with perfection of feature in the world, and they are not the ones that legend remembers. It was the light within, shining through her charming, imperfect features, that had made this Deirdre's face so lovely. No one else he had ever seen had anything like the magic of the lost Deirdre.

> Let all men go apart and mourn together—
> No man can ever love her. Not a man
> Can dream to be her lover. . . . No man say—
> What could one say to her? There are no words
> That one could say to her.

No, no words at all. And it was going to be impossible to go through with this. Harris knew it overwhelmingly just as his finger touched the buzzer. But the door opened almost instantly, and then it was too late.

Maltzer stood just inside, peering out through his heavy spectacles. You could see how tensely he had been waiting. Harris was a little shocked to see that the man was trembling. It was hard to think of the confident and imperturbable Maltzer, whom he had known briefly a year ago, as shaken like this. He wondered if Deirdre herself were as tremulous with sheer nerves—but it was not time yet to let himself think of that.

"Come in, come in," Maltzer said irritably. There was no reason for irritation. The year's work, so much of it in secrecy and solitude, must have tried him physically and mentally to the very breaking point.

"She all right?" Harris asked inanely, stepping inside.

"Oh yes . . . yes, *she's* all right." Maltzer bit his thumbnail and glanced over his shoulder at an inner door, where Harris guessed she would be waiting.

"No," Maltzer said, as he took an involuntary step toward it. "We'd better have a talk first. Come over and sit down. Drink?"

Harris nodded, and watched Maltzer's hands tremble as he tilted the decanter. The man was clearly on the very verge of collapse, and Harris felt a sudden cold uncertainty open up in him in the one place where until now he had been oddly confident.

"She *is* all right?" he demanded, taking the glass.

"Oh yes, she's perfect. She's so confident it scares me." Maltzer gulped his drink and poured another before he sat down.

"What's wrong, then?"

"Nothing, I guess. Or . . . well, I don't know. I'm not sure anymore. I've worked toward this meeting for nearly a year, but now—well, I'm not sure it's time yet. I'm just not sure."

He stared at Harris, his eyes large and indistinguishable behind the lenses. He was a thin, wire-taut man with all the bone and sinew showing plainly beneath the dark skin of his face. Thinner, now, than he had been a year ago when Harris saw him last.

"I've been too close to her," he said now. "I have no perspective anymore. All I can see is my own work. And I'm just not sure that's ready yet for you or anyone to see."

"She thinks so?"

"I never saw a woman so confident." Maltzer drank, the glass clicking on his teeth. He looked up suddenly through the distorting lenses. "Of course a failure now would mean—well, absolute collapse," he said.

Harris nodded. He was thinking of the year of incredibly painstaking work that lay behind this meeting, the immense fund of knowledge, of infinite patience, the secret collaboration of artists, sculptors, designers, scientists, and the genius of Maltzer governing them all as an orchestra conductor governs his players.

He was thinking too, with a certain unreasoning jealousy, of the strange, cold, passionless intimacy between Maltzer and Deirdre in that year, a closer intimacy than any two humans can ever have shared before. In a sense the Deirdre whom he saw in a few minutes would *be* Maltzer, just as he thought he detected in Maltzer now and then small mannerisms of inflection and motion that had been Deirdre's own. There had been between them a sort of unimaginable marriage stranger than anything that could ever have taken place before.

"—so many complications," Maltzer was saying in his worried voice with its faintest possible echo of Deirdre's lovely, cadenced rhythm. (The sweet, soft huskiness he would never hear again.) "There was shock, of course. Terrible shock. And a great fear of fire. We had to conquer that before we could take the first steps. But we did it. When you go in you'll probably find her sitting before the fire." He caught the startled question in Harris's eyes and smiled. "No, she can't feel the warmth now, of course. But she likes to watch the flames. She's mastered any abnormal fear of them quite beautifully."

"She can—" Harris hesitated. "Her eyesight's normal now?"

"Perfect," Maltzer said. "Perfect vision was fairly simple to provide. After all, that sort of thing has already been worked out, in other connections. I might even say her vision's a little better than perfect, from our own standpoint." He shook his head irritably. "I'm not worried about the mechanics of the thing. Luckily they got to her before the brain was touched at all. Shock was the only danger to her sensory centers, and we took care of all that first of all, as soon as communication could be established. Even so, it needed great courage on her part. Great courage." He was silent for a moment, staring into his empty glass.

"Harris," he said suddenly, without looking up, "have I made a mistake? Should we have let her die?"

Harris shook his head helplessly. It was an unanswerable question. It had tormented the whole world for a year now. There had been hundreds of answers and thousands of words written on the subject. Has anyone the right to preserve a brain alive when its body is destroyed? Even if a new body can be provided, necessarily so very unlike the old?

"It's not that she's—ugly—now," Maltzer went on hurriedly, as if afraid of an answer. "Metal isn't ugly. And Deirdre . . . well, you'll see. I tell you, I can't see myself. I know the whole mechanism so well— it's just mechanics to me. Maybe she's—grotesque, I don't know. Often I've wished I hadn't been on the spot, with all my ideas, just when the fire broke out. Or that it could have been anyone but Deirdre. She was so beautiful— Still, if it had been someone else I think the whole thing might have failed completely. It takes more than just an uninjured brain. It takes strength and courage beyond common, and—well, something more. Something—unquenchable. Deirdre has it. She's still Deirdre. In a way she's still beautiful. But I'm not sure anybody but myself could see that. And you know what she plans?"

"No—what?"

"She's going back on the air-screen."

Harris looked at him in stunned disbelief.

"She *is* still beautiful," Maltzer told him fiercely. "She's got courage, and a serenity that amazes me. And she isn't in the least worried or resentful about what's happened. Or afraid what the verdict of the public will be. But I am, Harris. I'm terrified."

They looked at each other for a moment more, neither speaking. Then Maltzer shrugged and stood up.

"She's in there," he said, gesturing with his glass.

Harris turned without a word, not giving himself time to hesitate. He crossed toward the inner door.

The room was full of a soft, clear, indirect light that climaxed in the fire crackling on a white tiled hearth. Harris paused inside the door, his heart beating thickly. He did not see her for a moment. It was a perfectly commonplace room, bright, light, with pleasant furniture, and flowers on the tables. Their perfume was sweet on the clear air. He did not see Deirdre.

Then a chair by the fire creaked as she shifted her weight in it. The high back hid her, but she spoke. And for one dreadful moment it was the voice of an automaton that sounded in the room, metallic, without inflection.

"Hel-lo—," said the voice. Then she laughed and tried again. And it was the old, familiar, sweet huskiness he had not hoped to hear again as long as he lived.

In spite of himself he said, "Deirdre!" and her image rose before him as if she herself had risen unchanged from the chair, tall, golden, swaying a little with her wonderful dancer's poise, the lovely, imperfect features lighted by the glow that made them beautiful. It was the cruelest thing his memory could have done to him. And yet the voice—after that one lapse, the voice was perfect.

"Come and look at me, John," she said.

He crossed the floor slowly, forcing himself to move. That instant's flash of vivid recollection had nearly wrecked his hard-won poise. He tried to keep his mind perfectly blank as he came at last to the verge of seeing what no one but Maltzer had so far seen or known about in its entirety. No one at all had known what shape would be forged to clothe the most beautiful woman on Earth, now that her beauty was gone.

He had envisioned many shapes. Great, lurching robot forms, cylindrical, with hinged arms and legs. A glass case with the brain floating in it and appendages to serve its needs. Grotesque visions, like nightmares come nearly true. And each more inadequate than the last, for what metal shape could possibly do more than house ungraciously the mind and brain that had once enchanted a whole world?

Then he came around the wing of the chair, and saw her.

The human brain is often too complicated a mechanism to function perfectly. Harris's brain was called upon to perform a very elaborate series of shifting impressions. First, incongruously, he remembered a curious inhuman figure he had once glimpsed leaning over the fence rail outside a farmhouse. For an instant the shape had stood up integrated, ungainly, impossibly human, before the glancing eye resolved it into an arrangement of brooms and buckets. What the eye had found only roughly humanoid, the suggestible brain had accepted fully formed. It was thus now, with Deirdre.

The first impression that his eyes and mind took from sight of her was shocked and incredulous, for his brain said to him unbelievingly, *"This is Deirdre! She hasn't changed at all!"*

Then the shift of perspective took over, and even more shockingly, eye and brain said, "No, not Deirdre—not human. Nothing but metal coils. Not Deirdre at all—" And that was the worst. It was like waking from a dream of someone beloved and lost, and facing anew, after that heartbreaking reassurance of sleep, the inflexible fact that nothing can bring the lost to life again. Deirdre was gone, and this was only machinery heaped in a flowered chair.

Then the machinery moved, exquisitely, smoothly, with a grace as familiar as the swaying poise he remembered. The sweet, husky voice of Deirdre said,

"It's me, John darling. It really is, you know."

And it was.

That was the third metamorphosis, and the final one. Illusion steadied and became factual, real. It was Deirdre.

He sat down bonelessly. He had no muscles. He looked at her speechless and unthinking, letting his senses take in the sight of her without trying to rationalize what he saw.

She was golden still. They had kept that much of her, the first impression of warmth and color which had once belonged to her sleek hair and the apricot tints of her skin. But they had had the good sense to go no farther. They had not tried to make a wax image of the lost Deirdre. (*No woman born / who was so beautiful—Not one so beautiful / of all the women born—*)

And so she had no face. She had only a smooth, delicately modeled ovoid for her head, with a . . . a sort of crescent-shaped mask across the frontal area where her eyes would have been if she had needed eyes. A narrow, curved quarter moon, with the horns turned upward. It was filled in with something translucent, like cloudy crystal, and tinted the aquamarine of the eyes Deirdre used to have. Through that, then, she saw the world. Through that she looked without eyes, and behind it, as behind the eyes of a human—she was.

Except for that, she had no features. And it had been wise of those who designed her, he realized now. Subconsciously he had been dreading some clumsy attempt at human features that might creak like a marionette's in parodies of animation. The eyes, perhaps, had had to open in the same place upon her head, and at the same distance apart, to make easy for her an adjustment to the stereoscopic vision she used to have. But he was glad they had not given her two eye-shaped openings with glass marbles inside them. The mask was better.

(Oddly enough, he did not once think of the naked brain that must lie inside the metal. The mask was symbol enough for the woman within. It was enigmatic; you did not know if her gaze was on you searchingly, or wholly withdrawn. And it had no variations of brilliance such as once had played across the incomparable mobility of Deirdre's face. But eyes, even human eyes, are as a matter of fact enigmatic enough. They have no expression except what the lids impart; they take all animation from the features. We automatically watch the eyes of the friend we speak with, but if he happens to be lying down so that he speaks across his shoulder and his face is upside-down to us, quite as automatically we watch the mouth. The gaze keeps shifting nervously between mouth and eyes in their reversed order, for it is the position in the face, not the feature itself, which we are accustomed to accept as the seat of the soul. Deirdre's mask was in that proper place; it was easy to accept it as a mask over eyes.)

She had, Harris realized as the first shock quieted, a very beautifully shaped head—a bare, golden skull. She turned it a little, gracefully upon her neck of metal, and he saw that the artist who shaped it had given her the most delicate suggestion of cheekbones, narrowing in the blankness below the mask to the hint of a human face. Not too much. Just enough so that when the head turned you saw by its modeling that it had moved, lending perspective and foreshortening to the expressionless golden helmet. Light did not slip uninterrupted as if over the surface of a golden egg. Brancusi himself had never made anything more simple or more subtle than the modeling of Deirdre's head.

But all expression, of course, was gone. All expression had gone up in the smoke of the theater fire, with the lovely, mobile, radiant features which had meant Deirdre.

As for her body, he could not see its shape. A garment hid her. But they had made no incongruous attempt to give her back the clothing that once had made her famous. Even the softness of cloth would have called the mind too sharply to the remembrance that no human body lay beneath the folds, nor does metal need the incongruity of cloth for its protection. Yet without garments, he realized, she would have looked oddly naked, since her new body was humanoid, not angular machinery.

The designer had solved his paradox by giving her a robe of very fine metal mesh. It hung from the gentle slope of her shoulders in straight, pliant folds like a longer Grecian chlamys, flexible, yet with weight enough of its own not to cling too revealingly to whatever metal shape lay beneath.

The arms they had given her were left bare, and the feet and ankles. And Maltzer had performed his greatest miracle in the limbs of the new Deirdre. It was a mechanical miracle basically, but the eye appreciated first that he had also showed supreme artistry and understanding.

Her arms were pale shining gold, tapered smoothly, without modeling, and flexible their whole length in diminishing metal bracelets fitting one inside the other clear down to the slim, round wrists. The hands were more nearly human than any other feature about her, though they, too, were fitted together in delicate, small sections that slid upon one another with the flexibility almost of flesh. The fingers' bases were solider than human, and the fingers themselves tapered to longer tips.

Her feet, too, beneath the tapering broader rings of the metal ankles, had been constructed upon the model of human feet. Their finely tooled sliding segments gave her an arch and a heel and a flexible forward section formed almost like the sollerets of medieval armor.

She looked, indeed, very much like a creature in armor, with her delicately plated limbs and her featureless head like a helmet with a visor of glass, and her robe of chain mail. But no knight in armor ever moved as Deirdre moved, or wore his armor upon a body of such inhumanly fine proportions. Only a knight from another world, or a knight of Oberon's court, might have shared that delicate likeness.

Briefly he had been surprised at the smallness and exquisite proportions of her. He had been expecting the ponderous mass of such robots as he had seen, wholly automatons. And then he realized that for them, much of the space had to be devoted to the inadequate mechanical brains that guided them about their duties. Deirdre's brain still preserved and proved the craftsmanship of an artisan far defter than man. Only the body was of metal, and it did not seem complex, though he had not yet been told how it was motivated.

Harris had no idea how long he sat staring at the figure in the cushioned chair. She was still lovely—indeed, she was still Deirdre—and as he looked, he let the careful schooling of his face relax. There was no need to hide his thoughts from her.

She stirred upon the cushions, the long, flexible arms moving with a litheness that was not quite human. The motion disturbed him as the body itself had not, and in spite of himself his face froze a little. He had the feeling that from behind the crescent mask she was watching him very closely.

Slowly she rose.

The motion was very smooth. Also it was serpentine, as if the body beneath the coat of mail were made in the same interlocking sections as her limbs. He had expected and feared mechanical rigidity; nothing had prepared him for this more-than-human suppleness.

She stood quietly, letting the heavy mailed folds of her garment settle about her. They fell together with a faint ringing sound, like small bells far off, and hung beautifully in pale golden, sculptured folds. He had risen automatically as she did. Now he faced her, staring. He had never seen her stand perfectly still, and she was not doing it now. She swayed just a bit, vitality burning inextinguishably in her brain as once it had burned in her body, and stolid immobility was as impossible to her as it had always been. The golden garment caught points of light from the fire and glimmered at him with tiny reflections as she moved.

Then she put her featureless helmeted head a little to one side, and he heard her laughter as familiar in its small, throaty, intimate sound as he had ever heard it from her living throat. And every gesture, every attitude, every flowing of motion into motion was so utterly Deirdre that the overwhelming illusion swept his mind again and this was the flesh-and-blood woman as clearly as if he saw her standing there whole once more, like the Phoenix from the fire.

"Well, John," she said in the soft, husky, amused voice he remembered perfectly. "Well, John, is it I?" She knew it was. Perfect assurance sounded in the voice. "The shock will wear off, you know. It'll be easier and easier as time goes on. I'm quite used to myself now. See?"

She turned away from him and crossed the room smoothly, with the old, poised dancer's glide, to the mirror that paneled one side of the room. And before it, as he had so often seen her preen before, he watched her preening now, running flexible metallic hands down the folds of her metal garment, turning to admire herself over one metal shoulder, making the mailed folds tinkle and sway as she struck an arabesque position before the glass.

His knees let him down into the chair she had vacated. Mingled shock and relief loosened all his muscles in him, and she was more poised and confident than he.

"It's a miracle," he said with conviction. "It's *you*. But I don't see how—" He had meant, "—how, without face or body—" but clearly he could not finish that sentence.

She finished it for him in her own mind and answered without self-consciousness. "It's motion, mostly," she said, still admiring her own suppleness in the mirror. "See?" And very lightly on her springy, armored feet she flashed through an enchaînement of brilliant steps, swinging round with a pirouette to face him. "That was what Maltzer and I worked out between us, after I began to get myself under control again." Her voice was somber for a moment, remembering a dark time in the past. Then she went on, "It wasn't easy, of course, but it was fascinating. You'll never guess how fascinating, John! We knew we couldn't work out anything like a facsimile of the way I used to look, so we had to find some other basis to build on. And motion is the other basis of recognition, after actual physical likeness."

She moved lightly across the carpet toward the window and stood looking down, her featureless face averted a little and the light shining across the delicately hinted curves of the cheekbones.

"Luckily," she said, her voice amused, "I never was beautiful. It was—well, vivacity, I suppose, and muscular coordination. Years and years of training, and all of it engraved here"—she struck her golden helmet a light, ringing blow with golden knuckles—"in the habit patterns grooved into my brain. So this body . . . did he tell you? . . . works entirely through the brain. Electromagnetic currents flowing along from ring to ring, like this." She rippled a boneless arm at him with a motion like flowing water. "Nothing holds me together—nothing!—except muscles of magnetic currents. And if I'd been somebody else—somebody who moved differently, why, the flexible rings would have moved differently too, guided by the impulse from another brain. I'm not conscious of doing anything I haven't always done. The same impulses that used to go out to my muscles go out now to—this." And she made a shuddering, serpentine motion of both arms at him, like a Cambodian dancer, and then laughed wholeheartedly, the sound of it ringing through the room with such full-throated merriment that he could not help seeing again the familiar face crinkled with pleasure, the white teeth shining. "It's all perfectly subconscious now," she told him. "It took lots of practice at first, of course, but now even my signature looks just as it always did—the coordination is duplicated that delicately." She rippled her arms at him again and chuckled.

"But the voice, too," Harris protested inadequately. "It's *your* voice, Deirdre."

"The voice isn't only a matter of throat construction and breath control, my darling Johnnie! At least, so Professor Maltzer assured me a year ago, and I certainly haven't any reason to doubt him!" She laughed again. She was laughing a little too much, with a touch of the bright, hysteric overexcitement he remembered so well. But if any woman ever had reason for mild hysteria, surely Deirdre had it now.

The laughter rippled and ended, and she went on, her voice eager. "He says voice control is almost wholly a matter of hearing what you produce, once you've got adequate mechanism, of course. That's why deaf people, with the same vocal cords as ever, let their voices change completely and lose all inflection when they've been deaf long enough. And luckily, you see, I'm not deaf!"

She swung around to him, the folds of her robe twinkling and ringing, and rippled up and up a clear, true scale to a lovely high note, and then cascaded down again like water over a falls. But she left him no time for applause. "Perfectly simple, you see. All it took was a little matter of genius from the professor to get it worked out for me! He started with a new variation of the old Vodor you must remember hearing about, years ago. Originally, of course, the thing was ponderous. You know how it worked—speech broken down to a few basic sounds and built up again in combinations produced from a keyboard. I think originally the sounds were a sort of *ktch* and a *shoosh*ing noise, but we've got it all worked to a flexibility and range quite as good as human now. All I do is—well, mentally play on the keyboard of

my . . . my sound-unit, I suppose it's called. It's much more complicated than that, of course, but I've learned to do it unconsciously. And
I regulate it by ear, quite automatically now. If you were—*here*—
instead of me, and you'd had the same practice, your own voice would
be coming out of the same keyboard and diaphragm instead of mine.
It's all a matter of the brain patterns that operated the body and now
operate the machinery. They send out very strong impulses that are
stepped up as much as necessary somewhere or other in here—" Her
hands waved vaguely over the mesh-robed body.

She was silent a moment, looking out the window. Then she turned
away and crossed the floor to the fire, sinking again into the flowered
chair. Her helmet-skull turned its mask to face him, and he could feel
a quiet scrutiny behind the aquamarine of its gaze.

"It's—odd," she said, "being here in this . . . this . . . instead of a
body. But not as odd or as alien as you might think. I've thought about
it a lot—I've had plenty of time to think—and I've begun to realize
what a tremendous force the human ego really is. I'm not sure I want
to suggest it has any mystical power it can impress on mechanical
things, but it does seem to have a power of some sort. It does instill
its own force into inanimate objects, and they take on a personality of
their own. People do impress their personalities on the houses they
live in, you know. I've noticed that often. Even empty rooms. And it
happens with other things, too, especially, I think, with inanimate
things that men depend on for their lives. Ships, for instance—they
always have personalities of their own.

"And planes—in wars you always hear of planes crippled too badly
to fly, but struggling back anyhow with their crews. Even guns acquire
a sort of ego. Ships and guns and planes are 'she' to the men who
operate them and depend on them for their lives. It's as if machinery
with complicated moving parts almost simulates life and does acquire
from the men who used it—well, not exactly life, of course—but a
personality. I don't know what. Maybe it absorbs some of the actual
electrical impulses their brains throw off, especially in times of stress.

"Well, after a while I began to accept the idea that this new body
of mine could behave at least as responsively as a ship or a plane.
Quite apart from the fact that my own brain controls its 'muscles.' I
believe there's an affinity between men and the machines they make.
They make them out of their own brains, really, a sort of mental
conception and gestation, and the result responds to the minds that
created them and to all human minds that understand and manipulate
them."

She stirred uneasily and smoothed a flexible hand along her mesh-robed metal thigh. "So this is myself," she said. "Metal—but me. And it grows more and more myself the longer I live in it. It's my house and the machine my life depends on, but much more intimately in each case than any real house or machine ever was before to any other human. And you know, I wonder if in time I'll forget what flesh felt like—my own flesh, when I touched it like this—and the metal against the metal will be so much the same I'll never even notice?"

Harris did not try to answer her. He sat without moving, watching her expressionless face. In a moment she went on.

"I'll tell you the best thing, John," she said, her voice softening to the old intimacy he remembered so well that he could see superimposed upon the blank skull the warm, intent look that belonged with the voice. "I'm not going to live forever. It may not sound like a—best thing—but it is, John. You know, for a while that was the worst of all, after I knew I was—after I woke up again. The thought of living on and on in a body that wasn't mine, seeing everyone I knew grow old and die, and not being able to stop—

"But Maltzer says my brain will probably wear out quite normally —except, of course, that I won't have to worry about looking old!— and when it gets tired and stops, the body I'm in won't be any longer. The magnetic muscles that hold it into my own shape and motions will let go when the brain lets go, and there'll be nothing but a . . . a pile of disconnected rings. If they ever assemble it again, it won't be me." She hesitated. "I like that, John," she said, and he felt from behind the mask a searching of his face.

He knew and understood that somber satisfaction. He could not put it into words; neither of them wanted to do that. But he understood. It was the conviction of mortality, in spite of her immortal body. She was not cut off from the rest of her race in the essence of their humanity, for though she wore a body of steel and they perishable flesh, yet she must perish too, and the same fears and faiths still united her to mortals and humans, though she wore the body of Oberon's inhuman knight. Even in her death she must be unique—dissolution in a shower of tinkling and clashing rings, he thought, and almost envied her the finality and beauty of that particular death—but afterward, oneness with humanity in however much or little awaited them all. So she could feel that this exile in metal was only temporary, in spite of everything.

(And providing, of course, that the mind inside the metal did not veer from its inherited humanity as the years went by. A dweller in a house may impress his personality upon the walls, but subtly the walls, too, may impress their own shape upon the ego of the man. Neither of them thought of that, at the time.)

Deirdre sat a moment longer in silence. Then the mood vanished and she rose again, spinning so that the robe belled out ringing about her ankles. She rippled another scale up and down, faultlessly and with the same familiar sweetness of tone that had made her famous.

"So I'm going right back on the stage, John," she said serenely. "I can still sing. I can still dance. I'm still myself in everything that matters, and I can't imagine doing anything else for the rest of my life."

He could not answer without stammering a little. "Do you think . . . will they accept you, Deirdre? After all—"

"They'll accept me," she said in that confident voice. "Oh, they'll come to see a freak at first, of course, but they'll stay to watch—Deirdre. And come back again and again just as they always did. You'll see, my dear."

But hearing her sureness, suddenly Harris himself was unsure. Maltzer had not been, either. She was so regally confident, and disappointment would be so deadly a blow at all that remained of her—

She was so delicate a being now, really. Nothing but a glowing and radiant mind poised in metal, dominating it, bending the steel to the illusion of her lost loveliness with a sheer self-confidence that gleamed through the metal body. But the brain sat delicately on its poise of reason. She had been through intolerable stresses already, perhaps more terrible depths of despair and self-knowledge than any human brain had yet endured before her, for—since Lazarus himself—who had come back from the dead?

But if the world did not accept her as beautiful, what then? If they laughed, or pitied her, or came only to watch a jointed freak performing as if on strings where the loveliness of Deirdre had once enchanted them, what then? And he could not be perfectly sure they would not. He had known her too well in the flesh to see her objectively even now, in metal. Every inflection of her voice called up the vivid memory of the face that had flashed its evanescent beauty in some look to match the tone. She was Deirdre to Harris simply because she had been so intimately familiar in every poise and attitude, through so many years. But people who knew her only slightly, or saw her for the first time in metal—what would they see?

A marionette? Or the real grace and loveliness shining through?

He had no possible way of knowing. He saw her too clearly as she had been to see her now at all, except so linked with the past that she was not wholly metal. And he knew what Maltzer feared, for Maltzer's psychic blindness toward her lay at the other extreme. He had never known Deirdre except as a machine, and he could not see her objectively any more than Harris could. To Maltzer she was pure metal, a robot his own hands and brain had devised, mysteriously animated by the mind of Deirdre, to be sure, but to all outward seeming a thing of metal solely. He had worked so long over each intricate part of her body, he knew so well how every jointure in it was put together, that he could not see the whole. He had studied many film records of her, of course, as she used to be, in order to gauge the accuracy of his facsimile, but this thing he had made was a copy only. He was too close to Deirdre to see her. And Harris, in a way, was too far. The indomitable Deirdre herself shone so vividly through the metal that his mind kept superimposing one upon the other.

How would an audience react to her? Where in the scale between these two extremes would their verdict fall?

For Deirdre, there was only one possible answer.

"I'm not worried," Deirdre said serenely, and spread her golden hands to the fire to watch lights dancing in reflection upon their shining surfaces. "I'm still myself. I've always had . . . well, power over my audiences. Any good performer knows when he's got it. Mine isn't gone. I can still give them what I always gave, only now with greater variations and more depths than I'd ever have done before. Why, look—" She gave a little wriggle of excitement.

"You know the arabesque principle—getting the longest possible distance from fingertip to toetip with a long, slow curve through the whole length? And the brace of the other leg and arm giving contrast? Well, look at me. I don't work on hinges now. I can make every motion a long curve if I want to. My body's different enough now to work out a whole new school of dancing. Of course there'll be things I used to do that I won't attempt now—no more dancing *sur les pointes*, for instance—but the new things will more than balance the loss. I've been practicing. Do you know I can turn a hundred fouettés now without a flaw? And I think I could go right on and turn a thousand, if I wanted."

She made the firelight flash on her hands, and her robe rang musically as she moved her shoulders a little. "I've already worked out one new dance for myself," she said. "God knows I'm no choreographer, but I did want to experiment first. Later, you know, really creative men like Massanchine or Fokhileff may want to do something entirely new for me—a whole new sequence of movements based on a new technique. And music—that could be quite different, too. Oh, there's no end to the possibilities! Even my voice has more range and power. Luckily I'm not an actress—it would be silly to try to play Camille or Juliet with a cast of ordinary people. Not that I couldn't, you know." She turned her head to stare at Harris through the mask of glass. "I honestly think I could. But it isn't necessary. There's too much else. Oh, I'm not worried!"

"Maltzer's worried," Harris reminded her.

She swung away from the fire, her metal robe ringing, and into her voice came the old note of distress that went with a furrowing of her forehead and a sidewise tilt of the head. The head went sidewise as it had always done, and he could see the furrowed brow almost as clearly as if flesh still clothed her.

"I know. And I'm worried about him, John. He's worked so awfully hard over me. This is the doldrums now, the letdown period, I suppose. I know what's on his mind. He's afraid I'll look just the same to the world as I look to him. Tooled metal. He's in a position no one ever quite achieved before, isn't he? Rather like God." Her voice rippled a little with amusement. "I suppose to God we must look like a collection of cells and corpuscles ourselves. But Maltzer lacks a god's detached viewpoint."

"He can't see you as I do, anyhow." Harris was choosing his words with difficulty. "I wonder, though—would it help him any if you postponed your debut awhile? You've been with him too closely, I think. You don't quite realize how near a breakdown he is. I was shocked when I saw him just now."

The golden head shook. "No. He's close to a breaking point, maybe, but I think the only cure's action. He wants me to retire and stay out of sight, John. Always. He's afraid for anyone to see me except a few old friends who remember me as I was. People he can trust to be—kind." She laughed. It was very strange to hear that ripple of mirth from the blank, unfeatured skull. Harris was seized with sudden panic at the thought of what reaction it might evoke in an audience of strangers. As if he had spoken the fear aloud, her voice denied it. "I don't need kindness. And it's no kindness to Maltzer to hide me under a bushel. He *has* worked too hard, I know. He's driven himself to a breaking point. But it'll be a complete negation of all he's worked for if I hide myself now. You don't know what a tremendous lot of genius and artistry went into me, John. The whole idea from the start was to re-create what I'd lost so that it could be proved that beauty and talent need not be sacrificed by the destruction of parts or all the body.

"It wasn't only for me that we meant to prove that. There'll be others who suffer injuries that once might have ruined them. This was to end all suffering like that forever. It was Maltzer's gift to the whole race as well as to me. He's really a humanitarian, John, like most great men. He'd never have given up a year of his life to this work if it had been for any one individual alone. He was seeing thousands of others beyond me as he worked. And I won't let him ruin all he's achieved because he's afraid to prove it now he's got it. The whole wonderful achievement will be worthless if I don't take the final step. I think his breakdown, in the end, would be worse and more final if I never tried than if I tried and failed."

Harris sat in silence. There was no answer he could make to that. He hoped the little twinge of shamefaced jealousy he suddenly felt did not show, as he was reminded anew of the intimacy closer than marriage which had of necessity bound these two together. And he knew that any reaction of his would in its way be almost as prejudiced as Maltzer's, for a reason at once the same and entirely opposite. Except that he himself came fresh to the problem, while Maltzer's viewpoint was colored by a year of overwork and physical and mental exhaustion.

"What are you going to do?" he asked.

She was standing before the fire when he spoke, swaying just a little so that highlights danced all along her golden body. Now she turned with a serpentine grace and sank into the cushioned chair beside her. It came to him suddenly that she was much more than humanly graceful—quite as much as he had once feared she would be less than human.

"I've already arranged for a performance," she told him, her voice a little shaken with a familiar mixture of excitement and defiance.

Harris sat up with a start. "How? Where? There hasn't been any publicity at all yet, has there? I didn't know—"

"Now, now, Johnnie," her amused voice soothed him. "You'll be handling everything just as usual once I get started back to work—that is, if you still want to. But this I've arranged for myself. It's going to be a surprise. I . . . I felt it had to be a surprise." She wriggled a little among the cushions. "Audience psychology is something I've always felt rather than known, and I do feel this is the way it ought to be done. There's no precedent. Nothing like this ever happened before. I'll have to go by my own intuition."

"You mean it's to be a complete surprise?"

"I think it must be. I don't want the audience coming in with preconceived ideas. I want them to see me exactly as I am now *first*, before they know who or what they're seeing. They must realize I can still give as good a performance as ever, before they remember and compare it with my past performances. I don't want them to come ready to pity my handicaps—I haven't got any!—or full of morbid curiosity. So I'm going on the air after the regular eight-o'clock telecast of the feature from Teleo City. I'm just going to do one specialty in the usual vaude program. It's all been arranged. They'll build up to it, of course, as the highlight of the evening, but they aren't to say who I am until the end of the performance—if the audience hasn't recognized me already, by then."

"Audience?"

"Of course. Surely you haven't forgotten they still play to a theater audience at Teleo City? That's why I want to make my debut there. I've always played better when there were people in the studio, so I could gauge reactions. I think most performers do. Anyhow, it's all arranged."

"Does Maltzer know?"

She wriggled uncomfortably. "Not yet."

"But he'll have to give his permission, too, won't he? I mean—"

"Now look, John! That's another idea you and Maltzer will have to get out of your minds. I don't belong to him. In a way he's just been my doctor through a long illness, but I'm free to discharge him whenever I choose. If there were ever any legal disagreement, I suppose he'd be entitled to quite a lot of money for the work he's done on my new body— for the body itself, really, since it's his own machine, in one sense. But he doesn't own it, or me. I'm not sure just how the question would be decided by the courts—there again, we've got a problem without precedent. The body may be his work, but the brain that makes it something more than a collection of metal rings is *me*, and he couldn't restrain me against my will even if he wanted to. Not legally, and not—" She hesitated oddly and looked away. For the first time Harris was aware of something beneath the surface of her mind which was quite strange to him.

"Well, anyhow," she went on, "that question won't come up. Maltzer and I have been much too close in the past year to clash over anything as essential as this. He knows in his heart that I'm right, and he won't try to restrain me. His work won't be completed until I do what I was built to do. And I intend to do it."

That strange little quiver of something—something un-Deirdre—which had so briefly trembled beneath the surface of familiarity stuck in Harris's mind as something he must recall and examine later. Now he said only,

"All right. I suppose I agree with you. How soon are you going to do it?"

She turned her head so that even the glass mask through which she looked out at the world was foreshortened away from him, and the golden helmet with its hint of sculptured cheekbone was entirely enigmatic.

"Tonight," she said.

Maltzer's thin hand shook so badly that he could not turn the dial. He tried twice and then laughed nervously and shrugged at Harris.

"You get her," he said.

Harris glanced at his watch. "It isn't time yet. She won't be on for half an hour."

Maltzer made a gesture of violent impatience. "Get it, get it!"

Harris shrugged a little in turn and twisted the dial. On the tilted screen above them, shadows and sound blurred together and then clarified into a somber medieval hall, vast, vaulted, people in bright costume moving like pygmies through its dimness. Since the play concerned Mary of Scotland, the actors were dressed in something approximating Elizabethan garb, but as every era tends to translate costume into terms of the current fashions, the women's hair was dressed in a style that would have startled Elizabeth, and their footgear was entirely anachronistic.

The hall dissolved and a face swam up into soft focus upon the screen. The dark, lush beauty of the actress who was playing the Stuart queen glowed at them in velvety perfection from the clouds of her pearl-strewn hair. Maltzer groaned.

"She's competing with *that*," he said hollowly.

"You think she can't?"

Maltzer slapped the chair arms with angry palms. Then the quivering of his fingers seemed suddenly to strike him, and he muttered to himself, "Look at 'em! I'm not even fit to handle a hammer and saw." But the mutter was an aside. "Of course she can't compete," he cried irritably. "She hasn't any sex. She isn't female anymore. She doesn't know that yet, but she'll learn."

Harris stared at him, feeling a little stunned. Somehow the thought had not occurred to him before at all, so vividly had the illusion of the old Deirdre hung about the new one.

"She's an abstraction now," Maltzer went on, drumming his palms upon the chair in quick, nervous rhythms. "I don't know what it'll do to her, but there'll be change. Remember Abelard? She's lost everything that made her essentially what the public wanted, and she's going to find it out the hard way. After that—" He grimaced savagely and was silent.

"She hasn't lost everything," Harris defended. "She can dance and sing as well as ever, maybe better. She still has grace and charm and—"

"Yes, but where did the grace and charm come from? Not out of the habit patterns in her brain. No, out of human contacts, out of all the things that stimulate sensitive minds to creativeness. And she's lost three of her five senses. Everything she can't see and hear is gone. One of the strongest stimuli to a woman of her type was the knowledge of sex competition. You know how she sparkled when a man came into the room? All that's gone, and it was an essential. You know how liquor stimulated her? She's lost that. She couldn't taste food or drink even if she needed it. Perfume, flowers, all the odors we respond to mean nothing to her now. She can't feel anything with tactual delicacy anymore. She used to surround herself with luxuries—she drew her stimuli from them—and that's all gone, too. She's withdrawn from all physical contacts."

He squinted at the screen, not seeing it, his face drawn into lines like the lines of a skull. All flesh seemed to have dissolved off his bones in the past year, and Harris thought almost jealously that even in that way he seemed to be drawing nearer Deirdre in her fleshlessness with every passing week.

"Sight," Maltzer said, "is the most highly civilized of the senses. It was the last to come. The other senses tie us in closely with the very roots of life; I think we perceive with them more keenly than we know. The things we realize through taste and smell and feeling stimulate directly, without a detour through the centers of conscious thought. You know how often a taste or odor will recall a memory to you so subtly you don't know exactly what caused it? We need those primitive senses to tie us in with nature and the race. Through those ties Deirdre drew her vitality without realizing it. Sight is a cold, intellectual thing compared with the other senses. But it's all she has to draw on now. She isn't a human being anymore, and I think what humanity is left in her will drain out little by little and never be replaced. Abelard, in a way, was a prototype. But Deirdre's loss is complete."

"She isn't human," Harris agreed slowly. "But she isn't pure robot either. She's something somewhere between the two, and I think it's a mistake to try to guess just where, or what the outcome will be."

"I don't have to guess," Maltzer said in a grim voice. "I know. I wish I'd let her die. I've done something to her a thousand times worse than the fire ever could. I should have let her die in it."

"Wait," said Harris. "Wait and see. I think you're wrong."

On the television screen Mary of Scotland climbed the scaffold to her doom, the gown of traditional scarlet clinging warmly to supple young curves as anachronistic in their way as the slippers beneath the gown, for—as everyone but playwrights knows—Mary was well into middle age before she died. Gracefully this latter-day Mary bent her head, sweeping the long hair aside, kneeling to the block.

Maltzer watched stonily, seeing another woman entirely.

"I shouldn't have let her," he was muttering. "I shouldn't have let her do it."

"So you really think you'd have stopped her if you could?" Harris asked quietly. And the other man after a moment's pause shook his head jerkily.

"No, I suppose not. I keep thinking if I worked and waited a little longer maybe I could make it easier for her, but—no, I suppose not. She's got to face them sooner or later, being herself." He stood up abruptly, shoving back his chair. "If she only weren't so . . . so frail. She doesn't realize how delicately poised her very sanity is. We gave her what we could—the artists and the designers and I, all gave our very best—but she's so pitifully handicapped even with all we could do. She'll always be an abstraction and a . . . a freak, cut off from the world by handicaps worse in their way than anything any human being ever suffered before. Sooner or later she'll realize it. And then—" He began to pace up and down with quick, uneven steps, striking his hands together. His face was twitching with a little tic that drew up one eye to a squint and released it again at irregular intervals. Harris could see how very near collapse the man was.

"Can you imagine what it's like?" Maltzer demanded fiercely. "Penned into a mechanical body like that, shut out from all human contacts except what leaks in by way of sight and sound? To know you aren't human any longer? She's been through shocks enough already. When that shock fully hits her—"

"Shut up," said Harris roughly. "You won't do her any good if you break down yourself. Look—the vaude's starting."

Great golden curtains had swept together over the unhappy Queen of Scotland and were parting again now, all sorrow and frustration wiped away once more as cleanly as the passing centuries had already expunged them. Now a line of tiny dancers under the tremendous arch of the stage kicked and pranced with the precision of little mechanical dolls too small and perfect to be real. Vision rushed down upon them and swept along the row, face after stiffly smiling face racketing by like fence pickets. Then the sight rose into the rafters and looked down upon them from a great height, the grotesquely foreshortened figures still prancing in perfect rhythm even from this inhuman angle.

There was applause from an invisible audience. Then someone came out and did a dance with lighted torches that streamed long, weaving ribbons of fire among clouds of what looked like cotton wool but was most probably asbestos. Then a company in gorgeous pseudo-period costumes postured its way through the new singing ballet form of dance, roughly following a plot which had been announced as *Les Sylphides*, but had little in common with it. Afterward the precision dancers came on again, solemn and charming as performing dolls.

Maltzer began to show signs of dangerous tension as act succeeded act. Deirdre's was to be the last, of course. It seemed very long indeed before a face in close-up blotted out the stage, and a master of ceremonies with features like an amiable marionette's announced a very special number as the finale. His voice was almost cracking with excitement—perhaps he, too, had not been told until a moment before what lay in store for the audience.

Neither of the listening men heard what it was he said, but both were conscious of a certain indefinable excitement rising among the audience, murmurs and rustlings and a mounting anticipation as if time had run backward here and knowledge of the great surprise had already broken upon them.

Then the golden curtains appeared again. They quivered and swept apart on long upward arcs, and between them the stage was full of a shimmering golden haze. It was, Harris realized in a moment, simply a series of gauze curtains, but the effect was one of strange and wonderful anticipation, as if something very splendid must be hidden in the haze. The world might have looked like this on the first morning of creation, before heaven and earth took form in the mind of God. It was a singularly fortunate choice of stage set in its symbolism, though

Harris wondered how much necessity had figured in its selection, for there could not have been much time to prepare an elaborate set.

The audience sat perfectly silent, and the air was tense. This was no ordinary pause before an act. No one had been told, surely, and yet they seemed to guess—

The shimmering haze trembled and began to thin, veil by veil. Beyond was darkness, and what looked like a row of shining pillars set in a balustrade that began gradually to take shape as the haze drew back in shining folds. Now they could see that the balustrade curved up from left and right to the head of a sweep of stairs. Stage and stairs were carpeted in black velvet; black velvet draperies hung just ajar behind the balcony, with a glimpse of dark sky beyond them trembling with dim synthetic stars.

The last curtain of golden gauze withdrew. The stage was empty. Or it seemed empty. But even through the aerial distances between this screen and the place it mirrored, Harris thought that the audience was not waiting for the performer to come on from the wings. There was no rustling, no coughing, no sense of impatience. A presence upon the stage was in command from the first drawing of the curtains; it filled the theater with its calm domination. It gauged its timing, holding the audience as a conductor with lifted baton gathers and holds the eyes of his orchestra.

For a moment everything was motionless upon the stage. Then, at the head of the stairs, where the two curves of the pillared balustrade swept together, a figure stirred.

Until that moment she had seemed another shining column in the row. Now she swayed deliberately, light catching and winking and running molten along her limbs and her robe of metal mesh. She swayed just enough to show that she was there. Then, with every eye upon her, she stood quietly to let them look their fill. The screen did not swoop to a close-up upon her. Her enigma remained inviolate and the television watchers saw her no more clearly than the audience in the theater.

Many must have thought her at first some wonderfully animate robot, hung perhaps from wires invisible against the velvet, for certainly she was no woman dressed in metal—her proportions were too thin and fine for that. And perhaps the impression of robotism was what she meant to convey at first. She stood quiet, swaying just a little, a masked and inscrutable figure, faceless, very slender in her robe that hung in folds as pure as a Grecian chlamys, though she did not look Grecian at all. In the visored golden helmet and the robe of

mail that odd likeness to knighthood was there again, with its implications of medieval richness behind the simple lines. Except that in
her exquisite slimness she called to mind no human figure in armor,
not even the comparative delicacy of a St. Joan. It was the chivalry
and delicacy of some other world implicit in her outlines.

A breath of surprise had rippled over the audience when she moved.
Now they were tensely silent again, waiting. And the tension, the
anticipation, was far deeper than the surface importance of the scene
could ever have evoked. Even those who thought her a manikin seemed
to feel the forerunning of greater revelations.

Now she swayed and came slowly down the steps, moving with a
suppleness just a little better than human. The swaying strengthened.
By the time she reached the stage floor she was dancing. But it was
no dance that any human creature could ever have performed. The
long, slow, languorous rhythms of her body would have been impossible to a figure hinged at its joints as human figures hinge. (Harris
remembered incredulously that he had feared once to find her jointed
like a mechanical robot. But it was humanity that seemed, by contrast,
jointed and mechanical now.)

The languor and the rhythm of her patterns looked impromptu, as
all good dances should, but Harris knew what hours of composition
and rehearsal must lie behind it, what laborious graving into her brain
of strange new pathways, the first to replace the old ones and govern
the mastery of metal limbs.

To and fro over the velvet carpet, against the velvet background,
she wove the intricacies of her serpentine dance, leisurely and yet with
such hypnotic effect that the air seemed full of looping rhythms, as if
her long, tapering limbs had left their own replicas hanging upon the
air and fading only slowly as she moved away. In her mind, Harris
knew, the stage was a whole, a background to be filled in completely
with the measured patterns of her dance, and she seemed almost to
project that completed pattern to her audience so that they saw her
everywhere at once, her golden rhythms fading upon the air long after
she had gone.

Now there was music, looping and hanging in echoes after her like
the shining festoons she wove with her body. But it was no orchestral
music. She was humming, deep and sweet and wordlessly, as she
glided her easy, intricate path about the stage. And the volume of the
music was amazing. It seemed to fill the theater, and it was not amplified by hidden loudspeakers. You could tell that. Somehow, until
you heard the music she made, you had never realized before the

subtle distortions that amplification puts into music. This was utterly pure and true as perhaps no ear in all her audience had ever heard music before.

While she danced, the audience did not seem to breathe. Perhaps they were beginning already to suspect who and what it was that moved before them without any fanfare of the publicity they had been half-expecting for weeks now. And yet, without the publicity, it was not easy to believe the dancer they watched was not some cunningly motivated manikin swinging on unseen wires about the stage.

Nothing she had done yet had been human. The dance was no dance a human being could have performed. The music she hummed came from a throat without vocal cords. But now the long, slow rhythms were drawing to their close, the pattern tightening in to a finale. And she ended as inhumanly as she had danced, willing them not to interrupt her with applause, dominating them now as she had always done. For her implication here was that a machine might have performed the dance, and a machine expects no applause. If they thought unseen operators had put her through those wonderful paces, they would wait for the operators to appear for their bows. But the audience was obedient. It sat silently, waiting for what came next. But its silence was tense and breathless.

The dance ended as it had begun. Slowly, almost carelessly, she swung up the velvet stairs, moving with rhythms as perfect as her music. But when she reached the head of the stairs, she turned to face her audience, and for a moment stood motionless, like a creature of metal, without volition, the hands of the operator slack upon its strings.

Then, startlingly, she laughed.

It was lovely laughter, low and sweet and full-throated. She threw her head back and let her body sway and her shoulders shake, and the laughter, like the music, filled the theater, gaining volume from the great hollow of the roof and sounding in the ears of every listener, not loud, but as intimately as if each sat alone with the woman who laughed.

And she was a woman now. Humanity had dropped over her like a tangible garment. No one who had ever heard that laughter before could mistake it here. But before the reality of who she was had quite time to dawn upon her listeners, she let the laughter deepen into music, as no human voice could have done. She was humming a familiar refrain close in the ear of every hearer. And the humming in turn swung into words. She sang in her clear, light, lovely voice:

"The yellow rose of Eden, is blooming in my heart—"

It was Deirdre's song. She had sung it first upon the airways a month before the theater fire that had consumed her. It was a commonplace little melody, simple enough to take first place in the fancy of a nation that had always liked its songs simple. But it had a certain sincerity, too, and no taint of the vulgarity of tune and rhythm that foredooms so many popular songs to oblivion after their novelty fades.

No one else was ever able to sing it quite as Deirdre did. It had been identified with her so closely that though for a while after her accident singers tried to make it a memorial for her, they failed so conspicuously to give it her unmistakable flair that the song died from their sheer inability to sing it. No one ever hummed the tune without thinking of her and the pleasant, nostalgic sadness of something lovely and lost.

But it was not a sad song now. If anyone had doubted whose brain and ego motivated this shining metal suppleness, they could doubt no longer. For the voice was Deirdre, and the song. And the lovely, poised grace of her mannerisms that made up recognition as certainly as sight of a familiar face.

She had not finished the first line of her song before the audience knew her.

And they did not let her finish. The accolade of their interruption was a tribute more eloquent than polite waiting could ever have been. First a breath of incredulity rippled over the theater, and a long, sighing gasp that reminded Harris irrelevantly as he listened of the gasp which still goes up from matinee audiences at the first glimpse of the fabulous Valentino, so many generations dead. But this gasp did not sigh itself away and vanish. Tremendous tension lay behind it, and the rising tide of excitement rippled up in little murmurs and spatterings of applause that ran together into one overwhelming roar. It shook the theater. The television screen trembled and blurred a little to the volume of that transmitted applause.

Silenced before it, Deirdre stood gesturing on the stage, bowing and bowing as the noise rolled up about her, shaking perceptibly with the triumph of her own emotion.

Harris had an intolerable feeling that she was smiling radiantly and that the tears were pouring down her cheeks. He even thought, just as Maltzer leaned forward to switch off the screen, that she was blowing kisses over the audience in the time-honored gesture of the grateful actress, her golden arms shining as she scattered kisses abroad from the featureless helmet, the face that had no mouth.

"Well?" Harris said, not without triumph.

Maltzer shook his head jerkily, the glasses unsteady on his nose so that the blurred eyes behind them seemed to shift.

"Of course they applauded, you fool," he said in a savage voice. "I might have known they would under this setup. It doesn't prove anything. Oh, she was smart to surprise them—I admit that. But they were applauding themselves as much as her. Excitement, gratitude for letting them in on a historic performance, mass hysteria—*you* know. It's from now on the test will come, and this hasn't helped any to prepare her for it. Morbid curiosity when the news gets out—people laughing when she forgets she isn't human. And they will, you know. There are always those who will. And the novelty wearing off. The slow draining away of humanity for lack of contact with any human stimuli anymore—"

Harris remembered suddenly and reluctantly the moment that afternoon which he had shunted aside mentally, to consider later. The sense of something unfamiliar beneath the surface of Deirdre's speech. Was Maltzer right? Was the drainage already at work? Or was there something deeper than this obvious answer to the question? Certainly she had been through experiences too terrible for ordinary people to comprehend. Scars might still remain. Or, with her body, had she put on a strange, metallic something of the mind, that spoke to no sense which human minds could answer?

For a few minutes neither of them spoke. Then Maltzer rose abruptly and stood looking down at Harris with an abstract scowl.

"I wish you'd go now," he said.

Harris glanced up at him, startled. Maltzer began to pace again, his steps quick and uneven. Over his shoulder he said,

"I've made up my mind, Harris. I've got to put a stop to this."

Harris rose. "Listen," he said. "Tell me one thing. What makes you so certain you're right? Can you deny that most of it's speculation—hearsay evidence? Remember, I talked to Deirdre, and she was just as sure as you are in the opposite direction. Have you any real reason for what you think?"

Maltzer took his glasses off and rubbed his nose carefully, taking a long time about it. He seemed reluctant to answer. But when he did, at last, there was a confidence in his voice Harris had not expected.

"I have a reason," he said. "But you won't believe it. Nobody would."
"Try me."

Maltzer shook his head. "Nobody *could* believe it. No two people were ever in quite the same relationship before as Deirdre and I have been. I helped her come back out of complete—oblivion. I knew her before she had voice or hearing. She was only a frantic mind when I first made contact with her, half insane with all that had happened and fear of what would happen next. In a very literal sense she was reborn out of that condition, and I had to guide her through every step of the way. I came to know her thoughts before she thought them. And once you've been that close to another mind, you don't lose the contact easily." He put the glasses back on and looked blurrily at Harris through the heavy lenses. "Deirdre is worried," he said. "I know it. You won't believe me, but I can—well, sense it. I tell you, I've been too close to her very mind itself to make any mistake. You don't see it, maybe. Maybe even she doesn't know it yet. But the worry's there. When I'm with her, I feel it. And I don't want it to come any nearer the surface of her mind than it's come already. I'm going to put a stop to this before it's too late."

Harris had no comment for that. It was too entirely outside his own experience. He said nothing for a moment. Then he asked simply, "How?"

"I'm not sure yet. I've got to decide before she comes back. And I want to see her alone."

"I think you're wrong," Harris told him quietly. "I think you're imagining things. I don't think you *can* stop her."

Maltzer gave him a slanted glance. "I can stop her," he said, in a curious voice. He went on quickly, "She has enough already—she's nearly human. She can live normally as other people live, without going back on the screen. Maybe this taste of it will be enough. I've got to convince her it is. If she retires now, she'll never guess how cruel her own audiences could be, and maybe that deep sense of— distress, uneasiness, whatever it is—won't come to the surface. It mustn't. She's too fragile to stand that." He slapped his hands together sharply. "I've got to stop her. For her own sake, I've got to do it!" He swung round again to face Harris. "Will you go now?"

Never in his life had Harris wanted less to leave a place. Briefly he thought of saying simply, "No I won't." But he had to admit in his own mind that Maltzer was at least partly right. This was a matter between Deirdre and her creator, the culmination, perhaps, of that year's long intimacy so like marriage that this final trial for supremacy was a need he recognized.

He would not, he thought, forbid the showdown if he could. Perhaps the whole year had been building up to this one moment between them in which one or the other must prove himself victor. Neither was very stable just now, after the long strain of the year past. It might very well be that the mental salvation of one or both hinged upon the outcome of the clash. But because each was so strongly motivated not by selfish concern but by solicitude for the other in this strange combat, Harris knew he must leave them to settle the thing alone.

He was in the street and hailing a taxi before the full significance of something Maltzer had said came to him. "*I can stop her,*" he had declared, with an odd inflection in his voice.

Suddenly Harris felt cold. Maltzer had made her—of course he could stop her if he chose. Was there some key in that supple golden body that could immobilize it at its maker's will? Could she be imprisoned in the cage of her own body? No body before in all history, he thought, could have been designed more truly to be a prison for its mind than Deirdre's, if Maltzer chose to turn the key that locked her in. There must be many ways to do it. He could simply withhold whatever source of nourishment kept her brain alive, if that were the way he chose.

But Harris could not believe he would do it. The man wasn't insane. He would not defeat his own purpose. His determination rose from his solicitude for Deirdre; he would not even in the last extremity try to save her by imprisoning her in the jail of her own skull.

For a moment Harris hesitated on the curb, almost turning back. But what could he do? Even granting that Maltzer would resort to such tactics, self-defeating in their very nature, how could any man on earth prevent him if he did it subtly enough? But he never would. Harris knew he never would. He got into his cab slowly, frowning. He would see them both tomorrow.

He did not. Harris was swamped with excited calls about yesterday's performance, but the message he was awaiting did not come. The day went by very slowly. Toward evening he surrendered and called Maltzer's apartment.

It was Deirdre's face that answered, and for once he saw no remembered features superimposed upon the blankness of her helmet. Masked and faceless, she looked at him inscrutably.

"Is everything all right?" he asked, a little uncomfortable.

"Yes, of course," she said, and her voice was a bit metallic for the first time, as if she were thinking so deeply of some other matter that she did not trouble to pitch it properly. "I had a long talk with Maltzer last night, if that's what you mean. You know what he wants. But nothing's been decided yet."

Harris felt oddly rebuffed by the sudden realization of the metal of her. It was impossible to read anything from face or voice. Each had its mask.

"What are you going to do?" he asked.

"Exactly as I'd planned," she told him, without inflection.

Harris floundered a little. Then, with an effort at practicality, he said, "Do you want me to go to work on booking, then?"

She shook the delicately modeled skull. "Not yet. You saw the reviews today, of course. They—*did* like me." It was an understatement, and for the first time a note of warmth sounded in her voice. But the preoccupation was still there, too. "I'd already planned to make them wait awhile after my first performance," she went on. "A couple of weeks, anyhow. You remember that little farm of mine in Jersey, John? I'm going over today. I won't see anyone except the servants there. Not even Maltzer. Not even you. I've got a lot to think about. Maltzer has agreed to let everything go until we've both thought things over. He's taking a rest, too. I'll see you the moment I get back, John. Is that all right?"

She blanked out almost before he had time to nod and while the beginning of a stammered argument was still on his lips. He sat there staring at the screen.

The two weeks that went by before Maltzer called him again were the longest Harris had ever spent. He thought of many things in the interval. He believed he could sense in that last talk with Deirdre something of the inner unrest that Maltzer had spoken of—more an abstraction than a distress, but some thought had occupied her mind which she would not—or was it that she could not?—share even with her closest confidants. He even wondered whether, if her mind was as delicately poised as Maltzer feared, one would ever know whether or not it had slipped. There was so little evidence one way or the other in the unchanging outward form of her.

Most of all he wondered what two weeks in a new environment would do to her untried body and newly patterned brain. If Maltzer were right, then there might be some perceptible—drainage—by the time they met again. He tried not to think of that.

Maltzer televised him on the morning set for her return. He looked very bad. The rest must have been no rest at all. His face was almost a skull now, and the blurred eyes behind their lenses burned. But he seemed curiously at peace, in spite of his appearance. Harris thought he had reached some decision, but whatever it was had not stopped his hands from shaking or the nervous tic that drew his face sidewise into a grimace at intervals.

"Come over," he said briefly, without preamble. "She'll be here in half an hour." And he blanked out without waiting for an answer.

When Harris arrived, Maltzer was standing by the window looking down and steadying his trembling hands on the sill.

"I can't stop her," he said in a monotone, and again without preamble. Harris had the impression that for two weeks his thoughts must have run over and over the same track, until any spoken word was simply a vocal interlude in the circling of his mind. "I couldn't do it. I even tried threats, but she knew I didn't mean them. There's only one way out, Harris." He glanced up briefly, hollow-eyed behind the lenses. "Never mind. I'll tell you later."

"Did you explain everything to her that you did to me?"

"Nearly all. I even taxed her with that . . . that sense of distress I *know* she feels. She denied it. She was lying. We both knew. It was worse after the performance than before. When I saw her that night, I tell you I *knew*—she senses something wrong, but she won't admit it." He shrugged. "Well—"

Faintly in the silence they heard the humming of the elevator descending from the helicopter platform on the roof. Both men turned to the door.

She had not changed at all. Foolishly, Harris was a little surprised. Then he caught himself and remembered that she would never change—never, until she died. He himself might grow white-haired and senile; she would move before him then as she moved now, supple, golden, enigmatic.

Still, he thought she caught her breath a little when she saw Maltzer and the depths of his swift degeneration. She had no breath to catch, but her voice was shaken as she greeted them.

"I'm glad you're both here," she said, a slight hesitation in her speech. "It's a wonderful day outside. Jersey was glorious. I'd forgotten how lovely it is in summer. Was the sanitarium any good, Maltzer?"

He jerked his head irritably and did not answer. She went on talking in a light voice, skimming the surface, saying nothing important.

This time Harris saw her as he supposed her audiences would, eventually, when the surprise had worn off and the image of the living

Deirdre faded from memory. She was all metal now, the Deirdre they would know from today on. And she was not less lovely. She was not even less human—yet. Her motion was a miracle of flexible grace, a pouring of suppleness along every limb. (From now on, Harris realized suddenly, it was her body and not her face that would have mobility to express emotion; she must act with her limbs and her lithe, robed torso.)

But there was something wrong. Harris sensed it almost tangibly in her inflections, her elusiveness, the way she fenced with words. This was what Maltzer had meant, this was what Harris himself had felt just before she left for the country. Only now it was strong—certain. Between them and the old Deirdre whose voice still spoke to them a veil of—detachment—had been drawn. Behind it she was in distress. Somehow, somewhere, she had made some discovery that affected her profoundly. And Harris was terribly afraid that he knew what the discovery must be. Maltzer was right.

He was still leaning against the window, staring out unseeingly over the vast panorama of New York, webbed with traffic bridges, winking with sunlit glass, its vertiginous distances plunging downward into the blue shadows of earth-level. He said now, breaking into the light-voiced chatter, "Are you all right, Deirdre?"

She laughed. It was lovely laughter. She moved lithely across the room, sunlight glinting on her musical mailed robe, and stooped to a cigarette box on a table. Her fingers were deft.

"Have one?" she said, and carried the box to Maltzer. He let her put the brown cylinder between his lips and hold a light to it, but he did not seem to be noticing what he did. She replaced the box and then crossed to a mirror on the far wall and began experimenting with a series of gliding ripples that wove patterns of pale gold in the glass. "Of course I'm all right," she said.

"You're lying."

Deirdre did not turn. She was watching him in the mirror, but the ripple of her motion went on slowly, languorously, undisturbed.

"No," she told them both.

Maltzer drew deeply on his cigarette. Then with a hard pull he unsealed the window and tossed the smoking stub far out over the gulfs below. He said,

"You can't deceive me, Deirdre." His voice, suddenly, was quite calm. "I created you, my dear. I know. I've sensed that uneasiness in you growing and growing for a long while now. It's much stronger today than it was two weeks ago. Something happened to you in the country. I don't know what it was, but you've changed. Will you admit to yourself what it is, Deirdre? Have you realized yet that you must not go back on the screen?"

"Why, no," said Deirdre, still not looking at him except obliquely, in the glass. Her gestures were slower now, weaving lazy patterns in the air. "No, I haven't changed my mind."

She was all metal—outwardly. She was taking unfair advantage of her own metalhood. She had withdrawn far within, behind the mask of her voice and her facelessness. Even her body, whose involuntary motions might have betrayed what she was feeling, in the only way she could be subject to betrayal now, she was putting through ritual motions that disguised it completely. As long as these looping, weaving patterns occupied her, no one had any way of guessing even from her motion what went on in the hidden brain inside her helmet.

Harris was struck suddenly and for the first time with the completeness of her withdrawal. When he had seen her last in this apartment, she had been wholly Deirdre, not masked at all, overflowing the metal with the warmth and ardor of the woman he had known so well. Since then—since the performance on the stage—he had not seen the familiar Deirdre again. Passionately, he wondered why. Had she begun to suspect even in her moment of triumph what a fickle master an audience could be? Had she caught, perhaps, the sound of whispers and laughter among some small portion of her watchers, though the great majority praised her?

Or was Maltzer right? Perhaps Harris's first interview with her had been the last bright burning of the lost Deirdre, animated by excitement and the pleasure of meeting after so long a time, animation summoned up in a last strong effort to convince him. Now she was gone, but whether in self-protection against the possible cruelties of human beings, or whether in withdrawal to metalhood, he could not guess. Humanity might be draining out of her fast, and the brassy taint of metal permeating the brain it housed.

Maltzer laid his trembling hand on the edge of the opened window and looked out. He said in a deepened voice, the querulous note gone for the first time:

"I've made a terrible mistake, Deirdre. I've done you irreparable harm." He paused a moment, but Deirdre said nothing. Harris dared not speak. In a moment Maltzer went on. "I've made you vulnerable, and given you no weapons to fight your enemies with. And the human race is your enemy, my dear, whether you admit it now or later. I think you know that. I think it's why you're so silent. I think you must have suspected it on the stage two weeks ago and verified it in Jersey while you were gone. They're going to hate you, after a while, because you are still beautiful, and they're going to persecute you because you are different—and helpless. Once the novelty wears off, my dear, your audience will be simply a mob."

He was not looking at her. He had bent forward a little, looking out the window and down. His hair stirred in the wind that blew very strongly up this high and whined thinly around the open edge of the glass.

"I meant what I did for you," he said, "to be for everyone who meets with accidents that might have ruined them. I should have known my gift would mean worse ruin than any mutilation could be. I know now that there's only one legitimate way a human being can create life. When he tries another way, as I did, he has a lesson to learn. Remember the lesson of the student Frankenstein? He learned, too. In a way, he was lucky—the way he learned. He didn't have to watch what happened afterward. Maybe he wouldn't have had the courage—I know I haven't."

Harris found himself standing without remembering that he rose. He knew suddenly what was about to happen. He understood Maltzer's air of resolution, his new, unnatural calm. He knew, even, why Maltzer had asked him here today, so that Deirdre might not be left alone. For he remembered that Frankenstein, too, had paid with his life for the unlawful creation of life.

Maltzer was leaning head and shoulders from the window now, looking down with almost hypnotized fascination. His voice came back to them remotely in the breeze, as if a barrier already lay between them.

Deirdre had not moved. Her expressionless mask, in the mirror, watched him calmly. She *must* have understood. Yet she gave no sign, except that the weaving of her arms had almost stopped now, she moved so slowly. Like a dance seen in a nightmare, under water.

It was impossible, of course, for her to express any emotion. The fact that her face showed none now should not, in fairness, be held against her. But she watched so wholly without feeling— Neither of them moved toward the window. A false step, now, might send him over. They were quiet, listening to his voice.

"We who bring life into the world unlawfully," said Maltzer, almost thoughtfully, "must make room for it by withdrawing our own. That seems to be an inflexible rule. It works automatically. The thing we create makes living unbearable. No, it's nothing you can help, my dear.

I've asked you to do something I created you incapable of doing. I made you to perform a function, and I've been asking you to forego the one thing you were made to do. I believe that if you do it, it will destroy you, but the whole guilt is mine, not yours. I'm not even asking you to give up the screen, anymore. I know you can't, and live. But I can't live and watch you. I put all my skill and all my love in one final masterpiece, and I can't bear to watch it destroyed. I can't live and watch you do only what I made you to do and ruin yourself because you must do it.

"But before I go, I have to make sure you understand." He leaned a little farther, looking down, and his voice grew more remote as the glass came between them. He was saying almost unbearable things now, but very distantly, in a cool, passionless tone filtered through wind and glass, and with the distant humming of the city mingled with it, so that the words were curiously robbed of poignancy. "I can be a coward," he said, "and escape the consequences of what I've done, but I can't go and leave you—not understanding. It would be even worse than the thought of your failure, to think of you bewildered and confused when the mob turns on you. What I'm telling you, my dear, won't be any real news—I think you sense it already, though you may not admit it to yourself. We've been too close to lie to each other, Deirdre—I know when you aren't telling the truth. I know the distress that's been growing in your mind. You are not wholly human, my dear. I think you know that. In so many ways, in spite of all I could do, you must always be less than human. You've lost the senses of perception that kept you in touch with humanity. Sight and hearing are all that remain, and sight, as I've said before, was the last and coldest of the senses to develop. And you're so delicately poised on a sort of thin edge of reason. You're only a clear, glowing mind animating a metal body, like a candle flame in a glass. And as precariously vulnerable to the wind."

He paused. "Try not to let them ruin you completely," he said after a while. "When they turn against you, when they find out you're more helpless than they—I wish I could have made you stronger, Deirdre. But I couldn't. I had too much skill for your good and mine, but not quite enough skill for that."

He was silent again, briefly, looking down. He was balanced precariously now, more than halfway over the sill and supported only by one hand on the glass. Harris watched with an agonized uncertainty, not sure whether a sudden leap might catch him in time or send him over. Deirdre was still weaving her golden patterns, slowly and unchangingly, watching the mirror and its reflection, her face and masked eyes enigmatic.

"I wish one thing, though," Maltzer said in his remote voice. "I wish—before I finish—that you'd tell me the truth, Deirdre. I'd be happier if I were sure I'd—reached you. Do you understand what I've said? Do you believe me? Because if you don't, then I know you're lost beyond all hope. If you'll admit your own doubt—and I know you do doubt—I can think there may be a chance for you after all. Were you lying to me, Deirdre? Do you know how . . . how wrong I've made you?"

There was silence. Then very softly, a breath of sound, Deirdre answered. The voice seemed to hang in midair, because she had no lips to move and localize it for the imagination.

"Will you listen, Maltzer?" she asked.

"I'll wait," he said. "Go on. Yes or no?"

Slowly she let her arms drop to her sides. Very smoothly and quietly she turned from the mirror and faced him. She swayed a little, making her metal robe ring.

"I'll answer you," she said. "But I don't think I'll answer that. Not with yes or no, anyhow. I'm going to walk a little, Maltzer. I have something to tell you, and I can't talk standing still. Will you let me move about without—going over?"

He nodded distantly. "You can't interfere from that distance," he said. "But keep the distance. What do you want to say?"

She began to pace a little way up and down her end of the room, moving with liquid ease. The table with the cigarette box was in her way, and she pushed it aside carefully, watching Maltzer and making no swift motions to startle him.

"I'm not—well, subhuman," she said, a faint note of indignation in her voice. "I'll prove it in a minute, but I want to say something else first. You must promise to wait and listen. There's a flaw in your argument, and I resent it. I'm not a Frankenstein monster made out of dead flesh. I'm myself—alive. You didn't create my life, you only preserved it. I'm not a robot, with compulsions built into me that I have to obey. I'm free-willed and independent, and, Maltzer—I'm human."

Harris had relaxed a little. She knew what she was doing. He had no idea what she planned, but he was willing to wait now. She was not the indifferent automaton he had thought. He watched her come to the table again, in a lap of her pacing, and stoop over it, her eyeless mask turned to Maltzer to make sure a variation of her movement did not startle him.

"I'm human," she repeated, her voice humming faintly and very sweetly. "Do you think I'm not?" she asked, straightening and facing them both. And then suddenly, almost overwhelmingly, the warmth and the old ardent charm were radiant all around her. She was robot no longer, enigmatic no longer. Harris could see as clearly as in their first meeting the remembered flesh still gracious and beautiful as her voice evoked his memory. She stood swaying a little, as she had always swayed, her head on one side, and she was chuckling at them both. It was such a soft and lovely sound, so warmly familiar.

"Of course I'm myself," she told them, and as the words sounded in their ears neither of them could doubt it. There was hypnosis in her voice. She turned away and began to pace again, and so powerful was the human personality which she had called up about her that it beat out at them in deep pulses, as if her body were a furnace to send out those comforting waves of warmth. "I have handicaps, I know," she said. "But my audiences will never know. I won't let them know. I think you'll believe me, both of you, when I say I could play Juliet just as I am now, with a cast of ordinary people, and make the world accept it. Do you think I could, John? Maltzer, don't you believe I could?"

She paused at the far end of her pacing path and turned to face them, and they both stared at her without speaking. To Harris she was the Deirdre he had always known, pale gold, exquisitely graceful in remembered postures, the inner radiance of her shining through metal as brilliantly as it had ever shone through flesh. He did not wonder, now, if it were real. Later he would think again that it might be only a disguise, something like a garment she had put off with her lost body, to wear again only when she chose. Now the spell of her compelling charm was too strong for wonder. He watched, convinced for the moment that she was all she seemed to be. She could play Juliet if she said she could. She could sway a whole audience as easily as she swayed him. Indeed, there was something about her just now more convincingly human than anything he had noticed before. He realized that in a split second of awareness before he saw what it was.

She was looking at Maltzer. He, too, watched, spellbound in spite of himself, not dissenting. She glanced from one to the other. Then she put back her head and laughter came welling and choking from her in a great, full-throated tide. She shook in the strength of it. Harris could almost see her round throat pulsing with the sweet low-pitched waves of laughter that were shaking her. Honest mirth, with a little derision in it.

Then she lifted one arm and tossed her cigarette into the empty fireplace.

Harris choked, and his mind went blank for one moment of blind denial. He had not sat here watching a robot smoke and accepting it as normal. He could not! And yet he had. That had been the final touch of conviction which swayed his hypnotized mind into accepting her humanity. And she had done it so deftly, so naturally, wearing her radiant humanity with such rightness, that his watching mind had not even questioned what she did.

He glanced at Maltzer. The man was still halfway over the window ledge, but through the opening of the window he, too, was staring in stupefied disbelief, and Harris knew they had shared the same delusion.

Deirdre was still shaking a little with laughter. "Well," she demanded, the rich chuckling making her voice quiver, "am I all robot, after all?"

Harris opened his mouth to speak, but he did not utter a word. This was not his show. The byplay lay wholly between Deirdre and Maltzer; he must not interfere. He turned his head to the window and waited.

And Maltzer for a moment seemed shaken in his conviction.

"You . . . you *are* an actress," he admitted slowly. "But I . . . I'm not convinced I'm wrong. I think—" He paused. The querulous note was in his voice again, and he seemed racked once more by the old doubts and dismay. Then Harris saw him stiffen. He saw the resolution come back, and understood why it had come. Maltzer had gone too far already upon the cold and lonely path he had chosen to turn back, even for stronger evidence than this. He had reached his conclusions only after mental turmoil too terrible to face again. Safety and peace lay in the course he had steeled himself to follow. He was too tired, too exhausted by months of conflict, to retrace his path and begin all over. Harris could see him groping for a way out, and in a moment he saw him find it.

"That was a trick," he said hollowly. "Maybe you could play it on a larger audience, too. Maybe you have more tricks to use. I might be wrong. But, Deirdre"—his voice grew urgent—"you haven't answered the one thing I've got to know. You can't answer it. You *do* feel— dismay. You've learned your own inadequacy, however well you can hide it from us—even from us. I *know*. Can you deny that, Deirdre?"

She was not laughing now. She let her arms fall, and the flexible golden body seemed to droop a little all over, as if the brain that a moment before had been sending out strong, sure waves of confidence had slackened its power, and the intangible muscles of her limbs slackened with it. Some of the glowing humanity began to fade. It receded within her and was gone, as if the fire in the furnace of her body were sinking and cooling.

"Maltzer," she said uncertainly, "I can't answer that—yet. I can't—"

And then, while they waited in anxiety for her to finish the sentence, she *blazed*. She ceased to be a figure in stasis—she *blazed*.

It was something no eyes could watch and translate into terms the brain could follow; her motion was too swift. Maltzer in the window was a whole long room-length away. He had thought himself safe at such a distance, knowing no normal human being could reach him before he moved. But Deirdre was neither normal nor human.

In the same instant she stood drooping by the mirror, she was simultaneously at Maltzer's side. Her motion negated time and destroyed space. And as a glowing cigarette tip in the dark describes closed circles before the eyes when the holder moves it swiftly, so Deirdre blazed in one continuous flash of golden motion across the room.

But curiously, she was not blurred. Harris, watching, felt his mind go blank again, but less in surprise than because no normal eyes and brain could perceive what it was he looked at.

(In that moment of intolerable suspense his complex human brain paused suddenly, annihilating time in its own way, and withdrew to a cool corner of its own to analyze in a flashing second what it was he had just seen. The brain could do it timelessly; words are slow. But he knew he had watched a sort of tesseract of human motion, a parable of fourth-dimensional activity. A one-dimensional point, moved through space, creates a two-dimensional line, which in motion creates a three-dimensional cube. Theoretically the cube, in motion, would produce a fourth-dimensional figure. No human creature had ever seen a figure of three dimensions moved through space and time before— until this moment. She had not blurred; every motion she made was distinct, but not like moving figures on a strip of film. Not like anything that those who use our language had ever seen before, or created words to express. The mind saw, but without perceiving. Neither words nor thoughts could resolve what happened into terms for human brains. And perhaps she had not actually and literally moved through the fourth dimension. Perhaps—since Harris was able to see her—it had been almost and not quite that unimaginable thing. But it was close enough.)

While to the slow mind's eye she was still standing at the far end of the room, she was already at Maltzer's side, her long, flexible fingers gentle but very firm upon his arms. She waited—

The room shimmered. There was sudden violent heat beating upon Harris's face. Then the air steadied again and Deirdre was saying softly, in a mournful whisper:

"I'm sorry—I had to do it. I'm sorry—I didn't mean you to know—"

Time caught up with Harris. He saw it overtake Maltzer too, saw the man jerk convulsively away from the grasping hands, in a ludicrously futile effort to forestall what had already happened. Even thought was slow, compared with Deirdre's swiftness.

The sharp outward jerk was strong. It was strong enough to break the grasp of human hands and catapult Maltzer out and down into the swimming gulfs of New York. The mind leaped ahead to a logical conclusion and saw him twisting and turning and diminishing with dreadful rapidity to a tiny point of darkness that dropped away through sunlight toward the shadows near the earth. The mind even conjured up a shrill, thin cry that plummeted away with the falling body and hung behind it in the shaken air.

But the mind was reckoning on human factors.

Very gently and smoothly, Deirdre lifted Maltzer from the windowsill and with effortless ease carried him well back into the safety of the room. She set him down before a sofa and her golden fingers unwrapped themselves from his arms slowly, so that he could regain control of his own body before she released him.

He sank to the sofa without a word. Nobody spoke for an unmeasurable length of time. Harris could not. Deirdre waited patiently. It was Maltzer who regained speech first, and it came back on the old track, as if his mind had not yet relinquished the rut it had worn so deep.

"All right," he said breathlessly. "All right, you can stop me this time. But I know, you see. I know! You can't hide your feeling from me, Deirdre. I know the trouble you feel. And next time—next time I won't wait to talk!"

Deirdre made the sound of a sigh. She had no lungs to expel the breath she was imitating, but it was hard to realize that. It was hard to understand why she was not panting heavily from the terrible exertion of the past minutes; the mind knew why but could not accept the reason. She was still too human.

"You still don't see," she said. "Think, Maltzer, think!"

There was a hassock beside the sofa. She sank upon it gracefully, clasping her robed knees. Her head tilted back to watch Maltzer's face. She saw only stunned stupidity on it now; he had passed through too much emotional storm to think at all.

"All right," she told him. "Listen—I'll admit it. You're right. I *am* unhappy. I do know what you said was true—but not for the reason you think. Humanity and I are far apart, and drawing farther. The gap will be hard to bridge. Do you hear me, Maltzer?"

Harris saw the tremendous effort that went into Maltzer's wakening. He saw the man pull his mind back into focus and sit up on the sofa with weary stiffness.

"You . . . you do admit it, then?" he asked in a bewildered voice.

Deirdre shook her head sharply.

"Do you still think of me as delicate?" she demanded. "Do you know I carried you here at arm's length halfway across the room? Do you realize you weigh *nothing* to me? I could"—she glanced around the room and gestured with sudden, rather appalling violence—"tear this building down," she said quietly. "I could tear my way through these walls, I think. I've found no limit yet to the strength I can put forth if I try." She held up her golden hands and looked at them. "The metal would break, perhaps," she said reflectively, "but then, I have no feeling—"

Maltzer gasped, *"Deirdre—"*

She looked up with what must have been a smile. It sounded clearly in her voice. "Oh, I won't. I wouldn't have to do it with my hands, if I wanted. Look—listen!"

She put her head back and a deep, vibrating hum gathered and grew in what one still thought of as her throat. It deepened swiftly and the ears began to ring. It was deeper, and the furniture vibrated. The walls began almost imperceptibly to shake. The room was full and bursting with a sound that shook every atom upon its neighbor with a terrible, disrupting force.

The sound ceased. The humming died. Then Deirdre laughed and made another and quite differently pitched sound. It seemed to reach out like an arm in one straight direction—toward the window. The opened panel shook. Deirdre intensified her hum, and slowly, with imperceptible jolts that merged into smoothness, the window jarred itself shut.

"You see?" Deirdre said. "You see?"

But still Maltzer could only stare. Harris was staring too, his mind beginning slowly to accept what she implied. Both were too stunned to leap ahead to any conclusions yet.

Deirdre rose impatiently and began to pace again, in a ringing of metal robe and a twinkling of reflected lights. She was pantherlike in her suppleness. They could see the power behind that lithe motion now; they no longer thought of her as helpless, but they were far still from grasping the truth.

"You were wrong about me, Maltzer," she said with an effort at patience in her voice. "But you were right, too, in a way you didn't guess. I'm not afraid of humanity. I haven't anything to fear from them. Why"—her voice took on a tinge of contempt—"already I've set a fashion in women's clothing. By next week you won't see a woman on the street without a mask like mine, and every dress that isn't cut like a chlamys will be out of style. I'm not afraid of humanity! I won't lose touch with them unless I want to. I've learned a lot—I've learned too much already."

Her voice faded for a moment, and Harris had a quick and appalling vision of her experimenting in the solitude of her farm, testing the range of her voice, testing her eyesight—could she see microscopically and telescopically?—and was her hearing as abnormally flexible as her voice?

"You were afraid I had lost feeling and scent and taste," she went on, still pacing with that powerful, tigerish tread. "Hearing and sight would not be enough, you think? But why do you think sight is the last of the senses? It may be the latest, Maltzer—Harris—*but why do you think it's the last?*"

She may not have whispered that. Perhaps it was only their hearing that made it seem thin and distant, as the brain contracted and would not let the thought come through in its stunning entirety.

"No," Deirdre said, "I haven't lost contact with the human race. I never will, unless I want to. It's too easy . . . too easy."

She was watching her shining feet as she paced, and her masked face was averted. Sorrow sounded in her soft voice now.

"I didn't mean to let you know," she said. "I never would have, if this hadn't happened. But I couldn't let you go believing you'd failed. You made a perfect machine, Maltzer. More perfect than you knew."

"But, Deirdre—," breathed Maltzer, his eyes fascinated and still incredulous upon her, "but, Deirdre, if we did succeed—what's wrong?

I can feel it now—I've felt it all along. You're so unhappy—you still are. Why, Deirdre?"

She lifted her head and looked at him, eyelessly, but with a piercing stare.

"Why are you so sure of that?" she asked gently.

"You think I could be mistaken, knowing you as I do? But I'm not Frankenstein . . . you say my creation's flawless. Then what—"

"Could you ever duplicate this body?" she asked.

Maltzer glanced down at his shaking hands. "I don't know. I doubt it. I—"

"Could anyone else?"

He was silent. Deirdre answered for him. "I don't believe anyone could. I think I was an accident. A sort of mutation halfway between flesh and metal. Something accidental and . . . and unnatural, turning off on a wrong course of evolution that never reaches a dead end. Another brain in a body like this might die or go mad, as you thought I would. The synapses are too delicate. You were—call it lucky—with me. From what I know now, I don't think a . . . a baroque like me could happen again." She paused a moment. "What you did was kindle the fire for the Phoenix, in a way. And the Phoenix rises perfect and renewed from its own ashes. Do you remember why it had to reproduce itself that way?"

Maltzer shook his head.

"I'll tell you," she said. "It was because there was only one Phoenix. Only one in the whole world."

They looked at each other in silence. Then Deirdre shrugged a little.

"He always came out of the fire perfect, of course. I'm not weak, Maltzer. You needn't let that thought bother you anymore. I'm not vulnerable and helpless. I'm not subhuman." She laughed dryly. "I suppose," she said, "that I'm—superhuman."

"But—not happy."

"I'm afraid. It isn't unhappiness, Maltzer—it's fear. I don't want to draw so far away from the human race. I wish I needn't. That's why I'm going back on the stage—to keep in touch with them while I can. But I wish there could be others like me. I'm . . . I'm lonely, Maltzer."

Silence again. Then Maltzer said, in a voice as distant as when he had spoken to them through glass, over gulfs as deep as oblivion: "Then I am Frankenstein, after all."

"Perhaps you are," Deirdre said very softly. "I don't know. Perhaps you are."

She turned away and moved smoothly, powerfully, down the room to the window. Now that Harris knew, he could almost hear the sheer power purring along her limbs as she walked. She leaned the golden forehead against the glass—it clinked faintly, with a musical sound—and looked down into the depths Maltzer had hung above. Her voice was reflective as she looked into those dizzy spaces which had offered oblivion to her creator.

"There's one limit I can think of," she said, almost inaudibly. "Only one. My brain will wear out in another forty years or so. Between now and then I'll learn . . . I'll change . . . I'll know more than I can guess today. I'll change— That's frightening. I don't like to think about that." She laid a curved golden hand on the latch and pushed the window open a little, very easily. Wind whined around its edge. "I could put a stop to it now, if I wanted," she said. "If I wanted. But I can't, really. There's so much still untried. My brain's human, and no human brain could leave such possibilities untested. I wonder, though . . . I do wonder—"

Her voice was soft and familiar in Harris's ears, the voice Deirdre had spoken and sung with, sweetly enough to enchant a world. But as preoccupation came over her a certain flatness crept into the sound. When she was not listening to her own voice, it did not keep quite to the pitch of trueness. It sounded as if she spoke in a room of brass, and echoes from the walls resounded in the tones that spoke there.

"I wonder," she repeated, the distant taint of metal already in her voice.

That Only a Mother

JUDITH MERRIL

Margaret reached over to the other side of the bed where Hank should have been. Her hand patted the empty pillow, and then she came altogether awake, wondering that the old habit should remain after so many months. She tried to curl up, cat-style, to hoard her own warmth, found she couldn't do it anymore, and climbed out of bed with a pleased awareness of her increasingly clumsy bulkiness.

Morning motions were automatic. On the way through the kitchenette, she pressed the button that would start breakfast cooking—the doctor had said to eat as much breakfast as she could—and tore the paper out of the facsimile machine. She folded the long sheet carefully to the "National News" section, and propped it on the bathroom shelf to scan while she brushed her teeth.

No accidents. No direct hits. At least none that had been officially released for publication. *Now, Maggie, don't get started on that. No accidents. No hits. Take the nice newspaper's word for it.*

The three clear chimes from the kitchen announced that breakfast was ready. She set a bright napkin and cheerful colored dishes on the table in a futile attempt to appeal to a faulty morning appetite. Then, when there was nothing more to prepare, she went for the mail, allowing herself the full pleasure of prolonged anticipation, because today there would *surely* be a letter.

There was. There were. Two bills and a worried note from her mother: "Darling. Why didn't you write and tell me sooner? I'm thrilled, of course, but, well, one hates to mention these things, but are you *certain* the doctor was right? Hank's been around all that uranium or thorium or whatever it is all these years, and I know you say he's a designer, not a technician, and he doesn't get near anything that might be dangerous, but you know he used to, back at Oak Ridge. Don't you think . . . well, of course, I'm just being a foolish old woman, and I don't want you to get upset. You know much more about it than I do, and I'm sure your doctor was right. He *should* know . . ."

Margaret made a face over the excellent coffee, and caught herself refolding the paper to the medical news.

Stop it, Maggie, stop it! The radiologist said Hank's job couldn't have exposed him. And the bombed area we drove past . . . No, no. Stop it, now! Read the social notes or the recipes, Maggie girl.

A well-known geneticist, in the medical news, said that it was possible to tell with absolute certainty, at five months, whether the child would be normal, or at least whether the mutation was likely to produce anything freakish. The worst cases, at any rate, could be prevented. Minor mutations, of course, displacements in facial features, or changes in brain structure could not be detected. And there had been some cases recently, of normal embryos with atrophied limbs that did not develop beyond the seventh or eighth month. But, the doctor concluded cheerfully, the *worst* cases could now be predicted and prevented.

"Predicted and prevented." We predicted it, didn't we? Hank and the others, they predicted it. But we didn't prevent it. We could have stopped it in '46 and '47. Now . . .

Margaret decided against the breakfast. Coffee had been enough for her in the morning for ten years; it would have to do for today. She buttoned herself into interminable folds of material that, the salesgirl had assured her, was the *only* comfortable thing to wear during the last few months. With a surge of pure pleasure, the letter and newspaper forgotten, she realized she was on the next to the last button. It wouldn't be long now.

The city in the early morning had always been a special kind of excitement for her. Last night it had rained, and the sidewalks were still damp-gray instead of dusty. The air smelled the fresher, to a city-bred woman, for the occasional pungency of acrid factory smoke. She walked the six blocks to work, watching the lights go out in the all-night hamburger joints, where the plate-glass walls were already catching the sun, and the lights go on in the dim interiors of cigar stores and dry-cleaning establishments.

The office was in a new Government building. In the rolovator, on the way up, she felt, as always, like a frankfurter roll in the ascending half of an old-style rotary toasting machine. She abandoned the air-foam cushioning gratefully at the fourteenth floor, and settled down behind her desk, at the rear of a long row of identical desks.

Each morning the pile of papers that greeted her was a little higher. These were, as everyone knew, the decisive months. The war might be won or lost on these calculations as well as any others. The manpower office had switched her here when her old expediter's job got to be too strenuous. The computer was easy to operate, and the work was absorbing, if not as exciting as the old job. But you didn't just stop working these days. Everyone who could do anything at all was needed.

And—she remembered the interview with the psychologist—*I'm probably the unstable type. Wonder what sort of neurosis I'd get sitting home reading that sensational paper . . .*

She plunged into the work without pursuing the thought.

February 18.

Hank darling,

Just a note—from the hospital, no less. I had a dizzy spell at work, and the doctor took it to heart. Blessed if I know what I'll do with myself lying in bed for weeks, just waiting—but Dr. Boyer seems to think it may not be so long.

There are too many newspapers around here. More infanticides all the time, and they can't seem to get a jury to convict any of them. It's the fathers who do it. Lucky thing you're not around, in case—

Oh, darling, that wasn't a very *funny* joke, was it? Write as often as you can, will you? I have too much time to think. But there really isn't anything wrong, and nothing to worry about.

Write often, and remember I love you.

Maggie.

SPECIAL SERVICE TELEGRAM

FEBRUARY 21, 1953

22:04 LK37G

FROM: TECH. LIEUT. H. MARVELL

X47-016 GCNY

TO: MRS. H. MARVELL

WOMEN'S HOSPITAL

NEW YORK CITY

HAD DOCTOR'S GRAM STOP WILL ARRIVE FOUR OH TEN STOP SHORT LEAVE STOP YOU DID IT MAGGIE STOP LOVE HANK

February 25.

Hank dear,

So you didn't see the baby either? You'd think a place this size would at least have visiplates on the incubators, so the fathers could get a look, even if the poor benighted mommas can't. They tell me I won't see her for another week, or maybe more—but of course, mother always warned me if I didn't slow my pace, I'd probably even have my babies too fast. Why must she *always* be right?

Did you meet that battle-ax of a nurse they put on here? I imagine they save her for people who've already had theirs, and don't let her get too near the prospectives—but a woman like that simply shouldn't be allowed in a maternity ward. She's obsessed with mutations, can't seem to talk about anything else. Oh, well, *ours* is all right, even if it was in an unholy hurry.

I'm tired. They warned me not to sit up so soon, but I *had* to write you. All my love, darling,

Maggie.

February 29.

Darling,

I finally got to see her! It's all true, what they say about new babies and the face that only a mother could love—but it's all there, darling, eyes, ears, and noses—no, only one!—all in the right places. We're so *lucky*, Hank.

I'm afraid I've been a rambunctious patient. I kept telling that hatchet-faced female with the mutation mania that I wanted to *see* the baby. Finally the doctor came in to "explain" everything to me, and talked a lot of nonsense, most of which I'm sure no one could have understood, any more than I did. The only thing I got out of it was that she didn't actually *have* to stay in the incubator; they just thought it was "wiser."

I think I got a little hysterical at that point. Guess I was more worried than I was willing to admit, but I threw a small fit about it. The whole business wound up with one of those hushed medical conferences outside the door, and finally the Woman in White said: "Well, we might as well. Maybe it'll work out better that way."

I'd heard about the way doctors and nurses in these places develop a God complex, and believe me it is as true figuratively as it is literally that a mother hasn't got a leg to stand on around here.

I *am* awfully weak, still. I'll write again soon. Love,

Maggie.

March 8.

Dearest Hank,

Well, the nurse was wrong if she told you that. She's an idiot anyhow. It's a girl. It's easier to tell with babies than with cats, and *I know*. How about Henrietta?

I'm home again, and busier than a betatron. They got *everything* mixed up at the hospital, and I had to teach myself how to bathe her and do just about everything else. She's getting prettier, too. When can you get a leave, a *real* leave?

Love,
Maggie.

May 26.

Hank dear,

You should see her now—and you shall. I'm sending along a reel of color movie. My mother sent her those nighties with draw-strings all over. I put one on, and right now she looks like a snow-white potato sack with that beautiful, beautiful flower-face blooming on top. Is that *me* talking? Am I a doting mother? But wait till you *see* her!

July 10.

. . . Believe it or not, as you like, but your daughter can talk, and I don't mean baby talk. Alice discovered it—she's a dental assistant in the WACs, you know—and when she heard the baby giving out what I thought was a string of gibberish, she said the kid knew words and sentences, but couldn't say them clearly because she has no teeth yet. I'm taking her to a speech specialist.

September 13.

. . . We have a prodigy for real! Now that all her front teeth are in, her speech is perfectly clear and—a new talent now—she can sing! I mean really carry a tune! At seven months! Darling, my world would be perfect if you could only get home.

November 19.

. . . at last. The little goon was so busy being clever, it took her all this time to learn to crawl. The doctor says development in these cases is always erratic . . .

SPECIAL SERVICE TELEGRAM

DECEMBER 1, 1953

08:47 LK59F

FROM: TECH. LIEUT. H. MARVELL

X47-016 GCNY

TO: MRS. H. MARVELL

APT. K-17

504 E. 19 ST.

N.Y. N.Y.

WEEK'S LEAVE STARTS TOMORROW STOP WILL ARRIVE AIRPORT TEN
OH FIVE STOP DON'T MEET ME STOP LOVE LOVE LOVE HANK

Margaret let the water run out of the bathinette until only a few inches
were left, and then loosed her hold on the wriggling baby.

"I think it was better when you were retarded, young woman," she
informed her daughter happily. "You *can't* crawl in a bathinette, you
know."

"Then why can't I go in the bathtub?" Margaret was used to her
child's volubility by now, but every now and then it caught her un-
awares. She swooped the resistant mass of pink flesh into a towel and
began to rub.

"Because you're too little, and your head is very soft, and bathtubs
are very hard."

"Oh. Then when can I go in the bathtub?"

"When the outside of your head is as hard as the inside, brainchild."
She reached toward a pile of fresh clothing. "I cannot understand,"
she added, pinning a square of cloth through the nightgown, "why a
child of your intelligence can't learn to keep a diaper on the way other
babies do. They've been used for centuries, you know, with perfectly
satisfactory results."

The child disdained to reply; she had heard it too often. She waited
patiently until she had been tucked, clean and sweet-smelling, into a
white-painted crib. Then she favored her mother with a smile that
inevitably made Margaret think of the first golden edge of the sun
bursting into a rosy predawn. She remembered Hank's reaction to the
color pictures of his beautiful daughter, and with the thought, realized
how late it was.

"Go to sleep, puss. When you wake up, you know, your *daddy* will
be here."

"Why?" asked the four-year-old mind, waging a losing battle to keep
the ten-month-old body awake.

Margaret went into the kitchenette and set the timer for the roast. She examined the table and got her clothes from the closet, new dress, new shoes, new slip, new everything, bought weeks before and saved for the day Hank's telegram came. She stopped to pull a paper from the facsimile and, with clothes and news, went into the bathroom and lowered herself gingerly into the steaming luxury of a scented tub.

She glanced through the paper with indifferent interest. Today at least there was no need to read the national news. There was an article by a geneticist. The same geneticist. Mutations, he said, were increasing disproportionately. It was too soon for recessives; even the first mutants, born near Hiroshima and Nagasaki in 1946 and 1947, were not old enough yet to breed. *But my baby's all right.* Apparently, there was some degree of free radiation from atomic explosions causing the trouble. *My baby's fine. Precocious, but normal.* If more attention had been paid to the first Japanese mutations, he said . . .

There was that little notice in the paper in the spring of '47. That was when Hank quit at Oak Ridge. "Only 2 or 3 percent of those guilty of infanticide are being caught and punished in Japan today . . ." *But* MY BABY's *all right.*

She was dressed, combed, and ready to the last light brush-on of lip paste, when the door chime sounded. She dashed for the door and heard for the first time in eighteen months the almost-forgotten sound of a key turning in the lock before the chime had quite died away.

"Hank!"

"Maggie!"

And then there was nothing to say. So many days, so many months, of small news piling up, so many things to tell him, and now she just stood there, staring at a khaki uniform and a stranger's pale face. She traced the features with the finger of memory. The same high-bridged nose, wide-set eyes, fine feathery brows; the same long jaw, the hair a little farther back now on the high forehead, the same tilted curve to his mouth. Pale . . . Of course, he'd been underground all this time. And strange, stranger because of lost familiarity than any newcomer's face could be.

She had time to think all that before his hand reached out to touch her, and spanned the gap of eighteen months. Now, again, there was nothing to say, because there was no need. They were together, and for the moment that was enough.

"Where's the baby?"

"Sleeping. She'll be up any minute."

No urgency. Their voices were as casual as though it were a daily exchange, as though war and separation did not exist. Margaret picked up the coat he'd thrown on the chair near the door and hung it carefully in the hall closet. She went to check the roast, leaving him to wander through the rooms by himself, remembering and coming back. She found him, finally, standing over the baby's crib.

She couldn't see his face, but she had no need to.

"I think we can wake her just this once." Margaret pulled the covers down and lifted the white bundle from the bed. Sleepy lids pulled back heavily from smoky brown eyes.

"Hello." Hank's voice was tentative.

"Hello." The baby's assurance was more pronounced.

He had heard about it, of course, but that wasn't the same as hearing it. He turned eagerly to Margaret. "She really can—?"

"Of course she can, darling. But what's more important, she can even do nice normal things like other babies do, even stupid ones. Watch her crawl!" Margaret set the baby on the big bed.

For a moment young Henrietta lay and eyed her parents dubiously.

"Crawl?" she asked.

"That's the idea. Your daddy is new around here, you know. He wants to see you show off."

"Then put me on my tummy."

"Oh, of course." Margaret obligingly rolled the baby over.

"What's the matter?" Hank's voice was still casual, but an undercurrent in it began to charge the air of the room. "I thought they turned over first."

"This baby"—Margaret would not notice the tension—"*This* baby does things when she wants to."

This baby's father watched with softening eyes while the head advanced and the body hunched up propelling itself across the bed.

"Why, the little rascal." He burst into relieved laughter. "She looks like one of those potato-sack racers they used to have on picnics. Got her arms pulled out of the sleeves already." He reached over and grabbed the knot at the bottom of the long nightie.

"I'll do it, darling." Margaret tried to get there first.

"Don't be silly, Maggie. This may be *your* first baby, but *I* had five kid brothers." He laughed her away, and reached with his other hand for the string that closed one sleeve. He opened the sleeve bow and groped for an arm.

"The way you wriggle," he addressed his child sternly, as his hand touched a moving knob of flesh at the shoulder, "anyone might think you are a worm, using your tummy to crawl on, instead of your hands and feet."

Margaret stood and watched, smiling. "Wait till you hear her sing, darling—"

His right hand traveled down from the shoulder to where he thought an arm would be, traveled down, and straight down, over firm small muscles that writhed in an attempt to move against the pressure of his hand. He let his fingers drift up again to the shoulder. With infinite care he opened the knot at the bottom of the nightgown. His wife was standing by the bed, saying, "She can do 'Jingle Bells,' and—"

His left hand felt along the soft knitted fabric of the gown, up toward the diaper that folded, flat and smooth, across the bottom end of his child. No wrinkles. No kicking. *No . . .*

"Maggie." He tried to pull his hands from the neat fold in the diaper, from the wriggling body. "Maggie." His throat was dry; words came hard, low and grating. He spoke very slowly, thinking the sound of each word to make himself say it. His head was spinning, but he had to *know* before he let it go. "Maggie, why . . . didn't you . . . tell me?"

"Tell you what, darling?" Margaret's poise was the immemorial patience of woman confronted with man's childish impetuosity. Her sudden laugh sounded fantastically easy and natural in that room; it was all clear to her now. "Is she wet? I didn't know."

She didn't know. His hands, beyond control, ran up and down the soft-skinned baby body, the sinuous, limbless body. *Oh God, dear God*—his head shook and his muscles contracted in a bitter spasm of hysteria. His fingers tightened on his child—*Oh God, she didn't know . . .*

Contagion

KATHERINE MacLEAN

It was like an Earth forest in the fall, but it was not fall. The forest leaves were green and copper and purple and fiery red, and a wind sent patches of bright greenish sunlight dancing among the leaf shadows.

The hunt party of the *Explorer* filed along the narrow trail, guns ready, walking carefully, listening to the distant, half-familiar cries of strange birds.

A faint crackle of static in their earphones indicated that a gun had been fired.

"Got anything?" asked June Walton. The helmet intercom carried her voice to the ears of the others without breaking the stillness of the forest.

"Took a shot at something," explained George Barton's cheerful voice in her earphones. She rounded a bend of the trail and came upon Barton standing peering up into the trees, his gun still raised. "It looked like a duck."

"This isn't Central Park," said Hal Barton, his brother, coming into sight. His green space suit struck an incongruous note against the bronze and red forest. "They won't all be ducks," he said soberly.

"Maybe some will be dragons. Don't get eaten by a dragon, June," came Max's voice quietly into her earphones. "Not while I still love you." He came out of the trees carrying the blood-sample kit and touched her glove with his, the grin on his ugly beloved face barely visible in the mingled light and shade. A patch of sunlight struck a greenish glint from his fishbowl helmet.

They walked on. A quarter of a mile back, the spaceship *Explorer* towered over the forest like a tapering skyscraper, and the people of the ship looked out of the viewplates at fresh winds and sunlight and clouds, and they longed to be outside.

But the likeness to Earth was danger, and the cool wind might be death, for if the animals were like Earth animals, their diseases might be like Earth diseases, alike enough to be contagious, different enough to be impossible to treat. There was warning enough in the past. Colonies had vanished, and traveled spaceways drifted with the corpses of ships which had touched on some plague planet.

The people of the ship waited while their doctors, in airtight space suits, hunted animals to test them for contagion.

The four medicos, for June Walton was also a doctor, filed through the alien homelike forest, walking softly, watching for motion among the copper and purple shadows.

They saw it suddenly, a lighter, moving copper patch among the darker browns. Reflex action swung June's gun into line, and behind her someone's gun went off with a faint crackle of static and made a hole in the leaves beside the specimen. Then for a while no one moved.

This one looked like a man, a magnificently muscled, leanly graceful, humanlike animal. Even in its callused bare feet, it was a head taller than any of them. Red-haired, hawk-faced, and darkly tanned, it stood breathing heavily, looking at them without expression. At its side hung a sheath knife, and a crossbow was slung across one wide shoulder.

They lowered their guns.

"It needs a shave," Max said reasonably in their earphones, and he reached up to his helmet and flipped the switch that let his voice be heard. "Something we could do for you, Mac?"

The friendly drawl was the first voice that had broken the forest sounds. June smiled suddenly. He was right. The strict logic of evolution did not demand beards; therefore a non-human would not be wearing a three-day growth of red stubble.

Still panting, the tall figure licked dry lips and spoke. "Welcome to Minos. The mayor sends greetings from Alexandria."

"English?" gasped June.

"We were afraid you would take off again before I could bring word to you . . . It's three hundred miles . . . We saw your scout plane pass twice, but we couldn't attract its attention."

June looked in stunned silence at the stranger leaning against the tree. Thirty-six light-years—thirty-six times six trillion miles of monotonous space travel—to be told that the planet was already settled! "We didn't know there was a colony here," she said. "It's not on the map."

"We were afraid of that," the tall bronze man answered soberly. "We have been here three generations and no traders have come."

Max shifted the kit strap on his shoulder and offered a hand. "My name is Max Stark, M.D. This is June Walton, M.D., Hal Barton, M.D., and George Barton, Hal's brother, also M.D."

"Patrick Mead is the name." The man smiled, shaking hands casually. "Just a hunter and bridge carpenter myself. Never met any medicos before."

The grip was effortless, but even through her air-proofed glove June could feel that the fingers that touched hers were as hard as padded steel.

"What—what is the population of Minos?" she asked.

He looked down at her curiously for a moment before answering. "Only one hundred and fifty." He smiled. "Don't worry, this isn't a city planet yet. There's room for a few more people." He shook hands with the Bartons quickly. "That is—you are people, aren't you?" he asked startlingly.

"Why not?" said Max with a poise that June admired.

"Well, you are all so—so—" Patrick Mead's eyes roamed across the faces of the group. "So varied."

They could find no meaning in that, and stood puzzled.

"I mean," Patrick Mead said into the silence, "all these—interesting different hair colors and face shapes and so forth—" He made a vague wave with one hand as if he had run out of words or was anxious not to insult them.

"Joke?" Max asked, bewildered.

June laid a hand on his arm. "No harm meant," she said to him over the intercom. "We're just as much of a shock to him as he is to us."

She addressed a question to the tall colonist on outside sound. "What should a person look like, Mr. Mead?"

He indicated her with a smile. "Like you."

June stepped closer and stood looking up at him, considering her own description. She was tall and tanned, like him; had a few freckles, like him; and wavy red hair, like his. She ignored the brightly humorous blue eyes.

"In other words," she said, "everyone on the planet looks like you and me?"

Patrick Mead took another look at their four faces and began to grin. "Like me, I guess. But I hadn't thought of it before, that people could have different colored hair or that noses could fit so many ways onto faces. Judging by my own appearance, I suppose any fool can walk on his hands and say the world is upside-down!" He laughed and sobered. "But then why wear space suits? The air is breathable."

"For safety," June told him. "We can't take any chances on plague."

Pat Mead was wearing nothing but his weapons, and the wind ruffled his hair. He looked comfortable, and they longed to take off the stuffy space suits and feel the wind against their own skins. Minos was like home, like Earth . . . But they were strangers.

"Plague," Pat Mead said thoughtfully. "We had one here. It came two years after the colony arrived and killed everyone except the Mead families. They were immune. I guess we look alike because we're all related, and that's why I grew up thinking that it is the only way people can look."

Plague. "What was the disease?" Hal Barton asked.

"Pretty gruesome, according to my father. They called it the melting sickness. The doctors died too soon to find out what it was or what to do about it."

"You should have trained more doctors, or sent to civilization for some." A trace of impatience was in George Barton's voice.

Pat Mead explained patiently, "Our ship, with the power plant and all the books we needed, went off into the sky to avoid the contagion, and never came back. The crew must have died." Long years of hardship were indicated by that statement, a colony with electric power gone and machinery stilled, with key technicians dead and no way to replace them. June realized then the full meaning of the primitive sheath knife and bow.

"Any recurrence of melting sickness?" asked Hal Barton.

"No."

"Any other diseases?"

"Not a one."

Max was eyeing the bronze red-headed figure with something approaching awe. "Do you think all the Meads look like that?" he said to June on the intercom. "I wouldn't mind being a Mead myself!"

Their job had been made easy by the coming of Pat. They went back to the ship laughing, exchanging anecdotes with him. There was nothing now to keep Minos from being the home they wanted except the melting sickness, and forewarned against it, they could take precautions.

The polished silver-and-black column of the *Explorer* seemed to rise higher and higher over the trees as they neared it. Then its symmetry blurred all sense of specific size as they stepped out from among the trees and stood on the edge of the meadow, looking up.

"Nice!" said Pat. "Beautiful!" The admiration in his voice was warming.

"It was a yacht," Max said, still looking up, "secondhand, an old-time beauty without a sign of wear. Synthetic diamond-studded control board and murals on the walls. It doesn't have the new speed drives, but it brought us thirty-six light-years in one and a half subjective years. Plenty good enough."

The tall tanned man looked faintly wistful, and June realized that he had never had access to a film library, never seen a movie, never experienced luxury. He had been born and raised on Minos without electricity.

"May I go aboard?" Pat asked hopefully.

Max unslung the specimen kit from his shoulder, laid it on the carpet of plants that covered the ground, and began to open it.

"Tests first," Hal Barton said. "We have to find out if you people still carry this so-called melting sickness. We'll have to de-microbe you and take specimens before we let you on board. Once on, you'll be no good as a check for what the other Meads might have."

Max was taking out a rack and a stand of preservative bottles and hypodermics.

"Are you going to jab me with those?" Pat asked with alarm.

"You're just a specimen animal to me, bud!" Max grinned at Pat Mead, and Pat grinned back. June saw that they were friends already, the tall pantherish colonist and the wry, black-haired doctor. She felt a stab of guilt because she loved Max and yet could pity him for being smaller and frailer than Pat Mead.

"Lie down," Max told him, "and hold still. We need two spinal-fluid samples from the back, a body-cavity one in front, and another from the arm."

Pat lay down obediently. Max knelt, and as he spoke, expertly swabbed and inserted needles with the smooth speed that had made him a fine nerve surgeon on Earth.

High above them the scout helioplane came out of an opening in the ship and angled off toward the west, its buzz diminishing. Then, suddenly, it veered and headed back, and Reno Ulrich's voice came tinnily from their earphones.

"What's that you've got? Hey, what are you docs doing down there?" He banked again and came to a stop, hovering fifty feet away. June could see his startled face looking through the glass at Pat.

Hal Barton switched to a narrow radio beam, explained rapidly, and pointed in the direction of Alexandria. Reno's plane lifted and flew away over the odd-colored forest.

"The plane will drop a note on your town, telling them you got through to us," Hal Barton told Pat, who was sitting up watching Max dexterously put the blood and spinal fluids into the right bottles without exposing them to air.

"We won't be free to contact your people until we know if they still carry melting sickness," Max added. "You might be immune so it doesn't show on you, but still carry enough germs—if that's what caused it—to wipe out a planet."

"If you do carry melting sickness," said Hal Barton, "we won't be able to mingle with your people until we've cleared them of the disease."

"Starting with me?" Pat asked.

"Starting with you," Max told him ruefully, "as soon as you step on board."

"More needles?"

"Yes, and a few little extras thrown in."

"Rough?"

"It isn't easy."

A few minutes later, standing in the stalls for space suit decontamination, being buffeted by jets of hot disinfectant, bathed in glares of sterilizing ultraviolet radiation, June remembered that and compared Pat Mead's treatment to theirs.

In the *Explorer*, stored carefully in sealed tanks and containers, was the ultimate, multipurpose cure-all. It was a solution of enzymes so like the key catalysts of the human cell nucleus that it caused chemical derangement and disintegration in any nonhuman cell. Nothing could live in contact with it but human cells; any alien intruder to the body would die. Nucleocat Cureall was its trade name.

But the cure-all alone was not enough for complete safety. Plagues had been known to slay too rapidly and universally to be checked by human treatment. Doctors are not reliable; they die. Therefore spaceways and interplanetary health law demanded that ship equipment for guarding against disease be totally mechanical in operation, rapid, and efficient.

Somewhere near them, in a series of stalls which led around and around like a rabbit maze, Pat was being herded from stall to stall by peremptory mechanical voices, directed to soap and shower, ordered to insert his arm into a slot which took a sample of his blood, given solutions to drink, bathed in germicidal ultraviolet, shaken by sonic blasts, breathing air thick with sprays of germicidal mists, being directed to put his arms into other slots where they were anesthetized and injected with various immunizing solutions.

Finally, he would be put in a room of high temperature and extreme dryness and instructed to sit for half an hour while more fluids were dripped into his veins through long thin tubes.

All legal spaceships were built for safety. No chance was taken of allowing a suspected carrier to bring an infection on board with him.

June stepped from the last shower stall into the locker room, zipped off her space suit with a sigh of relief, and contemplated herself in a wall mirror. Red hair, dark blue eyes, tall . . .

"I've got a good figure," she said thoughtfully.

Max turned at the door. "Why this sudden interest in your looks?" he asked suspiciously. "Do we stand here and admire you, or do we finally get something to eat?"

"Wait a minute." She went to a wall phone and dialed it carefully, using a combination from the ship's directory. "How're you doing, Pat?"

The phone picked up a hissing of water or spray. There was a startled chuckle. "Voices, too! Hello, June. How do you tell a machine to go spray itself?"

"Are you hungry?"

"No food since yesterday."

"We'll have a banquet ready for you when you get out," she told Pat and hung up, smiling. Pat Mead's voice had a vitality and enjoyment which made shipboard talk sound like sad artificial gaiety in contrast.

They looked into the nearby small laboratory where twelve squealing hamsters were protestingly submitting to a small injection each of Pat's blood. In most of them the injection was followed by one of antihistaminics and adaptives. Otherwise the hamster defense system would treat all nonhamster cells as enemies, even the harmless human blood cells, and fight back against them violently.

One hamster, the twelfth, was given an extra-large dose of adaptive so that if there were a disease, he would not fight it or the human cells and thus succumb more rapidly.

"How ya doing, George?" Max asked.

"Routine," George Barton grunted absently.

On the way up the long spiral ramps to the dining hall, they passed a viewplate. It showed a long scene of mountains in the distance on the horizon, and between them, rising step by step as they grew farther away, the low rolling hills, bronze and red with patches of clear green where there were fields.

Someone was looking out, standing very still, as if she had been there a long time—Bess St. Clair, a Canadian woman. "It looks like Winnipeg," she told them as they paused. "When are you doctors going to let us out of this barber pole? Look." She pointed. "See that patch of field on the south hillside, with the brook winding through it? I've staked that hillside for our house. When do we get out?"

Reno Ulrich's tiny scout plane buzzed slowly in from the distance and began circling lazily.

"Sooner than you think," Max told her. "We've discovered a castaway colony on the planet. They've done our tests for us by just living here. If there's anything here to catch, they've caught it."

"People on Minos?" Bess's handsome ruddy face grew alive with excitement.

"One of them is down in the medical department," June said. "He'll be out in twenty minutes."

"May I go see him?"

"Sure," said Max. "Show him the way to the dining hall when he gets out. Tell him we sent you."

"Right!" She turned and ran down the ramp like a small girl going to a fire. Max grinned at June and she grinned back. After a year and a half of isolation in space, everyone was hungry for the sight of new faces, the sound of unfamiliar voices.

They climbed the last two turns to the cafeteria and entered to a rich subdued blend of soft music and quiet conversation. The cafeteria was a section of the old dining room, left when the rest of the ship had been converted to living and working quarters, and it still had the original finely grained wood of the ceiling and walls, the sound absorbency, the soft-music spools, and the intimate small light at each table where people leisurely ate and talked.

They stood in line at the hot-foods counter, and behind her June could hear a girl's voice talking excitedly through the murmur of conversation.

"—new man, honest! I saw him through the viewplate when they came in. He's down in the medical department. A real frontiersman."

The line drew abreast of the counters, and she and Max chose three heaping trays, starting with hydroponic mushroom steak, raised in the growing trays of water and chemicals; sharp salad bowl with rose tomatoes and aromatic peppers; tank-grown fish with special sauce; four different desserts; and assorted beverages.

Presently they had three tottering trays successfully maneuvered to a table. Brant St. Clair came over. "I beg your pardon, Max, but they are saying something about Reno carrying messages to a colony of savages for the medical department. Will he be back soon, do you know?"

Max smiled up at him, his square face affectionate. Everyone liked the shy Canadian. "He's back already. We just saw him come in."

"Oh, fine." St. Clair beamed. "I had an appointment with him to go out and confirm what looks like a nice vein of iron to the northeast. Have you seen Bess? Oh—there she is." He turned swiftly and hurried away.

A very tall man with fiery red hair came in surrounded by an eagerly talking crowd of ship people. It was Pat Mead. He stood in the doorway alertly scanning the dining room. Sheer vitality made him seem even larger than he was. Sighting June, he smiled and began to thread toward their table.

"Look!" said someone. "There's the colonist!" Sheila, a pretty, jeweled woman, followed and caught his arm. "Did you *really* swim across a river to come here?"

Overflowing with goodwill and curiosity, people approached from all directions. "Did you actually walk three hundred miles? Come, eat with us. Let me help choose your tray."

Everyone wanted him to eat at their table, everyone was a specialist and wanted data about Minos. They all wanted anecdotes about hunting wild animals with a bow and arrow.

"He needs to be rescued," Max said. "He won't have a chance to eat."

June and Max got up firmly, edged through the crowd, captured Pat, and escorted him back to their table. June found herself pleased to be claiming the hero of the hour.

Pat sat in the simple, subtly designed chair and leaned back almost voluptuously, testing the way it gave and fitted itself to him. He ran his eyes over the bright tableware and heaped plates. He looked around at the rich grained walls and soft lights at each table. He said nothing, just looking and feeling and experiencing.

"When we build our town and leave the ship," June explained, "we will turn all the staterooms back into the lounges and ballrooms and cocktail bars that used to be inside. Then it will be beautiful."

Pat smiled, cocked his head to the music, and tried to locate its source. "It's good enough now. We only play music tapes once a week in city hall."

They ate, Pat beginning the first meal he had had in more than a day.

Most of the other diners finished when they were halfway through and began walking over, diffidently at first, then in another wave of smiling faces, handshakes, and introductions. Pat was asked about crops, about farming methods, about rainfall and floods, about farm animals and plant breeding, about the compatibility of imported Earth seeds with local ground, about mines and strata.

There was no need to protect him. He leaned back in his chair and drawled answers with the lazy ease of a panther; where he could think of no statistics, he would fill the gap with an anecdote. It showed that he enjoyed spinning campfire yarns and being the center of interest.

Between bouts of questions, he ate and listened to the music.

June noticed that the female specialists were prolonging the questions more than they needed, clustering around the table, laughing at his jokes, until presently Pat was almost surrounded by pretty faces, eager questions, and chiming laughs. Sheila the beautiful laughed most chimingly of all.

June nudged Max, and Max shrugged indifferently. It wasn't anything a man would pay attention to, perhaps. But June watched Pat for a moment more, then glanced uneasily back to Max. He was eating and listening to Pat's answers and did not feel her gaze. For some reason Max looked almost shrunken to her. He was shorter than she had realized; she had forgotten that he was only the same height as herself. She was aware of the clear lilting chatter of female voices increasing at Pat's end of the table.

"That guy's a menace," Max said, and laughed to himself, cutting another slice of hydroponic mushroom steak. "What's got you?" he added, glancing aside at her when he noticed her sudden stillness.

"Nothing," she said hastily, but she did not turn back to watching Pat Mead. She felt disloyal. Pat was only a superb animal. Max was the man she loved. Or—was he? Of course he was, she told herself angrily. They had gone colonizing together because they wanted to spend their lives together; she had never thought of marrying any other man. Yet the sense of dissatisfaction persisted, and along with it a feeling of guilt.

Len Marlow, the protein-tank-culture technician responsible for the mushroom steaks, had wormed his way into the group and asked Pat a question. Now he was saying, "I don't dig you, Pat. It sounds like you're putting the people into the tanks instead of the vegetables!" He glanced at them, looking puzzled. "See if you two can make anything of this. It sounds medical to me."

Pat leaned back and smiled, sipping a glass of hydroponic burgundy. "Wonderful stuff. You'll have to show us how to make it."

Len turned back to him. "You people live off the country, right? You hunt and bring in steaks and eat them, right? Well, say I have one of those steaks right here and I want to eat it, what happens?"

"Go ahead and eat it. It just wouldn't digest. You'd stay hungry."

"Why?" Len was aggrieved.

"Chemical differences in the basic protoplasm of Minos. Different amino linkages, left-handed instead of right-handed molecules in the carbohydrates, things like that. Nothing will be digestible here until you are adapted chemically by a little test-tube evolution. Till then you'd starve to death on a full stomach."

Pat's side of the table had been loaded with the dishes from two trays, but it was almost clear now and the dishes were stacked neatly to one side. He started on three desserts, thoughtfully tasting each in turn.

"Test-tube evolution?" Max repeated. "What's that? I thought you people had no doctors."

"It's a story." Pat leaned back again. "Alexander P. Mead, the head of the Mead clan, was a plant geneticist, a very determined personality, and no man to argue with. He didn't want us to go through the struggle of killing off all Minos plants and putting in our own, spoiling the face of the planet and upsetting the balance of its ecology. He decided that he would adapt our genes to this planet or kill us trying. He did it, all right."

"Did which?" asked June, suddenly feeling a sourceless prickle of fear.

"Adapted us to Minos. He took human cells—"

She listened intently, trying to find a reason for fear in the explanation. It would have taken many human generations to adapt to Minos by ordinary evolution, and that only at a heavy toll of death and hunger which evolution exacts. There was a shorter way: Human cells have the ability to return to their primeval condition of independence, hunting, eating, and reproducing alone.

Alexander P. Mead took human cells and made them into phagocytes. He put them through the hard savage school of evolution—a thousand generations of multiplication, hardship, and hunger, with the alien indigestible food always present, offering its reward of plenty to the cell that reluctantly learned to absorb it.

"Leukocytes can run through several thousand generations of evolution in six months," Pat Mead finished. "When they reached a point where they would absorb Minos food, he planted them back in the people he had taken them from."

"What was supposed to happen then?" Max asked, leaning forward.

"I don't know exactly how it worked. He never told anybody much about it, and when I was a little boy he had gone loco and was wandering ha-ha-ing around waving a test tube. Fell down a ravine and broke his neck at the age of eighty."

"A character," Max said.

Why was she afraid? "It worked, then?"

"Yes. He tried it on all the Meads the first year. The other settlers didn't want to be experimented on until they saw how it worked out. It worked. The Meads could hunt and plant while the other settlers were still eating out of hydroponics tanks."

"It worked," said Max to Len. "You're a plant geneticist and a tank-culture expert. There's a job for you."

"Uh-*uh!*" Len backed away. "It sounds like a medical problem to me. Human cell control—right up your alley."

"It is a one-way street," Pat warned. "Once it is done, you won't be able to digest ship food. I'll get no good from this protein. I ate it just for the taste."

Hal Barton appeared quietly beside the table. "Three of the twelve test hamsters have died," he reported, and turned to Pat. "Your people carry the germs of melting sickness, as you call it. The dead hamsters were injected with blood taken from you before you were de-infected. We can't settle here unless we de-infect everybody on Minos. Would they object?"

"We wouldn't want to give you folks germs." Pat smiled. "Anything for safety. But there'll have to be a vote on it first."

The doctors went to Reno Ulrich's table and walked with him to the hangar, explaining. He was to carry the proposal to Alexandria, mingle with the people, be persuasive, and wait for them to vote before returning. He was to give himself shots of cure-all every two hours on the hour or run the risk of disease.

Reno was pleased. He had dabbled in sociology before retraining as a mechanic for the expedition. "This gives me a chance to study their

mores." He winked wickedly. "I may not be back for several nights."
They watched through the viewplate as he took off, and then went
over to the laboratory for a look at the hamsters.

Three were alive and healthy, munching lettuce. One was the control; the other two had been given shots of Pat's blood from before he
entered the ship, but with no additional treatment. Apparently a hamster could fight off melting sickness easily if left alone. Three were
still feverish and ruffled, with a low red blood count, but recovering.
The three dead ones had been given strong shots of adaptive and
counterhistamine, so their bodies had not fought back against the
attack.

June glanced at the dead animals hastily and looked away again.
They lay twisted with a strange semi-fluid limpness, as if ready to
dissolve. The last hamster, which had been given the heaviest dose of
adaptive, had apparently lost all its hair before death. It was hairless
and pink, like a stillborn baby.

"We can find no microorganisms," George Barton said. "None at all.
Nothing in the body that should not be there. Leukosis and anemia.
Fever only for the ones that fought it off." He handed Max some
temperature charts and graphs of blood counts.

June wandered out into the hall. Pediatrics and obstetrics were her
field; she left the cellular research to Max and just helped him with
laboratory routine. The strange mood followed her out into the hall,
then abruptly lightened.

Coming toward her, busily telling a tale of adventure to the gorgeous
Sheila Davenport, was a tall, red-headed, magnificently handsome
man. It was his handsomeness which made Pat such a pleasure to
look upon and talk with, she guiltily told herself, and it was his tremendous vitality . . . It was like meeting a movie hero in the flesh, or
a hero out of the pages of a book—Deerslayer, John Clayton, Lord
Greystoke.

She waited in the doorway to the laboratory and made no move to
join them, merely acknowledged the two with a nod and a smile and
a casual lift of the hand. They nodded and smiled back.

"Hello, June," said Pat and continued telling his tale, but as they
passed he lightly touched her arm.

"You Tarzan?" she said mockingly and softly to his passing profile,
and knew that he had heard.

That night she had a nightmare. She was running down a long
corridor looking for Max, but every man she came to was a big

bronze man with red hair and bright-blue eyes who touched her arm.

The pink hamster! She woke suddenly, feeling as if alarm bells had been ringing, and listened carefully, but there was no sound. She had had a nightmare, she told herself, but alarm bells were still ringing in her unconscious. Something was wrong.

Lying still and trying to preserve the images, she groped for a meaning, but the mood faded under the cold touch of reason. Damn intuitive thinking! A pink hamster! Why did the unconscious have to be so vague? She fell asleep again and forgot.

They had lunch with Pat Mead that day, and after it was over, Pat delayed June with a hand on her shoulder and looked down at her.

"Me Tarzan, you Jane," he said and then turned away, answering the hails of a party at another table as if he had not spoken. She stood shaken, and then walked to the door where Max waited.

She was particularly affectionate with Max the rest of the day, and it pleased him. He would not have been if he had known why. She tried to forget Pat's reply.

June was in the laboratory with Max, watching the growth of a small tank culture of the alien protoplasm from a Minos weed and listening to Len Marlow pour out his troubles.

"And Elsie tags around after that big goof all day, listening to his stories. And then she tells me I'm just jealous, I'm imagining things!" He passed his hand across his eyes. "I came away from Earth to be with Elsie . . . I'm getting a headache. Look, can't you persuade Pat to cut it out, June? You and Max are his friends."

"Here, have an aspirin," June said. "We'll see what we can do."

"Thanks." Len picked up his tank culture and went out, not at all cheered.

Max sat brooding over the dials and meters at his end of the laboratory, apparently sunk in thought. When Len had gone, he spoke almost harshly. "Why encourage the guy? Why let him hope?"

"Found out anything about the differences in protoplasm?" she evaded.

"Why let him kid himself? What chance has he got against that hunk of muscle and smooth talk?"

"But Pat isn't after Elsie," she protested.

"Every scatterbrained woman on this ship is trailing after Pat with her tongue hanging out. Brant St. Clair is in the bar right now. He doesn't say what he is drinking about, but do you think Pat is resisting all these women crowding down on him?"

"There are other things besides looks and charm," she said, grimly trying to concentrate on a slide under her binocular microscope.

"Yeah, and whatever they are, Pat has them, too. Who's more competent to support a woman and a family on a frontier planet than a handsome bruiser who was born here?"

"I meant"—June spun around on her stool with unexpected passion—"there is old friendship, and there's loyalty and memories, and personality!" She was half shouting.

"They're not worth much on the secondhand market," Max said. He was sitting slumped on his lab stool, looking dully at his dials. "Now *I'm* getting a headache!" He smiled ruefully. "No kidding, a real headache. And over other people's troubles, yet!"

Other people's troubles . . . She got up and wandered out into the long curving halls. "Me Tarzan, you Jane," Pat's voice repeated in her mind. Why did the man have to be so overpoweringly attractive, so glaring a contrast to Max? Why couldn't the universe manage to run on without generating troublesome love triangles?

She walked up the curving ramps to the dining hall where they had eaten and drunk and talked yesterday. It was empty except for one couple talking forehead to forehead over cold coffee.

She turned and wandered down the long easy spiral of corridor to the pharmacy and dispensary. It was empty. George was probably in the test lab next door, where he could hear if he was wanted. The automatic vendor of harmless euphorics, stimulants, and opiates stood in the corner, brightly decorated in pastel abstract designs, with its automatic tabulator graph glowing above it.

Max had a headache, she remembered. She recorded her thumbprint in the machine and pushed the plunger for a box of aspirins, trying to focus her attention on the problem of adapting the people of the ship to the planet Minos. An aquarium tank with a faint solution of histamine would be enough to convert a piece of human skin into a community of voracious active phagocytes individually seeking something to devour, but could they eat enough to live away from the rich sustaining plasma of human blood?

After the aspirins, she pushed another plunger for something for herself. Then she stood looking at it, a small box with three pills in her hand—Theobromine, a heart strengthener and a confidence-giving euphoric all in one, something to steady shaky nerves. She had used it before only in emergency. She extended a hand and looked at it. It was trembling. Damn triangles!

While she was looking at her hand, there was a click from the automatic drug vendor. It summed the morning use of each drug in the vendors throughout the ship and recorded it in a neat addition to the end of each graph line. For a moment she could not find the green line for anodynes and the red line for stimulants, and then she saw that they went almost straight up.

There were too many being used—far too many to be explained by jealousy or psychosomatic peevishness. This was an epidemic, and only one disease was possible!

The disinfecting of Pat had not succeeded. Nucleocat Cureall, killer of all infections, had not cured! Pat had brought melting sickness into the ship with him!

Who had it?

The drug vendor glowed cheerfully, uncommunicative. She opened a panel in its side and looked in on restless interlacing cogs, and on the inside of the door she saw printed some directions . . . "To remove or examine records before reaching end of the reel . . ."

After a few fumbling minutes she had the answer. In the cafeteria at breakfast and lunch, thirty-eight men out of the forty-eight aboard ship had taken more than his norm of stimulant. Twenty-one had taken aspirin as well. The only woman who had made an unusual purchase was herself!

She remembered the hamsters that had thrown off the infection with a short sharp fever, and checked back in the records to the day before. There was a short rise in aspirin sales to women at late afternoon. The women were safe.

It was the men who had melting sickness!

Melting sickness killed in hours, according to Pat Mead. How long had the men been sick?

As she was leaving, Jerry came into the pharmacy, recorded his thumbprint and took a box of aspirin from the machine.

She felt all right. Self-control was working well, and it was possible still to walk down the corridor smiling at the people who passed. She took the emergency elevator to the control room and showed her credentials to the technician on watch.

"Medical Emergency." At a small control panel in the corner was a large red button, precisely labeled. She considered it and picked up the control-room phone. This was the hard part, telling someone, especially someone who had it—Max.

She dialed, and when the click on the end of the line showed he had picked up the phone, she told Max what she had seen.

"No women, just the men," he repeated. "That right?"

"Yes."

"Probably it's chemically alien, inhibited by one of the female hormones. We'll try sex hormone shots, if we have to. Where are you calling from?"

She told him.

"That's right. Give Nucleocat Cureall another chance. It might work this time. Push that button."

She went to the panel and pushed the large red button. Through the long height of the *Explorer,* bells woke to life and began to ring in frightened clangor, emergency doors thumped shut, mechanical apparatus hummed into life, and canned voices began to give rapid urgent directions.

A plague had come.

She obeyed the mechanical orders, went out into the hall, and walked in line with the others. The captain walked ahead of her and the gorgeous Sheila Davenport fell into step beside her. "I look like a positive hag this morning. Does that mean I'm sick? Are we all sick?"

June shrugged, unwilling to say what she knew.

Others came out of all rooms into the corridor, thickening the line. They could hear each room lock as the last person left it, and then, faintly, the hiss of disinfectant spray. Behind them, on the heels of the last person in line, segments of the ship slammed off and began to hiss.

They wound down the spiral corridor until they reached the medical-treatment section again, and there they waited in line.

"It won't scar my arms, will it?" asked Sheila apprehensively, glancing at her smooth, lovely arms.

The mechanical voice said, "Next. Step inside, please, and stand clear of the door."

"Not a bit," June reassured Sheila, and stepped into the cubicle.

Inside, she was directed from cubicle to cubicle and given the usual buffeting by sprays and radiation, had blood samples taken, and was injected with Nucleocat and a series of other protectives. At last she was directed through another door into a tiny cubicle with a chair.

"You are to wait here," commanded the recorded voice metallically. "In twenty minutes the door will unlock and you may then leave. All people now treated may visit all parts of the ship which have been protected. It is forbidden to visit any quarantine or unsterile part of the ship without permission from the medical officers."

Presently the door unlocked and she emerged into bright lights again, feeling slightly battered.

She was in the clinic. A few men sat on the edge of beds and looked sick. One was lying down. Brant and Bess St. Clair sat near each other, not speaking.

Approaching her was George Barton, reading a thermometer with a puzzled expression.

"What is it, George?" she asked anxiously.

"Some of the women have a slight fever, but it's going down. None of the fellows have any—but their white count is way up, their red count is way down, and they look sick to me."

She approached St. Clair. His usually ruddy cheeks were pale, his pulse was light and too fast, and his skin felt clammy. "How's the headache? Did the Nucleocat treatment help?"

"I feel worse, if anything."

"Better set up beds," she told George. "Get everyone back into the clinic."

"We're doing that," George assured her. "That's what Hal is doing."

She went back to the laboratory. Max was pacing up and down, absently running his hands through his black hair until it stood straight up. He stopped when he saw her face and scowled thoughtfully. "They are still sick?" It was more a statement than a question.

She nodded.

"The Cureall didn't cure this time," he muttered. "That leaves it up to us. We have melting sickness, and according to Pat and the hamsters, that leaves us less than a day to find out what it is and learn how to stop it."

Suddenly an idea for another test struck him and he moved to the worktable to set it up. He worked rapidly, with an occasional uncoordinated movement breaking his usual efficiency.

It was strange to see Max troubled and afraid.

She put on a laboratory smock and began to work. She worked in silence. The mechanicals had failed. Hal and George Barton were busy staving off death from the weaker cases and trying to gain time for Max and her to work. The problem of the plague had to be solved by the two of them alone. It was in their hands.

Another test, no results. Another test, no results. Max's hands were shaking and he stopped a moment to take stimulants.

She went into the ward for a moment, found Bess, and warned her quietly to tell the other women to be ready to take over if the men became too sick to go on. "But tell them calmly. We don't want to frighten the men." She lingered in the ward long enough to see the word spread among the women in a widening wave of paler faces and compressed lips; then she went back to the laboratory.

Another test. There was no sign of a microorganism in anyone's blood, merely a growing horde of leukocytes and phagocytes, prowling as if mobilized to repel invasion.

Len Marlow was wheeled in unconscious, with Hal Barton's written comments and conclusions pinned to the blanket.

"I don't feel so well myself," the assistant complained. "The air feels thick. I can't breathe."

June saw that his lips were blue. "Oxygen short," she told Max.

"Low red-corpuscle count," Max answered. "Look into a drop and see what's going on. Use mine; I feel the same way he does." She took two drops of Max's blood. The count was low, falling too fast.

Breathing is useless without the proper minimum of red corpuscles in the blood. People below that minimum die of asphyxiation although their lungs are full of pure air. The red-corpuscle count was falling too fast. The time she and Max had to work in was too short.

"Pump some more CO_2 into the air system," Max said urgently over the phone. "Get some into the men's end of the ward."

She looked through the microscope at the live sample of blood. It was a dark clear field and bright moving things spun and swirled through it, but she could see nothing that did not belong there.

"Hal," Max called over the general speaker system, "cut the other treatments, check for accelerating anemia. Treat it like monoxide poisoning—CO_2 and oxygen."

She reached into a cupboard under the worktable, located two cylinders of oxygen, cracked the valves, and handed one to Max and one to the assistant. Some of the bluish tint left the assistant's face as he breathed, and he went over to the patient with reawakened concern.

"Not breathing, Doc!"

Max was working at the desk, muttering equations of hemoglobin catalysis.

"Len's gone, Doc," the assistant said more loudly.

"Artificial respiration and get him into a regeneration tank," said June, not moving from the microscope. "Hurry! Hal will show you how. The oxidation and mechanical heart action in the tank will keep him going. Put anyone in a tank who seems to be dying. Get some women to help you. Give them Hal's instructions."

The tanks were ordinarily used to suspend animation in a nutrient bath during the regrowth of any diseased organ. They could preserve life in an almost totally destroyed body during the usual disintegration and regrowth treatments for cancer and old age, and they could encourage healing as destruction continued . . . but they could not prevent ultimate death as long as the disease was not conquered.

The drop of blood in June's microscope was a great dark field, and in the foreground, brought to gargantuan solidity by the stereo effect, drifted neat saucer shapes of red blood cells. They turned end for end, floating by the humped misty mass of a leukocyte which was crawling on the cover glass. There were not enough red corpuscles, and she felt that they grew fewer as she watched.

She fixed her eye on one, not blinking in fear that she would miss what might happen. It was a tidy red button, and it spun as it drifted, the current moving it aside in a curve as it passed by the leukocyte.

Then, abruptly, the cell vanished.

June stared numbly at the place where it had been. Where had it gone?

Behind her, Max was calling over the speaker system again: "Dr. Stark speaking. Any technician who knows anything about the life tanks, start bringing more out of storage and set them up. Emergency."

"We may need forty-seven," June said quietly. There were forty-seven men.

"We may need forty-seven," Max repeated to the ship in general. His voice did not falter. "Set them up along the corridor. Hook them in on extension lines."

His voice filtered back from the empty floors above in a series of dim echoes. What he had said meant that every man on board might be on the point of heart stoppage.

June looked blindly through the binocular microscope, trying to think. Out of the corner of her eye, she could see that Max was wavering and breathing more and more frequently of the pure, cold, burning oxygen of the cylinders. In the microscope she could see that there were fewer red cells left alive in the drop of his blood. The rate of fall was accelerating.

She didn't have to glance at Max to know how he would look—skin pale, black eyebrows and keen brown eyes slightly squinted in thought, a faint ironical grin twisting the bluing lips. Intelligent, thin, sensitive, his face was part of her mind. It was inconceivable that Max could die. He couldn't die. He couldn't leave her alone.

She forced her mind back to the problem. All the men of the *Explorer* were at the same point, wherever they were. Somehow losing blood, dying.

Moving to Max's desk, she spoke into the intercom system. "Bess, send a couple of women to look through the ship, room by room, with a stretcher. Make sure all the men are down here." She remembered Reno. "Sparks, heard anything from Reno? Is he back?"

Sparks replied weakly after a lag. "The last I heard from Reno was a call this morning. He was raving about mirrors, and Pat Mead's folks not being real people, just carbon copies, and claiming he was crazy; and I should send him the psychiatrist. I thought he was kidding. He didn't call back."

"Thanks, Sparks." Reno was dead.

Max dialed and spoke gasping over the phone. "Are you okay up there? Forget about engineering controls. Drop everything and head for the tanks while you can still walk. If your tank's not done, lie down next to it."

June went back to the worktable and whispered into her own phone. "Bess, send up a stretcher for Max. He looks pretty bad."

There had to be a solution. The life tanks could sustain life in a damaged body, encouraging it to regrow more rapidly, but they merely slowed death as long as the disease was not checked. The postponement could not last long, for destruction could go on steadily in the tanks until the nutritive solution would hold no life except the triumphant microscopic killers that caused melting sickness.

There were very few red blood corpuscles in the microscope field now, incredibly few. She tipped the microscope and they began to drift, spinning slowly. A lone corpuscle floated through the center. She watched it as the current swept it in an arc past the dim off-focus bulk of the leukocyte. There was a sweep of motion and it vanished.

For a moment it meant nothing to her; then she lifted her head from the microscope and looked around. Max sat at his desk, head in hand, his rumpled short black hair sticking out between his fingers at odd angles. A pencil and a pad scrawled with formulas lay on the desk before him. She could see his concentration in the rigid set of his shoulders. He was still thinking; he had not given up.

"Max, I just saw a leukocyte grab a red blood corpuscle. It was unbelievably fast."

"Leukemia," muttered Max without moving. "Galloping leukemia yet! That comes under the heading of cancer. Well, that's part of the answer. It might be all we need." He grinned feebly and reached for the speaker set. "Anybody still on his feet in there?" he muttered into it, and the question was amplified to a booming voice throughout the ship. "Hal, are you still going? Look, Hal, change all the dials, change the dials, set them to deep melt and regeneration. One week. This is like leukemia. Got it? This is like leukemia."

June rose. It was time for her to take over the job. She leaned across his desk and spoke into the speaker system. "Doctor Walton talking," she said. "This is to the women. Don't let any of the men work any more; they'll kill themselves. See that they all go into the tanks right away. Set the tank dials for deep regeneration. You can see how from the ones that are set."

Two exhausted and frightened women clattered in the doorway with a stretcher. Their hands were scratched and oily from helping to set up tanks.

"That order includes you," she told Max sternly and caught him as he swayed.

Max saw the stretcher bearers and struggled upright. "Ten more minutes," he said clearly. "Might think of an idea. Something not right in this setup. I have to figure how to prevent a relapse, how the thing started."

He knew more bacteriology than she did; she had to help him think. She motioned the bearers to wait, fixed a breathing mask for Max from a cylinder of CO_2 and one of oxygen. Max went back to his desk.

She walked up and down, trying to think, remembering the hamsters. The melting sickness, it was called. Melting. She struggled with an impulse to open a tank which held one of the men. She wanted to look in, see if that would explain the name.

Melting sickness . . .

Footsteps came and Pat Mead stood uncertainly in the doorway. Tall, handsome, rugged, a pioneer. "Anything I can do?" he asked.

She barely looked at him. "You can stay out of our way. We're busy."

"I'd like to help," he said.

"Very funny." She was vicious, enjoying the whip of her words. "Every man is dying because you're a carrier, and you want to help."

He stood nervously clenching and unclenching his hands. "A guinea pig, maybe. I'm immune. All the Meads are."

"Go away." God, why couldn't she think? What makes a Mead immune?

"Aw, let 'im alone," Max muttered. "Pat hasn't done anything." He went waveringly to the microscope, took a tiny sliver from his finger, suspended it in a slide, and slipped it under the lens with detached habitual dexterity. "Something funny going on," he said to June. "Symptoms don't feel right."

After a moment he straightened and motioned for her to look. "Leukocytes, phagocytes—" He was bewildered. "My own—"

She looked in, and then looked back at Pat in a growing wave of horror. "They're not your own, Max!" she whispered.

Max rested a hand on the table to brace himself, put his eye to the microscope, and looked again. June knew what he saw. Phagocytes, leukocytes, attacking and devouring his tissues in a growing incredible horde, multiplying insanely.

Not his phagocytes! Pat Mead's! The Meads' evolved cells had learned too much. They were contagious. And Pat Mead's . . . How much alike *were* the Meads? . . . Mead cells contagious from one to another, not a disease attacking or being fought, but acting as normal leukocytes in whatever body they were in! The leukocytes of tall, redheaded people, finding no strangeness in the bloodstream of any of the tall, redheaded people. No strangeness . . . A totipotent leukocyte finding its way into cellular wombs.

The womblike life tanks. For the men of the *Explorer*, a week's cure with deep melting to de-differentiate the leukocytes and turn them back to normal tissue, then regrowth and reforming from the cells that were there. From the cells that *were* there. *From the cells that were there* . . .

"Pat, the germs are your cells!"

Crazily, Pat began to laugh, his face twisted with sudden understanding. "I understand. I get it. I'm a contagious personality. That's funny, isn't it?"

Max rose suddenly from the microscope and lurched. Pat caught him as he fell, and the bewildered stretcher bearers carried him out to the tanks.

For a week June tended the tanks. The other women volunteered to help, but she refused. She said nothing, hoping her guess would not be true.

"Is everything all right?" Elsie asked her anxiously. "How is Len coming along?" Elsie looked haggard and worn, like all the women, from doing the work that the men had always done, and their own work too.

"He's fine," June said tonelessly, shutting tight the door of the tank room. "They're all fine."

"That's good," Elsie said, but she looked more frightened than before.

June firmly locked the tank-room door and the girl went away.

The other women had been listening, and now they wandered back to their jobs, unsatisfied by June's answer, but not daring to ask for the truth. They were there whenever June went into the tank room, and they were still there—or relieved by others, June was not sure—when she came out. And always some one of them asked the unvarying question for all the others, and June gave the unvarying answer. But she kept the key. No woman but herself knew what was going on in the life tanks.

Then the day of completion came. June told no one of the hour. She went into the room as on the other days, locked the door behind her, and there was the nightmare again. This time it was reality, and she wandered down a path between long rows of coffinlike tanks, calling, "Max! Max!" silently and looking into each one as it opened.

But each face she looked at was the same. Watching them dissolve and regrow in the nutrient solution, she had only been able to guess at the horror of what was happening. Now she knew.

They were all the same lean-boned, blond-skinned face, with a pin-feather growth of reddish down on cheeks and scalp. All horribly—and handsomely—the same.

A medical kit lay carelessly on the floor beside Max's tank. She stood near the bag. "Max," she said, and found her throat closing. The canned voice of the mechanical apparatus mocked her, speaking glibly about waking and sitting up. "I'm sorry, Max . . ."

The tall man with rugged features and bright blue eyes sat up sleepily and lifted an eyebrow at her, and ran his hand over his red-fuzzed head in a gesture of bewilderment. "What's the matter, June?" he asked drowsily.

She gripped his arm. "Max—"

He compared the relative size of his arm with her hand and said wonderingly, "You shrank."

"I know, Max. I know."

He turned his head and looked at his arms and legs, pale blond arms and legs with a down of red hair. He touched the thick left arm, squeezed a pinch of hard flesh. "It isn't mine," he said, surprised. "But I can feel it."

Watching his face was like watching a stranger mimicking and distorting Max's expressions. Max in fear. Max trying to understand what had happened to him, looking around at the other men sitting up in their tanks. Max feeling the terror that was in herself and all the men as they stared at themselves and their friends and saw what they had become.

"We're all Pat Mead," he said harshly. "All the Meads are Pat Mead. That's why he was surprised to see people who didn't look like himself."

"Yes, Max."

"Max," he repeated. "It's me, all right. The nervous system didn't change." His new blue eyes held hers. "I'm me inside. Do you love me, June?"

But she couldn't know yet. She had loved Max with the thin, ironic face, the rumpled black hair, and the twisted smile that never really hid his quick sympathy. Now he was Pat Mead. Could he also be Max? "Of course I still love you, darling."

He grinned. It was still the wry smile of Max, though fitting strangely on the handsome new blond face. "Then it isn't so bad. It might even be pretty good. I envied him this big, muscular body. If Pat or any of these Meads so much as looks at you, I'm going to knock his block off. Now I can do it."

She laughed and couldn't stop. It wasn't that funny. But it was still Max, trying to be unafraid, drawing on humor. Maybe the rest of the men would also be their old selves, enough so the women would not feel that their men were strangers.

Behind her, male voices spoke characteristically. She did not have to turn to know which was which: "This is one way to keep a guy from stealing your girl," that was Len Marlow; "I've got to write down reactions," Hal Barton; "Now I can really work that hillside vein of metal," St. Clair. Then others complaining, swearing, laughing bitterly at the trick that had been played on them and their flirting, tempted women. She knew who they were. Their women would know them apart too.

"We'll go outside," Max said. "You and I. Maybe the shock won't be so bad to the women after they see me." He paused. "You didn't tell them, did you?"

"I couldn't. I wasn't sure. I—was hoping I was wrong."

She opened the door and closed it quickly. There was a small crowd on the other side.

"Hello, Pat," Elsie said uncertainly, trying to look past them into the tank room before the door shut.

"I'm not Pat, I'm Max," said the tall man with the blue eyes and the fuzz-reddened skull. "Listen—"

"Good heavens, Pat, what happened to your hair?" Sheila asked.

"I'm Max," insisted the man with the handsome face and the sharp blue eyes. "Don't you get it? I'm Max Stark. The melting sickness is Mead cells. We caught them from Pat. They adapted us to Minos. They also changed us all into Pat Mead."

The women stared at him, at each other. They shook their heads.

"They don't understand," June said. "I couldn't have if I hadn't seen it happening, Max."

"It's Pat," said Sheila, dazedly stubborn. "He shaved off his hair. It's some kind of joke."

Max shook her shoulders, glaring down at her face. "I'm Max. Max Stark. They all look like me. Do you hear? It's funny, but it's not a joke. Laugh for us, for God's sake!"

"It's too much," said June. "They'll have to see."

She opened the door and let them in. They hurried past her to the tanks, looking at forty-six identical blond faces, beginning to call in frightened voices:

"Jerry!"

"Harry!"

"Lee, where are you, sweetheart—"

June shut the door on the voices that were growing hysterical, the women terrified and helpless, the men shouting to let the women know who they were.

"It isn't easy," said Max, looking down at his own thick muscles. "But you aren't changed and the other girls aren't. That helps."

Through the muffled noise and hysteria, a bell was ringing.

"It's the air lock," June said.

Peering in the viewplate were nine Meads from Alexandria. To all appearances, eight of them were Pat Mead at various ages, from fifteen to fifty, and the other was a handsome, leggy, redheaded girl who could have been his sister.

Regretfully, they explained through the voice tube that they had walked over from Alexandria to bring news that the plane pilot had contracted melting sickness there and had died.

They wanted to come in.

June and Max told them to wait and returned to the tank room. The men were enjoying their new height and strength, and the women were bewilderedly learning that they could tell one Pat Mead from another by voice, by gesture of face or hand. The panic was gone. In its place was acceptance of the fantastic situation.

Max called for attention. "There are nine Meads outside who want to come in. They have different names, but they're all Pat Mead."

They frowned or looked blank, and George Barton asked, "Why didn't you let them in? I don't see any problem."

"One of them," said Max soberly, "is a girl. *Patricia* Mead. The girl wants to come in."

There was a long silence while the implication settled to the fear center of the women's minds. Sheila the beautiful felt it first. She cried, "No! Please don't let her in!" There was real fright in her tone and the women caught it quickly.

Elsie clung to Len, begging, "You don't want me to change, do you, Len? You like me the way I am! Tell me you do!"

The other girls backed away. It was illogical, but it was human. June felt terror rising in herself. She held up her hand for quiet and presented the necessity to the group.

"Only half of us can leave Minos," she said. "The men cannot eat ship food; they've been conditioned to this planet. We women can go, but we would have to go without our men. We can't go outside without contagion, and we can't spend the rest of our lives in quarantine inside the ship. George Barton is right—there is no problem."

"But we'd be changed!" Sheila shrilled. "I don't want to become a Mead! I don't want to be somebody else!"

She ran to the inner wall of the corridor. There was a brief hesitation, and then, one by one, the women fled to that side, until there were only Bess, June, and four others left.

"See!" cried Sheila. "A vote! We can't let the girl in!"

No one spoke. To change, to be someone else—the idea was strange and horrifying. The men stood uneasily glancing at each other, as if looking into mirrors, and against the wall of the corridor the women watched in fear and huddled together, staring at the men. One man in forty-seven poses. One of them made a beseeching move toward Elsie and she shrank away.

"No, Len! I won't let you change me!"

Max stirred restlessly, the ironic smile that made his new face his own unconsciously twisting into a grimace of pity. "We men can't leave, and you women can't stay," he said bluntly. "Why not let Patricia Mead in. Get it over with!"

June took a small mirror from her belt pouch and studied her own face, aware of Max talking forcefully, the men standing silent, the women pleading. Her face . . . her own face with its dark-blue eyes, small nose, long mobile lips . . . the mind and the body are inseparable; the shape of a face is part of the mind. She put the mirror back.

"I'd kill myself!" Sheila was sobbing. "I'd rather die!"

"You won't die," Max was saying. "Can't you see there's only one solution—"

They were looking at Max. June stepped silently out of the tank room, and then turned and went to the air lock. She opened the valves that would let in Pat Mead's sister.

The Woman from Altair

LEIGH BRACKETT

I / *Ahrian*

What a great day it was for everybody, when David came home from
deep space. It was a day that will remain for a long while on the
calendar of the McQuarrie family, marked heavily in red.

We had driven down to the spaceport to meet him—myself, and
Bet, who was David's and my sister, just out of college, and David's
fiancée, a Miss Lewisham. The Miss Lewisham had family but no
money, and David had both, and that was as far as it went. She was
one of these handsome, shallow-eyed babes as perfectly machined as
a chunk of Bakelite, and just as human. Bet thought she was terrific.
She had spent hours getting herself up to be as like her as possible,
but it was all in vain. Bet's hair still behaved like hair, and blew.

The spaceport was swarming. Interplanetary flight had long ago
ceased to be a thing of breathless wonder to the populace, but starships
were still new and rare, and the men who flew them were still heroic.
Word had gone out that the *Anson McQuarrie* was due in from somewhere beyond the Pleiades, and there were thousands of people backed
up behind the barricades. I remember that there were flags, and somebody had prepared a speech.

"Isn't it wonderful!" said Bet, around a lump in her throat. "And all
for David."

"There are some other men on that ship, too," I said.

"Oh, you always have to be so nasty," she snapped. "David's the
captain, and the owner, too. And he deserves the reception."

"Uh-huh," I said, "and what's more, David himself would be the
last to disagree with you."

Officials were opening a way for us, and I shoved Bet along it with
the Miss Lewisham, who headed like a homing duck for the TV cameras. At about that moment a feminine voice hailed us, and Bet whirled
around, crying out, "Marthe!"

An extremely attractive young woman detached herself from a group of obvious reporters and joined us.

"I'm going to be quite shameless," she announced, "and presume on an old school friendship."

I liked the way she grinned and practically dared me to throw her out of the family circle. I should have done so, but didn't because of that cheeky grin, and that's how Marthe Walters came to be mixed up in this mess. I wished so desperately afterward that I had pushed her face in. But how is one to know?

Bet was offering explanations. "Marthe was a senior when I was a freshman, Rafe. Remember? That was when I was going to be a journalist." She rushed through the introductions, and memory clicked.

"Oh, yes," I said. "You're the Marthe Walters who does those profile sketches for *Public*."

"It's honest work, but it's a living."

"You've come to the right place. My brother has the devil and all of a profile."

She cocked her head on one side and gave me a peculiarly intelligent look. "Yours isn't so bad. And come to think of it, I've never heard of you."

"I'm the forgotten McQuarrie," I said. "The one who didn't go to space."

All this time we were being assisted onward to the place that had been reserved for the family. Bet was burbling, the Miss Lewisham was being statuesque and proud, and this bright-eyed intruder, Marthe, was thinking questions and trying to devise a politic way of asking them.

"You're David's older brother?"

"Ancient."

"And you're a McQuarrie, and you didn't go to space." She shook her head. "That's like being a fish, and refusing to swim."

"It's not Rafe's fault," said Bet, with that touch of womanly pity she could get in her voice sometimes. "How soon will he land, Rafe? I just can't wait!"

I was trying to figure out what color Marthe's eyes were. I got them pegged for blue, and then there was some change in the light or something, and they were green as seawater.

"Surely," she said, "you didn't wash out."

"No, it was noisier than that. I crashed. It was a light plane, but it came down heavy."

"He was on his way to the spaceport from the Academy," said Bet sadly. "He had his papers and everything, and was going out on his first voyage as a junior officer. The disappointment nearly killed Father, Rafe being the oldest son and everything. But then, he still had David."

"I see," said Marthe. She smiled at me, and this time it wasn't cheeky, but the sort of smile a man would like to see more of. "I'm sorry. I thought that walking stick was pure swank."

"It is," I told her, and laughed. "I think that's what really disgusts the family—I'm healthy as a horse. I only carry the thing to remind them that I'm supposed to be frail."

They were in radio communication with the *Anson McQuarrie*. The reports of position kept coming in, and an amplifier blatted them out. Men ran around looking harried, a million voices chattered, necks craned, the tension built up. The towers of Manhattan glittered mightily in the distance. Marthe and I talked. I think we talked about her.

A great roar went up. Bet screamed in my ear. There was a perfect frenzy of sound for a few moments, and then there was silence, and in it the sky split open like tearing silk. A speck of silver came whistling down the cleft, growing rapidly, becoming a huge graceful creature with tarnished flanks and star-dust on her nose, and pride in every rivet. Oh, she was beautiful, and she settled light as a moonbeam on the landing field that had been cleared of any lesser craft. The *Anson McQuarrie* was home.

I noticed then that Marthe had not been watching the ship at all. She was watching me.

"You," she said, "are a rather puzzling person."

"Does that bother you?"

"I don't like a book that has the whole story on the first page."

"Good," I said. "Then you won't like David. Come along. And oh, yes, any time you want to catch up on your reading—"

"There he is!" shrieked Bet. "There's David!"

The barricades were keeping back the crowds, and officials were forming a second line of defense against the mob of reporters. We, the family, were allowed to be first with our greetings. The underhatch had opened in that vast keel, the platform was run out, and a tall figure in absolutely impeccable uniform had emerged onto it. Bands played, thousands cheered, the TV cameras rolled, and David lifted his hand and smiled. A handsome beggar, my brother, with all the best points of the McQuarrie stock. I think he was a little annoyed when Bet flung herself up the steps and onto his neck. She mussed his collar badly.

I waved. The Miss Lewisham mounted to the platform, showing her splendid legs. She held out her arms graciously, prepared to grant

David the dignified kiss due a hero from his future wife. But David gave her a horrified look as though he had forgotten all about her, and his face turned six different shades of red.

He recovered magnificently. He caught those outstretched hands and shook them warmly, at the same time getting her off to one side so smoothly that she hardly realized it. Before she could say anything, he had spoken, to the world at large, with boyish pride.

"I have seen," he said, "many strange and precious things on the worlds of other stars. And I have brought back with me the most wonderful of them all. I want you to welcome her to Earth."

Here he turned to someone who had been waiting inside the hatch, and handed her out.

I don't think that any of us, least of all the Miss Lewisham, caught on for a moment. We were too busy, like everybody else, staring at the little creature who was clinging to David's hand.

She seemed incredibly small and fragile to be a grown woman, and yet that is what she was, and no mistake about it. She wore a very quaint drapery of some gossamer stuff that shimmered in the sunlight, and the lovely shape of her beneath it was something to wonder at. Her skin was perfectly white and beautiful, like fine porcelain, and her little face was pointed and fey-looking, with eyebrows that swept up toward her temples like two delicate feathers. Her hair was the color of amethysts. There was a great deal of it, piled high on her head in an intricate coiffure, and the lights in it were marvelous, as though every conceivable shade of that jewel had been melted and spun together and made alive. Her eyes, slanting under those sweeping brows, were the same color, but deeper, a true purple. They looked out in great bewilderment upon this noisy alien world.

"She is from Altair," said David. "Her name is Ahrian. She is my wife."

The reactions to that last simple statement were violent and more than a little confused. Sometime before the shouting died, and while Bet was still staring like an absolute idiot at her unexpected sister-in-law, the Miss Lewisham departed, with every hair still perfectly in place. Where her temper was, I don't know. The reporters stampeded, and no one and nothing could hold them back. The TV men were in transports when David kissed his little bride from Altair. I looked down at Marthe.

"I suppose," I said, "it wouldn't be any good asking you to go away now."

She said it wouldn't be. She was shivering slightly, like a wolf that has found a fat lamb asleep under its nose. "A woman from Altair," she whispered. "This isn't a story, it's a sensation."

"It's certainly a surprise for the family!"

"Poor little thing, she looks scared to death. Whatever you feel, don't take it out on her." Marthe glanced up at me, as though a sudden thought had occurred to her. "By the way," she asked, "is your brother quite right in the head?"

"I'm beginning to wonder," I said.

Up on the platform, the focus of the excitement, the new Mrs. David McQuarrie trembled against her husband and stared with those purple enigmatic eyes at the alien hosts of a world that was not her own.

II / *Stranger on Earth*

Grimly we set off on the ride home. I had managed to get Bet on one side and threaten her with bodily injury if she didn't keep her mouth shut. David himself, what with the exultation of homecoming and the sensation he had created with his dramatic announcement of marriage, was flying too high to notice any of us too much. He held Ahrian in the circle of his arm as if she had been a child, and talked to her, and soothed her, and pointed out this and that interesting thing along the road.

As she looked at the houses and trees, the hills and valleys, the sun and the sky, I couldn't help being sorry for her. In my younger days I had gone, as supercargo in my father's ships, to Venus and Mars and beyond the Belt to Jupiter. I knew what it was like to walk on alien soil. And she was so far away from home that even her familiar sun was gone.

She glanced at us now and then, with a kind of shy terror. Bet sulked and glowered, but I managed a smile, and Marthe patted Ahrian's hand. David had taught her English. She spoke it well, but with a curious rippling accent that made it sound like a foreign tongue.

Her voice was soft and low and very sweet. She did not talk much. Neither did we.

David barely noticed that we had a stranger with us. I had said vaguely that Marthe was a friend of mine, and he had nodded and forgot her. I was rather glad to have her along. There are times when families should not be alone together.

The McQuarrie place is built on top of a rise. The house is large, and was originally built almost two centuries ago, when old Anson

McQuarrie founded the family fortune with a fleet of ore carriers for the Lunar mines. There are old trees around it, and a thousand acres of land, and it is one of those places that exude from every pore a discreet odor of money.

Ahrian looked at it and said dutifully,

"It is very beautiful."

"Not quite the sort of place she's used to," David remarked to us. "But she'll love it."

I wondered if she would.

We all piled out of the car, and Marthe hesitated. She had been so completely absorbed in studying Ahrian that I doubt if she had thought of her own position at all. Now the sight of our rather hulking house seemed to daunt her.

"I think maybe I better go back now," she said. "I've imposed enough, and I've got a lot to go on. I'd like to really interview them both, but this is hardly the time for it."

"Oh, no," I told her emphatically. "You're staying. Bet's got to have somebody to yak to, and it isn't going to be me. You're her old school chum, remember?"

Marthe took a good look at Bet's furious countenance and muttered, "I have a feeling I'm going to hold this against you, Mr. McQuarrie."

She was so right. Except that I held it against myself, the other way round.

Suddenly Ahrian, who was a little distance up the walk with David, let out a quivering scream. David began to yell angrily for me. I went on to see what was the matter.

"It's only Buck," I said.

"Well, get him out of here. He's frightening Ahrian."

"She might as well get used to him now," I said, and took Buck by the collar. He was a very large dog, and one of the best I ever had. He didn't like Ahrian. I could feel him shiver, and the hair on his back bristled under my hand.

David was going to get ugly about it, and then Ahrian said, "It is that I have not before seen such a creature. It means no harm. Only it is uneasy."

She began to talk to Buck, in her own soft liquid tongue. Gradually his muscles stilled and the hackles flattened and the ears relaxed. His eyes had a puzzled look. Presently he stalked forward and laid his head in her hands.

Ahrian laughed. "You see? We are friends."

I looked at the dog. There was no joy in him. Ahrian took her small white hands from his head. Abruptly he turned and went away, running fast.

Ahrian said softly, "I have very much to learn."

"Just the same," said David, glaring at me, "you be careful with your confounded livestock." He swept Ahrian on up the walk. The door had been opened. David did the inevitable thing. He picked Ahrian up in his arms and bore her with a courtly flourish across the threshold.

"All I've got to say is," Bet snarled, "I hope they can't—I mean, I just couldn't bear it to have a little nephew with lavender hair!"

She stamped on into the house. I took Marthe firmly by the arm. "Bet can fix you up with suitable garments."

"What for?"

"We are having a dinner tonight, in David's honor. Formal, of course. There will be many people."

"How delightful," she said, and groaning, followed Bet.

That dinner may not have been delightful, but it certainly was not dull. The drawing rooms teemed with what Daisy Ashford would have referred to as costly people, all quite ill at ease. Ahrian, sitting at the table in the place that was to have been the Miss Lewisham's, was a little figure fashioned in some Dresden of Fairyland, dressed in a matchless tissue of pale gold and crowned with that incredibly beautiful hair.

The women didn't know how to deal with her, and the men were fascinated, and all in all it was not a successful social occasion. Late in the evening David made her sing. She had a curious stringed instrument from which she drew soft wandering music, and she sang songs of her own world that were sweet and very strange. Some of them didn't have any words. They told of the things that lie hid beyond mountains, and of the secrets oceans know, and of the long, still thoughts of deserts. But they were not the mountains or the deserts or the seas of Earth. Toward the end there came into her eyes two great crystal tears.

Soon after that I noticed that she had disappeared. David was holding the center of the stage with some thrilling recital of events beyond the stars, and it seemed to be up to me to look for her.

I found her at last, standing disconsolate on the steps that led down from the terrace into the garden. There were many shadows in it, and the shrubs rustled in the wind, so that it must have seemed a frightening place to her. There were clouds, I remember, veiling the sky.

She turned and looked at me. "Why did you come to me?"

"I thought perhaps you might be lonely."

"There is David," she answered. "Why might I be lonely?"

I could not see her face, except as a small blurred whiteness in the gloom. "Yes," I said, "you have David. But it's still possible to be sad."

She said, "I will not be sad." I could read nothing in the tone of her voice, either.

"Ahrian, you must try to understand us. We were upset today, because we hadn't expected you, and—well—" I tried, rather lamely, to explain how things had stood. "It wasn't anything personal. You're part of the family now, and we'll do all we can to make you welcome."

"The little one—she is full of anger."

"She's just a kid. Give her time. A month from now she'll be wanting to dye her hair to match yours." I held out my hand. "We have a custom here of clasping hands as a token of friendship. Will you take mine, Ahrian?"

She hesitated, a long, long moment. Then she said gravely, as if it were something I must remember, "I do not hate you, Rafe." She put her hand in mine, a fleeting touch as light and chill as the falling of a snowflake. Then she shivered. "It is cold on your world when the darkness comes."

"Is it always warm on yours?" We started toward the house, and looking down at her beside me, I thought I could understand why David had not been able to let her go.

She answered softly, "Yes, it is warm, and the moons are like bright lamps in the sky. The spires and the rooftops glisten, and there are dark leaves that shake out perfume—"

She broke off, too quickly, and said no more.

"You must love David very deeply to have come all this long way home with him."

"Love is indeed a great force," she murmured.

We went inside, and David claimed her again.

For several days I did not see much of Ahrian. I handle the financial end of the McQuarrie business, not because I like it but because I have to do something to justify the money I spend. David had brought back an invaluable cargo, some of it from worlds that, like Ahrian's, had never been touched before. I think we cleared around a million dollars on it, over and above the cost of the voyage.

I was so busy that I hardly had time to see Marthe. Strange, how important it had become to see Marthe, so quickly and without anything being said about it. She had left our house, of course, in high spirits over the inside stuff she had got for her articles. I had said,

"When will I see you again?" And she had answered, "Any time."
That's how it was—any time we could possibly make it.

One night, when by chance the family were all together at dinner,
Ahrian said shyly, "David, I have been thinking—"

Instantly he was all attention. He really did seem to adore her. I
will admit that I had a few sneaking suspicions, or perhaps it was only
a puzzled wonder, since David so far in his life had had only three
loves—starships, himself, and the McQuarrie name, in that order. But
his manner with Ahrian appeared to show that he had found the fourth.

"In my home," said Ahrian, "I had a small place that was my own,
in which I found much pleasure in fashioning little gifts for those I
loved. Only a very small place, David—might I have one here?"

David smiled at her and said that she might have anything there
was on Earth or the other planets, except the ugly clothes that might
be all right for Earthlings but were not for her. Ahrian smiled back,
asking, still with that shy hesitance, for some gemstones of small value,
and some fine wires of platinum and gold.

"Diamonds," said David. "Emeralds. All you like."

"No. I will have the crystal and the zircon. Uncut, please. I wish
to shape them myself."

"With those tiny hands? Very well, darling. I'll have them here
tomorrow."

Ahrian thanked him gravely and glanced across at me. "I am learning very quickly, Rafe. I have seen all your horses. They are a wonder
to me, so large and beautiful."

"If you like," I said, "I could teach you to ride."

"Perhaps on that very little one?"

I laughed and explained to her why a three-week foal was not
suitable for that. David said fiercely that he was not going to have
Ahrian trampled to death by one of my lubberly beasts, and forbade
anything of the sort.

After dinner I got Bet alone and asked her how she was making
out with Ahrian.

"Oh, I suppose it isn't her fault, but she gives me the creeps, Rafe!
She goes drifting around the place like a funny little shadow, and
sometimes the way she looks at you . . . I get the feeling she's studying
me—way deep inside, I mean. I don't like it—and I don't like her!"

"Well, try to be as nice as you can. The poor little critter must be
having a hard enough time of it. Remember we're as alien to her as
she is to us."

"She wanted to come," said Bet, without pity. I left her, and went off to keep a date with Marthe. . . .

III / *Gifts of—Love*

David fixed up a wonderful workshop for Ahrian, where she could make pretty trinkets to her heart's content. She would remain there for hours, humming softly to herself, letting no one, not even David, in to see what she was doing. She worked for weeks, and then one evening she came in to dinner with the pleased air of a child who has done a nice thing. I saw that she was carrying some light burden in a fold of her gown.

She was wearing a kind of tiara that went very well with her masses of amethystine hair and her curious little face. It was a delicate thing, exquisitely wrought of mingled wires of platinum and gold woven into a strange design of flowers and set with a flawless crystal that she had cut herself in a way that I had never seen a crystal cut before.

She strewed her small burden glittering on the tablecloth. "See! I have made a gift for everyone. You must wear them, or I shall be so unhappy!"

They were beautiful. For David and me she had made rings—for, as she said, we did not wear jewels as the men of her world did, and so she had had to be content with rings. For Bet there was a necklace, of a sort that no girl could resist if the devil himself had given it to her.

There was a chorus of astonished comment. David told Ahrian that she could make a fortune for herself if she would make and sell these things to the world. Ahrian shook her head.

"No. These are gifts and must be fashioned with a meaning from the heart. Otherwise I could not make them."

The stones were all most curiously cut.

It was exactly eight days after that giving of gifts that the thing happened.

David was away on some business in the city. Marthe was spending the weekend—Ahrian seemed an odd kind of chaperone, but we thought she would serve—and we had been taking a stroll in a wood that there is north of the house.

All of a sudden we heard the sound of someone screaming.

We started to run back toward the house. A scream has no identity, but somehow I knew this one came from Bet. Marthe got some distance ahead of me, and then she began to scream, too. There were other sounds mixed with the screaming. I made all the speed I could. Where the wood ended, there was a wide stretch of turf, with the house way at the back of it and here and there apple trees that were part of an old orchard.

Bet had got herself up into one of these old thorny veterans. Her clothes were torn and there were dabbles of blood on her face and dress. Her cries had ceased to have any meaning. In a minute she was going to faint.

My big dog Buck was under the tree. He leaped and sprang, and his teeth flashed like knives in the sunlight, snapping shut no more than a short inch beneath the limb Bet huddled on. He moaned as he leaped, a strange and dreadful sound as though he were being tortured and were pleading for release.

I shouted his name. He turned his head, gave me one pitiful look, and then he went back to trying to kill my sister. I was carrying the heavy blackthorn stick I used when I walked in the country. I hit him with the knob of it. Poor Buck! He was dead in a minute or two, as quick as I could make it, and he never tried to defend himself. I caught Bet as she tumbled out of the apple tree, and Marthe and I between us got her to the house.

Ahrian was there. She gave a little cry of horror and bent her head, and I remember the flash of crystal on her forehead in the dim hall. Servants came and took Bet. Marthe ran off somewhere to be sick, and I called town for David and a doctor.

For a while I was busy with brandy and restoratives. Presently Bet came around, more terrified than hurt. Her scratches had come mostly from climbing into the tree. She said she had been looking for Marthe and me, when suddenly Buck had appeared out of nowhere and, for no reason at all, tried to tear her throat out.

"I never did him any harm," she whimpered. "I like him, and he liked me. He must have gone mad."

I was glad when the doctor came and put her under for a while. Buck was taken away for autopsy. He was not rabid, nor was there a sign of any other disease. I had that stick burned up. I couldn't forget the way Buck had moaned, the way he had looked at me before he died. David had some bitter words to say, and I nearly hit him, which was unfair under the circumstances.

Anyway, the dog was dead, and Bet was all right. In time everybody's nerves calmed down, and even Bet got tired of talking about it. David had a birthday coming up. Ahrian made great preparations, asking us all incessant questions about how things should be done according to our customs, and adding a few of her own.

David liked lavishness, so there was another big dinner and a lot of people. Ahrian had gained confidence, and everybody had had time to gossip themselves out about her by now. It was a much more successful occasion than the first. Even some of the women decided not to hate her.

Marthe and I retired into the library for a little quiet lovemaking. Between times we discussed getting married. Through the closed doors we heard Ahrian singing for a while, not the longing heartsick things she had sung before, but something gay and wicked. When she stopped, there was only the usual buzz and chatter of people.

Some time went by, I don't know how much. Without any warning a terrible racket arose of horses squealing, and of yelling, and I remember thinking that the barns must be on fire.

I got outside in a hurry. The guests were beginning to pour out onto the veranda and peer curiously into the darkness to see what the trouble was. Among them, I noticed Ahrian with a cloak around her.

The stables and the big open paddocks are some distance from the house. Halfway there I saw Jamieson, my head groom, running toward me.

"It's Miss Bet," he gasped, white-faced and shaking. "Hurry!"

I hurried, but there was a cold, sick feeling in me that told me hurrying was no use.

There was an old brood mare, gentle as a kitten, long past her usefulness and pensioned off. She was Bet's especial pet, and old Hazel would muster up a stiff-legged canter from wherever she was to come and snuffle over her for sugar-lumps.

All the big floodlights were on. There was a confusion of men and horses and noise. Old Hazel was pressed up against the paddock fence, her coat dark with sweat, trembling in every muscle. There was blood on her legs. Bet was dead. In her long white party dress and her silver sandals she had come all the way down there and gone into the paddock, and the old mare had trampled her. It didn't make any sense at all. I kneeled there beside her in the dirt, and the necklace of zircons that Ahrian had given her glittered among the splashes of blood.

The men had got ropes on the mare now, and she began to thrash and scream like a crazy thing. Somebody handed me a gun, and I used it, all the time knowing that the poor old beast had no more killing in her than Buck had had.

It made no kind of sense. But Bet was dead.

It was a fine ending to a gay evening.

You know how it is with a kid sister. Sometimes she's a pest, and sometimes she's ridiculous, and she always talks too much, but even so— And it was such an ugly way to die.

David was going down to shoot every horse in the place. When I stopped him, he turned on me. There was a bad scene. They were my animals. One had tried, and one had succeeded, and that made me practically a murderer. I let it go, because he was hard hit, and so was I. But from then on there was a wall between me and my brother, and the hate he had against me over Bet's death seemed to grow day by day. I couldn't understand why. It seemed almost insane, but whatever shortcomings David had, insanity was not one of them.

We buried Bet, and no one wept more bitterly than Ahrian. She was David's loving comforter, and for the first time I was genuinely glad she was there.

IV / Star Dreams

On the night after the funeral I began to dream.

At first the dreams were brief and vague. But they got longer and clearer, until my days became nightmares and my nights an unbearable hell. Sleep became a torture. I dreamed of space.

The McQuarries are spacemen. From old Anson down the sons have flown the ships, and the daughters have married men who could fly ships, and the McQuarrie flag has been carried a long, long way. As far as I know, we never did anything more sinful than to get there first, but the McQuarrie ships have gained and held the richest cream of the trade between the worlds, and now they are breaking the trails between the stars.

I was a McQuarrie, and the oldest son to boot, and I had to go to space. That was a thing as inevitable as sunrise, and as little questioned. I went.

Now I dreamed of space. I was caught in it, quite alone, between the blackness and the blaze, with nothing above or below or around me but the cruel bright eyes of far-off suns to note my fall. I fell, through the millions of silent miles, turning over and over, voiceless, helpless, and when I had done falling the stars looked just the same, and it seemed I had not moved. I knew that I was going to fall forever and never be allowed to die, and at the end of forever the stars would not have changed.

They were ghastly dreams. Opiates only made them worse. I spent whole days riding, until both my horse and I were weary enough to drop, so that I might sleep. It was no good. I tried drinking, and that was no help either.

There was guilt in those dreams. One part of them recurred over and over—myself, knowing about the unending doom that waited for me out there beyond the sky, and running away from it, running like a hunted hare. Everywhere I turned, there was my father with his arms stretched wide, barring the way. His face was turned from me, and my fear lest he should suddenly see me and know the truth was as great in a different way as my fear of space. So I would creep away, but in the end there was no escape, and I was falling, falling down the timeless universe.

I didn't see Marthe. I didn't have the heart to see anybody. I began to think of death. It seemed preferable to a padded cell.

David relented enough to be worried. Ahrian hovered over me sweetly. I didn't tell them anything, of course, except that I was having trouble sleeping.

Then, curiously enough, Ahrian got mixed up in my nightmares. Not Ahrian herself, but her world, the world of Altair she had left for David.

That was strange, because she had spoken very little about her world. She had, in fact, refused to talk about it. David had not discussed it either, except from the standpoint of trade. Yet here I was, seeing it in detail, in sudden bright flashes that came without reason in the midst of my horrible plunging through space. I could see every leaf and flower, each single turret of a pale and gleaming city of which I knew the streets as well as I knew my own woods. I saw in detail the quaint shapes of the rooftops with the carving on them, and the wide plain of some feathery grass, the color of blue smoke, that sloped away toward an opalescent sea. I knew the separate colors of the several moons, and the particular perfume that came on the wind at the sinking of Altair.

This was so extremely odd that I mentioned it to Ahrian, not, of course, telling her that I had had other dreams as well. She gave a little start and said, "How strange!"

I went on to tell her some of the details, and suddenly she laughed and said, "But it is not so very strange, after all. I have told you all those things."

"When?" I said.

"Some few nights ago. You had had a number of drinks, Rafe, and perhaps you do not remember. I talked to you, thinking that it might help you to sleep, and it was of my own world that I talked."

That seemed as good an explanation as any; in fact, the only one. So I let it drop, and after that I dreamed no more of Ahrian's world.

I felt wretched about Marthe, but this wasn't a thing you dragged someone else into, especially someone you cared about. I put her off, and fought, not very gallantly, a fight I knew I was losing. I began to have blank periods during my waking hours. Once I found my horse on the edge of a cliff, with the dirt already sliding from under him. Another time I was looking at the sharp blade of my big pocketknife that had drawn a tentative line of red across my wrist.

I stopped riding. I stopped driving my car. I locked up all my guns and made Jamieson hide the key. I knew I ought to die, but I wasn't quite ready, not quite. . . .

Marthe came one day, unannounced and uninvited. She came into the house and found me, and politely shut the door in everyone's face. Then she came and stood in front of me.

"I want the truth, Rafe. What's gone wrong?"

I said something about not having felt well, assured her I was all right, thanked her for coming, and tried to put her out. She wouldn't be put.

"Look at me, Rafe. Is it because you don't love me?" She made me look at her, and presently she smiled and said, "I didn't think so."

I caught hold of her, then. After a while she whispered, "There's something evil in this house. I felt it when I came in the door. Something wicked!"

"Nonsense," I told her.

She clung to it, though, and cried a little, and swore at me because I had worried her. Then she stepped back and said flatly:

"You look like the devil. What is it, Rafe?"

"I don't quite know." Suddenly, perhaps because of what she had said, I wanted to be out of that house. Irrational? But I wasn't being rational then. "Let's take a walk. Maybe the air will clear my head."

We didn't go far. The last few weeks had worn me down badly, and every crack and jar I had in my frame was plaguing me. By the time we made it to a grassy knoll well away from the house and sat down, Marthe was looking genuinely frightened.

I hadn't meant to tell her anything. I had determined not to tell her. And, of course, I did tell her. I don't know what she made of it, because it wasn't very coherent, the dream part, but she got quite white and flung her arms around me.

"You need a psychiatrist," she said, "and a good doctor."

"I've had a doctor. And a psychiatrist isn't any good unless you're hiding something from yourself. I'm not."

"But there must be some reason for the dreams."

"It isn't any buried guilt. Listen, Marthe, I'll tell you something, and that will make two people in the world who know it. Maybe you won't think much of me after you hear it, but I'd have to tell you sometime and it better be now. That time my plane crashed, on the way to the spaceport. I crashed it myself. Deliberately, intentionally crashed it."

Her eyes widened. Before she could say anything, I rushed on.

"I never wanted to go to space. When I was a little kid, and my father would talk to me about it, I didn't want to go. I liked Earth. I liked dogs and horses and prowling in the woods. Above all, I resented being forced into a set mold that didn't fit me, just because generations of McQuarries had been poured into that mold. My father and I had some bitter words over that, when I was little.

"When I got older I still felt that way, but I'd discovered it wasn't any use to fight. Besides, I liked my father. You know how some men are—pride, family tradition, all that business. Space was his life. It meant more to him to have me be a spaceman than it did to me not to be one. So I went. I didn't like it. I hated it, as a matter of fact. But I kept my mouth shut. Then, coming back from Mars on that first voyage, we lost a man.

"He'd gone outside the hull to repair something, and his magnetic grapples didn't hold, and he drifted off. I saw him through the port, growing smaller and smaller as we left him behind, until he disappeared. You know how fast a spaceship moves at full acceleration? Even by the time we got the boats out it was too late. He's still there. He'll always be there.

"After that, I had a horror of space, the way some people used to have for the sea. It wasn't that I was afraid of getting killed, it was the emptiness, the dark and the cold and the silence, and the *waiting*. I hate being cooped in, and the ship was like an iron coffin. I tried to fight it. I made two more voyages, and I was sick for months after the second one. I didn't tell anybody why. Finally I went up to the Academy to get my ticket, and my father was proud and happy. Blast people's pride and their ideas that their children have to love just what they do! He gave me a berth on his flagship.

"I couldn't tell him the truth, and I couldn't go. I didn't have any right to—to ask men to depend on me and then maybe— So I crashed my plane. If I died, I wanted to do it decently and alone. If I didn't, I figured I'd get smashed up enough so that I couldn't pass a space-physical, and that would be that, with everybody's honor still intact. I guess God was on my side. Anyway, I judged the impact just right. After that, David carried the torch, and my father died happy."

We didn't talk for a while. I sat turning round and round on my finger the ring that Ahrian had given me. Presently Marthe said, "That explains it."

"What?"

"The look I saw in your face when David's ship came in. No regret, no envy. You didn't want to be where he was. But you were as proud of him as Bet was."

"He likes to strut a bit," I said, "but the son-of-a-gun is just as good as he thinks he is. Maybe better. I've talked to his men . . . Well, what about me?"

She said some things that did me more good than any psychiatry, and for the first time in weeks I began to think perhaps there was some hope in the world. We made up a little for all the time we had lost, and then Marthe became thoughtful again.

"Rafe, you started once to say something about Ahrian. Where does she come into this?"

"Nowhere, really." I told her about seeming to see Ahrian's world. "Turned out she'd described it to me, and imagination did the rest."

"I wonder."

She sat still and intent, and then she questioned me about those particular dreams, what Ahrian had said, what I had said, what I remembered. Finally I demanded to know what she was getting at.

"Has it ever occurred to you, Rafe, that all this trouble has come onto you since Ahrian came? All the tragic things there are no real explanations for—Buck, and the old mare, and Bet going down into the paddock in her white formal, a thing no woman in her right mind would do, and at that hour of the night! And now these nightmares that are driving you to—to— Oh, you didn't tell me that part of it, but I can see it in your face! It's all wrong, Rafe. It's all without reason."

"But what on earth could Ahrian have to do with it? That's just wild talk, Marthe."

"Is it? How do we know what the people of her world can do, what powers they may have?"

"But she loves David! Why would she want to destroy his family?"

"How do you know she loves him? Did she ever tell you so?"

"Yes." Then Ahrian's words came back to me, and I corrected myself. "No, come to think of it. She only said love was a great force. Hang it all, though, she came with him, didn't she? All the way to Earth."

For some reason, this talk was disturbing me deeply. It oppressed me, in that open empty place, and gave me a sense that someone was listening and that Marthe had better not say any more—for her own sake.

"That's all nonsense," I said roughly. "People can't send dreams on each other, or make people do things, or—or kill by remote control."

"People like us—no. But Ahrian isn't—people. I'm afraid of her, Rafe. She's strange, inside. Bet said the same thing."

"Woman talk."

"Maybe. Or maybe sometimes we're nearer the truth than men because we aren't ashamed to rely on the instincts God gave us. She's evil. She's filled the house with death."

Marthe shivered as though a cold wind had struck her, and suddenly she reached out and tore Ahrian's ring off my finger and threw it far away into the deep grass.

"I don't want anything of her about you. Nothing!"

Then it was my turn to shiver. Because the minute that ring was gone, so were the oppression and the vague fear, and my screwed-up nerves began to slacken off again.

Still I would not believe. I knew the power of suggestion, and considering the state I was in, none of my reactions would be worth a plugged nickel anyway.

"I still say this is all nonsense, Marthe. Ahrian's never shown the slightest sign of having any special 'power.' She's never been anything but sweet and friendly, and she follows David around like a spaniel. And there just isn't the shadow of a motive."

"I know how we can find out."

I stared at her. "How?"

"Those dreams you had of Ahrian's world. She couldn't have described all the details to you, and you couldn't have imagined all the rest of them exactly right. Someone who had been there would know. If the dreams were wrong, then Ahrian told the truth and they were nothing worse than dreams. But if they were right—*all* right—then they weren't dreams but memories from Ahrian's own mind, mixed in with the awful things she was sending to torture you."

I remembered that I hadn't had a single glimpse of that world since I mentioned it to Ahrian, which seemed an odd coincidence.

"Even so, how could she know how I felt about space? How could she— Oh, all right. We'll go ask David."

"No, not David! Not anyone who has anything to do with her. Besides, if she has some deep reason to hate David, *he* wouldn't be likely to tell us, would he?"

"So that's it. Don't you think maybe your reporter's mind is running away with you?"

"I'm trying to save your neck, you stubborn fool!" she snarled, between rage and tears.

I got up. "Come on, then. There's Griffith—he's observer on the *Anson McQuarrie,* and I know him fairly well." It occurred to me suddenly that Griffith hadn't been around since the night of the *Anson McQuarrie*'s landing, and I wondered why, since he had always been a good friend of David's. For some reason, that unimportant fact made me as curious as a woman to know why.

Marthe's car was in the drive. Ahrian called to us from the terrace, looking very lovely with her filmy skirts blowing around her and her hair full of those incredible purple gleamings in the sunlight. Marthe said she was going to take me for a drive, and Ahrian said it would do me good. They both smiled, and we drove away.

"Does she always wear that tiara?" asked Marthe.

"I don't know. She wears it a lot. Why?"

"It's extremely bad taste in the daytime."

"Part of her native costume, I reckon."

"She didn't have it when she came."

"No, she made it— Oh, who cares!" I yawned and went to sleep. I slept like a baby and never dreamed of anything. I was still asleep when Marthe stopped at the address in the city I had given her and only woke when she shook me half out of the car.

V / About Altair

Griffith was home. Spacemen are usually home between voyages, with their shoes off and their feet up, getting acquainted with their wives and kids. He seemed glad to see me, but not too glad. He asked how everything was, and I said, "Fine," and he said he'd been meaning to come up but he'd been too busy, and we both knew that neither statement was true. Then he said awkwardly that he was sorry about Bet, and I thanked him. When he couldn't think of any more ways to stall, he asked me what he could do for me.

"Well," I said, "my fiancée is wild to see the pictures you shot on the last voyage. New worlds, and all that." I explained to him who she was. "She's thinking of doing an article—how a special observer works, how the records are turned over to the government and the scientific bodies, and so on. I thought, as a special favor, you might be willing to show her the reels."

"Oh," he said, almost with a sigh of relief. "Sure, I'll be glad to."

He took us off to a small building at the rear of the house, where he had his photo lab and a projection room. He found the reels he wanted while chattering about some fine astronomical stuff that he'd been given an award for. Marthe asked him all the questions she could think of about his work, taking notes in a businesslike way. The projector began to hum. We watched.

The reels were magnificent. Griffith knew his job. Interstellar space came alive before us. Nebulae, clusters, unknown suns, glittering star streams, swept across the tridimensional screen in perfect reproduction of color.

We watched strange solar systems plunge toward us, and then the slow unveiling of individual planets as the *Anson McQuarrie* sank toward them. Some were dead and barren, some furiously alive, and some were peopled, not always by anything approaching the human. Each had its spectrum analysis and an exhaustive list of what ores and minerals might be found there, also atmosphere content, gravity, types and aspects of native flora and fauna.

In the fascination of watching, I almost forgot what I came for. Then—

It was there. The world, the country of my dream—Ahrian's world. Each leaf and flower and blade of grass, each shading of color, the gleaming city with the curious roofs, the plain that swept toward the opalescent sea.

I felt very sick and strange. I'm not sure what happened after that, but presently I was back in Griffith's house and Marthe was feeding me brandy. I asked for more, and when I stopped shaking I turned to Griffith, who was much upset.

"That was the second world of Altair," I said. "The home world of my brother's wife."

"Yes," said Griffith.

"What happened there?" I got up and went close to him, and he stepped back a little. "What happened between my brother and Ahrian?"

"You better ask David," he muttered and tried to turn away. I caught him.

"Tell me," I said. "Bet's already dead, so it's too late for her. But there's David—and me. For God's sake, Griff, you used to be his friend!"

"Yes," said Griffith slowly. "I used to be. I told him not to do what he did, but you know David." He made an angry, indecisive gesture, and then he looked at me. "She's such a little thing. How did she— I mean—"

"Never mind. Just tell me what David did to her. She didn't come with him of her own free will, did she?"

"No. Oh, he tried to make out that she did, but everybody knew better. To this day I don't know exactly what the deal was, but her people needed something, a particular chemical or drug, I think, and they must have needed it badly. The ship, of course, was heavily stocked with all sorts of chemicals and medical supplies—you know how useful David has found them before in establishing good relations with other races.

"If it isn't their kids, it's their cattle, or a crop blight, or polluted water, and they're always grateful when you can fix things up, especially the primitives. Well, Ahrian's people are far from primitive, but I guess they'd run out of the source for whatever it was. David was mighty secretive about the whole thing."

He hesitated, and I prodded him. "What you're trying to say is that David gave them the chemicals or drugs they needed in exchange for Ahrian. Bought her, in fact."

Griffith nodded. He seemed to feel a personal sense of shame about it, as though the act of service under David had made him a party to the crime.

"Blackmailed her would be closer to the truth," he said. "The ugliest part of it was that Ahrian was already pledged . . . At least, that's what I heard. Anyway, no, she didn't come of her own free will."

I think, if I had had David's neck between my hands then, I would have broken it. How evil a mess could a man make? And where were you going to put justice?

Marthe said to Griffith, "Did her people have any unusual abilities? It's very important, Mr. Griffith."

"Their culture is very complex, and we weren't there long enough to study it in detail. Also, there was the language barrier. But I'm pretty sure they're telepaths—many races are, you know—though to what extent I couldn't say."

"Telepaths," said Marthe softly, and looked at me. "Mr. Griffith, do the women there wear a sort of tiara, shaped like—" She described

Ahrian's headgear minutely, including the oddly cut crystal. "Habitually, I mean."

He stared at her as though he thought it was just like a woman to worry about fashions at a time like this. "Honestly, Miss Walters, I didn't notice. Both sexes go in for jewelry, and nearly all of them make it themselves, and nobody could keep track—" He halted, apparently struck by a sudden memory. "I did see a marriage ceremony, though, where little crowns like that were used as we use rings. The man and woman exchanged them, and as near as I could figure the words, the rite was called something like the One-Making."

"Thank you," said Marthe. "Thank you very much. Now I think I'd better get Rafe home."

I said something to Griffith, I'm not sure what, but he shook hands with me and seemed relieved. I sat in the car, thinking, and Marthe drove, not back toward the house, but to her apartment. She told me she'd be back in a minute and went off, taking the keys with her. I sat thinking, and my thoughts were not good. Marthe returned, carrying a small suitcase.

"What's that for?" I demanded.

"I'm staying with you."

"The devil you are!"

She faced me, with a look as level as a steel blade and just as unyielding. "You mean more to me than propriety, or my good name, or even my own skin. Is that clear? I am staying with you until this business is finished."

I roared at her. I pleaded with her. I explained that if Ahrian were out for me, she would be out for Marthe too, if she got in the way. I told her she'd only make it harder for me, worrying about her.

All the time I was roaring, pleading, and explaining, Marthe was driving out of town, immovable, maddening, and wonderful. Finally I gave up. I couldn't throw her out of the car. Even if I had, it wouldn't have prevented her coming.

She spoke at last. "Of course, you know there's a simple solution to all this—simple, logical, and safe."

"What?"

"Go away out of Ahrian's reach, and let David take his own consequences."

"He deserves it," I said savagely.

"But you won't go away."

"How can I, Marthe?" And I began to yell at her all over again because *she* wouldn't go.

"All right, that's settled. Now let's start thinking. Obviously, we can't go to the police."

"Hardly." It was frightening to consider what a hard-boiled cop would make out of a woman who had lavender hair and performed witchcraft. "You believe that tiara Ahrian wears has something to do with her—well, her power over other people's minds?"

"Possibly. I don't know. That's just it, Rafe—we don't *know,* and so we have to be suspicious of everything."

I remembered the unexplainable sensation I had had when Marthe threw that ring away. Could it have been a contact, a sort of focal point to concentrate the energy of her thought-waves which were, perhaps, amplified and controlled by the aid of that mesh of gold and platinum wires and that strangely faceted crystal? I remembered also the necklace of zircons that glittered on Bet's throat, the night she died.

These gifts must be fashioned with a meaning from the heart . . .

"I don't know what we're going to do, Rafe. Do you?"

"Face them with it, I suppose. Face them both. Drag it out in the open, anyway."

Marthe sighed, and we drove on in gloomy silence.

VI / *The Last Magic*

It was dark when we reached the house. Ahrian welcomed us with little cries of delight.

"I am so happy you have brought Marthe back with you. It has been too long since we have seen her."

"She's staying for a while," I said.

"How very nice. Since the little one is gone, I am lonely with no woman to talk to. Come, I will see that all is well in the room of guests."

"Where's David?" I asked.

"Oh, he has gone into the city and will not be back tonight. And my heart is sad, for I think that he has gone to talk of another voyage."

She took Marthe away. I followed, on the pretext of making sure that Marthe had everything she needed, and stayed until the arrival of the maid. Then I went and changed for dinner, cursing David.

I got a word alone with Marthe before we went down. "We'd better wait," I said. "I want to tackle them together. It's the only way I know to put David on his guard."

"Has he mentioned another voyage to you?" Marthe wanted to know.

I shook my head. "But then, he seldom mentions anything to me anymore."

"Ahrian's doing."

There didn't seem to be any doubt about that. David and I had never exactly loved one another, but there had certainly never been any real ill feeling between us, either. Since Bet's death, all that had been changed.

Ahrian put herself out to be nice to Marthe. If we hadn't known what we knew, it would have been a delightful evening. Instead, it was rather horrible. All the time I was remembering how I had felt out there on the hill and wondering how much Ahrian knew, or suspected, and what she might be going to do about it.

All at once she cried out, "Oh, Rafe, you have lost your ring!"

I told her some reasonably plausible lie. "I'm awfully sorry, Ahrian. You must make me another sometime."

She smiled. "There will be no need for that. Wait." She ran off. Marthe and I looked at each other, not daring to speak. Presently Ahrian came back, presumably from her workroom, carrying a cushion made of silk.

"See? I have made these for you both—a betrothal gift."

On the cushion were two rings, identical in design, one large, one small. The zircons made a pale glittering, like two wicked eyes that watched us.

"Will you not exchange them now? I should be so happy!"

Marthe was going to say something violent. I gave her a look that shut her up and thanked Ahrian profusely. It was one of those things. If she knew we suspected her and her gifts, that was that. But if she didn't know, I didn't want her to find out just yet.

"But," I said, "they are too beautiful for mere gifts. We'll save them for the wedding, Ahrian. We were planning on a double ring ceremony anyway, and these will be perfect. Won't they, Marthe?"

"Oh, yes," she said.

Ahrian beamed like a happy child, and murmured that her little trinkets weren't worthy of such an honor, and in that moment I began to doubt the whole crazy story again. No one could look so guileless and innocent and sweet as Ahrian did, and be guilty of the things we thought she was.

Marthe must have seen me wavering, because she said, "Rafe, darling, put them away where they'll be quite safe. I wouldn't want anything to happen to them before the wedding."

I took them up to my room and hid them in the farthest back corner of a bureau drawer under a pile of shirts. While I was up there alone, the most awful temptation came over me to put the big one on my finger—just to look at it, to admire the sparkle of the queerly cut stone and the wonderful filigree work of the band. What harm could there be in a ring?

I guess it was the very strength of that compulsion that saved me. I got scared. I slammed the drawer shut, locked it, and threw the key out the window. Then I turned around to find Marthe standing in the doorway.

"I wouldn't have let you put it on," she whispered. "But you see, Rafe? You see how right we were!"

I began to shake a bit. We started downstairs again, and Marthe said in my ear, "She knows. I'm sure she knows."

I agreed with her, and I was afraid. It shamed me to be afraid of such a frail little creature, but I was.

Marthe and I were both relieved when it came time to go to bed. It freed us from the weird necessity of making conversation with Ahrian. I had no intention of sleeping, but it was good to be away from her. Marthe's room was down the hall from mine, farther than I liked but plenty close enough to hear her if she called me.

I told her to leave the door open and yell like the devil if anything—anything at all—seemed wrong to her. I left mine open, too, and sat down in a chair where I could see the lighted hall. I wished I had a gun, but I didn't dare leave Marthe for all the time it would take to rouse out Jamieson and get the key. I picked out the heaviest stick I had and kept it in my hand.

The house was quiet, and nothing happened. The huge relic of a clock that stood on the stair landing chimed peacefully every fifteen minutes, and every hour it counted off the strokes in a deep, soft voice. I think the last time I heard it was half past two. I didn't mean to sleep. I had purposely drunk nothing but black coffee all evening. But I had been so long without sleep!

I remember getting up and walking down the hall to Marthe's door and glancing in at her, curled up in the big bed. After that things got dim. I don't believe that I slept very deeply, or very long, but it was enough. I dreamed with a terrible vividness of Marthe. She was standing in the garden, wrapped in a plaid bathrobe, and she was in danger, very great danger, and she needed me.

Starting up out of the chair, I listened for a moment. The house was silent, except for the clock ticking gently to itself on the landing. I ran down the hall and into Marthe's room. At first I thought she was still there, and then I saw that the shape in the bed was only a mockery of tumbled blankets. I called her. There was no answer. Calling, I ran down through the house, and there was no answer at all until I came out on the terrace above the shadowy garden. Then I heard her say my name.

She was standing in a patch of moonlight with the plaid robe wrapped around her, and her face was white as death. In a minute I had my arms around her and she was sobbing, asking if I were safe.

"I must have been dreaming, Rafe, but I thought you were somewhere out here, hurt, maybe dying."

She was in a terrible fright, and so was I. Because I knew who had sent those dreams—easy dreams to send, without any aids to telepathy, since with each of us the thought of danger to the other was right on top of our minds, conscious and screaming.

I wanted out of that garden.

We went up the steps together and onto the wide terrace, in that clear, white, damnable moonlight. From the long doors that opened into the library, David stepped and barred our way. He held a heavy double-barreled shotgun, and at that range he couldn't miss.

David.

He hadn't gone to town. He had been in his room all this time—waiting. His eyes were wide open, empty and bright, reflecting the cold fire of the moon.

Ahrian was with him.

I made some futile gesture of getting Marthe behind me, and I cried out, "David!" He turned his head a very little, like a man who hears a sound far off, and his brow puckered, but he did not speak.

Ahrian said softly, "I am sorry that it must be so, Rafe and Marthe. You are blameless, and you have been kind. If only Marthe had not sensed what was within me . . . But now it must be finished here, tonight."

"Ahrian," I said, and the twin black barrels of the shotgun watched me, and the stone of David's ring sparkled against the stock. "David did a wicked thing. We know about it—but does it give you the right to kill us all? Bet, and Marthe . . ."

"I made a promise to my gods," she whispered. "I had a mother and father, a brother, a sister—and more than all of them, though I loved them dearly, there was one who would have been my other self."

"I'll take you back," I said. "I'll send a ship out to Altair—only let Marthe go!"

"Could I go back as I am, as he has made me? Could I find my life again, with the blood that is already on me? No. I will take from David everything that he loves, even space itself, and in the end I will tell him how and why. Then—I will die."

"All right. All right, Ahrian. But why Marthe? She can't stop you. If David kills me, that's enough. He'll be tried for murder, the whole story will come out, and that will be the end of him whether he's convicted or not."

Ahrian smiled, a tender thing of ineffable sadness. "Marthe is speaking within herself, words that you should hear. Her body wishes much to live, but her heart says, 'Not without him,' and her heart is stronger. No, Rafe. If she lives, she will slip David out of the cage I have built for him. Now let us stop torturing each other!"

Her face contracted in a spasm of pain. She turned her head toward the motionless effigy of a man who stood beside her, and I saw the gun go up, and I knew this was the finish.

I shouted his name once more, pure reflex, and shoved Marthe aside as far as I could. David was twenty-five or thirty feet away. I bent over and began to run toward him. I didn't know why. It was hopeless, but it was all I could think of to do. The distance looked like thirty miles—and then I heard him moan. He was moaning the way old Buck had moaned that day, and his head was pulled back as though he were straining away from something. I knew he didn't *want* to kill me, even then.

Ahrian whispered. The crystal glowed in the moonlight, and there was in her face a magnificent and awful strength. David gave a low wail of agony. The cords stood out on the backs of his hands. The eyes of the woman from Altair blazed like purple stars. The gunstock settled into place, and David's finger curled in on the trigger.

Someone sped by me, off to one side and going like the wind. Someone in a plaid robe, headed not for David, but for Ahrian.

There was a scream, I don't know whose. Maybe mine. The gun let off, both barrels, right above my shoulder, and the hot metal seared my hand where I shoved the thing up at the last second so that it hit nothing but the treetops. David groaned and let it drop, and so did I. I reeled around, and there was Marthe leaning over the stone balustrade, shivering, sobbing, triumphant, holding in one hand the crystal tiara.

I carried Ahrian into the house. Her body, light and frail as a bird's, was broken. It was a long fall into the garden, and she had hit hard. Her hair had come loose and hung over my arm in a long thick pall, dark purple in the moonlight.

I laid her on the couch, as gently as I could. She looked up at me and said quite clearly, "The beasts I could force against their will. The human mind is stronger. With all my skill and care—a little too strong."

She was still a while, and then she whispered, "I am sad, Rafe, that I must die so far away from home."

That was all.

The shot had roused the servants, who began to straggle in from the far wing of the house. I told them that David thought he had heard prowlers and fired at them, and in the excitement Ahrian had fallen from the terrace. They believed it. Why not? David was still sitting out there, doubled up on the cold stone, looking at nothing. Somehow I couldn't speak to him, or touch him. I sent the servants to get him in, and told them to call the people who had to be called. Then I took Marthe up to her room.

"It'll be all right," I told her. "It was an accident. Let me tell the story. You won't even be named."

"I don't care," she said, in a strange harsh voice. "All I care about is you, and you're alive and safe." She put her arms around me, a fierce and painful grip. "I'm sorry I killed her, I didn't mean to, but I'd do it again, Rafe, I'd do it again—she wanted to kill you!" She caught her breath, still clinging to me, and then she began to cry. "You fool, oh you fool, rushing David like that to make him fire at you instead of me." She said some more things, and then her voice got faint. I put her on the bed and made her take a sedative, and presently she was asleep.

I left the maid with her and went downstairs. There were things I had to say to David.

That was how the McQuarrie tradition came to an end after two hundred years. Even the house is gone, for none of us could bear it any longer. David will never go to space again.

I'm glad. What did it gain the McQuarries? What has it ever gained men? Have men ever brought back more happiness from the stars? Will they ever?

Well, it's too late now to wonder about that. It's been too late, ever since the first skin-clad barbarian stared up at the moon and lusted for it. If Marthe and I have sons, I am afraid that McQuarries will go to space again.

Short in the Chest

MARGARET ST. CLAIR

The girl in the marine-green uniform turned up her hearing aid a trifle—they were all a little deaf, from the cold-war bombing—and with an earnest frown regarded the huxley that was seated across the desk from her.

"You're the queerest huxley I ever heard of," she said flatly. "The others aren't at all like you."

The huxley did not seem displeased at this remark. It took off its windowpane glasses, blew on them, polished them on a handkerchief, and returned them to its nose. Sonya's turning up the hearing aid had activated the short in its chest again; it folded its hands protectively over the top buttons of its dove-gray brocaded waistcoat.

"And in what way, my dear young lady, am I different from other huxleys?" it asked.

"Well—you tell me to speak to you frankly, to tell you exactly what is in my mind. I've only been to a huxley once before, but it kept talking about giving me the big, overall picture, and about using dighting* to transcend myself. It spoke about in-group love, and inter-group harmony, and it said our basic loyalty must be given to Defense, which in the cold-war emergency is the country itself.

"You're not like that at all, not at all philosophic. I suppose that's why they're called huxleys—because they're philosophic rob—I beg your pardon."

---

*In the past, I have been accused of making up some of the unusual words that appear in my stories. Sometimes this accusation has been justified; sometimes, as in "Vulcan's Dolls" (see *Plant Life of the Pacific World*), it has not. For the record, therefore, be it observed that "dight" is a Middle English word meaning, among other things, "to have intercourse with." (See *Poets of the English Language*, Auden and Pearson, Vol. 1, p. 173.) [See also *Webster's New International Dictionary*, unabridged version.] "Dight" was reintroduced by a late twentieth-century philologist who disliked the "sleep with" euphemism, and who saw that the language desperately needed a transitive verb that would be "good usage."—M.S.C.

"Go ahead and say it," the huxley encouraged. "I'm not shy. I don't mind being called a robot."

"I might have known. I guess that's why you're so popular. I never saw a huxley with so many people in its waiting room."

"I *am* a rather unusual robot," the huxley said, with a touch of smugness. "I'm a new model, just past the experimental stage, with unusually complicated relays. But that's beside the point. You haven't told me yet what's troubling you."

The girl fiddled nervously with the control of her hearing aid. After a moment she turned it down; the almost audible sputtering in the huxley's chest died away.

"It's about the pigs," she said.

"The pigs!" The huxley was jarred out of its mechanical calm. "You know, I thought it would be something about dighting," it said after a second. It smiled winningly. "It usually is."

"Well . . . it's about that too. But the pigs were what started me worrying. I don't know whether you're clear about my rank. I'm Major Sonya Briggs, in charge of the Zone Thirteen piggery."

"Oh," said the huxley.

"Yes . . . Like the other armed services, we Marines produce all our own food. My piggery is a pretty important unit in the job of keeping up the supply of pork chops. Naturally, I was disturbed when the newborn pigs refused to nurse.

"If you're a new robot, you won't have much on your memory coils about pigs. As soon as the pigs are born, we take them away from the sow—we use an aseptic scoop—and put them in an enclosure of their own with a big nursing tank. We have a recording of a sow grunting, and when they hear that, they're supposed to nurse. The sow gets an oestric, and after a few days she's ready to breed again. The system is supposed to produce a lot more pork than letting the baby pigs stay with the sow in the old-fashioned way. But as I say, lately they've been refusing to nurse.

"No matter how much we step up the grunting record, they won't take the bottle. We've had to slaughter several litters rather than let them starve to death. And at that the flesh hasn't been much good— too mushy and soft. As you can easily see, the situation is getting serious."

"Um," the huxley said.

"Naturally, I made full reports. Nobody has known what to do. But when I got my dighting slip a couple of times ago, in the space marked 'Purpose,' besides the usual rubber-stamped 'To reduce inter-service tension,' somebody had written in: 'To find out from Air their solution of the neonatal pig nutrition problem.'

"So I knew my dighting opposite number in Air was not only supposed to reduce inter-group tension, but also I was supposed to find out from him how Air got its newborn pigs to eat." She looked down, fidgeting with the clasp of her musette bag.

"Go on," said the huxley with a touch of severity. "I can't help you unless you give me your full confidence."

"Is it true that the dighting system was set up by a group of psychologists after they'd made a survey of inter-service tension? After they'd found that Marine was feuding with Air, and Air with Infantry, and Infantry with Navy, to such an extent that it was cutting down overall Defense efficiency? They thought that sex relations would be the best of all ways of cutting down hostility and replacing it with friendly feelings, so they started the dighting plan?"

"You know the answers to those questions as well as I do," the huxley replied frostily. "The tone of your voice when you asked them shows that they are to be answered with 'Yes.' You're stalling, Major Briggs."

"It's so unpleasant . . . What do you want me to tell you?"

"Go on in detail with what happened after you got your blue dighting slip."

She shot a glance at him, flushed, looked away again, and began talking rapidly. "The slip was for next Tuesday. I hate Air for dighting, but I thought it would be all right. You know how it is—there's a particular sort of kick in feeling oneself change from a cold sort of loathing into being eager and excited and in love with it. After one's had one's Watson, I mean.

"I went to the neutral area Tuesday afternoon. He was in the room when I got there, sitting in a chair with his big feet spread out in front of him, wearing one of those loathsome leather jackets. He stood up politely when he saw me, but I knew he'd just about as soon cut my throat as look at me, since I was Marine. We were both armed, naturally."

"What did he look like?" the huxley broke in.

"I really didn't notice. Just that he was Air. Well, anyway, we had a drink together. I've heard they put cannabis in the drinks they serve you in the neutral areas, and it might be true. I didn't feel nearly so hostile to him after I'd finished my drink. I even managed to smile, and he managed to smile back. He said, 'We might as well get started, don't you think?' So I went in the head.

"I took off my things and left my gun on the bench beside the washbasin. I gave myself my Watson in the thigh."

"The usual Watson?" the huxley asked as she halted. "Oestric and anti-concipient injected subcutaneously from a sterile ampoule?"

"Yes. He'd had his Watson too, the priapic, because when I got back . . ." She began to cry.

"What happened after you got back?" the huxley queried after she had cried for a while.

"I just wasn't any good. No good at all. The Watson might have been so much water for all the effect it had. Finally he got sore. He said, 'What's the matter with you? I might have known anything Marine was in would get loused up.'

"That made me angry, but I was too upset to defend myself. 'Tension reduction!' he said. 'This is a fine way to promote inter-service harmony. I'm not only not going to sign the checking out sheet, I'm going to file a complaint against you to your group.' "

"Oh, my," said the huxley.

"Yes, wasn't it terrible? I said, 'If you file a complaint, I'll file a countercharge. You didn't reduce *my* tension, either.'

"We argued about it for a while. He said that if I filed countercharges there'd be a trial and I'd have to take pentathol and then the truth would come out. He said it wasn't his fault; he'd been ready.

"I knew that was true, so I began to plead with him. I reminded him of the cold war, and how the enemy were about to take Venus, when all we had was Mars. I talked to him about loyalty to Defense, and I asked him how he'd feel if he was kicked out of Air. And finally, after what seemed like hours, he said he wouldn't file charges. I guess he felt sorry for me. He even agreed to sign the checking out sheet.

"That was that. I went back to the head and put on my clothes, and we both went out. We left the room at different times, though, because we were too angry to smile at each other and look happy. Even as it was, I think some of the neutral area personnel suspected us."

"Is that what's been worrying you?" the huxley asked when she seemed to have finished.

"Well . . . I can trust you, can't I? You really won't tell?"

"Certainly I won't. Anything told to a huxley is a privileged communication. The first amendment applies to us, if to no other profession."

"Yes, I remember there was a supreme court decision about freedom of speech . . ." She swallowed, choked, and swallowed again. "When I got my next dighting slip," she said bravely, "I was so upset I applied for a gyn. I hoped the doctor would say there was something physically wrong with me, but he said I was in swell shape. He said, 'A girl like you ought to be mighty good at keeping inter-service tension down.' So there wasn't any help there.

"Then I went to a huxley, the huxley I was telling you about. It talked philosophy to me. That wasn't any help either. So—finally— well, I stole an extra Watson from the lab."

There was a silence. When she saw that the huxley seemed to have digested her revelation without undue strain, she went on, "I mean, an extra Watson beyond the one I was issued. I couldn't endure the thought of going through another dight like the one before. There was quite a fuss about the ampoule's being missing. The dighting drugs are under strict control. But they never did find out who'd taken it."

"And did it help you? The double portion of oestric?" the huxley asked. It was prodding at the top buttons of its waistcoat with one forefinger, rather in the manner of one who is not quite certain he feels an itch.

"Yes, it did. Everything went off well. He—the man—said I was a nice girl, and Marine was a good service, next to Infantry, of course. He was Infantry. I had a fine time myself, and last week when I got a request sheet from Infantry asking for some pig pedigrees, I went ahead and initialed it. That tension reduction does work. I've been feeling awfully jittery, though. And yesterday I got another blue dighting slip.

"What am I to do? I can't steal another Watson. They've tightened up the controls. And even if I could, I don't think one extra would be enough. This time I think it would take *two*."

She put her head down on the arm of her chair, gulping desperately.

"You don't think you'd be all right with just one Watson?" the huxley asked after an interval. "After all, people used to dight habitually without any Watsons at all."

"That wasn't inter-service dighting. No, I don't think I'd be all right. You see, this time it's with Air again. I'm supposed to try to find out about porcine nutrition. And I've always particularly hated Air."

She twisted nervously at the control of her hearing aid. The huxley gave a slight jump. "Ah—well, of course you might resign," it said in a barely audible voice.

Sonya—in the course of a long-continued struggle there is always a good deal of cultural contamination, and if there were girls named Sonya, Olga, and Tatiana in Defense, there were girls named Shirley and Mary Beth to be found on the enemy's side—Sonya gave him an incredulous glance. "You must be joking. I think it's in very poor taste. I didn't tell you my difficulties for you to make fun of me."

The huxley appeared to realize that it had gone too far. "Not at all, my dear young lady," it said placatingly. It pressed its hands to its bosom. "Just a suggestion. As you say, it was in poor taste. I should have realized that you'd rather die than not be Marine."

"Yes, I would."

She turned the hearing aid down again. The huxley relaxed. "You may not be aware of it, but difficulties like yours are not entirely unknown," it said. "Perhaps, after a long course of oestrics, antibodies are built up. Given a state of initial physiological reluctance, a forced sexual response might . . . But you're not interested in all that. You want help. How about taking your troubles to somebody higher? Taking them all the way up?"

"You mean—the CO?"

The huxley nodded.

Major Briggs's face flushed scarlet. "I can't do that! I just can't! No nice girl would. I'd be too ashamed." She beat on her musette bag with one hand and began to sob.

Finally she sat up. The huxley was regarding her patiently. She opened her bag, got out cosmetics and mirror, and began to repair emotion's ravages. Then she extracted an electronically powered vibro-needle from the depths of her bag and began crafting away on some indeterminate white garment.

"I don't know what I'd do without my crafting," she said in explanation. "These last few days, it's all that's kept me sane. Thank goodness it's fashionable to do crafting now. Well. I've told you all about my troubles. Have you any ideas?"

The huxley regarded her with faintly protruding eyes. The vibro-needle clicked away steadily, so steadily that Sonya was quite unaware of the augmented popping in the huxley's chest. Besides, the noise was of a frequency that her hearing aid didn't pick up any too well.

The huxley cleared its throat. "Are you sure your dighting difficulties are really your fault?" it asked in an oddly altered voice.

"Why—I suppose so. After all, there's been nothing wrong with the men either time." Major Briggs did not look up from her work.

"Yes, physiologically. But let's put it this way. And I want you to remember, my dear young lady, that we're both mature, sophisticated individuals, and that I'm a huxley, after all. Supposing your dighting date had been with . . . somebody in . . . Marine. Would you have had any difficulty with it?"

Sonya Briggs put down her crafting, her cheeks flaming. "With a group brother? You have no right to talk to me like that!"

"Now, now. You must be calm."

The sputtering in the huxley's chest was by now so loud that only Sonya's emotion could have made her deaf to it. It was also so well-established that even her laying down the vibro-needle had had no effect on it.

"Don't be offended," the huxley went on in its unnatural voice. "I was only putting a completely hypothetical case."

"Then . . . supposing it's understood that it's completely hypothetical and I would never, never dream of doing a thing like that . . . then, I don't suppose I'd have had any trouble with it." She picked up the needle once more.

"In other words, it's not your fault. Look at it this way. You're Marine."

"Yes." The girl's head went up proudly. "I'm Marine."

"Yes. And that means you're a hundred times—a thousand times—better than any of these twerps you've been having to dight with. Isn't that true? Just in the nature of things. Because you're Marine."

"Why—I guess it is. I never thought of it before like that."

"But you can see it's true now, when you think of it. Take that date you had with the man from Air. How could it be your fault that you couldn't respond to him, somebody from *Air*? Why, it was his fault—it's as plain as the nose on your face—*his* fault for being from a repulsive service like Air!"

Sonya was looking at the huxley with parted lips and shining eyes. "I never thought of it before," she breathed. "But it's true. You're right. You're wonderfully, wonderfully right!"

"Of course I am," said the huxley smugly. "I was built to be right. Now, let's consider this matter of your next date."

"Yes, let's."

"You'll go to the neutral area, as usual. You'll be wearing your miniBAR won't you?"

"Yes, of course. We always go in armed."

"Good. You'll go to the head and undress. You'll give yourself your Watson. If it works—"

"It won't. I'm almost sure of that."

"Hear me out. As I was saying, if it works, you'll dight. If it doesn't, you'll be carrying your miniBAR."

"Where?" asked Sonya, frowning.

"Behind your back. You want to give him a chance. But not too good a chance. If the Watson doesn't work—" the huxley paused for dramatic effect—"*get out your gun and shoot him. Shoot him through the heart.* Leave him lying up against a bulkhead. Why should you go through a painful scene like the one you just described for the sake of a yuk from Air?"

"Yes—but—" Sonya had the manner of one who, while striving to be reasonable, is none too sure that reasonableness can be justified. "That wouldn't reduce inter-service tension effectively."

"My dear young lady, why should inter-service tension be reduced at the expense of Marine? Besides, you've got to take the big, overall view. Whatever benefits Marine, benefits Defense."

"Yes . . . That's true . . . I think you've given me good advice."

"Of course I have! One thing more. After you shoot him, leave a note with your name, sector, and identity number on it. You're not ashamed of it."

"No . . . No . . . But I just remembered. How can he give me the pig formula when he's dead?"

"He's just as likely to give it to you dead as he was when he was alive. Besides, think of the humiliation of it. You, Marine, having to lower yourself to wheedle a thing like that out of Air! Why, he ought to be proud, honored, to give the formula to you."

"Yes, he ought." Sonya's lips tightened. "I won't take any nonsense from him," she said. "Even if the Watson works and I dight him, I'll shoot him afterwards. Wouldn't you?"

"Of course. Any girl with spirit would."

Major Briggs glanced at her watch. "Twenty past! I'm overdue at the piggery right now. Thank you so much." She beamed at him. "I'm going to take your advice."

"I'm glad. Good-bye."

"Good-bye."

She walked out of the room, humming, "From the halls of Montezuma . . ."

Left alone, the huxley interchanged its eyes and nose absently a couple of times. It looked up at the ceiling speculatively, as if it wondered when the bombs from Air, Infantry, and Navy were going to come crashing down. It had had interviews with twelve young women so far, and it had given them all the same advice it had given Major Briggs. Even a huxley with a short in its chest might have foreseen that the final result of its counseling would be catastrophic for Marine.

It sat a little while longer, repeating to itself, "Poppoff, Poppoff, Papa, potatoes, poultry, prunes and prism, prunes and prism."

Its short was sputtering loudly and cheerfully; it hunted around on the broadcast sound band until it found a program of atonal music that covered the noise successfully. Though its derangement had reached a point that was not far short of insanity, the huxley still retained a certain cunning.

Once more it repeated, "Poppoff Poppoff," to itself. Then it went to the door of its waiting room and called in its next client.

The Anything Box

ZENNA HENDERSON

I suppose it was about the second week of school that I noticed Sue-lynn particularly. Of course, I'd noticed her name before and checked her out automatically for maturity and ability and probable performance the way most teachers do with their students during the first weeks of school. She had checked out mature and capable and no worry as to performance as I had pigeonholed her—setting aside for the moment the little nudge that said, "Too quiet"—with my other no-worrys until the fluster and flurry of the first days had died down a little.

I remember my noticing day. I had collapsed into my chair for a brief respite from guiding hot little hands through the intricacies of keeping a Crayola within reasonable bounds and the room was full of the relaxed, happy hum of a pleased class as they worked away, not realizing that they were rubbing "blue" into their memories as well as onto their papers. I was meditating on how individual personalities were beginning to emerge among the thirty-five or so heterogeneous first graders I had, when I noticed Sue-lynn—really noticed her—for the first time.

She had finished her paper—far ahead of the others as usual—and was sitting at her table facing me. She had her thumbs touching in front of her on the table and her fingers curving as though they held something between them—something large enough to keep her fingertips apart and angular enough to bend her fingers as if for corners. It was something pleasant that she held—pleasant and precious. You could tell that by the softness of her hold. She was leaning forward a little, her lower ribs pressed against the table, and she was looking, completely absorbed, at the table between her hands. Her face was relaxed and happy. Her mouth curved in a tender half-smile, and as I watched, her lashes lifted and she looked at me with a warm share-the-pleasure look. Then her eyes blinked and the shutters came down inside them. Her hand flicked into the desk and out. She pressed her thumbs to her forefingers and rubbed them slowly together. Then she laid one hand over the other on the table and looked down at them with the air of complete denial and ignorance children can assume so devastatingly.

The incident caught my fancy and I began to notice Sue-lynn. As I consciously watched her, I saw that she spent most of her free time staring at the table between her hands, much too unobtrusively to catch my busy attention. She hurried through even the funnest of fun papers and then lost herself in looking. When Davie pushed her down at recess, and blood streamed from her knee to her ankle, she took her bandages and her tear-smudged face to that comfort she had so readily—if you'll pardon the expression—at hand and emerged minutes later, serene and dry-eyed. I think Davie pushed her down because of her Looking. I know the day before he had come up to me, red-faced and squirming.

"Teacher," he blurted. "She Looks!"

"Who looks?" I asked absently, checking the vocabulary list in my book, wondering how on earth I'd missed *where,* one of those annoying *wh* words that throw the children for a loss.

"Sue-lynn. She Looks and Looks!"

"At you?" I asked.

"Well . . ." He rubbed a forefinger below his nose, leaving a clean streak on his upper lip, accepted the proffered Kleenex, and put it in his pocket. "She looks at her desk and tells lies. She says she can see . . ."

"Can see what?" My curiosity picked up its ears.

"Anything," said Davie. "It's her Anything Box. She can see anything she wants to."

"Does it hurt you for her to Look?"

"Well," he squirmed. Then he burst out: "She says she saw me with a dog biting me because I took her pencil—she said." He started a pell-mell verbal retreat. "She *thinks* I took her pencil. I only found—" His eyes dropped. "I'll give it back."

"I hope so," I smiled. "If you don't want her to look at you, then don't do things like that."

"Durn girls," he muttered and clomped back to his seat.

So I think he pushed her down the next day to get back at her for the dog bite.

Several times after that I wandered to the back of the room, casually in her vicinity, but always she either saw or felt me coming and the quick sketch of her hand disposed of the evidence. Only once I thought I caught a glimmer of something—but her thumb and forefinger brushed in sunlight, and it must have been just that.

Children don't retreat for no reason at all, and, though Sue-lynn did not follow any overt pattern of withdrawal, I started to wonder about her. I watched her on the playground, to see how she tracked there. That only confused me more.

She had a very regular pattern. When the avalanche of children first descended at recess, she avalanched along with them and nothing in the shrieking, running, dodging mass resolved itself into a withdrawn Sue-lynn. But after ten minutes or so, she emerged from the crowd, tousle-haired, rosy-cheeked, smutched with dust, one shoelace dangling and, through some alchemy that I coveted for myself, she suddenly became untousled, undusty, and unsmutched. And there she was, serene and composed on the narrow little step at the side of the flight of stairs just where they disappeared into the base of the pseudo-Corinthian column that graced Our Door and her cupped hands received whatever they received and her absorption in what she saw became so complete that the bell came as a shock every time.

And each time, before she joined the rush to Our Door, her hand would sketch a gesture to her pocket, if she had one, or to the tiny ledge that extended between the hedge and the building. Apparently she always had to put the Anything Box away, but never had to go back to get it.

I was so intrigued by her putting whatever it was on the ledge that once I actually went over and felt along the grimy little outset. I sheepishly followed my children into the hall, wiping the dust from my fingertips, and Sue-lynn's eyes brimmed amusement at me without her mouth's smiling. Her hands mischievously squared in front of her and her thumbs caressed a solidness as the line of children swept into the room.

I smiled too because she was so pleased with having outwitted me. This seemed to be such a gay withdrawal that I let my worry die down. Better this manifestation than any number of other ones that I could name.

Someday, perhaps, I'll learn to keep my mouth shut. I wish I had before that long afternoon when we primary teachers worked together in a heavy cloud of ditto fumes, the acrid smell of India ink, drifting cigarette smoke, and the constant current of chatter, and I let Alpha get me started on what to do with our behavior problems. She was all raunched up about the usual rowdy loudness of her boys and the eternal clack of her girls, and I—bless my stupidity—gave her Sue-lynn as an example of what should be our deepest concern rather than the outbursts from our active ones.

"You mean she just sits and looks at nothing?" Alpha's voice grated into her questioning tone.

"Well, I can't see anything," I admitted. "But apparently she can."

"But that's having hallucinations!" Her voice went up a notch. "I read a book once—"

"Yes." Marlene leaned across the desk to flick ashes into the ashtray. "So we have heard and heard and heard."

"Well!" sniffed Alpha. "It's better than *never* reading a book."

"We're waiting," Marlene leaked smoke from her nostrils, "for the day when you read another book. This one must have been uncommonly long."

"Oh, I don't know." Alpha's forehead wrinkled with concentration. "It was only about—" Then she reddened and turned her face angrily away from Marlene.

"Apropos of *our* discussion—," she said pointedly. "It sounds to me like that child has a deep personality disturbance. Maybe even a psychotic—whatever—" Her eyes glistened faintly as she turned the thought over.

"Oh, I don't know," I said, surprised into echoing her words at my sudden need to defend Sue-lynn. "There's something about her. She doesn't have that apprehensive, hunched-shoulder, don't-hit-me-again air about her that so many withdrawn children have." And I thought achingly of one of mine from last year that Alpha had now and was verbally bludgeoning back into silence after all my work with him. "She seems to have a happy, adjusted personality, only with this odd little . . . *plus*."

"Well, I'd be worried if she were mine," said Alpha. "I'm glad all my kids are so normal." She sighed complacently. "I guess I really haven't anything to kick about. I seldom ever have problem children except wigglers and yakkers, and a holler and a smack can straighten them out."

Marlene caught my eye mockingly, tallying Alpha's class with me, and I turned away with a sigh. To be so happy—well, I suppose ignorance does help.

"You'd better do something about that girl," Alpha shrilled as she left the room. "She'll probably get worse and worse as time goes on. Deteriorating, I think the book said."

I had known Alpha a long time and I thought I knew how much of her talk to discount, but I began to worry about Sue-lynn. Maybe this *was* a disturbance that was more fundamental than the usual run-of-the-mill that I had met up with. Maybe a child *can* smile a soft, contented smile and still have little maggots of madness flourishing somewhere inside.

Or, by gorry! I said to myself defiantly, maybe she *does* have an Anything Box. Maybe she *is* looking at something precious. Who am I to say no to anything like that?

An Anything Box! What could you see in an Anything Box? Heart's desire? I felt my own heart lurch—just a little—the next time Sue-lynn's hands curved. I breathed deeply to hold me in my chair. If it was *her* Anything Box, I wouldn't be able to see my heart's desire in it. Or would I? I propped my cheek up on my hand and doodled aimlessly on my time-schedule sheet. How on earth, I wondered—not for the first time—do I manage to get myself off on these tangents?

Then I felt a small presence at my elbow and turned to meet Sue-lynn's wide eyes.

"Teacher?" The word was hardly more than a breath.

"Yes?" I could tell that for some reason Sue-lynn was loving me dearly at the moment. Maybe because her group had gone into new books that morning. Maybe because I had noticed her new dress, the ruffles of which made her feel very feminine and lovable, or maybe just because the late autumn sun lay so golden across her desk. Anyway, she was loving me to overflowing, and since, unlike most of the children, she had no casual hugs or easy moist kisses, she was bringing her love to me in her encompassing hands.

"See my box, Teacher? It's my Anything Box."

"Oh, my!" I said. "May I hold it?"

After all, I have held—tenderly or apprehensively or bravely—tiger magic, live rattlesnakes, dragon's teeth, poor little dead butterflies, and two ears and a nose that dropped off Sojie one cold morning—none of which I could see any more than I could the Anything Box. But I took the squareness from her carefully, my tenderness showing in my fingers and my face.

And I received weight and substance and actuality!

Almost I let it slip out of my surprised fingers, but Sue-lynn's apprehensive breath helped me catch it and I curved my fingers around the precious warmness and looked down, down, past a faint shimmering, down into Sue-lynn's Anything Box.

I was running barefoot through the whispering grass. The swirl of my skirts caught the daisies as I rounded the gnarled apple tree at the corner. The warm wind lay along each of my cheeks and chuckled in my ears. My heart outstripped my flying feet and melted with a rush of delight into warmness as his arms—

I closed my eyes and swallowed hard, my palms tight against the Anything Box. "It's beautiful!" I whispered. "It's wonderful, Sue-lynn. Where did you get it?"

Her hands took it back hastily. "It's mine," she said defiantly. "It's mine."

"Of course," I said. "Be careful now. Don't drop it."

She smiled faintly as she sketched a motion to her pocket. "I won't." She patted the pocket on her way back to her seat.

Next day she was afraid to look at me at first for fear I might say something or look something or in some way remind her of what must seem like a betrayal to her now, but after I only smiled my usual smile, with no added secret knowledge, she relaxed.

A night or so later when I leaned over my moon-drenched windowsill and let the shadow of my hair hide my face from such ebullient glory, I remembered about the Anything Box. Could I make one for myself? Could I square off this aching waiting, this outreaching, this silent cry inside me, and make it into an Anything Box? I freed my hands and brought them together thumb to thumb, framing a part of the horizon's darkness between my upright forefingers. I stared into the empty square until my eyes watered. I sighed, and laughed a little, and let my hands frame my face as I leaned out into the night. To have magic so near—to feel it tingle off my fingertips and then to be so bound that I couldn't receive it. I turned away from the window—turning my back on brightness.

It wasn't long after this that Alpha succeeded in putting sharp points of worry back in my thoughts of Sue-lynn. We had ground duty together, and one morning when we shivered while the kids ran themselves rosy in the crisp air, she sizzed in my ear.

"Which one is it? The abnormal one, I mean."

"I don't have any abnormal children," I said, my voice sharpening before the sentence ended because I suddenly realized whom she meant.

"Well, I call it abnormal to stare at nothing." You could almost taste the acid in her words. "Who is it?"

"Sue-lynn," I said reluctantly. "She's playing on the bars now."

Alpha surveyed the upside-down Sue-lynn whose brief skirts were belled down from her bare pink legs and half covered her face as she swung from one of the bars by her knees. Alpha clutched her wizened blue hands together and breathed on them. "She looks normal enough," she said.

"She *is* normal!" I snapped.

"*Well,* bite my head off!" cried Alpha. "You're the one that said she wasn't, not me—or is it 'not I'? I never could remember. Not me? Not I?"

The bell saved Alpha from a horrible end. I never knew a person so serenely unaware of essentials and so sensitive to trivia. But she had succeeded in making me worry about Sue-lynn again, and the worry exploded into distress a few days later.

Sue-lynn came to school sleepy-eyed and quiet. She didn't finish any of her work and she fell asleep during rest time. I cussed TV and drive-ins and assumed a night's sleep would put it right. But next day Sue-lynn burst into tears and slapped Davie clear off his chair.

"Why, Sue-lynn!" I gathered Davie up in all his astonishment and took Sue-lynn's hand. She jerked it away from me and flung herself at Davie again. She got two handfuls of his hair and had him out of my grasp before I knew it. She threw him bodily against the wall with a flip of her hands, then doubled up her fists and pressed them to her streaming eyes. In the shocked silence of the room, she stumbled over to Isolation and, seating herself, back to the class, on the little chair, she leaned her head into the corner and sobbed quietly in big gulping sobs.

"What on earth goes on?" I asked the stupefied Davie who sat spraddle-legged on the floor fingering a detached tuft of hair. "What did you do?"

"I only said 'Robber Daughter,' " said Davie. "It said so in the paper. My mama said her daddy's a robber. They put him in jail cause he robbered a gas station." His bewildered face was trying to decide whether or not to cry. Everything had happened so fast that he didn't know yet if he was hurt.

"It isn't nice to call names," I said weakly. "Get back into your seat. I'll take care of Sue-lynn later."

He got up and sat gingerly down in his chair, rubbing his ruffled hair, wanting to make more of a production of the situation but not knowing how. He twisted his face experimentally to see if he had tears available and had none.

"Durn girls," he muttered and tried to shake his fingers free of a wisp of hair.

I kept my eye on Sue-lynn for the next half hour as I busied myself with the class. Her sobs soon stopped and her rigid shoulders relaxed. Her hands were softly in her lap, and I knew she was taking comfort from her Anything Box. We had our talk together later, but she was so completely sealed off from me by her misery that there was no communication between us. She sat quietly watching me as I talked, her hands trembling in her lap. It shakes the heart, somehow, to see the hands of a little child quiver like that.

That afternoon I looked up from my reading group, startled, as though by a cry, to catch Sue-lynn's frightened eyes. She looked around bewildered and then down at her hands again—her empty hands. Then she darted to the Isolation corner and reached under the chair. She went back to her seat slowly, her hands squared to an unseen weight. For the first time, apparently, she had had to go get the Anything Box. It troubled me with a vague unease for the rest of the afternoon.

Through the days that followed while the trial hung fire, I had Sue-lynn in attendance bodily, but that was all. She sank into her Anything Box at every opportunity. And always, if she had put it away somewhere, she had to go back for it. She roused more and more reluctantly from these waking dreams, and there finally came a day when I had to shake her to waken her.

I went to her mother, but she couldn't or wouldn't understand me, and made me feel like a frivolous gossipmonger taking her mind away from her husband, despite the fact that I didn't even mention him— or maybe because I didn't mention him.

"If she's being a bad girl, spank her," she finally said, wearily shifting the weight of a whining baby from one hip to another and pushing her tousled hair off her forehead. "Whatever you do is all right by me. My worrier is all used up. I haven't got any left for the kids right now."

Well, Sue-lynn's father was found guilty and sentenced to the State Penitentiary and school was less than an hour old the next day when Davie came up, clumsily a-tiptoe, braving my wrath for interrupting a reading group, and whispered hoarsely, "Sue-lynn's asleep with her eyes open again, Teacher."

We went back to the table and Davie slid into his chair next to a completely unaware Sue-lynn. He poked her with a warning finger. "I told you I'd tell on you."

And before our horrified eyes, she toppled, as rigidly as a doll, sideways off the chair. The thud of her landing relaxed her, and she lay limp on the green asphalt tile—a thin paper doll of a girl, one hand still clenched open around something. I pried her fingers loose and almost wept to feel enchantment dissolve under my heavy touch. I carried her down to the nurse's room and we worked over her with wet towels and prayer and she finally opened her eyes.

"Teacher," she whispered weakly.

"Yes, Sue-lynn." I took her cold hands in mine.

"Teacher, I almost got in my Anything Box."

"No," I answered. "You couldn't. You're too big."

"Daddy's there," she said. "And where we used to live."

I took a long, long look at her wan face. I hope it was genuine concern for her that prompted my next words. I hope it wasn't envy or the memory of the niggling nagging of Alpha's voice that put firmness in my voice as I went on. "That's playlike," I said. "Just for fun."

Her hands jerked protestingly in mine. "Your Anything Box is just for fun. It's like Davie's cow pony that he keeps in his desk or Sojie's jet plane, or when the big bear chases all of you at recess. It's fun-for-play, but it's not for real. You mustn't think it's for real. It's only play."

"No!" she denied. "*No!*" she cried frantically and, hunching herself up on the cot, peering through her tear-swollen eyes, she scrabbled under the pillow and down beneath the rough blanket that covered her.

"Where is it?" she cried. "Where is it? Give it back to me, Teacher!"

She flung herself toward me and pulled open both my clenched hands.

"Where did you put it? Where did you put it?"

"There is no Anything Box," I said flatly, trying to hold her to me and feeling my heart breaking along with hers.

"You took it!" she sobbed. "You took it away from me!" And she wrenched herself out of my arms.

"Can't you give it back to her?" whispered the nurse. "If it makes her feel so bad? Whatever it is—"

"It's just imagination," I said, almost sullenly. "I can't give her back something that doesn't exist."

Too young! I thought bitterly. Too young to learn that heart's desire is only playlike.

Of course the doctor found nothing wrong. Her mother dismissed the matter as a fainting spell and Sue-lynn came back to class next day, thin and listless, staring blankly out the window, her hands palm down on the desk. I swore by the pale hollow of her cheek that never, *never* again would I take any belief from anyone without replacing it with something better. What had I given Sue-lynn? What had she better than I had taken from her? How did I know but that her Anything Box was on purpose to tide her over rough spots in her life like this? And what now, now that I had taken it from her?

Well, after a time she began to work again, and later, to play. She came back to smiles, but not to laughter. She puttered along quite satisfactorily except that she was a candle blown out. The flame was gone wherever the brightness of belief goes. And she had no more sharing smiles for me, no overflowing love to bring to me. And her shoulder shrugged subtly away from my touch.

Then one day I suddenly realized that Sue-lynn was searching our classroom. Stealthily, casually, day by day she was searching, covering every inch of the room. She went through every puzzle box, every lump of clay, every shelf and cupboard, every box and bag. Methodically she checked behind every row of books and in every child's desk until finally, after almost a week, she had been through everything in the place except my desk. Then she began to materialize suddenly at my elbow every time I opened a drawer. And her eyes would probe quickly and sharply before I slid it shut again. But if I tried to intercept her looks, they slid away and she had some legitimate errand that had brought her up to the vicinity of the desk.

She believes it again, I thought hopefully. She won't accept the fact that her Anything Box is gone. She wants it again.

But it *is* gone, I thought drearily. It's really-for-true gone.

My head was heavy from troubled sleep, and sorrow was a weariness in all my movements. Waiting is sometimes a burden almost too heavy to carry. While my children hummed happily over their fun-stuff, I brooded silently out the window until I managed a laugh at myself. It was a shaky laugh that threatened to dissolve into something else, so I brisked back to my desk.

As good a time as any to throw out useless things, I thought, and to see if I can find that colored chalk I put away so carefully. I plunged my hands into the wilderness of the bottom right-hand drawer of my desk. It was deep with a huge accumulation of anything—just anything—that might need a temporary hiding place. I knelt to pull out leftover Jack Frost pictures and a broken bean shooter, a chewed red ribbon, a roll of cap-gun ammunition, one striped sock, six Numbers papers, a rubber dagger, a copy of *The Gospel According to St. Luke,* a miniature coal shovel, patterns for jack-o'-lanterns, and a pink plastic pelican. I retrieved my Irish linen hankie I thought lost forever and Sojie's report card that he had told me solemnly had blown out of his hand and landed on a jet and broke the sound barrier so loud that it busted all to flitters. Under the welter of miscellany, I felt a squareness. Oh, happy! I thought, this *is* where I put the colored chalk! I cascaded papers off both sides of my lifting hands and shook the box free.

We were together again. Outside, the world was an enchanting wilderness of white, the wind shouting softly through the windows, tapping wet, white fingers against the warm light. Inside all the worry and waiting, the apartness and loneliness were over and forgotten, their hugeness dwindled by the comfort of a shoulder, the warmth of clasping hands—and nowhere, nowhere was the fear of parting, nowhere the need to do without again. This was the happy ending. This was—

This was Sue-lynn's Anything Box!

My racing heart slowed as the dream faded . . . and rushed again at the realization. I had it here! In my junk drawer! It had been here all the time!

I stood up shakily, concealing the invisible box in the flare of my skirts. I sat down and put the box carefully in the center of my desk, covering the top of it with my palms lest I should drown again in delight. I looked at Sue-lynn. She was finishing her fun paper, competently but unjoyously. Now would come her patient sitting with quiet hands until told to do something else.

Alpha would approve. And very possibly, I thought, Alpha would, for once in her limited life, be right. We may need "hallucinations" to keep us going—all of us but the Alphas—but when we go so far as to try to force ourselves, physically, into the never-never land of heart's desire . . .

I remembered Sue-lynn's thin rigid body toppling doll-like off its chair. Out of her deep need she had found—or created? Who could tell?—something too dangerous for a child. I could so easily bring the brimming happiness back to her eyes—but at what a possible price!

No, I had a duty to protect Sue-lynn. Only maturity—the maturity born of the sorrow and loneliness that Sue-lynn was only beginning to know—could be trusted to use an Anything Box safely and wisely.

My heart thudded as I began to move my hands, letting the palms slip down from the top to shape the sides of—

I had moved them back again before I really saw, and I have now learned almost to forget that glimpse of what heart's desire is like when won at the cost of another's heart.

I sat there at the desk trembling and breathless, my palms moist, feeling as if I had been on a long journey away from the little schoolroom. Perhaps I had. Perhaps I had been shown all the kingdoms of the world in a moment of time.

"Sue-lynn," I called. "Will you come up here when you're through?"

She nodded unsmilingly and snipped off the last paper from the edge of Mistress Mary's dress. Without another look at her handiwork, she carried the scissors safely to the scissors box, crumpled the scraps of paper in her hand, and came up to the wastebasket by the desk.

"I have something for you, Sue-lynn," I said, uncovering the box.

Her eyes dropped to the desktop. She looked indifferently up at me. "I did my fun paper already."

"Did you like it?"

"Yes." It was a flat lie.

"Good," I lied right back. "But look here." I squared my hands around the Anything Box.

She took a deep breath and the whole of her little body stiffened.

"I found it," I said hastily, fearing anger. "I found it in the bottom drawer."

She leaned her chest against my desk, her hands caught tightly between, her eyes intent on the box, her face white with the aching want you see on children's faces pressed to Christmas windows.

"Can I have it?" she whispered.

"It's yours," I said, holding it out.

Still she leaned against her hands, her eyes searching my face. "Can I have it?" she asked again.

"Yes!" I was impatient with this anticlimax. "But—"

Her eyes flickered. She had sensed my reservation before I had. "But you must never try to get into it again."

"OK," she said, the word coming out on a long relieved sigh. "OK, Teacher."

She took the box and tucked it lovingly into her small pocket. She turned from the desk and started back to her table. My mouth quirked with a small smile. It seemed to me that everything about her had suddenly turned upward—even the ends of her straight taffy-colored hair. The subtle flame about her that made her Sue-lynn was there again. She scarcely touched the floor as she walked.

I sighed heavily and traced on the desktop with my finger a probable size for an Anything Box. What would Sue-lynn choose to see first? How like a drink after a drought it would seem to her.

I was startled as a small figure materialized at my elbow. It was Sue-lynn, her fingers carefully squared before her.

"Teacher," she said softly, all the flat emptiness gone from her voice. "Anytime you want to take my Anything Box, you just say so."

I groped through my astonishment and incredulity for words. She couldn't possibly have had time to look into the Box yet.

"Why, thank you, Sue-lynn," I managed. "Thanks a lot. I would like very much to borrow it sometime."

"Would you like it now?" she asked, proffering it.

"No, thank you," I said, around the lump in my throat. "I've had a turn already. You go ahead."

"OK," she murmured. Then—"Teacher?"

"Yes?"

Shyly she leaned against me, her cheek on my shoulder. She looked up at me with her warm, unshuttered eyes, then both arms were suddenly around my neck in a brief awkward embrace.

"Watch out!" I whispered, laughing into the collar of her blue dress. "You'll lose it again!"

"No I won't," she laughed back, patting the flat pocket of her dress. "Not ever, ever again!"

Death Between the Stars

MARION ZIMMER BRADLEY

They asked me about it, of course, before I boarded the starship. All through the Western sector of the Galaxy, few rules are stricter than the one dividing human from nonhuman, and the little captain of the *Vesta*—he was Terran, too, and proud in the black leather of the Empire's merchant-man forces—hemmed and hawed about it, as much as was consistent with a spaceman's dignity.

"You see, Miss Vargas," he explained, not once but as often as I would listen to him, "this is not, strictly speaking, a passenger ship at all. Our charter is only to carry cargo. But, under the terms of our franchise, we are required to transport an occasional passenger, from the more isolated planets where there is no regular passenger service. Our rules simply don't permit us to discriminate, and the Theradin reserved a place on this ship for our last voyage."

He paused, and reemphasized, "We have only the one passenger cabin, you see. We're a cargo ship, and we are not allowed to make any discrimination between our passengers."

He looked angry about it. Unfortunately, I'd run up against that attitude before. Some Terrans won't travel on the same ship with nonhumans even when they're isolated in separate ends of the ship.

I understood his predicament, better than he thought. The Theradin seldom travel in space. No one could have foreseen that Haalvordhen, the Theradin from Samarra, who had lived on the forsaken planet of Deneb IV for eighteen of its cycles, would have chosen this particular flight to go back to its own world.

At the same time, I had no choice. I had to get back to an Empire planet—*any* planet—where I could take a starship for Terra. With war about to explode in the Procyon sector, I had to get home before communications were knocked out altogether. Otherwise—well, a Galactic war can last up to eight hundred years. By the time regular transport service was reestablished, I wouldn't be worrying about getting home.

The *Vesta* could take me well out of the dangerous sector, and all the way to Samarra—Sirius Seven—which was, figuratively speaking, just across the street from the Solar System and Terra. Still, it was a questionable solution. The rules about segregation are strict, the anti-discriminatory laws are stricter, and the Theradin had made a prior reservation.

The captain of the *Vesta* couldn't have refused him transportation, even if fifty human Terran women had been left stranded on Deneb IV. And sharing a cabin with the Theradin was ethically, morally, and socially out of the question. Haalvordhen was a nonhuman telepath; and no human in his right senses will get any closer than necessary even to a human telepath. As for a nonhuman one—

And yet, what other way was there?

The captain said tentatively, "We *might* be able to squeeze you into the crewmen's quarters—" He paused uneasily and glanced up at me.

I bit my lip, frowning. That was worse yet. "I understand," I said slowly, "that this Theradin—Haalvordhen—has offered to allow me to share *its* quarters."

"That's right. But, Miss Vargas—"

I made up my mind in a rush. "I'll do it," I said. "It's the best way, all around."

At the sight of his scandalized face, I almost regretted my decision. It was going to cause an interplanetary scandal, I thought wryly. A human woman—and a Terran citizen—spending forty days in space and sharing a cabin with a nonhuman!

The Theradin, although male in form, had no single attribute which one could remotely refer to as sex. But of course that wasn't the problem. The nonhuman were specifically prohibited from mingling with the human races. Terran custom and taboo were binding, and I faced, resolutely, the knowledge that by the time I got to Terra, the planet might be made too hot to hold me.

Still, I told myself defiantly, it was a big Galaxy. And conditions weren't normal just now and that made a big difference. I signed a substantial check for my transportation and made arrangements for the shipping and stowing of what few possessions I could safely transship across space.

But I still felt uneasy when I went aboard the next day—so uneasy that I tried to bolster up my flagging spirits with all sorts of minor comforts. Fortunately, the Theradin were oxygen breathers, so I knew there would be no trouble about atmosphere mixtures or the air pressure to be maintained in the cabin. And the Theradin were Type Two nonhumans, which meant that the acceleration of a hyperspeed ship would knock my shipmate into complete prostration without special drugs. In fact, he would probably stay drugged in his skyhook during most of the trip.

The single cabin was far up toward the nose of the starship. It was a queer little spherical cubbyhole, a nest. The walls were foam-padded all around the sphere, for passengers never develop a spaceman's skill at maneuvering their bodies in free fall, and cabins had to be designed so that an occupant, moving unguardedly, would not dash out his or her brains against an unpadded surface. Spaced at random on the inside of the sphere were three skyhooks—nested cradles on swinging pivots—into which the passenger was snugged during blastoff in shock-absorbing foam and a complicated Garensen pressure apparatus and was thus enabled to sleep secure without floating away.

A few screw-down doors were marked LUGGAGE. I immediately unscrewed one door and stowed my personal belongings in the bin. Then I screwed the top down securely and carefully fastened the padding over it. Finally, I climbed around the small cubbyhole, seeking to familiarize myself with it before my unusual roommate arrived.

It was about fourteen feet in diameter. A sphincter lock opened from the narrow corridor to cargo bays and crewmen's quarters, while a second led into the cabin's functional equivalent of a bathroom. Plant-bound men and women are always surprised and a little shocked when they see the sanitary arrangements on a spaceship. But once they've tried to perform normal bodily functions in free fall, they understand the peculiar equipment very well.

I've made six trips across the Galaxy in as many cycles. I'm practically an old hand, and can even wash my face in freefall without drowning. The trick is to use a sponge and suction. But, by and large, I understand perfectly why spacemen, between planets, usually look a bit unkempt.

I stretched out on the padding of the main cabin, and waited with growing uneasiness for the nonhuman to show. Fortunately, it wasn't long before the diaphragm on the outer sphincter lock expanded and a curious, peaked face peered through.

"Vargas Miss Hel-len?" said the Theradin in a sibilant whisper.

"That's my name," I replied instantly. I pulled upward, and added, quite unnecessarily, "You are Haalvordhen, of course."

"Such is my identification," confirmed the alien, and the long, lean, oddly muscled body squirmed through after the peaked head. "It is kind, Vargas Miss, to share accommodation under this necessity."

"It's kind of you," I said vigorously. "We've all got to get home before this war breaks out!"

"That war may be prevented, I have all hope," the nonhuman said. He spoke comprehensibly in Galactic Standard, but expressionlessly, for the vocal cords of the Theradins are located in an auxiliary pair of inner lips, and their voices seem reedy and lacking in resonance to human ears.

"Yet know you, Vargas Miss, they would have hurled me from this ship to make room for an Empire citizen, had you not been heart-kind to share."

"Good heavens!" I exclaimed, shocked, "I didn't know that!"

I stared at him, disbelieving. The captain couldn't have legally done such a thing—or even seriously have entertained the thought. Had he been trying to intimidate the Theradin into giving up his reserved place?

"I-I was meaning to thank *you*," I said, to cover my confusion.

"Let us thank we-other, then, and be in accord," the reedy voice mouthed.

I looked the nonhuman over, unable to hide completely my curiosity. In form the Theradin was vaguely humanoid—but only vaguely—for the squat arms terminated in mittened "hands" and the long, sharp face was elfin and perpetually grimacing.

The Theradin have no facial muscles to speak of, and no change of expression or of vocal inflection is possible for them. Of course, being telepathic, such subtleties of visible or auditory expression would be superfluous on the face of it.

I felt—as yet—none of the revulsion which the mere presence of the Theradin was *supposed* to inspire. It was not much different from being in the presence of a large humanoid animal. There was nothing inherently fearful about the alien. Yet he was a telepath—and of a nonhuman breed my species had feared for a thousand years.

Could he read my mind?

"Yes," said the Theradin from across the cabin. "You must forgive me. I try to put up barrier, but it is hard. You broadcast your thought so strong it is impossible to shut it out." The alien paused. "Try not to be embar-rass. It bother me, too."

Before I could think of anything to say to that, a crew member in black leather thrust his head, unannounced, through the sphincter and said with an air of authority, "In skyhooks, please." He moved confidently into the cabin. "Miss Vargas, can I help you strap down?" he asked.

"Thanks, but I can manage," I told him.

Hastily I clambered into the skyhook, buckling the inner straps and fastening the suction tubes of the complicated Garensen apparatus across my chest and stomach. The nonhuman was awkwardly drawing his hands from their protective mittens and struggling with the Garensens.

Unhappily, the Theradin have a double thumb, and handling the small-size Terran equipment is an almost impossibly delicate task. It is made more difficult by the fact that the flesh of their "hands" is mostly thin mucous membrane which tears easily on contact with leather and raw metal.

"Give Haalvordhen a hand," I urged the crewman. "I've done this dozens of times!"

I might as well have saved my breath. The crewman came and assured himself that *my* straps and tubes and cushions were meticulously tightened. He took what seemed to me a long time, and used his hands somewhat excessively. I lay under the heavy Garensen equipment, too inwardly furious to even give him the satisfaction of protest.

It was far too long before he finally straightened and moved toward Haalvordhen's skyhook. He gave the alien's outer straps only a perfunctory tug or two and then turned his head to grin at me with a totally uncalled-for familiarity.

"Blastoff in ninety seconds," he said, and wriggled himself rapidly out through the lock.

Haalvordhen exploded in a flood of Samarran which I could not follow. The vehemence of his voice, however, was better than a dictionary. For some strange reason I found myself sharing his fury. The unfairness of the whole procedure was shameful. The Theradin had paid passage money and deserved in any case the prescribed minimum of decent attention.

I said forthrightly, "Never mind the fool, Haalvordhen. Are you strapped down all right?"

"I don't know," he replied despairingly. "The equipment is unfamiliar—"

"Look—" I hesitated, but in common decency I had to make the gesture. "If I examine carefully my own Garensens, can you read my mind and see how they should be adjusted?"

He mouthed, "I'll try," and immediately I fixed my gaze steadily on the apparatus.

After a moment, I felt a curious sensation. It was something like the faint, sickening feeling of being touched and pushed about, against my will, by a distasteful stranger.

I tried to control the surge of almost physical revulsion. No wonder that humans kept as far as possible from the telepathic races. . . .

And then I saw—did I *see*, I wondered, or was it a direct telepathic interference with my perceptions?—a second image superimpose itself on the Garensens into which I was strapped. And the realization was so disturbing that I forgot the discomfort of the mental rapport completely.

"You aren't nearly fastened in," I warned. "You haven't begun to fasten the suction tubes—oh, *damn* the man. He must have seen in common humanity—" I broke off abruptly and fumbled in grim desperation with my own straps. "I think there's just time—"

But there wasn't. With appalling suddenness a violent clamor—the final warning—hit my ears. I clenched my teeth and urged frantically: "Hang on! Here we go!"

And then the blast hit us! Under the sudden sickening pressure I felt my lungs collapse and struggled to remain upright, choking for breath. I heard a queer, gagging grunt from the alien, and it was far more disturbing than a human scream would have been. Then the second shock wave struck with such violence that I screamed aloud in completely human terror. Screamed—and blacked out.

I wasn't unconscious very long. I'd never collapsed during takeoff before, and my first fuzzy emotion when I felt the touch of familiar things around me again was one of embarrassment. What had happened? Then, almost simultaneously, I became reassuringly aware that we were in free fall and that the crewman who had warned us to alert ourselves was stretched out on the empty air near my skyhook. He looked worried.

"Are you all right, Miss Vargas?" he asked, solicitously. "The blastoff wasn't any rougher than usual—"

"I'm all right," I assured him woozily. My shoulders jerked and the Garensens shrieked as I pressed upward, undoing the apparatus with tremulous fingers. "What about the Theradin?" I asked urgently. "His Garensens weren't fastened. You barely glanced at them."

The crewman spoke slowly and steadily, with a deliberation I could not mistake. "Just a minute, Miss Vargas," he said. "Have you forgotten? I spent *every moment* of the time I was in here fastening the Theradin's belts and pressure equipment."

He gave me a hand to assist me up, but I shook it off so fiercely that I flung myself against the padding on the opposite side of the cabin. I caught apprehensively at a handhold and looked down at the Theradin.

Haalvordhen lay flattened beneath the complex apparatus. His peaked pixie face was shrunken and ghastly, and his mouth looked badly bruised. I bent closer, then jerked upright with a violence that sent me cascading back across the cabin, almost into the arms of the crewman.

"You must have fixed those belts *just now,*" I said accusingly. "They *were not* fastened before blastoff! It's malicious criminal negligence, and if Haalvordhen dies—"

The crewman gave me a slow, contemptuous smile. "It's my word against yours, sister," he reminded me.

"In common decency, in common humanity—" I found that my voice was hoarse and shaking, and could not go on.

The crewman said humorlessly, "I should think you'd be glad if the geek died in blastoff. You're awfully concerned about the geek—and you know how *that* sounds?"

I caught the frame of the skyhook and anchored myself against it. I was almost too faint to speak. "What were you trying to do?" I brought out at last. "*Murder* the Theradin?"

The crewman's baleful gaze did not shift from my face. "Suppose you close your mouth," he said, without malice but with an even inflection that was far more frightening. "If you don't, we may have to close it for you. I don't think much of humans who fraternize with geeks."

I opened and shut my mouth several times before I could force myself to reply. All I finally said was, "You know, of course, that I intend to speak to the captain."

"Suit yourself." He turned and strode contemptuously toward the door. "We'd have been doing you a favor if the geek had died in blastoff. But, as I say, suit yourself. I think your geek's alive, anyhow. They're hard to kill."

I clutched the skyhook, unable to move, while he dragged his body through the sphincter lock and it contracted behind him.

Well, I thought bleakly, I had known what I would be letting myself in for when I'd made the arrangement. And since I was already committed, I might as well see if Haalvordhen was alive or dead. Resolutely

I bent over his skyhook, angling sharply to brace myself in free fall.

He wasn't dead. While I looked, I saw the bruised and bleeding "hands" flutter spasmodically. Then, abruptly, the alien made a queer, rasping noise. I felt helpless, and for some reason I was stirred to compassion.

I bent and laid a hesitant hand on the Garensen apparatus, which was now neatly and expertly fastened. I was bitter about the fact that for the first time in my life I had lost consciousness! Had I not done so, the crewman could not have so adroitly covered his negligence. But it was important to remember that the circumstance would not have helped Haalvordhen much either.

"Your feelings do you nothing but credit!" The reedy, flat voice was almost a whisper. "If I may trespass once more on your kindness— can you unfasten these instruments again?"

I bent to comply, asking helplessly as I did so, "Are you sure you're all right?"

"Very far from all right," the alien mouthed, slowly and without expression.

I had the feeling that he resented being compelled to speak aloud, but I didn't think I could stand that telepath touch again. The alien's flat, slitted eyes watched me while I carefully unfastened the suction tubes and cushioning devices.

At this distance I could see that the eyes had lost their color and that the raw "hands" were flaccid and limp. There were also heavily discolored patches about the alien's throat and head. He pronounced, with a terribly thick effort:

"I should have—been drugged. Now it's too late. *Argha maci—*" The words trailed off into blurred Samarran, but the discolored patch in his neck still throbbed sharply, and the hands twitched in an agony which, being dumb, seemed the more fearful.

I clung to the skyhook, dismayed at the intensity of my own emotion. I thought that Haalvordhen had spoken again when the sharp jolt of command sounded, clear and imperative, in my brain.

"Procalamine!" For an instant the shock was all I could feel—the shock, and the overwhelming revulsion at the telepathic touch. There was no hesitation or apology in it now, for the Theradin was fighting for his life. Again the sharp, furious command came: *"Give me procalamine!"*

And with a start of dismay I realized that most nonhumans needed the drug, which was kept on all spaceships to enable them to live in free fall.

Few nonhuman races have the stubbornly persistent heart of the Terrans, which beats by muscular contraction alone. The circulation of the Theradin, and similar races, is dependent on gravity to keep the vital fluid pulsing. Procalamine gives their main blood organ just enough artificial muscular spasm to keep the blood moving and working.

Hastily I propelled myself into the "bathroom"—wiggled hastily through the diaphragm and unscrewed the top of the bin marked First Aid. Neatly pigeonholed beneath transparent plastic were sterile bandages, antiseptics clearly marked Human and—separately, for the three main types of nonhuman races, in one deep bin—the small plastic globules of vital stimulants.

I sorted out two purple fluorescent ones—little globes marked *procalamine*—and looked at the warning, in raised characters on the globule. It read: For Administration by Qualified Space Personnel Only. A touch of panic made my diaphragm catch. Should I call the *Vesta*'s captain or one of the crew?

Then a cold certainty grew in me. If I did, Haalvordhen wouldn't get the stimulant he needed. I sorted out a fluorescent needle for nonhuman integument, pricked the globule, and sucked the dose into the needle. Then, with its tip still enclosed in the plastic globe, I wriggled myself back to where the alien still lay loosely confined by one of the inner straps.

Panic touched me again, with the almost humorous knowledge that I didn't know where to inject the stimulant and that a hypodermic injection in space presents problems which only space-trained men are able to cope with. But I reached out notwithstanding and gingerly picked up one of the unmittened "hands." I didn't stop to think how I knew that this was the proper site for the injection. I was too overcome with strong physical loathing.

Instinct from man's remote past on Earth told me to drop the non-human flesh and cower, gibbering and howling as my simian antecedents would have done. The raw membrane was feverishly hot and unpleasantly slimy to touch. I fought rising queasiness as I tried to think how to steady him for the injection.

In free fall there is no steadiness, no direction. The hypodermic needle, of course, worked by suction, but piercing the skin would be the big problem. Also, I was myself succumbing to the dizziness of no-gravity flight and realized coldly that if I couldn't make the injection in the next few minutes, I wouldn't be able to accomplish it at all.

For a minute I didn't care, a primitive part of myself reminding me that if the alien died, I'd be rid of a detestable cabinmate and have a decent trip between planets.

Then, stubbornly, I threw off the temptation. I steadied the needle in my hand, trying to conquer the disorientation which convinced me that I was looking both up and down at the Theradin.

My own center of gravity seemed to be located in the pit of my stomach, and I fought the familiar space voyaging instinct to curl up in the fetal position and float. I moved slightly closer to the Theradin. I knew that if I could get close enough, our two masses would establish a common center of gravity and I would have at least a temporary orientation while I made the injection.

The maneuver was unpleasant, for the alien seemed unconscious, flaccid and still, and mere physical closeness to the creature was repellent. The feel of the thick, wettish "hand" pulsing feebly in my own was almost sickeningly intimate. But at last I managed to maneuver myself close enough to establish a common center of gravity between us—an axis on which I seemed to hover briefly suspended.

I pulled Haalvordhen's "hand" into this weight center in the bare inches of space between us, braced the needle, and resolutely stabbed with it.

The movement disturbed the brief artificial gravity, and Haalvordhen floated and bounced a little weightlessly in his skyhook. The "hand" went sailing back, the needle recoiling harmlessly. I swore out loud, now quite foolishly angry, and my own jerky movement of annoyance flung me partially across the cabin.

Inching slowly back, I tried to grit my teeth but only succeeded with a snap that jarred my skull. In tense anger, I seized Haalvordhen's "hand," which had almost stopped its feverish pulsing, and with a painfully slow effort—any quick or sudden movement would have thrown me, in recoil, across the cabin again—I wedged Haalvordhen's "hand" under the strap and anchored it there.

It twitched faintly—the Theradin was apparently still sensible to pain—and my stomach rose at that sick pulsing. But I hooked my feet under the skyhook's frame and flung my free arm down and across the alien, holding tight to the straps that confined him.

Still holding him thus wedged down securely, I jabbed again with the needle. It touched, pricked—and then, in despair, I realized it could not penetrate the Theradin integument without weight and pressure behind it.

I was too absorbed now in what had to be done to care just how I did it. So I wrenched forward with a convulsive movement that threw me, full-length, across the alien's body. Although I still had no weight, the momentum of the movement drove the hypodermic needle deeply into the flesh of the "hand."

I pressed the catch, then picked myself up slowly and looked around to see the crewman who had jeered at me with his head thrust through the lock again, regarding me with the distaste he had displayed toward the Theradin from the first. To him I was lower than the Theradin, having degraded myself by close contact with a nonhuman.

Under that frigid, contemptuous stare, I was unable to speak. I could only silently withdraw the needle and hold it up. The rigid look of condemnation altered just a little, but not much. He remained silent, looking at me with something halfway between horror and accusation.

It seemed years, centuries, eternities that he clung there, just looking at me, his face an elongated ellipse above the tight collar of his black leathers. Then, without even speaking, he slowly withdrew his head and the lock contracted behind him, leaving me alone with my sickening feeling of contamination and an almost hysterical guilt.

I hung the needle up on the air, curled myself into a ball, and, entirely unstrung, started sobbing like a fool.

It must have been a long time before I managed to pull myself together, because before I even looked to see whether Haalvordhen was still alive, I heard the slight buzzing noise which meant that it was a meal period and that food had been sent through the chute to our cabin. I pushed the padding listlessly aside and withdrew the heat-sealed containers—one set colorless, the other set nonhuman fluorescent.

Tardily conscious of what a fool I'd been making of myself, I hauled my rations over to the skyhook and tucked them into a special slot, so that they wouldn't float away. Then, with a glance at the figure stretched out motionless beneath the safety strap of the other skyhook, I shrugged, pushed myself across the cabin again, and brought the fluorescent containers to Haalvordhen.

He made a weary, courteous noise which I took for acknowledgment. By now heartily sick of the whole business, I set them before him with a bare minimum of politeness and withdrew to my own skyhook, occupying myself with the always-ticklish problem of eating in free fall.

At last I drew myself up to return the containers to the chute, knowing we wouldn't leave the cabin during the entire trip. Space, on a starship, is held to a rigid minimum. There is simply no room for untrained outsiders moving around in the cramped ship, perhaps getting dangerously close to critically delicate equipment, and the crew is far too busy to stop and keep an eye on rubbernecking tourists.

In an emergency, passengers can summon a crewman by pressing a call-button. Otherwise, as far as the crew was concerned, we were in another world.

I paused in midair to Haalvordhen's skyhook. His containers were untouched, and I felt moved to say, "Shouldn't you try to eat something?"

The flat voice had become even weaker and more rasping now, and the nonhuman's careful enunciation was slurred. Words of his native Samarran intermingled with queer turns of phrase which I expected were literally rendered from mental concepts.

"Heart-kind of you, *thakkava* Varga Miss, but late. Haalvordhen-I deep in grateful wishing—" A long spate of Samarran, thickly blurred, followed, then as if to himself, "Theradin-we, die nowhere only on Samarra, and only a little time ago Haalvordhen-I knowing must die, and must returning to home planet. *Saata.* Knowing to return and die there where Theradin-we around dying—" The jumble of words blurred again, and the limp "hands" clutched spasmodically, in and out.

Then, in a queer, careful tone, the nonhuman said, "But I am not living to return where I can stop-die. Not so long Haalvordhen-I be lasting, although Vargas-you Miss be helping most like *real* instead of alien. Sorry your people be most you unhelping—" he stopped again, and with a queer little grunting noise, continued, "Now Haalvordhen-I be giving Vargas-you stop-gift of heritage, be needful it is."

The flaccid form of the nonhuman suddenly stiffened, went rigid. The drooping lids over the Theradin's eyes seemed to unhood themselves, and in a spasm of fright I tried to fling myself backward. But I did not succeed. I remained motionless, held in a dumb fascination.

I felt a sudden, icy cold, and the sharp physical nausea crawled over me again at the harsh and sickening touch of the alien on my mind, not in words this time, but in a rapport even closer—a hateful touch so intimate that I felt my body go limp in helpless fits and spasms of convulsive shuddering under the deep, hypnotic contact.

Then a wave of darkness almost palpable surged up in my brain. I tried to scream, "*Stop it, stop it!*" And a panicky terror flitted in my last conscious thought through my head. *This is why, this is the reason humans and telepaths don't mix—*

And then a great dark door opened under my senses and I plunged again into unconsciousness.

It was not more than a few seconds, I suppose, before the blackness swayed and lifted and I found myself floating, curled helplessly in mid-air, and seeing, with a curious detachment, the Theradin's skyhook below me. Something in the horrid limpness of that form stirred me wide awake.

With a tight band constricting my breathing, I arrowed downward. I had never seen a dead Theradin before, but I needed no one to tell me that I saw one now. The constricting band still squeezed my throat in dry gasps, and in a frenzy of hysteria I threw myself wildly across the cabin, beating and battering on the emergency button, shrieking and sobbing and screaming. . . .

They kept me drugged all the rest of the trip. Twice I remember waking and shrieking out things I did not understand myself, before the stab of needles in my arm sent me down into comforting dreams again. Near the end of the flight, while my brain was still fuzzy, they made me sign a paper, something to do with witnessing that the crew held no responsibility for the Theradin's death.

It didn't matter. There was something clear and cold and shrewd in my mind, behind the surface fuzziness, which told me I must do exactly what they wanted, or I would find myself in serious trouble with the Terran authorities. At the time I didn't even care about that and supposed it was the drugs. Now, of course, I know the truth.

When the ship made planetfall at Samarra, I had to leave the *Vesta* and transship for Terra. The *Vesta*'s little captain shook me by the hand and carefully avoided my eyes, without mentioning the dead Theradin. I had the feeling—strange, how clear it was to my perceptions—that he regarded me in the same way he would regard a loaded time bomb that might explode at any moment.

I knew he was anxious to hurry me aboard a ship for Terra. He offered me special reservations on a linocruiser at a nominal price, with the obvious lie that he owned a part interest in it. Detachedly I listened to his floundering lies, ignored the hand he offered again, and told a lie or two of my own. He was angry. I knew he didn't want me to linger on Samarra.

Even so, he was glad to be rid of me.

Descending at last from the eternal formalities of the Terran landing zone, I struck out quickly across the port city and hailed a Theradin ground car. The Theradin driving it looked at me curiously, and in a buzzing voice informed me that I could find a human conveyance at the opposite corner. Surprised at myself, I stopped to wonder what I was doing. And then—

And then I identified myself in a way the Theradin could not mistake. He was nearly as surprised as I was. I clambered into the car, and he drove me to the queer, block-shaped building which my eyes had never seen before but which I now knew as intimately as the blue sky of Terra.

Twice, as I crossed the twisting ramp, I was challenged. Twice, with the same shock of internal surprise, I answered the challenge correctly.

At last I came before a Theradin whose challenge crossed mine like a sure, sharp lance, and the result was startling. The Theradin Haalvamphrenan leaned backward twice in acknowledgment and said—not in words—"Haalvordhen!"

I answered in the same fashion. "Yes. Due to certain blunders, I could not return to our home planet and was forced to use the body of this alien. Having made the transfer unwillingly, under necessity, I now see certain advantages. Once within this body, it does not seem at all repulsive, and the host is highly intelligent and sympathetic.

"I regret the feeling that I am distasteful to you, dear friend. But, consider. I can now contribute my services as messenger and courier, without discrimination by these mind-blind Terrans. The law which prevents Theradin from dying on any other planet should now be changed."

"Yes, yes," the other acquiesced, quickly grasping my meaning. "But now to personal matters, my dear Haalvordhen. Of course your possessions are held intact for you."

I became aware that I possessed five fine residences upon the planet, a private lake, a grove of Theirry-trees, and four hattel-boats. Inheritance among the Theradin, of course, is dependent upon continuity of the mental personality, regardless of the source of the young. When any Theradin died, transferring his mind into a new and younger host, the new host at once possessed all of those things which had belonged to the former personality. Two Theradin, unsatisfied with their individual wealth, sometimes pooled their personalities into a single host-body, thus accumulating modest fortunes.

Continuity of memory, of course, was perfect. As Helen Vargas, I had certain rights and privileges as a Terran citizen, certain possessions, certain family rights, certain Empire privileges. And as Haalvordhen, I was made free of Samarra as well.

In a sense of strict justice, I "told" Haalvamphrenan how the original host had died. I gave him the captain's name. I didn't envy him, when the *Vesta* docked again at Samarra.

"On second thought," Haalvamphrenan said reflectively, "I shall merely commit suicide in his presence."

Evidently, Helen-Haalvordhen-I had a very long and interesting life ahead of me.

So did all the other Theradin.

The Ship Who Sang

ANNE McCAFFREY

She was born a thing and as such would be condemned if she failed to pass the encephalograph test required of all newborn babies. There was always the possibility that though the limbs were twisted, the mind was not, that though the ears would hear only dimly, the eyes see vaguely, the mind behind them was receptive and alert.

The electroencephalogram was entirely favorable, unexpectedly so, and the news was brought to the waiting, grieving parents. There was the final, harsh decision: to give their child euthanasia or permit it to become an encapsulated "brain," a guiding mechanism in any one of a number of curious professions. As such, their offspring would suffer no pain, live a comfortable existence in a metal shell for several centuries, performing unusual service to Central Worlds.

She lived and was given a name, Helva. For her first three vegetable months she waved her crabbed claws, kicked weakly with her clubbed feet and enjoyed the usual routine of the infant. She was not alone, for there were three other such children in the big city's special nursery. Soon they all were removed to Central Laboratory School, where their delicate transformation began.

One of the babies died in the initial transferral, but of Helva's "class," seventeen thrived in the metal shells. Instead of kicking feet, Helva's neural responses started her wheels; instead of grabbing with hands, she manipulated mechanical extensions. As she matured, more and more neural synapses would be adjusted to operate other mechanisms that went into the maintenance and running of a spaceship. For Helva was destined to be the "brain" half of a scout ship, partnered with a man or a woman, whichever she chose, as the mobile half. She would be among the elite of her kind. Her initial intelligence tests registered above normal and her adaptation index was unusually high. As long as her development within her shell lived up to expectations, and there were no side-effects from the pituitary tinkering, Helva would live a rewarding, rich, and unusual life, a far cry from what she would have faced as an ordinary, "normal" being.

However, no diagram of her brain patterns, no early IQ tests recorded certain essential facts about Helva that Central must eventually learn. They would have to bide their official time and see, trusting that the massive doses of shell-psychology would suffice her, too, as the necessary bulwark against her unusual confinement and the pressures of her profession. A ship run by a human brain could not run rogue or insane with the power and resources Central had to build into their scout ships. Brain ships were, of course, long past the experimental stages. Most babies survived the perfected techniques of pituitary manipulation that kept their bodies small, eliminating the necessity of transfers from smaller to larger shells. And very, very few were lost when the final connection was made to the control panels of ship or industrial combine. Shell-people resembled mature dwarfs in size whatever their natal deformities were, but the well-oriented brain would not have changed places with the most perfect body in the Universe.

So, for happy years, Helva scooted around in her shell with her classmates, playing such games as Stall, Power-Seek, studying her lessons in trajectory, propulsion techniques, computation, logistics, mental hygiene, basic alien psychology, philology, space history, law, traffic, codes: all the et ceteras that eventually became compounded into a reasoning, logical, informed citizen. Not so obvious to her, but of more importance to her teachers, Helva ingested the precepts of her conditioning as easily as she absorbed her nutrient fluid. She would one day be grateful to the patient drone of the subconscious-level instruction.

Helva's civilization was not without busy, do-good associations, exploring possible inhumanities to terrestrial as well as extraterrestrial citizens. One such group—Society for the Preservation of the Rights of Intelligent Minorities—got all incensed over shelled "children" when Helva was just turning fourteen. When they were forced to, Central Worlds shrugged its shoulders, arranged a tour of the Laboratory Schools, and set the tour off to a big start by showing the members case histories, complete with photographs. Very few committees ever looked past the first few photos. Most of their original objections about "shells" were overridden by the relief that these hideous (to them) bodies *were* mercifully concealed.

Helva's class was doing fine arts, a selective subject in her crowded program. She had activated one of her microscopic tools, which she would later use for minute repairs to various parts of her control panel. Her subject was large—a copy of *The Last Supper*—and her canvas, small—the head of a tiny screw. She had tuned her sight to the proper degree. As she worked she absentmindedly crooned, producing a curious sound. Shell-people used their own vocal cords and diaphragms, but sound issued through microphones rather than mouths. Helva's hum, then, had a curious vibrancy, a warm, dulcet quality even in its aimless chromatic wanderings.

"Why, what a lovely voice you have," said one of the female visitors.

Helva "looked" up and caught a fascinating panorama of regular, dirty craters on a flaky pink surface. Her hum became a gurgle of surprise. She instinctively regulated her "sight" until the skin lost its cratered look and the pores assumed normal proportions.

"Yes, we have quite a few years of voice training, madam," remarked Helva calmly. "Vocal peculiarities often become excessively irritating during prolonged interstellar distances and must be eliminated. I enjoyed my lessons."

Although this was the first time that Helva had seen unshelled people, she took this experience calmly. Any other reaction would have been reported instantly.

"I meant that you have a nice singing voice . . . dear," the lady said.

"Thank you. Would you like to see my work?" Helva asked politely. She instinctively sheered away from personal discussions, but she filed the comment away for further meditation.

"Work?" asked the lady.

"I am currently reproducing *The Last Supper* on the head of a screw."

"Oh, I say," the lady twittered.

Helva turned her vision back to magnification and surveyed her copy critically. "Of course, some of my color values do not match the old Master's and the perspective is faulty, but I believe it to be a fair copy."

The lady's eyes, unmagnified, bugged out.

"Oh, I forget," and Helva's voice was really contrite. If she could have blushed, she would have. "You people don't have adjustable vision."

The monitor of this discourse grinned with pride and amusement as Helva's tone indicated pity for the unfortunate.

"Here, this will help," said Helva, substituting a magnifying device in one extension and holding it over the picture.

In a kind of shock, the ladies and gentlemen of the committee bent to observe the incredibly copied and brilliantly executed *Last Supper* on the head of a screw.

"Well," remarked one gentleman who had been forced to accompany his wife, "the good Lord can eat where angels fear to tread."

"Are you referring, sir," asked Helva politely, "to the Dark Age discussions of the number of angels who could stand on the head of a pin?"

"I had that in mind."

"If you substitute 'atom' for 'angel,' the problem is not insoluble, given the metallic content of the pin in question."

"Which you are programmed to compute?"

"Of course."

"Did they remember to program a sense of humor, as well, young lady?"

"We are directed to develop a sense of proportion, sir, which contributes the same effect."

The good man chortled appreciatively and decided the trip was worth his time.

If the investigation committee spent months digesting the thoughtful food served them at the Laboratory School, they left Helva with a morsel as well.

"Singing" as applicable to herself required research. She had, of course, been exposed to and enjoyed a music-appreciation course that had included the better-known classical works, such as *Tristan und Isolde, Candide, Oklahoma!,* and *Le nozze di Figaro,* along with the atomic-age singers, Birgit Nilsson, Bob Dylan, and Geraldine Todd, as well as the curious rhythmic progressions of the Venusians, Capellan visual chromatics, the sonic concerti of the Altairians and Reticulan croons. But "singing" for any shell-person posed considerable technical difficulties. Shell-people were schooled to examine every aspect of a problem or situation before making a prognosis. Balanced properly between optimism and practicality, the nondefeatist attitude of the shell-people led them to extricate themselves, their ships, and personnel, from bizarre situations. Therefore to Helva, the problem that she couldn't open her mouth to sing, among other restrictions, did not bother her. She would work out a method, bypassing her limitations, whereby she could sing.

She approached the problem by investigating the methods of sound reproduction through the centuries, human and instrumental. Her own sound-production equipment was essentially more instrumental than vocal. Breath control and the proper enunciation of vowel sounds within the oral cavity appeared to require the most development and practice. Shell-people did not, strictly speaking, breathe. For their purposes, oxygen and other gases were not drawn from the surrounding atmosphere through the medium of lungs but sustained artificially by solution in their shells. After experimentation, Helva discovered that she could manipulate her diaphragmic unit to sustain tone. By relaxing the throat muscles and expanding the oral cavity well into the frontal sinuses, she could direct the vowel sounds into the most felicitous position for proper reproduction through her throat microphone. She compared the results with tape recordings of modern singers and was not unpleased, although her own tapes had a peculiar quality about them, not at all unharmonious, merely unique. Acquiring a repertoire from the Laboratory library was no problem to one trained to perfect recall. She found herself able to sing any role and any song which struck her fancy. It would not have occurred to her that it was curious for a female to sing bass, baritone, tenor, mezzo, soprano, and coloratura as she pleased. It was, to Helva, only a matter of the correct reproduction and diaphragmatic control required by the music attempted.

If the authorities remarked on her curious avocation, they did so among themselves. Shell-people were encouraged to develop a hobby so long as they maintained proficiency in their technical work.

On the anniversary of her sixteenth year, Helva was unconditionally graduated and installed in her ship, the XH-834. Her permanent titanium shell was recessed behind an even more indestructible barrier in the central shaft of the scout ship. The neural, audio, visual, and sensory connections were made and sealed. Her extendibles were diverted, connected, or augmented, and the final, delicate-beyond-description brain taps were completed while Helva remained anesthetically unaware of the proceedings. When she woke, she *was* the ship. Her brain and intelligence controlled every function from navigation to such loading as a scout ship of her class needed. She could take care of herself and her ambulatory half in any situation already recorded in the annals of Central Worlds and any situation its most fertile minds could imagine.

Her first actual flight, for she and her kind had made mock flights on dummy panels since she was eight, showed her to be a complete master of the techniques of her profession. She was ready for her great adventures and the arrival of her mobile partner.

There were nine qualified scouts sitting around collecting base pay the day Helva reported for active duty. There were several missions that demanded instant attention, but Helva had been of interest to several department heads in Central for some time and each bureau chief was determined to have her assigned to *his* section. No one had remembered to introduce Helva to the prospective partners. The ship always chose its own partner. Had there been another "brain" ship at the base at the moment, Helva would have been guided to make the first move. As it was, while Central wrangled among itself, Robert Tanner sneaked out of the pilots' barracks, out to the field, and over to Helva's slim metal hull.

"Hello, anyone at home?" Tanner said.

"Of course," replied Helva, activating her outside scanners. "Are you my partner?" she asked hopefully, as she recognized the Scout Service uniform.

"All you have to do is ask," he retorted in a wistful tone.

"No one has come. I thought perhaps there were no partners available and I've had no directives from Central."

Even to herself Helva sounded a little self-pitying, but the truth was she was lonely, sitting on the darkened field. She had always had the company of other shells and more recently, technicians by the score. The sudden solitude had lost its momentary charm and become oppressive.

"No directives from Central is scarcely a cause for regret, but there happen to be eight other guys biting their fingernails to the quick just waiting for an invitation to board you, you beautiful thing."

Tanner was inside the central cabin as he said this, running appreciative fingers over her panel, the scout's gravity-chair, poking his head into the cabins, the galley, the head, the pressured-storage compartments.

"Now, if you want to goose Central and do *us* a favor all in one, call up the barracks and let's have a ship-warming partner-picking party. Hmmmm?"

Helva chuckled to herself. He was so completely different from the occasional visitors or the various Laboratory technicians she had encountered. He was so gay, so assured, and she was delighted by his suggestion of a partner-picking party. Certainly it was not against anything in her understanding of regulations.

"Cencom, this is XH-834. Connect me with Pilot Barracks."

"Visual?"

"Please."

A picture of lounging men in various attitudes of boredom came on her screen.

"This is XH-834. Would the unassigned scouts do me the favor of coming aboard?"

Eight figures were galvanized into action, grabbing pieces of wearing apparel, disengaging tape mechanisms, disentangling themselves from bedsheets and towels.

Helva dissolved the connection while Tanner chuckled gleefully and settled down to await their arrival.

Helva was engulfed in an unshell-like flurry of anticipation. No actress on her opening night could have been more apprehensive, fearful, or breathless. Unlike the actress, she could throw no hysterics, china objets d'art, or greasepaint to relieve her tension. She could, of course, check her stores for edibles and drinks, which she did, serving Tanner from the virgin selection of her commissary.

Scouts were colloquially known as "brawns" as opposed to their ship "brains." They had to pass as rigorous a training program as the brains and only the top 1 percent of each contributory world's highest scholars were admitted to Central Worlds Scout Training Program. Consequently the eight young men who came pounding up the gantry into Helva's hospitable lock were unusually fine-looking, intelligent, well-coordinated, and well-adjusted young men, looking forward to a slightly drunken evening, Helva permitting, and all quite willing to do each other dirt to get possession of her.

Such a human invasion left Helva mentally breathless, a luxury she thoroughly enjoyed for the brief time she felt she should permit it.

She sorted out the young men. Tanner's opportunism amused but did not specifically attract her; the blond Nordsen seemed too simple; dark-haired Alatpay had a kind of obstinacy for which she felt no compassion; Mir-Ahnin's bitterness hinted an inner darkness she did not wish to lighten, although he made the biggest outward play for her attention. Hers was a curious courtship—this would be only the first of several marriages for her, for brawns retired after seventy-five years of service, or earlier if they were unlucky. Brains, their bodies safe from any deterioration, were indestructible. In theory, once a shell-person had paid off the massive debt of early care, surgical adaptation, and maintenance charges, he or she was free to seek employment elsewhere. In practice, shell-people remained in the Service until they chose to self-destruct or died in line of duty. Helva had actually spoken to one shell-person 322 years old. She had been so awed by the contact she hadn't presumed to ask the personal questions she had wanted to.

Her choice of a brawn did not stand out from the others until

Tanner started to sing a scout ditty recounting the misadventures of the bold, dense, painfully inept Billy Brawn. An attempt at harmony resulted in cacophony and Tanner wagged his arms wildly for silence.

"What we need is a roaring good lead tenor. Jennan, besides palming aces, what do you sing?"

"Sharp," Jennan replied with easy good humor.

"If a tenor is absolutely necessary, I'll attempt it," Helva volunteered.

"My good *woman*," Tanner protested.

"Sound your A," said Jennan, laughing.

Into the stunned silence that followed the rich, clear, high A, Jennan remarked quietly, "Such an A Caruso would have given the rest of his notes to sing."

It did not take them long to discover her full range.

"All Tanner asked for was one roaring good lead tenor," Jennan said jokingly, "and our sweet mistress supplied us an entire repertory company. The boy who gets this ship will go far, far, far."

"To the Horsehead Nebula?" asked Nordsen, quoting an old Central saw.

"To the Horsehead Nebula and back, we shall make beautiful music," said Helva, chuckling.

"Together," Jennan said. "Only you'd better make the music and, with my voice, I'd better listen."

"I rather imagined it would be I who listened," suggested Helva.

Jennan executed a stately bow with an intricate flourish of his crushbrimmed hat. He directed his bow toward the central control pillar where Helva *was*. Her own personal preference crystallized at that precise moment and for that particular reason: Jennan, alone of the men, had addressed his remarks directly at her physical presence, regardless of the fact that he knew she could pick up his image wherever he was in the ship and regardless of the fact that her body was behind massive metal walls. Throughout their partnership, Jennan never failed to turn his head in her direction no matter where he was in relation to her. In response to this personalization, Helva at that moment and from then on always spoke to Jennan only through her central mike, even though that was not always the most efficient method.

Helva didn't know that she fell in love with Jennan that evening. As she had never been exposed to love or affection, only the drier cousins, respect and admiration, she could scarcely have recognized her reaction to the warmth of his personality and thoughtfulness. As a shell-person, she considered herself remote from emotions largely connected with physical desires.

"Well, Helva, it's been swell meeting you," said Tanner suddenly as she and Jennan were arguing about the baroque quality of "Come All Ye Sons of Art." "See you in space sometime, you lucky dog, Jennan. Thanks for the party, Helva."

"You don't have to go so soon?" asked Helva, realizing belatedly that she and Jennan had been excluding the others from this discussion.

"Best man won," Tanner said wryly. "Guess I'd better go get a tape on love ditties. Might need 'em for the next ship, if there're any more at home like you."

Helva and Jennan watched them leave, both a little confused.

"Perhaps Tanner's jumping to conclusions?" Jennan asked.

Helva regarded him as he slouched against the console, facing her shell directly. His arms were crossed on his chest and the glass he held had been empty for some time. He was handsome—they all were—but his watchful eyes were unwary, his mouth assumed a smile easily, his voice (to which Helva was particularly drawn) was resonant, deep, and without unpleasant overtones or accent.

"Sleep on it, at any rate, Helva. Call me in the morning if it's your opt."

She called him at breakfast, after she had checked her choice through Central. Jennan moved his things aboard, received their joint commission, had his personality and experience file locked into her reviewer, gave her the coordinates of their first mission. The XH-834 officially became the JH-834.

Their first mission was a dull but necessary crash priority (Medical got Helva), rushing a vaccine to a distant system plagued with a virulent spore disease. They had only to get to Spica as fast as possible.

After the initial, thrilling forward surge at her maximum speed, Helva realized her muscles were to be given less of a workout than her brawn on this tedious mission. But they did have plenty of time for exploring each other's personalities. Jennan, of course, knew what Helva was capable of as a ship and partner, just as she knew what she could expect from him. But these were only facts, and Helva looked forward eagerly to learning that human side of her partner which could not be reduced to a series of symbols. Nor could the give-and-take of two personalities be learned from a book. It had to be experienced.

"My father was a scout, too, or is that programmed?" began Jennan their third day out.

"Naturally."

"Unfair, you know. You've got all my family history and I don't know one blamed thing about yours."

"I've never known either," Helva said. "Until I read yours, it hadn't occurred to me I must have one, too, someplace in Central's files."

Jennan snorted. "Shell psychology!"

Helva laughed. "Yes, and I'm even programmed against curiosity about it. You'd better be, too."

Jennan ordered a drink, slouched into the gravity couch opposite her, put his feet on the bumpers, turning himself idly from side to side on the gimbals.

"Helva—a made-up name . . ."

"With a Scandinavian sound."

"You aren't blond," Jennan said positively.

"Well, then, there're dark Swedes."

"And blond Turks and this one's harem is limited to one."

"Your woman in purdah, yes, but you can comb the pleasure houses—" Helva found herself aghast at the edge to her carefully trained voice.

"You know," Jennan interrupted her, deep in some thought of his own, "my father gave me the impression he was a lot more married to his ship, the Silvia, than to my mother. I know I used to think Silvia was my grandmother. She was a low number, so she must have been a great-great-grandmother at least. I used to talk to her for hours."

"Her registry?" asked Helva, unwittingly jealous of everyone and anyone who had shared his hours.

"422. I think she's TS now. I ran into Tom Burgess once."

Jennan's father had died of a planetary disease, the vaccine for which his ship had used up in curing the local citizens.

"Tom said she'd got mighty tough and salty. You lose your sweetness and I'll come back and haunt you, girl," Jennan threatened.

Helva laughed. He startled her by stamping up to the column panel, touching it with light, tender fingers.

"I *wonder* what you look like," he said softly, wistfully.

Helva had been briefed about this natural curiosity of scouts. She didn't know anything about herself and neither of them ever would or could.

"Pick any form, shape, and shade and I'll be yours obliging," she countered, as training suggested.

"Iron Maiden, I fancy blondes with long tresses," and Jennan pantomimed Lady Godiva–like tresses. "Since you're immolated in titanium, I'll call you Brunehilde, my dear," and he made his bow.

With a chortle, Helva launched into the appropriate aria just as Spica made contact.

"What'n'ell's that yelling about? Who are you? And unless you're Central Worlds Medical, go away. We've got a plague. No visiting privileges."

"My ship is singing, we're the JH-834 of Worlds, and we've got your vaccine. What are our landing coordinates?"

"Your *ship* is singing?"

"The greatest SATB in organized space. Any request?"

The JH-834 delivered the vaccine but no more arias and received immediate orders to proceed to Leviticus IV. By the time they got there, Jennan found a reputation awaiting him and was forced to defend the 834's virgin honor.

"I'll stop singing," murmured Helva contritely as she ordered up poultices for his third black eye in a week.

"You will not," Jennan said through gritted teeth. "If I have to black eyes from here to the Horsehead to keep the snicker out of the title, we'll be the ship who sings."

After the "ship who sings" tangled with a minor but vicious narcotic ring in the Lesser Magellanics, the title became definitely respectful. Central was aware of each episode and punched out a "special interest" key on JH-834's file. A first-rate team was shaking down well.

Jennan and Helva considered themselves a first-rate team, too, after their tidy arrest.

"Of all the vices in the universe, I *hate* drug addiction," Jennan remarked as they headed back to Central Base. "People can go to hell quick enough without that kind of help."

"Is that why you volunteered for Scout Service? To redirect traffic?"

"I'll bet my official answer's on your review."

"In far too flowery wording. 'Carrying on the traditions of my family, which has been proud of four generations in Service,' if I may quote you your own words."

Jennan groaned. "I was *very* young when I wrote that. I certainly hadn't been through Final Training. And once I was in Final Training, my pride wouldn't let me fail . . .

"As I mentioned, I used to visit Dad on board the Silvia and I've a very good idea she might have had her eye on me as a replacement for my father because I had had massive doses of scout-oriented propaganda. It took. From the time I was seven, I was going to be a scout or else." He shrugged as if deprecating a youthful determination that had taken a great deal of mature application to bring to fruition.

"Ah, so? Scout Sahir Silan on the JS-422 penetrating into the Horse-head Nebula?"

Jennan chose to ignore her sarcasm.

"With *you*, I may even get that far. But even with Silvia's nudging *I* never daydreamed myself *that* kind of glory in my wildest flights of fancy. I'll leave the whoppers to your agile brain henceforth. I have in mind a smaller contribution to space history."

"So modest?"

"No. Practical. We also serve, et cetera." He placed a dramatic hand on his heart.

"Glory hound!" scoffed Helva.

"Look who's talking, my Nebula-bound friend. At least I'm not greedy. There'll only be one hero like my dad at Parsaea, but I *would* like to be remembered for some kudos. Everyone does. Why else do or die?"

"Your father died on his way back from Parsaea, if I may point out a few cogent facts. So he could never have known he was a hero for damming the flood with his ship. Which kept the Parsaean colony from being abandoned. Which gave them a chance to discover the antipar-alytic qualities of Parsaea. Which *he* never knew."

"I know," said Jennan softly.

Helva was immediately sorry for the tone of her rebuttal. She knew very well how deep Jennan's attachment to his father had been. On his review a note was made that he had rationalized his father's loss with the unexpected and welcome outcome of the Affair at Parsaea.

"Facts are not human, Helva. My father was and so am I. And *basically*, so are you. Check over your dial, 834. Amid all the wires attached to you is a heart, an underdeveloped human heart. Ob-viously!"

"I apologize, Jennan," she said.

Jennan hesitated a moment, threw out his hands in acceptance, and then tapped her shell affectionately.

"If they ever take us off the milk runs, we'll make a stab at the Nebula, huh?"

As so frequently happened in the Scout Service, within the next hour they had orders to change course, not to the Nebula, but to a recently colonized system with two habitable planets, one tropical, one glacial. The sun, named Ravel, had become unstable; the spectrum was that of a rapidly expanding shell, with absorption lines rapidly displacing toward violet. The augmented heat of the primary had already forced evacuation of the nearer world, Daphnis. The pattern of spectral emissions gave indication that the sun would sear Chloe as well. All ships in the immediate spatial vicinity were to report to Disaster Headquarters on Chloe to effect removal of the remaining colonists.

The JH-834 obediently presented itself and was sent to outlying areas on Chloe to pick up scattered settlers who did not appear to appreciate the urgency of the situation. Chloe, indeed, was enjoying the first temperatures above freezing since it had been flung out of its parent. Since many of the colonists were religious fanatics who had settled on rigorous Chloe to fit themselves for a life of pious reflection, Chloe's abrupt thaw was attributed to sources other than a rampaging sun.

Jennan had to spend so much time countering specious arguments that he and Helva were behind schedule on their way to the fourth and last settlement.

Helva jumped over the high range of jagged peaks that surrounded and sheltered the valley from the former raging snows as well as the present heat. The violent sun with its flaring corona was just beginning to brighten the deep valley as Helva dropped down to a landing.

"They'd better grab their toothbrushes and hop aboard," Helva said. "HQ says speed it up."

"All women," remarked Jennan in surprise as he walked down to meet them. "Unless the men on Chloe wear furred skirts."

"Charm 'em but pare the routine to the bare essentials. And turn on your two-way private."

Jennan advanced smiling, but his explanation of his mission was met with absolute incredulity and considerable doubt as to his authenticity. He groaned inwardly as the matriarch paraphrased previous explanations of the warming sun.

"Revered mother, there's been an overload on that prayer circuit and the sun is blowing itself up in one obliging burst. I'm here to take you to the spaceport at Rosary—"

"That Sodom?" The worthy woman glowered and shuddered disdainfully at his suggestion. "We thank you for your warning but we have no wish to leave our cloister for the rude world. We must go about our morning meditation, which has been interrupted—"

"It'll be permanently interrupted when that sun starts broiling you. You must come now," Jennan said firmly.

"Madame," said Helva, realizing that perhaps a female voice might carry more weight in this instance than Jennan's very masculine charm.

"Who spoke?" cried the nun, startled by the bodiless voice.

"I, Helva, the ship. Under my protection you and your sisters-in-faith may enter safely and be unprofaned by association with a male. I will guard you and take you safely to a place prepared for you."

The matriarch peered cautiously into the ship's open port. "Since only Central Worlds is permitted the use of such ships, I acknowledge that you are not trifling with us, young man. However, we are in no danger here."

"The temperature at Rosary is now ninety-nine degrees," said Helva. "As soon as the sun's rays penetrate directly into this valley, it will also be ninety-nine degrees, and it is due to climb to approximately one hundred eighty degrees today. I notice your buildings are made of wood with moss chinking. Dry moss. It should fire around noontime."

The sunlight was beginning to slant into the valley through the peaks, and the fierce rays warmed the restless group behind the matriarch. Several opened the throats of their furry parkas.

"Jennan," said Helva privately to him, "our time is very short."

"I can't leave them, Helva. Some of those girls are barely out of their teens."

"Pretty, too. No wonder the matriarch doesn't want to get in."

"Helva."

"It will be the Lord's will," said the matriarch stoutly and turned her back squarely on rescue.

"To burn to death?" shouted Jennan as she threaded her way through her murmuring disciples.

"They want to be martyrs? Their opt, Jennan," said Helva dispassionately. "We must leave and that is no longer a matter of option."

"How can I leave, Helva?"

"Parsaea?" Helva asked tauntingly as he stepped forward to grab one of the women. "You can't drag them *all* aboard and we don't have time to fight it out. Get on board, Jennan, or I'll have you on report."

"They'll die," muttered Jennan dejectedly as he reluctantly turned to climb on board.

"You can risk only so much," Helva said sympathetically. "As it is we'll just have time to make a rendezvous. Lab reports a critical speedup in spectral evolution."

Jennan was already in the air lock when one of the younger women, screaming, rushed to squeeze in the closing port. Her action set off the others. They stampeded through the narrow opening. Even crammed back to breast, there was not enough room inside for all the women. Jennan broke out space suits for the three who would have to remain with him in the air lock. He wasted valuable time explaining to the matriarch that she must put on the suit because the air lock had no independent oxygen or cooling units.

"We'll be caught," said Helva in a grim tone to Jennan on their private connection. "We've lost eighteen minutes in this last-minute rush. I am now overloaded for maximum speed and I must attain maximum speed to outrun the heat wave."

"Can you lift? We're suited."

"Lift? Yes," she said, doing so. "Run? I stagger."

Jennan, bracing himself and the women, could feel her sluggishness as she blasted upward. Heartlessly, Helva applied thrust as long as she could, despite the fact that the gravitational force mashed her cabin passengers brutally and crushed two fatally. It was a question of saving as many as possible. The only one for whom she had any concern was Jennan and she was in desperate terror about his safety. Airless and uncooled, protected by only one layer of metal, not three, the air lock was not going to be safe for the four trapped there, despite their space suits. These were only the standard models, not built to withstand the excessive heat to which the ship would be subjected.

Helva ran as fast as she could but the incredible wave of heat from the explosive sun caught them halfway to cold safety.

She paid no heed to the cries, moans, pleas, and prayers in her cabin. She listened only to Jennan's tortured breathing, to the missing throb in his suit's purifying system and the sucking of the overloaded cooling unit. Helpless, she heard the hysterical screams of his three companions as they writhed in the awful heat. Vainly, Jennan tried to calm them, tried to explain they would soon be safe and cool if they could be still and endure the heat. Undisciplined by their terror and torment, they tried to strike out at him despite the close quarters. One flailing arm became entangled in the leads to his power pack and the damage was quickly done. A connection, weakened by heat and the dead weight of the arm, broke.

For all the power at her disposal, Helva was helpless. She watched as Jennan fought for his breath, as he turned his head beseechingly toward *her,* and died.

Only the iron conditioning of her training prevented Helva from swinging around and plunging back into the cleansing heart of the exploding sun. Numbly she made rendezvous with the refugee convoy.

She obediently transferred her burned, heat-prostrated passengers to the assigned transport.

"I will retain the body of my scout and proceed to the nearest base for burial," she informed Central dully.

"You will be provided escort," was the reply.

"I have no need of escort."

"Escort is provided, XH-834," she was told curtly. The shock of hearing Jennan's initial severed from her call number cut off her half-formed protest. Stunned, she waited by the transport until her screens showed the arrival of two other slim brain ships. The cortege proceeded homeward at unfunereal speeds.

"834? The ship who sings?"

"I have no more songs."

"Your scout was Jennan."

"I do not wish to communicate."

"I'm 422."

"Silvia?"

"Silvia died a long time ago. I'm 422. Currently MS," the ship rejoined curtly. "AH-640 is our other friend, but Henry's not listening in. Just as well—he wouldn't understand it if you wanted to turn rogue. But I'd stop *him* if he tried to deter you."

"Rogue?" The term snapped Helva out of her apathy.

"Sure. You're young. You've got power for years. Skip. Others have done it. 732 went rogue twenty years ago after she lost her scout on a mission to that white dwarf. Hasn't been seen since."

"I never heard about rogues."

"As it's exactly the thing we're conditioned against, you sure wouldn't hear about it in school, my dear," 422 said.

"Break conditioning?" cried Helva, anguished, thinking longingly of the white, white furious hot heart of the sun she had just left.

"For you I don't think it would be hard at the moment," 422 said quietly, her voice devoid of her earlier cynicism. "The stars are out there, winking."

"Alone?" cried Helva from her heart.

"Alone!" 422 confirmed bleakly.

Alone with all of space and time. Even the Horsehead Nebula would not be far enough away to daunt her. Alone with a hundred years to live with her memories and nothing . . . nothing more.

"Was Parsaea worth it?" she asked 422 softly.

"Parsaea?" 422 repeated, surprised. "With his father? Yes. We were there, at Parsaea when we were needed. Just as you . . . and his

son . . . were at Chloe. When you were needed. The crime is not knowing where need is and not being there."

"But *I* need *him*. Who will supply my need?" said Helva bitterly. . . .

"834," said 422 after a day's silent speeding, "Central wishes your
report. A replacement awaits your opt at Regulus Base. Change course
accordingly."

"A replacement?" That was certainly not what she needed . . . a
reminder inadequately filling the void Jennan left. Why, her hull was
barely cool of Chloe's heat. Atavistically, Helva wanted time to mourn
Jennan.

"Oh, none of them are impossible if *you're* a good ship," 422 remarked philosophically. "And it is just what you need. The sooner the
better."

"You told them I wouldn't go rogue, didn't you?" Helva said.

"The moment passed you even as it passed me after Parsaea, and
before that, after Glen Arthur, and Betelgeuse."

"We're conditioned to go on, aren't we? We *can't* go rogue. You were
testing."

"Had to. Orders. Not even Psych knows why a rogue occurs. Central's very worried, and so, daughter, are your sister ships. I asked to
be your escort. I . . . don't want to lose you both."

In her emotional nadir, Helva could feel a flood of gratitude for
Silvia's rough sympathy.

"We've all known this grief, Helva. It's no consolation, but if we
couldn't feel with our scouts, we'd only be machines wired for sound."

Helva looked at Jennan's still form stretched before her in its shroud
and heard the echo of his rich voice in the quiet cabin.

"Silvia! I *couldn't* help him," she cried from her soul.

"Yes, dear, I know," 422 murmured gently and then was quiet.

The three ships sped on, wordless, to the great Central Worlds base
at Regulus. Helva broke silence to acknowledge landing instructions
and the officially tendered regrets.

The three ships set down simultaneously at the wooded edge where
Regulus's gigantic blue trees stood sentinel over the sleeping dead in
the small Service cemetery. The entire Base complement approached
with measured step and formed an aisle from Helva to the burial
ground. The honor detail, out of step, walked slowly into her cabin.
Reverently they placed the body of her dead love on the wheeled bier,
covered it honorably with the deep-blue, star-splashed flag of the

Service. She watched as it was driven slowly down the living aisle, which closed in behind the bier in last escort.

Then, as the simple words of interment were spoken, as the atmosphere planes dipped in tribute over the open grave, Helva found voice for her lonely farewell.

Softly, barely audible at first, the strains of the ancient song of evening and requiem swelled to the final poignant measure until black space itself echoed back the sound of the song the ship sang.

When I Was Miss Dow

SONYA DORMAN HESS

These hungry, mother-haunted people come and find us living in what they like to call crystal palaces, though really we live in glass places, some of them highly ornamented and others plain as paper. They come first as explorers, and perhaps realize we are a race of one sex only, rather amorphous beings of proteide; and we, even baby I, are Protean also, being able to take various shapes at will. One sex, one brain lobe, we live in more or less glass bridges over the humanoid chasm, eating, recreating, attending races, and playing other games like most living creatures.

Eventually, we're all dumped into the cell banks and reproduced once more.

After the explorers comes the colony of miners and scientists; the Warden and some of the other elders put on faces to greet them, agreeing to help with the mining of some ores, even giving them a koota or two as they become interested in our racing dogs. They set up their places of life, pop up their machines, bang-bang, chug-chug; we put on our faces, forms, smiles, and costumes. I am old enough to learn to change my shape too.

The Warden says to me, "It's about time you made a change, yourself. Some of your friends are already working for these people, bringing home credits and sulfas."

My Uncle (by the Warden's fourth conjunction) made himself over at the start, being one of the first to realize how it could profit us.

I protest to the Warden, "I'm educated and trained as a scholar. You always say I must remain deep in my mathematics and other studies."

My Uncle says, "You have to do it. There's only one way for us to get along with them," and he runs his fingers through his long blond hair. My Uncle's not an educated person, but highly placed politically, and while Captain Dow is around, my Uncle retains this particular shape. The captain is shipping out soon, then Uncle will find some other features, because he's already warned it's unseemly for him to be chasing around in the face of a girl after the half-bearded boys from the spaceships. I don't want to do this myself, wasting so much time, when the fourteen decimals even now are clicking on my mirrors.

The Warden says, "We have a pattern from a female botanist, she ought to do for you. But before we put you into the pattern tank, you'll have to approximate another brain lobe. They have two."

"I know," I say sulkily. A botanist. A she.

"Into the tank," the Warden says to me without mercy, and I am his to use as he believes proper.

I spend four days in the tank absorbing the female Terran pattern. When I'm released, the Warden tells me, "Your job is waiting for you. We went to a lot of trouble to arrange it." He sounds brusque, but perhaps this is because he hasn't conjoined for a long time. The responsibilities of being Warden of Mines and Seeds come first, long before any social engagement.

I run my fingers through my brunette curls and notice my Uncle is looking critically at me. "Haven't you made yourself rather old?" he asks.

"Oh, he's all right," the Warden says. "Thirty-three isn't badly matched to the Doctor, as I understand it."

Dr. Arnold Proctor, the colony's head biologist, is busy making radiograph pictures (with his primitive X rays) of skeletal structures: murger birds, rodents, and our pets and racers, the kootas. Dogs, to the Terrans, who are fascinated by them. We breed them primarily for speed and stamina, but some of them carry a gene for an inherited structural defect which cripples them, and they have to be destroyed before they are full grown. The Doctor is making a special study of kootas.

He gets up from his chair when I enter the office. "I'm Miss Dow, your new assistant," I say, hoping my long fingernails will stand up to the pressure of punchkeys on the computer, since I haven't had much practice in retaining foreign shapes. I'm still in uncertain balance between myself and Martha Dow, who is also myself. But one does not have two lobes for nothing, I discover.

"Good morning. I'm glad you're here," the Doctor says.

He is a nice, pink man with silver hair, soft-spoken, intelligent. I'm pleased, as we work along, to find he doesn't joke and wisecrack like so many of the Terrans, though I am sometimes whimsical, I like music and banquets as well as my studies.

Though absorbed in his work, Dr. Proctor isn't rude to interrupters. A man of unusual balance, coming as he does from a culture which sends out scientific parties that are 90 percent of one sex, when their species provides them with two. At first meeting he is dedicated but agreeable, and I'm charmed.

"Dr. Proctor," I ask him one morning, "is it possible for you to radiograph my koota? She's very fine, from the fastest stock available, and I'd like to breed her."

"Yes, yes, of course," he promises with his quick, often absent smile. "By all means. You wish to breed only the best." It's typical of him to assume we're all as dedicated as he.

My Uncle's not pleased. "There's nothing wrong with your koota," he says. "What do you want to X-ray her for? Suppose he finds something is wrong? You'll be afraid to race or breed her, and she won't be replaced. Besides, your interest in her may make him suspicious."

"Suspicious of what?" I ask, but my Uncle won't say, so I ask him, "Suppose she's bred and her pups are cripples?"

The Warden says, "You're supposed to have your mind on your work, not on racing. The koota was just to amuse you when you were younger."

I lean down and stroke her head, which is beautiful, and she breathes a deep and gentle breath in response.

"Oh, let him go," my Uncle says wearily. He's getting disgusted because they didn't intend for me to bury myself in a laboratory or a computer room without making more important contacts. But a scholar is born with a certain temperament and has an introspective nature, and as I'm destined eventually to replace the Warden, naturally I prefer the life of the mind.

"I must say," my Uncle remarks, "you look the image of a Terran female. Is the work interesting?"

"Oh, yes, fascinating," I reply, and he snorts at my lie, since we both know it's dull and routine, and most of my time is spent working out the connections between my two brain lobes, which still present me with some difficulty.

My koota bitch is subjected to a pelvic radiograph. Afterward, I stand on my heels in the small, darkened cubicle, looking at the film on the viewing screen. There he stands too, with his cheekbones emerald in the peculiar light, and his hair, which is silver in daylight, looks phosphorescent. I resist this. I am resisting this Doctor with the X-ray eyes who can examine my marrow with ease. He sees Martha's marrow, every perfect corpuscle of it.

You can't imagine how comforting it is to be so transparent. There's no need to pretend, adjust, advance, retreat, or discuss the oddities of my planet. We are looking at the X-ray film of my prized racer and companion to determine the soundness of her hip joints, yet I suspect the doctor, platinum-green and tall as a tower, is piercing my reality with his educated gaze. He can see the blood flushing my surfaces. I don't need to do a thing but stand up straight so the crease of fat at my waist won't distort my belly button, the center of it all.

"You see?" he says. I do see, looking at the film in this darkness where perfection or disaster may be viewed, and I'm twined in the paradox which confronts me here. The darker the room, the brighter the screen and the clearer the picture. Less light! and the truth becomes more evident. Either the koota is properly jointed and may be bred without danger of passing the gene on to her young, or she is not properly jointed and cannot be used. Less light, more truth! And the Doctor is green sculpture—a little darker and he would be a bronze—but his natural color is pink alabaster.

"You see," the Doctor says, and I do try to see. He points his wax pencil at one hip joint on the film, and says, "A certain amount of osteoarthritic build-up is already evident. The cranial rim is wearing down, she may go lame. She'll certainly pass the defect on to some of her pups, if she's bred."

This koota has been my playmate and friend for a long time. She retains a single form, that of koota, full of love and beautiful speed; she has been a source of pleasure and pride.

Dr. Proctor, of the pewter hair, will discuss the anatomical defects of the koota in a gentle and cultivated voice. I am disturbed. There shouldn't be any need to explain the truth, which is evident. Yet it seems that to comprehend the exposures, I require a special education. It's said that the more you have seen, the quicker you are to sort the eternal verities into one pile and the dismal illusions into another. How is it that sometimes the Doctor wears a head which resembles that of a koota, with a splendid muzzle and noble brow?

Suddenly, he gives a little laugh and points the end of the wax pencil at my navel, announcing, "There. There, it is essential that the belly button onto the pelvis, or you'll bear no children." Thoughts of offspring had occurred to me. But weren't we discussing my racer? The radiograph film is still clipped to the view screen, and upon it, spread-eagled, appears the bony Rorschach of my koota bitch, her hip joints expressing doom.

I wish the Doctor would put on the daylight. I come to the conclusion that there's a limit to how much truth I can examine, and the more I submit to the conditions necessary for examining it, the more unhappy I become.

Dr. Proctor is a man of such perfect integrity that he continues to talk about bones and muscles until I'm ready to scream for mercy. He has done something unusual and probably prohibited, but he's not aware of it. I mean it must be prohibited in his culture, where it seems they play on each other, but not with each other. I'm uneasy, fluctuating.

He snaps two switches. Out goes the film and on goes the sun, making my eyes stream with grateful tears, although he's so adjusted to these contrasts he doesn't so much as blink. Floating in the sunshine, I've become opaque; he can't see anything but my surface tensions, and I wonder what he does in his spare time. A part of me seems to tilt, or slide.

"There, there, oh dear, Miss Dow," he says, patting my back, rubbing my shoulder blades. His forearms and fingers extend gingerly. "You do want to breed only the best, don't you?" he asks. I begin within me a compulsive ritual of counting the elements; it's all I can do to keep communications open between my brain lobes. I'm suffering from eclipses; one goes dark, the other lights up like a new saloon, that one goes dark, the other goes nova.

"There, there," the Doctor says, distressed because I'm quivering and trying to keep the connections open; I have never felt clogged before. They may have to put me back into the pattern tank.

Profoundly disturbed, I lift my face, and he gives me a kiss. Then I'm all right, balanced again, one lobe composing a concerto for virtix flute, the other one projecting, "Oh Arnie, oh Arnie." Yes, I'm okay for the shape I'm in. He's marking off my joints with his wax pencil (the marks of which can be easily erased from the film surface) and he's mumbling, "It's essential, oh yes, it's essential."

Finally, he says, "I guess all of us colonists are lonely here," and I say, "Oh yes, aren't we," before I realize the enormity of the Warden's manipulations, and what a lot I have to learn. Evidently the Warden triple-carded me through the Colony Punch Center as a Terran. I lie and say, "Oh yes, yes. Oh, Arnie, put out the light," for we may find some more truth.

"Not here," Arnie says, and of course he's right, this is a room for study, for cataloging obvious facts, not a place for carnival. There are not many places for it, I discover with surprise. Having lived in glass all my life, I expect everyone else to be as comfortable there as I am. But this isn't so.

Just the same, we find his quarters, after dark, to be comfortable and free of embarrassment. You wouldn't think a dedicated man of his age would be so vigorous, but I find out he spends his weekends at the recreation center hitting a ball with his hand. The ball bounces back off a wall and he hits it and hits it. Though he's given that up now because we're together on weekends.

"You're more than an old bachelor like me deserves," he tells me.

"Why are you an old bachelor?" I ask him. I do wonder why, if it's something not to be.

He tries to explain it to me. "I'm not a young man. I wouldn't make a good husband, I'm afraid. I like to work late, to be undisturbed. In my leisure time, I like to make wood carvings. Sometimes I go to bed with the sun and sometimes I'm up working all night. And then children. No. I'm lucky to be an old bachelor," he says.

Arnie carves kaku wood, which has a brilliant grain and is soft enough to permit easy carving. He's working on a figure of a murger bird, whittling lengthwise down the wood so the grain, wavy, full of flowing, wedge-shaped lines, will represent the feathers. The lamplight shines on his hair and the crinkle of his eyelids as he looks down, and carves, whittles, turns. He's absorbed in what he doesn't see there, but he's projecting what he wants to see. It's the reverse of what he must do in the viewing room. I begin to suffer a peculiar pain, located in the nerve cluster between my lungs. He's not talking to me. He's not caressing me. He's forgotten I'm here, and like a false projection, I'm beginning to fade. In another hour perhaps the film will become blank. If he doesn't see me, then am I here?

He's doing just what I do when busy with one of my own projects, and I admire the intensity with which he works: it's magnificent. Yes, I'm jealous of it, I burn with rage and jealousy, he has abandoned me to be Martha and I wish I were myself again, free in shape and single in mind. Not this sack of mud clinging to another. Yet he's teaching me that it's good to cling to another. I'm exhausted from strange disciplines. Perhaps he's tired too; I see that sometimes he kneads the muscles of his stomach with his hands, and closes his eyes.

The Warden sits me down on one of my rare evenings home and talks angrily. "You're making a mistake," he says. "If the Doctor finds out what you are, you'll lose your job with the Colony. Besides, we never supposed you'd have a liaison with only one man. You were supposed to start with the Doctor and go on from there. We need every credit you can bring in. And by the way, you haven't done well on that score lately. Is he stingy?"

"Of course he isn't."

"But all you bring home in credits is your pay."

I can think of no reply. It's true the Warden has a right to use me in whatever capacity will serve us all best, as I will use others when I'm a Warden, but he and my Uncle spend half the credits from my job on sulfadiazole, to which they've become addicted.

"You've no sense of responsibility," the Warden says. Perhaps he's coming close to time for conjunction again, and this makes him more concerned about my stability.

My Uncle says, "Oh, he's young, leave him alone. As long as he turns over most of those pay credits to us. Though what he uses the remainder for, I'll never know."

I use it for clothes at the Colony Exchange. Sometimes Arnie takes me out for an evening, usually to the Laugh Tree Bar, where the space crews, too, like to relax. The bar is the place to find joy babies, young, pretty, planet-born girls who work at the Colony Punch Center during the day and spend their evenings here competing for the attention of the officers. Sitting here with Arnie, I can't distinguish a colonist's daughter from one of my friends or relatives. They wouldn't know me, either.

Once, at home, I try to talk with a few of these friends about my feelings. But I discover that whatever female patterns they've borrowed are superficial ones; none of them bother to grow an extra lobe, but merely tuck the Terran pattern into a corner of their own for handy reference. They are most of them on sulfas. Hard and shiny toys, they skip like pebbles over the surface of the colonists' lives.

Then they go home, revert to their own free forms, and enjoy their mathematics, colors, compositions, and seedings.

"Why me?" I demand of the Warden. "Why two lobes? Why me?"

"We felt you'd be more efficient," he answers. "And while you're here, which you seldom are these days, you'd better revert to other shapes. Your particles may be damaged if you hold that female form too long."

Oh, but you don't know, I want to tell him. You don't know I'll hold it forever. If I'm damaged or dead, you'll put me into the cell banks, and you'll be amazed, astonished, terrified, to discover that I come out complete, all Martha. I can't be changed.

"You little lump of protagon," my Uncle mumbles bitterly. "You'll never amount to anything, you'll never be a Warden. Have you done any of your own work recently?"

I say, "Yes, I've done some crystal divisions, and regrown them in nonestablished patterns." My Uncle's in a bad mood, as he's kicking sulfa and his nerve tissue is addled. I'm wise to speak quietly to him, but he still grumbles.

"I can't understand why you like being a two-lobed pack of giggles. I couldn't wait to get out of it. And you were so dead against it to begin with."

"Well, I have learned," I start to say, but can't explain what it is I'm still learning, and close my eyes. Part of it is that on the line between the darkness and the brightness it's easiest to float. I've never wanted to practice only easy things. My balance is damaged. I never had to balance. It's not a term or concept I understand even now, at home, in free form. Some impress of Martha's pattern lies on my own brain cells. I suspect it's permanent damage, which gives me joy. That's what I mean about not understanding it; I am taught to strive for perfection, how can I be pleased with this, which may be a catastrophe?

Arnie carves on a breadth of kaku wood, bringing out to the surface a seascape. Knots become clots of spray, a flaw becomes windblown spume. I want to be Martha. I'd like to go to the Laugh Tree with Arnie, for a good time; I'd like to learn to play cards with him.

You see what happens: Arnie is, in his way, like my original self, and I hate that part of him, since I've given it up to be Martha. Martha makes him happy, she is chocolate to his appetite, pillow for his weariness.

I turn for company to my koota. She's the color of morning, her chest juts out like an ax blade, her ribs spring up and back like wings, her eyes are large and clear as she returns my gaze. Yet she's beyond hope; in a little time, she'll be lame; she can't race anymore, she must not mother a litter. I turn to her and she gazes back into my eyes, dreaming of speed and wind on the sandy beaches where she has run.

"Why don't you read some tapes?" Arnie suggests to me, because I'm restless and I disturb him. The koota lies at my feet. I read tapes. Every evening in his quarters Arnie carves, I read tapes, the broken racer lies at my feet. I pass through Terran history this way. When the clown tumbles into the tub, I laugh. Terran history is full of clowns and tubs; at first it seems that's all there is, but you learn to see beneath the comic costumes.

While I float on that taut line, the horizon between light and dark, where it's so easy, I begin to sense what is under the costumes: staggering down the street dead drunk on a sunny afternoon with everyone laughing at you; hiding under the veranda because you made blood come out of Pa's face; kicking a man when he's in the gutter because you've been kicked and have to pass it on. Terrans have something called tragedy. It's what one of them called being a poet in the body of a cockroach.

"Have you heard the rumor?" Arnie asks, putting down the whittling tool. "Have you heard that some of the personnel in Punch Center aren't really humans?"

"Not really?" I ask, putting away the tape. We have no tragedy. In my species, family relationships are based only on related gene patterns; they are finally dumped into the family bank and a new relative is created from the old. It's one form of ancient history multiplying itself, but it isn't tragic. The koota, her utility destroyed by a recessive gene, lies sleeping at my feet. Is this tragedy? But she is a single form, she can't regenerate a lost limb, or exfoliate brain tissue. She can only return my gaze with her steadfast and affectionate one.

"What are they, then?" I ask Arnie. "If they're not human?"

"The story is that the local life-forms aren't as we really see them. They've put on faces, like ours, to deal with us. And some of them have filtered into personnel."

Filtered! As if I were a virus.

I say, "But they must be harmless. No harm has come to anyone."

"We don't know that for a fact," Arnie replies.

"You look tired," I say, and he comes to me to be soothed, to be loved in his flesh, his single form, his search for the truth in the darkness of the viewing cubicle. At present he's doing studies of murger birds. Their spinal cavities are large, air-filled ovals, and their bone is extremely porous, which permits them to soar to great heights.

The koota no longer races on the windblown beaches; she lies at our feet, looking into the distance. The wall must be transparent to her eyes, I feel that beyond it she sees clearly how the racers go, down the long, bright curve of sand in the morning sun. She sighs and lays her head down on her narrow, delicate paws.

Arnie says, "I seem to be tired all the time," and kneads the muscles of his chest. He puts his head down on my breasts. "I don't think the food's agreeing with me lately."

"Do you suffer pains?" I ask curiously.

"Suffer," he says, "what kind of nonsense is that, with analgesics. No. I don't suffer. I just don't feel well."

He's absorbed in murger birds, kaku wood, he descends into the dark and rises up like a rocket across the horizon into the thin clarity above. While I float. I no longer dare to breathe, I'm afraid of disturbing everything. I do not want anything. His head lies on my breast and I will not disturb him.

"Oh. My God," Arnie says, and I know what it's come to, even before he begins to choke, and his muscles leap although I hold him in my arms. I know his heart is choking on massive doses of blood; the brilliance fades from his eyes and they begin to go dark while I tightly hold him. If he doesn't see me as he dies, will I be here?

I can feel, under my fingers, how rapidly his skin cools. I must put him down, here with his carvings and his papers, and I must go home. But I lift Arnie in my arms, and call the koota, who gets up rather stiffly. It's long after dark, and I carry him slowly, carefully, home to what he called a crystal palace, where the Warden and my Uncle are teaching each other to play chess with a set some space captain gave them in exchange for seed crystals. They sit in a bloom of light, sparkling, their old brains bent over the chessmen, as I breathe open the door and carry Arnie in.

First, my Uncle gives me just a glance, but then another glance, and a hard stare. "Is that the Doctor?" he asks.

I put Arnie down and hold one of his cold hands. "Warden," I say, on my knees, on eye level with the chessboard and its carved men. "Warden, can you put him in one of the banks?"

The Warden turns to look at me, as hard as my Uncle. "You've become deranged, trying to maintain two lobes," he says. "You cannot reconstitute or re-create a Terran by our methods, and you must know it."

"Over the edge, over the edge," my Uncle says, now a blond, six-foot, hearty male Terran, often at the Laugh Tree with one of the joy babies. He enjoys life, his own or someone else's. I have too, I suppose. Am I fading? I am, really, just one of Arnie's projections, a form on a screen in his mind. I am not, really, Martha. Though I tried.

"We can't have him here," the Warden says. "You'd better get him out of here. You couldn't explain a corpse like that to the colonists, if they came looking for him. They'll think we did something to him. It's nearly time for my next conjunction, do you want your nephew to arrive in disgrace? The Uncles will drain his bank."

The Warden gets up and comes over to me. He takes hold of my dark curls and pulls me to my feet. It hurts my physical me, which is Martha, God knows, Arnie, I'm Martha, it seems to me. "Take him back to his quarters," the Warden says to me. "And come back here immediately. I'll try to see you back to your own pattern, but it may be too late. In part, I blame myself. If you must know. So I will try."

Yes, yes, I want to say to him; as I was, dedicated, free; turn me back into myself, I never wanted to be anyone else, and now I don't know if I am anyone at all. The light's gone from his eyes and he doesn't see me.

I pick him up and breathe the door out and go back through the night to his quarters, where the lamp still burns. I'm going to leave him here, where he belongs. Before I go, I pick up the small carving of the murger bird and take it with me, home to my glass bridge where at the edge of the mirrors the decimals are still clicking perfectly, clicking out known facts; an octagon can be reduced, the planet turns at such a degree on its axis, to see the truth you must have light of some sort, but to see the light you must have darkness of some sort. I can no longer float on the horizon between the two because that horizon has disappeared. I've learned to descend, and to rise, and descend again.

I'm able to revert without help to my own free form, to reabsorb the extra brain tissue. The sun comes up and it's bright. The night comes down and it's dark. I'm becoming somber, and a brilliant student. Even my Uncle says I'll be a good Warden, when the time comes.

The Warden goes to conjunction; from the cell banks a nephew is lifted out. The koota lies dreaming of races she has run in the wind. It is our life, and it goes on, like the life of other creatures.

The Food Farm

KIT REED

So here I am, warden-in-charge, fattening them up for our leader, Tommy Fango; here I am laying on the banana pudding and the milk-shakes and the cream-and-brandy cocktails, going about like a technician, gauging their effect on haunch and thigh when all the time it is I who love him, I who could have pleased him eternally if only life had broken differently. But I am scrawny now, I am swept like a leaf around corners, battered by the slightest wind. My elbows rattle against my ribs and I have to spend half the day in bed so a gram or two of what I eat will stay with me, for if I do not, the fats and creams will vanish, burned up in my own insatiable furnace, and what little flesh I have will melt away.

Cruel as it may sound, I know where to place the blame.

It was vanity, all vanity, and I hate them most for that. It was not my vanity, for I have always been a simple soul; I reconciled myself early to reinforced chairs and loose garments, to the spattering of remarks. Instead of heeding them I plugged in, and I would have been happy to let it go at that, going through life with my radio in my bodice, for while I never drew cries of admiration, no one ever blanched and turned away.

But they were vain and in their vanity my frail father, my pale, scrawny mother saw me not as an entity but as a reflection on them-selves. I flush with shame to remember the excuses they made for me. "She takes after May's side of the family," my father would say, denying any responsibility. "It's only baby fat," my mother would say, jabbing her elbow into my soft flank. "Nelly is big for her age." Then she would jerk furiously, pulling my voluminous smock down to cover my knees. That was when they still consented to be seen with me. In that period they would stuff me with pies and roasts before we went anywhere, filling me up so I would not gorge myself in public. Even so I had to take thirds, fourths, fifths and so I was a humiliation to them.

In time I was too much for them and they stopped taking me out; they made no more attempts to explain. Instead they tried to think of ways to make me look better; the doctors tried the fool's poor battery of pills; they tried to make me join a club. For a while my mother and I did exercises; we would sit on the floor, she in a black leotard, I in my smock. Then she would do the brisk one-two, one-two and I would make a few passes at my toes. But I had to listen, I had to plug in, and after I was plugged in, naturally I had to find something to eat; Tommy might sing and I always ate when Tommy sang, and so I would leave her there on the floor, still going one-two, one-two. For a while after that they tried locking up the food. Then they began to cut into my meals.

That was the cruelest time. They would refuse me bread, they would plead and cry, plying me with lettuce and telling me it was all for my own good. My own good. Couldn't they hear my vitals crying out? I fought, I screamed, and when that failed I suffered in silent obedience until finally hunger drove me into the streets. I would lie in bed, made brave by the Monets and Barry Arkin and the Philadons coming in over the radio, and Tommy (there was never enough; I heard him a hundred times a day and it was never enough; how bitter that seems now!). I would hear them and then when my parents were asleep I would unplug and go out into the neighborhood. The first few nights I begged, throwing myself on the mercy of passersby and then plunging into the bakery, bringing home everything I didn't eat right there in the shop. I got money quickly enough; I didn't even have to ask. Perhaps it was my bulk, perhaps it was my desperate subverbal cry of hunger; I found I had only to approach and the money was mine. As soon as they saw me, people would whirl and bolt, hurling a purse or wallet into my path as if to slow me in my pursuit; they would be gone before I could even express my thanks. Once I was shot at. Once a stone lodged itself in my flesh.

At home my parents continued with their tears and pleas. They persisted with their skim milk and their chops, ignorant of the life I lived by night. In the daytime I was complaisant, dozing between snacks, feeding on the sounds which played in my ear, coming from the radio concealed in my dress. Then, when night fell, I unplugged; it gave a certain edge to things, knowing I would not plug in again until I was ready to eat. Some nights this only meant going to one of the caches in my room, bringing forth bottles and cartons and cans. On other nights I had to go into the streets, finding money where I could. Then I would lay in a new supply of cakes and rolls and baloney from the delicatessen and several cans of ready-made frosting and perhaps a flitch of bacon or some ham; I would toss in a basket of oranges to ward off scurvy and a carton of candy bars for quick energy. Once I had enough I would go back to my room, concealing food here and there, rearranging my nest of pillows and comforters. I would open the first pie or the first half-gallon of ice cream and then, as I began, I would plug in.

You had to plug in; everybody that mattered was plugged in. It was our bond, our solace, and our power, and it wasn't a matter of being distracted, or occupying time. The sound was what mattered, that and the fact that fat or thin, asleep or awake, you were important when you plugged in, and you knew that through fire and flood and adversity, through contumely and hard times there was this single bond, this common heritage; strong or weak, eternally gifted or wretched and ill-loved, we were all plugged in.

Tommy, beautiful Tommy Fango, the others paled to nothing next to him. Everybody heard him in those days; they played him two or three times an hour, but you never knew when it would be, so you were plugged in and listening hard every living moment; you ate, you slept, you drew breath for the moment when they would put on one of Tommy's records, you waited for his voice to fill the room. Cold cuts and cupcakes and game hens came and went during that period in my life, but one thing was constant: I always had a cream pie thawing and when they played the first bars of "When a Widow" and Tommy's voice first flexed and uncurled, I was ready, I would eat the cream pie during Tommy's midnight show. The whole world waited in those days; we waited through endless sunlight, through nights of drumbeats and monotony, we all waited for Tommy Fango's records, and we waited for that whole unbroken hour of Tommy, his midnight show. He came on live at midnight in those days; he sang, broadcasting from the Hotel Riverside, and that was beautiful, but more important, he talked, and while he was talking he made everything all right. Nobody was lonely when Tommy talked; he brought us all together on that midnight show, he talked and made us powerful, he talked, and finally he sang. You have to imagine what it was like, me in the night, Tommy, the pie. In a while I would go to a place where I had to live on Tommy and only Tommy, to a time when hearing Tommy would bring back the pie, all the poor lost pies . . .

Tommy's records, his show, the pie . . . that was perhaps the happiest period of my life. I would sit and listen and I would eat and eat and eat. So great was my bliss that it became torture to put away the food at daybreak; it grew harder and harder for me to hide the cartons and the cans and the bottles, all the residue of my happiness. Perhaps a bit of bacon fell into the register; perhaps an egg rolled under the bed and began to smell. All right, perhaps I did become careless, continuing my revels into the morning, or I may have been thoughtless enough to leave a jelly roll unfinished on the rug. I became aware that they were watching, lurking just outside my door, plotting as I ate. In time they broke in on me, weeping and pleading, lamenting over every ice-cream carton and crumb of pie; then they threatened. Finally they restored the food they had taken from me in the daytime, thinking to curtail my eating at night. Folly. By that time I needed it all, I shut myself in with it and would not listen. I ignored their cries of hurt pride, their outpourings of wounded vanity, their puny little threats. Even if I had listened, I could not have forestalled what happened next.

I was so happy that last day. There was a Smithfield ham, mine, and I remember a jar of cherry preserves, mine, and I remember bacon, pale and white on Italian bread. I remember sounds downstairs and before I could take warning, an assault, a company of uniformed attendants, the sting of a hypodermic gun. Then the ten of them closed in and grappled me into a sling, or net, and heaving and straining, they bore me down the stairs. I'll never forgive you, I cried, as they bundled me into the ambulance. I'll never forgive you, I bellowed, as my mother in a last betrayal took away my radio, and I cried out one last time, as my father removed a hambone from my breast: I'll never forgive you. And I never have.

It is painful to describe what happened next. I remember three days of horror and agony, of being too weak, finally, to cry out or claw the walls. Then at last I was quiet and they moved me into a sunny, pastel, chintz-bedizened room. I remember that there were flowers on the dresser and someone watching me.

"What are you in for?" she said.

I could barely speak for weakness. "Despair."

"Hell with that," she said, chewing. "You're in for food."

"What are you eating?" I tried to raise my head.

"Chewing. Inside of the mouth. It helps."

"I'm going to die."

"Everybody thinks that at first. I did." She tilted her head in an attitude of grace. "You know, this is a very exclusive school."

Her name was Ramona, and as I wept silently, she filled me in. This was a last resort for the few who could afford to send their children here. They prettied it up with a schedule of therapy, exercise, massage; we would wear dainty pink smocks and talk of art and theater; from time to time we would attend classes in elocution and hygiene. Our parents would say with pride that we were away at Faircrest, an elegant finishing school; we knew better—it was a prison and we were being starved.

"It's a world I never made," said Ramona, and I knew that her parents were to blame, even as mine were. Her mother liked to take the children into hotels and casinos, wearing her thin daughters like a garland of jewels. Her father followed the sun on his private yacht, with the pennants flying and his children on the fantail, lithe and tanned. He would pat his flat, tanned belly and look at Ramona in disgust. When it was no longer possible to hide her, he gave in to blind pride. One night they came in a launch and took her away. She had been here six months now and had lost almost a hundred pounds. She must have been monumental in her prime; she was still huge.

"We live from day to day," she said. "But you don't know the worst."

"My radio," I said in a spasm of fear. "They took away my radio."

"There is a reason," she said. "They call it therapy."

I was mumbling in my throat, in a minute I would scream.

"Wait." With ceremony, she pushed aside a picture and touched a tiny switch and then, like sweet balm for my panic, Tommy's voice flowed into the room.

When I was quiet she said, "You only hear him once a day."

"No."

"But you can hear him any time you want to. You hear him when you need him most."

But we were missing the first few bars and so we shut up and listened, and after "When a Widow" was over we sat quietly for a moment, her resigned, me weeping, and then Ramona threw another switch and the Sound filtered into the room, and it was almost like being plugged in.

"Try not to think about it."

"I'll die."

"If you think about it you *will* die. You have to learn to use it instead. In a minute they will come with lunch," Ramona said and as The Screamers sang sweet background, she went on in a monotone: "A chop. One lousy chop with a piece of lettuce and maybe some gluten bread. I pretend it's a leg of lamb, that works if you eat very, very slowly and think about Tommy the whole time; then if you look at your picture of Tommy you can turn the lettuce into anything you want, Caesar salad or a whole smorgasbord, and if you say his name over and over you can pretend a whole bombe or torte if you want to and . . ."

"I'm going to pretend a ham and kidney pie and a watermelon filled with chopped fruits and Tommy and I are in the Rainbow Room and we're going to finish up with Fudge Royale . . ." I almost drowned in my own saliva; in the background I could almost hear Tommy, and I could hear Ramona saying, "Capon, Tommy would like capon, canard à l'orange, Napoleons, tomorrow we will save Tommy for lunch and listen while we eat . . ." and I thought about that, I thought about listening and imagining whole cream pies and I went on, ". . . lemon pie, rice pudding, a whole Edam cheese . . . I think I'm going to live."

The matron came in the next morning at breakfast, and stood as she would every day, tapping red fingernails on one svelte hip, looking on in revulsion as we fell on the glass of orange juice and the hard-boiled egg. I was too weak to control myself; I heard a shrill sniveling sound and realized only from her expression that it was my own voice: "Please, just some bread, a stick of butter, anything, I could lick the dishes if you'd let me, only please don't leave me like this, please . . ." I can still see her sneer as she turned her back.

I felt Ramona's loyal hand on my shoulder. "There's always toothpaste, but don't use too much at once or they'll come and take it away from you."

I was too weak to rise and so she brought it and we shared the tube and talked about all the banquets we had ever known, and when we got tired of that, we talked about Tommy, and when that failed, Ramona went to the switch and we heard "When a Widow," and that helped for a while, and then we decided that tomorrow we would put off "When a Widow" until bedtime because then we would have something to look forward to all day. Then lunch came and we both wept.

It was not just hunger: after a while the stomach begins to devour itself and the few grams you toss it at mealtimes assuage it, so that in time the appetite itself begins to fail. After hunger comes depression. I lay there, still too weak to get about, and in my misery I realized that they could bring me roast pork and watermelon and Boston cream pie without ceasing; they could gratify all my dreams and I would only

202 ★ KIT REED

weep helplessly, because I no longer had the strength to eat. Even then, when I thought I had reached rock bottom, I had not comprehended the worst. I noticed it first in Ramona. Watching her at the mirror, I said, in fear, "You're thinner."

She turned with tears in her eyes. "Nelly, I'm not the only one."

I looked around at my own arms and saw that she was right: there was one less fold of flesh above the elbow; there was one less wrinkle at the wrist. I turned my face to the wall and all Ramona's talk of food and Tommy did not comfort me. In desperation she turned on Tommy's voice, but as he sang I lay back and contemplated the melting of my own flesh.

"If we stole a radio, we could hear him again," Ramona said, trying to soothe me. "We could hear him when he sings tonight."

Tommy came to Faircrest on a visit two days later, for reasons that I could not then understand. All the other girls lumbered into the assembly hall to see him, thousands of pounds of agitated flesh. It was that morning that I discovered I could walk again, and I was on my feet, struggling into the pink tent in a fury to get to Tommy, when the matron intercepted me.

"Not you, Nelly."

"I have to get to Tommy. I have to hear him sing."

"Next time, maybe." With a look of naked cruelty she added, "You're a disgrace. You're still too gross."

I lunged, but it was too late; she had already shot the bolt. And so I sat in the midst of my diminishing body, suffering while every other girl in the place listened to him sing. I knew then that I had to act; I would regain myself somehow, I would find food and regain my flesh and then I would go to Tommy. I would use force if I had to, but I would hear him sing. I raged through the room all that morning, hearing the shrieks of five hundred girls, the thunder of their feet, but even when I pressed myself against the wall, I could not hear Tommy's voice.

Yet Ramona, when she came back to the room, said the most interesting thing. It was some time before she could speak at all, but in her generosity she played "When a Widow" while she regained herself, and then she spoke: "He came for something, Nelly. He came for something he didn't find."

"Tell about what he was wearing. Tell what his throat did when he sang."

"He looked at all the *before* pictures, Nelly. The matron was trying to make him look at the *afters*, but he kept looking at the *befores* and shaking his head and then he found one and put it in his pocket and if he hadn't found it, he wasn't going to sing."

I could feel my spine stiffen. "Ramona, you've got to help me. I must go to him."

That night we staged a daring break. We clubbed the attendant when he brought dinner, and once we had him under the bed we ate all the chops and gluten bread on his cart and then we went down the corridor, lifting bolts, and when we were a hundred strong we locked the matron in her office and raided the dining hall, howling and eating everything we could find. I ate that night, how I ate, but even as I ate, I was aware of a fatal lightness in my bones, a failure in capacity, and so they found me in the frozen-food locker, weeping over a chain of link sausage, inconsolable because I understood that they had spoiled it for me, they with their chops and their gluten bread; I could never eat as I once had, I would never be myself again.

In my fury I went after the matron with a ham hock, and when I had them all at bay I took a loin of pork for sustenance and I broke out of that place. I had to get to Tommy before I got any thinner; I had to try. Outside the gate I stopped a car and hit the driver with the loin of pork and then I drove to the Hotel Riverside, where Tommy always stayed. I made my way up the fire stairs on little cat feet and when the valet went to his suite with one of his velveteen suits I followed, quick as a tigress, and the next moment I was inside. When all was quiet, I tiptoed to his door and stepped inside.

He was magnificent. He stood at the window, gaunt and beautiful; his blond hair fell to his waist and his shoulders shriveled under a heartbreaking double-breasted pea-green velvet suit. He did not see me at first; I drank in his image and then, delicately, cleared my throat. In the second that he turned and saw me, everything seemed possible.

"It's you." His voice throbbed.

"I had to come."

Our eyes fused and in that moment I believed that we two could meet, burning as a single, lambent flame, but in the next second his face had crumpled in disappointment; he brought a picture from his pocket, a fingered, cracked photograph, and he looked from it to me and back at the photograph, saying, "My darling, you've fallen off."

"Maybe it's not too late," I cried, but we both knew I would fail.

And fail I did, even though I ate for days, for five desperate, heroic weeks; I threw pies into the breech, fresh hams and whole sides of beef, but those sad days at the food farm, the starvation and the drugs have so upset my chemistry that it cannot be restored; no matter what

I eat I fall off and I continue to fall off; my body is a halfway house for foods I can no longer assimilate. Tommy watches, and because he knows he almost had me, huge and round and beautiful, Tommy mourns. He eats less and less now. He eats like a bird and lately he has refused to sing; strangely, his records have begun to disappear.

And so a whole nation waits.

"I almost had her," he says, when they beg him to resume his midnight shows; he will not sing, he won't talk, but his hands describe the mountain of woman he has longed for all his life.

And so I have lost Tommy, and he has lost me, but I am doing my best to make it up to him. I own Faircrest now, and in the place where Ramona and I once suffered, I use my skills on the girls Tommy wants me to cultivate. I can put twenty pounds on a girl in a couple of weeks and I don't mean bloat, I mean solid fat. Ramona and I feed them up and once a week we weigh and I poke the upper arm with a special stick and I will not be satisfied until the stick goes in and does not rebound because all resiliency is gone. Each week I bring out my best and Tommy shakes his head in misery because the best is not yet good enough; none of them are what I once was. But one day the time and the girl will be right—would that it were me—the time and the girl will be right and Tommy will sing again. In the meantime, the whole world waits; in the meantime, in a private wing well away from the others, I keep my special cases; the matron, who grows fatter as I watch her. And Mom. And Dad.

The Heat Death of the Universe

PAMELA ZOLINE

1. ONTOLOGY: That branch of metaphysics which concerns itself with the problems of the nature of existence or being.

2. Imagine a pale blue morning sky, almost green, with clouds only at the rims. The earth rolls and the sun appears to mount, mountains erode, fruits decay, the Foraminifera adds another chamber to its shell, babies' fingernails grow as does the hair of the dead in their graves, and in egg timers the sands fall and the eggs cook on.

3. Sarah Boyle thinks of her nose as too large, though several men have cherished it. The nose is generous and performs a well-calculated geometric curve, at the arch of which the skin is drawn very tight and a faint whiteness of bone can be seen showing through, it has much the same architectural tension and sense of mathematical calculation as the day-after-Thanksgiving breastbone on the carcass of turkey; her maiden name was Sloss, mixed German, English, and Irish descent; in grade school she was very bad at playing softball and, besides being chosen last for the team, was always made to play center field, no one could ever hit to center field; she loves music best of all the arts, and of music, Bach, J. S.; she lives in California, though she grew up in Boston and Toledo.

4. BREAKFAST TIME AT THE BOYLES' HOUSE ON LA FLORIDA STREET, ALAMEDA, CALIFORNIA, THE CHILDREN DEMAND SUGAR FROSTED FLAKES.

With some reluctance Sarah Boyle dishes out Sugar Frosted Flakes to her children, already hearing the decay set in upon the little milk-white teeth, the bony whine of the dentist's drill. The dentist is a short, gentle man with a mustache who sometimes reminds Sarah of an uncle who lives in Ohio. One bowl per child.

5. If one can imagine it considered as an abstract object by members of a totally separate culture, one can see that the cereal box might seem a beautiful thing. The solid rectangle is neatly joined and classical in proportions, on it are squandered wealths of richest colors, virgin blues, crimsons, dense ochres, precious pigments once reserved for sacred paintings and as cosmetics for the blind faces of marble gods. Giant size. Net Weight 16 ounces, 250 grams. "They're tigeriffic!" says Tony the Tiger. The box blats promises: Energy, Nature's Own Goodness, an endless pubescence. On its back is a mask of William Shakespeare to be cut out, folded, worn by thousands of tiny Shakespeares in Kansas City, Detroit, Tucson, San Diego, Tampa. He appears at once more kindly and somewhat more vacant than we are used to seeing him. Two or more of the children lay claim to the mask, but Sarah puts off that Solomon's decision until such time as the box is empty.

6. A notice in orange flourishes states that a Surprise Gift is to be found somewhere in the package, nestled amongst the golden flakes. So far it has not been unearthed, and the children request more cereal than they wish to eat, great yellow heaps of it, to hurry the discovery. Even so, at the end of the meal, some layers of flakes remain in the box and the Gift must still be among them.

7. There is even a Special Offer of a secret membership, code, and magic ring; these to be obtained by sending in the box top with 50¢.

8. Three offers on one cereal box. To Sarah Boyle this seems to be oversell. Perhaps something is terribly wrong with the cereal and it must be sold quickly, got off the shelves before the news breaks. Perhaps it causes a special, cruel Cancer in little children. As Sarah Boyle collects the bowls printed with bunnies and baseball statistics, still slopping half full of milk and wilted flakes, she imagines *in her mind's eye* the headlines, "Nation's Small Fry Stricken, Fate's Finger Sugar-Coated, Lethal Sweetness Socks Tots."

9. Sarah Boyle is a vivacious and intelligent young wife and mother, educated at a fine Eastern college, proud of her growing family, which keeps her busy and happy around the house.

10. BIRTHDAY.

Today is the birthday of one of the children. There will be a party in the late afternoon.

11. CLEANING UP THE HOUSE. ONE.

Cleaning up the kitchen. Sarah Boyle puts the bowls, plates, glasses, and silverware into the sink. She scrubs at the stickiness on the yellow-marbled Formica table with a blue synthetic sponge, a special blue which we shall see again. There are marks of children's hands in various sizes printed with sugar and grime on all the table's surfaces. The marks catch the light; they appear and disappear according to the position of the observing eye. The floor sweepings include a triangular half of toast spread with grape jelly, bobby pins, a green Band-Aid, flakes, a doll's eye, dust, dog's hair, and a button.

12. Until we reach the statistically likely planet and begin to converse with whatever green-faced, teleporting denizens thereof—considering only this shrunk and communication-ravaged world—can we any more postulate a separate culture? Viewing the metastasis of Western Culture it seems progressively less likely. Sarah Boyle imagines a whole world which has become like California, all topographical imperfections sanded away with the sweet-smelling burr of the plastic surgeon's cosmetic polisher; a world populace dieting, leisured, similar in pink and mauve hair and rhinestone shades. A land Cunt Pink and Avocado Green, brassiered and girdled by monstrous complexities of Super Highways, a California endless and unceasing, embracing and transforming the entire globe, California, California!

13. INSERT ONE. ON ENTROPY.

ENTROPY: A quantity introduced in the first place to facilitate the calculations, and to give clear expressions to the results of thermodynamics. Changes of entropy can be calculated only for a reversible process, and may then be defined as the ratio of the amount of heat taken up to the absolute temperature at which the heat is absorbed. Entropy changes for actual irreversible processes are calculated by postulating equivalent theoretical reversible changes. The entropy of a system is a measure of its degree of disorder. The total entropy of any isolated system can never decrease in any change; it must either increase (irreversible process) or remain constant (reversible process). The total entropy of the Universe therefore is increasing, tending towards a maximum, corresponding to complete disorder of the particles in it (assuming that it may be regarded as an isolated system). See *heat death of the Universe*.

14. CLEANING UP THE HOUSE. TWO.

Washing the baby's diapers. Sarah Boyle writes notes to herself all over the house; a mazed wild script larded with arrows, diagrams, pictures; graffiti on every available surface in a desperate/heroic attempt to index, record, bluff, invoke, order, and placate. On the fluted and flowered white plastic lid of the diaper bin she has written in Blushing Pink Nitetime lipstick a phrase to ward off fumy ammoniac despair. "The nitrogen cycle is the vital round of organic and inorganic exchange on earth. The sweet breath of the Universe." On the wall by the washing machine are Yin and Yang signs, mandalas, and the words, "Many young wives feel trapped. It is a contemporary socio-logical phenomenon which may be explained in part by a gap between changing living patterns and the accommodation of social services to these patterns." Over the stove she has written "Help, Help, Help, Help, Help."

15. Sometimes she numbers or letters the things in a room, writing the assigned character on each object. There are 819 separate move-able objects in the living room, counting books. Sometimes she labels objects with their names, or with false names; thus on her bureau the hairbrush is labeled HAIRBRUSH, the cologne, COLOGNE, the hand cream, CAT. She is passionately fond of children's dictionaries, en-cyclopedias, ABCs, and all reference books, transfixed and comforted at their simulacra of a complete listing and ordering.

16. On the door of a bedroom are written two definitions from refer-ence books, "GOD: An object of worship"; HOMEOSTASIS: Main-tenance of constancy of internal environment."

17. Sarah Boyle washes the diapers, washes the linen, Oh Saint Veronica, changes the sheets on the baby's crib. She begins to put away some of the toys, stepping over and around the organizations of playthings which still seem inhabited. There are various vehicles, and articles of medicine, domesticity, and war; whole zoos of stuffed ani-mals, bruised and odorous with years of love; hundreds of small figures, plastic animals, cowboys, cars, spacemen, with which the children make sub and supra worlds in their play. One of Sarah's favorite toys is the Baba, the wooden Russian doll which, opened, reveals a smaller but otherwise identical doll, which opens to reveal, etc., a lesson in infinity at least to the number of seven dolls.

18. Sarah Boyle's mother has been dead for two years. Sarah Boyle thinks of music as the formal articulation of the passage of time, and of Bach as the most poignant rendering of this. Her eyes are sometimes the color of the aforementioned kitchen sponge. Her hair is natural spaniel brown; months ago on an hysterical day she dyed it red, so

now it is two-toned with a stripe in the middle, like the painted walls of slum buildings or old schools.

19. INSERT TWO. THE HEAT DEATH OF THE UNIVERSE.

The second law of thermodynamics can be interpreted to mean that the ENTROPY of a closed system tends toward a maximum and that its available ENERGY tends toward a minimum. It has been held that the Universe constitutes a thermodynamically closed system, and if this were true it would mean that a time must finally come when the Universe "unwinds" itself, no energy being available for use. This state is referred to as the "heat death of the Universe." It is by no means certain, however, that the Universe can be considered as a closed system in this sense.

20. Sarah Boyle pours out a Coke from the refrigerator and lights a cigarette. The coldness and sweetness of the thick brown liquid make her throat ache and her teeth sting briefly, sweet juice of my youth, her eyes glass with the carbonation, she thinks of the Heat Death of the Universe. A logarithmic of those late summer days, endless as the Irish serpent twisting through jeweled manuscripts forever, tail in mouth, the heat pressing, bloating, doing violence. The Los Angeles sky becomes so filled and bleached with detritus that it loses all color and silvers like a mirror, reflecting back the fricasseeing earth. Everything becoming warmer and warmer, each particle of matter becoming more agitated, more excited until the bonds shatter, the glues fail, the deodorants lose their seals. She imagines the whole of New York City melting like a Dali into a great chocolate mass, a great soup, the Great Soup of New York.

21. CLEANING UP THE HOUSE. THREE.

Beds made. Vacuuming the hall, a carpet of faded flowers, vines, and leaves, which endlessly wind and twist into each other in a fevered and permanent ecstasy. Suddenly the vacuum blows instead of sucks, spewing marbles, dolls' eyes, dust, crackers. An old trick. "Oh my god," says Sarah. The baby yells on cue for attention/changing/food. Sarah kicks the vacuum cleaner and it retches and begins working again.

22. AT LUNCH ONLY ONE GLASS OF MILK IS SPILLED.

At lunch only one glass of milk is spilled.

23. The plants need watering, Geranium, Hyacinth, Lavender, Avocado, Cyclamen. Feed the fish, happy fish with china castles and

mermaids in the bowl. The turtle looks more and more unwell and is probably dying.

24. Sarah Boyle's blue eyes, how blue? Bluer far and of a different quality than the Nature metaphors which were both engine and fuel to so much of precedent literature. A fine, modern, acid, synthetic blue; the shiny cerulean of the skies on postcards sent from lush subtropics, the natives grinning ivory ambivalent grins in their dark faces; the promising, fat, unnatural blue of the heavy tranquilizer capsule; the cool, mean blue of that fake kitchen sponge; the deepest, most unbelievable azure of the tiled and mossless interiors of California swimming pools. The chemists in their kitchens cooked, cooled, and distilled this blue from thousands of colorless and wonderfully constructed crystals, each one unique and nonpareil; and now that color hisses, bubbles, burns in Sarah's eyes.

25. INSERT THREE. ON LIGHT.
    LIGHT: Name given to the agency by means of which a viewed object influences the observer's eyes. Consists of electromagnetic radiation within the wavelength range 4×10^{-5} cm. to 7×10^{-5} cm. approximately; variations in the wavelength produce different sensations in the eye, corresponding to different colors. See *color vision*.

26. LIGHT AND CLEANING THE LIVING ROOM.
    All the objects (819) and surfaces in the living room are dusty, gray common dust as though this were the den of a giant, molting mouse. Suddenly quantities of waves or particles of very strong sunlight speed in through the window, and everything incandesces, multiple rainbows. Poised in what has become a solid cube of light, like an ancient insect trapped in amber, Sarah Boyle realizes that the dust is indeed the most beautiful stuff in the room, a manna for the eyes. Duchamp, that father of thought, has set with fixative some dust which fell on one of his sculptures, counting it as part of the work. "That way madness lies, says Sarah," says Sarah. The thought of ordering a household on Dada principles balloons again. All the rooms would fill up with objects, newspapers and magazines would compost, the potatoes in the rack, the canned green beans in the garbage can would take new heart and come to life again, reaching out green shoots toward the sun. The plants would grow wild and wind into a jungle around the house, splitting plaster, tearing shingles, the garden would enter in at the door. The goldfish would die, the birds would die, we'd have them

stuffed; the dog would die from lack of care, and probably the children—all stuffed and sitting around the house, covered with dust.

27. INSERT FOUR. DADA.

DADA (Fr., hobby-horse) was a nihilistic precursor of Surrealism, invented in Zurich during World War I, a product of hysteria and shock lasting from about 1915 to 1922. It was deliberately anti-art and anti-sense, intended to outrage and scandalize, and its most characteristic production was the reproduction of the "Mona Lisa" decorated with a mustache and the obscene caption LHOOQ (read: *elle a chaud au cul*) "by" Duchamp. Other manifestations included Arp's collages of colored paper cut out at random and shuffled, ready-made objects such as the bottle drier and the bicycle wheel "signed" by Duchamp, Picabia's drawings of bits of machinery with incongruous titles, incoherent poetry, a lecture given by thirty-eight lecturers in unison, and an exhibition in Cologne in 1920, held in an annex to a café lavatory, at which a chopper was provided for spectators to smash the exhibits with—which they did.

28. TIME PIECES AND OTHER MEASURING DEVICES.

In the Boyle house there are four clocks; three watches (one a Mickey Mouse watch which does not work); two calendars and two engagement books; three rulers, a yard stick; a measuring cup; a set of red plastic measuring spoons, which includes a tablespoon, a teaspoon, a one-half teaspoon, one-fourth teaspoon, and one-eighth teaspoon; an egg timer; an oral thermometer and a rectal thermometer; a Boy Scout compass; a barometer in the shape of a house, in and out of which an old woman and an old man chase each other forever without fulfillment; a bathroom scale; an infant scale; a tape measure which can be pulled out of a stuffed felt strawberry; a wall on which the children's heights are marked; a metronome.

29. Sarah Boyle finds a new line in her face after lunch while cleaning the bathroom. It is as yet barely visible, running from the midpoint of her forehead to the bridge of her nose. By inward curling of her eyebrows she can etch it clearly as it will come to appear in the future. She marks another mark on the wall where she has drawn out a scoring area. Face Lines and Other Intimations of Mortality, the heading says. There are thirty-two marks, counting this latest one.

30. Sarah Boyle is a vivacious and witty young wife and mother, educated at a fine Eastern college, proud of her growing family, which keeps her happy and busy around the house, involved in many hobbies

and community activities, and only occasionally given to obsessions concerning Time/Entropy/Chaos and Death.

31. Sarah Boyle is never quite sure how many children she has.

32. Sarah thinks from time to time; Sarah is occasionally visited with this thought; at times this thought comes upon Sarah, that there are things to be hoped for, accomplishments to be desired beyond the mere reproductions, mirror reproduction of one's kind. The babies. Lying in bed at night sometimes the memory of the act of birth, always the hue and texture of red plush theater seats, washes up; the rending which always, at a certain intensity of pain, slipped into landscapes, the sweet breath of the sweating nurse. The wooden Russian doll has bright, perfectly round red spots on her cheeks, she splits in the center to reveal a doll smaller but in all other respects identical with round bright red spots on her cheeks, etc.

33. How fortunate for the species, Sarah muses or is mused, that children are as ingratiating as we know them. Otherwise they would soon be salted off for the leeches they are, and the race would extinguish itself in a fair sweet flowering, the last generation's massive achievement in the arts and pursuits of high civilization. The finest women would have their tubes tied off at the age of twelve, or perhaps refrain altogether from the Act of Love? All interests would be bent to a refining and perfecting of each febrile sense, each fluid hour, with no more cowardly investment in immortality via the patchy and too often disappointing vegetables of one's own womb.

34. INSERT FIVE. LOVE.
    LOVE: A typical sentiment involving fondness for, or attachment to, an object, the idea of which is emotionally colored whenever it arises in the mind, and capable, as Shand has pointed out, of evoking any one of a whole gamut of primary emotions, according to the situation in which the object is placed, or represented; often, and by psychoanalysts always, used in the sense of *sex-love* or even *lust* (q.v.).

35. Sarah Boyle has at times felt a unity with her body, at other times a complete separation. The mind/body duality considered. The time/ space duality considered. The male/female duality considered. The matter/energy duality considered. Sometimes, at extremes, her Body seems to her an animal on a leash, taken for walks in the park by her Mind. The lampposts of experience. Her arms are lightly freckled, and when she gets very tired the places under her eyes became violet.

36. Housework is never completed, the chaos always lurks ready to encroach on any area left unweeded, a jungle filled with dirty pans and the roaring of giant stuffed toy animals suddenly turned savage. Terrible glass eyes.

37. SHOPPING FOR THE BIRTHDAY CAKE.

Shopping in the supermarket with the baby in front of the cart and a larger child holding on. The light from the ice-cube-tray-shaped fluorescent lights is mixed blue and pink and brighter, colder, and cheaper than daylight. The doors swing open just as you reach out your hand for them, Tantalus, moving with a ghastly quiet swing. Hot dogs for the party. Potato chips, gumdrops, a paper tablecloth with birthday designs, hot-dog buns, catsup, mustard, piccalilli, balloons, instant coffee Continental style, dog food, frozen peas, ice cream, frozen lima beans, frozen broccoli in butter sauce, paper birthday hats, paper napkins in three colors, a box of Sugar Frosted Flakes with a Wolfgang Amadeus Mozart mask on the back, bread, pizza mix. The notes of a just graspable music filter through the giant store, for the most part bypassing the brain and acting directly on the liver, blood, and lymph. The air is delicately scented with aluminum. Half-and-half cream, tea bags, bacon, sandwich meat, strawberry jam. Sarah is in front of the shelves of cleaning products now, and the baby is beginning to whine. Around her are whole libraries of objects, offering themselves. Some of that same old hysteria that had incarnadined her hair rises up again, and she does not refuse it. There is one moment when she can choose direction, like standing on a chalk-drawn X, a hot cross bun, and she does not choose calm and measure. Sarah Boyle begins to pick out, methodically, deliberately, and with a careful ecstasy, one of every cleaning product which the store sells. Window Cleaner, Glass Cleaner, Brass Polish, Silver Polish, Steel Wool, eighteen different brands of Detergent, Disinfectant, Toilet Cleanser, Water Softener, Fabric Softener, Drain Cleanser, Spot Remover, Floor Wax, Furniture Wax, Car Wax, Carpet Shampoo, Dog Shampoo, Shampoo for people with dry, oily, and normal hair, for people with dandruff, for people with gray hair. Toothpaste, Tooth Powder, Denture Cleaner, Deodorants, Antiperspirants, Antiseptics, Soaps, Cleansers, Abrasives, Oven Cleaners, Makeup Removers. When the same products appear in different sizes Sarah takes one of each size. For some products she accumulates whole little families of containers: a giant Father bottle of shampoo, a Mother bottle, an Older Sister bottle just smaller than the Mother bottle, and a very tiny Baby Brother bottle. Sarah fills three shopping carts and has to have help wheeling them all down the aisles. At the check-out counter her laughter and hysteria keep threatening to overflow as the pale blond clerk with no eyebrows like the "Mona Lisa" pretends normality and disinterest. The bill comes to $57.53 and Sarah has to write a check. Driving home, the baby strapped in the drive-a-cot and the paper bags bulging in the backseat, she cries.

38. BEFORE THE PARTY.

Mrs. David Boyle, mother-in-law of Sarah Boyle, is coming to the party of her grandchild. She brings a toy, a yellow wooden duck on a string, made in Austria; the duck quacks as it is pulled along the floor. Sarah is filling paper cups with gumdrops and chocolates, and Mrs. David Boyle sits at the kitchen table and talks to her. She is talking about several things, she is talking about her garden, which is flourishing except for a plague of rare black beetles, thought to have come from Hong Kong, which are undermining some of the most delicate growths at the roots and feasting on the leaves of other plants. She is talking about a sale of household linens, which she plans to attend on the following Tuesday. She is talking about her neighbor who has Cancer and is wasting away. The neighbor is a Catholic woman who had never had a day's illness in her life until the Cancer struck, and now she is, apparently, failing with dizzying speed. The doctor says her body's chaos, chaos, cells running wild all over, says Mrs. David Boyle. When I visited her she hardly *knew* me, can hardly *speak,* can't keep herself *clean,* says Mrs. David Boyle.

39. Sometimes Sarah can hardly remember how many cute, chubby little children she has.

40. When she used to stand out in center field far away from the other players, she used to make up songs and sing them to herself.

41. She thinks of the end of the world by ice.

42. She thinks of the end of the world by water.

43. She thinks of the end of the world by nuclear war.

44. There must be more than this, Sarah Boyle thinks, from time to time. What could one do to justify one's passage? Or less ambitiously, to change, even in the motion of the smallest mote, the course and circulation of the world? Sometimes Sarah's dreams are of heroic girth, a new symphony using laboratories of machinery and all invented instruments, at once giant in scope and intelligible to all, to heal the

bloody breach; a series of paintings which would transfigure and astonish and calm the frenzied art world in its panting race; a new novel that would refurbish language. Sometimes she considers the mystical, the streaky and random, and it seems that one change, no matter how small, would be enough. Turtles are supposed to live for many years. To carve a name, date, and perhaps a word of hope upon a turtle's shell, then set him free to wend the world, surely this one act might cancel out absurdity?

45. Mrs. David Boyle has a faint mustache, like Duchamp's "Mona Lisa."

46. THE BIRTHDAY PARTY.
Many children, dressed in pastels, sit around the long table. They are exhausted and overexcited from games fiercely played, some are flushed and wet, others unnaturally pale. This general agitation and the paper party hats they wear combine to make them appear a dinner party of debauched midgets. It is time for the cake. A huge chocolate cake in the shape of a rocket and launching pad and covered with blue and pink icing is carried in. In the hush the birthday child begins to cry. He stops crying, makes a wish, and blows out the candles.

47. One child will not eat hot dogs, ice cream, or cake, and asks for cereal. Sarah pours him out a bowl of Sugar Frosted Flakes, and a moment later he chokes. Sarah pounds him on the back and out spits a tiny green plastic snake with red glass eyes, the Surprise Gift. All the children want it.

48. AFTER THE PARTY THE CHILDREN ARE PUT TO BED.
Bath time. Observing the nakedness of children, pink and slippery as seals, squealing as seals, now the splashing, grunting, and smacking of cherry flesh on raspberry flesh reverberate in the pearl-tiled steamy cubicle. The nakedness of children is so much more absolute than that of the mature. No musky curling hair to indicate the target points, no knobbly clutch of plane and fat and curvature to ennoble this prince of beasts. All well-fed naked children appear edible. Sarah's teeth hum in her head with memory of bloody feastings, prehistory. Young humans appear too like the young of other species for smugness, and the comparison is not even in their favor, they are much the most peeled and unsupple of those young. Such pinkness, such utter nuded pinkness; the orifices neatly incised, rimmed with a slightly deeper rose, the incessant demands for breast, time, milks of many sorts.

49. INSERT SIX. WEINER ON ENTROPY.

In Gibbs's Universe order is least probable, chaos most probable. But while the Universe as a whole, if indeed there is a whole Universe, tends to run down, there are local enclaves whose direction seems opposed to that of the Universe at large and in which there is a limited and temporary tendency for organization to increase. Life finds its home in some of these enclaves.

50. Sarah Boyle imagines, in her mind's eye, cleaning and ordering the whole world, even the Universe. Filling the great spaces of space with a marvelous sweet-smelling, deep-cleansing foam. Deodorizing rank caves and volcanoes. Scrubbing rocks.

51. INSERT SEVEN. TURTLES.

Many different species of carnivorous Turtles live in the fresh waters of the tropical and temperate zones of various continents. Most northerly of the European Turtles (extending as far as Holland and Lithuania) is the European Pond Turtle (*Emys orbicularis*). It is from eight to ten inches long and may live a hundred years.

52. CLEANING UP AFTER THE PARTY.

Sarah is cleaning up after the party. Gumdrops and melted ice cream surge off paper plates, making holes in the paper tablecloth through the printed roses. A fly has died a splendid death in a pool of strawberry ice cream. Wet jelly beans stain all they touch, finally becoming themselves colorless, opaque white like flocks of tamed or sleeping maggots. Plastic favors mount half-eaten pieces of blue cake. Strewn about are thin strips of fortune papers from the Japanese poppers. Upon them are printed strangely assorted phrases selected by apparently unilingual Japanese. Crowds of delicate yellow people spending great chunks of their lives in producing these most ephemeral of objects, and inscribing thousands of fine papers with absurd and incomprehensible messages. "The very hairs of your head are all numbered," reads one. Most of the balloons have popped. Someone has planted a hot dog in the daffodil pot. A few of the helium balloons have escaped their owners and now ride the ceiling. Another fortune paper reads, "Emperor's horses meet death worse, numbers, numbers."

53. She is very tired, violet under the eyes, mauve beneath the eyes. Her uncle in Ohio used to get the same marks under his eyes. She goes to the kitchen to lay the table for tomorrow's breakfast, then she sees that in the turtle's bowl the turtle is floating, still, on the surface of the water. Sarah Boyle pokes at it with a pencil, but it does not

move. She stands for several minutes looking at the dead turtle on the surface of the water. She is crying again.

54. She begins to cry. She goes to the refrigerator and takes out a carton of eggs, white eggs, extra large. She throws them one by one onto the kitchen floor, which is patterned with strawberries in squares. They break beautifully. There is a Secret Society of Dentists, all mustached, with Special Code and Magic Rings. She begins to cry. She takes up three bunny dishes and throws them against the refrigerator, they shatter, and then the floor is covered with shards, chunks of partial bunnies, an ear, an eye here, a paw; Stockton, California; Acton, California; Chico, California; Redding, California; Glen Ellen, California; Cadiz, California; Angels Camp, California; Half Moon Bay. The total ENTROPY of the Universe therefore is increasing, tending towards a maximum, corresponding to complete disorder of the particles in it. She is crying, her mouth is open. She throws a jar of grape jelly and it smashes the window over the sink. Her eyes are blue. She begins to open her mouth. It has been held that the Universe constitutes a thermodynamically closed system, and if this were true it would mean that a time must finally come when the Universe "unwinds" itself, no energy being available for use. This state is referred to as the "heat death of the Universe." Sarah Boyle begins to cry. She throws a jar of strawberry jam against the stove, enamel chips off, and the stove begins to bleed. Bach had twenty children, how many children has Sarah Boyle? Her mouth is open. Her mouth is opening. She turns on the water and fills the sinks with detergent. She writes on the kitchen wall, "William Shakespeare has Cancer and lives in California." She writes, "Sugar Frosted Flakes are the Food of the Gods." The water foams up in the sink, overflowing, bubbling onto the strawberry floor. She is about to begin to cry. Her mouth is opening. She is crying. She cries. How can one ever tell whether there are one or many fish? She begins to break glasses and dishes, she throws cups and cooking pots and jars of food, which shatter and break and spread over the kitchen. The sand keeps falling, very quietly, in the egg timer. The old man and woman in the barometer never catch each other. She picks up eggs and throws them into the air. She begins to cry. She opens her mouth. The eggs arch slowly through the kitchen, like a baseball, hit high against the spring sky, seen from far away. They go higher and higher in the stillness, hesitate at the zenith, then begin to fall away slowly, slowly, through the fine, clear air.

The Power of Time

JOSEPHINE SAXTON

"It shouldn't present much difficulty if you approach it in a positive way," I said to the Chief of the Mohawks, Flying Spider. "Your tribe is expert in this kind of thing. All you have to do is number the parts, get it translated in terms of a computer jigsaw multidimensional complex, get the land measured out and prepared in advance—new sewage systems and so on, flood the Trent and the Soar to form an island—aw, cummarn Spider, you can do it. . . ."

My power complex that I never thought about, working on his power complex that he nurtured and lived by. He was very powerful and his tribe had worked for five hundred years to make it so, and other tribes too; time was when Flying Spider's ancestors had been a very small minority, working high above the streets of New York, building on higher bits, repairing, cleaning. Work other people would not do, nor could do; the Mohawks took naturally to heights. Yes, Flying Spider was powerful all right: he owned the whole of Manhattan Island. His ancestors had sold out for twenty-four dollars worth of trinkets, and he had bought it back for an unimaginable sum. He didn't only own the land either, but every stone of every building, every plate of glass, scrap of metal, nut, bolt, electric wire. He owned all the companies, too, except for DuPont on the eleventh floor of the Empire State who had a special concession in return for making all the Tribal Costumes free of charge and before any other order. Like Spider for instance always wore full regalia, masses of gorgeous feathers but rain- and stain-proofed; you could have poured printing ink all over him and it would have brushed off when dry. Not that anyone would ever do such a thing, not to Flying Spider. So Spider was powerful and rich, and so was I. There were only about a hundred of us as rich as that, all descended from former depressed peoples and groups, like about five generations back my great-multi-great grandmother was secretary to the Stir-crazy Housewives League of Loughborough Ltd., England.

That's what I call progress, I mean, out of the sixteen million or so people left on this planet after the Great Emigrations, I should end up being one of the Elite. Everybody else lived well, too, but we hundred or so Top People decided how well. I not only wanted to get one up on Spider though (that's just a kind of hobby we had, buying things from each other and then proving them more valuable than the price paid), I wanted Manhattan Island for myself. You see, my family have always had a kind of thing about Manhattan, it's been a kind of Mecca for them although I can't say why; it has just been a thing to sit at Mother's knee and listen to tales of Manhattan. Families have things like that. But I had never been there. Yes, I know it sounds a bit odd what with travel so easy, anti-grav sledge would have got me there in half an hour but not only had I always been rich and powerful I had always been—well, English Eccentric, which is a type you probably never heard of but in my case it took the form of never leaving the village where I was born. Travel never appealed to me; 3-D-TV was as much of the outside world as I wanted to experience. I had everything I wanted right there in East Leake, which was Reservation Country for the Ancient Britons, a small village that made two leaps in its development; first in the thirteenth century when it got itself built round the church, and second around the twentieth when they added a few thousand houses, a supermarket, a library, and a health-center. And a couple of boutiques, which were places where the women bought clothes. Crazy, and kind of nice.

So I was already thirty-four when I had this whim to see something different. In spite of its niceness it was very, very dull around East Leake. Mudflats, forest with sparse red deer, Nottingham City for occasional outings—oh, I think I'd seen Robin Hood's Oak just once too often, and that, in case you were wondering, is an ancient monument to some guy who represented a depressed minority, some very long time back. It was a kind of nostalgia got me, I think, those traditional tales of Manhattan; it was said that my great-multi-great grandmother had actually been there. I have a pair of her false eyelashes set in Lucite, they look like underwater caterpillars, and I'd been looking at them . . .

Well I'll explain to you quite straight now just in case you haven't got it. What I wanted to do was buy the whole of Manhattan Island and have it re-erected on the site of East Leake, a village between Nottingham and Loughborough, in England. It was only a matter of marking every piece correctly and sticking piece A onto piece B.

"Okay, okay it's a challenge. I'll transact. Let's say the entire thing including inhabitants within six weeks, in working order?"

"That's what I had in mind, Spider. Is that your earliest delivery date?"

She finished typing the last letter of the day as Secretary of the Stir-crazy Housewives League of Loughborough Ltd. and went to look out of the window for a while, through the cotton mandalas of Nottingham lace. Mailman should be due, more mail, please let there be more mail. There was, in lieu of telephone messages. Her husband didn't like telephones, they made him too accessible from work at the weekends, and in any case, they were expensive.

CONGRATULATIONS ON BEING WINNER OF ONE WEEK IN NEW YORK. YOUR GUESS NUMBER OF SUGAR TWEETIES IN ONE TON ACCURATE AB-SOLUTELY NOT COUNTING PLASTIC TURKEYS WHICH WAS THE CATCH. OUR REP WILL CALL TO ARRANGE TICKETS RESERVATIONS ESCORTS TO SUIT YOU.

After the initial shock and fuss there were envious good-byes, passionate kisses that were expressions of perfect trust in fidelity that betrayed a horror of betrayal, after all, she's a good-looking woman for her age, all those escorts laid on, standing in line to take her out, Manhattan at her feet for a week. Brand-new white tweed suit, huge straw hat, export-reject shoes that looked like perfects. Lucky woman zooming up to thirty thousand feet, far above the cat-spit of the rest of the Stir-crazies. Worried about things like her ankles swelling at the altitude, being struck by lightning, being struck dumb with shyness on arrival, her hair and complexion reacting badly to the New York air and water, all figment nightmares that began to dissolve even as lunch was served on the plane, and the man in the next seat told her what it was like for a month on a Greek island, what it is like in St. Louis where he owned a chain of supermarkets. Oh, she thought, it must be marvelous to be an American and travel a lot. He was stopping over in New York to take in culture in the form of off-Broadway plays, one must not allow the mind to stagnate. Nope. Nossir. Accent blossoming even before landing.

The JFK Airport, two valises at her feet, hands clutching purse, raincoat, passport, tickets, just standing there wondering what to do. More people in one place than she has ever seen before, and how they rush around, how worried they look. The temperature is in the nineties and humid, her face shines, she prickles all over. And with fear, too, not just heat, for she can sense something horrible and her stomach contracts around the warmed-up Stroganoff that the air-hostess gave her. What is it that is so evil? It vibrates everywhere; it is in the very breath of the place. The organizers of the competition arrived to whisk her off in a yellow taxi driven by a big handsome Negro who seemed oblivious of the fact that there were other cars on the street, thousands of them. The noise was incredible, car horns going all the time, tires screeching—a thing one never heard in England, but in America they always seemed to corner on brakes and two wheels, people calling, traffic rumble, subway roar coming up out of the ground, police sirens. Police sirens, does that mean someone has been murdered? Could be. And then it seemed to her that she could smell and hear the vibrations of Hell, she could see how it had all come to be, suddenly one day the lid of the Pit had crumbled up because of the pressure, and all this had come oozing up out of the earth, materialized as City. Oh, no, I want to go home, I wish I had never come, my husband, my children, take me back. . . .

But she never said it aloud, kept smiling and looking and asking, kept the false eyelashes fluttering. The hotel room they gave her was clean and comfortable, and she would be fetched next morning to go on a tour of the Fifth Avenue dress shops followed by lunch at the Russian Tea Room near Carnegie Hall. No sleep to speak of because it took several hours to unpack her things, find her soap and brushes, even though they had been efficiently packed. She felt kind of not herself at all in some funny way, was it—disoriented? Dangerous sort of state to be in, nothing that was back home in England seemed real, her family seemed like dim photographs, East Leake was just a very tiny unimportant place. But the next day things improved.

There were pancakes stuffed with goats-milk cream cheese, caviar, and sour cream, and vodka for lunch, the kind of food that one could cook up out of recipe books at home but by no means obtain when eating out. She began to feel better, the center of a great deal of unaccustomed attention, and it was all very pleasant. The escort for that day was charming and intelligent with golden ginger hair, a soft, silky-looking beard, and impeccable manners. They discussed Russian literature as far as she was able, although she blessed the time she had spent years before forcing herself to read *Crime and Punishment,* because she could remember details of the book that he did not, which made her feel very good indeed. He told her that the trimmings on the central chandelier of the restaurant were Christmas witch-balls from six years previous. So they were fallible and human in America even if it was a Russian place. It certainly was not all noise and machinery and rush and food in cans . . .

A conducted tour of the East Fifty-seventh Street art galleries in the afternoon, an introduction to kinetic art. Glass globe on black cube, inside the globe a long symmetrical loop of neon that moved backwards and forwards changing from red to blue in a regular rhythm, caused swelling and receding patterns on and in the glass globe, gave a hooting bleep that went into her ears and bounced off the inside of her skull. Regularly. She stood watching it entranced, she had never seen the like. . . . It was hypnotic, compelling, it seemed to catch one up, one floated one did, who did? Timeless space, bodiless, beautiful, and it had a message. Buy me and take me home. But three thousand dollars was more than she would ever have all at one time, and the money she had won was meant to be spent in dress and cosmetic shops. Her escort dragged her away from the artwork, allowing her a glimpse of large steel sequins revolving on black velvet, catching the pulsing lights from the glass globe, it was sensuous, like a woman dancing. She felt so very much more relaxed and at home in the city by the end of the second day; she had only needed rest after the flight. What a city it was, a unique creation of Man. Nowhere else exactly like it on Earth; that fact in itself was exciting.

"Yes, sure, Spider, it's the perfect site for it. A disused gypsum mine right under the hill, stretches over an area of approximately three hundred square miles, you can use what you like of it to suspend the sewers and subways and all of that in, it'll be a cinch, I mean, East Leake is built over a vast cavern, you won't have any blasting to do at all and it's like the Rock of Ages for strength, they don't even get a split in the wallpaper from subsidence, and you won't need to flood much of Nottingham to get it all in, I was talking to the surveyors only this morning, you see, there's no problem at all, don't make any. Down to the eleventh floor and DuPont giving trouble? Build them a solid concrete base with elevator, and when the whole building is transported put DuPont's floor back onto that, they'll have everything they're legally entitled to but who else will care? Anybody else grumbles at coming to England, offer them the same treatment, tell 'em they can stay behind. They'll come to their senses, what business are they going to do on Manhattan Desert Island?"

I was really flying with the idea, it was taking shape already only a couple of days after I had signed the deal with Spider. I had had to sell out thousands of square miles of Finland to do it, but as I had no intention of going there I did not care. I had never been to Manhattan, it was coming to me! I sorted it out with the town councils and started on the evacuation of all the inhabitants in the area, and when we actually got the measurements it included West Leake, Sutton Bonington, Hoton and Costock, Stanford, and part of Bunny. But as I pointed out to them as I worked it out on my desk IBM—what was their problem? They would benefit. I was having it seen to that everyone got a better house than the one they were leaving, that new factories and shops would be built, that their whole standard of living would improve not to mention the retirement pensions for every head of household inconvenienced. They might have been Ancient Britons on Reservation Country, but they were open to reason if it smelled of comfort. By the time I had finished talking to them, they couldn't wait for the subsonic rasers to move in.

Everybody stand back! The alarm hooters making all of Sherwood Forest tremble, all of Charnwood shake. And then, the strange drone that was almost a silence, quite quickly, the whole area I needed to re-erect Manhattan on became dust, which was of course siphoned off to my breeze-block factory in Yorkshire. "I may create chaos at times, but I have never liked waste," I said to a Flying Spider stunned with admiration.

"I do believe you have genius," he said to me. That's what I call progress, I thought. It had only been a matter of weeks since our first head-on meetings and he had thought me unadventurous and neurotic with my dislike of travel, and hopeless at buying and selling. That compliment from him made me feel fabulous. A powerful fella, Flying Spider.

The escort for the day was a delight to be with: a large young man with long hair and mustaches that would have twirled themselves had he not kept on so doing, smiling the while and occasionally allowing one eye to slide inwards creating an effect that somehow enhanced him. Wild, like a pirate. In smart places he wore a silk tie, polished shoes, and neat socks to his dark suit and light-blue shirt, and in downtown bars he brought out from his briefcase a pair of leather sandals and a scarlet handkerchief. He would swagger in with the scarf around his head, shirt ripped open, and sandals on his feet, grinning wildly so that she went along with everything he said instead of pausing to think him slightly nutty. Such a man in East Leake, oh, they would think him so strange! They talked about the literary scene, authors like John Barth and Donald Barthelme, the poems of Sonya Dorman, and Nabokov's entry into the world of science fiction. The man was only doing escort duty to make money, his true ambition was to be a writer. She made mental notes to read up things all winter and to see if her husband could be persuaded to wear a pirate-style hand-kerchief around the house and to give a lecture to the Stir-crazies on New Wave writing in America. She was beginning to feel light-headed and elated and could logically refer her state of mind to the vodka and Camparis he bought her on the strength of the competition expense account, and yet it was not just quite that. It reminded her of the first evenings she had spent out with her husband before they had married. She looked around her and everything seemed so wonderful. It was the authentic feeling: falling in love.

"Well, if DuPont won't come across, and it means that there will only be one hundred and nineteen floors to the Empire State, then I have to have it built right on top of the hill, on the site of Adastral House, you know? Appropriate name, no? Yes, I do insist, I want it to be as tall as it was, higher above actual sea level than its original site. Think of the view! On a clear day I'll be able to see as far as Northampton or Derby, depending on which way I look. Right over the new rivers, and by the way, the flooding went well, the new course stood up to the inundating perfectly, there's not a ripple difference in the shape of the water around New Manhattan, the currents run exactly right, you can move the ferry tomorrow, check that the tollgates on the tunnels and bridges are sorted out properly, like the Pennsylvania lane will now be the lane for North Wales. We'll make twopence or so, too, people will drive down from Edinburgh to ride on the ferry at night, it's quite spectacular I hear." Spider was delighted with me, I could tell from the way he laughed. He liked women with imagination. He told me that already the city was in pieces and stored on the Palisades and the Poconos in the order of re-erection and that whole blocks of masonry were continually on their way across the Atlantic by anti-grav sledge. They had been obliged to use subsonic rasers on whole tracts of forest, but if I wanted fast delivery, then they hadn't time to store out in Arizona. The thing was worked out to split-second timing, just about. Spider wanted to show me how efficient he was; I was sorry about the forest, but I appreciated his efforts. I gave orders to have the area replanted at the first opportunity. I took a two-seater sledge myself to watch the foundations of the Empire State being relaid right on the site I had specified. I hovered around for hours and could hardly explain to myself why I felt so scared. I put it down to excitement. After all, it was no mean thing I had set in motion. It was a First, all right. I couldn't sleep that night even though the luxury houseboat I had fixed up on the East River, formerly the Trent, was as comfortable a place as any I had ever known. I was not to sleep properly for many nights although I was not to know it at the time. And it was sound-proofed too against the twenty-four-hour activity of anti-grav sledges homing in with the next bit of the jigsaw, armies of fiberglass and old-time concrete mixers, the clang of scaffolding, blowtorches, cranes, lorries, drills, and other machinery. So it wasn't the noise that kept me awake. Every day I went floating out over the growing city to watch, checking the avenues with a map just for the hell of it; it looked like scum and lichen at first with square mushrooms sprouting here and there. But as time passed it began to take more shape, glossy yellow sunrises would reflect off flight after flight of glass, some of the smaller buildings even had flags flying from their tops and people began to move in. Every hour a new sledge arrived and furniture and boxes and people began to settle themselves back into their homes, shops, and offices. Faces appeared at the windows to see what the view was like from the new location. Most of them looked disappointed for they looked out on exactly the same bricks and barred windows of places like West Eighty-eighth as they ever had, although one old fellow swore we had planted his withered acacia a foot out of true because his Siamese cat was used to jumping out of his fifth-floor window onto the branch, and the first time it tried it, it fell to its death. I was sorry about the cat but I had to prove that the tree was correctly placed by showing him the plan of his backyard with every stone numbered and in its right slot including the drain, which matched with the duplicate sewage system they had built. Actually the sewage system was only duplicate where it joined the outer world, down there it was completely redesigned, much bigger and faster with a built-in rat-gassing system. My idea, of course, but I had paid to have it invented. Offer enough money and people will invent anything, in working order. So, no rats and no spilling sewers. The people of Manhattan would like me, I thought, and even at that point they did not seem particularly per-turbed. Life for them would go on much as usual, and if they wanted to take vacations in America rather than England they only had to apply for free transport. I had all that worked out; with my kind of money it was easy. Oh yes!

What I particularly liked to watch were the spidermen working high up. They were like anti-grav pussycats; height just did not scare them.

Way out on girders they poised with spanners and blowtorches and scorned a safe place even to eat lunch. I floated past them and sometimes one would acknowledge my presence with a grave nod of his magnificent head. Spider's tribe didn't have to work, of course, but it was in their blood and they loved it. For hundreds of years they had spent most of their waking hours hundreds of feet up over city streets, why stop? There was a thrilling moment when they had finally got the Big One (my name for the Empire State Building) right up and perfect with the exception of the elusive eleventh floor. There was one of those blazing sunsets and I flashed past at about the sixtieth and got like scarlet fluorescent blood flung in my eyes followed by a brilliant blue-sky reflection and I instinctively reversed to take the sight again and again, faster and faster, oh I had been missing kicks up until then, it began to be very real that I owned a city, red blue, red blue went the sky off my towers of glass until the greenish clouds of evening came and I descended, blown clean out of my mind with exultation. I lay in bed that night still seeing the flash of color, and it was something like someone was trying to get a message through to me and my ears began to sing. I knew I was overtired and a little disoriented; my surroundings were completely strange, there were bound to be side effects. I got up before dawn and looked out on the river. Somewhere near the island there should have been a thing called the Statue of Liberty, but I had forgotten to include it in the deal. Anyway, I thought, who wants sculpture that size, I had the whole of the Guggenheim and all that stuff to myself if I wanted Art, it all belonged to me and besides I didn't want to reopen negotiations with Spider at that point, he would think me inefficient. I was just a little depressed about the whole project around that time I must admit, but I put it down to extended impatience. Six weeks was seeming like an awful long time to realize a dream, but as Spider said:

"You don't want the Chase Manhattan in Battery Park or Penn Station under the elephants in the Natural History Museum, do you? Give us time, we'll put it together truly pretty. Nobody who lives there will know any different, it's all *organized*." And the way he said that word *organized* gave me a cool thrill of horrified admiration for him; I mean, one knew that he meant every word he said, that when he had spoken it was so.

"Okay, Chief," I murmured, and a gleam of something reached me from him. I was outpowered by Flying Spider, but I was still the one with the imagination.

"What shall we do next after this is over?" he asked me.

"How about putting the Taj Mahal on top of Ayers Rock in Australia?" He was a bit disgusted at that.

"I meant something new and original. Like we consider a merger of some kind, both our companies working together?"

I still don't know how I kept my head cool, it was fantastic. A merger! Him and me!

"Good idea, Chief," I said, and didn't sleep that night either. That was sheer happiness kept me awake though. It suddenly seemed as if I had been dreaming a dream for centuries, and it was beginning to come true.

There were two days of the Competition Trip left, and she was feeling just wonderful. She wondered how she could ever have felt that the city was frightful, it must have been the shock of impact, so very many people crammed into one small island. She was with an escort in Le Mistral, which was one of New York's best restaurants, and she was slightly drunk and very happy. He was a delight to be with, charming and considerate, leading the conversation this way and that, pouring out the vintage claret that he had chosen whilst yet consulting her on his choice. She had said:

"Well, actually what I usually have at home is red plonk," and he had admitted that it could be fine stuff but he thought that night they should have something a little better. They drank it with squabs that had been stewed in a rich brown cream sauce full of olives and she marveled at the perfect crispness of the accompanying salad. In restaurants salad was usually a bit limp. This stuff was rampant with life. They talked much also about the beauty of the big city by night, and by the time they had got round to the fresh fruit salad in kirsch and then the excellent coffee she was truly flying with well-being, happiness, joy. Her companion was stunningly handsome and beautifully bronzed, probably he took his holidays in Bermuda or somewhere fabulous like that. A noble profile, jet-black hair.

"Where did you get that wonderful tan from?" she asked him, and he smiled with no hint of acid, and explained that it was not a tan as she would see if they were in daylight, he was a full-blooded Mohawk Indian, and by day he worked as a spiderman high up on the skyscrapers, he only did the escort job at night to make extra money for his family. His wife was sick with a disease of the spleen and medical bills were steep. But, he said, they were not to talk of that, he had something wonderful to show her. The sixty-fifth floor, the Rainbow Room. Huge windows through which he indicated a fabulous view.

Somehow at that moment they had become unprofessional and clasped hands, and she could hardly breathe for the shock of what she saw, it was so beautiful. The mist was below them in the canyons, moving towards them menacing and amorphous was the Empire State Building like an insect presence from Outer Space, a glittering treasure in the sky. Just coming in to land, perpetually coming nearer. She spread out her hands to it and was stunned by the mystery of architecture that is unearthly and unreal and wished a deep wish in her heart, to come one day and live in Manhattan where she felt at home and loved.

And loved! By the city of course, because she was in love with it.

"City of dreams, I love you," and maybe he heard or maybe not, but he was professional escort again, pointing out the East River with the lights on it, the bridges. But he was again holding one of her hands, to steady her, she tottered and he was rock steady, it was his job to fly high and reach ground safely.

Chief Flying Spider apologized for being one day late with the goods. It was DuPont's fault, they had decided at the last minute that they wanted to come in on the move, and so the problem of how to insert their offices back into the Big One had to be solved. I came up with the unique idea of floating it all the way across the Atlantic on several layers of anti-grav sledges all inter-computerized so that there would be no hangups like the entire thing sliding down into the fathoms. DuPont resented losing working time and I wanted them in but fast so it seemed obvious to me to float the entire thing over at one blast, typewriters and computers clocking away, temporary short-wave telephones installed, elevator doors double locked. About fifteen thousand anti-grav units were fastened all the way up to the top of the Big One from the twelfth floor up and lasers sliced through the entire floor just above the ceilings of the tenth, and at the precise preset moment up it went like a plumb line sweet and perfect and in slid DuPont still yakking on the phone and hardly a drop of coffee spilled. Electricity and plumbing were put back onto permanent supply and every sliver of wood was checked for perfect fit. Mortar was injected where necessary and unbreakable steel rods slipped in like pins, down laser-bored holes full of resin, which were then given an electromagnetic charge which sealed the two joins stronger than they had originally been. All the windows were tested for warp, we didn't want glass exploding in people's faces, but there was no strain anywhere. Spider thought I was rather bright to have thought of doing it that way and

I thought him pretty bright to have accomplished what I had dreamed. Together, after the merger we knew we would do things together that would shake the world. There were then only a few things to check, like making sure that all the commuters had been given good homes in the surrounding English countryside. That department of the scheme was sure all was well, but I wanted everything checked and double checked before I declared the place officially in working order and mine. Already the subways were roaring and I was very pleased with those.

The escort for that last night was a very nice man who was to take her out to dinner and then the theater. They were to see three one-act plays in an off-Broadway theater and she looked forward to the evening very much. She had taken especial care with her makeup and dress. She wore a white velvet trouser-suit with trailing medieval sleeves and a diamanté belt at high waist level, a thing she could never have worn in East Leake. Her husband had helped her to choose her clothes for the trip, and as she placed a Juliet cap of rhinestones on her hair she noticed that she pined for him less every day and thought with horror of going back home to the flat village and the Stir-crazies secretarial work and the housework and having nobody interesting to talk to . . . oh, it was going to be so dreadful—she belonged here, in Manhattan, this was her true home. But she told herself not to be selfish and silly, of course she loved her husband and her home, and the Stir-crazies were making real progress like nursery schools for children over two years, trips out once a month, equal pay. And this was just a trip, she was lucky, not to be greedy . . . greedy people risked losing everything.

All during dinner she told her escort about the previous evening when she had stood on the sixty-fifth floor in an ecstatic condition, she rattled on all during the excellent crepes stuffed with spinach and ham, and the coffee, and went on about the incredible beauty of New York City, Manhattan Island, Isle of Dreams, right up until the curtain went up on the first play. During the intervals she told her escort about the escort of the previous evening, that he was a Mohawk, that he was beautiful, that his wife was sick. Her escort smiled kindly, and from superior age and experience forbore to point out that his lady for the evening was in love not only with the City but with a man. If he did not say anything, then she would arrive home safely not knowing the fact herself. He took her to a soda fountain for some iced tea, offered her lime sherbet but she could not eat. He sent her home in a cab and there at the door of the hotel stood her Mohawk in brown denim overalls, moccasins, and a blue-check shirt. She needed no telling, no prompting as to the state of her mind, she knew what she wanted. They both wanted the same, they talked about it in her hotel room. They wanted to live together in Manhattan, they wanted to forget that they had other lives. They kissed a few times and lay back on the bed, dizzy and reeling from the sheer delight of kissing in a state of new love. And shocked at the impact they would make on several lives if they went one bit further. He spoke of his wife who would sicken and die if she knew he made love with any other woman, his children who would be damaged if he left them; she spoke of her husband to whom she felt wedded forever, she felt wedding vows were sacred if old-fashioned, she thought about her children and saw destruction and grief looming, she thought of her house and it crumbled to dust in her vision of how it would be if she allowed herself to love this man who felt so right in her arms. He left silently and she did not weep, nor sleep either. Lay there murmuring:

"Seductive city I love you, every building, every stone, every splinter I love it all, the river round you, the great buildings, the canyons, and the smell and the taste and the feel of the hard stone sidewalk I love you so . . ." Turn the love over to inanimate objects, transmute it, somehow, make it into a memory only, so that I can live at home in peace with myself. . . .

At dawn she went out for a coffee in a drugstore unafraid of jostling and screeching tires and sirens, let them, let it, nothing can hurt me now, oh let anything try to hurt me now!

Spider called me:

"It's all yours, the whole works complete with trash in the gutter and roaches. Wanna conducted tour?" I picked up the Lucite block with the false eyelashes of my great-multi-great grandmother in it. I swear the damn things moved. Like crawled, or winked. Horrible but I couldn't help laughing, after all I had hardly slept for six weeks, where I got the energy from I did not know. It's amazing what a sense of accomplishment can do for the nervous system. I put the Lucite block back down on some papers on my desk and told Spider no, not the conducted tour just yet, first I had a crazy thing I wanted to do, which was fly the Atlantic on an anti-grav and take a look at Manhattan Island all bleak and bare. He thought I was crazy.

"The first trip you take outside your own backyard and what do you go and see . . . it's all happening *here!* The trouble I went to make it so . . ."

"I know, I know, it's just a feeling I have, I want to."

I hung up on him and knew I was nervous about the merger, for one thing. Our combined powers might be too much I felt, maybe we could accomplish some awful things between us, it worried me a bit. But I wasn't going to say anything, and first I had to check a few points. On the TV they were interviewing the former residents of New Jersey and places like that where all the commuters had lived who now lived on the outskirts of Leicester and Derby. Even at that it was a shorter commute and what with the inconvenience-money I was paying them they felt very happy, there was a noticeable lack of sentimentality over their homeland, the weather would be a slight problem until the weather bureau checked with Ecology to get the summers fixed without damage. I wanted it hot and humid in those New York summer streets, and they wanted the sun to ripen corn and peaches in their weekend houses. They would have it, soon, soon. Meetings were shown between old inhabitants and the new influx, and it seemed that mainly they would get on together very nicely. Both groups felt to have benefited.

"After all," said one housewife who had lived on Roulstone Crescent, which was now swallowed up by the intersection of Broadway and Seventh, "it will be nice to ride into New York of an evening and go to the flicks, there warn't much choice before."

It was all set, it was mine. There would be the official company meeting to sign the merger. Before I set off for my trip I called Spider.

"By the way, what were you thinking of doing with the site of Old Manhattan?"

"I thought I might do a repro. Ancient Indian Reservation . . ."

"See you later," I said, smiling.

She stayed awake every moment until she got back home. The plane journey had been fabulous, intense blue runway lights, the lights of the city from the air, an electric storm, and black silk clouds ripping on the wings, the whole sky illuminated like her sudden discovery of a new love, plunged into cloud like its loss. But then straight up to the sight of the stars, and when the air-hostess asked her if she wanted a drink she refused, saying that she wanted to be clearheaded for the dawn. Ahead into pale liquid glass containing one bright star, permitting herself one physically exploding thought of him and how it might have been and then, landing, forbidding herself ever to think of him again, because she knew that if she did something utterly dreadful might happen.

I hovered about over the desolate site of Manhattan and wondered why I had come, it had been a crazy thing to do. It was utterly dreary and kind of haunted looking, the earth flat brick dust, everything flattened or filled in, all the foundations and subways, everything, smooth wreckage. Still, Spider would replant it and make it as it had been in ancient times, it would be a fine natural place one day soon. I made for home, slinging the sledge into top speed so I was back home in under two hours, round trip. I was in a state of nerves and so did not land straight away, but took a float around first. I was under the impression at first that it was my nerves and lack of sleep playing me up. The skyline was trembling. Moving around idiotically. And then I began shouting meaningless warnings. Buildings were toppling over sideways and I was only just in time to avoid the steel cupola of the Woolworth building as it glided past me like a falling rocket and exploded into scales somewhere down an abyss. I sent my sledge straight up at top speed and then began to circle, switched the controls over to automatic-avoid, and watched everything. It was the gypsum mine caving in, of course, it had been roofed firm for thousands of years but this was just too much. All the engineers and consultants had said it would be fine, but dammit, they had been wrong. Maybe it was the subsonic lasers had done unseen damage, maybe it was my wanting the Big One right on top of the hill at the thinnest point of the cave roof, I don't know. The sound was softened at that height and in the closed dome, but I knew what it sounded like. All that screaming and shouting and crying out, yells of disbelief and horror, echoes of explosions as power lines hit subway cars, fires everywhere, gas leaks, whole tops of skyscrapers falling into the street and bursting like fruit, yellow cabs like beetles under bricks, flat, horns howling into silence, and then the sucking downwards, a thousand feet of sparkling white gypsum grinding against itself and spreading back miles of surrounding yellow clay, the pressure so great that Beacon Hill ten miles away became three feet higher above sea level. And then I saw him, right near the top of the Big One, outside and hanging onto the steel fence around the parapet on the eighty-sixth floor. He was waving to me and the building swayed back and forth, back and forth as its foundations worked their way down through the crystals, crushing lower towards the thousand feet of waiting black space. I homed in, aware of vast winds and flashes of light, scarlet blue, scarlet blue, explosions, sunset, dust and fire and electricity in the air like natural forces were endorsing what was happening. I strapped myself in and opened the door and could hardly breathe because of gas and dust and smoke rising and the wind full of it forcing its way into my chest and we could not hear each other at all. I tried, I got close enough to the parapet for it to brush me, I tried, I reached out, I screamed at him to jump, I knew he could do it if I hovered steady, but I had forgotten the automatic-avoid system was still switched on. He leapt into empty space and I zoomed out of the way of his falling body. Down it went over and over, I stayed to watch the island sink, like the lid of the Great Pit was taken off, the void claiming its own again, it was a triumphal roar, a greedy sucking, closing over it, the Abyss eating up what was its rightful property.

It was a long time ago and on Earth. I emigrated. I had no money left and no friends, no home, no choice. I don't have anything much now, no power. I didn't have any then, I have never had any. Or I would have made everything go very differently.

False Dawn

CHELSEA QUINN YARBRO

Most of the bodies were near the silos and storage tanks, where the defenders had retreated in the end. Caught between the Pirates and the Sacramento, they had been wiped out to a man. Mixed in with a few Pirate bodies Thea saw an occasional CD uniform. The cops had gone over at last.

She moved through the stench of the tumbled, looted corpses cautiously, carefully. She had not survived for her twenty-six years being foolhardy.

After dark she made her way east into Chico—what was left of it. Here the Pirates had revenged themselves on the few remaining townspeople. There were men, terribly mutilated men, hanging by their heels from lampposts, turning as they swung. And there were women.

One of the women wasn't dead yet. Her ravaged body hung naked from a broken billboard. Her legs were splayed wide and anchored with ropes. Her legs and belly were bloody, there were heavy bruises on her face and breasts, and she had been branded with a large M for mutant.

When Thea came near her, she jerked in her bonds and shrieked laughter that ended in a shuddering wail. *Don't let me ever get like that,* Thea thought, watching the woman's spasmodic thrusts with her hips. *Not like that.*

There was a movement down the street and Thea froze. She could not run without being seen and she could not wait if it were Pirates. She moved slowly, melting into the shadow of a gutted building, disappearing into the darkness as she kept watch.

The creatures that appeared were dogs; lean, wretched things with red-rimmed eyes and raised hackles. Thea had seen enough of the wild dogs to know that these were hunting meat. In the woman they found it. The largest of the dogs approached her on his belly, whining a little. He made a quick dash and nipped the leg nearest him. Aside from a long howl of laughter the woman did nothing. Emboldened, the dog came toward her, taking a more decisive bite from the leg. The response was a jerk and a scream followed by low laughter. The other dogs grew bolder. Each began to make quick, bouncing attacks, taking token bits of flesh from her legs and feet, growing ever bolder when they met with no resistance.

Thea watched stonily from the shadows, fitting a quarrel to her makeshift crossbow. Then she braced her forearm and pulled the trigger.

The high sobbing laughter was cut off with a bubble and a sigh as the quarrel bit into the woman's neck. There was no sound then but the snarling dogs.

In the deep shadows of the alley, Thea moved away from the dogs. *I'd forgot about that,* she said to herself accusingly. *There will be more dogs. And rats,* she thought, after a moment.

As she walked, she tightened her crossbow again and fitted another quarrel to it. *She probably wasn't a mutant,* she let herself think. *Probably she was just healthy.* She didn't want to consider what the Pirates would do to Thea herself, genetically altered as she was.

The sound of the dogs died behind her in the empty, littered streets. Here and there she saw piles of bodies, some dead from fighting, others from more sinister things. The M brand was on many of them. Twice she saw the unmistakable signs of New Leprosy on the blind faces, skin scaled over and turning the silver that allied it with the old disease. But unlike the first leprosy the new variety *was* contagious. And the Pirates had carried it away with them.

She chafed her dark, hard skin, long since burned to a red-brown. So far she had been lucky and had resisted most of the new diseases; but she knew that the luck would eventually run out, even for her. Even if she found the Gold Lake Settlement and they accepted her.

After more than an hour of walking, she left Chico behind, striking eastward through ruined fields and swampland. The last crops had been forced from the ground and now the stalks crisscrossed underfoot like great soggy snakes. A heavy phosphorescence hung over the marshland, a light that did not illuminate or warm. Thea did not know the source of it, but she avoided the spot. Since the Sacramento Disaster four years ago, the valley had ceased to be safe land. Before the levees had crumbled, it had been a haven from the pollution around it. Now, with the delta a reeking chemical quagmire, the upper river was slowly surrendering to the spreading contamination.

She stumbled and saw a dead cat at her feet. Animals had been at it: the chest gaped and the eye sockets were empty, but the fur was healthy. She shook her head at the waste of it. Bending closer, she noticed with surprise that the front paws were the tawny-orange of regenerated tissue. Maybe it had been virally mutated, as she had been. Or maybe the virus was catching. A lot of other things sure were catching. Shaking her head again, she dragged some rotting stalks over the little carcass, knowing it for the empty gesture it was even as she did it.

The ground grew soggier as she went, the old stalks becoming a vile goo, and sticky. She looked ahead for firmer ground and saw an oily stretch of water moving sluggishly under the wan moon. Beyond was the stunted fuzz of what had been cattails. Sliding the nictitating membranes over her eyes, she dropped to her knees and moved forward, her crossbow at the ready. The river was not a friendly place.

Once she heard a pig rooting along the bank and she stopped. Those pigs that were still alive were dangerous and hungry. Eventually it crashed away up the bank and Thea began paddling again. *One thing to say for the Disaster,* she thought as the stinking water surged around her. *It killed a lot of insects.*

Then she reached the cattails and slipped in among them for cover. There was a kind of protection that would last her until first light, when she would have to find higher ground. She found a hummock and curled up on it for a few hours' sleep.

The dawn brought more animals to the river, and a few foraging Pirates who swept by in their modified open vans. They had rifles and took three shots for two carcasses—the pig from the night before and an ancient horse with broken knees.

"Bring 'em in! Bring 'em in!" hollered the one in the lead van.

"Give me a hand, you snot-fucking Mute!"

The first gave a shout. "Montague gave you hauling this week. Cox didn't change that. *I* didn't have maggots in my pack." He snorted mockingly and revved the engine.

"You know what you have to do if you waste fuel," the one doing the hauling said gleefully.

"Just you shove it!" shouted the first, panic in his voice. "I don't want to hear no threats from you. I could drop you right now."

"Then you'd have to do the hauling," reminded the second laconically, then added, "Cox says Montague's dead, anyway."

"Him and his guard," the one on the bank said, as if it were a curse. "They tried to stop Wilson and me when we got that Mute kid out of the cellar. Said to leave him alone. A rotten Mute! Montague—he was crazy."

They were silent but for the whir of the engines and the sound of the dead animals being dragged through the mud.

Thea huddled in the cattails, hardly daring to breathe. She had seen Cloverdale after they had sacked it, in the days before Montague had organized them under that ironic rallying cry, "Survive!"

"That's one," said the first.

"Lick your cock."

Again there was silence until the one doing the hauling let out a scream.

"What's the matter?" demanded the one at the vans.

"Water spiders!" the other shrieked in terror. "Dozens of 'em!" And he made a horrible sound in his throat.

From her protection in the cattails, Thea watched, crouching, fright in her eyes. Water spiders were nothing to mess with, even for her. She clung to the reeds around her and watched for the hard, shiny bodies with the long hooked mandibles filled with paralyzing venom. Three of them could kill you in less than ten minutes. Dozens, and you didn't have a chance at all.

The voice-rending shouts had stopped, and soon a body drifted aimlessly by, with the spiders climbing over the face toward the eyes. Thea turned away.

Up on the bank there was a cough and the motor whizzed as the Pirate on the van drove off too fast.

Thea waited until the body had slid out of sight around a bend in the river before she moved free from the cattails. Then she ran off through the brushy undergrowth, not pausing to look for Pirates or for spiders. Her knees were uncertain as jelly and her fright made her light-headed. She ran frantically until she was on higher ground; there she stopped and breathed.

She had come about half a mile from the river in those few minutes, and had left a wake like a timber run through the underbrush. There was nothing to concern her about that: it could easily have been caused by an animal and would not be investigated. But the hunting party meant that the Pirates were still around, maybe camped. She had to get away from them, or she would end up like the woman in Chico. *Not like that.* She shuddered.

She guessed that the Pirates were camped near the river, within walking distance of Chico, so she started off to the southeast, keeping to the cover of the trees. The scrub oaks were gone, but the hardier fruit trees had run riot. Thea knew that if she had to, she could climb into the trees and pick off the Pirates one by one with her crossbow until they killed her. That would take time. And she needed time.

By midday she had put several miles between herself and the Pirates. The river lay below her, a greasy brown smudge. The east fork of the Sacramento was dying.

That was when she found the makeshift silo. Some farmer in the hills, maybe one of the old communes, had built a silo to store his grain, and there it stood: lopsided, rusty, but safe and dry. A haven for the night, and perhaps a base for a couple of days. It would be a good place to come back to after scouting the hills for the best way into the sierra and Gold Lake.

She walked around the silo carefully, looking for the door and for the farmhouse it had once belonged to. The farmhouse turned out to be a charred shell. The silo was the only thing left standing where once there had been a house, chicken coops, and a barn. She shook her head and swung the door open.

In the next instant she was reeling back. "Stupid, stupid!" she said aloud. "Stupid." For there was a man in the silo, waving something at her. She started to run, angry and frustrated.

"No! No!" the voice followed her. "Don't run away! Wait!" It got louder. "That's my arm!"

Thea stopped. His arm. "What?" she yelled back.

"It's my arm. They cut it off." The words made a weird echo in the corrugated walls of the silo. "Last week."

She started back toward the sound. "Who did?"

"The Pirates. In Chico." He was getting weaker, and his words came irregularly. "I got this far."

She stood in the doorway looking down at him. "Why'd you keep it?"

He drew in a breath. "They were looking for a man with only one arm. So I sewed this in my jacket. I can't get any further without help," he finished.

"Well, you better bury it," she told him, casting a glance at the thing.

He met her eyes. "I can't."

Thea looked him over carefully. He was ten, fifteen years older than she was, with a stocky body made gaunt with hunger and pain. His wide face was deeply lined and grimy. The clothes he wore were torn and filthy, but had once been expensive, she could tell.

"How long you been here?" she asked him.

"I think three days."

"Oh." From the state of the arm that was about right. She pointed to the stump. "How does it feel? Infected?"

He frowned. "I don't think so. Not much. It itches."

She accepted this for the moment. "Where were you going? You got a place to go?"

"I was trying to get into the mountains."

Thea considered, and her first impulse was to run, to leave this man to rot or live as it happened. But she hesitated. Gold Lake was a long way away, and getting there would be hard.

"I got medicine," she said, making up her mind. "You can have some of it. Not all, 'cause it's mine and I might need it. But you can have a little."

He looked at her, his rumpled face puzzled. "Thank you," he said, unused to the words.

"I got parapenicillin and a little sporomicin. Which one do you want?"

"The penicillin."

"I got some ascorbic tablets for later," she added, looking thoughtfully at the stump of his arm as she came into the silo. There had been infection, but it was clearing and the skin was the tawny-orange color of regenerating tissue. "You left-handed?"

"Yes."

"You're lucky."

After releasing the crossbow and storing the quarrel, she shrugged out of her pack, putting it down carefully, not too close to the man. He still had one good arm and he had admitted he was left-handed. "What's your name?" she asked as she dug into the bag.

"Seth Pearson," he said with slight hesitation.

She looked at him sharply. "It says David Rossi on your neck tags. Which is it?"

"It doesn't matter. Whichever one you like."

Thea looked away. "Okay. That's the way we'll do it, Rossi." She handed him a packet, worn but intact. "That's the penicillin. You'll have to eat it, I don't have any needles." Then she added, "It tastes terrible. Here." She handed him a short, flat stick of jerky. "Venison and tough. It'll take the taste away." She put her pack between them and sat on the floor. When the man had managed to choke down the white slime, she said, "Tomorrow I'm going east. You can come with me if you can keep up. There's one more bad river ahead, and you might have to swim it. It's rocky and fast. So you better make up your

mind tonight." Then she took two more pieces of jerky out of her pack
and ate them in a guarded silence.

The north wind bit through them as they walked; the sun was bright
but cold. The gentle slope grew gradually steeper and they climbed
more slowly, saying nothing and keeping wary eyes on the bushes that
littered the slopes. By midafternoon they were walking over the crumbling trunks of large pine trees that had fallen, victims of smog. The
dust from the dead trees blew in plumes around them, stinging their
eyes and making them sneeze. Yet still they climbed.

The going got slower and slower until they called a halt in the lee
of a huge stump. Rossi braced his good shoulder and held out his
tattered jacket to protect them from the wind.

"Are you all right?" Thea asked him when she had caught her
breath. "You're the wrong color."

"Just a little winded." He nodded. "I'm . . . still weak."

"Yeah," she said, looking covertly at his stump. The color was deep-
ening. "You're getting better."

His feet slid suddenly on the rolling dust and he grabbed out to her
to keep from falling.

She stepped back. "Don't do that."

As he regained his footing, he looked at her in some surprise. "Why?"
he asked gently.

"Don't you touch me." She grabbed at her crossbow defensively.

He frowned, his eyes troubled, then his brow cleared. "I won't." In
those two words he had great understanding. He knew the world that
Thea lived in as well as she did.

With a look of defiance she tightened the crossbow's straps on her
arm, never taking her eyes from the man. "I can shoot this real fast,
Rossi. Remember that."

Whatever he might have said was lost. "Hold it right there," came
the voice from behind them.

Aside from the exchange of quick, frightened glances, they did not
move.

"That's right." There was a puff of dust, and another, then a young
man in a ruined CD uniform stood in front of them, a rifle cradled in
his arms. "I knew I'd catch you," he said aloud to himself. "I been
following you all morning."

Thea edged closer to Rossi.

"You people come out from Chico, right?" He bounced the weapon
he carried.

"No."

"What about you?" he demanded of Thea.

"No."

He looked back toward Rossi, an unpleasant smile on his face. "What about you . . . Rossi, is it? Sure you didn't come through Chico? I heard a guy named Rossi was killed outside Orland."

"I don't know about that."

"They said he was trying to save Montague when Cox took over. You know anything about that? Rossi?"

"No."

The younger man laughed. "Hey, don't you lie to me, Rossi. You lie to me and I'm going to kill you."

In the shadow, Thea slowly put a quarrel into her crossbow, keeping as much out of sight as she could.

"You're going to kill us anyway, so why does it matter if we lie?" Rossi was asking.

"Listen," the CD man began. "What's that?" he said, looking squarely at Thea. "What are you doing?" And he reached out, grabbing her by the arm and jerking her off her feet. "You bitch-piece!" He kicked savagely into her shoulder, just once. Then Rossi put himself between them. "Move!"

"No. You want me to move, you'll have to kill me." He said to Thea, without turning, "Did he hurt you?"

"Some," she admitted. "I'll be okay."

"She your woman? Is she?"

Rossi rose slowly, forcing the man with the rifle to move back. "No. She's nobody's woman."

At that the other man giggled. "I bet she needs it. I bet she's real hungry for it."

Thea closed her eyes to hide the indignation in her. If this was to be rape, being *used* . . . She opened her eyes when Rossi's hand touched her shoulder.

"You try any more dumb things like that, cunt, and that's going to be the end. Understand?"

"Yes," she mumbled.

"And what will Cox say when he finds out what you're doing?" Rossi asked.

"Cox won't say nothing!" the CD man spat.

"So you deserted." Rossi nodded at the guilt in the man's face. "That was stupid."

"You shut up!" He leaned toward them. "You are going to take me out of here, wherever you're going. If anybody spots us, or we get trapped, I am going to make both of you look like a butcher shop. You got that? . . . HUH?"

"You stink," said Thea.

For a moment there was anger in the young, hard eyes, then he grabbed her face with one hand. "Not yet, not yet." His grip tightened. "You want some of that, you're gonna have to beg for it, real hard. You're gonna have to suck it out of me. Right?" He looked defiantly at Rossi. "Right?" he repeated.

"Let her go."

"You want her?"

"Leave her alone."

"All right," he said with a little nod. He stepped back from her. "Later, huh? When you've thought it over."

Rossi looked at the CD man. "I'll be close, Thea. Just call."

As the two men stared at each other, Thea wanted to run from both of them, to the protection of the destroyed forest. But she could not escape on an open hillside. She rubbed her shoulder gingerly and went to Rossi's side.

"I'm a better choice," the CD man mocked her. "My name's Lastly. You can call me that, bitch-piece. Don't call me anything else."

She said nothing as she looked up the hillside.

Rossi's voice was soft. "Don't try it now. There's cover up ahead and I'll get him into a fight."

With deep surprise she turned to him. "Truly? You'd do that?"

He would have gone on, but Lastly shoved them apart. "I don't want none of that. You don't whisper when I'm around, hear? You got anything to say, you speak up."

"I wanted to piss," said Rossi.

Lastly giggled again. "Oh, no. Not for a while. You aren't gonna leave a trail. Got that?"

With a shrug Rossi led the long walk toward the trees.

"What was that?" Lastly turned the barrel of his gun toward the sound that surged through the underbrush.

The ululation rose and fell through the trees, lonely and terrible.

"Dogs," said Rossi bluntly. "They're hunting."

In the deep shadows of dusk the scattered trees seemed to grow together, surrounding the three people who moved through the gloom. The sound came again, closer and sharper.

"Where are they?"

Thea looked back at him. "A ways off yet. You can't shoot them until they get close."

"We got to get out of here," Lastly said in fear. "Right? We got to find someplace safe."

Rossi squinted up at the fading sky. "I'd say we have another hour yet. After that, we'd better climb trees."

"But they're rotten," Lastly protested.

"They're better than dogs," Rossi reminded him.

But Lastly wasn't listening. "There used to be camps around here, didn't there? We got to find them. No dogs gonna come into camp."

"You fool," said Rossi dispassionately.

"No talking. I don't want to hear it." Lastly's gun wavered in front of Rossi.

"Then you both stop it," Thea put in quietly. "The dogs can hear you."

All fell silent. In a moment Rossi said, "Thea's right. If we're quiet, we might find one of your camps in time."

"You get moving, then," Lastly said hurriedly. "Right now."

It had been a summer cabin once, when people still had summer cabins. The view below it had been of pine forests giving way to the fertile swath of the valley. Now it stood in a clearing surrounded by rotting trees, above the spreading contamination of the river. Oddly enough the windows were still intact.

"We can stay here," Rossi said after circling the cabin. "The back porch is screened and we can get the door off its hinges."

"We can get through the window," Lastly said eagerly.

"If it's broken, so can the dogs." When this had sunk in, Rossi went on. "The back is secure. We'll be able to protect ourselves."

"You two get it done," Lastly ordered, pointing the rifle toward the rear porch. "Get it done fast."

As Thea and Rossi struggled with the door, Lastly straddled the remains of a picket fence. "Say, you see what Cox did to that Mute in Chico? Took the skin right off him, hey. Cox, he's gonna get rid of all the Mutes—just you wait."

"Yes," said Rossi as he pulled at a rusted hinge.

"Know what? Montague wanted to save 'em. You hear about that, Rossi? Why would someone want to do that? Huh? Why'd any real man save Mutes?"

Rossi didn't answer.

"I asked you something . . . Rossi. You tell me."

"Maybe he thought they were the only ones worth saving."

"What about you, bitch-piece? You save a Mute?" He bounced on the fence as he stroked his rifle.

With a look of pure disgust, Thea said, "Just me, Lastly. I'm saving me."

"What you saving for me? I got something for you . . ."

"The door's off," Rossi interrupted, pulling it aside. "We can go in now."

Mice had got into the house, eating the dried fruits and flour that had been stored in the ample kitchen. But there were cans left, filled with food Thea could hardly remember. Pots and pans hung on the wall, mostly rusty, but a few made of enamelware and ready for use. The stove was a wood-burner.

"Look at it," Rossi said, his eyes lingering on the cupboards and their precious contents. "Enough to take with us for later."

"Damn, it's perfect. I'm gonna have it right tonight. Hot food, and a bath and all the ways I want it." He glanced slyly from Rossi to Thea.

"Smoke might bring the Pirates," said Rossi with a sour smile. "Have you thought of that?"

"It's nighttime, Rossi. They ain't coming up here till morning."

Thea had wandered around the kitchen. "There's no wood, anyway. That table is plastic."

They all stood for a moment, then Lastly announced, "You heard the lady, Rossi. There's no wood. You gonna get it for her, right? Right?"

"I'll go," said Thea quickly.

"Oh, no."

"But he can't work with one arm."

"If he takes his time, bitch-piece."

"What about you, Lastly?" Rossi asked evenly. "You're able and you've got the gun."

"And let you two lock me out with the dogs? I ain't dumb, Rossi." He moved around the table. "It's you, Rossi. You're it." He shoved a chair at him. "Catch your breath, 'cause you're going out there."

"Not without Thea."

Lastly made his now familiar giggle. "Want it for yourself, huh? She ain't putting it out to you. She wants a man. Not you."

Thea gave Rossi a pleading look. "Let me lock myself in the side room. Then both of you can go."

"Right!" said Lastly unexpectedly. "The bitch-piece is right. We lock her up and we get the wood. Rossi?"

"If that's what you want, Thea."

She nodded. "Yes."

"I'll see you later?" he asked her, his deep eyes on hers.

"I hope so," she answered.

"Come on, bitch-piece. We're going to lock you up." He took her by the arm, half dragging her through the main room of the cabin to the side room. "There you are," he said, thrusting her inside. "Your own boudoir. You keep nice and warm while you wait." And he slammed the door. There was a distinct sound as Thea pushed the lock home.

She sat in the bedroom, huddled on the bare mattress in the center of the room, listening for the sound of the men. She had wanted to run from them, but she felt tired and helpless now. As time passed, she slumped and slid until she stretched on the bed, asleep.

"You were supposed to get ready. I told you to get ready," said the harsh voice above her. "You knew I'd be back." She was pulled roughly onto her back and pinned there by a sudden weight across her body.

Barely awake, Thea pushed against the man, hands and feet seeking vulnerable places.

"Shut UP!" Lastly growled, his hand slamming across her face. When Thea cried out, he hit her again. "You listen, cunt; you're for me. You think I'm letting a Mute-fucker like Montague get you? Huh?" He struck her arms back, catching her wrists in a length of rope. "We taught him and his pervs a lesson at Chico. You hear?" He pulled the rope taut against the bed slats. "This time I'm getting mine. Right?"

With a sob of pure fury Thea launched herself at Lastly, teeth bared and legs twisting.

"No, you don't." Lastly giggled. This time his fist caught her on the side of the head and she fell back, dizzy and sick. "Don't give me a hard time, cunt. It makes it worse for you." Rope looped her left ankle and then her right, to be tied under the mattress. Angrily Thea pulled at the ropes.

"Don't," Lastly said, coming near her. "You do that any more and I'm going to hurt you. See this?" He put a small knife up close to her face. "I got it in the kitchen. It's real sharp. You give me any more trouble and I'm gonna carve you up some, till you learn some manners."

"No."

Ignoring this, Lastly began to cut off her jacket. When he had ripped that from her, he slit the seams on her leather pants. As he pulled these away, she twisted in the ropes.

Immediately he was across her. "I told you." He put the knife to her, catching one nipple between the blade and his thumb. "I could peel this off, you know?" He pressed harder. The knife bit into her flesh. "No noise, cunt. You be quiet or I take it all off."

In the sudden sharp pain the nictitating membranes closed over her eyes.

And Lastly saw. "Mute! Shit! You lousy Mute!" There was something like triumph in his voice. She cried out as he pulled the wrinkled bit of flesh from her. Blood spread over her breast.

With a shout Lastly wiggled his pants down to his knees and in one quick movement pushed into her. Forcing himself deeper, laughing, he said, "Montague's Mute! I'm gonna ruin you." Falling forward, he fastened his teeth on her sound breast.

At that she screamed. He brought his head up. "You do that again, Mute, and this one comes off with my teeth." He hit her in the mouth as he came.

In the next moment he was off her, torn out of her and slammed against the wall.

"You filthy! . . ." Rossi, his hand in Lastly's hair, hit him into the wall again. There was an audible crack and Lastly slumped.

Then he came back to the bed. "Oh, God, Thea," he said softly. "I never meant it to be like this." He knelt beside her, not touching her. "I'm sorry." It was as if he were apologizing for the world. Gently he untied her, speaking to her as he did. When he freed her, she huddled on the bed in silent tears which shook her wholly.

Finally she turned to him, shame in her eyes. "I wanted you. I wanted you," she said and turned away.

In wonder he rose. "I have one arm and a price on my head."

"I wanted you," she said again, not daring to look at him.

"My name," he said very quietly, "is Evan Montague." And he waited, looking away from her.

Then he felt her hand on his. "I wanted you."

He turned to her, holding her hand, not daring to touch her. She drew him down beside her, but pulled back from him. "He hurt me," she said numbly.

"Here I tried to save everybody and couldn't even save you," he whispered bitterly. He looked at her, at her bloody breasts and bruised face, at the deep scratches on her thighs. "Let me get your medicine . . ."

"No." She grabbed at his hand frantically. "Don't leave me."

With what might have been a smile he sat holding her hand while she shivered and the blood dried, until they heard the sound of engines, like a distant hive.

"They're looking for him. Or me," Montague said.

She nodded. "Do we have to leave?"

"Yes."

"If we stay?"

"They'll kill me. Not you, though . . . And you are a mutant, aren't you?"

She understood and shook spasmodically. "Don't let them. Kill me. Kill me. Please."

The terror in her face alarmed him. He pulled her fingers to his lips, kissing them. "I will. I promise, Thea." Then he changed. "No. We're getting out of here. We're going to live as long as we can."

Sighing, Lastly collapsed, his head at a strange angle.

"Come on," Montague said.

With an effort Thea rose to her feet, holding on to his arm until the dizziness passed. "I need clothes."

He looked about the room, to the dresser that was encircled with ropes. "There?" he asked, going to it and pulling the drawers. The clothes were for children, but Thea was small enough to wear some of them. With determination she struggled into heavy canvas jeans, but balked at a sweater or jacket. "I can't," she whispered.

"Shush," he said. They heard the sounds of the motors getting nearer.

"What time is it?" she asked.

"Early. It's gray in the east."

"We've got to go. My pack . . ."

"Leave it," he said brusquely. "Neither you nor I can carry it."

"My crossbow . . ."

"In the kitchen. Put it on my arm. If you load it, I can fire." He bundled a jacket under his arm. "You'll want this later."

The engines grew louder. "I thought that was the way," Montague said ironically. "I was a fool." He went to the window and opened it. "This way. And straight into the trees."

"Evan!" she called as the cold morning air brushed the raw places on her breast. "Evan!"

"Can you make it? You've got to," he said as he came to her side.

"Yes. But slowly."

"All right." He took her hand, feeling her fingers and the crossbow warm in the morning cold. "We'll go slowly for a while."

As they climbed away into the dying forest and the dark, the sounds of the engines grew loud behind them, shutting out the noise of their escape and sending the wild dogs howling away from them into the cold gray light before dawn.

Nobody's Home

JOANNA RUSS

After she had finished her work at the North Pole, Jannina came down to the Red Sea refineries, where she had family business, jumped to New Delhi for dinner, took a nap in a public hotel in Queensland, walked from the hotel to the station, bypassed the Leeward Islands (where she thought she might go, but all the stations were busy), and met Charley to watch the dawn over the Carolinas.

"Where've you *been,* dear C?"

"Tanzania. And you're married."

"No."

"I heard you were married," he said. "The Lees told the Smiths who told the Kerguelens who told the Utsumbés, and we get around, we Utsumbés. A new wife, they said. I didn't know you were especially fond of women."

"I'm not. She's my husbands' wife. And we're not married yet, Charley. She's had hard luck. A first family started in '35, two husbands burned out by an overload while arranging transportation for a concert—of all things, pushing papers, you know!—and the second divorced her, I think, and she drifted away from the third (a big one), and there was some awful quarrel with the fourth, people chasing people around tables, I don't know."

"Poor woman."

In the manner of people joking and talking lightly they had drawn together, back to back, sitting on the ground and rubbing their shoulders and the backs of their heads together. Jannina said sorrowfully, "What lovely hair you have, Charley Utsumbé, like metal mesh."

"All we Utsumbés are exceedingly handsome." They linked arms. The sun, which anyone could chase around the world now, see it rise or set twenty times a day, fifty times a day—if you wanted to spend your life like that—rose dripping out of the cypress swamp. There was nobody around for miles. Mist drifted up from the pools and low places.

"My God," he said, "it's summer! I have to be at Tanga now."

"What?" said Jannina.

"One loses track," he said apologetically. "I'm sorry, love, but I have unavoidable business at home. Tax labor."

"But why summer, why did its being summer . . ."

"Train of thought! Too complicated." And already they were out of key, already the mild affair was over, there having come between them the one obligation that can't be put off to the time you like, or the place you like; off he'd go to plug himself into a road-mender or a doctor, though it's of some advantage to mend all the roads of a continent at one time.

She sat cross-legged on the station platform, watching him enter the booth and set the dial. He stuck his head out the glass door. "Come with me to Africa, lovely lady!"

She thumbed her nose at him. "You're only a passing fancy, Charley U!" He blew a kiss, enclosed himself in the booth, and disappeared. (The transmatter field is larger than the booth, for obvious reasons; the booth flicks on and off several million times a second and so does not get transported itself, but it protects the machinery from the weather and it keeps people from losing elbows or knees or slicing the ends off a package or a child. The booths at the cryogenics center at the North Pole have exchanged air so often with those of warmer regions that each has its own microclimate; leaves and seeds, plants and earth are piled about them. The notes pinned to the door said, Don't Step on the Grass! Wish to Trade Pawlownia Sapling for Sub-Arctic Canadian Moss; Watch Your Goddamn Bare Six-Toed Feet! Wish Amateur Cellist for Quartet, Six Months' Rehearsal Late Uhl with Reciter; I Lost a Squirrel Here Yesterday, Can You Find It Before It Dies? Eight Children Will Be Heartbroken—Cecilia Ching, Buenos Aires.)

Jannina sighed and slipped on her glass woolly; nasty to get back into clothes, but home was cold. You never knew where you might go, so you carried them. Years ago (she thought) I came here with someone in the dead of winter, either an unmatched man or someone's starting spouse—only two of us, at any rate—and we waded through the freezing water and danced as hard as we could and then proved we could sing and drink beer in a swamp at the same time, Good Lord! And then went to the public resort on the Ile de la Cité to watch professional plays, opera, games—you have to be good to get in there!—and got into some clothes because it was chilly after sundown in September—no, wait, it was Venezuela—and watched the lights come out and smoked like mad at a café table and tickled the robot waiter and pretended we were old, really old, perhaps a hundred and fifty . . . Years ago!

But *was* it the same place? she thought, and dismissing the incident forever, she stepped into the booth, shut the door, and dialed home: the Himalayas. The trunk line was clear. The branch stop was clear. The family's transceiver (located in the anteroom behind two doors, to keep the task of heating the house within reasonable limits) had damn well better be clear, or somebody would be blown right into the vestibule. Momentum- and heat-compensators kept Jannina from arriving home at seventy degrees Fahrenheit internal temperature (seven degrees lost for every mile you teleport upward) or too many feet above herself (rise to the east, drop going west; to the north or south you are apt to be thrown right through the wall of the booth). Someday (thought Jannina) everybody will decide to let everybody live in decent climates. But not yet. Not this everybody.

She arrived home singing "The World's My Backyard, Yes, the World Is My Oyster," a song that had been popular in her first youth, some seventy years before.

The Komarovs' house was hardened foam with an automatic inside line to the school near Naples. It was good to be brought up on your own feet. Jannina passed through; the seven-year-olds lay with their heads together and their bodies radiating in a six-person asterisk. In this position (which was supposed to promote mystical thought) they played Barufaldi, guessing the identity of famous dead personages through anagrammatic sentences, the first letters of the words of which (unscrambled into aphorisms or proverbs) simultaneously spelled out a moral and a series of Goedel numbers (in a previously agreed-upon code) which . . .

"Oh, my darling, how felicitous is the advent of your appearance!" cried a boy (hard to take, the polysyllabic stage). "Embrace me, dearest maternal parent! Unite your valuable upper limbs about my eager person!"

"Vulgar!" said Jannina, laughing.

"*Non sum filius tuus?*" said the child.

"No, you're not my body-child. You're my godchild. Your mother bequeathed me to you when she died. What are you learning?"

"The eternal parental question," he said, frowning. "How to run a helicopter. How to prepare food from its actual, revolting, raw constituents. Can I go now?"

"*Can* you?" she said. "Nasty imp!"

"Good," he said. "I've made you feel guilty. Don't *do* that," and as she tried to embrace him, he ticklishly slid away. "The robin walks quietly up the branch of the tree," he said breathlessly, flopping back on the floor.

"That's not an aphorism." (Another Barufaldi player.)

"It is."

"It isn't."

"It is."

"It isn't."

"It is."

"It—"

The school vanished; the antechamber appeared. In the kitchen Chi Komarov was rubbing the naked back of his sixteen-year-old son. Parents always kissed each other; children always kissed each other. She touched foreheads with the two men and hung her woolly on the hook by the ham radio rig. Someone was always around. Jannina flipped the cover off her wrist chronometer: standard regional time, date, latitude-longitude, family computer hookup clear. "At my age I ought to remember these things," she said. She pressed the computer hookup: Ann at tax labor in the schools, bit-a-month plan, regular Ann; Lee with three months to go, five years off, heroic Lee; Phuong in Paris, still rehearsing; C.E. gone, won't say where, spontaneous C.E.; Ilse making some repairs in the basement, not a true basement, but the room farthest down the hillside. She went up the stairs and then came down and put her head around at the living-and-swimming room. Through the glass wall one could see the mountains. Old Al, who had joined them late in life, did a bit of gardening in the brief summers, and generally stuck around the place. Jannina beamed. "Hullo, Old Al!" Big and shaggy, a rare delight, his white body hair. She sat on his lap. "Has she come?"

"The new one? No," he said.

"Shall we go swimming?"

He made an expressive face. "No, dear," he said. "I'd rather go to Naples and watch the children fly helicopters. I'd rather go to Nevada and fly them myself. I've been in the water all day, watching a very dull person restructure coral reefs and experiment with polyploid polyps."

"You mean *you* were doing it."

"One gets into the habit of working."

"But you didn't have to!"

"It was a private project. Most interesting things are."

She whispered in his ear.

With happily flushed faces, they went into Old Al's inner garden and locked the door.

Jannina, temporary family representative, threw the computer helmet over her head and, thus plugged in, she cleaned house, checked food supplies, did a little of the legal business entailed by a family of eighteen adults (two triplet marriages, a quad, and a group of eight). She felt very smug. She put herself through by radio to Himalayan HQ (above two thousand meters) and hooking computer to computer—a very odd feeling, like an urge to sneeze that never comes off—extended a formal invitation to one Leslie Smith ("Come stay, why don't you?"), notifying every free Komarov to hop it back and fast. Six hikers might come for the night—backpackers. More food. First thunderstorm of the year in Albany, New York (North America). Need an extra two rooms by Thursday. Hear the Palnatoki are moving. Can't use a room. Can't use a kitten. Need the geraniums back, Mrs. Adam, Chile. The best maker of hand-blown glass in the world has killed in a duel the second-best maker of hand-blown glass for joining the movement toward ceramics. A bitter struggle is foreseen in the global economy. Need a lighting designer. Need fifteen singers and electric pansensicon. Standby tax labor xxxxxpj through xxxyq to Cambaluc, great tectogenic—

With the guilty feeling that one always gets gossiping with a computer, for it's really not reciprocal, Jannina flipped off the helmet. She went to get Ilse. Climbing back through the white foam room, the purple foam room, the green foam room, everything littered with plots and projects of the clever Komarovs or the even cleverer Komarov children, stopping at the baby room for Ilse to nurse her baby, Jannina danced staidly around studious Ilse. They turned on the nursery robot and the television screen. Ilse drank beer in the swimming room, for her milk. She worried her way through the day's record of events—faults in the foundation, some people who came from Chichester and couldn't find C.E. so one of them burst into tears, a new experiment in genetics coming around the gossip circuit, an execrable set of equations from some imposter in Bucharest.

"A duel!" said Jannina.

They both agreed it was shocking. And what fun. A new fashion. You had to be a little mad to do it. Awful.

The light went on over the door to the tunnel that linked the house to the antechamber, and very quickly, one after another, as if the branch line had just come free, eight Komarovs came into the room. The light flashed again; one could see three people debouch one after the other, persons in boots, with coats, packs, and face masks over their woollies. They were covered with snow, either from the mountain terraces above the house or from some other place, Jannina didn't know. They stamped the snow off in the antechamber and hung their clothes outside. "Good heavens, you're not circumcised!" cried someone. There was as much handshaking and embracing all around as at a wedding party. Velet Komarov (the short, dark one) recognized Fung Pao-Yu and swung her off her feet. People began to joke, tentatively stroking one another's arms. "Did you have a good hike? Are you a good hiker, Pao-Yu?" said Velet. The light over the antechamber went on again, though nobody could see a thing, since the glass was steamed over from the collision of hot with cold air. Old Al stopped, halfway into the kitchen. The baggage receipt chimed, recognized only by family ears—upstairs a bundle of somebody's things, ornaments, probably, for the missing Komarovs were still young and the young are interested in clothing, were appearing in the baggage receptacle. "Ann or Phuong?" said Jannina. "Five to three, anybody? Match me!" but someone strange opened the door of the booth and peered out. Oh, a dizzying sensation. She was painted in a few places, which was awfully odd because really it was old-fashioned; and why do it for a family evening? It was a stocky young woman. It was an awful mistake (thought Jannina). Then the visitor made her second mistake.

"I'm Leslie Smith," she said. But it was more through clumsiness than being rude. Chi Komarov (the tall, blond one) saw this instantly, and snatching off his old-fashioned spectacles, he ran to her side and patted her, saying teasingly, "Now, haven't we met? Now, aren't you married to someone I know?"

"No, no," said Leslie Smith, flushing with pleasure.

He touched her neck. "Ah, you're a tightrope dancer!"

"Oh, no!" exclaimed Leslie Smith.

"*I'm* a tightrope dancer," said Chi. "Would you believe it?"

"But you're too—too *spiritual*," said Leslie Smith hesitantly.

"Spiritual, how do you like that, family, spiritual?" he cried, delighted (a little more delighted, thought Jannina, than the situation really called for), and he began to stroke her neck.

"What a lovely neck you have," he said.

This steadied Leslie Smith. She said, "I like tall men," and allowed herself to look at the rest of the family. "Who are these people?" she said, though one was afraid she might really mean it.

Fung Pao-Yu to the rescue: "Who are these people? Who are they, indeed! I doubt if they are anybody. One might say, 'I have met these people,' but has one? What existential meaning would such a statement convey? I myself, now, I have met them. I have been introduced to them. But they are like the Sahara. It is all wrapped in mystery. I doubt if they even have names," etc. etc. Then lanky Chi Komarov disputed possession of Leslie Smith with Fung Pao-Yu, and Fung Pao-Yu grabbed one arm and Chi the other; and she jumped up and down fiercely; so that by the time the lights dimmed and the food came, people were feeling better—or so Jannina judged. So embarrassing and delightful to be eating fifteen to a room! "We Komarovs are famous for eating whatever we can get whenever we can get it," said Velet proudly. Various Komarovs in various places, with the three hikers on cushions and Ilse at full length on the rug. Jannina pushed a button with her toe and the fairy lights came on all over the ceiling. "The children did that," said Old Al. He had somehow settled at Leslie Smith's side and was feeding her so-chi from his own bowl. She smiled up at him. "We once," said a hiking companion of Fung Pao-Yu's, "arranged a dinner in an amphitheater where half of us played servants to the other half, with forfeits for those who didn't show. It was the result of a bet. Like the bad old days. Did you know there were once *five billion people* in this world?"

"The gulls," said Ilse, "are mating on the Isle of Skye." There were murmurs of appreciative interest. Chi began to develop an erection and everyone laughed. Old Al wanted music and Velet didn't; what might have been a quarrel was ended by Ilse's furiously boxing their ears. She stalked off to the nursery.

"Leslie Smith and I are both old-fashioned," said Old Al, "because neither of us believes in gabbing. Chi—your theater?"

"We're turning people away." He leaned forward earnestly, tapping his fingers on his crossed knees. "I swear, some of them are threatening to commit suicide."

"It's a choice," said Velet reasonably.

Leslie Smith had dropped her bowl. They retrieved it for her.

"Aiy, I remember—" said Pao-Yu. "What I remember! We've been eating dried mush for three days, tax-issue. Did you know one of my dads killed himself?"

"No!" said Velet, surprised.

"Years ago," said Pao-Yu. "He said he refused to live to see the time when chairs were reintroduced. He also wanted further genetic engineering, I believe, for even more intelligence. He did it out of spite,

I'm sure. I think he wrestled a shark. Jannina, is this tax-issue food? Is it this year's style tax-issue sauce?"

"No, next year's," said Jannina snappishly. Really, some people! She slipped into Finnish, to show up Pao-Yu's pronunciation. "Isn't that so?" she asked Leslie Smith.

Leslie Smith stared at her.

More charitably Jannina informed them all, in Finnish, that the Komarovs had withdrawn their membership in a food group, except for Ann, who had taken out an individual, because what the dickens, who had the time? And tax-issue won't kill you. As they finished, they dropped their dishes into the garbage field and Velet stripped a layer off the rug. In that went, too. Indulgently Old Al began a round: "Red."

"Sun," said Pao-Yu.

"The Red Sun Is," said one of the triplet Komarovs.

"The Red Sun Is—High," said Chi.

"The Red Sun Is High, The," Velet said.

"The Red Sun Is High, The Blue—" Jannina finished. They had come to Leslie Smith, who could either complete it or keep it going. She chose to declare for complete, not shyly (as before) but simply by pointing to Old Al.

"The red sun is high, the blue," he said. "Subtle! Another: *Ching*."

"*Nü.*"

"*Ching nü ch'i.*"

"*Ching nü ch'i ch'u.*"

"*Ssu.*"

"*Wo.*"

"*Ssu wo yü.*"

It had got back to Leslie Smith again. She said, "I can't do that."

Jannina got up and began to dance—I'm nice in my nasty way, she thought. The others wandered toward the pool and Ilse reappeared on the nursery monitor screen, saying, "I'm coming down."

Somebody said, "What time is it in the Argentine?"

"Five A.M."

"I think I want to go."

"Go, then."

"I go."

"Go well."

The red light over the antechamber door flashed and went out.

"Say, why'd you leave your other family?" said Ilse, settling near Old Al where the wall curved out. Ann, for whom it was evening, would be home soon; Chi, who had just got up a few hours back in western America, would stay somewhat longer; nobody ever knew Old Al's schedule and Jannina herself had lost track of the time. She would stay up until she felt sleepy. She followed a rough twenty-eight-hour day, Phuong (what a nuisance that must be at rehearsals!) a twenty-two hour one, Ilse six hours up, six hours dozing. Jannina nodded, heard the question, and shook herself awake.

"I didn't leave them. They left me."

There was a murmur of sympathy around the pool.

"They left me because I was stupid," said Leslie Smith. Her hands were clasped passively in her lap. She looked very genteel in her blue body paint, a stocky young woman with small breasts. One of the triplet Komarovs, flirting in the pool with the other two, choked. The non-aquatic members of the family crowded around Leslie Smith, touching her with little, soft touches; they kissed her and exposed to her all their unguarded surfaces, their bellies, their soft skins. Old Al kissed her hands. She sat there, oddly unmoved. "But I *am* stupid," she said. "You'll find out."

Jannina put her hands over her ears. "A masochist!" Leslie Smith looked at Jannina with a curious, stolid look. Then she looked down and absently began to rub one blue-painted knee.

"Luggage!" shouted Chi, clapping his hands together, and the triplets dashed for the stairs.

"No, I'm going to bed," said Leslie Smith, "I'm tired," and quite simply, she got up and let Old Al lead her through the pink room, the blue room, the turtle-and-pet room (temporarily empty), the trash room, and all the other rooms, to the guest room with the view that looked out over the cold hillside to the terraced plantings below.

"The best maker of hand-blown glass in the world," said Chi, "has killed in a duel the second-best maker of hand-blown glass in the world."

"For joining the movement to ceramics," said Ilse, awed. Jannina felt a thrill: this was the bitter stuff under the surface of life, the fury that boiled up. A bitter struggle is foreseen in the global economy. Good old tax-issue stuff goes toddling along, year after year. She was, thought Jannina, extraordinarily grateful to be living now, to be in such an extraordinary world, to have so long to go before her death. So much to do!

Old Al came back into the living room. "She's in bed."

"Well, which of us—?" said the triplet-who-had-choked, looking mischievously around from one to the other.

Chi was about to volunteer, out of his usual conscientiousness, thought Jannina, but then she found herself suddenly standing up, and then just as suddenly sitting down again. "I just don't have the nerve," she said.

Velet Komarov walked on his hands toward the stairs, then somersaulted, and vanished, climbing. Old Al got off the hand-carved chest he had been sitting on and fetched a can of ale from it. He levered off the top and drank. Then he said, "She really is stupid, you know." Jannina's skin crawled.

"Oooh," said Pao-Yu. Chi betook himself to the kitchen and returned with a paper folder. It was coated with frost. He shook it, then impatiently dropped it in the pool. The redheaded triplet swam over and took it. "Smith, Leslie," he said. "Adam Two, Leslie. Yee, Leslie. Schwarzen, Leslie."

"What on earth does the woman *do* with herself besides get married?" exclaimed Pao-Yu.

"She drove a hovercraft," said Chi, "in some out-of-the-way places around the Pacific until the last underground stations were completed. Says when she was a child she wanted to drive a truck."

"Well, you can," said the redheaded triplet, "can't you? Go to Arizona or the Rockies and drive on the roads. The sixty-mile-an-hour road. The thirty-mile-an-hour road. Great artistic recreation."

"That's not work," said Old Al.

"Couldn't she take care of children?" said the redheaded triplet. Ilse sniffed.

"Stupidity's not much of a recommendation for that," Chi said. "Let's see—no children. No, of course not. Overfulfilled her tax work on quite a few routine matters here. Kim, Leslie. Went to Moscow and contracted a double with some fellow, didn't last. Registered as a singleton, but that didn't last, either. She said she was lonely, and they were exploiting her."

Old Al nodded.

"Came back and lived informally with a theater group. Left them. Went into psychotherapy. Volunteered for several experimental, intelligence-enhancing programs, was turned down—hum!—sixty-five come the winter solstice, muscular coordination average, muscular development above average, no overt mental pathology, empathy average, prognosis: poor. No, wait a minute, it says, 'More of the same.' Well, that's the same thing."

"What I want to know," added Chi, raising his head, "is who met Miss Smith and decided we needed the lady in this Ice Palace of ours?"

Nobody answered. Jannina was about to say, "Ann, perhaps?" but as she felt the urge to do so—surely it wasn't right to turn somebody off like that, *just* for that!—Chi (who had been flipping through the dossier) came to the last page, with the tax-issue stamp absolutely unmistakable, woven right into the paper.

"The computer did," said Pao-Yu, and she giggled idiotically.

"Well," said Jannina, jumping to her feet, "tear it up, my dear, or give it to me, and I'll tear it up for you. I think Miss Leslie Smith deserves from us the same as we'd give to anybody else, and I—for one—intend to go *right up there* . . ."

"After Velet," said Old Al dryly.

"*With* Velet, if I must," said Jannina, raising her eyebrows, "and if you don't know what's due a guest, Old Daddy, I do, and I intend to provide it. Lucky I'm keeping house this month, or you'd probably feed the poor woman nothing but seaweed."

"You won't like her, Jannina," said Old Al.

"I'll find that out for myself," said Jannina with some asperity, "and I'd advise you to do the same. Let her garden with you, Daddy. Let her squirt the foam for the new rooms. And now," she glared around at them, "I'm going to clean *this* room, so you'd better hop it, the lot of you," and dashing into the kitchen, she had the computer helmet on her head and the hoses going before they had even quite cleared the area of the pool. Then she took the helmet off and hung it on the wall. She flipped the cover off her wrist chronometer and satisfied herself as to the date. By the time she got back to the living room there was nobody there, only Leslie Smith's dossier lying on the carved chest. There was Leslie Smith; there was all of Leslie Smith. Jannina knocked on the wall cupboard and it revolved, presenting its openable side; she took out chewing gum. She started chewing and read about Leslie Smith.

Q: What have you seen in the last twenty years that you particularly liked?

A: I don't . . . the museum, I guess. At Oslo. I mean the . . . the mermaid and the children's museum, I don't care if it's a children's museum.

Q: Do you like children?

A: Oh, no.

(No disgrace in *that*, certainly, thought Jannina.)

Q: But you liked the children's museum.

A: Yes, sir . . . Yes . . . I liked those little animals, the fake ones, in the . . . the . . .

Q: The crèche?

A: Yes. And I liked the old things from the past, the murals with the flowers on them, they looked so real.

(Dear God!)

Q: You said you were associated with a theater group in Tokyo. Did you like it?

A: No . . . yes, I don't know.

Q: Were they nice people?

A: Oh, yes. They were awfully nice. But they got mad at me, I suppose . . . You see . . . well, I don't seem to get things quite right, I suppose. It's not so much the work, because I do that all right, but the other . . . the little things. It's always like that.

Q: What do you think is the matter?

A: You . . . I think you know.

Jannina flipped through the rest of it: Normal, normal, normal. Miss Smith was as normal as could be. Miss Smith was stupid. Not even very stupid. It was too damned bad. They'd probably have enough of Leslie Smith in a week, the Komarovs; yes, we'll have enough of her (Jannina thought), never able to catch a joke or a tone of voice, always clumsy, however willing, but never happy, never at ease. You can get a job for her, but what else can you get for her? Jannina glanced down at the dossier, already bored.

Q: You say you would have liked to live in the old days. Why is that? Do you think it would have been more adventurous, or would you like to have had lots of children?

A: I . . . you have no right . . . You're condescending.

Q: I'm sorry. I suppose you mean to say that then you would have been of above-average intelligence. You would, you know.

A: I know. I looked it up. Don't condescend to me.

Well, it *was* too damned bad! Jannina felt tears rise in her eyes. What had the poor woman done? It was just an accident, that was the horror of it, not even a tragedy, as if everyone's forehead had been stamped with the word "Choose" except for Leslie Smith's. She needs money, thought Jannina, thinking of the bad old days when people did things for money. Nobody could take to Leslie Smith. She wasn't insane enough to stand for being hurt or exploited. She wasn't clever enough to interest anybody. She certainly wasn't feebleminded; they couldn't very well put her into a hospital for the feebleminded or the brain-injured; in fact (Jannina was looking at the dossier again) they had tried to get her to work there, and she had taken a good, fast swing at the supervisor. She had said the people there were "hideous" and "revolting." She had no particular mechanical aptitudes. She had no particular interests. There was not even anything for her to read or watch; how could there be? She seemed (back at the dossier) to spend most of her time either working or going on public tours of exotic places, coral reefs and places like that. She enjoyed aqualung diving, but didn't do it often because that got boring. And that was that. There was, all in all, very little one could do for Leslie Smith. You might even say that in her own person she represented all the defects of the bad old days. Just imagine a world made up of such creatures! Jannina yawned. She slung the folder away and padded into the kitchen. Pity Miss Smith wasn't good-looking, also a pity that she was too well balanced (the folder said) to think that cosmetic surgery would make that much difference. Good for you, Leslie, you've got some sense, anyhow. Jannina, half-asleep, met Ann in the kitchen, beautiful, slender Ann reclining on a cushion with her so-chi and melon. Dear old Ann. Jannina nuzzled her brown shoulder. Ann poked her.

"Look," said Ann, and she pulled from the purse she wore at her waist a tiny fragment of cloth, stained rusty brown.

"What's that?"

"The second-best maker of hand-blown glass—oh, you know about it—well, this is his blood. When the best maker of hand-blown glass in the world had stabbed to the heart the second-best maker of hand-blown glass in the world, and cut his throat, too, some small children steeped handkerchiefs in his blood, and they're sending pieces all over the world."

"Good God!" cried Jannina.

"Don't worry, my dear," said lovely Ann, "it happens every decade or so. The children say they want to bring back cruelty, dirt, disease, glory, and hell. Then they forget about it. Every teacher knows that." She sounded amused. "I'm afraid I lost my temper today, though, and walloped your godchild. It's in the family, after all."

Jannina remembered when she herself had been much younger and Annie, barely a girl, had come to live with them. Ann had played at being a child and had put her head on Jannina's shoulder, saying, "Jannie, tell me a story." So Jannina now laid her head on Ann's breast and said, "Annie, tell me a story."

Ann said, "I told my children a story today, a creation myth. Every creation myth has to explain how death and suffering came into the world, so that's what this one is about. In the beginning, the first man and the first woman lived very contentedly on an island until one day they began to feel hungry. So they called to the turtle who holds up the world to send them something to eat. The turtle sent them a mango and they ate it and were satisfied, but the next day they were hungry again.

" 'Turtle,' they said, 'send us something to eat.' So the turtle sent them a coffee berry. They thought it was pretty small, but they ate it anyway and were satisfied. The third day they called on the turtle again and this time the turtle sent them two things: a banana and a stone. The man and woman did not know which to choose, so they asked the turtle which they should eat. 'Choose,' said the turtle. So they chose the banana and ate that, but they used the stone for a game of catch. Then the turtle said, 'You should have chosen the stone. If you had chosen the stone, you would have lived forever, but now that you have chosen the banana, Death and Pain have entered the world, and it is not I that can stop them.' "

Jannina was crying. Lying in the arms of her old friend, she wept bitterly, with a burning sensation in her chest and the taste of death and ashes in her mouth. It was awful. It was horrible. She remembered the embryo shark she had seen when she was three, in the Auckland Cetacean Research Center, and how she had cried then. She didn't know what she was crying about. "Don't, don't!" she sobbed.

"Don't what?" said Ann affectionately. "Silly Jannina!"

"Don't, don't," cried Jannina, "don't, it's true, it's true!" and she went on in this way for several more minutes. Death had entered the world. Nobody could stop it. It was ghastly. She did not mind for herself but for others, for her godchild, for instance. He was going to die. He was going to suffer. Nothing could help him. Duel, suicide, or old age, it was all the same. "This life!" gasped Jannina. "This awful life!" The thought of death became entwined somehow with Leslie Smith, in bed upstairs, and Jannina began to cry afresh, but eventually the thought of Leslie Smith calmed her. It brought her back to herself. She wiped her eyes with her hand. She sat up.

"Do you want a smoke?" said beautiful Ann, but Jannina shook her head. She began to laugh. Really, the whole thing was quite ridiculous.

"There's this Leslie Smith," she said, dry-eyed. "We'll have to find a tactful way to get rid of her. It's idiotic, in this day and age."

And she told lovely Annie all about it.

The Funeral

KATE WILHELM

No one could say exactly how old Madam Westfall was when she finally died. At least one hundred twenty, it was estimated. At the very least. For twenty years Madam Westfall had been a shell containing the very latest products of advances made in gerontology, and now she was dead. What lay on the viewing dais was merely a painted, funereally garbed husk.

"She isn't real," Carla said to herself. "It's a doll or something. It isn't really Madam Westfall." She kept her head bowed, and didn't move her lips, but she said the words over and over. She was afraid to look at a dead person. *The second time they slaughtered all those who bore arms, unguided, mindless now, but lethal with the arms caches that they used indiscriminately.* Carla felt goose bumps along her arms and legs. She wondered if anyone else had been hearing the old Teacher's words.

The line moved slowly, all the girls in their long gray skirts had their heads bowed, their hands clasped. The only sound down the corridor was the sush-sush of slippers on plastic flooring, the occasional rustle of a skirt.

The Viewing Room had a pale green, plastic floor, frosted-green plastic walls, and floor-to-ceiling windows that were now slits of brilliant light from a westering sun. All the furniture had been taken from the room, all the ornamentation. There were no flowers, nothing but the dais, and the bedlike box covered by a transparent shield. And the Teachers. Two at the dais, others between the light strips, at the doors. Their white hands clasped against black garb, heads bowed, hair slicked against each head, straight parts emphasizing bilateral symmetry. The Teachers didn't move, didn't look at the dais, at the girls parading past it.

Carla kept her head bowed, her chin tucked almost inside the V of her collarbone. The serpentine line moved steadily, very slowly. "She isn't real," Carla said to herself, desperately now.

She crossed the line that was the cue to raise her head; it felt too heavy to lift, her neck seemed paralyzed. When she did move, she heard a joint crack, and although her jaws suddenly ached, she couldn't relax.

The second green line. She turned her eyes to the right and looked at the incredibly shrunken, hardly human mummy. She felt her stomach lurch and for a moment she thought she was going to vomit. "She isn't real. It's a doll. She isn't real!" The third line. She bowed her head, pressed her chin hard against her collarbone, making it hurt. She couldn't swallow now, could hardly breathe. The line proceeded to the South Door and through it into the corridor.

She turned left at the South Door, and with her eyes downcast, started the walk back to her genetics class. She looked neither right nor left, but she could hear others moving in the same direction, slippers on plastic, the swish of a skirt, and when she passed by the door to the garden she heard laughter of some Ladies who had come to observe the viewing. She slowed down.

She felt the late sun hot on her skin at the open door and with a sideways glance, not moving her head, she looked quickly into the glaring greenery, but could not see them. Their laughter sounded like music as she went past the opening.

"That one, the one with the blue eyes and straw-colored hair. Stand up, girl."

Carla didn't move, didn't realize she was being addressed until a Teacher pulled her from her seat.

"Don't hurt her! Turn around, girl. Raise your skirts, higher. Look at me, child. Look up, let me see your face . . ."

"She's too young for choosing," said the Teacher, examining Carla's bracelet. "Another year, Lady."

"A pity. She'll coarsen in a year's time. The fuzz is so soft right now, the flesh so tender. Oh, well . . ." She moved away, flicking a red skirt about her thighs, her red-clad legs narrowing to tiny ankles, flashing silver slippers with heels that were like icicles. She smelled . . . Carla didn't know any words to describe how she smelled. She drank in the fragrance hungrily.

"Look at me, child. Look up, let me see your face . . ." The words sang through her mind over and over. At night, falling asleep she thought of the face, drawing it up from the deep black, trying to hold it in focus: white skin, pink cheek ridges, silver eyelids, black lashes longer than she had known lashes could be, silver-pink lips, three silver spots—one at the corner of her left eye, another at the corner of her mouth, the third like a dimple in the satiny cheek. Silver hair that was loose, in waves about her face, that rippled with life of its own when she moved. If only she had been allowed to touch the hair, to run her finger over that cheek . . . The dream that began with the music of the Lady's laughter, ended with the nightmare of her other words: "She'll coarsen in a year's time . . ."

After that Carla had watched the changes take place on and within her body, and she understood what the Lady had meant. Her once smooth legs began to develop hair; it grew under her arms, and, most shameful, it sprouted as a dark, coarse bush under her belly. She wept. She tried to pull the hairs out, but it hurt too much, and made her skin sore and raw. Then she started to bleed, and she lay down and waited to die, and was happy that she would die. Instead, she was ordered to the infirmary and was forced to attend a lecture on feminine hygiene. She watched in stony-faced silence while the Doctor added the new information to her bracelet. The Doctor's face was smooth and pink, her eyebrows pale, her lashes so colorless and stubby that they were almost invisible. On her chin was a brown mole with two long hairs. She wore a straight blue-gray gown that hung from her shoulders to the floor. Her drab hair was pulled back tightly from her face, fastened in a hard bun at the back of her neck. Carla hated her. She hated the Teachers. Most of all she hated herself. She yearned for maturity.

Madam Westfall had written: Maturity brings grace, beauty, wisdom, happiness. Immaturity means ugliness, unfinished beings with potential only, wholly dependent upon and subservient to the mature citizens.

There was a True-False quiz on the master screen in front of the classroom. Carla took her place quickly and touch-typed her ID number on the small screen of her machine.

She scanned the questions, and saw that they were all simple declarative statements of truth. Her stylus ran down the True column of her answer screen and it was done. She wondered why they were killing time like this, what they were waiting for. Madam Westfall's death had thrown everything off schedule.

Paperlike brown skin, wrinkled and hard, with lines crossing lines, vertical, horizontal, diagonal, leaving little islands of flesh, hardly enough to coat the bones. Cracked voice, incomprehensible: *they took away the music from the air . . . voices from the skies . . . erased pictures that move . . . boxes that sing and sob . . .* Crazy talk. And, . . . *only one left that knows. Only one.*

Madam Trudeau entered the classroom and Carla understood why the class had been personalized that period. The Teacher had been waiting for Madam Trudeau's appearance. The girls rose hurriedly. Madam Trudeau motioned for them to be seated once more.

"The following girls attended Madam Westfall during the past five years." She read from a list. Carla's name was included on her list. On finishing it, she asked, "Is there anyone who attended Madam Westfall whose name I did not read?"

There was a rustle from behind Carla. She kept her gaze fastened on Madam Trudeau. "Name?" the Teacher asked.

"Luella, Madam."

"You attended Madam Westfall? When?"

"Two years ago, Madam. I was a relief for Sonya, who became ill suddenly."

"Very well." Madam Trudeau added Luella's name to her list. "You will all report to my office at eight A.M. tomorrow morning. You will be excused from classes and duties at that time. Dismissed." With a bow she excused herself to the class Teacher and left the room.

Carla's legs twitched and ached. Her swim class was at eight each morning and she had missed it, had been sitting on the straight chair for almost two hours, when finally she was told to go into Madam Trudeau's office. None of the other waiting girls looked up when she rose and followed the attendant from the anteroom. Madam Trudeau was seated at an oversized desk that was completely bare, with a mirrorlike finish. Carla stood before it with her eyes downcast, and she could see Madam Trudeau's face reflected from the surface of the desk. Madam Trudeau was looking at a point over Carla's head, unaware that the girl was examining her features.

"You attended Madam Westfall altogether seven times during the past four years, is that correct?"

"I think it is, Madam."

"You aren't certain?"

"I . . . I don't remember, Madam."

"I see. Do you recall if Madam Westfall spoke to you during any of those times?"

"Yes, Madam."

"Carla, you are shaking. Are you frightened?"

"No, Madam."

"Look at me, Carla."

Carla's hands tightened, and she could feel her fingernails cutting into her hands. She thought of the pain, and stopped shaking. Madam Trudeau had pasty, white skin, with peaked black eyebrows, sharp black eyes, black hair. Her mouth was wide and full, her nose long and narrow. As she studied the girl before her, it seemed to Carla that something changed in her expression, but she couldn't say what it was, or how it now differed from what it had been a moment earlier. A new intensity perhaps, a new interest.

"Carla, I've been looking over your records. Now that you are fourteen it is time to decide on your future. I shall propose your name for the Teachers' Academy on the completion of your current courses. As my protégé, you will quit the quarters you now occupy and attend me in my chambers . . ." She narrowed her eyes. "What is the matter with you, girl? Are you ill?"

"No, Madam. I . . . I had hoped . . . I mean, I designated my choice last month. I thought . . ."

Madam Trudeau looked to the side of her desk where a records screen was lighted. She scanned the report, and her lips curled derisively. "A Lady. You would be a Lady!" Carla felt a blush fire her face, and suddenly her palms were wet with sweat. Madam Trudeau laughed, a sharp barking sound. She said, "The girls who attended Madam Westfall in life, shall attend her in death. You will be on duty in the Viewing Room for two hours each day, and when the procession starts for the burial services in Scranton, you will be part of the entourage. Meanwhile, each day for an additional two hours immediately following your attendance in the Viewing Room you will meditate on the words of wisdom you have heard from Madam Westfall, and you will write down every word she ever spoke in your presence. For this purpose there will be placed a notebook and a pen in your cubicle, which you will use for no other reason. You will discuss this with no one except me. You, Carla, will prepare to move to my quarters immediately, where a learning cubicle will be awaiting you. Dismissed."

Her voice became sharper as she spoke, and when she finished the words were staccato. Carla bowed and turned to leave.

"Carla, you will find that there are certain rewards in being chosen as a Teacher."

Carla didn't know if she should turn and bow again, or stop where she was, or continue. When she hesitated, the voice came again, shorter, raspish. "Go. Return to your cubicle."

The first time, they slaughtered only the leaders, the rousers, . . . would be enough to defuse the bomb, leave the rest silent and powerless and malleable . . .

Carla looked at the floor before her, trying to control the trembling in her legs. Madam Westfall hadn't moved, hadn't spoken. She was dead, gone. The only sound was the sush-sush of slippers. The green plastic floor was a glare that hurt her eyes. The air was heavy and smelled of death. Smelled the Lady, drank in the fragrance, longed to touch her. Pale, silvery pink lips, soft, shiny, with two high peaks on the upper lip. The Lady stroked her face with fingers that were soft and cool and gentle . . . *when their eyes become soft with unspeakable desires and their bodies show signs of womanhood, then let them have their duties chosen for them, some to bear the young for the society, some to become Teachers, some Nurses, Doctors, some to be taken as Lovers by the citizens, some to be . . .*

Carla couldn't control the sudden start that turned her head to look at the mummy. The room seemed to waver, then steadied again. The tremor in her legs became stronger, harder to stop. She pressed her knees together hard, hurting them where bone dug into flesh and skin. Fingers plucking at the coverlet. Plucking bones, brown bones with horny nails.

Water. Girl, give me water. Pretty, pretty. You would have been killed, you would have. Pretty. The last time they left no one over ten. No one at all. Ten to twenty-five.

Pretty. Carla said it to herself. Pretty. She visualized it as p-r-i-t-y. *Pity* with an *r*. Scanning the dictionary for p-r-i-t-y. Nothing. Pretty. *Afraid of shiny, pretty faces. Young, pretty faces.*

The trembling was all through Carla. Two hours. Eternity. She had stood here forever, would die here, unmoving, trembling, aching. A sigh and the sound of a body falling softly to the floor. Soft body crumbling so easily. Carla didn't turn her head. It must be Luella. So frightened of the mummy. She'd had nightmares every night since Madam Westfall's death. What made a body stay upright, when it fell so easily? Take it out, the thing that held it together, and down, down. Just to let go, to know what to take out and allow the body to fall like that into sleep. Teachers moved across her field of vision, two of them in their black gowns. Sush-sush. Returned with Luella, or someone, between them. No sound. Sush-sush.

The new learning cubicle was an exact duplicate of the old one. Cot, learning machine, chair, partitioned-off commode and washbasin. And new, the notebook and pen. Carla had never had a notebook and pen before. There was the stylus that was attached to the learning machine, and the lighted square in which to write, that then vanished into the machine. She turned the blank pages of the notebook, felt the paper between her fingers, tore a tiny corner off one of the back pages, examined it closely, the jagged edge, the texture of the fragment; she tasted it. She studied the pen just as minutely; it had a pointed, smooth end, and it wrote black. She made a line, stopped to admire it, and crossed it with another line. She wrote very slowly, "Carla," started to put down her number, the one on her bracelet, then stopped in confusion. She never had considered it before, but she had no last name, none that she knew. She drew three heavy lines over the two digits she had put down.

At the end of the two hours of meditation she had written her name a number of times, had filled three pages with it, in fact, and had written one of the things that she could remember hearing from the gray lips of Madam Westfall: "Non-citizens are the property of the state."

The next day the citizens started to file past the dais. Carla breathed deeply, trying to sniff the fragrance of the passing Ladies, but they were too distant. She watched their feet, clad in shoes of rainbow colors: pointed toes, stiletto heels; rounded toes, carved heels; satin, sequined slippers . . . And just before her duty ended for the day, the Males started to enter the room.

She heard a gasp, Luella again. She didn't faint this time, merely gasped once. Carla saw the feet and legs at the same time, and she looked up to see a male citizen. He was very tall and thick and was dressed in the blue and white clothing of a Doctor of Law. He moved into the sunlight and there was a glitter from gold at his wrists, and his neck, and the gleam of a smooth polished head. He turned past the dais and his eyes met Carla's. She felt herself go light-headed and hurriedly she ducked her head and clenched her hands. She thought he was standing still, looking at her, and she could feel her heart thumping hard. Her relief arrived then and she crossed the room as fast as she could without appearing indecorous.

Carla wrote: "Why did he scare me so much? Why have I never seen a Male before? Why does everyone else wear colors while the girls and the Teachers wear black and gray?"

She drew a wavering line-figure of a man, and stared at it, and then x-ed it out. Then she looked at the sheet of paper with dismay. Now she had four ruined sheets of paper to dispose of.

Had she angered him by staring? Nervously she tapped on the paper and tried to remember what his face had been like. Had he been frowning? She couldn't remember. Why couldn't she think of anything to write for Madam Trudeau? She bit the end of the pen and then wrote slowly, very carefully: *Society may dispose of its property as it chooses, following discussion with at least three members, and following permission which is not to be arbitrarily denied.*

Had Madam Westfall ever said that? She didn't know, but she had to write something, and that was the sort of thing that Madam Westfall had quoted at great length. She threw herself down on the cot and stared at the ceiling. For three days she had kept hearing the Madam's dead voice, but now when she needed to hear her again, nothing.

Sitting in the straight chair, alert for any change in the position of the ancient one, watchful, afraid of the old Teacher. Cramped, tired, and sleepy. Half listening to mutterings, murmurings of exhaled and inhaled breaths that sounded like words that made no sense. . . . *Mama said hide child, hide don't move and Stevie wanted a razor for his birthday and Mama said you're too young, you're only nine and he said no Mama I'm thirteen don't you remember and Mama said hide child hide don't move at all and they came in hating pretty faces . . .*

Carla sat up and picked up the pen again, then stopped. When she heard the words, they were so clear in her head, but as soon as they ended, they faded away. She wrote: "hating pretty faces . . . hide child . . . only nine." She stared at the words and drew a line through them.

Pretty faces. Madam Westfall had called her pretty, pretty.

The chimes for social hour were repeated three times and finally Carla opened the door of her cubicle and took a step into the anteroom where the other protégés already had gathered. There were five. Carla didn't know any of them, but she had seen all of them from time to time in and around the school grounds. Madam Trudeau was sitting on a high-backed chair that was covered with black. She blended into it, so that only her hands and her face seemed apart from the chair, dead white hands and face. Carla bowed to her and stood uncertainly at her own door.

"Come in, Carla. It is social hour. Relax. This is Wanda, Louise, Stephanie, Mary, Dorothy." Each girl inclined her head slightly as her name was mentioned. Carla couldn't tell afterward which name went with which girl. Two of them wore the black-striped overskirt that meant they were in the Teachers' Academy. The other three still wore the gray of the lower school, as did Carla, with black bordering the hems.

"Carla doesn't want to be a Teacher," Madam Trudeau said drily. "She prefers the paint box of a Lady." She smiled with her mouth only. One of the academy girls laughed. "Carla, you are not the first to envy the paint box and the bright clothes of the Ladies. I have something to show you. Wanda, the film."

The girl who had laughed touched a button on a small table and on one of the walls a picture was projected. Carla caught her breath. It was a Lady, all gold and white, gold hair, gold eyelids, filmy white gown that ended just above her knees. She turned and smiled, holding out both hands, flashing jeweled fingers, long, gleaming nails that came to points. Then she reached up and took off her hair.

Carla felt that she would faint when the golden hair came off in the Lady's hands, leaving short, straight brown hair. She placed the gold hair on a ball, and then, one by one, stripped off the long gleaming nails, leaving her hands just hands, bony and ugly. The Lady peeled off her eyelashes and brows, and then patted a brown, thick coating of something on her face, and, with its removal, revealed pale skin with wrinkles about her eyes, with hard, deep lines aside her nose down to her mouth that had also changed, had become small and mean. Carla wanted to shut her eyes, turn away, and go back to her cubicle, but she didn't dare move. She could feel Madam Trudeau's stare, and the gaze seemed to burn.

The Lady took off the swirling gown, and under it was a garment Carla never had seen before that covered her from her breasts to her thighs. The stubby fingers worked at fasteners, and finally got the garment off, and there was her stomach, bigger, bulging, with cruel red lines where the garment had pinched and squeezed her. Her breasts drooped almost to her waist. Carla couldn't stop her eyes, couldn't make them not see, couldn't make herself not look at the rest of the repulsive body.

Madam Trudeau stood up and went to her door. "Show Carla the other two films." She looked at Carla then and said, "I order you to watch. I shall quiz you on the contents." She left the room.

The other two films showed the same Lady at work. First with a protégé, then with a male citizen. When they were over Carla stumbled back to her cubicle and vomited repeatedly until she was exhausted. She had nightmares that night.

How many days, she wondered, have I been here now? She no longer trembled, but became detached almost as soon as she took her place between two of the tall windows. She didn't try to catch a whiff of the fragrance of the Ladies, or try to get a glimpse of the Males. She had chosen one particular spot in the floor on which to concentrate, and she didn't shift her gaze from it.

They were old and full of hate, and they said, let us remake them in our image, and they did.

Madam Trudeau hated her, despised her. Old and full of hate . . .

"Why were you not chosen to become a Woman to bear young?"

"I am not fit, Madam. I am weak and timid."

"Look at your hips, thin, like a Male's hips. And your breasts, small and hard." Madam Trudeau turned away in disgust. "Why were you not chosen to become a Professional, a Doctor, or a Technician?"

"I am not intelligent enough, Madam. I require many hours of study to grasp the mathematics."

"So. Weak, frail, not too bright. Why do you weep?"

"I don't know, Madam. I am sorry."

"Go to your cubicle. You disgust me."

Staring at a flaw in the floor, a place where an indentation distorted the light, creating one very small oval shadow, wondering when the ordeal would end, wondering why she couldn't fill the notebook with the many things that Madam Westfall had said, things that she could remember here, and could not remember when she was in her cubicle with pen poised over the notebook.

Sometimes Carla forgot where she was, found herself in the chamber of Madam Westfall, watching the ancient one struggle to stay alive, forcing breaths in and out, refusing to admit death. Watching the incomprehensible dials and tubes and bottles of fluids with lowering levels, watching needles that vanished into flesh, tubes that disappeared under the bedclothes, that seemed to writhe now and again with a secret life, listening to the mumbling voice, the groans and sighs, the meaningless words.

Three times they rose against the children and three times slew them until there were none left, none at all because the contagion had spread and all over ten were infected and carried radios . . .

Radios? A disease? Infected with radios, spreading it among young people?

And Mama said hide child hide and don't move and put this in the cave too and don't touch it.

Carla's relief came and numbly she walked from the Viewing Room. She watched the movement of the black border of her skirt as she walked, and it seemed that the blackness crept up her legs, enveloped her middle, climbed her front until it reached her neck, and then it strangled her. She clamped her jaws hard and continued to walk her measured pace.

The girls who had attended Madam Westfall in life were on duty throughout the school ceremonies after the viewing. They were required to stand in a line behind the dais. There were eulogies to the patience and firmness of the first Teacher. Eulogies to her wisdom in setting up the rules of the school. Carla tried to keep her attention on the speakers, but she was so tired and drowsy that she heard only snatches. Then she was jolted into awareness. Madam Trudeau was talking.

". . . a book that will be the guide to all future Teachers, showing them the way through personal tribulations and trials to achieve the serenity that was Madam Westfall's. I am honored by this privilege, in choosing me and my apprentices to accomplish this end . . ."

Carla thought of the gibberish that she had been putting down in her notebook and she blinked back tears of shame. Madam Trudeau should have told them why she wanted the information. She would have to go back over it all and destroy all the nonsense that she had written down.

Late that afternoon the entourage formed that would accompany Madam Westfall to her final ceremony in Scranton, her native city, where her burial would return her to her family.

Madam Trudeau had an interview with Carla before departure. "You will be in charge of the other girls," she said. "I expect you to maintain order. You will report any disturbance, or any infringement of rules immediately, and if that is not possible, if I am occupied, you will personally impose order in my name."

"Yes, Madam."

"Very well. During the journey the girls will travel together in a compartment of the tube. Talking will be permitted, but no laughter, no childish play. When we arrive at the Scranton home, you will be given rooms with cots. Again you will all comport yourselves with the dignity of the office which you are ordered to fulfill at this time."

Carla felt excitement mount within her as the girls lined up to take their places along the sides of the casket. They went with it to a closed limousine where they sat knee to knee, unspeaking, hot, to be taken over smooth highways for an hour to the tube. Madam Westfall had refused to fly in life, and was granted the same rights in death, so her body was to be transported from Wilmington to Scranton by the rocket tube. As soon as the girls had accompanied the casket to its car and were directed to their own compartment, their voices raised in a babble. It was the first time any of them had left the school grounds since entering them at the age of five.

Ruthie was going to work in the infants' wards, and she turned faintly pink and soft looking when she talked about it. Luella was a music apprentice already, having shown skill on the piano at an early age. Lorette preened herself slightly and announced that she had been chosen as a Lover by a Gentleman. She would become a Lady one day. Carla stared at her curiously, wondering at her pleased look, wondering if she had not been shown the films yet. Lorette was blue-eyed, with pale hair, much the same build as Carla. Looking at her, Carla could imagine her in soft dresses, with her mouth painted, her hair covered by the other hair that was cloud soft and shiny . . . She looked at the girl's cheeks flushed with excitement at the thought of her future, and she knew that with or without the paint box, Lorette would be a Lady whose skin would be smooth, whose mouth would be soft . . .

"The fuzz is so soft now, the flesh so tender." She remembered the scent, the softness of the Lady's hands, the way her skirt moved about her red-clad thighs.

She bit her lip. But she didn't want to be a Lady. She couldn't ever think of them again without loathing and disgust. She was chosen to be a Teacher.

They said it is the duty of society to prepare its non-citizens for citizenship but it is recognized that there are those who will not meet the requirements and society itself is not to be blamed for those occasional failures that must accrue.

She took out her notebook and wrote the words in it.

"Did you just remember something else she said?" Lisa asked. She was the youngest of the girls, only ten, and had attended Madam Westfall one time. She seemed to be very tired.

Carla looked over what she had written, and then read it aloud. "It's from the school rules book," she said. "Maybe changed a little, but the same meaning. You'll study it in a year or two."

Lisa nodded. "You know what she said to me? She said I should go hide in the cave, and never lose my birth certificate. She said I should never tell anyone where the radio is." She frowned. "Do you know what a cave is? And a radio?"

"You wrote it down, didn't you? In the notebook?"

Lisa ducked her head. "I forgot again. I remembered it once and then forgot again until now." She searched through her cloth travel bag for her notebook and when she didn't find it, she dumped the contents on the floor to search more carefully. The notebook was not there.

"Lisa, when did you have it last?"

"I don't know. A few days ago. I don't remember."

"When Madam Trudeau talked to you the last time, did you have it then?"

"No. I couldn't find it. She said if I didn't have it the next time I was called for an interview, she'd whip me. But I can't find it!" She broke into tears and threw herself down on her small heap of belongings. She beat her fists on them and sobbed. "She's going to whip me and I can't find it. I can't. It's gone."

Carla stared at her. She shook her head. "Lisa, stop that crying. You couldn't have lost it. Where? There's no place to lose it. You didn't take it from your cubicle, did you?"

The girl sobbed louder. "No. No. No. I don't know where it is."

Carla kneeled by her and pulled the child up from the floor to a squatting position. "Lisa, what did you put in the notebook? Did you play with it?"

Lisa turned chalky white and her eyes became very large, then she closed them, no longer weeping.

"So you used it for other things? Is that it? What sort of things?"

Lisa shook her head. "I don't know. Just things."

"All of it? The whole notebook?"

"I couldn't help it. I didn't know what to write down. Madam Westfall said too much. I couldn't write it all. She wanted to touch me and I was afraid of her and I hid under the chair and she kept calling me, 'Child, come here don't hide, I'm not one of them. Go to the cave and take it with you.' And she kept reaching for me with her hands. I . . . they were like chicken claws. She would have ripped me apart with them. She hated me. She said she hated me. She said I should have been killed with the others, why wasn't I killed with the others."

Carla, her hands hard on the child's shoulders, turned away from the fear and despair she saw on the girl's face. Ruthie pushed past her and hugged the child.

"Hush, hush, Lisa. Don't cry now. Hush. There, there."

Carla stood up and backed away. "Lisa, what sort of things did you put in the notebook?"

"Just things that I like. Snowflakes and flowers and designs."

"All right. Pick up your belongings and sit down. We must be nearly there. It seems like the tube is stopping."

Again they were shown from a closed compartment to a closed limousine and whisked over countryside that remained invisible to them. There was a drizzly rain falling when they stopped and got out of the car.

The Westfall house was a three-storied, pseudo-Victorian wooden building, with balconies and cupolas, and many chimneys. There was scaffolding about it, and one of the three porches had been torn away and was being replaced as restoration of the house, turning it into a national monument, progressed. The girls accompanied the casket to a gloomy, large room where the air was chilly and damp, and scant lighting cast deep shadows. After the casket had been positioned on the dais which also had accompanied it, the girls followed Madam Trudeau through narrow corridors, up narrow steps, to the third floor where two large rooms had been prepared for them, each containing seven cots.

Madam Trudeau showed them the bathroom that would serve their needs, told them good night, and motioned Carla to follow her. They descended the stairs to a second floor room that had black, massive furniture: a desk, two straight chairs, a bureau with a wavery mirror over it, and a large canopied bed.

Madam Trudeau paced the black floor silently for several minutes without speaking, then she swung around and said, "Carla, I heard every word that silly little girl said this afternoon. She drew pictures in her notebook! This is the third time the word cave has come up in reports of Madam Westfall's mutterings. Did she speak to you of caves?"

Carla's mind was whirling. How had she heard what they had said? Did maturity also bestow magical abilities? She said, "Yes, Madam, she spoke of hiding in a cave."

"Where is the cave, Carla? Where is it?"

"I don't know, Madam. She didn't say."

Madam Trudeau started to pace once more. Her pale face was drawn in lines of concentration that carved deeply into her flesh, two furrows straight up from the inner brows, other lines at the sides of her nose, straight to her chin, her mouth tight and hard. Suddenly she sat down and leaned back in the chair. "Carla, in the last four or five years Madam Westfall became childishly senile; she was no longer living in the present most of the time, but was reliving incidents in her past. Do you understand what I mean?"

Carla nodded, then said hastily, "Yes, Madam."

"Yes. Well, it doesn't matter. You know that I have been commissioned to write the biography of Madam Westfall, to immortalize her writings and her utterances. But there is a gap, Carla. A large gap in our knowledge, and until recently it seemed that the gap never would be filled in. When Madam Westfall was found as a child, wandering in a dazed condition, undernourished, almost dead from exposure, she did not know who she was, where she was from, anything about her past at all. Someone had put an identification bracelet on her arm, a steel bracelet that she could not remove, and that was the only clue there was about her origins. For ten years she received the best medical care and education available, and her intellect sparkled brilliantly, but she never regained her memory."

Madam Trudeau shifted to look at Carla. A trick of the lighting made her eyes glitter like jewels. "You have studied how she started her first school with eight students, and over the next century developed her teaching methods to the point of perfection that we now employ throughout the nation, in the Males' school as well as the Females'. Through her efforts Teachers have become the most respected of all citizens and the schools the most powerful of all institutions." A mirthless smile crossed her face, gone almost as quickly as it formed, leaving the deep shadows, lines, and the glittering eyes. "I honored you more than you yet realize when I chose you for my protégé."

The air in the room was too close and dank, smelled of moldering wood and unopened places. Carla continued to watch Madam Trudeau, but she was feeling light-headed and exhausted and the words seemed interminable to her. The glittering eyes held her gaze and she said nothing. The thought occurred to her that Madam Trudeau would take Madam Westfall's place as head of the school now.

"Encourage the girls to talk, Carla. Let them go on as much as they want about what Madam Westfall said, lead them into it if they stray from the point. Written reports have been sadly deficient." She stopped and looked questioningly at the girl. "Yes? What is it?"

"Then . . . I mean after they talk, are they to write? . . . Or should I try to remember and write it all down?"

"There will be no need for that," Madam Trudeau said. "Simply let them talk as much as they want."

"Yes, Madam."

"Very well. Here is a schedule for the coming days. Two girls on duty in the Viewing Room at all times from dawn until dark, yard exercise in the enclosed garden behind the building if the weather permits, kitchen duty, and so on. Study it, and direct the girls to their duties. On Saturday afternoon everyone will attend the burial, and on Sunday we return to the school. Now go."

Carla bowed, and turned to leave. Madam Trudeau's voice stopped her once more. "Wait, Carla. Come here. You may brush my hair before you leave."

Carla took the brush in numb fingers and walked obediently behind Madam Trudeau, who was loosening hair clasps that restrained her heavy black hair. It fell down her back like a dead snake, uncoiling slowly. Carla started to brush it.

"Harder, girl. Are you so weak that you can't brush hair?"

She plied the brush harder until her arm became heavy and then Madam Trudeau said, "Enough. You are a clumsy girl, awkward and stupid. Must I teach you everything, even how to brush one's hair properly?" She yanked the brush from Carla's hand and now there were two spots of color on her cheeks and her eyes were flashing. "Get out. Go! Leave me! On Saturday immediately following the funeral you will administer punishment to Lisa for scribbling in her notebook. Afterward report to me. And now get out of here!"

Carla snatched up the schedule and backed across the room, terrified of the Teacher who seemed demoniacal suddenly. She bumped into the other chair and nearly fell down. Madam Trudeau laughed shortly and cried, "Clumsy, awkward! You would be a Lady! You?"

Carla groped behind her for the doorknob and finally escaped into the hallway, where she leaned against the wall trembling too hard to move on. Something crashed into the door behind her and she stifled a scream and ran. The brush. Madam had thrown the brush against the door.

Madam Westfall's ghost roamed all night, chasing shadows in and out of rooms, making the floors creak with her passage, echoes of her voice drifting in and out of the dorm where Carla tossed restlessly. Twice she sat upright in fear, listening intently, not knowing why. Once Lisa cried out and she went to her and held her hand until the child quieted again. When dawn lighted the room Carla was awake and standing at the windows looking at the ring of mountains that encircled the city. Black shadows against the lesser black of the sky, they darkened, and suddenly caught fire from the sun striking their tips. The fire spread downward, went out and became merely light on the leaves that were turning red and gold. Carla turned from the view, unable to explain the pain that filled her. She awakened the first two girls who were to be on duty with Madam Westfall and after their quiet departure, returned to the window. The sun was all the way up now, but its morning light was soft; there were no hard outlines anywhere. The trees were a blend of colors with no individual boundaries, and rocks and earth melted together and were one. Birds were singing with the desperation of summer's end and winter's approach.

"Carla?" Lisa touched her arm and looked up at her with wide, fearful eyes. "Is she going to whip me?"

"You will be punished after the funeral," Carla said, stiffly. "And I should report you for touching me, you know."

The child drew back, looking down at the black border on Carla's skirt. "I forgot." She hung her head. "I'm . . . I'm so scared."

"It's time for breakfast, and after that we'll have a walk in the gardens. You'll feel better after you get out in the sunshine and fresh air."

"Chrysanthemums, dahlias, marigolds. No, the small ones there, with the brown fringes . . ." Luella pointed out the various flowers to the other girls. Carla walked in the rear, hardly listening, trying to keep her eye on Lisa, who also trailed behind. She was worried about the child. She had not slept well, had eaten no breakfast, and was so pale and wan that she didn't look strong enough to take the short garden walk with them.

Eminent personages came and went in the gloomy old house and huddled together to speak in lowered voices. Carla paid little attention to them. "I can change it after I have some authority," she said to a still inner self who listened and made no reply. "What can I do now? I'm property. I belong to the state, to Madam Trudeau and the school. What good if I disobey and am also whipped? Would that help any? I won't hit her hard." The inner self said nothing, but she thought she could hear a mocking laugh come from the mummy that was being honored.

They had all those empty schools, miles and miles of school halls where no feet walked, desks where no students sat, books that no students scribbled up, and they put the children in them and they could see immediately who couldn't keep up, couldn't learn the new ways and they got rid of them. Smart. Smart of them. They were smart and had the goods and the money and the hatred. My God, they hated. That's who wins, who hates most. And is more afraid. Every time.

Carla forced her arms not to move, her hands to remain locked before her, forced her head to stay bowed. The voice now went on and on and she couldn't get away from it.

. . . rained every day, cold freezing rain and Daddy didn't come back and Mama said, hide child, hide in the cave where it's warm, and don't move no matter what happens, don't move. Let me put it on your arm, don't take it off, never take it off show it to them if they find you show them make them look . . .

Her relief came and Carla left. In the wide hallway that led to the back steps she was stopped by a rough hand on her arm. "Damme, here's a likely one. Come here, girl. Let's have a look at you." She was spun around and the hand grasped her chin and lifted her head. "Did I say it! I could spot her all the way down the hall, now couldn't I. Can't hide what she's got with long skirts and that skinny hairdo, now can you? Didn't I spot her!" He laughed and turned Carla's head to the side and looked at her in profile, then laughed even louder.

She could see only that he was red faced, with bushy eyebrows, and thick gray hair. His hand holding her chin hurt, digging into her jaws at each side of her neck.

"Victor, turn her loose," the cool voice of a female said then. "She's been chosen already. An apprentice Teacher."

He pushed Carla from him, still holding her chin, and he looked down at the skirts with the broad black band at the bottom. He gave her a shove that sent her into the opposite wall. She clutched at it for support.

"Whose pet is she?" he said darkly.

"Trudeau's."

He turned and stamped away, not looking at Carla again. He wore the blue and white of a Doctor of Law. The female was a Lady in pink and black.

"Carla. Go upstairs." Madam Trudeau moved from an open doorway and stood before Carla. She looked up and down the shaking girl. "Now do you understand why I apprenticed you before this trip? For your own protection."

They walked to the cemetery on Saturday, a bright, warm day with golden light and the odor of burning leaves. Speeches were made, Madam Westfall's favorite music was played, and the services ended. Carla dreaded returning to the dormitory. She kept a close watch on Lisa who seemed but a shadow of herself. Three times during the night she had held the girl until her nightmares subsided, and each time she had stroked her fine hair and soft cheeks and murmured to her quieting words, and she knew it was only her own cowardice that prevented her saying that it was she who would administer the whipping. The first shovelful of earth was thrown on top the casket and everyone turned to leave the place, when suddenly the air was filled with raucous laughter, obscene chants, and wild music. It ended almost as quickly as it started, but the group was frozen until the mountain air became unnaturally still. Not even the birds were making a sound following the maniacal outburst.

Carla had been unable to stop the involuntary look that she cast about her at the woods that circled the cemetery. Who? Who would dare? Only a leaf or two stirred, floating downward on the gentle air effortlessly. Far in the distance a bird began to sing again, as if the evil spirits that had flown past were now gone.

"Madam Trudeau sent this up for you," Luella said nervously, handing Carla the rod. It was plastic, three feet long, thin, flexible. Carla looked at it and turned slowly to Lisa. The girl seemed to be swaying back and forth.

"I am to administer the whipping," Carla said. "You will undress now."

Lisa stared at her in disbelief, and then suddenly she ran across the room and threw herself on Carla, hugging her hard, sobbing. "Thank you, Carla. Thank you so much. I was so afraid, you don't know how afraid. Thank you. How did you make her let you do it? Will you be punished, too? I love you so much, Carla." She was incoherent in her relief and she flung off her gown and underwear and turned around.

Her skin was pale and soft, rounded buttocks, dimpled just above the fullness. She had no waist yet, no breasts, no hair on her baby body. Like a baby she had whimpered in the night, clinging tightly to Carla, burying her head in the curve of Carla's breasts.

Carla raised the rod and brought it down, as easily as she could. Anything was too hard. There was a red welt. The girl bowed her head lower but didn't whimper. She was holding the back of a chair, and it jerked when the rod struck.

It would be worse if Madam Trudeau was doing it, Carla thought.

She would try to hurt, would draw blood. Why? Why? The rod was hanging limply, and she knew it would be harder on both of them if she didn't finish it quickly. She raised it and again felt the rod bite into flesh, sending the vibration into her arm, through her body.

Again. The girl cried out, and a spot of blood appeared on her back. Carla stared at it in fascination and despair. She couldn't help it. Her arm wielded the rod too hard and she couldn't help it. She closed her eyes a moment, raised the rod, and struck again. Better. But the vibrations that had begun with the first blow increased, and she felt dizzy, and couldn't keep her eyes off the spot of blood that was trailing down the girl's back. Lisa was weeping now, her body was shaking. Carla felt a responsive tremor start within her.

Eight, nine. The excitement that stirred her was unnameable, unknowable, never before felt like this. Suddenly she thought of the Lady who had chosen her once, and scenes of the film she had been forced to watch flashed through her mind . . . *remake them in our image.* She looked about in that moment frozen in time, and she saw the excitement on some of the faces, on others fear, disgust, and revulsion. Her gaze stopped on Helga, who had her eyes closed, whose body was moving rhythmically. She raised the rod and brought it down as hard as she could, hitting the chair with a noise that brought everyone out of her own kind of trance. A sharp, cracking noise that was a finish.

"Ten!" she cried and threw the rod across the room.

Lisa turned and through brimming eyes, red, swollen, ugly with crying, said, "Thank you, Carla. It wasn't so bad."

Looking at her Carla knew hatred. It burned through her, distorted the image of what she saw. Inside her body the excitement found no outlet, and it flushed her face, made her hands numb, and filled her with hatred. She turned and fled.

Before Madam Trudeau's door, she stopped a moment, took a deep breath, and knocked. After several moments the door opened and Madam Trudeau came out. Her eyes were glittering more than ever, and there were two spots of color on her pasty cheeks.

"It is done? Let me look at you." Her fingers were cold and moist when she lifted Carla's chin. "Yes, I see. I see. I am busy now. Come back in half an hour. You will tell me about it. Half an hour." Carla never had seen a genuine smile on the Teacher's face before, and now when it came, it was more frightening than her frown was. Carla didn't move, but she felt as if every cell in her body had tried to pull back.

She bowed and turned to leave. Madam Trudeau followed her a

step and said in a low vibrant voice, "You felt it, didn't you? You know now, don't you?"

"Madam Trudeau, are you coming back?" The door behind her opened, and one of the Doctors of Law appeared there.

"Yes, of course." She turned and went back to the room.

Carla let herself into the small enclosed area between the second and third floor, then stopped. She could hear the voices of girls coming down the stairs, going on duty in the kitchen, or outside for evening exercises. She stopped to wait for them to pass, and she leaned against the wall tiredly. This space was two and a half feet square perhaps. It was very dank and hot. From here she could hear every sound made by the girls on the stairs. Probably that was why the second door had been added, to muffle the noise of those going up and down. The girls had stopped on the steps and were discussing the laughter and obscenities they had heard in the cemetery.

Carla knew that it was her duty to confront them, to order them to their duties, to impose proper silence on them in public places, but she closed her eyes and pressed her hand hard on the wood behind her for support and wished they would finish their childish prattle and go on. The wood behind her started to slide.

She jerked away. A sliding door? She felt it and ran her finger along the smooth paneling to the edge where there was now a six-inch opening as high as she could reach down to the floor. She pushed the door again and it slid easily, going between the two walls. When the opening was wide enough she stepped through it. The cave! She knew it was the cave that Madam Westfall had talked about incessantly.

The space was no more than two feet wide, and very dark. She felt the inside door and there was a knob on it, low enough for children to reach. The door slid as smoothly from the inside as it had from the outside. She slid it almost closed and the voices were cut off, but she could hear other voices, from the room on the other side of the passage. They were not clear. She felt her way farther, and almost fell over a box. She held her breath as she realized that she was hearing Madam Trudeau's voice:

"... be there. Too many independent reports of the old fool's babbling about it for there not to be something to it. Your men are incompetent."

"Trudeau, shut up. You scare the living hell out of the kids, but you don't scare me. Just shut up and accept the report. We've been over every inch of the hills for miles, and there's no cave. It was over a hundred years ago. Maybe there was one that the kids played in, but it's gone now. Probably collapsed."

"We have to be certain, absolutely certain."

"What's so important about it anyway? Maybe if you would give us more to go on we could make more progress."

"The reports state that when the militia came here, they found only Martha Westfall. They executed her on the spot without questioning her first. Fools! When they searched the house, they discovered that it was stripped. No jewels, no silver, diaries, papers. Nothing. Steve Westfall was dead. Dr. Westfall dead. Martha. No one has ever found the articles that were hidden, and when the child again appeared, she had true amnesia that never yielded to attempts to penetrate it."

"So, a few records, diaries. What are they to you?" There was silence, then he laughed. "The money! He took all his money out of the bank, didn't he."

"Don't be ridiculous. I want records, that's all. There's a complete ham radio, complete. Dr. Westfall was an electronics engineer as well as a teacher. No one could begin to guess how much equipment he hid before he was killed."

Carla ran her hand over the box, felt behind it. More boxes.

"Yeah, yeah. I read the reports, too. All the more reason to keep the search nearby. For a year before the end a close watch was kept on the house. They had to walk to wherever they hid the stuff. And I can just say again that there's no cave around here. It fell in."

"I hope so," Madam Trudeau said.

Someone knocked on the door, and Madam Trudeau called, "Come in."

"Yes, what is it? Speak up, girl."

"It is my duty to report, Madam, that Carla did not administer the full punishment ordered by you."

Carla's fists clenched hard. Helga.

"Explain," Madam Trudeau said sharply.

"She only struck Lisa nine times, Madam. The last time she hit the chair."

"I see. Return to your room."

The man laughed when the girl closed the door once more. "Carla is the golden one, Trudeau? The one who wears a single black band?"

"The one you manhandled earlier, yes."

"Insubordination in the ranks, Trudeau? Tut, tut. And your reports all state that you never have any rebellion. Never."

Very slowly Madam Trudeau said, "I have never had a student who didn't abandon any thoughts of rebellion under my guidance. Carla will be obedient. And one day she will be an excellent Teacher. I know the signs."

Carla stood before the Teacher with her head bowed and her hands clasped together. Madam Trudeau walked around her without touching her, then sat down and said, "You will whip Lisa every day for a week, beginning tomorrow."

Carla didn't reply.

"Don't stand mute before me, Carla. Signify your obedience immediately."

"I . . . I can't, Madam."

"Carla, any day that you do not whip Lisa, I will. And I will also whip you double her allotment. Do you understand?"

"Yes, Madam."

"You will inform Lisa that she is to be whipped every day, by one or the other of us. Immediately."

"Madam, please . . ."

"You speak out of turn, Carla!"

"I, Madam, please don't do this. Don't make me do this. She is too weak . . ."

"She will beg you to do it, won't she, Carla. Beg you with tears flowing to be the one, not me. And you will feel the excitement and the hate and every day you will feel it grow strong. You will want to hurt her, want to see blood spot her bare back. And your hate will grow until you won't be able to look at her without being blinded by your own hatred. You see, I know, Carla. I know all of it."

Carla stared at her in horror. "I won't do it. I won't."

"I will."

They were old and full of hatred for the shiny young faces, the bright hair, the straight backs, and strong legs and arms. They said: let us remake them in our image and they did.

Carla repeated Madam Trudeau's words to the girls gathered in the two sleeping rooms on the third floor. Lisa swayed and was supported by Ruthie. Helga smiled.

That evening Ruthie tried to run away and was caught by two of the blue-clad Males. The girls were lined up and watched as Ruthie was stoned. They buried her without a service on the hill where she had been caught.

After dark, lying on the cot open-eyed, tense, Carla heard Lisa's whisper close to her ear. "I don't care if you hit me, Carla. It won't hurt like it does when she hits me."

"Go to bed, Lisa. Go to sleep."

"I can't sleep. I keep seeing Ruthie. I should have gone with her. I wanted to, but she wouldn't let me. She was afraid there would be Males on the hill watching. She said if she didn't get caught, then I should try to follow her at night." The child's voice was flat, as if shock had dulled her sensibilities.

Carla kept seeing Ruthie too. Over and over she repeated to herself: I should have tried it. I'm cleverer than she was. I might have escaped. I should have been the one. She knew it was too late now. They would be watching too closely.

An eternity later she crept from her bed and dressed quietly. Soundlessly she gathered her own belongings, and then collected the notebooks of the other girls, and the pens; and she left the room. There were dim lights on throughout the house as she made her way silently down stairs and through corridors. She left a pen by one of the outside doors, and very cautiously made her way back to the tiny space between the floors. She slid the door open and deposited everything else she carried inside the cave. She tried to get to the kitchen for food, but stopped when she saw one of the Officers of Law. She returned soundlessly to the attic rooms and tiptoed among the beds to Lisa's cot. She placed one hand over the girl's mouth and shook her awake with the other.

Lisa bolted upright, terrified, her body stiffened convulsively. With her mouth against the girl's ear Carla whispered, "Don't make a sound. Come on." She half-led, half-carried the girl to the doorway, down the stairs, and into the cave and closed the door.

"You can't talk here, either," she whispered. "They can hear." She spread out the extra garments she had collected and they lay down together, her arms tight about the girl's shoulders. "Try to sleep," she whispered. "I don't think they'll find us here. And after they leave, we'll creep out and live in the woods. We'll eat nuts and berries . . ."

The first day they were jubilant at their success and they giggled and muffled the noise with their skirts. They could hear all the orders being issued by Madam Trudeau: guards in all the halls, on the stairs, at the door to the dorm to keep other girls from trying to escape also. They could hear all the interrogations, of the girls, the guards who had not seen the escapees. They heard the mocking voice of the Doctor of Law deriding Madam Trudeau's boasts of absolute control.

The second day Carla tried to steal food for them, and, more important, water. There were blue-clad Males everywhere. She returned empty-handed. During the night Lisa whimpered in her sleep and

Carla had to stay awake to quiet the child who was slightly feverish.

"You won't let her get me, will you?" she begged over and over.

The third day Lisa became too quiet. She didn't want Carla to move from her side at all. She held Carla's hand in her hot, dry hand and now and then tried to raise it to her face, but she was too weak now. Carla stroked her forehead.

When the child slept Carla wrote in the notebooks, in the dark, not knowing if she wrote over other words, or on blank pages. She wrote her life story, and then made up other things to say. She wrote her name over and over, and wept because she had no last name. She wrote nonsense words and rhymed them with other nonsense words. She wrote of the savages who had laughed at the funeral and she hoped they wouldn't all die over the winter months. She thought that probably they would. She wrote of the golden light through green-black pine trees and of birds' songs and moss underfoot. She wrote of Lisa lying peacefully now at the far end of the cave amidst riches that neither of them could ever have comprehended. When she could no longer write, she drifted in and out of the golden light in the forest, listening to the birds' songs, hearing the raucous laughter that now sounded so beautiful.

Of Mist, and Grass, and Sand

VONDA N. McINTYRE

The little boy was frightened. Gently, Snake touched his hot forehead. Behind her, three adults stood close together, watching, suspicious, afraid to show their concern with more than narrow lines around their eyes. They feared Snake as much as they feared their only child's death. In the dimness of the tent, the flickering lamplights gave no reassurance.

The child watched with eyes so dark the pupils were not visible, so dull that Snake herself feared for his life. She stroked his hair. It was long and very pale, a striking color against his dark skin, dry and irregular for several inches near the scalp. Had Snake been with these people months ago, she would have known the child was growing ill.

"Bring my case, please," Snake said.

The child's parents started at her soft voice. Perhaps they had expected the screech of a bright jay, or the hissing of a shining serpent. This was the first time Snake had spoken in their presence. She had only watched when the three of them had come to observe her from a distance and whisper about her occupation and her youth; she had only listened, and then nodded, when finally they came to ask her help. Perhaps they had thought she was mute.

The fair-haired young man lifted her leather case. He held the satchel away from his body, leaning to hand it to her, breathing shallowly with nostrils flared against the faint smell of musk in the dry desert air. Snake had almost accustomed herself to the kind of uneasiness he showed; she had already seen it often.

When Snake reached out, the young man jerked back and dropped the case. Snake lunged and barely caught it, gently set it on the felt floor, and glanced at him with reproach. His husband and his wife came forward and touched him to ease his fear. "He was bitten once," the dark and handsome woman said. "He almost died." Her tone was not of apology, but of justification.

"I'm sorry," the younger man said. "It's—" He gestured toward her; he was trembling, and trying visibly to control the reactions of his fear. Snake glanced down at her shoulder, where she had been unconsciously aware of the slight weight and movement. A tiny serpent, thin as the finger of a baby, slid himself around her neck to show his narrow head below her short black curls. He probed the air with his trident tongue in a leisurely manner, out, up and down, in, to savor the taste of the smells. "It's only Grass," Snake said. "He cannot harm you." If he were bigger, he might frighten; his color was pale green, but the scales around his mouth were red, as if he had just feasted as a mammal eats, by tearing. He was, in fact, much neater.

The child whimpered. He cut off the sound of pain; perhaps he had been told that Snake, too, would be offended by crying. She only felt sorry that his people refused themselves such a simple way of easing fear. She turned from the adults, regretting their terror of her, but unwilling to spend the time it would take to convince them their reactions were unjustified. "It's all right," she said to the little boy. "Grass is smooth, and dry, and soft, and if I left him to guard you, even death could not reach your bedside." Grass poured himself into her narrow, dirty hand, and she extended him toward the child. "Gently." He reached out and touched the sleek scales with one fingertip. Snake could sense the effort of even such a simple motion, yet the boy almost smiled.

"What are you called?"

He looked quickly toward his parents, and finally they nodded. "Stavin," he whispered. He had no strength or breath for speaking.

"I am Snake, Stavin, and in a little while, in the morning, I must hurt you. You may feel a quick pain, and your body will ache for several days, but you will be better afterward."

He stared at her solemnly. Snake saw that though he understood and feared what she might do, he was less afraid than if she had lied to him. The pain must have increased greatly, as his illness became more apparent, but it seemed that others had only reassured him, and hoped the disease would disappear or kill him quickly.

Snake put Grass on the boy's pillow and pulled her case nearer. The lock opened at her touch. The adults still could only fear her; they had had neither time nor reason to discover any trust. The wife was old enough that they might never have another child, and Snake could tell by their eyes, their covert touching, their concern, that they loved this one very much. They must, to come to Snake in this country.

It was night, and cooling. Sluggish, Sand slid out of the case, moving his head, moving his tongue, smelling, tasting, detecting the warmth of bodies.

"Is that—?" The older husband's voice was low, and wise, but terrified, and Sand sensed the fear. He drew back into striking position and sounded his rattle softly.

Snake spoke, moving her hand, and extended her arm. The pit viper relaxed and flowed around and around her slender wrist to form black and tan bracelets. "No," she said. "Your child is too ill for Sand to help. I know it is hard, but please try to be calm. This is a fearful thing for you, but it is all I can do."

She had to annoy Mist to make her come out. Snake rapped on the bag and finally poked her twice. Snake felt the vibration of sliding scales, and suddenly the albino cobra flung herself into the tent. She moved quickly, yet there seemed to be no end to her. She reared back and up. Her breath rushed out in a hiss. Her head rose well over a meter above the floor. She flared her wide hood. Behind her, the adults gasped, as if physically assaulted by the gaze of the tan spectacle design on the back of Mist's hood. Snake ignored the people and spoke to the great cobra, focusing her attention by her words. "Ah, thou. Furious creature. Lie down; 'tis time for thee to earn thy dinner. Speak to this child, and touch him. He is called Stavin." Slowly, Mist relaxed her hood, and allowed Snake to touch her. Snake grasped her firmly behind the head and held her so she looked at Stavin. The cobra's silver eyes picked up the yellow of the lamplight. "Stavin," Snake said, "Mist will only meet you now. I promise that this time she will touch you gently."

Still, Stavin shivered when Mist touched his thin chest. Snake did not release the serpent's head, but allowed her body to slide against the boy's. The cobra was four times longer than Stavin was tall. She curved herself in stark white loops across his swollen abdomen, extending herself, forcing her head toward the boy's face, straining against Snake's hands. Mist met Stavin's frightened stare with the gaze of lidless eyes. Snake allowed her a little closer.

Mist flicked out her tongue to taste the child.

The younger husband made a small, cut-off, frightened sound. Stavin flinched at it, and Mist drew back, opening her mouth, exposing her fangs, audibly thrusting her breath through her throat. Snake sat back on her heels, letting out her own breath. Sometimes, in other places, the kinfolk could stay while she worked. "You must leave," she said gently. "It's dangerous to frighten Mist."

"I won't—"

"I'm sorry. You must wait outside."

Perhaps the younger husband, perhaps even the wife, would have made the indefensible objections and asked the answerable questions, but the older man turned them and took their hands and led them away.

"I need a small animal," Snake said as he lifted the tent flap. "It must have fur, and it must be alive."

"One will be found," he said, and the three parents went into the glowing night. Snake could hear their footsteps in the sand outside.

Snake supported Mist in her lap and soothed her. The cobra wrapped herself around Snake's narrow waist, taking in her warmth. Hunger made the cobra even more nervous than usual, and she was hungry, as was Snake. Coming across the black sand desert, they had found sufficient water, but Snake's traps were unsuccessful. The season was summer, the weather was hot, and many of the furry tidbits Sand and Mist preferred were estivating. When the serpents missed their regular meal, Snake began a fast as well.

She saw with regret that Stavin was more frightened now. "I am sorry to send your parents away," she said. "They can come back soon."

His eyes glistened, but he held back the tears. "They said to do what you told me."

"I would have you cry, if you are able," Snake said. "It isn't such a terrible thing." But Stavin seemed not to understand, and Snake did not press him; she knew that his people taught themselves to resist a difficult land by refusing to cry, refusing to mourn, refusing to laugh. They denied themselves grief and allowed themselves little joy, but they survived.

Mist had calmed to sullenness. Snake unwrapped her from her waist and placed her on the pallet next to Stavin. As the cobra moved, Snake guided her head, feeling the tension of the striking muscles. "She will touch you with her tongue," she told Stavin. "It might tickle, but it will not hurt. She smells with it, as you do with your nose."

"With her tongue?"

Snake nodded, smiling, and Mist flicked out her tongue to caress Stavin's cheek. Stavin did not flinch; he watched, his child's delight in knowledge briefly overcoming pain. He lay perfectly still as Mist's long tongue brushed his cheeks, his eyes, his mouth. "She tastes the sickness," Snake said. Mist stopped fighting the restraint of her grasp and drew back her head. Snake sat on her heels and released the cobra, who spiraled up her arm and laid herself across her shoulders.

"Go to sleep, Stavin," Snake said. "Try to trust me, and try not to fear the morning."

Stavin gazed at her for a few seconds, searching for truth in Snake's pale eyes. "Will Grass watch?"

She was startled by the question, or rather, by the acceptance behind the question. She brushed his hair from his forehead and smiled a smile that was tears just beneath the surface. "Of course." She picked Grass up. "Thou wilt watch this child and guard him." The snake lay quiet in her hand, and his eyes glittered black. She laid him gently on Stavin's pillow.

"Now sleep."

Stavin closed his eyes, and the life seemed to flow out of him. The alteration was so great that Snake reached out to touch him, then saw that he was breathing, slowly, shallowly. She tucked a blanket around him and stood up. The abrupt change in position dizzied her; she staggered and caught herself. Across her shoulders, Mist tensed.

Snake's eyes stung and her vision was oversharp, fever-clear. The sound she imagined she heard swooped in closer. She steadied herself against hunger and exhaustion, bent slowly, and picked up the leather case. Mist touched her cheek with the tip of her tongue.

She pushed aside the tent flap and felt relief that it was still night. She could stand the heat, but the brightness of the sun curled through her, burning. The moon must be full; though the clouds obscured everything, they diffused the light so the sky appeared gray from horizon to horizon. Beyond the tents, groups of formless shadows projected from the ground. Here, near the edge of the desert, enough water existed so clumps and patches of bush grew, providing shelter and sustenance for all manner of creatures. The black sand, which sparkled and blinded in the sunlight, at night was like a layer of soft soot. Snake stepped out of the tent, and the illusion of softness disappeared; her boots slid crunching into the sharp hard grains.

Stavin's family waited, sitting close together between the dark tents that clustered in a patch of sand from which the bushes had been ripped and burned. They looked at her silently, hoping with their eyes, showing no expression in their faces. A woman somewhat younger than Stavin's mother sat with them. She was dressed, as they were, in a long loose robe, but she wore the only adornment Snake had seen among these people: a leader's circle, hanging around her neck on a leather thong. She and the older husband were marked close kin by their similarities: sharp-cut planes of face, high cheekbones, his hair white and hers graying early from deep black, their eyes the dark brown best suited for survival in the sun. On the ground by their feet, a small black animal jerked sporadically against a net and infrequently gave a shrill weak cry.

"Stavin is asleep," Snake said. "Do not disturb him, but go to him if he wakes."

The wife and young husband rose and went inside, but the older man stopped before her. "Can you help him?"

"I hope we may. The tumor is advanced, but it seems solid." Her own voice sounded removed, slightly hollow, as if she were lying. "Mist will be ready in the morning." She still felt the need to give him reassurance, but she could think of none.

"My sister wished to speak with you," he said, and left them alone without introduction, without elevating himself by saying that the tall woman was the leader of this group. Snake glanced back, but the tent flap fell shut. She was feeling her exhaustion more deeply, and across her shoulders Mist was, for the first time, a weight she thought heavy.

"Are you all right?"

Snake turned. The woman moved toward her with a natural elegance made slightly awkward by advanced pregnancy. Snake had to look up to meet her gaze. She had small fine lines at the corners of her eyes, as if she laughed, sometimes, in secret. She smiled, but with concern. "You seem very tired. Shall I have someone make you a bed?"

"Not now," Snake said, "not yet. I won't sleep until afterward."

The leader searched her face, and Snake felt a kinship with her in their shared responsibility.

"I understand, I think. Is there anything we can give you? Do you need aid with your preparations?"

Snake found herself having to deal with the questions as if they were complex problems. She turned them in her tired mind, examined them, dissected them, and finally grasped their meanings. "My pony needs food and water—"

"It is taken care of."

"And I need someone to help me with Mist. Someone strong. But it's more important that they aren't afraid."

The leader nodded. "I would help you," she said, and smiled again, a little. "But I am a bit clumsy of late. I will find someone."

"Thank you."

Somber again, the older woman inclined her head and moved slowly toward a small group of tents. Snake watched her go, admiring her grace. She felt small and young and grubby in comparison.

Sand began to unwrap himself from her wrist. Feeling the

anticipatory slide of scales on her skin, she caught him before he could drop to the ground. Sand lifted the upper half of his body from her hands. He flicked out his tongue, peering toward the little animal, feeling its body heat, smelling its fear. "I know thou art hungry," Snake said, "but that creature is not for thee." She put Sand in the case, lifted Mist from her shoulder, and let her coil herself in her dark compartment.

The small animal shrieked and struggled again when Snake's diffuse shadow passed over it. She bent and picked it up. The rapid series of terrified cries slowed and diminished and finally stopped as she stroked it. Finally it lay still, breathing hard, exhausted, staring up at her with yellow eyes. It had long hind legs and wide pointed ears, and its nose twitched at the serpent smell. Its soft black fur was marked off in skewed squares by the cords of the net.

"I am sorry to take your life," Snake told it. "But there will be no more fear, and I will not hurt you." She closed her hand gently around it, and stroking it, grasped its spine at the base of its skull. She pulled once, quickly. It seemed to struggle briefly, but it was already dead. It convulsed; its legs drew up against its body, and its toes curled and quivered. It seemed to stare up at her, even now. She freed its body from the net.

Snake chose a small vial from her belt pouch, pried open the animal's clenched jaws, and let a single drop of the vial's cloudy preparation fall into its mouth. Quickly she opened the satchel again and called Mist out. The cobra came slowly, slipping over the edge, hood closed, sliding in the sharp-grained sand. Her milky scales caught the thin light. She smelled the animal, flowed to it, touched it with her tongue. For a moment Snake was afraid she would refuse dead meat, but the body was still warm, still twitching reflexively, and she was very hungry. "A tidbit for thee." Snake spoke to the cobra, a habit of solitude. "To whet thy appetite." Mist nosed the beast, reared back and struck, sinking her short fixed fangs into the tiny body, biting again, pumping out her store of poison. She released it, took a better grip, and began to work her jaws around it; it would hardly distend her throat. When Mist lay quiet, digesting the small meal, Snake sat beside her and held her, waiting.

She heard footsteps in the coarse sand.

"I'm sent to help you."

He was a young man, despite a scatter of white in his black hair. He was taller than Snake and not unattractive. His eyes were dark, and the sharp planes of his face were further hardened because his hair was pulled straight back and tied. His expression was neutral.

"Are you afraid?"

"I will do as you tell me."

Though his form was obscured by his robe, his long fine hands showed strength.

"Then hold her body, and don't let her surprise you." Mist was beginning to twitch from the effects of the drugs Snake had put in the small animal. The cobra's eyes stared, unseeing.

"If it bites—"

"Hold, quickly!"

The young man reached, but he had hesitated too long. Mist writhed, lashing out, striking him in the face with her tail. He staggered back, at least as surprised as hurt. Snake kept a close grip behind Mist's jaws and struggled to catch the rest of her as well. Mist was no constrictor, but she was smooth and strong and fast. Thrashing, she forced out her breath in a long hiss. She would have bitten anything she could reach. As Snake fought with her, she managed to squeeze the poison glands and force out the last drops of venom. They hung from Mist's fangs for a moment, catching light as jewels would; the force of the serpent's convulsions flung them away into the darkness. Snake struggled with the cobra, aided for once by the sand, on which Mist could get no purchase. Snake felt the young man behind her grabbing for Mist's body and tail. The seizure stopped abruptly, and Mist lay limp in their hands.

"I am sorry—"

"Hold her," Snake said. "We have the night to go."

During Mist's second convulsion, the young man held her firmly and was of some real help. Afterward, Snake answered his interrupted question. "If she were making poison and she bit you, you would probably die. Even now her bite would make you ill. But unless you do something foolish, if she manages to bite, she will bite me."

"You would benefit my cousin little, if you were dead or dying."

"You misunderstand. Mist cannot kill me." She held out her hand so he could see the white scars of slashes and punctures. He stared at them, and looked into her eyes for a long moment, then looked away.

The bright spot in the clouds from which the light radiated moved westward in the sky; they held the cobra like a child. Snake found herself half dozing, but Mist moved her head, dully attempting to evade restraint, and Snake woke herself abruptly. "I must not sleep," she said to the young man. "Talk to me. What are you called?"

As Stavin had, the young man hesitated. He seemed afraid of her, or of something. "My people," he said, "think it unwise to speak our names to strangers."

"If you consider me a witch, you should not have asked my aid. I know no magic, and I claim none."

"It's not a superstition," he said. "Not as you might think. We're not afraid of being bewitched."

"I can't learn all the customs of all the people on this earth, so I keep my own. My custom is to address those I work with by name." Watching him, Snake tried to decipher his expression in the dim light.

"Our families know our names, and we exchange names with those we would marry."

Snake considered that custom and thought it would fit badly on her. "No one else? Ever?"

"Well . . . a friend might know one's name."

"Ah," Snake said. "I see. I am still a stranger, and perhaps an enemy."

"A *friend* would know my name," the young man said again. "I would not offend you, but now you misunderstand. An acquaintance is not a friend. We value friendship highly."

"In this land one should be able to tell quickly if a person is worth calling 'friend.' "

"We take friends seldom. Friendship is a great commitment."

"It sounds like something to be feared."

He considered that possibility. "Perhaps it's the betrayal of friendship we fear. That is a very painful thing."

"Has anyone ever betrayed you?"

He glanced at her sharply, as if she had exceeded the limits of propriety. "No," he said, and his voice was as hard as his face. "No friend. I have no one I call friend."

His reaction startled Snake. "That's very sad," she said, and grew silent, trying to comprehend the deep stresses that could close people off so far, comparing her loneliness of necessity and theirs of choice. "Call me Snake," she said finally, "if you can bring yourself to pronounce it. Saying my name binds you to nothing."

The young man seemed about to speak; perhaps he thought again that he had offended her, perhaps he felt he should further defend his customs. But Mist began to twist in their hands, and they had to hold her to keep her from injuring herself. The cobra was slender for her length, but powerful, and the convulsions she went through were more severe than any she had ever had before. She thrashed in Snake's grasp and almost pulled away. She tried to spread her hood, but Snake held her too tightly. She opened her mouth and hissed, but no poison dripped from her fangs.

She wrapped her tail around the young man's waist. He began to pull her and turn, to extricate himself from her coils.

"She's not a constrictor," Snake said. "She won't hurt you. Leave her—"

But it was too late; Mist relaxed suddenly and the young man lost his balance. Mist whipped herself away and lashed figures in the sand. Snake wrestled with her alone while the young man tried to hold her, but she curled herself around Snake and used the grip for leverage. She started to pull herself from Snake's hands. Snake threw them both backward into the sand; Mist rose above her, openmouthed, furious, hissing. The young man lunged and grabbed her just beneath her hood. Mist struck at him, but Snake, somehow, held her back. Together they deprived Mist of her hold and regained control of her. Snake struggled up, but Mist suddenly went quite still and lay almost rigid between them. They were both sweating; the young man was pale under his tan, and even Snake was trembling.

"We have a little while to rest," Snake said. She glanced at him and noticed the dark line on his cheek where, earlier, Mist's tail had slashed him. She reached up and touched it. "You'll have a bruise," she said. "But it will not scar."

"If it were true that serpents sting with their tails, you would be restraining both the fangs and the stinger, and I'd be of little use."

"Tonight I'd need someone to keep me awake, whether or not they helped me with Mist." Fighting the cobra produced adrenaline, but now it ebbed, and her exhaustion and hunger were returning, stronger.

"Snake . . ."

"Yes?"

He smiled quickly, half-embarrassed. "I was trying the pronunciation."

"Good enough."

"How long did it take you to cross the desert?"

"Not very long. Too long. Six days."

"How did you live?"

"There is water. We traveled at night, except yesterday, when I could find no shade."

"You carried all your food?"

She shrugged. "A little." And wished he would not speak of food.

"What's on the other side?"

"More sand, more bush, a little more water. A few groups of people, traders, the station I grew up and took my training in. And farther on, a mountain with a city inside."

"I would like to see a city. Someday."

"The desert can be crossed."

He said nothing, but Snake's memories of leaving home were recent enough that she could imagine his thoughts.

The next set of convulsions came, much sooner than Snake had expected. By their severity, she gauged something of the stage of Stavin's illness and wished it were morning. If she were to lose him, she would have it done, and grieve, and try to forget. The cobra would have battered herself to death against the sand if Snake and the young man had not been holding her. She suddenly went completely rigid, with her mouth clamped shut and her forked tongue dangling.

She stopped breathing.

"Hold her," Snake said. "Hold her head. Quickly, take her, and if she gets away, run. Take her! She won't strike at you now, she could only slash you by accident."

He hesitated only a moment, then grasped Mist behind the head. Snake ran, slipping in the deep sand, from the edge of the circle of tents to a place where bushes still grew. She broke off dry thorny branches that tore her scarred hands. Peripherally she noticed a mass of horned vipers, so ugly they seemed deformed, nesting beneath the clump of desiccated vegetation; they hissed at her: she ignored them. She found a narrow hollow stem and carried it back. Her hands bled from deep scratches.

Kneeling by Mist's head, she forced open the cobra's mouth and pushed the tube deep into her throat, through the air passage at the base of Mist's tongue. She bent close, took the tube in her mouth, and breathed gently into Mist's lungs.

She noticed: the young man's hands, holding the cobra as she had asked; his breathing, first a sharp gasp of surprise, then ragged; the sand scraping her elbows where she leaned; the cloying smell of the fluid seeping from Mist's fangs; her own dizziness, she thought from exhaustion, which she forced away by necessity and will.

Snake breathed and breathed again, paused, and repeated, until Mist caught the rhythm and continued it unaided.

Snake sat back on her heels. "I think she'll be all right," she said. "I hope she will." She brushed the back of her hand across her forehead. The touch sparked pain: she jerked her hand down and agony slid along her bones, up her arm, across her shoulder, through her chest, enveloping her heart. Her balance turned on its edge. She fell, tried to catch herself but moved too slowly, fought nausea and vertigo and almost succeeded, until the pull of the earth seemed to slip away in pain and she was lost in darkness with nothing to take a bearing by.

She felt sand where it had scraped her cheek and her palms, but it was soft. "Snake, can I let go?" She thought the question must be for someone else, while at the same time she knew there was no one else to answer it, no one else to reply to her name. She felt hands on her, and they were gentle; she wanted to respond to them, but she was too tired. She needed sleep more, so she pushed them away. But they held her head and put dry leather to her lips and poured water into her throat. She coughed and choked and spat it out.

She pushed herself up on one elbow. As her sight cleared, she realized she was shaking. She felt as she had the first time she was snake-bit, before her immunities had completely developed. The young man knelt over her, his water flask in his hand. Mist, beyond him, crawled toward the darkness. Snake forgot the throbbing pain. "Mist!" She slapped the ground.

The young man flinched and turned, frightened; the serpent reared up, her head nearly at Snake's standing eye level, her hood spread, swaying, watching, angry, ready to strike. She formed a wavering white line against black. Snake forced herself to rise, feeling as though she were fumbling with the control of some unfamiliar body. She almost fell again, but held herself steady. "Thou must not go to hunt now," she said. "There is work for thee to do." She held out her right hand to the side, a decoy to draw Mist if she struck. Her hand was heavy with pain. Snake feared, not being bitten, but the loss of the contents of Mist's poison sacs. "Come here," she said. "Come here, and stay thy anger." She noticed blood flowing down between her fingers, and the fear she felt for Stavin was intensified. "Didst thou bite me, creature?" But the pain was wrong: poison would numb her, and the new serum only sting . . .

"No," the young man whispered from behind her.

Mist struck. The reflexes of long training took over. Snake's right hand jerked away, her left grabbed Mist as she brought her head back. The cobra writhed a moment, and relaxed. "Devious beast," Snake said. "For shame." She turned and let Mist crawl up her arm and over her shoulder, where she lay like the outline of an invisible cape and dragged her tail like the edge of a train.

"She did not bite me?"

"No," the young man said. His contained voice was touched with awe. "You should be dying. You should be curled around the agony, and your arm swollen purple. When you came back—" He gestured toward her hand. "It must have been a bush viper."

Snake remembered the coil of reptiles beneath the branches and touched the blood on her hand. She wiped it away, revealing the double puncture of a snakebite among the scratches of the thorns. The wound was slightly swollen. "It needs cleaning," she said. "I shame myself by falling to it." The pain of it washed in gentle waves up her arm, burning no longer. She stood looking at the young man, looking around her, watching the landscape shift and change as her tired eyes tried to cope with the low light of setting moon and false dawn. "You held Mist well, and bravely," she said to the young man. "I thank you."

He lowered his gaze, almost bowing to her. He rose and approached her. Snake put her hand gently on Mist's neck so she would not be alarmed.

"I would be honored," the young man said, "if you would call me Arevin."

"I would be pleased to."

Snake knelt down and held the winding white loops as Mist crawled slowly into her compartment. In a little while, when Mist had stabilized, by dawn, they could go to Stavin.

The tip of Mist's white tail slid out of sight. Snake closed the case and would have risen, but she could not stand. She had not quite shaken off the effects of the new venom. The flesh around the wound was red and tender, but the hemorrhaging would not spread. She stayed where she was, slumped, staring at her hand, creeping slowly in her mind toward what she needed to do, this time for herself.

"Let me help you. Please."

He touched her shoulder and helped her stand. "I'm sorry," she said. "I'm so in need of rest . . ."

"Let me wash your hand," Arevin said. "And then you can sleep. Tell me when to awaken you—"

"I can't sleep yet." She collected herself, straightened, tossed the damp curls of her short hair off her forehead. "I'm all right now. Have you any water?"

Arevin loosened his outer robe. Beneath it he wore a loincloth and a leather belt that carried several leather flasks and pouches. His body was lean and well-built, his legs long and muscular. The color of his skin was slightly lighter than the sun-darkened brown of his face. He brought out his water flask and reached for Snake's hand.

"No, Arevin. If the poison gets in any small scratch you might have, it could infect."

She sat down and sluiced lukewarm water over her hand. The water dripped pink to the ground and disappeared, leaving not even a damp spot visible. The wound bled a little more, but now it only ached. The poison was almost inactivated.

"I don't understand," Arevin said, "how it is that you're unhurt. My younger sister was bitten by a bush viper." He could not speak as uncaringly as he might have wished. "We could do nothing to save her—nothing we have would even lessen her pain."

Snake gave him his flask and rubbed salve from a vial in her belt pouch across the closing punctures. "It's a part of our preparation," she said. "We work with many kinds of serpents, so we must be immune to as many as possible." She shrugged. "The process is tedious and somewhat painful." She clenched her fist; the film held, and she was steady. She leaned toward Arevin and touched his abraded cheek again. "Yes . . ." She spread a thin layer of the salve across it. "That will help it heal."

"If you cannot sleep," Arevin said, "can you at least rest?"

"Yes," she said. "For a little while."

Snake sat next to Arevin, leaning against him, and they watched the sun turn the clouds to gold and flame and amber. The simple physical contact with another human being gave Snake pleasure, though she found it unsatisfying. Another time, another place, she might do something more, but not here, not now.

When the lower edge of the sun's bright smear rose above the horizon, Snake rose and teased Mist out of the case. She came slowly, weakly, and crawled across Snake's shoulders. Snake picked up the satchel, and she and Arevin walked together back to the small group of tents.

Stavin's parents waited, watching for her, just outside the entrance of their tent. They stood in a tight, defensive, silent group. For a moment Snake thought they had decided to send her away. Then, with regret and fear like hot iron in her mouth, she asked if Stavin had died. They shook their heads and allowed her to enter.

Stavin lay as she had left him, still asleep. The adults followed her with their stares, and she could smell fear. Mist flicked out her tongue, growing nervous from the implied danger.

"I know you would stay," Snake said. "I know you would help, if you could, but there is nothing to be done by any person but me. Please go back outside."

They glanced at each other, and at Arevin, and she thought for a moment that they would refuse. Snake wanted to fall into the silence and sleep. "Come, cousins," Arevin said. "We are in her hands." He opened the tent flap and motioned them out. Snake thanked him with nothing more than a glance, and he might almost have smiled. She turned toward Stavin, and knelt beside him. "Stavin—" She touched his forehead; it was very hot. She noticed that her hand was less steady than before. The slight touch awakened the child. "It's time," Snake said.

He blinked, coming out of some child's dream, seeing her, slowly recognizing her. He did not look frightened. For that Snake was glad; for some other reason she could not identify, she was uneasy.

"Will it hurt?"

"Does it hurt now?"

He hesitated, looked away, looked back. "Yes."

"It might hurt a little more. I hope not. Are you ready?"

"Can Grass stay?"

"Of course," she said.

And realized what was wrong.

"I'll come back in a moment." Her voice changed so much, she had pulled it so tight, that she could not help but frighten him. She left the tent, walking slowly, calmly, restraining herself. Outside, the parents told her by their faces what they feared.

"Where is Grass?" Arevin, his back to her, started at her tone. The younger husband made a small grieving sound and could look at her no longer.

"We were afraid," the older husband said. "We thought it would bite the child."

"I thought it would. It was I. It crawled over his face, I could see its fangs—" The wife put her hands on the younger husband's shoulders, and he said no more.

"Where is he?" She wanted to scream; she did not.

They brought her a small open box. Snake took it and looked inside.

Grass lay cut almost in two, his entrails oozing from his body, half turned over, and as she watched, shaking, he writhed once, and flicked his tongue out once, and in. Snake made some sound too low in her throat to be a cry. She hoped his motions were only reflex, but she picked him up as gently as she could. She leaned down and touched her lips to the smooth green scales behind his head. She bit him quickly, sharply, at the base of the skull. His blood flowed cool and salty in her mouth. If he was not dead, she had killed him instantly.

She looked at the parents, and at Arevin; they were all pale, but she had no sympathy for their fear, and cared nothing for shared grief. "Such a small creature," she said. "Such a small creature, who could only give pleasure and dreams." She watched them for a moment more, then turned toward the tent again.

"Wait—" She heard the older husband move up close behind her. He touched her shoulder; she shrugged away his hand. "We will give you anything you want," he said, "but leave the child alone."

She spun on him in a fury. "Should I kill Stavin for your stupidity?" He seemed about to try to hold her back. She jammed her shoulder hard into his stomach and flung herself past the tent flap. Inside, she kicked over the satchel. Abruptly awakened, and angry, Sand crawled out and coiled himself. When the younger husband and the wife tried to enter, Sand hissed and rattled with a violence Snake had never heard him use before. She did not even bother to look behind her. She ducked her head and wiped her tears on her sleeve before Stavin could see them. She knelt beside him.

"What's the matter?" He could not help but hear the voices outside the tent, and the running.

"Nothing, Stavin," Snake said. "Did you know we came across the desert?"

"No," he said, with wonder.

"It was very hot, and none of us had anything to eat. Grass is hunting now. He was very hungry. Will you forgive him and let me begin? I will be here all the time."

He seemed so tired; he was disappointed, but he had no strength for arguing. "All right." His voice rustled like sand slipping through the fingers.

Snake lifted Mist from her shoulders and pulled the blanket from Stavin's small body. The tumor pressed up beneath his rib cage, distorting his form, squeezing his vital organs, sucking nourishment from him for its own growth, poisoning him with its wastes. Holding Mist's head, Snake let her flow across him, touching and tasting him. She had to restrain the cobra to keep her from striking; the excitement had agitated her. When Sand used his rattle, the vibrations made her flinch. Snake stroked her, soothing her; trained and bred-in responses began to return, overcoming the natural instincts. Mist paused when her tongue flicked the skin above the tumor, and Snake released her.

The cobra reared, and struck, and bit as cobras bite, sinking her fangs their short length once, releasing, instantly biting again for a better purchase, holding on, chewing at her prey. Stavin cried out, but he did not move against Snake's restraining hands.

Mist expended the contents of her venom sacs into the child and released him. She reared up, peered around, folded her hood, and slid across the mats in a perfectly straight line toward her dark close compartment.

"It's done, Stavin."

"Will I die now?"

"No," Snake said. "Not now. Not for many years, I hope." She took a vial of powder from her belt pouch. "Open your mouth." He complied, and she sprinkled the powder across his tongue. "That will help the ache." She spread a pad of cloth across the series of shallow puncture wounds without wiping off the blood.

She turned from him.

"Snake? Are you going away?"

"I will not leave without saying good-bye. I promise."

The child lay back, closed his eyes, and let the drug take him.

Sand coiled quiescently on the dark matting. Snake patted the floor to call him. He moved toward her and suffered himself to be replaced in the satchel. Snake closed it and lifted it, and it still felt empty. She heard noises outside the tent. Stavin's parents and the people who had come to help them pulled open the tent flap and peered inside, thrusting sticks in even before they looked.

Snake set down her leather case. "It's done."

They entered. Arevin was with them too; only he was empty-handed. "Snake—" He spoke through grief, pity, confusion, and Snake could not tell what he believed. He looked back. Stavin's mother was just behind him. He took her by the shoulder. "He would have died without her. Whatever happens now, he would have died."

She shook his hand away. "He might have lived. It might have gone away. We—" She could speak no more for hiding tears.

Snake felt the people moving, surrounding her. Arevin took one step toward her and stopped, and she could see he wanted her to defend herself. "Can any of you cry?" she said. "Can any of you cry for me and my despair, or for them and their guilt, or for small things and their pain?" She felt tears slip down her cheeks.

They did not understand her; they were offended by her crying. They stood back, still afraid of her, but gathering themselves. She no longer needed the pose of calmness she had used to deceive the child. "Ah, you fools." Her voice sounded brittle. "Stavin—"

Light from the entrance struck them. "Let me pass." The people in front of Snake moved aside for their leader. She stopped in front of Snake, ignoring the satchel her foot almost touched. "Will Stavin live?" Her voice was quiet, calm, gentle.

"I cannot be certain," Snake said, "but I feel that he will."

"Leave us." The people understood Snake's words before they did their leader's; they looked around and lowered their weapons, and finally, one by one, they moved out of the tent. Arevin remained. Snake felt the strength that came from danger seeping from her. Her knees collapsed. She bent over the satchel with her face in her hands. The older woman knelt in front of her before Snake could notice or prevent her. "Thank you," she said. "Thank you. I am so sorry . . ." She put her arms around Snake and drew her toward her, and Arevin knelt beside them, and he embraced Snake too. Snake began to tremble again, and they held her while she cried.

Later she slept, exhausted, alone in the tent with Stavin, holding his hand. The people had caught small animals for Sand and Mist. They had given her food and supplies and sufficient water for her to bathe, though the last must have strained their resources.

When she awakened, Arevin lay sleeping nearby, his robe open in the heat, a sheen of sweat across his chest and stomach. The sternness in his expression vanished when he slept; he looked exhausted and vulnerable. Snake almost woke him, but stopped, shook her head, and turned to Stavin.

She felt the tumor and found that it had begun to dissolve and shrivel, dying, as Mist's changed poison affected it. Through her grief Snake felt a little joy. She smoothed Stavin's pale hair back from his face. "I would not lie to you again, little one," she whispered, "but I must leave soon. I cannot stay here." She wanted another three days' sleep to finish fighting off the effects of the bush viper's poison, but she would sleep somewhere else. "Stavin?"

He half woke, slowly. "It doesn't hurt anymore," he said.

"I am glad."

"Thank you . . ."

"Good-bye, Stavin. Will you remember later on that you woke up, and that I did stay to say good-bye?"

"Good-bye," he said, drifting off again. "Good-bye, Snake. Good-bye, Grass." He closed his eyes.

Snake picked up the satchel and stood gazing down at Arevin. He did not stir. Half grateful, half regretful, she left the tent.

Dusk approached with long, indistinct shadows; the camp was hot and quiet. She found her tiger-striped pony tethered with food and water. New, full water-skins bulged on the ground next to the saddle, and desert robes lay across the pommel, though Snake had refused any payment. The tiger-pony whickered at her. She scratched his striped ears, saddled him, and strapped her gear on his back. Leading him, she started west, the way she had come.

"Snake—"

She took a breath and turned back to Arevin. He was facing the sun; it turned his skin ruddy and his robe scarlet. His streaked hair flowed loose to his shoulders, gentling his face. "You must leave?"

"Yes."

"I hoped you would not leave before . . . I hoped you would stay, for a time . . ."

"If things were different, I might have stayed."

"They were frightened—"

"I told them Grass couldn't hurt them, but they saw his fangs and they didn't know he could only give dreams and ease dying."

"But can't you forgive them?"

"I can't face their guilt. What they did was my fault, Arevin. I didn't understand them until too late."

"You said it yourself, you can't know all the customs and all the fears."

"I'm crippled," she said. "Without Grass, if I can't heal a person, I cannot help at all. I must go home and face my teachers, and hope they'll forgive my stupidity. They seldom give the name I bear, but they gave it to me—and they'll be disappointed."

"Let me come with you."

She wanted to; she hesitated and cursed herself for that weakness. "They may take Mist and Sand and cast me out, and you would be cast out too. Stay here, Arevin."

"It wouldn't matter."

"It would. After a while, we would hate each other. I don't know you, and you don't know me. We need calmness, and quiet, and time to understand each other well."

He came toward her and put his arms around her, and they stood embracing for a moment. When he raised his head, there were tears on his cheeks. "Please come back," he said. "Whatever happens, please come back."

"I will try," Snake said. "Next spring, when the winds stop, look for me. The spring after that, if I do not come, forget me. Wherever I am, if I live, I will forget you."

"I will look for you," Arevin said, and he would promise no more.

Snake picked up her pony's lead and started across the desert.

The Women Men Don't See

JAMES TIPTREE, JR.

I see her first while the Mexicana 727 is barreling down to Cozumel
Island. I come out of the can and lurch into her seat, saying, "Sorry,"
at a double female blur. The near blur nods quietly. The younger one
in the window seat goes on looking out. I continue down the aisle,
registering nothing. Zero. I never would have looked at them or
thought of them again.

Cozumel airport is the usual mix of panicky Yanks dressed for the
sand pile and calm Mexicans dressed for lunch at the Presidente. I
am a used-up Yank dressed for serious fishing; I extract my rods and
duffel from the riot and hike across the field to find my charter pilot.
One Captain Estéban has contracted to deliver me to the bonefish flats
of Bélise three hundred kilometers down the coast.

Captain Estéban turns out to be four feet nine of mahogany Maya
puro. He is also in a somber Mayan snit. He tells me my Cessna is
grounded somewhere and his Bonanza is booked to take a party to
Chetumal.

Well, Chetumal is south; can he take me along and go on to Bélise
after he drops them? Gloomily he concedes the possibility—*if* the other
party permits, and *if* there are not too many *equipajes*.

The Chetumal party approaches. It's the woman and her young
companion—daughter?—neatly picking their way across the gravel
and yucca apron. Their Ventura two-suiters, like themselves, are small,
plain, and neutral-colored. No problem. When the captain asks if I
may ride along, the mother says mildly, "Of course," without looking
at me.

I think that's when my inner tilt-detector sends up its first faint
click. How come this woman has already looked me over carefully
enough to accept on her plane? I disregard it. Paranoia hasn't been
useful in my business for years, but the habit is hard to break.

As we clamber into the Bonanza, I see the girl has what could be an attractive body if there was any spark at all. There isn't. Captain Estéban folds a serape to sit on so he can see over the cowling and runs a meticulous check-down. And then we're up and trundling over the turquoise Jell-O of the Caribbean into a stiff south wind.

The coast on our right is the territory of Quintana Roo. If you haven't seen Yucatán, imagine the world's biggest absolutely flat green-gray rug. An empty-looking land. We pass the white ruin of Tulum and the gash of the road to Chichén Itzá, a half-dozen coconut plantations, and then nothing but reef and low scrub jungle all the way to the horizon, just about the way the conquistadores saw it four centuries back.

Long strings of cumulus are racing at us, shadowing the coast. I have gathered that part of our pilot's gloom concerns the weather. A cold front is dying on the henequen fields of Mérida to the west, and the south wind has piled up a string of coastal storms: what they call *llovisnos*. Estéban detours methodically around a couple of small thunderheads. The Bonanza jinks, and I look back with a vague notion of reassuring the women. They are calmly intent on what can be seen of Yucatán. Well, they were offered the copilot's view, but they turned it down. Too shy?

Another *llovisno* puffs up ahead. Estéban takes the Bonanza upstairs, rising in his seat to sight his course. I relax for the first time in too long, savoring the latitudes between me and my desk, the week of fishing ahead. Our captain's classic Maya profile attracts my gaze: forehead sloping back from his predatory nose, lips and jaw stepping back below it. If his slant eyes had been any more crossed, he couldn't have made his license. That's a handsome combination, believe it or not. On the little Maya chicks in their minishifts with iridescent gloop on those cockeyes, it's also highly erotic. Nothing like the oriental doll thing; these people have stone bones. Captain Estéban's old grandmother could probably tow the Bonanza. . . .

I'm snapped awake by the cabin hitting my ear. Estéban is barking into his headset over a drumming racket of hail; the windows are dark gray.

One important noise is missing—the motor. I realize Estéban is fighting a dead plane. Thirty-six hundred; we've lost two thousand feet.

He slaps tank switches as the storm throws us around; I catch something about *gasolina* in a snarl that shows his big teeth. The Bonanza reels down. As he reaches for an overhead toggle, I see the fuel gauges are high. Maybe a clogged gravity feed line, I've heard of dirty gas down here. He drops the set; it's a million to one nobody can read us through the storm at this range anyway. Twenty-five hundred—going down.

His electric feed pump seems to have cut in: the motor explodes—quits—explodes—and quits again for good. We are suddenly out of the bottom of the clouds. Below us is a long white line almost hidden by rain: the reef. But there isn't any beach behind it, only a big meandering bay with a few mangrove flats—and it's coming up at us fast.

This is going to be bad, I tell myself with great unoriginality. The women behind me haven't made a sound. I look back and see they're braced down with their coats by their heads. With a stalling speed around eighty, all this isn't much use, but I wedge myself in.

Estéban yells some more into his set, flying a falling plane. He is doing one jesus job, too—as the water rushes up at us he dives into a hair-raising turn and hangs us into the wind—with a long pale ridge of sandbar in front of our nose.

Where in hell he found it I never know. The Bonanza mushes down, and we belly-hit with a tremendous tearing crash—bounce—hit again—and everything slews wildly as we flat-spin into the mangroves at the end of the bar. Crash! Clang! The plane is wrapping itself into a mound of strangler fig with one wing up. The crashing quits with us all in one piece. And no fire. Fantastic.

Captain Estéban prys open his door, which is now in the roof. Behind me a woman is repeating quietly, "Mother. Mother." I climb up the floor and find the girl trying to free herself from her mother's embrace. The woman's eyes are closed. Then she opens them and suddenly lets go, sane as soap. Estéban starts hauling them out. I grab the Bonanza's aid kit and scramble out after them into brilliant sun and wind. The storm that hit us is already vanishing up the coast.

"Great landing, Captain."

"Oh, yes! It was beautiful." The women are shaky, but no hysteria. Estéban is surveying the scenery with the expression his ancestors used on the Spaniards.

If you've been in one of these things, you know the slow-motion inanity that goes on. Euphoria, first. We straggle down the fig tree and out onto the sandbar in the roaring hot wind, noting without alarm that there's nothing but miles of crystalline water on all sides. It's only a foot or so deep, and the bottom is the olive color of silt. The distant shore around us is all flat mangrove swamp, totally uninhabitable.

"Bahía Espíritu Santo." Estéban confirms my guess that we're down in that huge water wilderness. I always wanted to fish it.

"What's all that smoke?" The girl is pointing at plumes blowing around the horizon.

"Alligator hunters," says Estéban. Maya poachers have left burn-offs in the swamps. It occurs to me that any signal fires we make aren't going to be too conspicuous. And I now note that our plane is well-buried in the mound of fig. Hard to see it from the air.

Just as the question of how the hell we get out of here surfaces in my mind, the older woman asks composedly, "If they didn't hear you, Captain, when will they start looking for us? Tomorrow?"

"Correct," Estéban agrees dourly. I recall that air-sea rescue is fairly informal here. Like, keep an eye open for Mario, his mother says he hasn't been home all week.

It dawns on me we may be here quite some while.

Furthermore, the diesel-truck noise on our left is the Caribbean piling back into the mouth of the bay. The wind is pushing it at us, and the bare bottoms on the mangroves show that our bar is covered at high tide. I recall seeing a full moon this morning in—believe it, St. Louis—which means maximal tides. Well, we can climb up in the plane. But what about drinking water?

There's a small splat! behind me. The older woman has sampled the bay. She shakes her head, smiling ruefully. It's the first real expression on either of them; I take it as the signal for introductions. When I say I'm Don Fenton from St. Louis, she tells me their name is Parsons, from Bethesda, Maryland. She says it so nicely I don't at first notice we aren't being given first names. We all compliment Captain Estéban again.

His left eye is swelled shut, an inconvenience beneath his attention as a Maya, but Mrs. Parsons spots the way he's bracing his elbow in his ribs.

"You're hurt, Captain."

"*Roto*—I think is broken." He's embarrassed at being in pain. We get him to peel off his Jaime shirt, revealing a nasty bruise on his superb dark bay torso.

"Is there tape in that kit, Mr. Fenton? I've had a little first-aid training."

She begins to deal competently and very impersonally with the tape. Miss Parsons and I wander to the end of the bar and have a conversation which I am later to recall acutely.

"Roseate spoonbills," I tell her as three pink birds flap away.

"They're beautiful," she says in her tiny voice. They both have tiny voices. "He's a Mayan Indian, isn't he? The pilot, I mean."

"Right. The real thing, straight out of the Bonampak murals. Have you seen Chichén and Uxmal?"

"Yes. We were in Mérida. We're going to Tikal in Guatemala . . . I mean, we were."

"You'll get there." It occurs to me the girl needs cheering up. "Have they told you that Maya mothers used to tie a board on the infant's forehead to get that slant? They also hung a ball of tallow over its nose to make the eyes cross. It was considered aristocratic."

She smiles and takes another peek at Estéban. "People seem different in Yucatán," she says thoughtfully. "Not like the Indians around Mexico City. More, I don't know, independent."

"Comes from never having been conquered. Mayas got massacred and chased a lot, but nobody ever really flattened them. I bet you didn't know that the last Mexican-Maya war ended with a negotiated truce in 1935."

"No!" Then she says seriously, "I like that."

"So do I."

"The water is really rising very fast," says Mrs. Parsons gently from behind us.

It is, and so is another *llovisno*. We climb back into the Bonanza. I try to rig my parka for a rain catcher, which blows loose as the storm hits fast and furious. We sort a couple of malt bars and my bottle of Jack Daniel's out of the jumble in the cabin and make ourselves reasonably comfortable. The Parsons take a sip of whiskey each, Estéban and I considerably more. The Bonanza begins to bump soggily. Estéban makes an ancient one-eyed Mayan face at the water seeping into his cabin and goes to sleep. We all nap.

When the water goes down, the euphoria has gone with it, and we're very, very thirsty. It's also damn near sunset. I get to work with a bait-casting rod and some treble hooks and manage to foul-hook four small mullets. Estéban and the women tie the Bonanza's midget life raft out in the mangroves to catch rain. The wind is parching hot. No planes go by.

Finally another shower comes over and yields us six ounces of water apiece. When the sunset envelopes the world in golden smoke, we squat on the sandbar to eat wet raw mullet and Instant Breakfast crumbs. The women are now in shorts, neat but definitely not sexy.

"I never realized how refreshing raw fish is," Mrs. Parsons says pleasantly. Her daughter chuckles, also pleasantly. She's on Mama's far side away from Estéban and me. I have Mrs. Parsons figured now:

Mother Hen protecting only chick from male predators. That's all right with me. I came here to fish.

But something is irritating me. The damn women haven't complained once, you understand. Not a peep, not a quaver, no personal manifestations whatever. They're like something out of a manual.

"You really seem at home in the wilderness, Mrs. Parsons. You do much camping?"

"Oh, goodness no." Diffident laugh. "Not since my Girl Scout days. Oh, look—are those man-o'-war birds?"

Answer a question with a question. I wait while the frigate birds sail nobly into the sunset.

"Bethesda . . . Would I be wrong in guessing you work for Uncle Sam?"

"Why, yes. You must be very familiar with Washington, Mr. Fenton. Does your work bring you there often?"

Anywhere but on our sandbar the little ploy would have worked. My hunter's gene twitches.

"Which agency are you with?"

She gives up gracefully. "Oh, just GSA records. I'm a librarian."

Of course. I know her now, all the Mrs. Parsonses in records divisions, accounting sections, research branches, personnel and administration offices. Tell Mrs. Parsons we need a recap on the external service contracts for fiscal '73. So Yucatán is on the tours now? Pity . . . I offer her the tired little joke. "You know where the bodies are buried."

She smiles deprecatingly and stands up. "It does get dark quickly, doesn't it?"

Time to get back into the plane.

A flock of ibis are circling us, evidently accustomed to roosting in our fig tree. Estéban produces a machete and a Maya string hammock. He proceeds to sling it between tree and plane, refusing help. His machete stroke is noticeably tentative.

The Parsons are taking a pee behind the tail vane. I hear one of them slip and squeal faintly. When they come back over the hull, Mrs. Parsons asks, "Might we sleep in the hammock, Captain?"

Estéban splits an unbelieving grin. I protest about rain and mosquitoes.

"Oh, we have insect repellent and we do enjoy fresh air."

The air is rushing by about force five and colder by the minute.

"We have our raincoats," the girl adds cheerfully.

Well, okay, ladies. We dangerous males retire inside the damp cabin. Through the wind I hear the women laugh softly now and then, apparently cosy in their chilly ibis roost. A private insanity, I decide. I know myself for the least threatening of men; my non-charisma has been in fact an asset jobwise, over the years. Are they having fantasies about Estéban? Or maybe they really are fresh-air nuts. . . . Sleep comes for me in invisible diesels roaring by on the reef outside.

We emerge dry-mouthed into a vast windy salmon sunrise. A diamond chip of sun breaks out of the sea and promptly submerges in cloud. I go to work with the rod and some mullet bait while two showers detour around us. Breakfast is a strip of wet barracuda apiece.

The Parsons continue stoic and helpful. Under Estéban's direction they set up a section of cowling for a gasoline flare in case we hear a plane, but nothing goes over except one unseen jet droning toward Panama. The wind howls, hot and dry and full of coral dust. So are we.

"They look first in the sea," Estéban remarks. His aristocratic frontal slope is beaded with sweat; Mrs. Parsons watches him concernedly. I watch the cloud blanket tearing by above, getting higher and dryer and thicker. While that lasts nobody is going to find us, and the water business is now unfunny.

Finally I borrow Estéban's machete and hack a long light pole. "There's a stream coming in back there, I saw it from the plane. Can't be more than two, three miles."

"I'm afraid the raft's torn." Mrs. Parsons shows me the cracks in the orange plastic; irritatingly, it's a Delaware label.

"All right," I hear myself announce. "The tide's going down. If we cut the good end off that air tube, I can haul water back in it. I've waded flats before."

Even to me it sounds crazy.

"Stay by plane," Estéban says. He's right, of course. He's also clearly running a fever. I look at the overcast and taste grit and old barracuda. The hell with the manual.

When I start cutting up the raft, Estéban tells me to take the serape. "You stay one night." He's right about that, too; I'll have to wait out the tide.

"I'll come with you," says Mrs. Parsons calmly.

I simply stare at her. What new madness has got into Mother Hen? Does she imagine Estéban is too battered to be functional? While I'm being astounded, my eyes take in the fact that Mrs. Parsons is now quite rosy around the knees, with her hair loose and a sunburn starting on her nose. A trim, in fact a very neat shading-forty.

"Look, that stuff is horrible going. Mud up to your ears and water over your head."

"I'm really quite fit and I swim a great deal. I'll try to keep up. Two would be much safer, Mr. Fenton, and we can bring more water."

She's serious. Well, I'm about as fit as a marshmallow at this time of winter, and I can't pretend I'm depressed by the idea of company. So be it.

"Let me show Miss Parsons how to work this rod."

Miss Parsons is even rosier and more windblown, and she's not clumsy with my tackle. A good girl, Miss Parsons, in her nothing way. We cut another staff and get some gear together. At the last minute Estéban shows how sick he feels: he offers me the machete. I thank him, but, no; I'm used to my Wirkkala knife. We tie some air into the plastic tube for a float and set out along the sandiest looking line.

Estéban raises one dark palm. *"Buen viaje."* Miss Parsons has hugged her mother and gone to cast from the mangrove. She waves. We wave.

An hour later we're barely out of waving distance. The going is purely god-awful. The sand keeps dissolving into silt you can't walk on or swim through, and the bottom is spiked with dead mangrove spears. We flounder from one pothole to the next, scaring up rays and turtles and hoping to god we don't kick a moray eel. Where we're not soaked in slime, we're desiccated, and we smell like the Old Cretaceous.

Mrs. Parsons keeps up doggedly. I only have to pull her out once. When I do so, I notice the sandbar is now out of sight.

Finally we reach the gap in the mangrove line I thought was the creek. It turns out to open into another arm of the bay, with more mangroves ahead. And the tide is coming in.

"I've had the world's lousiest idea."

Mrs. Parsons only says mildly, "It's so different from the view from the plane."

I revise my opinion of the Girl Scouts, and we plow on past the mangroves toward the smoky haze that has to be shore. The sun is setting in our faces, making it hard to see. Ibises and herons fly up around us, and once a big permit spooks ahead, his fin cutting a rooster tail. We fall into more potholes. The flashlights get soaked. I am having fantasies of the mangrove as universal obstacle; it's hard to recall I ever walked down a street, for instance, without stumbling over or under or through mangrove roots. And the sun is dropping, down, down.

Suddenly we hit a ledge and fall over it into a cold flow.

"The stream! It's fresh water!"

We guzzle and gargle and douse our heads; it's the best drink I remember. "Oh my, oh my—!" Mrs. Parsons is laughing right out loud.

"That dark place over to the right looks like real land."

We flounder across the flow and follow a hard shelf, which turns into solid bank and rises over our heads. Shortly there's a break beside a clump of spiny bromels, and we scramble up and flop down at the top, dripping and stinking. Out of sheer reflex my arm goes around my companion's shoulder—but Mrs. Parsons isn't there; she's up on her knees peering at the burnt-over plain around us.

"It's so good to see land one can walk on!" The tone is too innocent. *Noli me tangere.*

"Don't try it." I'm exasperated; the muddy little woman, what does she think? "That ground out there is a crust of ashes over muck, and it's full of stubs. You can go in over your knees."

"It seems firm here."

"We're in an alligator nursery. That was the slide we came up. Don't worry, by now the old lady's doubtless on her way to be made into handbags."

"What a shame."

"I better set a line down in the stream while I can still see."

I slide back down and rig a string of hooks that may get us breakfast. When I get back Mrs. Parsons is wringing muck out of the serape.

"I'm glad you warned me, Mr. Fenton. It *is* treacherous."

"Yeah." I'm over my irritation; god knows I don't want to *tangere* Mrs. Parsons, even if I weren't beat down to mush. "In its quiet way, Yucatán is a tough place to get around in. You can see why the Mayas built roads. Speaking of which—look!"

The last of the sunset is silhouetting a small square shape a couple of kilometers inland: a Maya *ruina* with a fig tree growing out of it.

"Lot of those around. People think they were guard towers."

"What a deserted-feeling land."

"Let's hope it's deserted by mosquitoes."

We slump down in the 'gator nursery and share the last malt bar, watching the stars slide in and out of the blowing clouds. The bugs aren't too bad; maybe the burn did them in. And it isn't hot anymore, either—in fact, it's not even warm, wet as we are. Mrs. Parsons continues tranquilly interested in Yucatán and unmistakably uninterested in togetherness.

Just as I'm beginning to get aggressive notions about how we're going to spend the night if she expects me to give her the serape, she stands up, scuffs at a couple of hummocks and says, "I expect this is as good a place as any, isn't it, Mr. Fenton?"

With which she spreads out the raft bag for a pillow and lies down on her side in the dirt with exactly half the serape over her and the other corner folded neatly open. Her small back is toward me.

The demonstration is so convincing that I'm halfway under my share of serape before the preposterousness of it stops me.

"By the way. My name is Don."

"Oh, of course." Her voice is graciousness itself. "I'm Ruth."

I get in not quite touching her, and we lie there like two fish on a plate, exposed to the stars and smelling the smoke in the wind and feeling things underneath us. It is absolutely the most intimately awkward moment I've had in years.

The woman doesn't mean one thing to me, but the obtrusive recessiveness of her, the defiance of her little rump eight inches from my fly—for two pesos I'd have those shorts down and introduce myself. If I were twenty years younger, if I wasn't so bushed . . . But the twenty years and the exhaustion are there, and it comes to me wryly that Mrs. Ruth Parsons has judged things to a nicety. If I *were* twenty years younger, she wouldn't be here. Like the butterfish that float around a sated barracuda, only to vanish away the instant his intent changes, Mrs. Parsons knows her little shorts are safe. Those firmly filled little shorts, so close . . .

A warm nerve stirs in my groin—and just as it does I become aware of a silent emptiness beside me. Mrs. Parsons is imperceptibly inching away. Did my breathing change? Whatever, I'm perfectly sure that if my hand reached, she'd be elsewhere—probably announcing her intention to take a dip. The twenty years bring a chuckle to my throat, and I relax.

"Good night, Ruth."

"Good night, Don."

And believe it or not, we sleep, while the armadas of the wind roar overhead.

Light wakes me—a cold white glare.

My first thought is 'gator hunters. Best to manifest ourselves as *turistas* as fast as possible. I scramble up, noting that Ruth has dived under the bromel clump.

"*Quién estás? A socorro!* Help, *señores!*"

No answer except the light goes out, leaving me blind.

I yell some more in a couple of languages. It stays dark. There's a vague scrabbling, whistling sound somewhere in the burn-off. Liking everything less by the minute, I try a speech about our plane having crashed and we need help.

A very narrow pencil of light flicks over us and snaps off.

"Eh-ep," says a blurry voice and something metallic twitters. They for sure aren't locals. I'm getting unpleasant ideas.

"Yes, help!"

Something goes *crackle-crackle whish-whish*, and all sounds fade away.

"What the holy hell!" I stumble toward where they were.

"Look." Ruth whispers behind me. "Over by the ruin."

I look and catch a multiple flicker which winks out fast.

"A camp?"

And I take two more blind strides. My leg goes down through the crust and a spike spears me just where you stick the knife in to unjoint a drumstick. By the pain that goes through my bladder I recognize that my trick kneecap has caught it.

For instant basket case you can't beat kneecaps. First you discover your knee doesn't bend anymore, so you try putting some weight on it and a bayonet goes up your spine and unhinges your jaw. Little grains of gristle have got into the sensitive bearing surface. The knee tries to buckle and can't, and mercifully you fall down.

Ruth helps me back to the serape.

"What a fool, what a godforgotten imbecile—"

"Not at all, Don. It was perfectly natural." We strike matches; her fingers push mine aside, exploring. "I think it's in place, but it's swelling fast. I'll lay a wet handkerchief on it. We'll have to wait for morning to check the cut. Were they poachers, do you think?"

"Probably," I lie. What I think they were is smugglers.

She comes back with a soaked bandanna and drapes it on. "We must have frightened them. That light . . . it seemed so bright."

"Some hunting party. People do crazy things around here."

"Perhaps they'll come back in the morning."

"Could be."

Ruth pulls up the wet serape, and we say good night again. Neither of us are mentioning how we're going to get back to the plane without help.

I lie staring south where Alpha Centauri is blinking in and out of the overcast and cursing myself for the sweet mess I've made. My first idea is giving way to an even less pleasing one.

Smuggling, around here, is a couple of guys in an outboard meeting a shrimp boat by the reef. They don't light up the sky or have some kind of swamp buggy that goes whoosh. Plus a big camp . . . paramilitary-type equipment?

I've seen a report of Guévaristo infiltrators operating on the British Honduran border, which is about a hundred kilometers—sixty miles—south of here. Right under those clouds. If that's what looked us over, I'll be more than happy if they don't come back . . .

I wake up in pelting rain, alone. My first move confirms that my leg is as expected—a giant misplaced erection bulging out of my shorts. I raise up painfully to see Ruth standing by the bromels, looking over the bay. Solid wet nimbus is pouring out of the south.

"No planes today."

"Oh, good morning, Don. Should we look at that cut now?"

"It's minimal." In fact the skin is hardly broken, and no deep puncture. Totally out of proportion to the havoc inside.

"Well, they have water to drink," Ruth says tranquilly. "Maybe those hunters will come back. I'll go see if we have a fish—that is, can I help you in any way, Don?"

Very tactful. I emit an ungracious negative, and she goes off about her private concerns.

They certainly are private, too; when I recover from my own sanitary efforts, she's still away. Finally I hear splashing.

"It's a big fish!" More splashing. Then she climbs up the bank with a three-pound mangrove snapper—and something else.

It isn't until the messy work of filleting the fish that I begin to notice.

She's making a smudge of chaff and twigs to singe the fillets, small hands very quick, tension in that female upper lip. The rain has eased off for the moment; we're sluicing wet but warm enough. Ruth brings me my fish on a mangrove skewer and sits back on her heels with an odd breathy sigh.

"Aren't you joining me?"

"Oh, of course." She gets a strip and picks at it, saying quickly, "We either have too much salt or too little, don't we? I should fetch some brine." Her eyes are roving from nothing to no place.

"Good thought." I hear another sigh and decide the Girl Scouts need an assist. "Your daughter mentioned you've come from Mérida. Have you seen much of Mexico?"

"Not really. Last year we went to Mazatlán and Cuernavaca . . ." She puts the fish down, frowning.

"And you're going to see Tikal. Going to Bonampak too?"

"No." Suddenly she jumps up, brushing rain off her face. "I'll bring you some water, Don."

She ducks down the slide, and after a fair while comes back with a full bromel stalk.

"Thanks." She's standing above me, staring restlessly round the horizon.

"Ruth, I hate to say it, but those guys are not coming back and it's probably just as well. Whatever they were up to, we looked like trouble. The most they'll do is tell someone we're here. That'll take a day or two to get around, we'll be back at the plane by then."

"I'm sure you're right, Don." She wanders over to the smudge fire.

"And quit fretting about your daughter. She's a big girl."

"Oh, I'm sure Althea's all right . . . They have plenty of water now." Her fingers drum on her thigh. It's raining again.

"Come on, Ruth. Sit down. Tell me about Althea. Is she still in college?"

She gives that sighing little laugh and sits. "Althea got her degree last year. She's in computer programming."

"Good for her. And what about you, what do you do in GSA Records?"

"I'm in Foreign Procurement Archives." She smiles mechanically, but her breathing is shallow. "It's very interesting."

"I know a Jack Wittig in Contracts, maybe you know him?"

It sounds pretty absurd, there in the 'gator slide.

"Oh, I've met Mr. Wittig. I'm sure he wouldn't remember me."

"Why not?"

"I'm not very memorable."

Her voice is factual. She's perfectly right, of course. Who was that woman, Mrs. Jannings, Janny, who coped with my per diem for years? Competent, agreeable, impersonal. She had a sick father or something. But dammit, Ruth is a lot younger and better-looking. Comparatively speaking.

"Maybe Mrs. Parsons doesn't want to be memorable."

She makes a vague sound, and I suddenly realize Ruth isn't listening to me at all. Her hands are clenched around her knees, she's staring inland at the ruin.

"Ruth. I tell you our friends with the light are in the next county by now. Forget it, we don't need them."

Her eyes come back to me as if she'd forgotten I was there, and she nods slowly. It seems to be too much effort to speak. Suddenly she cocks her head and jumps up again.

"I'll go look at the line, Don. I thought I heard something—" She's gone like a rabbit.

While she's away I try getting up onto my good leg and the staff. The pain is sickening; knees seem to have some kind of hot line to the stomach. I take a couple of hops to test whether the Demerol I have in my belt would get me walking. As I do so, Ruth comes up the bank with a fish flapping in her hands.

"Oh, no, Don! *No!*" She actually clasps the snapper to her breast.

"The water will take some of my weight. I'd like to give it a try."

"You mustn't!" Ruth says quite violently and instantly modulates down. "Look at the bay, Don. One can't see a thing."

I teeter there, tasting bile and looking at the mingled curtains of sun and rain driving across the water. She's right, thank god. Even with two good legs we could get into trouble out there.

"I guess one more night won't kill us."

I let her collapse me back onto the gritty plastic, and she positively bustles around, finding me a chunk to lean on, stretching the serape on both staffs to keep rain off me, bringing another drink, grubbing for dry tinder.

"I'll make us a real bonfire as soon as it lets up, Don. They'll see our smoke, they'll know we're all right. We just have to wait." Cheery smile. "Is there any way we can make you more comfortable?"

Holy Saint Stercuilius: playing house in a mud puddle. For a fatuous moment I wonder if Mrs. Parsons has designs on me. And then she lets out another sigh and sinks back onto her heels with that listening look. Unconsciously her rump wiggles a little. My ear picks up the operative word: *wait.*

Ruth Parsons is waiting. In fact, she acts as if she's waiting so hard it's killing her. For what? For someone to get us out of here, what else? . . . But why was she so horrified when I got up to try to leave? Why all this tension?

My paranoia stirs. I grab it by the collar and start idly checking back. Up to when whoever it was showed up last night, Mrs. Parsons was, I guess, normal. Calm and sensible, anyway. Now's she's humming like a high wire. And she seems to want to stay here and wait. Just as an intellectual pastime, why?

322 ★ JAMES TIPTREE, JR.

Could she have intended to come here? No way. Where she planned to be was Chetumal, which is on the border. Come to think, Chetumal is an odd way round to Tikal. Let's say the scenario was that she's meeting somebody in Chetumal. Somebody who's part of an organization. So now her contact in Chetumal knows she's overdue. And when those types appeared last night, something suggests to her that they're part of the same organization. And she hopes they'll put one and one together and come back for her?

"May I have the knife, Don? I'll clean the fish."

Rather slowly I pass the knife, kicking my subconscious. Such a decent ordinary little woman, a good Girl Scout. My trouble is that I've bumped into too many professional agilities under the careful stereotypes. *I'm not very memorable . . .*

What's in Foreign Procurement Archives? Wittig handles classified contracts. Lots of money stuff; foreign currency negotiations, commodity price schedules, some industrial technology. Or—just as a hypothesis—it could be as simple as a wad of bills back in that modest beige Ventura, to be exchanged for a packet from, say, Costa Rica. If she were a courier, they'd want to get at the plane. And then what about me and maybe Estéban? Even hypothetically, not good.

I watch her hacking at the fish, forehead knotted with effort, teeth in her lip. Mrs. Ruth Parsons of Bethesda, this thrumming, private woman. How crazy can I get? *They'll see our smoke . . .*

"Here's your knife, Don. I washed it. Does the leg hurt very badly?"

I blink away the fantasies and see a scared little woman in a mangrove swamp.

"Sit down, rest. You've been going all out."

She sits obediently, like a kid in a dentist chair.

"You're stewing about Althea. And she's probably worried about you. We'll get back tomorrow under our own steam, Ruth."

"Honestly, I'm not worried at all, Don." The smile fades; she nibbles her lip, frowning out at the bay.

"You know, Ruth, you surprised me when you offered to come along. Not that I don't appreciate it. But I rather thought you'd be concerned about leaving Althea alone with our good pilot. Or was it only me?"

This gets her attention at last.

"I believe Captain Estéban is a very fine type of man."

The words surprise me a little. Isn't the correct line more like "I trust Althea," or even, indignantly, "Althea is a good girl"?

"He's a man. Althea seemed to think he was interesting."

She goes on staring at the bay. And then I notice her tongue flick out and lick that prehensile upper lip. There's a flush that isn't sunburn around her ears and throat too, and one hand is gently rubbing her thigh. What's she seeing, out there in the flats?

Oho.

Captain Estéban's mahogany arms clasping Miss Althea Parsons's pearly body. Captain Estéban's archaic nostrils snuffling in Miss Parsons's tender neck. Captain Estéban's copper buttocks pumping into Althea's creamy upturned bottom . . . The hammock, very bouncy. Mayas know all about it.

Well, well. So Mother Hen has her little quirks.

I feel fairly silly and more than a little irritated. *Now* I find out. But even vicarious lust has much to recommend it, here in the mud and rain. I settle back, recalling that Miss Althea the computer programmer had waved good-bye very composedly. Was she sending her mother to flounder across the bay with me so she can get programmed in Maya? The memory of Honduran mahogany logs drifting in and out of the opalescent sand comes to me. Just as I am about to suggest that Mrs. Parsons might care to share my rain shelter, she remarks serenely, "The Mayas seem to be a very fine type of people. I believe you said so to Althea."

The implications fall on me with the rain. *Type.* As in breeding, bloodline, sire. Am I supposed to have certified Estéban not only as a stud but as a genetic donor?

"Ruth, are you telling me you're prepared to accept a half-Indian grandchild?"

"Why, Don, that's up to Althea, you know."

Looking at the mother, I guess it is. Oh, for mahogany gonads.

Ruth has gone back to listening to the wind, but I'm not about to let her off that easy. Not after all that *noli me tangere* jazz.

"What will Althea's father think?"

Her face snaps around at me, genuinely startled.

"Althea's father?" Complicated semismile. "He won't mind."

"He'll accept it too, eh?" I see her shake her head as if a fly were bothering her, and add with a cripple's malice: "Your husband must be a very fine type of a man."

Ruth looks at me, pushing her wet hair back abruptly. I have the impression that mousy Mrs. Parsons is roaring out of control, but her voice is quiet.

"There isn't any Mr. Parsons, Don. There never was. Althea's father was a Danish medical student . . . I believe he has gained considerable prominence."

"Oh." Something warns me not to say I'm sorry. "You mean he doesn't know about Althea?"

"No." She smiles, her eyes bright and cuckoo.

"Seems like rather a rough deal for her."

"I grew up quite happily under the same circumstances."

Bang, I'm dead. Well, well, well. A mad image blooms in my mind: generations of solitary Parsons women selecting sires, making impregnation trips. Well, I hear the world is moving their way.

"I better look at the fish line."

She leaves. The glow fades. *No.* Just no, no contact. Good-bye, Captain Estéban. My leg is very uncomfortable. The hell with Mrs. Parsons's long-distance orgasm.

We don't talk much after that, which seems to suit Ruth. The odd day drags by. Squall after squall blows over us. Ruth singes up some more fillets, but the rain drowns her smudge; it seems to pour hardest just as the sun's about to show.

Finally she comes to sit under my sagging serape, but there's no warmth there. I doze, aware of her getting up now and then to look around. My subconscious notes that she's still twitchy. I tell my subconscious to knock it off.

Presently I wake up to find her penciling on the water-soaked pages of a little notepad.

"What's that, a shopping list for alligators?"

Automatic polite laugh. "Oh, just an address. In case we—I'm being silly, Don."

"Hey." I sit up, wincing. "Ruth, quit fretting. I mean it. We'll all be out of this soon. You'll have a great story to tell."

She doesn't look up. "Yes . . . I guess we will."

"Come on, we're doing fine. There isn't any real danger here, you know. Unless you're allergic to fish?"

Another good-little-girl laugh, but there's a shiver in it.

"Sometimes I think I'd like to go . . . really far away."

To keep her talking I say the first thing in my head.

"Tell me, Ruth. I'm curious why you would settle for that kind of lonely life, there in Washington? I mean, a woman like you—"

"—should get married?" She gives a shaky sigh, pushing the notebook back in her wet pocket.

"Why not? It's the normal source of companionship. Don't tell me you're trying to be some kind of professional man-hater."

"Lesbian, you mean?" Her laugh sounds better. "With my security rating? No, I'm not."

"Well, then. Whatever trauma you went through, these things don't last forever. You can't hate all men."

The smile is back. "Oh, there wasn't any trauma, Don, and I *don't* hate men. That would be as silly as—as hating the weather." She glances wryly at the blowing rain.

"I think you have a grudge. You're even spooky of me."

Smooth as a mouse bite she says, "I'd love to hear about your family, Don."

Touché. I give her the edited version of how I don't have one any-more, and she says she's sorry, how sad. And we chat about what a good life a single person really has, and how she and her friends enjoy plays and concerts and travel, and one of them is head cashier for Ringling Brothers, how about that?

But it's coming out jerkier and jerkier like a bad tape, with her eyes going round the horizon in the pauses and her face listening for some-thing that isn't my voice. What's wrong with her? Well, what's wrong with any furtively unconventional middle-aged woman with an empty bed. And a security clearance. An old habit of mind remarks unkindly that Mrs. Parsons represents what is known as the classic penetration target.

"—so much more opportunity now." Her voice trails off.

"Hurrah for women's lib, eh?"

"The lib?" Impatiently she leans forward and tugs the serape straight. "Oh, that's doomed."

The apocalyptic word jars my attention.

"What do you mean, doomed?"

She glances at me as if I weren't hanging straight either and says vaguely, "Oh . . ."

"Come on, why doomed? Didn't they get that equal rights bill?"

Long hesitation. When she speaks again her voice is different.

"Women have no rights, Don, except what men allow us. Men are more aggressive and powerful, and they run the world. When the next real crisis upsets them, our so-called rights will vanish like—like that smoke. We'll be back where we always were: property. And whatever has gone wrong will be blamed on our freedom, like the fall of Rome was. You'll see."

Now all this is delivered in a gray tone of total conviction. The last time I heard that tone, the speaker was explaining why he had to keep his file drawers full of dead pigeons.

"Oh, come on. You and your friends are the backbone of the system; if you quit, the country would come to a screeching halt before lunch."

No answering smile.

"That's fantasy." Her voice is still quiet. "Women don't work that way. We're a—a toothless world." She looks around as if she wanted to stop talking. "What women do is survive. We live by ones and twos in the chinks of your world-machine."

"Sounds like a guerrilla operation." I'm not really joking, here in the 'gator den. In fact, I'm wondering if I spent too much thought on mahogany logs.

"Guerrillas have something to hope for." Suddenly she switches on the jolly smile. "Think of us as opossums, Don. Did you know there are opossums living all over? Even in New York City."

I smile back with my neck prickling. I thought I was the paranoid one.

"Men and women aren't different species, Ruth. Women do everything men do."

"Do they?" Our eyes meet, but she seems to be seeing ghosts between us in the rain. She mutters something that could be "My Lai" and looks away. "All the endless wars . . ." Her voice is a whisper. "All the huge authoritarian organizations for doing unreal things. Men live to struggle against each other; we're just part of the battlefield. It'll never change unless you change the whole world. I dream sometimes of—of going away—" She checks and abruptly changes voice. "Forgive me, Don, it's so stupid saying all this."

"Men hate wars too, Ruth," I say as gently as I can.

"I know." She shrugs and climbs to her feet. "But that's your problem, isn't it?"

End of communication. Mrs. Ruth Parsons isn't even living in the same world with me.

I watch her move around restlessly, head turning toward the ruins. Alienation like that can add up to dead pigeons, which would be GSA's problem. It could also lead to believing some joker who's promising to change the whole world. Which could just probably be my problem if one of them was over in that camp last night, where she keeps looking. *Guerrillas have something to hope for?* . . .

Nonsense. I try another position and see that the sky seems to be clearing as the sun sets. The wind is quieting down at last too. Insane to think this little woman is acting out some fantasy in this swamp. But that equipment last night was no fantasy; if those lads have some connection with her, I'll be in the way. You couldn't find a handier spot to dispose of the body. Maybe some Guévaristo is a fine type of man?

Absurd. Sure. The only thing more absurd would be to come through the wars and get myself terminated by a mad librarian's boyfriend on a fishing trip.

A fish flops in the stream below us. Ruth spins around so fast she hits the serape. "I better start the fire," she says, her eyes still on the plain and her head cocked, listening.

All right, let's test.

"Expecting company?"

It rocks her. She freezes, and her eyes come swiveling around at me like a film-take captioned Fright. I can see her decide to smile.

"Oh, one never can tell!" She laughs weirdly, the eyes not changed. "I'll get the—the kindling." She fairly scuttles into the brush.

Nobody, paranoid or not, could call *that* a normal reaction.

Ruth Parsons is either psycho or she's expecting something to happen—and it has nothing to do with me; I scared her pissless.

Well, she could be nuts. And I could be wrong, but there are some mistakes you only make once.

Reluctantly I unzip my body-belt, telling myself that if I think what I think, my only course is to take something for my leg and get as far as possible from Mrs. Ruth Parsons before whoever she's waiting for arrives.

In my belt also is a .32-caliber asset Ruth doesn't know about—and it's going to stay there. My longevity program leaves the shoot-outs to TV and stresses being somewhere else when the roof falls in. I can spend a perfectly safe and also perfectly horrible night out in one of those mangrove flats . . . Am I insane?

At this moment Ruth stands up and stares blatantly inland with her hand shading her eyes. Then she tucks something into her pocket, buttons up, and tightens her belt.

That does it.

I dry-swallow two 100-mg tabs, which should get me ambulatory and still leave me wits to hide. Give it a few minutes. I make sure my compass and some hooks are in my own pocket and sit waiting while Ruth fusses with her smudge fire, sneaking looks away when she thinks I'm not watching.

The flat world around us is turning into an unearthly amber and violet light show as the first numbness seeps into my leg. Ruth has crawled under the bromels for more dry stuff; I can see her foot. Okay. I reach for my staff.

Suddenly the foot jerks, and Ruth yells—or rather, her throat makes that *Uh-uh-hhh* that means pure horror. The foot disappears in a rattle of bromel stalks.

I lunge upright on the crutch and look over the bank at a frozen scene.

Ruth is crouching sideways on the ledge, clutching her stomach. They are about a yard below, floating on the river in a skiff. While I was making up my stupid mind, her friends have glided right under my ass. There are three of them.

They are tall and white. I try to see them as men in some kind of white jumpsuits. The one nearest the bank is stretching out a long white arm toward Ruth. She jerks and scuttles farther away.

The arm stretches after her. It stretches and stretches. It stretches two yards and stays hanging in air. Small black things are wiggling from its tip.

I look where their faces should be and see black hollow dishes with vertical stripes. The stripes move slowly . . .

There is no more possibility of their being human—or anything else I've ever seen. What has Ruth conjured up?

The scene is totally silent. I blink, blink—this cannot be real. The two in the far end of the skiff are writhing those arms around an apparatus on a tripod. A weapon? Suddenly I hear the same blurry voice I heard in the night.

"Guh-give," it groans. "G-give . . ."

Dear God, it's real, whatever it is. I'm terrified. My mind is trying not to form a word.

And Ruth—Jesus, of course—Ruth is terrified too; she's edging along the bank away from them, gaping at the monsters in the skiff, who are obviously nobody's friends. She's hugging something to her body. Why doesn't she get over the bank and circle back behind me?

"G-g-give." That wheeze is coming from the tripod. "Pee-eeze give." The skiff is moving upstream below Ruth, following her. The arm undulates out at her again, its black digits looping. Ruth scrambles to the top of the bank.

"Ruth!" My voice cracks. "Ruth, get over here behind me!"

She doesn't look at me, only keeps sidling farther away. My terror detonates into anger.

"Come back here!" With my free hand I'm working the .32 out of my belt. The sun has gone down.

She doesn't turn but straightens up warily, still hugging the thing. I see her mouth working. Is she actually trying to *talk* to them?

"Please . . ." She swallows. "Please speak to me. I need your help."

"RUTH!!"

At this moment the nearest white monster whips into a great S-curve and sails right onto the bank at her, eight feet of snowy rippling horror.

And I shoot Ruth.

I don't know that for a minute—I've yanked the gun up so fast that my staff slips and dumps me as I fire. I stagger up, hearing Ruth scream, "No! No! No!"

The creature is back down by his boat, and Ruth is still farther away, clutching herself. Blood is running down her elbow.

"Stop it, Don! They aren't attacking you!"

"For god's sake! Don't be a fool, I can't help you if you won't get away from them!"

No reply. Nobody moves. No sound except the drone of a jet passing far above. In the darkening stream below me, the three white figures shift uneasily; I get the impression of radar dishes focusing. The word spells itself in my head: *Aliens*.

Extraterrestrials.

What do I do, call the President? Capture them single-handed with my peashooter? . . . I'm alone in the arse end of nowhere with one leg and my brain cuddled in meperidine hydrochloride.

"Prrr-eese," their machine blurs again. "Wa-wat hep . . ."

"Our plane fell down," Ruth says in a very distinct, eerie voice. She points up at the jet, out toward the bay. "My—my child is there. Please take us *there* in your boat."

Dear god. While she's gesturing, I get a look at the thing she's hugging in her wounded arm. It's metallic, like a big glimmering distributor head. What—?

Wait a minute. This morning: when she was gone so long, she could have found that thing. Something they left behind. Or dropped. And she hid it, not telling me. That's why she kept going under that bromel clump—she was peeking at it. Waiting. And the owners came back and caught her. They want it. She's trying to bargain, by god.

"—Water." Ruth is pointing again. "Take us. Me. And him."

The black faces turn toward me, blind and horrible. Later on I may be grateful for that "us." Not now.

"Throw your gun away, Don. They'll take us back." Her voice is weak.

"Like hell I will. You—who are you? What are you doing here?"

"Oh god, does it matter? He's frightened," she cries to them. "Can you understand?"

She's as alien as they, there in the twilight. The beings in the skiff are twittering among themselves. Their box starts to moan.

"Ss-stu-dens," I make out. "S-stu-ding . . . not—huh-arm-ing . . . w-we . . . buh . . ." It fades into garble and then says "G-give . . . we . . . g-go . . ."

Peace-loving cultural-exchange students—on the interstellar level now. Oh, no.

"Bring that thing here, Ruth—right now!"

But she's starting down the bank toward them saying, "Take me."

"Wait! You need a tourniquet on that arm."

"I know. Please put the gun down, Don."

She's actually at the skiff, right by them. They aren't moving.

"Jesus Christ." Slowly, reluctantly, I drop the .32. When I start down the slide, I find I'm floating; adrenaline and Demerol are a bad mix.

The skiff comes gliding toward me, Ruth in the bow clutching the thing and her arm. The aliens stay in the stern behind their tripod, away from me. I note the skiff is camouflaged tan and green. The world around us is deep shadowy blue.

"Don, bring the water bag!"

As I'm dragging down the plastic bag, it occurs to me that Ruth really is cracking up, the water isn't needed now. But my own brain seems to have gone into overload. All I can focus on is a long white rubbery arm with black worms clutching the far end of the orange tube, helping me fill it. This isn't happening.

"Can you get in, Don?" As I hoist my numb legs up, two long white pipes reach for me. *No you don't.* I kick and tumble in beside Ruth. She moves away.

A creaky hum starts up, it's coming from a wedge in the center of the skiff. And we're in motion, sliding toward dark mangrove files.

I stare mindlessly at the wedge. Alien technological secrets? I can't see any, the power source is under that triangular cover, about two feet long. The gadgets on the tripod are equally cryptic, except that one has a big lens. Their light?

As we hit the open bay the hum rises, and we start planing faster and faster still. Thirty knots? Hard to judge in the dark. Their hull seems to be a modified trihedral much like ours, with a remarkable absence of slap. Say twenty-two feet. Schemes of capturing it swirl in my mind. I'll need Estéban.

Suddenly a huge flood of white light fans out over us from the tripod, blotting out the aliens in the stern. I see Ruth pulling at a belt around her arm, still hugging the gizmo.

"I'll tie that for you."

"It's all right."

The alien device is twinkling or phosphorescing slightly. I lean over to look, whispering, "Give that to me, I'll pass it to Estéban."

"No!" She scoots away, almost over the side. "It's theirs, they need it!"

"What? Are you crazy?" I'm so taken aback by this idiocy I literally stammer. "We have to, we—"

"They haven't hurt us. I'm sure they could." Her eyes are watching me with feral intensity; in the light her face has a lunatic look. Numb as I am, I realize that the wretched woman is poised to throw herself over the side if I move. With the alien thing.

"I think they're gentle," she mutters.

"For Christ's sake, Ruth, they're *aliens!*"

"I'm used to it," she says absently. "There's the island! Stop! Stop here!"

The skiff slows, turning. A mound of foliage is tiny in the light. Metal glints—the plane.

"Althea! Althea! Are you all right?"

Yells, movement on the plane. The water is high, we're floating over the bar. The aliens are keeping us in the lead with the light hiding them. I see one pale figure splashing toward us and a dark one behind, coming more slowly. Estéban must be puzzled by that light.

"Mr. Fenton is hurt, Althea. These people brought us back with the water. Are you all right?"

"A-okay." Althea flounders up, peering excitedly. "You all right? Whew, that light!" Automatically I start handing her the idiotic water bag.

"Leave that for the captain," Ruth says sharply. "Althea, can you climb in the boat? Quickly, it's important."

"Coming."

"No, no!" I protest, but the skiff tilts as Althea swarms in. The aliens twitter, and their voice box starts groaning. "Gu-give . . . now . . . give . . ."

"*Qué llega?*" Estéban's face appears beside me, squinting fiercely into the light.

"Grab it, get it from her—that thing she has—" but Ruth's voice rides over mine. "Captain, lift Mr. Fenton out of the boat. He's hurt his leg. Hurry, please."

"Goddamn it, wait!" I shout, but an arm has grabbed my middle. When a Maya boosts you, you go. I hear Althea saying, "Mother, your arm!" and fall onto Estéban. We stagger around in water up to my waist; I can't feel my feet at all.

When I get steady, the boat is yards away. The two women are head-to-head, murmuring.

"Get them!" I tug loose from Estéban and flounder forward. Ruth stands up in the boat facing the invisible aliens.

"Take us with you. Please. We want to go with you, away from here."

"Ruth! Estéban, get that boat!" I lunge and lose my feet again. The aliens are chirruping madly behind their light.

"Please take us. We don't mind what your planet is like; we'll learn—we'll do anything! We won't cause any trouble. Please. Oh *please*." The skiff is drifting farther away.

"Ruth! Althea! Are you crazy? Wait—" But I can only shuffle night-marelike in the ooze, hearing that damn voice box wheeze, "N-not come . . . more . . . not come . . ." Althea's face turns to it, open-mouthed grin.

"Yes, we understand," Ruth cries. "We don't want to come back. Please take us with you!"

I shout and Estéban splashes past me shouting too, something about radio.

"Yes-s-s," groans the voice.

Ruth sits down suddenly, clutching Althea. At that moment Estéban grabs the edge of the skiff beside her.

"Hold them, Estéban! Don't let her go."

He gives me one slit-eyed glance over his shoulder, and I recognize his total uninvolvement. He's had a good look at that camouflage paint and the absence of fishing gear. I make a desperate rush and slip again. When I come up Ruth is saying, "We're going with these people, Captain. Please take your money out of my purse, it's in the plane. And give this to Mr. Fenton."

She passes him something small; the notebook. He takes it slowly.

"Estéban! No!"

He has released the skiff.

"Thank you so much," Ruth says as they float apart. Her voice is shaky; she raises it. "There won't be any trouble, Don. Please send the cable. It's to a friend of mine, she'll take care of everything." Then she adds the craziest touch of the entire night. "She's a grand person, she's director of nursing training at NIH."

As the skiff drifts out, I hear Althea add something that sounds like "Right on."

Sweet Jesus . . . Next minute the humming has started; the light is receding fast. The last I see of Mrs. Ruth Parsons and Miss Althea Parsons is two small shadows against that light, like two opossums. The light snaps off, the hum deepens—and they're going, going, gone away.

In the dark water beside me, Estéban is instructing everybody in general to *chingarse* themselves.

"Friends, or something," I tell him lamely. "She seemed to want to go with them."

He is pointedly silent, hauling me back to the plane. He knows what could be around here better than I do, and Mayas have their own longevity program. His condition seems improved. As we get in, I notice the hammock has been repositioned.

In the night—of which I remember little—the wind changes. And at seven-thirty next morning a Cessna buzzes the sandbar under cloudless skies.

By noon we're back in Cozumel. Captain Estéban accepts his fees and departs laconically for his insurance wars. I leave the Parsons's bags with the Caribe agent, who couldn't care less. The cable goes to a Mrs. Priscilla Hayes Smith, also of Bethesda. I take myself to a medico and by three P.M. I'm sitting on the Cabañas terrace with a fat leg and a double Margarita, trying to believe the whole thing.

The cable said:

ALTHEA AND I TAKING EXTRAORDINARY OPPORTUNITY FOR TRAVEL. GONE SEVERAL YEARS. PLEASE TAKE CHARGE OUR AFFAIRS. LOVE, RUTH.

She'd written it that afternoon, you understand.

I order another double, wishing to hell I'd gotten a good look at that gizmo. Did it have a label, Made by Betelgeusians? No matter how weird it was, *how* could a person be crazy enough to imagine—?

Not only that but to hope, to plan? *If I could only go away* . . . That's what she was doing, all day. Waiting, hoping, figuring how to get Althea. To go sight unseen to an alien world . . .

With the third Margarita I try a joke about alienated women, but my heart's not in it. And I'm certain there won't be any bother, any trouble at all. Two human women, one of them possibly pregnant, have departed for, I guess, the stars; and the fabric of society will never show a ripple. I brood: Do all Mrs. Parsons's friends hold themselves in readiness for any eventuality, including leaving Earth? And will Mrs. Parsons somehow one day contrive to send for Mrs. Priscilla Hayes Smith, that grand person?

I can only send for another cold one, musing on Althea. What suns will Captain Estéban's sloe-eyed offspring, if any, look upon? "Get in, Althea, we're taking off for Orion." "A-okay, Mother." Is that some system of upbringing? *We survive by ones and twos in the chinks of your world-machine . . . I'm used to aliens . . .* She'd meant every word. Insane. How could a woman choose to live among unknown monsters, to say good-bye to her home, her world?

As the Margaritas take hold, the whole mad scenario melts down to the image of those two small shapes sitting side by side in the receding alien glare.

Two of our opossums are missing.

The Warlord of Saturn's Moons

ELEANOR ARNASON

Here I am, a silver-haired maiden lady of thirty-five, a feeder of stray cats, a window-ledge gardener, well on my way to the African violet and antimacassar stage. I can see myself at fifty, fat and a little crazy, making cucumber sandwiches for tea, and I view my future with mixed feelings. Whatever became of my childhood ambitions: joining the space patrol; winning a gold medal at the Olympics; climbing Mount Everest alone in my bathing suit, sustained only by my indomitable will and strange psychic arts learned from Hindu mystics? The saddest words of tongue or pen are something-or-other what might have been, I think. I light up a cigar and settle down to write another chapter of *The Warlord of Saturn's Moons*. A filthy habit you say, though I'm not sure if you're referring to smoking cigars or writing science fiction. True, I reply, but both activities are pleasurable, and we maiden ladies lead lives that are notoriously short on pleasure.

So back I go to the domes of Titan and my redheaded heroine deathraying down the warlord's minions. Ah, the smell of burning flesh, the spectacle of blackened bodies collapsing. Even on paper it gets a lot of hostility out of you, so that your nights aren't troubled by dreams of murder. Terribly unrestful, those midnight slaughters and waking shaking in the darkness, your hands still feeling pressure from grabbing the victim or fighting off the murderer.

Another escape! In a power-sledge, my heroine races across Titan's methane snow, and I go and make myself tea. There's a paper on the kitchen table, waiting to tell me all about yesterday's arsons, rapes, and bloody murders. Quickly I stuff it into the garbage pail. Outside, the sky is hazy. Another high-pollution day, I think. I can see incinerator smoke rising from the apartment building across the street, which means there's no air alert yet. Unless, of course, they're breaking the law over there. I fling open a cabinet and survey the array of teas. Earl Grey? I ponder, or Assam? Gunpowder? Jasmine? Gen Mai Cha?

Or possibly an herb tea: sassafras, mint, Irish moss, or mu. Deciding on Assam, I put water on, then go back to write an exciting chase through the icy Titanian mountains. A pursuer's sledge goes over a precipice and, as my heroine hears his long shriek on her radio, my teakettle starts shrieking. I hurry into the kitchen. Now I go through the tea-making ceremony: pouring boiling water into the pot, sloshing the water around and pouring it out, measuring the tea in, pouring more boiling water on top of the tea. All the while my mind is with my heroine, smiling grimly as she pilots the power-sledge between bare cliffs. Above her in the dark sky is the huge crescent of Saturn, a shining white line slashing across it—the famous rings. While the tea steeps, I wipe off a counter and wash a couple of mugs. I resist a sudden impulse to pull the newspaper out from among the used tea leaves and orange peelings. I already know what's in it. The Detroit murder count will exceed 1,000 again this year; the war in Thailand is going strong; most of Europe is out on strike. I'm far better off on Titan with my heroine, who is better able to deal with her problems than I am to deal with mine. A deadly shot, she has also learned strange psychic arts from Hindu mystics, which give her great strength, endurance, mental alertness, and a naturally pleasant body odor. I wipe my hands and look at them, noticing the bitten fingernails, the torn cuticles. My heroine's long, slender, strong hands have two-inch nails filed to a point and covered with a plastic paint that makes them virtually unbreakable. When necessary, she uses them as claws. Her cuticles, of course, are in perfect condition.

I pour myself a cup of tea and return to the story. Now my heroine is heading for the mountain hideout where her partner waits: a tall, thin, dour fellow with one shining steel prosthetic hand. She doesn't know his name and she suspects he himself may have forgotten it. He insists on being called 409, his number on the prison asteroid from which he has escaped. She drives as quickly as she dares, thinking of his long face, burned almost black by years of strong radiation on Mars and in space, so the white webbing of scars on its right side shows up clearly. His eyes are gray, so pale they seem almost colorless. As I write about 409, I find myself stirred by the same passion that stirs my heroine. I begin to feel uneasy, so I stop and drink some tea. I can see I'm going to have trouble with 409. It's never wise to get too involved with one's characters. Besides, I'm not his type. I imagine the way he'd look at me, indifference evident on his dark, scarred face. I could, of course, kill him off. My heroine would then spend the rest of the story avenging him, though she'd never get to the real murderer—me. But this solution, while popular among writers, is unfair.

I go into the kitchen, extract a carrot from a bunch in the icebox, clean it, and eat it. After that, I write the heroine's reunion with 409. Neither of them is demonstrative. They greet each other with apparent indifference and retire to bed. I skip the next scene. How can I watch that redheaded hussy in bed with the man I'm beginning to love? I continue the story at the moment when their alarm bell rings, and they awake to find the warlord's rocket planes have landed all around their hideout. A desperate situation! 409 suggests that he make a run for it in their rocket plane. While the warlord's minions pursue him, my heroine can sneak away in the power-sledge. The plan has little chance of success, but they can think of none better. They bid farewell to one another, and my heroine goes to wait in the sledge for the signal telling her 409 has taken off. As she waits, smoking a cigar, she thinks of what little she knows about 409. He was a fighter pilot in the war against the Martian colony and was shot down and captured. While in prison something happened to him that he either can't remember or refuses to talk about, and, when the war ended and he was released, he became a criminal. As for herself, she had been an ordinary sharp-shooter and student of Hindu mysticism, a follower of Swami Bluestone of the Brooklyn Vedic Temple and Rifle Range. Then she discovered by accident the warlord's plot to overthrow the government of Titan, the only one of Saturn's satellites not under his control. With her information about the plot, the government may still be saved. She has to get to Titan City with the microfilm dot!

The alarm bell rings, and she feels the ground shake as 409's plane takes off. Unfortunately, I'm writing the story from my heroine's point of view. I want to describe 409 blasting off, the warlord's rocket planes taking off after him, chasing him as he flies through the narrow, twisting valleys, the planes' rockets flaring red in the valley shadows and missiles exploding into yellow fireballs. All through this, of course, 409's scarred face remains tranquil and his hands move quickly and surely over the plane's controls. His steel prosthetic hand gleams in the dim light from the dials. But I can't put this in the story, since my heroine sees none of it as she slides off in the opposite direction, down a narrow trail hidden by overhanging cliffs.

I am beginning to feel tense, I don't know why. Possibly 409's dilemma is disturbing me. He's certainly in danger. In any case, my tea is cold. I turn on the radio, hoping for some relaxing rock music, and go to get more tea. But it's twenty to the hour, time for the news, and I get the weekend body count: two men found dead in suspected west-side dope house, naked body of woman dragged out of Detroit River. I hurry back and switch to a country music station. On it, someone's singing about how he intends to leave the big city and go back down south. As I go back into the kitchen, I think:

> Carry me back to Titan.
> That's where I want to be.
> I want to repose
> On the methane snows
> At the edge of a frozen sea.

I pour out the old tea and refill the cup with tea that's hot.

The radio begins to make that awful beepity-beep-beepity sound that warns you the news is coming up. I switch back to the rock station, where the news is now over. I'm safe for another fifty-five minutes, unless there's a special news flash to announce a five-car pileup or an especially ghastly murder.

The plan works! For my heroine, at least. She doesn't know yet if 409 got away. She speeds off unpursued. The power-sledge's heating system doesn't quite keep her warm, and the landscape around her is forbidding: bare cliffs and narrow valleys full of methane snow, overhead the dark blue sky. Saturn has set, and the tiny sun is rising, though she can't see it yet. On the high mountains the ice fields begin to glitter with its light. On she races, remembering how she met 409 in the slums of The Cup on Ganymede, as she fled the warlord's assassins. She remembers being cornered with no hope of escape. Then behind the two assassins a tall figure appeared, and the shining steel hand smashed down on the back of one assassin's head. As the other assassin turned, he got the hand across his face. A moment or two more, and both the assassins were on the ground, unconscious. Then she saw 409's twisted grin for the first time and his colorless eyes appraising her.

There I go, I think, getting all heated up over 409. The radio is beginning to bother me, so I shut it off and relight my cigar. I find myself wishing that men like 409 really existed. Increasingly in recent years, I've found real men boring. Is it possible, as some scientists argue, that the Y chromosome produces an inferior human being? There certainly seem to be far fewer interesting men than interesting women. But theories arguing that one kind of human being is naturally inferior make me anxious. I feel my throat muscles tightening and the familiar tense, numb feeling spreading across my face and my upper back. Quickly I return to my story.

Now out on the snowy plain, my heroine can see the transparent domes of Titan City ahead of her, shining in the pale sunlight. Inside the domes the famous pastel towers rise, their windows reflecting the sun. Her power-sledge speeds down the road, through the drifts that half cover it. Snow sprays up on either side of the sledge, so my heroine has trouble seeing to the left and right. As a result, it's some time before she sees the power-sledges coming up behind her on the right. At the same moment that she looks over and sees them, their sleek silver bodies shining in the sunlight and snow-sprays shooting up around them, her radio begins to go beep-beep-beep. She flicks it on. The voice of Janos Black, the warlord's chief agent on Titan, harsh and slurred by a thick Martian accent, tells her the bad news: 409's plane has been shot down. He ejected before it crashed. Even now the warlord's men are going after the ejection capsule, which is high on a cliff, wedged between a rock spire and the cliff wall. Janos offers her a trade: 409 for the microdot. But Janos may well be lying; 409 may have gotten away or else been blown up. She feels a sudden constriction of her throat at the thought of 409 dead. She flicks off the radio and pushes the power-sledge up to top speed. She realizes as she does so that 409 is unlikely to fare well if Janos gets ahold of him. Janos's wife and children died of thirst after the great Martian network of pipelines was blown apart by Earther bombs, and Janos knows that 409 was a pilot in the Earther expeditionary force.

I write another exciting chase, this one across the snowy plain toward the pink, green, blue, and yellow towers of Titan City. The warlord's power-sledges are gaining. Their rockets hit all around my heroine's sledge, and fire and black smoke erupt out of the snow. Swearing in a low monotone, she swings the sledge back and forth in a zigzag evasive pattern.

I stop to puff on my cigar and discover it's gone out again. My tea is cold. But the story's beginning at last to interest me. I keep on writing.

As my heroine approaches the entrance to Titan City, she's still a short distance ahead of her pursuers. Her radio beeps. It's Janos Black again. He tells her his men have gotten to the ejection capsule and are lowering it down the cliff. Any minute now, they'll have it down where they can open it and get 409 out.

Ignoring Janos, she concentrates on slowing her sledge and bringing it through the city's outer gate into the air lock. A moment or two later, she's safe. But what about 409?

Frankly, I don't know. I stand and stretch, decide to take a bath, and go to turn the water on. The air pollution must be worse than I originally thought. I have the dopey feeling I get on the days when the pollution is really bad. I look out the window. Dark gray smoke is still coming out of the chimneys across the street. Maybe I should call the Air Control number (dial AIR-CARE) and complain. But it takes a peculiar kind of person to keep on being public-spirited after it becomes obvious it's futile. I decide to put off calling Air Control and water my plants instead. Every bit of oxygen helps, I think. I check the bathtub—it's not yet half full—and go back to writing. After a couple of transitional paragraphs, my heroine finds herself in the antechamber to the Titan Council's meeting room. There is a man there, standing with his back to her. He's tall and slender, and his long hair is a shade between blond and gray. He turns and she recognizes the pale, delicate-looking face. This is Michael Stelladoro, the warlord of Saturn's moons. His eyes, she notices, are as blue as cornflowers, and he has a delightful smile. He congratulates her on escaping his power-sledges, then tells her that his men have gotten 409 out of the ejection capsule. He is still alive and as far as they can determine uninjured. They have given 409 a shot of Sophamine. At this my heroine gasps with horror. Sophamine, she knows, is an extremely powerful tranquilizer used to control schizophrenia. One dose is enough to make most people dependent on it, and withdrawal takes the form of a nightmarish psychotic fugue. The warlord smiles his delightful smile and turns on the radio he has clipped to his belt. A moment later my heroine hears 409's voice telling her that he has in fact been captured. He sounds calm and completely uninterested in his situation. That, she knows, is the Sophamine. It hasn't affected his perception of reality. He knows where he is and what is likely to happen to him, but he simply doesn't care. When the Sophamine wears off, all the suppressed emotions will well up, so intense that the only way he'll be able to deal with them will be to go insane, temporarily at least.

The warlord tells her he regrets having to use the Sophamine, but he was certain that 409 would refuse to talk unless he was either drugged or tortured, and there simply wasn't enough time to torture him.

"You fiend!" my heroine cries.

The warlord smiles again, as delightfully as before, and says if she gives the microdot to the Titan Council, he will turn 409 over to Janos

Black, who will attempt to avenge on him all the atrocities committed by the Earthers on Mars.

What can she do? As she wonders, the door to the meeting room opens, and she is asked to come in. For a moment, she thinks of asking the Titanians to arrest the warlord. Almost as if he's read her mind, he tells her there's no point in asking the Titanians to arrest him. He has diplomatic immunity and a warfleet waiting for him to return.

She turns to go into the meeting room. "I'll tell Janos the good news," the warlord says softly and turns his radio on.

She hesitates, then thinks, a man this evil must be stopped, no matter what the cost. She goes into the meeting room.

I remember the bathwater, leap up, and run into the bathroom. The tub is brim-full and about to overflow. I turn off the tap, let out some of the water, and start to undress. After I climb into the tub, I wonder how I'm going to get 409 out of the mess he's in. Something will occur to me. I grab the bar of soap floating past my right knee.

After bathing, I put on a pink and silver muumuu and make a fresh pot of tea. Cleanliness is next to godliness, I think as I sit down to write.

My heroine tells her story to the Titan Council and produces the microdot. On it is the warlord's plan for taking over the government of Titan and a list of all the Titanian officials he has subverted. The president of the council thanks her kindly and tells her that they already have a copy of the microdot, obtained for them by an agent of theirs who has infiltrated the warlord's organization. "Oh no! Oh no!" my heroine cries. Startled, the president asks her what's wrong. She explains that she has sacrificed her partner, her love, to bring them the information they already had. "Rest easy," the president says. "Our agent is none other than Janos Black. He won't harm 409."

Thinking of Janos's family dying of thirst in an isolated settlement, my heroine feels none too sure of this. But there's nothing left for her to do except hope.

After that, I describe her waiting in Titan City for news of 409, wandering restlessly through the famous gardens, barely noticing the beds of Martian sandflowers, the blossoming magnolia trees, the pools of enormous silver carp. Since the warlord now knows that the Titan Council knows about his schemes, the council moves quickly to arrest the officials he's subverted. The newscasts are full of scandalous revelations, and the warlord leaves Titan for his home base on Tethys, another one of Saturn's moons. My heroine pays no attention to the newscasts or to the excited conversations going on all around her. She

thinks of the trip she and 409 made from Ganymede to Titan in a
stolen moon-hopper, remembering 409's hands on the ship's controls,
the way he moved in zero-G, his colorless eyes, and his infrequent,
twisted smile. Cornball, I think, but leave the passage in. I enjoy
thinking about 409 as much as my heroine does.

After two days, Janos Black arrives in a police plane. 409 is with
him. Janos comes to see my heroine to bring her the news of their
arrival. He's a tall man with a broad chest and spindly arms and legs.
His face is ruddy and Slavic, and his hair is prematurely white. He
tells her that he kept 409 prisoner in the warlord's secret headquarters
in the Titanian mountains till the Titanian police moved in and arrested
everybody.

"Then he's all right," she cries joyfully.

Janos shakes his head.

"Why not?"

"The Sophamine," Janos explains. "When it wore off, he got hit
with the full force of all his repressed feelings, especially, I think, the
feelings he had about the war on Mars. Think of all that anger and
terror and horror and guilt flooding into his conscious mind. He tried
to kill himself. We stopped him, and he almost killed a couple of us in
the process. By we, I mean myself and the warlord's men; this happened before the police moved in. We had to give him another shot of
Sophamine. He's still full of the stuff. From what I've heard, the doctors
want to keep giving it to him. They think the first shot of Sophamine
he got destroyed his old system of dealing with his more dangerous
emotions, which are now overwhelming him. The doctors say on
Sophamine he can function more or less normally. Off it, they think
he'll be permanently insane."

"You planned this!" she cries.

Janos shakes his head. "The warlord gave the order, miss. I only
obeyed it. But I didn't mind this time. I didn't mind."

I stop to drink some tea. Then I write the final scene in the chapter:
my heroine's meeting with 409. He's waiting for her in a room at the
Titan City Hospital. The room is dark. He sits by the window looking
out at the tall towers blazing with light and at the dome above them,
which reflects the towers' light so it's impossible to look through it at
the sky. She can see his dark shape and the red tip of the cigar he
smokes.

"Do you mind if I turn on the lights?" she asks.

"No."

She finds the button and presses it. The ceiling begins to glow. She looks at 409. He lounges in his chair, his feet up on a table. She realizes it's the first time she's seen him look really relaxed. Before this, he's always seemed tense, even when asleep.

"How are you?" she asks.

"Fine." His voice sounds tranquil and indifferent.

She can't think of anything to say. He looks at her, his dark, scarred face expressionless. Finally he says, "Don't let it bother you. I feel fine." He pauses. She still can't think of anything to say. He continues. "The pigs don't want me for anything here on Titan. I think I'll be able to stay."

"What're you going to do here?"

"Work, I guess. The doctors say I can hold down a job if I keep taking Sophamine." He draws on the cigar, so the tip glows red, then blows out the smoke. He's looking away from her at the towers outside the window. She begins weeping. He looks back at her. "I'm all right. Believe me, I feel fine."

But she can't stop weeping.

Enough for today, I think and put down my pencil. Tomorrow, I'll figure out a way to get 409 off Sophamine. Where there's life there's hope and so forth, I tell myself.

The Day Before the Revolution

URSULA K. LE GUIN

In memoriam, Paul Goodman, 1911–1972

The speaker's voice was as loud as empty beer trucks in a stone street, and the people at the meeting were jammed up close, cobblestones, that great voice booming over them. Taviri was somewhere on the other side of the hall. She had to get to him. She wormed and pushed her way among the dark-clothed, close-packed people. She did not hear the words, nor see the faces: only the booming, and the bodies pressed one behind the other. She could not see Taviri, she was too short. A broad black-vested belly and chest loomed up, blocking her way. She must get through to Taviri. Sweating, she jabbed fiercely with her fist. It was like hitting stone, he did not move at all, but the huge lungs let out right over her head a prodigious noise, a bellow. She cowered. Then she understood that the bellow had not been at her. Others were shouting. The speaker had said something, something fine about taxes or shadows. Thrilled, she joined the shouting—"Yes! Yes!"—and shoving on, came out easily into the open expanse of the Regimental Drill Field in Parheo. Overhead the evening sky lay deep and colorless, and all around her nodded the tall weeds with dry, white, close-floreted heads. She had never known what they were called. The flowers nodded above her head, swaying in the wind that always blew across the fields in the dusk. She ran among them, and they whipped lithe aside and stood up again swaying, silent. Taviri stood among the tall weeds in his good suit, the dark gray one that made him look like a professor or a play actor, harshly elegant. He did not look happy, but he was laughing, and saying something to her. The sound of his voice made her cry, and she reached out to catch hold of his hand, but she did not stop, quite. She could not stop. "Oh, Taviri," she said, "it's just on there!" The queer sweet smell of the white weeds was heavy as she went on. There were thorns, tangles underfoot, there were slopes, pits. She feared to fall, she stopped.

———

Sun, bright morning-glare, straight in the eyes, relentless. She had forgotten to pull the blind last night. She turned her back on the sun, but the right side wasn't comfortable. No use. Day. She sighed twice, sat up, got her legs over the edge of the bed, and sat hunched in her nightdress looking down at her feet.

The toes, compressed by a lifetime of cheap shoes, were almost square where they touched each other and bulged out above in corns; the nails were discolored and shapeless. Between the knoblike ankle bones ran fine, dry wrinkles. The brief little plain at the base of the toes had kept its delicacy, but the skin was the color of mud, and knotted veins crossed the instep. Disgusting. Sad, depressing. Mean. Pitiful. She tried on all the words, and they all fit, like hideous little hats. Hideous: yes, that one too. To look at oneself and find it hideous, what a job! But then, when she hadn't been hideous, had she sat around and stared at herself like this? Not much! A proper body's not an object, not an implement, not a belonging to be admired, it's just you, yourself. Only when it's no longer you, but yours, a thing owned, do you worry about it—Is it in good shape? Will it do? Will it last?

"Who cares?" said Laia fiercely, and stood up.

It made her giddy to stand up suddenly. She had to put out her hand to the bedtable, for she dreaded falling. At that, she thought of reaching out to Taviri, in the dream.

What had he said? She could not remember. She was not sure if she had even touched his hand. She frowned, trying to force memory. It had been so long since she had dreamed about Taviri; and now not even to remember what he had said!

It was gone, it was gone. She stood there hunched in her nightdress, frowning, one hand on the bedtable. How long was it since she had thought of him—let alone dreamed of him—even thought of him, as "Taviri"? How long since she had said his name?

Asieo said. When Asieo and I were in prison in the North. Before I met Asieo. Asieo's theory of reciprocity. Oh yes, she talked about him, talked about him too much no doubt, maundered, dragged him in. But as "Asieo," the last name, the public man. The private man was gone, utterly gone. There were so few left who had even known him. They had all used to be in jail. One laughed about it in those days, all the friends in all the jails. But they weren't even there, these days. They were in the prison cemeteries. Or in the common graves.

"Oh, oh my dear," Laia said out loud, and she sank down onto the bed again because she could not stand up under the remembrance of those first weeks in the Fort, in the cell, those first weeks of the nine years in the Fort in Drio, in the cell, those first weeks after they told her that Asieo had been killed in the fighting in Capitol Square and had been buried with the Fourteen Hundred in the lime-ditches behind Oring Gate. In the cell. Her hands fell into the old position on her lap, the left clenched and locked inside the grip of the right, the right thumb working back and forth a little pressing and rubbing on the knuckle of the left first finger. Hours, days, nights. She had thought of them all, each one, each one of the Fourteen Hundred, how they lay, how the quicklime worked on the flesh, how the bones touched in the burning dark. Who touched him? How did the slender bones of the hand lie now? Hours, years.

"Taviri, I have never forgotten you!" she whispered, and the stupidity of it brought her back to morning light and the rumpled bed. Of course she hadn't forgotten him. These things go without saying between husband and wife. There were her ugly old feet flat on the floor again, just as before. She had got nowhere at all, she had gone in a circle. She stood up with a grunt of effort and disapproval, and went to the closet for her dressing gown.

The young people went about the halls of the House in becoming immodesty, but she was too old for that. She didn't want to spoil some young man's breakfast with the sight of her. Besides, they had grown up in the principle of freedom of dress and sex and all the rest, and she hadn't. All she had done was invent it. It's not the same.

Like speaking of Asieo as "my husband." They winced. The word she should use as a good Odonian, of course, was "partner." But why the hell did she have to be a good Odonian?

She shuffled down the hall to the bathrooms. Mairo was there, washing her hair in a lavatory. Laia looked at the long, sleek, wet hank with admiration. She got out of the House so seldom now that she didn't know when she had last seen a respectably shaven scalp, but still the sight of a full head of hair gave her pleasure, vigorous pleasure. How many times had she been jeered at, *Longhair, Longhair,* had her hair pulled by policemen or young toughs, had her hair shaved off down to the scalp by a grinning soldier at each new prison? And then had grown it all over again, through the fuzz, to the frizz, to the curls, to the mane . . . In the old days. For God's love, couldn't she think of anything today but the old days?

Dressed, her bed made, she went down to commons. It was a good breakfast, but she had never got her appetite back since the damned stroke. She drank two cups of herb tea, but couldn't finish the piece of fruit she had taken. How she had craved fruit as a child, badly enough to steal it; and in the Fort—oh for God's love, stop it! She smiled and replied to the greetings and friendly inquiries of the other breakfasters and big Aevi who was serving the counter this morning. It was he who had tempted her with the peach. "Look at this, I've been saving it for you," and how could she refuse? Anyway she had always loved fruit, and never got enough; once when she was six or seven she had stolen a piece off a vendor's cart in River Street. But it was hard to eat when everyone was talking so excitedly. There was news from Thu, real news. She was inclined to discount it at first, being wary of enthusiasms, but after she had read the article in the paper, and read between the lines of it, she thought, with a strange kind of certainty, deep but cold, Why, this is it; it has come. And in Thu, not here. Thu will break before this country does; the Revolution will first prevail there. As if that mattered! There will be no more nations. And yet it did matter somehow, it made her a little cold and sad—envious, in fact. Of all the infinite stupidities. She did not join in the talk much, and soon got up to go back to her room, feeling sorry for herself. She could not share their excitement. She was out of it, really out of it. It's not easy, she said to herself in justification, laboriously climbing the stairs, to accept being out of it when you've been in it, in the center of it, for fifty years. Oh for God's love. Whining!

She got the stairs and the self-pity behind her, entering her room. It was a good room, and it was good to be by herself. It was a great relief. Even if it wasn't strictly fair. Some of the kids in the attics were living five to a room no bigger than this. There were always more people wanting to live in an Odonian House than could be properly accommodated. She had this big room all to herself only because she was an old woman who had had a stroke. And maybe because she was Odo. If she hadn't been Odo, but merely the old woman with a stroke, would she have had it? Very likely. After all, who the hell wanted to room with a drooling old woman? But it was hard to be sure. Favoritism, elitism, leader-worship, they crept back and cropped out everywhere. But she had never hoped to see them eradicated in her lifetime, in one generation; only Time works the great changes. Meanwhile this was a nice, large, sunny room, proper for a drooling old woman who had started a world revolution.

Her secretary would be coming in an hour to help her dispatch the day's work. She shuffled over to the desk, a beautiful, big piece, a present from the Noi Cabinetmakers' Syndicate because somebody had heard her remark once that the only piece of furniture she had ever really longed for was a desk with drawers and enough room on top . . . damn, the top was practically covered with papers with notes clipped to them, mostly in Noi's small clear handwriting: Urgent.— Northern Provinces.—Consult w/R.T.?

Her own handwriting had never been the same since Asieo's death. It was odd, when you thought about it. After all, within five years after his death she had written the whole *Analogy*. And there were those letters, which the tall guard with the watery gray eyes, what was his name, never mind, had smuggled out of the Fort for her for two years. *The Prison Letters* they called them now, there were a dozen different editions of them. All that stuff, the letters, which people kept telling her were so full of "spiritual strength"—which probably meant she had been lying herself blue in the face when she wrote them, trying to keep her spirits up—and the *Analogy*, which was certainly the solidest intellectual work she had ever done, all of that had been written in the Fort in Drio, in the cell, after Asieo's death. One had to do something, and in the Fort they let one have paper and pens. . . . But it had all been written in the hasty, scribbling hand which she had never felt was hers, not her own like the round, black scrollings of the manuscript of *Society Without Government*, forty-five years old. Taviri had taken not only her body's and her heart's desire to the quicklime with him, but even her good clear handwriting.

But he had left her the Revolution.

How brave of you to go on, to work, to write, in prison, after such a defeat for the Movement, after your partner's death, people had used to say. Damn fools. What else had there been to do? Bravery, courage—what was courage? She had never figured it out. Not fearing, some said. Fearing yet going on, others said. But what could one do but go on? Had one any real choice, ever?

To die was merely to go on in another direction.

If you wanted to come home you had to keep going on, that was what she meant when she wrote, "True journey is return," but it had never been more than an intuition, and she was farther than ever now from being able to rationalize it. She bent down, too suddenly, so that she grunted a little at the creak in her bones, and began to root in a bottom drawer of the desk. Her hand came to an age-softened folder and drew it out, recognizing it by touch before sight confirmed: the manuscript of *Syndical Organization in Revolutionary Transition*. He had printed the title on the folder and written his name under it, Taviri Odo Asieo, IX 741. There was an elegant handwriting, every letter well-formed, bold, and fluent. But he had preferred to use a voiceprinter. The manuscript was all in voiceprint, and high quality, too, hesitancies adjusted and idiosyncrasies of speech normalized. You couldn't see there how he had said "o" deep in his throat as they did on the North Coast. There was nothing of him there but his mind. She had nothing of him at all except his name written on the folder. She hadn't kept his letters, it was sentimental to keep letters. Besides, she never kept anything. She couldn't think of anything that she had ever owned for more than a few years, except this ramshackle old body, of course, and she was stuck with that. . . .

Dualizing again. "She" and "it." Age and illness made one dualist, made one escapist; the mind insisted, *It's not me, it's not me.* But it was. Maybe the mystics could detach mind from body, she had always rather wistfully envied them the chance, without hope of emulating them. Escape had never been her game. She had sought for freedom here, now, body and soul.

First self-pity, then self-praise, and here she still sat, for God's love, holding Asieo's name in her hand, why? Didn't she know his name without looking it up? What was wrong with her? She raised the folder to her lips and kissed the handwritten name firmly and squarely, replaced the folder in the back of the bottom drawer, shut the drawer, and straightened up in the chair. Her right hand tingled. She scratched it, and then shook it in the air, spitefully. It had never quite got over the stroke. Neither had her right leg, or right eye, or the right corner of her mouth. They were sluggish, inept, they tingled. They made her feel like a robot with a short circuit.

And time was getting on, Noi would be coming, what had she been doing ever since breakfast?

She got up so hastily that she lurched, and grabbed at the chairback to make sure she did not fall. She went down the hall to the bathroom and looked in the big mirror there. Her gray knot was loose and droopy, she hadn't done it up well before breakfast. She struggled with it a while. It was hard to keep her arms up in the air. Amai, running in to piss, stopped and said, "Let me do it!" and knotted it up tight and neat in no time, with her round, strong, pretty fingers, smiling and silent. Amai was twenty, less than a third of Laia's age. Her parents had both been members of the Movement, one killed in the insurrection of '60, the other still recruiting in the South Provinces. Amai had grown up in Odonian Houses, born to the Revolution, a true daughter of anarchy. And so quiet and free and beautiful a child, enough to make you cry when you thought: this is what we worked for, this is what we meant, this is it, here she is, alive, the kindly, lovely future.

Laia Asieo Odo's right eye wept several little tears, as she stood between the lavatories and the latrines having her hair done up by the daughter she had not borne; but her left eye, the strong one, did not weep, nor did it know what the right eye did.

She thanked Amai and hurried back to her room. She had noticed, in the mirror, a stain on her collar. Peach juice, probably. Damned old dribbler. She didn't want Noi to come in and find her with drool on her collar.

As the clean shirt went on over her head, she thought, What's so special about Noi?

She fastened the collar-frogs with her left hand, slowly.

Noi was thirty or so, a slight, muscular fellow with a soft voice and alert dark eyes. That's what was special about Noi. It was that simple. Good old sex. She had never been drawn to a fair man or a fat one, or the tall fellows with big biceps, never, not even when she was fourteen and fell in love with every passing fart. Dark, spare, and fiery, that was the recipe. Taviri, of course. This boy wasn't a patch on Taviri for brains, nor even for looks, but there it was: she didn't want him to see her with dribble on her collar and her hair coming undone.

Her thin, gray hair.

Noi came in, just pausing in the open doorway—my God, she hadn't even shut the door while changing her shirt!—She looked at him and saw herself. The old woman.

You could brush your hair and change your shirt, or you could wear last week's shirt and last night's braids, or you could put on cloth of gold and dust your shaven scalp with diamond powder. None of it would make the slightest difference. The old woman would look a little less, or a little more, grotesque.

One keeps oneself neat out of mere decency, mere sanity, awareness of other people.

And finally even that goes, and one dribbles unashamed.

"Good morning," the young man said in his gentle voice.

"Hello, Noi."

No, by God, it was *not* out of mere decency. Decency be damned. Because the man she had loved, and to whom her age would not have mattered—because he was dead, must she pretend she had no sex? Must she suppress the truth, like a damned puritan authoritarian? Even six months ago, before the stroke, she had made men look at her and like to look at her; and now, though she could give no pleasure, by God she could please herself.

When she was six years old, and Papa's friend Gadeo used to come by to talk politics with Papa after dinner, she would put on the gold-colored necklace that Mama had found on a trash-heap and brought home for her. It was so short that it always got hidden under her collar where nobody could see it. She liked it that way. She knew she had it on. She sat on the doorstep and listened to them talk, and knew that she looked nice for Gadeo. He was dark, with white teeth that flashed. Sometimes he called her "pretty Laia." "There's my pretty Laia!" Sixty-six years ago.

"What? My head's dull. I had a terrible night." It was true. She had slept even less than usual.

"I was asking if you'd seen the papers this morning."

She nodded.

"Pleased about Soinehe?"

Soinehe was the province in Thu which had declared its secession from the Thuvian State last night.

He was pleased about it. His white teeth flashed in his dark, alert face. Pretty Laia.

"Yes. And apprehensive."

"I know. But it's the real thing, this time. It's the beginning of the end of the Government in Thu. They haven't even tried to order troops into Soinehe, you know. It would merely provoke the soldiers into rebellion sooner, and they know it."

She agreed with him. She herself had felt that certainty. But she could not share his delight. After a lifetime of living on hope because there is nothing but hope, one loses the taste for victory. A real sense of triumph must be preceded by real despair. She had unlearned despair a long time ago. There were no more triumphs. One went on.

"Shall we do those letters today?"

"All right. Which letters?"

"To the people in the North," he said without impatience.

"In the North?"

"Parheo, Oaidun."

She had been born in Parheo, the dirty city on the dirty river. She had not come here to the capital till she was twenty-two and ready to bring the Revolution. Though in those days, before she and the others had thought it through, it had been a very green and puerile revolution. Strikes for better wages, representation for women. Votes and wages—Power and Money, for the love of God! Well, one does learn a little, after all, in fifty years.

But then one must forget it all.

"Start with Oaidun," she said, sitting down in the armchair. Noi was at the desk ready to work. He read out excerpts from the letters she was to answer. She tried to pay attention and succeeded well enough that she dictated one whole letter and started on another. "Remember that at this stage your brotherhood is vulnerable to the threat of . . . no, to the danger . . . to . . ." She groped till Noi suggested, "The danger of leader-worship?"

"All right. And that nothing is so soon corrupted by power-seeking as altruism. No. And that nothing corrupts altruism—no. Oh for God's love you know what I'm trying to say, Noi, you write it. They know it too, it's just the same old stuff, why can't they read my books!"

"Touch," Noi said gently, smiling, citing one of the central Odonian themes.

"All right, but I'm tired of being touched. If you'll write the letter I'll sign it, but I can't be bothered with it this morning." He was looking at her with a little question or concern. She said, irritable, "There is something else I have to do!"

When Noi had gone she sat down at the desk and moved the papers about, pretending to be doing something, because she had been startled, frightened, by the words she had said. She had nothing else to do. She never had had anything else to do. This was her work: her lifework. The speaking tours and the meetings and the streets were out of reach for her now, but she could still write, and that was her work. And anyhow if she had had anything else to do, Noi would have known it; he kept her schedule, and tactfully reminded her of things, like the visit from the foreign students this afternoon.

Oh, damn. She liked the young, and there was always something to learn from a foreigner, but she was tired of new faces and tired of being on view. She learned from them, but they didn't learn from her; they had learnt all she had to teach long ago, from her books, from the Movement. They just came to look, as if she were the Great Tower in Rodarred, or the Canyon of the Tulaevea. A phenomenon, a monument. They were awed, adoring. She snarled at them: Think your own thoughts!—That's not anarchism, that's mere obscurantism.— You don't think liberty and discipline are incompatible, do you?—They accepted their tonguelashing meekly as children, gratefully, as if she were some kind of All-Mother, the idol of the Big Sheltering Womb. She! She who had mined the shipyards at Seissero, and had cursed Premier Inoilte to his face in front of a crowd of seven thousand, telling him he would have cut off his own balls and had them bronzed and sold as souvenirs, if he thought there was any profit in it—she who had screeched, and sworn, and kicked policemen, and spat at priests, and pissed in public on the big brass plaque in Capitol Square that said Here Was Founded the Sovereign Nation State of A-Io, etc., etc., *psssssss* to all that! And now she was everybody's grandmama, the dear old lady, the sweet old monument, come worship at the womb. The fire's out, boys, it's safe to come up close.

"No, I won't," Laia said out loud. "I will not." She was not self-conscious about talking to herself, because she always had talked to herself. "Laia's invisible audience," Taviri had used to say, as she went through the room muttering. "You needn't come, I won't be here," she told the invisible audience now. She had just decided what it was she had to do. She had to go out. To go into the streets.

It was inconsiderate to disappoint the foreign students. It was erratic, typically senile. It was un-Odonian. *Psssss* to all that. What was the good working for freedom all your life and ending up without any freedom at all? She would go out for a walk.

"What is an anarchist? One who, choosing, accepts the responsibility of choice."

On the way downstairs she decided, scowling, to stay and see the foreign students. But then she would go out.

They were very young students, very earnest: doe-eyed, shaggy, charming creatures from the Western Hemisphere, Benbili and the Kingdom of Mand, the girls in white trousers, the boys in long kilts, warlike and archaic. They spoke of their hopes. "We in Mand are so very far from the Revolution that maybe we are near it," said one of the girls, wistful and smiling: "The Circle of Life!" and she showed the extremes meeting, in the circle of her slender, dark-skinned fingers. Amai and Aevi served them white wine and brown bread, the hospitality of the House. But the visitors, unpresumptuous, all rose to take their leave after barely half an hour. "No, no, no," Laia said, "stay here, talk with Aevi and Amai. It's just that I get stiff sitting down, you see. I have to change about. It has been so good to meet you, will you come back to see me, my little brothers and sisters, soon?" For her heart went out to them, and theirs to her, and she exchanged kisses all round, laughing, delighted by the dark young cheeks, the affectionate eyes, the scented hair, before she shuffled off. She was really a little tired, but to go up and take a nap would be a defeat. She had wanted to go out. She would go out. She had not been alone outdoors since—when? since winter! before the stroke. No wonder she was getting morbid. It had been a regular jail sentence. Outside, the streets, that's where she lived.

She went quietly out the side door of the House, past the vegetable patch, to the street. The narrow strip of sour city dirt had been beautifully gardened and was producing a fine crop of beans and *ceëa*, but Laia's eye for farming was unenlightened. Of course it had been clear that anarchist communities, even in the time of transition, must work toward optimal self-support, but how that was to be managed in the way of actual dirt and plants wasn't her business. There were farmers and agronomists for that. Her job was the streets, the noisy, stinking streets of stone, where she had grown up and lived all her life, except for the fifteen years in prison.

She looked up fondly at the facade of the House. That it had been built as a bank gave peculiar satisfaction to its present occupants. They kept their sacks of meal in the bombproof money-vault, and aged their cider in kegs in safe-deposit boxes. Over the fussy columns that faced the street, carved letters still read, National Investors and Grain Factors Banking Association. The Movement was not strong on names. They had no flag. Slogans came and went as the need did. There was always the Circle of Life to scratch on walls and pavements where Authority would have to see it. But when it came to names they were indifferent, accepting and ignoring whatever they got called, afraid of being pinned down and penned in, unafraid of being absurd. So this best known and second oldest of all the cooperative Houses had no name except The Bank.

It faced on a wide and quiet street, but only a block away began the Temeba, an open market, once famous as a center for black market psychogenics and teratogenics, now reduced to vegetables, second-hand clothes, and miserable sideshows. Its crapulous vitality was gone, leaving only half-paralyzed alcoholics, addicts, cripples, hucksters, and fifth-rate whores, pawnshops, gambling dens, fortune-tellers, body-sculptors, and cheap hotels. Laia turned to the Temeba as water seeks its level.

She had never feared or despised the city. It was her country. There would not be slums like this if the Revolution prevailed. But there would be misery. There would always be misery, waste, cruelty. She had never pretended to be changing the human condition, to be Mama taking tragedy away from the children so they won't hurt themselves. Anything but. So long as people were free to choose, if they chose to drink flybane and live in sewers, it was their business. Just so long as it wasn't the business of Business, the source of profit and the means of power for other people. She had felt all that before she knew anything; before she wrote the first pamphlet, before she left Parheo, before she knew what "capital" meant, before she'd been farther than River Street where she played roll-taggie kneeling on scabby knees on the pavement with the other six-year-olds, she had known it: that she, and the other kids, and her parents, and their parents, and the drunks and whores and all of River Street, were at the bottom of something—were the foundation, the reality, the source.

But will you drag civilization down into the mud? cried the shocked decent people, later on, and she had tried for years to explain to them that if all you had was mud, then if you were God you made it into human beings, and if you were human you tried to make it into houses where human beings could live. But nobody who thought he was better than mud would understand. Now, water seeking its level, mud to mud, Laia shuffled through the foul, noisy street, and all the ugly weakness of her old age was at home. The sleepy whores, their lacquered hair arrangements dilapidated and askew, the one-eyed woman wearily yelling her vegetables to sell, the halfwit beggar slapping flies, these were her countrywomen. They looked like her, they were all sad, disgusting, mean, pitiful, hideous. They were her sisters, her own people.

She did not feel very well. It had been a long time since she had walked so far, four or five blocks, by herself, in the noise and push and stinking summer heat of the streets. She had wanted to get to Koly Park, the triangle of scruffy grass at the end of the Temeba, and sit there for a while with the other old men and women who always sat there, to see what it was like to sit there and be old; but it was too far. If she didn't turn back now, she might get a dizzy spell, and she had a dread of falling down, falling down and having to lie there and look up at the people come to stare at the old woman in a fit. She turned and started home, frowning with effort and self-disgust. She could feel her face very red, and a swimming feeling came and went in her ears. It got a bit much, she was really afraid she might keel over. She saw a doorstep in the shade and made for it, let herself down cautiously, sat, sighed.

Nearby was a fruit seller, sitting silent behind his dusty, withered stock. People went by. Nobody bought from him. Nobody looked at her. Odo, who was Odo? Famous revolutionary, author of *Community, The Analogy*, etc., etc. She, who was she? An old woman with gray hair and a red face sitting on a dirty doorstep in a slum, muttering to herself.

True? Was that she? Certainly it was what anybody passing her saw. But was it she, herself, any more than the famous revolutionary, etc., was? No. It was not. But who was she, then?

The one who loved Taviri.

Yes. True enough. But not enough. That was gone; he had been dead so long.

"Who am I?" Laia muttered to her invisible audience, and they knew the answer and told it to her with one voice. She was the little girl with scabby knees, sitting on the doorstep staring down through the dirty golden haze of River Street in the heat of late summer, the six-year-old, the sixteen-year-old, the fierce, cross, dream-ridden girl, untouched, untouchable. She was herself. Indeed she had been the tireless worker and thinker, but a bloodclot in a vein had taken that woman away from her. Indeed she had been the lover, the swimmer in the midst of life, but Taviri, dying, had taken that woman away with him. There was nothing left, really, but the foundation. She had come home; she had never left home. "True voyage is return." Dust and mud and a doorstep in the slums. And beyond, at the far end of the street, the field full of tall dry weeds blowing in the wind as night came.

"Laia! What are you doing here? Are you all right?"

One of the people from the House, of course, a nice woman, a bit fanatical and always talking. Laia could not remember her name though she had known her for years. She let herself be taken home, the woman talking all the way. In the big cool common room (once occupied by tellers counting money behind polished counters supervised by armed guards) Laia sat down in a chair. She was unable just as yet to face climbing the stairs, though she would have liked to be alone. The woman kept on talking, and other excited people came in. It appeared that a demonstration was being planned. Events in Thu were moving so fast that the mood here had caught fire, and something must be done. Day after tomorrow, no, tomorrow, there was to be a march, a big one, from Old Town to Capitol Square—the old route. "Another Ninth Month Uprising," said a young man, fiery and laughing, glancing at Laia. He had not even been born at the time of the Ninth Month Uprising, it was all history to him. Now he wanted to make some history of his own. The room had filled up. A general meeting would be held here, tomorrow, at eight in the morning. "You must talk, Laia."

"Tomorrow? Oh, I won't be here tomorrow," she said brusquely. Whoever had asked her smiled, another one laughed, though Amai glanced round at her with a puzzled look. They went on talking and shouting. The Revolution. What on earth had made her say that? What a thing to say on the eve of the Revolution, even if it was true.

She waited her time, managed to get up, for all her clumsiness, to slip away unnoticed among the people busy with their planning and excitement. She got to the hall, to the stairs, and began to climb them one by one. "The general strike," a voice, two voices, ten voices were saying in the room below, behind her. "The general strike," Laia muttered, resting for a moment on the landing. Above, ahead, in her room, what awaited her? The private stroke. That was mildly funny. She started up the second flight of stairs, one by one, one leg at a time, like a small child. She was dizzy, but she was no longer afraid to fall. On ahead, on there, the dry white flowers nodded and whispered in the open fields of evening. Seventy-two years and she had never had time to learn what they were called.

The Family Monkey

LISA TUTTLE

William

I was sitting with Florrie on the porch of her Daddy's house, watching the night get darker and wondering about making a move. I was at that time living in a boardinghouse in Nacogdoches, and Florrie's father had made me an offer to work for him that came complete with a house to live in. I didn't know if I wanted to be that much obligated to the man: I still thought I might want to go back to Tennessee, and maybe I'd be better with nothing to keep me here.

But then there was Florrie. I still can't figure why I was so interested in that scrawny little old girl, but I was. I guess there weren't too many women in Texas then, but still—most of the time Florrie didn't seem more than a child. But it was those other times that made me wonder, and made me wait, staying on in Texas, a place I didn't much like and didn't at all belong in.

I was just deciding that moving a little closer to her there on the porch couldn't do no harm when there was a sudden flash in the sky, much brighter than any falling star ever was. It began to drop, leaving a streaky, glowing trail behind as it blazed brighter and then disappeared into the pines.

"What was that?" Florrie asked, already standing.

"Falling star?" I got up beside her.

"If it was, it must have fallen right over in the graveyard, it was so big and bright," Florrie said. Then, "Let's go see! I'd love to see a star up close!"

I thought I'd like to see a star up close myself, not that Florrie gave me any time to agree or disagree. She just took off into the woods and I followed after as best I could. I ran into a lot of things in those dark woods. I tried to take hold of Florrie's hand, but she was impatient with me and pushed me off, saying there wasn't room for but one on this path, and that was true. It wasn't much of a path, and it must have been made by children, or elves, because below the shoulders I was fine, but I kept running head-on into hanging vines and protruding branches. I scratched my face up pretty good, and I guess I was lucky not to lose an eye. And Florrie really trotted through those woods, although I kept calling to her to slow up.

Halfway there it suddenly dawned on me. "Hey, Florrie, how're we goin' to see anything? It'll be pitch black in that old graveyard, and we didn't bring a lantern."

"If you'll hurry we can get there before the star burns itself out. We'll see by the light of that."

So I saved my breath for keeping up with her, not wanting to be lost in the woods without a light *or* a girl.

"There—is that it?"

I came up close behind her and looked where she was pointing. Whatever it was had sure enough landed right in the graveyard, but if it was a star or not we couldn't tell, for it had burned itself out. The night grew thicker around us and about all you could make out was a big, odd-angled, collapsed shape, like a barn some giant had pitched across a pasture. Whatever it was, it had no business being in that graveyard.

"What is it?" Florrie whispered, but I had no inclination to find out. Because suddenly, maybe foolishly, I was wondering if something might not come crawling out of the wreckage.

"Let's leave it be," I whispered back. "We can come out in the morning and have a good look. It's too dark now."

"If we wait till morning something might happen to it," she objected. "I'll just run back and fetch a lantern. You stay here and watch it."

"Why don't I go for the lantern?"

"You might get lost. I can go quicker'n you."

"Why don't we both go?"

"You afraid?" she asked, suddenly understanding.

"Of course not!" I said real quick.

"Then just wait here." And she took off running, and what could I do but stay? I didn't want her to think me a coward, and besides, she was right—I would have got lost in those woods.

Now, I am not the type who gets nervous about graveyards, after dark or otherwise. I don't believe in ghosts, and back in Tennessee there was a girl I used to take to a graveyard to court, so I have a kind of fondness for the places. The thing that was bothering me was that thing which didn't belong there, that chunk of star or whatever it was that had fallen out of the sky.

And as I sat there, staring at it (I couldn't see anything, but I didn't like the idea of turning my back on it), I started to hear something—a scratchy, grating sound that seemed to poke at the roots of my teeth and needle me just under my skin—and yet, although it didn't seem to make any sense at the time, I wasn't at all sure that I was hearing anything. It was a noise my body sensed more than heard, a noise that was somehow a part of me, inside, like the sound of my own blood pounding in my ears when everything else is silent.

I wanted to break and run, but there was something—and it was something more than fearing Florrie's scorn, it was a kind of compulsion—that wouldn't let me. So I stood there sweating, and argued with my feet, which seemed to want to drag me over closer to that thing.

"Mr. Peacock?" Florrie, with a light, burst out of the brush. "Oh, you weren't going to explore it without me?"

I saw that my feet had done a pretty good job despite my arguments.

"Why, no ma'am," I said, but she wasn't paying attention to me. She held the lantern up and we looked.

The thing which had fallen from the sky was of some dull metal. We could feel the heat from it, and the ground around was charred. I couldn't make out what it was, but I thought: It's a flying machine, and it's come from far away. And then forgot.

"What's that?" Florrie asked, whispering again.

There was a hole in the thing, deep blackness the lantern light didn't touch, gouged out of the silvery metal. Then I saw what Florrie meant. Something was moving inside the darkness, inside the metal thing. Something was trying to get out.

You might have expected a woman to go crazy then, and Florrie did, but not at all in the way you'd expect. She didn't grab me, and she didn't scream, and she didn't faint or cry or run for home. She said, "We gotta help him, Billy." Her voice was urgent, and she started walking toward the hole without fear or hesitation.

Most of all I noticed that she called me Billy. Then I noticed she'd said "him"—"We gotta help him"—and with all that noticing, I hardly paid any attention to the fact that I was agreeing and going with her, reaching in (carefully, avoiding the edges) and catching hold of something, someone, and pulling it out. I was scared, but I couldn't stop doing the thing that scared me. The flesh beneath my fingers didn't feel like the flesh of any man, but it was no animal we grappled with. He was stuck, and we knew we were hurting him, but we knew we had to get him out. It had to be done: the urgency was as great as if this had been my mother pinned beneath a rockslide.

And then we got him out and stretched on the grass. He looked enough like a man—in that he wasn't a dog or a horse—but even in the lantern light it was plain he wasn't human. He was some kind of freak or monster. His skin was too big on him. It hung like a sheet draped over his bones, the way the skin of a fat man, suddenly starved, might hang. It was rough and pebbly to the touch, and later, in daylight, we saw that he was a greenish-gray color all over. His eyes were too round, and there was something funny about the eyelids, and he didn't have a regular nose but only a couple of slits with flaps of flesh over them in the center of his face. It gave me a real creepy feeling all over when I saw what he was doing with his throat—blowing out a sort of translucent bubble of skin, the way a certain kind of lizard does.

I wished we hadn't come. I wished like anything we hadn't come.

"We'll have to get him to shelter so we can look after him," Florrie said. She stared down at the creature. I looked at her, not wanting to look at it. I wondered why she sounded so sure of herself, and why she wasn't scared.

Her face was tight, like she was hurting and trying not to let it bother her. "I wish I knew rightly what to do," she said quietly. "I know what's wrong, and I know what would make him worse, but . . . maybe there isn't anything I can do to make it better, maybe there isn't anything anyone *here* can do for him now. But we can try—we can make him more comfortable, at least. We'll have to fix up some kind of stretcher, to bring him up to the house. I'll go—"

"You? Why don't I?"

She looked at me scornfully. "Because you can't just go and get things out of my house without a lot of questions, that's why."

"What does it matter? If we're going to take him up there any-way—"

"We're not."

"You said—"

"Your house, not mine."

"My house! We can't carry him all the way to town, to a board-inghouse—"

"The guest house. That's what I meant. You'll be moving in soon, and we can keep him hidden there until he gets better."

"What makes you so sure I'm going to move in?"

"Now, Billy, don't be like that. We're just wasting time. Somebody might come and see."

"Well, so what if somebody does come?" I was getting pretty exasperated with her. "So what? Why can't we take him to your house? We could get the doctor, since you're so concerned about his health."

I stopped short of saying what else I thought—that this thing would be better off dead, that it didn't belong. Something like it would be easier explained away and forgotten once it was dead. Tuck him down in the graveyard among bodies too far gone to have any complaints about their company.

Florrie straightened slightly and said flatly, "My daddy shot a nigger once for comin' round on his property. He doesn't hardly think niggers are people, so you can guess what he'd have to say about this one. He'd kill him like an animal and feel less guilt. Now you just wait right here while I go get some things."

"Why should I? Why should I wait here with this old monster?"

"Billy, you just have to." She looked at me with her gray eyes shining in the lantern light, and I saw she wasn't a child at all. So I put my arm around her and made to kiss her, and she punched me in the gut.

Then she went off into the woods again while I was still hunched over. I started swearing, but I didn't go after her, and I didn't go off on my own. I stayed there with that thing, just like she wanted me to. Just like it wanted me to.

And we took it up to the guest house, and she tended it and nursed it, and just as she'd said, I moved into the house and went to work for her father and never made it back to Tennessee. And in time I married her, despite that gut-punch, and despite the way she had of bossing me. Pete—as we called the monster after the only sound, the only real sound, we ever heard him make, a sort of *ppppp-ttttt* sound in his throat—became a part of the family and no longer seemed like such a monster. In time, he looked just as natural to us as any other person did, although he never stopped making me uneasy. It really unsettled me the way he and Florrie seemed to understand each other, whereas he and I were always strangers to each other. Our kids, when they came in time, loved Pete, and he was good with them.

I guess in all it's been good, it's worked out. I've made a home for myself here and a name, friends, and family. I think about the Tennessee hills sometimes—it's too flat here, and too dusty, even in the piney woods, for my taste—and I miss them, and the people I used to know. But they're all dead now probably, or gone away, and if I was to go back there wouldn't be anyone that knew me. This is my place now, even if I still don't much like it.

Adaptation

At first it seemed only an oddity that they left him alone during the hours of darkness. At first, he was too immersed in his pain to notice how life around him slowed and consciousness moved to another level.

There was much to learn, once he had mended (as much as he would ever mend) and could turn his attention to things outside his body. Sleep intrigued him—it was strange to him.

Life was very boring here for him, injured and out of touch with his own people. He searched hungrily for new interests, knowing that he must keep himself going, keep himself intrigued, or die. Something had happened to him in the crash which made it harder for him to think. His mind seemed wrapped in gauze now; he was limited. He could not communicate with these creatures, could not understand nor be understood except on the fuzziest, most imprecise and primitive levels. He was frustrated by the multitude of things he could no longer do, some of them simple things learned in childhood. There were ranges and heights now forever barred to him.

He continued work with the limited mental equipment left to him. He tried to go on being a scholar, to give his life some meaning.

Sleep: it fascinated him. Here was something which might be important, a mental-spiritual state alien to his people. All of these creatures slept: What did it mean? What did they take from their journey through it every night?

To find out, he set about trying to fall asleep, to study the phenomenon at first hand. But he had no experience and no knowledge to draw upon. How to attain it? How to abandon oneself to it? It took him years to learn—but he had years. And when, finally, he had it:

He couldn't get back. It rushed upon him, swallowed him whole; he was wrapped, weighted, and sinking, and it was beyond all fighting. He had wanted this: why then did he now want so desperately to fight it? What instinct was this which prompted him to hold off?

But it was too late. He was lost to sleep, swathed in it like the humans who had rescued him.

If sleep were frightening, the dreams were worse. He could not control them, and they were not his. He'd fallen into a pit, the abyss mankind kept hidden behind the curtain of sleep.

He wandered through the dreams of others, not even of his own kind, was caught in them, and forced to play them out. Gave nightmares as well as received them as he shambled through the sleeping world.

Woke to the sun, terrified. Felt pity for the human race, a rush of gratitude for his own mental structure. He would never, he vowed, sleep again.

But the next night the battle began again. Sleep had him now. He'd made the mistake of learning it, and once learned, it would not be unlearned. It gripped him already with the force of undeniable habit.

Every night he fought it as long as he could, but it always overpowered him, submerged him, and every morning he dragged himself, shivering, out of the strange and terrifying sea of human sleep.

He was not, and could not be, human. The sharing of humanity's nightmares did not make him more human, yet it made him less than what he had once been. He forgot things; memories were lost, replaced by new learnings and by the useless memories, grafted on during sleep, of others. He changed and adapted, worn down by the numbing effects of day after day of living in this new, limited, and limiting world.

Emily

I looked through the dust-streaked window at the sunlit pine forest and could almost smell the baked resinous scent of the country where I had grown up. New York was far away now. I was bone weary and longing for the jouncing train ride to end. Just then I didn't care that it was Texas I was going to, not Paris; I simply wanted to be at rest.

My fingers brushed the cover of the book in my lap. The poems of Byron. Paul had given me that book. I heard his voice again, and wondered if anyone would ever again say my name the way he had said it.

I put the book inside the brown valise at my feet. In the bottom of that valise lay two hundred pages written out in my best hand: my unfinished novel. Unfinished, because I felt the hypocrisy of writing about love when I knew nothing about it, yet I wanted to write about nothing else.

The train was crawling along now. The Nacogdoches station would not be far away. It was good that I had come to Texas; it would be better for me—more real and less romantic—than Paris could have been.

In Texas I would learn to write about something other than love. I would relearn the important things, forgotten since childhood.

When Florrie embraced me, holding me close in her strong, capable arms, it seemed Mama was alive again, and I could become a little girl. Was this my little sister?

"Emma Kate! Oh, honey, how are you? It's so good to have you back home again!"

I hugged and kissed her a little awkwardly through being out of practice. "I'm just fine; I'm just fine, Florrie." I felt like crying and saw there were tears shining in Florrie's eyes, too.

"It's just so good to have you back!" One more squeeze and she moved reluctantly. "Now, where's the porter with your bags? Oh, Billy's got them. Come on, now—we'll get you home and out of those stiff clothes." It did me good to hear Florrie rattling on. "Now, we'll have a good long talk once you're settled in. I hope you're going to stay a good long while? No, no; we'll talk about all that later."

Billy hugged me, and it seemed strange to me that he was family now. I'd not set eyes on him since the day he and Florrie wed. And their children! It startled me a bit to see their four children. Florrie had been getting on with her life while I had been up in New York, teaching and playing at being an intellectual.

Billy loaded my things into the wagon with the children and helped me into the seat up front, between himself and Florrie. Then he clucked to the horses and we started off, slow and swaying. I looked out at the dusty road, the scrubby pines, the clapboard houses, the poorly dressed people, the animals. It seemed foreign to me after the man-made world of New York City.

The road wound through the forest, and the trees gave shelter from the sun and hid the straggling remains of the town. But the forest wasn't as deep as I remembered it. There were vast bare patches, ugly and denuded of trees: the harvest of the family lumber mill. The land was scarred, as by a forest fire, with tiny saplings pushing up bravely to stitch closed the wound. The old landmarks were gone and I couldn't be certain how far we were from home.

Florrie continued to talk and sometimes I listened. Finally she patted my knee. "Here. Almost home." The horse tugged us wearily around one last bend. Home. "Ain't it nice?"

I had imagined, somehow, that they would still be living in the old bride's house, although Florrie's letters had been rich with details of the building of their new home.

"It's lovely, Florrie," I said, and hugged her.

The house was large and sturdy, yet managed to have some style, a certain gentle elegance. It was painted white and the windows, upstairs and down, were decorated with green shutters like many of the houses in New Orleans. The little bridal house, a log cabin, still stood, not far across the sloping lawn. It had been Billy and Florrie's first home, but once the children started coming it must have quickly become more cramped than cozy.

A colored woman came out of the side door as we rolled up the looping ribbon of driveway, hurrying toward us and beaming. This was Mattie, who hugged me while Florrie told me what a great help Mattie was with the children and the chores.

I looked suddenly from Mattie's dark face to my sister's smile. "Where's Daddy?"

Florrie's smile tightened. "We'll go see him as soon as you get cleaned up." She took my arm and walked me up toward the house, Billy following behind with my bags, the children scattering like a flock of birds uncaged.

"I thought he might have come up here to meet me," I said.

"Well, we asked him to supper, of course, but he won't come up here. He's as stubborn as he ever was. He don't like niggers around the place."

Of course. Why had I thought he would mellow with age?

"It's not so much Mattie and Tom," Florrie said. "They're help—he might get used to ignoring them. But it's Pete he won't forgive us for."

"Who's Pete?" I didn't want to see my father. Every word Florrie said made me more certain.

"Pete," said Florrie. Her voice was odd. "Didn't I tell you about Pete? I suppose I never did. Well, you'll meet him by and by."

We entered by the back door, walking into a warm, good-smelling kitchen. But Florrie didn't give me time to gaze around, walking me quickly through a dark-wood hall and up uncarpeted stairs. "Right now you'd best get freshened up and go over to Daddy's. You know how cranky waiting makes him."

I did know, and I didn't like discovering that I still feared his anger.

My room was fresh and airy-feeling, from the white curtains sprigged with green to the patchwork quilt on the big brass bed. But I couldn't lie down on that bed for a nap; I couldn't even take a bath. Now that I knew Daddy was waiting for me, I became rushed and clumsy, knocking over the china pitcher after I had poured water into the washbowl—almost breaking it, but it landed on the rag rug instead of the floor, spilling out the rest of the water but not cracking.

I washed my face, neck, hands—trembling and trying not to as I changed my travel-stained dress for a clean one. I was a grown woman. Say what he liked, he could not make me a girl again.

"Emily?" It was Florrie, peeking around the door. She hurried in and embraced me. "Oh, honey, don't be nervous!"

"Isn't it silly?" I said, trying to laugh. "I've faced down angry parents and the headmaster at my school, but I'm afraid to see my own father. You were always the only one of us who could stand up to him, Florrie. I had to leave the state to be free of him."

We hugged again, and I clung to her a moment, trying to absorb some of her courage before I went to face our father.

He was waiting for me on the porch of the house I had grown up in. It was smaller in life than in memory, but he was not.

"It's about time you got here. Gossiping up there with your sister, I suppose."

"Hello, Daddy."

He got up to embrace me. We held each other awkwardly. I tried to kiss him, and his cheek rasped against mine.

"Come in and take dinner with me."

The kitchen, too, was smaller than I remembered it, and it was dirty, as it had never been when my mother was alive. Dinner was cornbread, beans, and ham, eaten sitting at the wooden table my father had built. It was much too large for the two of us, but I suppose he didn't see any need to build himself a smaller one when this one would do. He cooked and cleaned for himself now—Florrie might have done more for him, but I suspected it came down to a battle of wills between them.

We didn't speak much while we ate. That was my father's way. But the weight of the things we would say lay heavily on my tongue and I didn't eat much.

He commented on that, of course.

"Find a taste for fancy foods while you were up north?"

"I'm just not very hungry."

He wiped up the last few beans and sauce from his plate with a hunk of cornbread, washed that down with a gulp of iced tea, and settled back heavily in his chair, the wood complaining at his weight.

"Well," he said. "So you've come home. You given up on schoolteaching?"

I had known the question would come, but I had hoped for more time to think about it, time to talk with Florrie.

"I don't know if I've given up," I said. "I might just be here on a visit. Maybe I could see about getting a job near here—maybe do some tutoring." His eyes mocked me. He didn't believe me. He demanded some further explanation of myself and, unnerved, I made a mistake. I blurted out something I had meant to keep secret from him. "I thought I would do some writing while I'm here. I'm writing a novel."

His reaction was what I had known it would be: laughter, an out-raged snort of laughter. "So now you want to be a writer. Why didn't you stay in New York with all those other writers, with all those intellectuals?"

"I may go back," I said. "I told you I hadn't really decided yet. I . . ."

But he wasn't listening; he never listened to me. "You thought that since the life you chose for yourself didn't work out you'd come back here where your family would take care of you and you could play at writing without having to worry about getting a living from it. You could play at being an intellectual without having to prove yourself. You're like your mother, Emmie."

There were tears in my eyes, and I concentrated on not letting them fall.

He was silent, as I was—perhaps because he was sorry, or because he was thinking of my mother. Then he sighed and shook his head. "You shoulda got married, Emmie. You scared 'em all off with your learning and your books. Now you know you need a husband—but you might have done better to stay in New York, because there aren't any men in Texas who are gonna want a thirty-two-year-old spinster with too much book learning."

I wanted to refute him. I wanted to be cool and precise and witty—to laugh in his face as I told him how wrong he was, that I had never wanted to marry, and that I had known far more of life than he ever had. That I had seen great actors on the New York stage, had been driven about in a motorcar, had conversed once at a party with Dr. William James and his brother, the novelist, Mr. Henry James, had heard Samuel Clemens lecture, and had won the love of a fine man who would, I was certain, be known as a writer someday.

But actors, according to my father, were immoral; he wouldn't know who William James or Henry James or Samuel Clemens were; motorcars were a silly fad; and this fine, undiscovered writer who loved me was a married man.

And I was a spinster, as he said, and I was getting old, and I had come back to Texas where my book learning meant nothing and my father was still my father and could preach to me as he chose. I was silent for a long while, on the verge of tears as I stared down as the cold lumps of food on my plate.

He began to feel more kindly toward me in my defeat. "Well, Emmie," he said. "There have been spinsters that led worthwhile lives before you. Now that you're back home you can make yourself useful by looking after me and caring for this house. It needs a woman's hand—I can't do woman's work, myself. And your sister and I, we just can't get along in the same house together. She's too strong-willed for a woman." He chuckled, rather pleased. "She's too much like me, I guess."

I no longer wanted to cry. I wanted to scream. Terror crept into my throat, choking me. Take my mother's place? Be bullied and bossed by my father until that far distant day when he allowed himself to die?

"What d'you say, Emmie? You can move right into your old room—have it to yourself now that Florrie has a house of her own. You can even work on that novel of yours in your spare time if you like." He was growing benevolent, almost jolly, with the prospect of capturing me once again.

I shook my head wildly, unable to speak, and raised my face to his. I suppose the wild animal look in my eyes, my terror, must have shocked him: the smile slid right off his face.

"Now see here, Emily Kate, you're not a child anymore. You've got some duties, and since you never married, your duties are still to me. You can't just flutter through life like a butterfly—for one thing, you haven't got the looks or the spirit to get away with it. And your sister don't have room for you, and she don't need you. She'll have another child one of these days and need your room for it. You don't know nothing about babies, so you won't be any help there." He spoke ponderously, leaning and bumping against me with his words, sure of wearing me down, just as a horse will hit against a door with a worn latch until the door falls open before the animal's dumb persistence.

I clung to the thought that this time I must not give in, I must not let him wear me down. I was not demanding anything from him, only trying to keep my freedom. I would not come back under his roof and be imprisoned; I did not owe him that much.

"Or maybe you plan on trying to teach in town? Well, you could try, but they like to have men—a woman can't handle some of these rough country boys. Also, I think they've got enough teachers already—they don't need to hire somebody who's practically a stranger. And people will talk, they'll sure wonder why this nice maiden lady is letting her old daddy live alone and uncared for. Maybe, they'll say, she ain't really such a nice—"

I suddenly recalled my last major confrontation with my father. How I had wanted to go to school, to go East and earn a degree, and how my father had cornered me and knocked down every one of my reasons for going, telling me what a fool I was to consider it, telling me there wasn't enough money, telling me I was needed at home, telling me it wasn't fair to my sister, telling me I would never be any good, telling me women didn't need to know much, telling me if I liked to read I could read at home, and I, numbed into silence simply by the power of his presence, had begun to nod along with him, seeing my dreams char and burn to ash. And then—

"Harold."

We had both turned at the unfamiliar sound of the name, and the unfamiliar steel in the familiar soft voice. My mother had been un-smiling. "Harold," she said again, she who always called him Darlin' or Husband or Hal-honey. "I want to talk to you. Emma-honey, go help Florrie out back."

I was slow in doing what I was told, lingering to hear what my gentle mother could do against my powerful father.

"Harold, the girl is going to school. That is already settled. She is going to have a chance. She's smart, and we can well afford to send her and we aren't going to deny her this one thing that she wants. It's her life and I won't let you ruin it."

I could hardly believe that was my soft, wheedle-tongued mother speaking. Perhaps my father was as startled as me, for instead of bullying her into tears as I had seen him do many times before, he let her have her way. I did go to school; my mother had freed me.

But now my mother was dead. She couldn't fight my battles for me any longer.

"And if you want to write a book—why, honey, you can go right ahead and write it. I won't stop you. All I ask is that you keep the house clean, do my mending, and cook meals for the two of us. That's certainly not much to ask." My father was sure this battle was already won.

"It is too much to ask," I said grimly. I moved, rather shakily, out of my chair and away from the table. I had to get out; I was terrified that he would raise his voice to me and I'd start crying. "I won't keep house for you, Daddy. I've got to live my own life—I'm grown-up now." I didn't feel grown-up at all. "You can get yourself a maid if you want someone to cook your meals. I didn't come back to Texas to be your slave."

"Now, Emma Kate, that's no way to talk to your father—" There was the barest trace of uncertainty beneath the bluster. My rebellion, small as it was, had shaken him.

"I've got to go now," I said. "I told Florrie I'd come right back. We have a lot to discuss." I backed toward the door, keeping out of his reach, afraid he might try to stop me physically.

But he had decided to let me go this time. Shaking his head like an old dog bothered by flies, he said, "We'll talk about this some more when you've settled down. You're still tired from your journey and you need a chance to rest and give some thought to your life. There's plenty of time to work things out—you can move in here whenever you like. This is always your home, Emma Kate."

The trace of gentleness—which I knew to be a trap—almost undid me, but I managed to get out onto the porch before I tossed my quavering good-bye at him.

And then I ran back through the woods—ran like my father's little girl, and not at all like the aging spinster who had just defied him.

Florrie looked up from the game she played on the lawn with two of her children, concern on her features at the sight of me as I burst through the trees: red-faced, panting, hair straggling like a hoyden's. She got up at once, with a word to her children, and hurried to my side.

"Emmie, honey," she said, gripping my arm.

"I'm all right. I . . . ran . . . through the woods . . . all the way . . . back." My panting slowed as we walked up the lawn to the house.

"What happened?"

I shook my head.

Upstairs in my room, I washed my face and combed out my hair while Florrie began to unpack my bags, laying out fresh clothes for me.

"Florrie, he wants me to move in with him again. He wants everything to be just as if I had never escaped from him, as if I didn't have all my learning. He thinks I owe my life to him simply because I've never married." I began to pant again, this time with emotion.

Florrie took me in her arms and held me tightly. "Hush now, honey."

"He—he said you don't have room for me here and no one else wants me—"

"Emmie, stop it. You know we love you and you'll always be welcome here, just as long as you want. Don't let him scare you so. You're doing just fine with your life and it's foolish for you to worry about what he thinks."

I pulled away from her and busied myself unpacking. "I—I know that, Florrie. But he goes on at me so . . . I'm afraid that one day I'll agree with him—he'll bully me into moving into his house—and then I won't ever be free again. I can't take it, Florrie. I think I've got a life of my own and a mind of my own, but then he yells at me and I go all over like a little child again."

"You're tired," Florrie said gently. "Just tell yourself that you have your own life to live and it doesn't matter what he says. You'll start believing it after a while."

"It's hard to do," I said. "I'm not like you, Florrie. I never could stand up to him—I could only run away. I haven't got your backbone. I'm more like Mama—I let him wear me down."

"Emily." I looked at her. "Don't underestimate yourself *or* Mama. You are more like Mama than I am, but Mama was never weak. She was gentle, and she let Daddy have his way when it would keep peace, but for anything important—she wouldn't stop fighting until she had won. Remember how she stood up for you when you wanted to go to college? She faced Daddy down because—"

"Yes," I said. "I thought of that today. But she fought Daddy for *me*. She fought to protect us because she loved us. But she would never fight for something on her own behalf. She'd go without anything, put up with anything, unless it hurt us. And then she'd go to war. But for herself, she wouldn't raise a finger. And I'm afraid that I'm like that. Perhaps I might protect my child, if I had one, but I don't know how to fight to save myself."

Florrie looked at me with love and pain in her eyes, and I looked back. In a moment we might dissolve into tears, I thought, and to break the tension I said briskly, "Come now, Florrie. I need to get these things put away and then I would love a nice hot bath."

"You could take your bath now," she suggested. "And I could put away the rest of your things."

I shook my head. "No. If we work together, it will give us a chance to talk. Oh, Florrie, I've missed talking with you so! There's so much that never gets said in a letter."

"You're right," Florrie said a little ruefully. "Why, I somehow never could tell you about Pete. But you'll meet him later."

"Florrie, don't tease me! Who is Pete? When will I meet him?"

"In the morning. But now you tell me something. What made you decide to leave New York? You always sounded so happy there, from your letters, at least. Busy, working, meeting people. Did something happen, to change that? Why did you leave?"

As she spoke, by coincidence, I had in my hand the book of Byron's poems Paul had given me, and was casting about for a way of introducing him into the conversation. I turned to face her, and perhaps it was in my expression.

"A man, Emily?" she asked softly.

"He was married."

"Oh, Emily . . ." Her arms went around me and again she held me tightly, comforting me. She drew back and looked at me tenderly. "Poor darling. Do you want to talk about it?"

We sat down side by side on the bed, holding hands, and I was reminded of confidences exchanged in childhood. Many years had passed since then and now, married and the mother of children, Florrie seemed the older.

"He was a teacher," I said. "We had similar interests. We met to talk about our work, about poetry and philosophy. We both wanted to be writers ourselves someday, and we showed each other work we didn't dare show anyone else. We criticized each other, both honestly and gently, and helped each other become better writers.

"I thought it was a platonic friendship. I met his wife and she didn't like me—she was jealous of what I shared with her husband. I thought she was foolish to be jealous: Paul and I had the sort of friendship two men would be fortunate to have."

"And then you realized you were in love with him?"

I looked at her without surprise—it was the natural assumption— and shook my head. "No. One evening he confessed his love for me. Of course, I told him I did not return his feelings."

Florrie squeezed my hand.

"I thought we could continue to be friends," I said. "I thought that if I discouraged him, and kept talk away from romance, we could still be friends. Perhaps I should have refused to see him, but I didn't want to lose his friendship, and since I didn't love him, somehow I didn't believe he really loved me." I didn't feel proud of myself, telling Florrie. My own excuses sounded feeble in my ears. Perhaps I had been leading him on, afraid he might be my last chance for a different kind of life, afraid to let him go.

"Finally he—he offered to leave his wife for me. He wanted to take me with him to Paris. Morality is different there, and it would be easier for us to live together. And of course, he knew I longed to see Europe.

So I left. I had to. I gave up my job and came back here because otherwise he would have talked me into it. Otherwise I would have given in, and let him ruin his life."

Florrie sighed. "Oh, Emily, how noble of you."

Noble. That was a word Paul had used, too—misunderstanding. I thought coward would be more apt.

"But I didn't love him," I said to Florrie. "I wasn't being noble. If I had really loved him"—loved, in the way of a novel heroine—"really, wholeheartedly loved him, then I wouldn't have hesitated. I would have given myself to him, Florrie; I would have run away with him at once."

That is what I believed. And, later, when I was alone, I thought more on my ideal of love, and wondered if I would ever experience anything I would think worthy of the name. There would be—could be—no questions and no doubts, as there had been with Paul. Neither law nor morals would keep me from the man I loved; I would stop at nothing, I would do anything he asked, give myself utterly.

I sat up in bed, brooding on the question of love. The house was quiet, everyone asleep. I had thought I would sleep, but although I was bone weary, my body eager to slide into the healing lake of sleep, my mind was still active, jumping between thoughts of my father, thoughts of the career I had left behind, thoughts of Paul, thoughts of what love would mean to me.

I got up, then, and went to the bottom drawer of the dresser, where I had stored my unfinished novel. I lifted out the manuscript, remembering all the time that had gone into the writing and rewriting of the pages. I carried it to the bedside table and perched on the bed with it in my lap and began to read it by the light of the lamp.

It was the story of a perfect love between a man and a woman: the man an idealized Paul, the woman an idealized Me. I had been halted in my writing because, since I did not intend the novel to be a tragedy, I did not know where to go with this perfect love.

As I read over the pages of my novel, these pages that were the best I could write, my cheeks began to blaze. I felt feverish and unhappy, embarrassed by the prose. I imagined my father coming upon the manuscript and reading it and laughing. I imagined Florrie being kind. I felt a sudden revulsion toward Paul, who had encouraged me in this sickly, silly fantasy about love.

I knew nothing about love and probably never would. I was, as my father had said, a thirty-two-year-old spinster, and my ideas about love had come from books. How many of those books had been written by others who knew as little as I?

I put the pages aside, my hands trembling, feeling sick at heart. I could not go on with it. I had thought to build a new life in these pages, and they would be better as ash.

This thought firmly in mind, I rose and took the pile of paper to the washstand and there I burned it, page by page. The sight of the flame licking at the first page, the curling of the paper, the way the writing changed color and disappeared, word by word, invigorated me. I would start fresh, write about something new, but not until I knew something to write about. I would forget this novel as if it had never existed. I would not write something my father could laugh at—until I could write something good and strong and true I would write nothing at all. I would give up my pretensions.

The second page went quickly. I burned my finger on the third. On the fortieth I felt a sudden sick surge of regret: what if I was wrong? But the fortieth burned, too, and the forty-first—which I paused to read—made me certain again.

Halfway through, a wave of exhaustion made me sway, and I feared I might swoon. But I was determined to see it through. I burned my fingers again, several times, but I saw every page of my novel become ash.

I woke in the morning feeling hollow inside, with the certainty that something that was important to me was gone forever. I opened my eyes and remembered the novel. It was for the best, I thought. I did not regret it.

I had slept late, being so exhausted from the events of the preceding day, and breakfast had already been cleared away when I came downstairs.

"Mattie will fix you whatever you like for breakfast," Florrie said, kissing me on the cheek. "I thought you needed all the sleep you could get."

"I feel much better," I said, although I didn't. I felt drained and wished I were still asleep.

Florrie joined me in the kitchen for a cup of tea while I ate the scrambled eggs and sausage Mattie had fried up for me. I was just beginning to relax, to consider telling Florrie what I had done with my novel, when the door flew open and Florrie's eldest boy, Joe Bob, burst in.

"Young man, is that any way to come into a house?" Florrie said indignantly.

He grinned and looked at me. "Grandaddy says he wants you to go over and have a talk with him."

I lost all my appetite. Florrie looked at me sharply. "Now, Emmie. You eat a good breakfast first. You don't have to go hoppin' over there every time he says 'frog.' You need a chance to relax and get your strength up. And I want you to meet Pete first, anyway."

"Very well," I said dully. I could not face my father so soon. First I had to adjust to my life without the novel—my life without writing. I had to rebuild. It would be fatal if my father began arguing at me again while I was without supports. I had nothing left to help me resist: I could only cling with determination to the idea of not giving in, of not going to live in my father's house again, and hope that would be sufficient to carry me through all his attacks.

I pushed my eggs around on the plate, then looked at Florrie. "I can't eat," I said. "Really, I'm too nervous."

She bit her lip, then nodded. "All right. I'll take you to meet Pete. He'll make you feel better."

I laughed out of nervousness. "Really? I'm intrigued. Does this Pete-person have another name?"

"No," she said with a mysterious smile. "Come."

We went down the wide stretch of lawn dotted with pine trees and scrub oaks to the little cabin where Florrie and Billy had lived when they were first wed.

Florrie rapped sharply on the door once, then opened it, and we stepped into the dark cabin. The sudden change from daylight dimmed my sight and I could only make out somebody moving slowly and uncertainly in the far corner.

"Pete, it's Florrie. I've brought my sister Emily to meet you."

At that first meeting I thought him very old. He moved with difficulty, shuffling and awkward as if plagued by pain and weakness. He was too small, the way an old man will seem shrunk down to his bones, although he was no shorter than me. I gave him my hand when Florrie pronounced my name, and felt the long, hard, thin fingers move lightly over my palm, as if reading it, the way a blind person might. But I didn't think he was blind, for the big round eyes shone, and looked directly into mine.

Except for those eyes—which were beautiful, but not normal in a human face—he was, I thought, very ugly. I thought at first he had no nose, and revulsion rose in me, only to be smothered at once by pity, or something like it, flowing smooth and heavy as molasses into my mind and drowning the revulsion before it was fully formed. I realized then that he did have a nose, but it wasn't like the noses I was used to: nothing more than a couple of slits with flaps of flesh over them.

The three of us went to the big table beside one window. Florrie and I sat and Pete disappeared into the kitchen. I looked at Florrie but I said nothing. I had questions, but for the moment they didn't matter.

Pete returned with a teapot and three cups and saucers, setting the tray down carefully on the table before Florrie, who poured out the tea and served us all.

I had a chance to examine Pete more closely now. His skin hung in folds and wrinkles from his slight frame, like an exaggeration of the shrinkage of age, but I no longer thought he was old, nor did I think he was ugly. He could not be compared with anyone else within my experience, so he was neither ugly nor beautiful, but only himself.

We sipped our tea and smiled at one another, and after a quarter of an hour Florrie rose and indicated that it was time for us to go. It was only then that I realized we had none of us spoken since the greeting, and Pete had never spoken at all. And yet never had I felt so comfortable and so instantly at ease with a stranger as I had these past fifteen minutes.

Florrie and I said good-bye, and Pete nodded at us and blinked his bright eyes.

"You liked him," Florrie said as we started back up to the house.

"Yes. Florrie . . . who *is* he?"

"I don't know," she said, as if it did not matter. "I think Billy and I saved his life. And after that . . . he's just stayed with us." She was silent then, as we passed the two older children who were tumbling about on the grass. Just before we reached the house she spoke again.

"I would hate to have him leave. He's closer than kin."

I took a nap before supper and Florrie came upstairs to wake me, sitting beside me on the bed and gently touching my face.

I opened my eyes, feeling the dream fading past recall already. "I dreamed about Pete," I said, struggling to hold it.

Florrie nodded. "We all do. Good or bad?"

"Good." The dream was gone, not even an image remained, but I was left with a feeling of warmth toward him.

"My dreams about him are good ones, too. Sometimes I think—" she broke off.

"That he dreams about us, too?" I ventured.

Florrie nodded. "Mostly our dreams are good—sometimes the others have nightmares. I never do. But Sarah Jane"—that was her four-year-old—"has nightmares all the time about him. For some reason she is terrified of him. The other children love him and always want to play with him, but Sarah Jane cries whenever she sees him. I don't know why that is."

I couldn't understand it either. Pete might be frightening to a child only at first sight—he radiated such an air of harmlessness, of gentleness, that his looks soon became unimportant.

"I wonder if we give him nightmares," I said.

The next morning I did something I had not done since my college days: took out my sketchpad and went outside to draw. Later, perhaps, I might return to my watercolors, I thought. Since I had abandoned my novel I needed something to fill the gap.

I took a canvas chair and set it beneath a large shade tree, not far from Florrie and the baby. I chose to sketch them: mother with child in sunlight.

I had not been long at work when I saw Pete traveling toward me in his slow, painful hobble—as if he fought against great weights with every step. He stood beside me and watched with interest as my fingers—now somewhat crippled by his regard—created penciled figures on the page.

Mysteriously aware of his presence, the other two children (but not, of course, Sarah Jane) came running around the side of the house to play at being mountain goats upon poor Pete. I saw one of the dogs, a hunting hound who had been running with the children, turn tail at the sight of Pete and slink off out of sight.

Wondering a little uneasily why dogs should fear Pete, I continued my sketch until it was done. It was crude, and I was annoyed by my clumsiness, but Pete seemed pleased. He indicated that he wanted the pad and pencil, and when I gave them to him he hunkered down in the grass and set to work.

He was not especially skilled, yet I knew the first face for mine; next, Florrie's; then his own. They were not technically very good, yet there was a spark of life in them, something which made it obvious whom they represented.

Now, as I watched, he began to draw a story. Florrie—a very young Florrie—and a younger Billy; a starry night; a falling star; a crumpled, crashed vehicle—a flying machine, grounded in a graveyard.

I was so absorbed by what he was showing me that I scarcely noticed when Florrie took the baby back up to the house. He drew me pictures of another land and, with a sudden shock, I recognized the landscape of my dreams the night before. I stopped his hand with mine and made him look at me, but his eyes were not human, and I could read nothing in them.

"Emily Katherine!" Like a whip cracked above my head. I jerked up and saw my father standing some yards away. There it was again, that fear out of childhood. My stomach contracted and my mind, in old habit, nervously tried to recall what I had done that he would consider wrong.

"Come here, missy, I want to talk to you."

Whatever I had done, it was very bad indeed. My hands and feet felt like blocks of ice as I rose and walked to him. He grasped my arm, not gently, and marched me away.

"I know they preach nigger-loving up north," he said. "But you're a daughter of mine and I won't—I'd a damn sight sooner see you cuddlin' up to the biggest, blackest nigger in Texas than what I just saw." His voice was thick with fury, and his fingers gouged my arm.

"Daddy, don't!" I tried to pull away. "What are you talking about?" I knew my voice was weak and shrill, and I couldn't stop shaking. I hated him then, for making me so afraid.

"I'm talking about that monster. It's bad enough that Florrie and Billy keep it—it's too much to see you nose to nose and making cow eyes at it. Can't you see that thing ain't human? It's an animal, and it doesn't belong here. It should be killed, just like you'd kill a snake, so it can't spread its poison around."

"Don't you call Pete a monster," I said, nearly in tears. "And don't you insinuate—"

"I ain't insinuating. I'm *telling*. That monster is trouble, and you'd better keep away from it. If I ever see you cuddlin' up to that thing again—"

"Stop it!"

He let go of my arm. "Emily, you just do what your Daddy says and keep away from that thing. Don't talk to it, don't touch it, and don't sit with it. Or you'll be sorry. I'll make sure you're sorry."

Tears blinded me. He always reduced me to that, the child's refuge. I had never been able to defy my father except by running away. I was certain he thought I'd gone to New York only to run away from him, because I would never be an adult in his eyes.

When I walked back to the house I wasn't thinking of Florrie but of Pete. I wanted the peace his presence could give me, and I wanted to disobey my father. So I changed direction, and went toward the little house where Pete lived, and saw him waiting for me on the porch. And when I saw him—the dear, already familiar, not-human ugliness of him—something like a bolt of pain went through me. And, although I have never fainted in my life, I thought that I would faint then, standing on the wooden porch, staring at Pete.

He touched my arm and we went into the house together. I felt dazed and clumsy—I felt too large, as if all my skin had suddenly swollen, and my clothes were painfully constricting. Pete led me out of the main room and into the back room, his bedroom. It was small and familiar. As children, Florrie and I had come here to play games with our dolls. It seemed very bare now, empty of the personal possessions one would expect to find. There was only the bed against one wall, and a chair beside the window, and an old rag rug on the floor. I looked at the window, which, although screened with vines, let in filtered sunlight. Sensing my concern, Pete crossed to the window and closed the shutters. I heard the small, wooden click as they closed together.

I wanted to speak to him. He seemed suddenly a stranger, standing across the room in the dim light. He came closer, and I could see his features again, and they were as well known as if I had seen them every day of my life. I no longer wanted to spoil our shared silence with words.

He placed his hand, palm down, against my bosom, on the stiff, smooth fabric of my dress, meaning: let me feel what you are.

I turned my back on him to disrobe. The rustling of our clothing as we removed it filled the room with the sound of birds taking flight.

And my heart was one of those birds, trapped and left behind, fluttering in terror as I climbed naked into bed. Pete lay his head against my breast, listening, and then he knelt and stroked me slowly with the flat of one hand, soothing me as if I'd been a horse.

When I had stopped shivering (although I was still breathing fast and deep) he climbed into bed and pressed himself close to me. His skin was peppered roughly all over with what seemed to be goose bumps, and he was so cool to the touch that I wondered if he was frightened, too. The possibility made me feel better. It made us seem more alike.

I closed my eyes, expecting to be kissed. I had been kissed before. But his lips never touched mine: instead, I felt his breath warm against the skin of my face and a gentle, fluttering touch, which I later realized was the flaps of his nostrils moving in and out as he sniffed me.

Gradually, I warmed to him, and began to crave the friction of his cool, pebbly flesh against mine. I kept my eyes tightly shut, not daring to open them. I had glimpsed something, his male member, sprouting from the juncture of his legs, a frightening purplish vegetable. I felt it, warmer than the rest of his flesh, graze my leg now and then as he sniffed me and stroked me and rubbed his body against mine.

I could do nothing. I wanted to touch him, but I was afraid. I lay very still, hands clenched at my sides, clenched with wanting and with terror. I wished that I could faint, that it would end, that I would understand what to do. I thought I might cry, and made a soft sound in my throat. I was excited, desperate, and dreadfully confused, in a turmoil of conflicting desires. I moaned again, asking for his help.

Then he moved away from me, and my eyes flashed open. "Pete."

He looked at me and I couldn't read his eyes. What did he want? What was he thinking? I noticed how green his skin looked in the dim, filtered light, and saw how the hairless skin hung from his bones. I saw what he was. And I didn't faint, or scream, or roll away from his touch. Instead, most improbably, I felt a surging up of love. It ran through my veins like blood, heating me, making me brave enough to half sit up and lean forward. I caught his hand and pulled him closer. I tried not to think of my nakedness, and tried not to see the thing growing between his legs. When he took me in his arms I closed my eyes again, my mind rioting with senseless dream images, my thoughts a pathless jungle.

He parted my legs with his hands and I thought my heart would leap through my mouth. No—I didn't want this—I only wanted—I wanted to be alone—I wanted him—I *did* want this, the physical joining as well as the spiritual—but I didn't, yet—

I cried out in pain, although it was really only discomfort, and he stopped hurting me at once.

When he shifted position, my legs fell back together. Tears trickled from beneath my tightly shut lids, tears of fear and shame, and he licked them away.

He began stroking me again, and I realized his fingertips had warmed. They were raspily pleasant, like the tongue of a cat. They moved between my legs, caressing me more and more intimately until my legs fell apart and my body moved and I moaned and thought in strange, rapid jagged images, and my breath came as quickly as my thoughts, and I forgot about him and about my fear, it was as if I were alone with myself in my own bed, and so I clenched my teeth, my back arched, and I screamed silently, silently inside my head, bursting all the brilliant balloons of my thoughts.

Far away, yet very close, I felt him moving, and then the cool, rough length of his body was pressed along the length of mine and as I rocked toward sleep I was content. I seemed to feel Pete with my mind as well as with my body—we approached sleep together and his mind was joined to mine in a way our bodies had not been. His mind, I thought, was soothing mine as his hands had soothed my body. I was very sleepy and it was pleasant, even if utterly foreign to me, to be so close to another. So close, falling asleep together.

Then my father's face—a memory or a dream—shattered the moment, and I struggled to wake.

But I could not move, could not even open my eyes. As I fought it, I was drawn more deeply into the dream.

I saw my father sitting in his kitchen, cleaning out the gun he used for shooting squirrel and rabbit. But I knew, with the absolute certainty we have in dreams, that he did not intend to go hunting for his dinner this evening. His thoughts were open to me: I knew that he would go to some of the local men he knew, men ready to be frightened by the threat different-colored skin posed to their property and their women. My father thought of me: a spinster whose virginity had made her crazy, easy prey for the monster he now intended to kill, or at the least, to torture and geld and drive out of the county.

I was humiliated by the vision my father had of me and, for a moment, I blazed with hatred.

His fingers tightened on the gun in his lap, and his face twitched. Had my hatred done that? He tried to set the gun aside, but could not. Rejoicing in my power, I made him stand.

My father got the bullets and loaded the gun—not at my direction but of his own accord. I watched, knowing that he was thinking of Pete. His face was ugly with hate and anger, and his eyes whipped around the kitchen in restless search, as if he felt Pete's presence.

The gun moved like a live thing in his hands. My father began to struggle, straining against the will of the gun to point at his own legs.

I fought against him, silently and fiercely. I had Pete's force to magnify my own. I won't let you shoot him, I told my father. I'll kill you before I let you kill Pete.

The gun barrel shifted and for a moment I thought my father had won and taken control. Then I made him raise the gun. The position he held it in was unnatural and uncomfortable.

"Emily!" He said my name as if it were a curse. He was demanding, not pleading. He still thought he could command me, and he would not acknowledge my power.

The gun was at his heart. I could have killed him if I chose.

"Emily!" The tone that could make me tremble, even in dreams.

The barrel shifted slightly, caught between his will and mine, caught by my indecisiveness.

I shot him, and felt, for one impossible moment, the bullet tearing through his flesh.

I fainted then, or slept.

When I woke, feeling sick and miserable, Pete was dressed and sitting beside the window. I dressed myself and left the house without speaking. He did not once turn to look at me.

I was the one who found my father lying in a pool of his own blood. It is likely that no one else would have stopped by to visit, and if I had not gone when I did, he would have died.

It was natural that I should be the one to stay with him and look after him until he was completely well again. Everyone said how fortunate it was that I had come home. And, after my father was healed, it seemed for the best that I continue to live in his house. After all, the house was too much work for a man alone, and Florrie, with another baby on the way, could use the room I had occupied.

My father said that he had accidentally shot himself while cleaning his gun—not knowing it was loaded. He never spoke, to me or anyone else, of our struggle, so perhaps it was only a dream. I still get dreams sometimes from Pete, but that's the only time I am close to him. He makes me uncomfortable now, and I avoid him, except in my dreams. And no one would say that we can control what we do in our dreams.

Living and Dying

The new woman, Florrie's sister, was a surprise. She was open and vulnerable, beaming her needs, her wants, her fears at him with more intensity than he'd ever felt from a human being. He didn't have to search—she gave him herself.

And, he realized within moments of meeting her, he was capable of fulfilling her needs.

The understanding shook him out of his dullness. Was it possible that he would not remain a stranger forever? That he could know communion with one of these beings?

He both desired and feared the possible union. Like sleep, which had so fascinated him at first, might this not also prove a trap? To grow closer to one of them was to risk becoming too human, to risk losing what he really was. He would not be human, then, but only a freak.

But it might be worth the risk. If he were doomed to spend the rest of his life among humans, he must make the most of it. He must try to become involved with human society since his own kind was lost to him, and not remain on the edges of life. He could read them now with ease and he could send feelings to control them, but the idea of *real* communication tempted him strongly. Emily's own open hunger struck a responsive chord in him. How lonely he was. How he missed his own kind. Were he home, he would be choosing his lifemate now.

With that thought came such a strong urge that he made himself ignore all the things which made her strange, almost repugnant, to him, and concentrated on the likenesses.

He began by making himself known to her. First he sent a dream, and then followed that up with pictures when she was awake, telling her, however crudely, that he had come from another world.

But there was no time for the slow, leisurely courtship he had planned. She came to him in desperate need, projecting the idea that he was in danger from her father. Everything else had to wait. There was no time for the slow understanding which might lead eventually and naturally to a physical union. It was now or never.

Things moved so rapidly on this world! He would try to adjust to this different pace and hope that later they could be mated mind-to-mind. First, he would give her what she wanted.

It might have worked, but for Emily's fear. The fear rolled off her in a dreadful stench, bewildering him and making his genitals shrink in dismay. Fear had no place in lovemaking, and although with the room dim and his vision relaxed, she might almost have been one of his own kind, her fear incapacitated him.

Yet she still desired him. She needed him—he could feel that—and when she reached out for him he tried, limbs trembling with confusion, to ignore her fear. He tried to give her what she wanted. And then he hurt her, and the pain and fear undid him completely.

What sort of creature was this to feel pain and fear and still desire? He suddenly saw her as if in a blaze of light, body and feelings both hideously clear. She was an animal, an alien, a beast, a monster, unnatural and loathsome.

But although he no longer had any desire for her, he could feel *her* needs, and he reacted almost instinctively to satisfy them. He brought her to orgasm with his hand, meanwhile holding his emotions firmly in check, knowing that despite his urge to run, there was nowhere he could go.

He pushed her into deep sleep, knowing that he would have to follow, and cast about in search of the danger her thoughts had warned him of. He didn't want to think about what he had done, what he had, however briefly, wanted to share with this creature. He would never again consider mating with a human being. He was a castaway and had better get used to the life of a hermit and not think of coupling with beasts.

And so the years passed in solitude of his own devising. He saw few humans and cared for none of them. Billy died, and Florrie after him, and he mourned neither. Others were born who continued to let him live in the little house and brought him food and occasional company, thinking of him as a strange old family servant—an odd but uninteresting responsibility. So he lived out his life like a prison sentence and struggled against the involvement of dreams—knowing more about these people than he cared to, more involved than he wanted to be—and the nightly tyranny of sleep.

And then one was born who, even in infancy, was different, who made herself felt. She had a potential he had found in none of the humans he had encountered. She stirred something in him, an interest he had thought safely dead. And perhaps because he was of an age to be raising a child of his own, were he home, he took an interest in this child, and began to teach it and to nurture its strange talent.

He wove dreams for the child. He gave of himself to her, spending his nights in her dreams, becoming teacher and spiritual father to a child who became, under his care, something less or more than human.

Jody

As soon as I got off the bus I threw my thoughts on ahead to Pete, to see where he was and what he was feeling. And because it was a beautiful, blue-skyed day and I felt itchy and cramped and grouchy from sitting in school with a bunch of stupid kids and teachers, none of whom knew the things *I* knew, I started running just as soon as my feet hit the dusty side road which led off the highway through the woods toward home.

But something was different. I found Pete's mind, like always, but this time he pushed me away. His thoughts were all rolling around. I couldn't understand, and he wouldn't help me. Was it fear? Anger? Suddenly I realized that he was feeling joy. Joy—an almost unbearable excitement—and he didn't want to share it with me.

I realized I had stopped stock-still in the road, my mouth probably hanging open, and I started myself up again. My heart was lurching around like a dying fish. I didn't know what was going on, but it had to be something terrible. I couldn't even remember the last time Pete had pushed me out of his mind.

The walk down that interminable dusty road, striped with pine shadows and blazing sunlight, was the most painful I ever took. I don't think I was reacting just to his pushing me away—I think I knew already, knew without understanding why, that this was the end of Pete and me.

There were a whole bunch of strange cars pulled up on the circular gravel drive and when I walked into the front hall the air was blue with smoke and ringing with voices.

They were all in the living room. They went on with their talking at first, not noticing me in the doorway. My folks were there, and my sister and her junior politician boyfriend had driven in from Austin, and there were reporters with cameras and tape recorders and some senior politicians and some very quiet men who couldn't be anything but plainclothed police. And Pete was there, the center of it all, sitting in the antique Italian chair that nobody but company ever got to sit in, with reporters buzzing like flies around a cow pattie.

I sent a cry out to Pete, but his wall was still up. My sister Mary Beth quit chatting to some woman, turned, and saw me.

"Jody! Thank goodness you're finally here. I was thinking of sending Duane in his car up to school to fetch you." Even while she was glad to see me, I could feel her automatic assessment and disapproval of the way I looked. She couldn't understand how I could be so tacky as to wear baggy blue jeans, a shirt with a rip under one arm, and dusty boots to school. I made a face at her for her thoughts, and she looked a little shaken. She gripped my arm too tightly and whispered at me, "Jody, behave! There are some very important people here today and they're interested in Pete."

"So what?" I felt sick. This was it. This was finally it. Somehow the government had found out and come to take Pete away. And Pete was just sitting there like a stone, ignoring me. He was going to let them take him away.

"Honey, are you all right?"

I must really have looked terrible for Mary Beth to overlook my rudeness. "Yeah," I said. "What's going on?"

Instead of answering me, Mary Beth spoke to the whole room. "Everybody," she said brightly, the sorority girl at a club meeting, "Jody's come home from school. She'll be able to help us out—you see, she's always been able to communicate with Pete better than anyone else can. It's a special talent she has."

They were all staring at me. A flashbulb flared.

"You can all go to hell," I said, but I said it so low, my chin down, blinking from the flash, that I don't think anyone but Mary Beth heard. Her long nails pressed warningly into my flesh.

I stared at the ground. I wasn't going to let them take Pete away. Mary Beth would have to do a lot more than pinch me to get me to talk.

"Jody," said my mother, her voice threatening in the most civilized manner. "No one is going to hurt Pete. We have just learned that Pete comes from another planet. And his friends—"

"You aren't his friends!" I cried. "None of you are! Pete doesn't have any friends except me!"

My mind was running around like a hamster on a wheel, trying to think of a way to get Pete and myself away. I knew how to drive even though I wasn't old enough for a license, so if I could get somebody's keys—

Pete came into my mind then. Maybe he'd been paying attention to me all along, even though I couldn't feel him. He ended my fantasy with a bang. He showed me himself surrounded by others who looked like him: his own people. They were his friends, not us, and they had found him at last, and come to take him home. And Pete was happy. Overwhelmingly, unbearably relieved to leave his exile and go home again.

He was leaving *me,* though. Not simply this world, which had been his prison for so long, but *me.* And he was happy.

Pete laid a comfort-touch on me, but I evaded it easily. His heart wasn't really in it. He was so consumed by his own joy that my sadness was a minor irritation to him, that's all. He no longer had any time for me.

My mother and Mary Beth's boyfriend were taking it in turns to tell me what I already knew, but I was too numb to tell them to save their breaths. I didn't care about the details of "first contact," the landing and the discovery. I didn't care what had been on TV or what was happening anywhere else in the world.

"Mary Beth and I just happened to have the television on while we were having breakfast this morning—" Duane stopped suddenly, blushing. The biggest event in history had just happened and that fool thought people still cared if he and Mary Beth had spent the night together.

"And there they were," said Mary Beth, quickly filling in for him. She would make a good little wife. "We couldn't believe it at first.

Duane thought it was a hoax, but I said, 'Why, that looks like Pete! Our own funny old Pete!'

"So Duane, after I'd told him about Pete, and after what the announcer said about these alien visitors looking for their lost comrade, well, Duane said maybe he should call up his friend in the governor's office, and maybe also call the TV station, and . . ."

I turned around to leave. I wanted to be by myself.

"Jody, we haven't finished," Mary Beth said.

"I already know all that," I said.

"But everyone's been waiting for you," said Duane. "Can't you tell us what Pete's thinking about all this?"

I looked at them all, and at Pete who was bobbing gently in the good chair like a slightly dotty old man. The membrane at his neck was billowing gently and flaring orange. Since the photographer wasn't going crazy, I guessed this was nothing new to him, although it was to me. It was a sign of extreme emotion, I knew, but I had never seen it before.

"He's very happy," I said finally. "He's very, very happy that his friends have come for him at last, and he can't wait to go home again. That's all. He doesn't have anything he needs to say, except to his friends." Then I went upstairs to my room and closed the door.

My mother came up a few hours later with some sandwiches and a piece of cake and glass of milk on a tray.

"I thought you'd like something to eat," she said, setting the tray down on my dresser.

"Thanks," I said, scooting across the bed to reach the food on the dresser. I was hungry and wished I wasn't. It didn't seem right that my whole life could be breaking up and I was still getting hungry at the usual times. I broke off a piece of the cake and tasted it.

My mother sat down on the bed beside me. "Jody," she said carefully. "You understand Pete awfully well. Do you—that is, I heard that his friends all speak, uh, with their minds. They don't make any sounds, but it seems that we are able to hear them anyway . . . at least, that's what I've heard it's like. Can you do that? When you know what Pete wants, are you reading his mind?"

"When he lets me," I said. My mother has been frightened of me since I was just a baby, although that's not something she can admit even to herself.

"Can you—," she stopped. She would never believe me if I answered her now, so I waited. "He speaks to you through, um, telepathic conversation?" She gave the word an odd emphasis, so I suspected she was imitating someone else.

"Yeah, I guess. Sort of," I said.

"Why can't he talk to the rest of us like that, then? These other aliens talk to everyone mind-to-mind. Why do you suppose Pete can't?"

I looked at her in surprise. I'd always taken it for granted that I was special in being able to understand Pete.

She steeled herself. "Jody, can you read our minds, too?"

"No," I said. "Look, I can only read Pete's mind when he lets me. He sort of gives it to me. I send my thoughts back to him. I don't know how I do it—I guess he taught me how when I was such a little baby that I can't remember. But when he doesn't want me to, I can't. And I can't read anyone else. It's like I can hear Pete, but nobody else is talking the way he is."

"I see." My mother bent her dark head to examine her well-kept nails. "I thought—well, you sometimes seem to know what I'm thinking or what I'm going to say, and I thought maybe—"

"I can't read your mind," I said. "I guess I'm just real observant. I sort of put things together from how you move and what I know about you." This was true, but I didn't tell her about the dreams. I wasn't going to tell her I could go into her dreams at night, or that it was her dreams which let me know so much about her, so much more than she knew about me.

"These aliens," I said, wondering about these creatures who could, unlike Pete, make themselves so widely understood, "when are they getting here?"

"They'll arrive sometime tomorrow," she said. "They're being flown in with some government people, reporters, secret service, the whole lot. This is a big deal, you realize." She looked at me curiously. "Have you always known what Pete is?"

"Sure."

"And you never told anyone. Why?"

"Why should I?"

She looked at me in silence. "Poor Jody. Pete's always been very special to you, hasn't he?"

That didn't deserve an answer.

My mother looked as if she wanted to put her arms around me, as if she wanted to get into my mind. "Try not to take it so hard," she said. "Of course you'll miss him, but you know it will be best for him.

He wants to go home, where he belongs, to be among his own people. Think of how he must feel."

I closed my eyes and tried to block out her voice. I wished she would just shut up and go away. She didn't know anything. She couldn't possibly understand. I almost hated her.

I heard her sigh and get off the bed. "Okay. Try to get some sleep, Jody. You'll feel better."

I twisted my head away when she bent down to kiss me, and she left without another word. I was already going away myself, reaching out for Pete. He was in his house and, I thought, by himself. His thoughts were strung taut and vibrating slightly. I couldn't get ahold of anything. He wasn't pushing me away this time, he just wasn't paying attention.

Then there was something—a bit like static, and like a small electric shock—and I sat up in bed, trembling and alone. I was nowhere near Pete. And I knew what had happened, what it meant. Pete had been talking with someone else.

I didn't want anyone to see me and stop me, try to interfere or try to help, so I was very careful as I crept down the back stairs and out the kitchen door. To get to Pete's little house I had to pass in front of the lighted living-room window. It was nearly twilight, and I might be seen, so I ran and cast the image of a dog about me so that anyone looking out of the window would think one of the dogs had run past.

I found Pete in his bedroom, sitting on the cane-bottom, straight-backed chair beside the useless window. The window was a mass of vines and I could barely make out Pete's shape in the darkness.

"Pete?" I didn't try to touch his mind, knowing he might still be locked in communication with one of his people. I hadn't liked the feeling when I bumped into it before. I hadn't liked it one little bit.

I waited in the dark for Pete to respond. I didn't mind the wait. I was starting to feel better, calmer. I was fooling myself, of course, since nothing had changed, but just being with Pete was a tremendous relief after the confusion and loneliness of the afternoon.

He touched my mind with a question. A familiar touch, but strange. He was different: he was happy. I felt uncomfortable, wondering if what I had always thought normal for him had been a constant state of unhappiness, or loneliness, or sickness. I felt guilty. I had never been able to make him happy.

But that wasn't my fault; I couldn't be expected to do that—he sent the impressions rapidly. He had been lonely, and physically sick as a reaction to our atmosphere, and psychically sick with longing for home and friends. I had made him as happy as it was possible for him to be on this strange planet. But that wasn't enough. He was going home now, to be among his own kind again.

"What about me?" I was so upset I spoke aloud. "I'm like you—you made me be like you. I'm different from everybody else. I can't stay here if you're gone. *You* know what it's like—imagine how lonely I'll be! It isn't fair, it isn't right for you to go off and leave me after you've made me into a freak."

He tried to calm me—this was always his first defense against the destructive emotions of humankind. But I wasn't just another human; I knew how to evade his touch.

"Don't leave me," I said. "I can't stand it if you go. I won't have anybody, and I won't even have the hope you had, that someday my people might come for me, because you are my only people. There's only you and me, Pete. We belong together. Don't leave me here with strangers. Take me with you, please, Pete. We have to be together."

He did love me; I know he did. And he must have seen what it would be like for me if he left me. He couldn't condemn me to a worse loneliness than his own—he had too much compassion. True, I would be a stranger among his people, but I was a stranger among my own. At least I could have him.

Pete agreed. He would take me home with him.

By first light the place was like a fairground or the site of a rock concert. Newspeople and security littered the grounds around the house, and there were plenty of gawkers who had to be run off by the police. I was up early after spending the night with Pete. He had shared memories of his home planet with me, and although this was something he had done before, there was a new meaning and excitement to them now, because I would see all those things for myself, very soon. When at last I slept, I dreamed alone. Pete held me in his arms, but he lay wakeful through the night.

I hung around with my mother in the kitchen while I waited for the motorcade bearing the aliens to arrive from the airfield. I helped her and Mary Beth make coffee and sandwiches and hoped they wouldn't realize the mood I was trying to subdue had changed from sorrow to excitement. I couldn't let them suspect or they would try to stop me. I would have to watch for my chance and escape. I might not even be able to say good-bye.

I saw the short strand of black cars from the kitchen window and dashed out the door, running hard through the woods, afraid of being left behind despite Pete's promise.

The porch and grounds around Pete's house were swarming with people, and just as I got there I felt them focus their attention as the motorcade pulled up in a fine mist of dirt and gravel.

I craned as eagerly as anyone else to see the first alien step out of the car, but of course to me they were not aliens, but my own, adopted, people.

Pete, I thought, at the sight of the first one, and my mind leaped forward in greeting. But it was not Pete. Instead of his familiar mass, my mind touched something cold and unintelligible and was rebuffed.

There were three of them, and they all looked exactly the same. They wore form-fitting, skinlike suits which hid their sexual differences and protected them from the poisons which irritated Pete's skin.

Pete came out of the house, moving slowly as always, his neck-membrane flaring brightly with his emotions. The onlookers moved away as he came down the porch steps, and his alien brothers (or sisters?) came forward. All four merged in a long, silent embrace. It went on for minutes, and as I watched I felt miserable: uncomfortable, unhappy, abandoned, and repelled.

Then one of the aliens spoke. It was strange, because although I knew I was hearing it in my mind, the way that I heard Pete, I knew that this communication was not private. Everyone there heard it, too.

"We thank you people for your hospitality and kindness in caring for our injured brother. We will take him home with us now, and trouble you no further."

I felt a hand on my shoulder and twisted around to see my parents, Mary Beth, and Duane. I shrugged off my father's protective touch.

"Pete," I muttered, and thought at him fiercely. Look at me, think of me, tell them about me. Tell them I am going, too. Tell them I'm like you.

He didn't respond, and I ran to him and hugged him tightly. Pete, tell them! Tell them you can't leave me!

I felt the cold mind-touch of one of the other aliens, and then he spoke: not directly to me, but to everyone. "Child, you can't come with us. You must stay here with your own kind."

I was outraged. "Pete," I commanded. "Tell them."

Reluctantly he gave me his thoughts: He had asked them, and they had said no. They would not take me. It was not allowed.

I was shocked to think of Pete having to ask permission, to see Pete as more of a child than I was. I realized that he had not even insisted. He was as weak and uncertain as a long-time hospital patient, bending before the doctor's decision. It was not allowed. Didn't he *care?*

My mother touched my shoulder. "Darling. Let us all say good-bye to Pete, now. We'll miss him too, you know."

No one could miss Pete the way I would, but I stepped back as she wanted.

My mother hesitated a moment, a little timid now that this old friend of the family had been revealed as an alien. But, after all, she had known him since childhood, so she conquered her fear and hugged him. My father shook Pete's hand and patted his shoulder as if he were one of his workers about to leave on a long journey. My sister, a smile fixed politely on her face, hugged Pete for the first and last time in her life. Pete put his hands out as if he wanted to talk to them at last, to say something important before he left. Then he looked at me, and I saw the wattles of skin at his neck darken and wave slightly, about to flare.

That terrified me, that sight of emotion, for I knew it meant Pete was sad to leave me, which meant that he really *was* going to leave me. This was the end, with no escape.

Suddenly I was crying, for the first time in years, and I threw myself at Pete. "Take me with you . . . Oh, please, take me with you," I begged, with mind and voice and body. I didn't want to be left alone. All my life, Pete had been there for me. I couldn't bear it if he left; I had to go with him. He *was* my life.

Pete stood still, simply suffering my embrace, until I stopped crying. I let go of him, then, thinking of another chance. Trying to breathe normally, trying to sound calm, I turned back to my family.

"Let me go with him," I said. "Just in the car, up to the highway. To give me time to say good-bye. Please. The driver can let me out on the highway." Away from my family, I thought, I could make the other humans forget I was there. If the aliens saw what I could do, they might agree to take me. Pete would be on my side—I could make him be.

My mother looked unwilling—she must have known I would desert her and all the earth for Pete—but I concentrated on making her forget that, making her feel nothing but my need, and at last she nodded reluctantly at the driver and the security men by the car. "It's up to them," she said.

I looked at the man I figured to have the most power—it showed in the way he stood—and gave him everything I had. I tried to fix in his mind the idea that it would be stupid to leave me, good to take me along to keep Pete happy. They must take me, in fact, because—

One of the aliens intercepted my projection, snapped it up like a frog taking a fly from the air. They all three stared at me with their unreadable, alien expressions, and they looked nothing at all like Pete.

"Ma'am," said the man I'd been aiming my plea at, "I don't think it would be a good idea." He looked at my mother, not me. "There'll be a lot of sightseers up by the highway, maybe even some crazies with guns. It might not be safe or wise to stop there. I'm afraid I'll have to say no. Your daughter can say her good-byes here." He smiled.

I knew it was over, then, and I hated them all. Even Pete, who had done nothing at all to keep me. I would have fought for him, I would have faced all the armies of Earth to keep him by me, and he couldn't even argue with his friends.

That was the last of Pete for me. He made no effort to reach me with his mind as they drove him away, although I'm sure he could have done so. But he didn't. When they took him into space I knew it because I felt a shock and then a numbness. And then I knew about being alone. No more Pete. No more mind-talk. Ever.

I'm alone among these humans just like Pete was. At night I wander through their dreams, oppressed by their limits, missing Pete, who could show me things I cannot see alone.

I wonder sometimes if Pete is as lonely as I am. Sometimes I start to think that he'll come back for me. I know that's probably crazy, and I can't count on it, but I do think about it. It's all I have to hope for. I'm just afraid that he'll leave it too late. I could spend my whole life waiting for him, and die before he returns. But I'll wait forever, if I have to. That's all I can do. Pete made me his friend because he was lonely. He had no right to abandon me as he did—that was just too cruel. But I'll forgive him when he comes back.

My parents think that I miss Pete the way I would miss a friend or relative who went away, and they think that I will get over it in time. They think I can forget. They don't realize I lost my life.

They bought me a monkey, a bribe to cheer me up. What a joke. It almost makes me cry to look at it, sitting there on my bed and picking at things with its tiny hands, wearing a face no animal should wear, staring at me with those sorrowful, wise, and stupid eyes, wishing I'd pretend to be its mother and teach it the ways of our tribe.

Reunion

He was not accustomed to such excitement, not when it came from within himself. He had stopped hoping and become resigned to his way of life, and he had forgotten so much. After so long he could barely control his thoughts and some of the more embarrassing body functions also evaded control: limbs twitched or spasmed at moments, the neck membrane bloomed and sank in meaningless indications. Worst of all, he still had the embarrassing habit of sleep. But his fellows assured him that all would be well. Once he was safely home they would cure him and make him whole again.

He was grateful to his fellows, for he knew how awkward he was for them. It would have been easier for them all if he'd had the grace to die, instead of surviving as a defective. But they would do their duty by him, and take him home, back to real life again.

His thoughts turning more and more toward home, he had no time for the humans. Jody was a burden—not as easy to shed as the others. She clung to him and made leave-taking a less than perfect joy. He knew his fellows scorned him for his relationship with her. There was something sick and perverted in feeling such affection for an animal, no matter how lonely he had been, and he felt too ashamed of himself to try to explain how it had happened, how Jody was special, not like most of her kind.

He didn't like feeling uneasy. He wanted to get back to the life that was interrupted so long ago with the minimum of fuss. So he submerged his will and let the others tell him what to do. He was, after all, still an invalid, badly injured in the crash and malformed and malnourished by the years of living on this unhealthy alien planet.

The humans, seen now through the eyes of his fellows, were ugly again, unfamiliar with their smooth, plump-almost-to-skin-bursting bodies, and they made him shrink with distaste.

Jody, still, was Jody, and he was sorry to leave her. But it wasn't possible to take her along, even as a pet. She would not be able to adjust and survive, as he had. The shock, if it did not kill her, would make her life a misery.

He did try to tell the others that she was different, but they responded that she was not different enough. She was a freak among her own people, but she was still only human.

Of course he had to leave her. There had never really been any question about it. Despite his injuries and changes, he knew where he belonged. Soon, he would be home among friends and family, he would be cured and resume his life. Jody, despite her limited life span, would also adjust, he thought. She was young, and she would draw comfort from her own kind and forget him. It was right and proper for a being to be among its own kind.

View from a Height

JOAN D. VINGE

Saturday, the 7th

I want to know why those pages were missing! How am I supposed to keep up with my research if they leave out pages—?

(*Long sighing noise.*)

Listen to yourself, Emmylou: You're listening to the sound of fear. It was an oversight, you know that. Nobody did it to you on purpose. Relax, you're getting Fortnight Fever. Tomorrow you'll get the pages, and an apology too, if Harvey Weems knows what's good for him.

But still, five whole pages; and the table of contents. How could you miss *five* pages? And the table of contents.

How do I know there hasn't been a coup? The Northwest's finally taken over completely, and they're censoring the media— And like the Man without a Country, everything they send me from now on is going to have holes cut in it.

In *Science*?

Or maybe Weems has decided to drive me insane—?

Oh, my God . . . it would be a short trip. Look at me. I don't have any fingernails left.

("*Arrwk. Hello, beautiful. Hello? Hello?*")

("*Ozymandias! Get out of my hair, you devil.*" *Laughter.* "Polly want a cracker? Here . . . gently! That's a boy.")

It's beautiful when he flies. I never get tired of watching him, or looking at him, even after twenty years. Twenty years. . . . What did the *psittacidae* do, to win the right to wear a rainbow as their plumage? Although the way we've hunted them for it, you could say it was a mixed blessing. Like some other things.

Twenty years. How strange it sounds to hear those words, and know they're true. There are gray hairs when I look in the mirror. Wrinkles starting. And Weems is bald! Bald as an egg, and all squinty behind his spectacles. How did we get that way, without noticing it? Time is both longer and shorter than you think, and usually all at once.

Twelve days is a long time to wait for somebody to return your call. Twenty years is a long time gone. But I feel somehow as though it was only last week that I left home. I keep the circuits clean, going over them and over them, showing those mental home movies until I could almost step across, sometimes, into that other reality. But then I always look down, and there's that tremendous abyss full of space and time, and I realize I can't, again. You can't go home again.

Especially when you're almost one thousand astronomical units out in space. Almost there, the first rung of the ladder. Next Thursday is the day. Oh, that bottle of champagne that's been waiting for so long. Oh, the parallax view! I have the equal of the best astronomical equipment in all of near-Earth space at my command, and a view of the universe that no one has ever had before; and using them has made me the only astrophysicist ever to win a PhD in deep space. Talk about your fieldwork.

Strange to think that if the Forward Observatory had massed less than its thousand-plus tons, I would have been replaced by a machine. But because the installation is so large, I in my infinite human flexibility, even with my infinite human appetite, become the most efficient legal tender. And the farther out I get the more important my own ability to judge what happens, and respond to it, becomes. The first—and maybe the last—manned interstellar probe, on a one-way journey into infinity . . . into a universe unobscured by our own system's gases and dust . . . equipped with eyes that see everything from gamma to ultralong wavelengths, and ears that listen to the music of the spheres.

And Emmylou Stewart, the captive audience. Adrift on a star . . . if you hold with the idea that all the bits of inert junk drifting through space, no matter how small, have star potential. Dark stars, with brilliance in their secret hearts, only kept back from letting it shine by Fate, which denied them the critical mass to reach their kindling point.

Speak of kindling: the laser beam just arrived to give me my daily boost, moving me a little faster, so I'll reach a little deeper into the universe. Blue sky at bedtime; I always was a night person. I'm sure they didn't design the solar sail to filter light like the sky . . . but I'm glad it happened to work out that way. Sky-blue was always my passion—the color, texture, fluid purity of it. This color isn't exactly right; but it doesn't matter, because I can't remember how anymore.

This sky is a sun-catcher. A big blue parasol. But so was the original, from where I used to stand. The sky is a blue parasol . . . did anyone ever say that before, I wonder? If anyone knows, speak up—

Is anyone even listening? Will anyone ever be?

("Who cares, anyway? Come on, Ozzie—climb aboard. Let's drop down to the observation porch while I do my meditation, and try to remember what days were like.")

Weems, damn it, I want satisfaction!

Sunday, the 8th

That idiot. That intolerable moron—how could he do that to me? After all this time, wouldn't you think he'd know me better than that? To keep me waiting for twelve days, wondering and afraid: twelve days of all the possible stupid paranoias I could weave with my idle hands and mind, making myself miserable, asking for trouble—

And then giving it to me. God, he must be some kind of sadist! If I could only reach him, and hurt him the way I've hurt these past hours—

Except that I know the news wasn't his fault, and that he didn't mean to hurt me . . . and so I can't even ease my pain by projecting it onto him.

I don't know what I would have done if his image hadn't been six days stale when it got here. What would I have done, if he'd been in earshot when I was listening; what would I have said? Maybe no more than I did say.

What can you say, when you realize you've thrown your whole life away?

He sat there behind his faded blotter, twiddling his pen, picking up his souvenir moon rocks and laying them down—looking for all the world like a man with a time bomb in his desk drawer—and said, "Now don't worry, Emmylou. There's no problem . . ." Went on saying it, one way or another, for five minutes; until I was shouting, "What's *wrong*, damn it?"

"I thought you'd never even notice the few pages . . ." with that sidling smile of his. And while I'm muttering, "I may have been in solitary confinement for twenty years, Harvey, but it hasn't turned my brain to mush," he said,

"So maybe I'd better explain, first—" and the look on his face; oh, the look on his face. "There's been a biomed breakthrough. If you were here on Earth, you . . . well, your body's immune responses could be . . . made normal . . ." And then he looked down, as though he could really see the look on my own face.

Made normal. Made normal. It's all I can hear. I was born with no natural immunities. No defense against disease. No help for it. No. *No, no, no;* that's all I ever heard, all my life on Earth. Through the plastic walls of my sealed room; through the helmet of my sealed suit. . . . And now it's all changed. They could cure me. But I can't go home. I knew this could happen; I knew it had to happen someday. But I chose to ignore that fact, and now it's too late to do anything about it.

Then why can't I forget that I could have been f-free. . . .

. . . I didn't answer Weems today. Screw Weems. There's nothing to say. Nothing at all.

I'm so tired.

Monday, the 9th

Couldn't sleep. It kept playing over and over in my mind. . . . Finally took some pills. Slept all day, feel like hell. Stupid. And it didn't go away. It was waiting for me, still waiting, when I woke up.

It isn't fair—!

I don't feel like talking about it.

Tuesday, the 10th

Tuesday, already. I haven't done a thing for two days. I haven't even started to check out the relay beacon, and that damn thing has to be dropped off this week. I don't have any strength; I can't seem to move, I just sit. But I have to get back to work. Have to . . .

Instead I read the printout of the article today. Hoping I'd find a flaw! If that isn't the greatest irony of my entire life. For two decades I prayed that somebody would find a cure for me. And for two more decades I didn't care. Am I going to spend the next two decades hating it, now that it's been found?

No . . . hating myself. I could have been free, they could have cured me; if only I'd stayed on Earth. If only I'd been patient. But now it's too late . . . by twenty *years*.

I want to go home. I want to go home. . . . But you can't go home again. Did I really say that, so blithely, so recently? *You* can't: You,

Emmylou Stewart. You are in prison, just like you have always been in prison.

It's all come back to me so strongly. Why me? Why must I be the ultimate victim— In all my life I've never smelled the sea wind, or plucked berries from a bush and eaten them, right there! Or felt my parents' kisses against my skin, or a man's body. . . . Because to me they were all deadly things.

I remember when I was a little girl, and we still lived in Victoria— I was just three or four, just at the brink of understanding that I was the only prisoner in my world. I remember watching my father sit polishing his shoes in the morning, before he left for the museum. And me smiling, so deviously, "Daddy . . . I'll help you do that, if you let me come out—"

And he came to the wall of my bubble and put his arms into the hugging gloves, and said, so gently, "No." And then he began to cry. And I began to cry too, because I didn't know why I'd made him unhappy. . . .

And all the children at school, with their "spaceman" jokes, pointing at the freak; all the years of insensitive people asking the same stupid questions every time I tried to go out anywhere . . . worst of all, the ones who weren't stupid, or insensitive. Like Jeffrey . . . no, I will not think about Jeffrey! I couldn't let myself think about him then. I could never afford to get close to a man, because I'd never be able to touch him. . . .

And now it's too late. Was I controlling my fate, when I volunteered for this one-way trip? Or was I just running away from a life where I was always helpless; helpless to escape the things I hated, helpless to embrace the things I loved?

I pretended this was different, and important . . . but was that really what I believed? No! I just wanted to crawl into a hole I couldn't get out of, because I was so afraid.

So afraid that one day I would unseal my plastic walls, or take off my helmet and my suit; walk out freely to breathe the air, or wade in a stream, or touch flesh against flesh . . . and die of it.

So now I've walled myself into this hermetically sealed tomb for a living death. A perfectly sterile environment, in which my body will not even decay when I die. Never having really lived, I shall never really die, dust to dust. A perfectly sterile environment; in every sense of the word.

I often stand looking at my body in the mirror after I take a shower.

Hazel eyes, brown hair in thick waves with hardly any gray . . . and a good figure; not exactly stacked, but not unattractive. And no one has ever seen it that way but me. Last night I had the Dream again . . . I haven't had it for such a long time . . . this time I was sitting on a carved wooden beast in the park beside the Provincial Museum in Victoria; but not as a child in my suit. As a college girl, in white shorts and a bright cotton shirt, feeling the sun on my shoulders, and— Jeffrey's arms around my waist. . . . We stroll along the bayside hand in hand, under the Victorian lampposts with their bright hanging flower baskets, and everything I do is fresh and spontaneous and full of the moment. But always, always, just when he holds me in his arms at last, just as I'm about to . . . I wake up.

When we die, do we wake out of reality at last, and all our dreams come true? When I die . . . I will be carried on and on into the timeless depths of uncharted space in this computerized tomb, unmourned and unremembered. In time all the atmosphere will seep away; and my fair corpse, lying like Snow White's in inviolate sleep, will be sucked dry of moisture, until it is nothing but a mummified parchment of shriveled leather and bulging bones. . . .

("*Hello? Hello, baby? Good night. Yes, no, maybe . . . Awk. Food time!*")

("Oh, Ozymandias! Yes, yes, I know . . . I haven't fed you, I'm sorry. I know, I know . . .")

(*Clinks and rattles.*)

Why am I so selfish? Just because I can't eat, I expect him to fast, too. . . . No. I just forgot.

He doesn't understand, but he knows something's wrong; he climbs the lamp pole like some tripodal bem, using both feet and his beak, and stares at me with that glass-beady bird's eye, stares and stares and mumbles things. Like a lunatic! Until I can hardly stand not to shut him in a cupboard, or something. But then he sidles along my shoulder and kisses me—such a tender caress against my cheek, with that hooked prehensile beak that could crush a walnut like a grape— to let me know that he's worried, and he cares. And I stroke his feathers to thank him and tell him that it's all right . . . but it's not. And he knows it.

Does he ever resent his life? Would he, if he could? Stolen away from his own kind, raised in a sterile bubble to be a caged bird for a caged human. . . .

I'm only a bird in a gilded cage. I want to go home.

Wednesday, the 11th

Why am I keeping this journal? Do I really believe that sometime some alien being will find this, or some starship from Earth's glorious future will catch up to me . . . glorious future, hell. Stupid, selfish, short-sighted fools. They ripped the guts out of the space program after they sent me away, no one will ever follow me now. I'll be lucky if they don't declare me dead and forget about me.

As if anyone would care what a woman all alone on a lumbering space probe thought about day after day for decades, anyway. What monstrous conceit.

I did lubricate the bearings on the big scope today. I did that much. I did it so that I could turn it back toward Earth . . . toward the sun . . . toward the whole damn system. Because I can't even see it, all crammed into the space of two moon diameters, even Pluto; and too dim and small and far away below me for my naked eyes, anyway. Even the sun is no more than a gaudy star that doesn't even make me squint. So I looked for them with the scope. . . .

Isn't it funny how when you're a child you see all those drawings and models of the solar system with big, lumpy planets and golden wakes streaming around the sun. Somehow you never get over ex-pecting it to look that way in person. And here I am, one thousand astronomical units north of the solar pole, gazing down from a great height . . . and it doesn't look that way at all. It doesn't look like any-thing; even through the scope. One great blot of light, and all the pale tiny diamond chips of planets and moons around it, barely distinguish-able from half a hundred undistinguished stars trapped in the same arc of blackness. So meaningless, so insignificant . . . so disappointing.

Five hours I spent, today, listening to my journal, looking back and trying to find—something, I don't know, something I suddenly don't have anymore.

I had it at the start. I was disgusting; Pollyanna Grad-student skip-ping and singing through the rooms of my very own observatory. It seemed like heaven, and a lifetime spent in it couldn't possibly be long enough for all that I was going to accomplish, and discover. I'd never be bored, no, not me. . . .

And there was so much to learn about the potential of this place, before I got out to where it supposedly would matter, and there would be new things to turn my wonderful extended senses toward . . . while I could still communicate easily with my dear mentor Dr. Weems, and the world. (Who'd ever have thought, when the lecherous old goat was my thesis advisor at Harvard, and making jokes to his other grad students about "the lengths some women will go to to protect their virginity" that we would have to spend a lifetime together.)

There was Ozymandias's first word . . . and my first birthday in space, and my first anniversary . . . and my doctoral degree at last, printed out by the computer with scrolls made of little *x*'s and taped up on the wall. . . .

Then day and night and day and night, beating me black and blue with blue and black . . . my fifth anniversary, my eighth, my decade. I crossed the magnetopause, to become truly the first voyager in interstellar space . . . but by then there was no one left to *talk* to anymore, to really share the experience with. Even the radio and television broadcasts drifting out from Earth were diffuse and rare; there were fewer and fewer contacts with the reality outside. The plodding routines, the stupefying boredom—until sometimes I stood screaming down the halls just for something new; listening to the echoes that no one else would ever hear and pretending they'd come to call; trying so hard to believe there was something to hear that wasn't *my* voice, *my* echo, or Ozymandias making a mockery of it.

("*Hello, beautiful. That's a crock. Hello, hello?*")

("Ozymandias, get *away* from me—")

But always I had that underlying belief in my mission: that I was here for a purpose, for more than my own selfish reasons, or NASA's (or whatever the hell they call it now), but for Humanity, and Science. Through meditation I learned the real value of inner silence and thought that by creating an inner peace I had reached equilibrium with the outer silences. I thought that meditation had disciplined me, I was in touch with my self and with the soul of the cosmos. . . . But I haven't been able to meditate since—it happened. The inner silence fills up with my own anger screaming at me, until I can't remember what peace sounds like.

And what have I really discovered, so far? Almost nothing. Nothing worth wasting my analysis or all my fine theories—or my freedom—on. Space is even emptier than anyone dreamed, you could count on both hands the bits of cold dust or worldlet I've passed in all this time, lost souls falling helplessly through near-perfect vacuum . . . all of us together. With my absurdly long astronomical tape measure I have fixed precisely the distance to NGC 2419 and a few other features, and from that made new estimates about a few more distant ones. But I have not detected a miniature black hole insatiably vacuuming up the vacuum; I have not pierced the invisible clouds that shroud the ultralong wavelengths like fog; I have not discovered that life exists beyond the Earth in even the most tentative way. Looking back at the solar system I see nothing to show definitively that we even exist, anymore. All I hear anymore when I scan is electromagnetic noise, no coherent thought. Only Weems every twelfth night, like the last man alive. . . . Christ, I still haven't answered him.

Why bother? Let him sweat. Why bother with any of it. Why waste my precious time.

Oh, my precious time. . . . Half a lifetime left that could have been mine, on Earth.

Twenty years—I came through them all all right. I thought I was safe. And after twenty years, my facade of discipline and self-control falls apart at a touch. What a self-deluded hypocrite I've been. Do you know that I said the sky was like a blue parasol eighteen years ago? And probably said it again fifteen years ago, and ten, and five—

Tomorrow I pass 1000 AUs.

Thursday, the 12th

I burned out the scope. I burned out the scope. I left it pointing toward the Earth, and when the laser came on for the night it shone right down the scope's throat and burned it out. I'm so ashamed. . . . Did I do it on purpose, subconsciously?

("Good night starlight. Arrk. Good night. Good . . .")

("Damn it, I want to hear another human voice—!")

(Echoing, "voice, voice, voice, voice . . .")

When I found out what I'd done I ran away. I ran and ran through the halls. . . . But I only ran in a circle: This observatory, my prison, myself . . . I can't escape. I'll always come back in the end, to this green-walled room with its desk and its terminals, its cupboards crammed with a hundred thousand dozens of everything, toilet paper and magnetic tape and oxygen tanks. . . . And I can tell you exactly how many steps it is to my bedroom or how long it took me to crochet the afghan on the bed . . . how long I've sat in the dark and silence, setting up an exposure program or listening for the feeble pulse of a radio galaxy two billion light-years away. There will never be anything different, or anything more.

When I finally came back here, there was a message waiting. Weems, grinning out at me half-bombed from the screen—"Congratulations," he cried, "on this historic occasion! Emmylou, we're having a little celebration here at the lab; mind if we join you in yours, one thousand astronomical units from home—?" I've never seen him drunk. They really must have meant to do something nice for me, planning it all six days ahead. . . .

To celebrate I shouted obscenities I didn't even know I knew at him, until my voice was broken and my throat was raw.

Then I sat at my desk for a long time with my jackknife lying open in my hand. Not wanting to die—I've always been too afraid of death for that—but wanting to hurt myself. I wanted to make a fresh hurt, to take my attention off the terrible thing that is sucking me into myself like an imploding star. Or maybe just to punish myself, I don't know. But I considered the possibility of actually cutting myself quite calmly; while some separate part of me looked on in horror. I even pressed the knife against my flesh . . . and then I stopped and put it away. It hurts too much.

I can't go on like this. I have duties, obligations, and I can't face them. What would I do without the emergency automechs? . . . But it's the rest of my life, and they can't go on doing my job for me forever—

Later.

I just had a visitor. Strange as that sounds. Stranger yet—it was Donald Duck. I picked up half of a children's cartoon show today, the first coherent piece of nondirectional, unbeamed television broadcast I've recorded in months. And I don't think I've ever been happier to see anyone in my life. What a nice surprise, so glad you could drop by. . . . Ozymandias loves him; he hangs upside down from his swing under the cabinet with a cracker in one foot, cackling away and saying, "Give us a kiss, *smack-smack-smack*." . . . We watched it three times. I even smiled, for a while; until I remembered myself. It helps. Maybe I'll watch it again until bedtime.

Friday, the 13th

Friday the Thirteenth. Amusing. Poor Friday the Thirteenth, what did it ever do to deserve its reputation? Even if it had any power to make my life miserable, it couldn't hold a candle to the rest of this week. It seems like an eternity since last weekend.

I repaired the scope today; replaced the burned-out parts. Had to suit up and go outside for part of the work . . . I haven't done any outside maintenance for quite a while. Odd how both exhilarating and terrifying it always is when I first step out of the air lock, utterly alone, into space. You're entirely on your own, so far away from any possibility of help, so far away from anything at all. And at that moment you doubt yourself, suddenly, terribly . . . just for a moment.

But then you drag your umbilical out behind you and clank along the hull in your magnetized boots that feel so reassuringly like lead ballast. You turn on the lights and look for the trouble, find it, and get to work; it doesn't bother you anymore. . . . When your life seems to have torn loose and be drifting free, it creates a kind of sea anchor to work with your hands; whether it's doing some mindless routine chore or the most intricate of repairs.

There was a moment of panic, when I actually saw charred wires and melted metal, when I imagined the damage was so bad that I couldn't repair it again. It looked so final, so—masterful. I clung there by my feet and whimpered and clenched my hands inside my gloves, like a great shining baby, for a while. But then I pulled myself down and began to pry here and unscrew there and twist a component free . . . and little by little I replaced everything. One step at a time; the way we get through life.

By the time I'd finished I felt quite calm, for the first time in days; the thing that's been trying to choke me to death this past week seemed to falter a little at my demonstration of competence. I've been breathing easier since then; but I still don't have much strength. I used up all I had just overcoming my own inertia.

But I shut off the lights and hiked around the hull for a while afterwards—I couldn't face going back inside just then: Looking at the black convex dish of the solar sail I'm embedded in, up at the radio antenna's smaller dish occluding stars as the observatory's cylinder wheels endlessly at the hub of the spinning parasol. . . .

That made me dizzy, and so I looked out into the starfields that lie on every side. Even with my own poor, unaugmented senses there's so much more to see out here, unimpeded by atmosphere or dust, undominated by any sun's glare. The brilliance of the Milky Way, the depths of star and nebula and farthest galaxy breathlessly suspended . . . as I am. The realization that I'm lost for eternity in an uncharted sea.

Strangely, although that thought aroused a very powerful emotion when it struck me, it wasn't a negative one at all: It was from another scale of values entirely; like the universe itself. It was as if the universe itself stretched out its finger to touch me. And in touching me, singling me out, it only heightened my awareness of my own insignificance.

That was somehow very comforting. When you confront the absolute indifference of magnitudes and vistas so overwhelming, the swollen ego of your self-important suffering is diminished. . . .

And I remembered one of the things that was always so important to me about space—that here *any*one has to put on a spacesuit before they step outside. We're all aliens, no one better equipped to survive than another. I am as normal as anyone else, out here.

I must hold on to that thought.

Saturday, the 14th

There is a reason for my being here. There is a reason.

I was able to meditate earlier today. Not in the old way, the usual way, by emptying my mind. Rather by letting the questions fill up the space, not fighting them; letting them merge with my memories of all that's gone before. I put on music, that great mnemonic stimulator; letting the images that each tape evoked free-associate and interact.

And in the end I could believe again that my being here was the result of a free choice. No one forced me into this. My motives for volunteering were entirely my own. And I was given this position because NASA believed that I was more likely to be successful in it than anyone else they could have chosen.

It doesn't matter that some of my motives happened to be unresolved fear or wanting to escape from things I couldn't cope with. It really doesn't matter. Sometimes retreat is the only alternative to destruction, and only a madman can't recognize the truth of that. Only a madman. . . . Is there anyone "sane" on Earth who isn't secretly a fugitive from something unbearable somewhere in their life? And yet they function normally.

If they ran, they ran toward something, too, not just away. And so did I. I had already chosen a career as an astrophysicist before I ever dreamed of being a part of this project. I could have become a medical researcher instead, worked on my own to find a cure for my condition. I could have grown up hating the whole idea of space and "spacemen," stumbling through life in my damned ugly sterile suit. . . .

But I remember when I was six years old, the first time I saw a film of suited astronauts at work in space . . . they looked just like me! And no one was laughing. How could I help but love space, then?

(And how could I help but love Jeffrey, with his night-black hair, and his blue flightsuit with the starry patch on the shoulder. Poor Jeffrey, poor Jeffrey, who never even realized his own dream of space before they cut the program out from under him. . . . I will not talk about Jeffrey. I will not.)

Yes, I could have stayed on Earth, and waited for a cure! I knew even then there would have to be one, someday. It was both easier and harder to choose space, instead of staying.

And I think the thing that really decided me was that those people had faith enough in me and my abilities to believe that I could run this observatory and my own life smoothly for as long as I lived. Billions of dollars and a thousand tons of equipment resting on me; like Atlas holding up his world.

Even Atlas tried to get rid of his burden; because no matter how vital his function was, the responsibility was still a burden to him. But he took his burden back again too, didn't he; for better or worse. . . .

I worked today. I worked my butt off getting caught up on a week's worth of data processing and maintenance, and I'm still not finished. Discovered while I was at it that Ozymandias had used those missing five pages just like the daily news: crapped all over them. My sentiments exactly! I laughed and laughed.

I think I may live.

Sunday, the 15th

The clouds have parted.

That's not rhetorical—among my fresh processed data is a series of photo reconstructions in the ultralong wavelengths. And there's a gap in the obscuring gas up ahead of me, a break in the clouds that extends thirty or forty light-years. Maybe fifty! Fantastic. What a view. What a view I have from here of everything, with my infinitely extended vision: of the way ahead, of the passing scene—or looking back toward Earth.

Looking back. I'll never stop looking back and wishing it could have been different. That at least there could have been two of me, one to be here, one who could have been normal, back on Earth; so that I wouldn't have to be forever torn in two by regrets—

("Hello. What's up, doc? Avast!")

("Hey, watch it! If you drink, don't fly.")

Damn bird . . . If I'm getting maudlin, it's because I had a party today. Drank a whole bottle of champagne. Yes, I had *the* party . . . we did, Ozymandias and I. Our private 1000 AU celebration. Better late than never, I guess. At least we did have something concrete to celebrate—the photos. And if the celebration wasn't quite as merry as it could have been, still I guess it will probably seem like it was when I look back on it from the next one, at 2000 AUs. They'll be coming faster now, the celebrations. I may even live to celebrate 8000. What the hell, I'll shoot for 10,000—

After we finished the champagne . . . Ozymandias thinks '98 was a great year, thank God he can't drink as fast as I can . . . I put on my Strauss waltzes, and the *Barcarolle:* Oh, the Berlin Philharmonic; their touch is what a lover's kiss must be. I threw the view outside onto the big screen, a ballroom of stars, and danced with my shadow. And part of the time I wasn't dancing above the abyss in a jumpsuit and head-phones, but waltzing in yards of satin and lace across a ballroom floor in nineteenth-century Vienna. What I wouldn't give to be *there* for a moment out of time. Not for a lifetime, or even a year, but just for an evening; just for one waltz.

Another thing I shall never do. There are so many things we can't do, any of us, for whatever the reasons—time, talent, life's callous whims. We're all on a one-way trip into infinity. If we're lucky, we're given some life's work we care about, or some person. Or both, if we're very lucky.

And I do have Weems. Sometimes I see us like an old married couple, who have grown to a tolerant understanding over the years. We've never been soul mates, God knows, but we're comfortable with each others' silences. . . .

I guess it's about time I answered him.

About the Authors

Eleanor Arnason published her first science fiction story in 1973; her short fiction has appeared in *New Worlds, Orbit, Asimov's Science Fiction,* and *Amazing Stories.* Her novels include *The Sword Smith* (1978), *To the Resurrection Station* (1986), *Daughter of the Bear King* (1987), and *Ring of Swords* (1993). Her novel *A Woman of the Iron People,* published in 1991, was honored with a James Tiptree, Jr., Memorial Award.

Eleanor Arnason has published both fantasy and science fiction, and comments about both genres:

> Science fiction deals with the effect of science and technology on people. Fantasy deals with the things that have been devalued in industrial society: emotion, intuition, personal loyalty, the sense that human beings are part of the natural world. Both are ways to analyze the changes caused by industrialization, to understand what has been lost and what has been gained. (From "On Writing Science Fiction," in *Women of Vision,* edited by Denise Du Pont [New York: St. Martin's Press, 1988])

Leigh Brackett was known and loved for her colorful adventure stories. Her novels include *The Sword of Rhiannon* (1953), *The Nemesis from Terra* (1961), *The Big Jump* (1955), *The Ginger Star* (1974), and the book many critics consider her best, *The Long Tomorrow* (1955). She also wrote screenplays for the motion picture director Howard Hawks, among them *The Big Sleep* (1946) and *Rio Bravo* (1958). She died in 1978 while working on the screenplay of *The Empire Strikes Back,* the second of George Lucas's Star Wars movies.

Leigh Brackett was married to science fiction writer Edmond Hamilton and had this to say about their different ways of working:

Writing is a uniquely personal and solitary endeavor. . . . But when you're being constantly exposed to another way of doing it, a bit of that will rub off.

Ed always knew the last line of a story before he wrote the first one, and every line he wrote aimed straight at that target. I used the opposite method—write an opening and let it grow. . . .

I began to realize that this method was not in any sense an artistic virtue; all it meant was that I didn't know how to construct a story. . . . I was in such a hurry to get to the wonderful adventures thronging in my mind that I couldn't be bothered with the bones of the thing . . . after a certain length of time I began to understand how Ed put a story together, and found myself doing the same thing. So if he learned a little bit of style from me, I learned a whole lot about structure from him. (From "Afterword," in *The Best of Leigh Brackett*, edited by Edmond Hamilton [New York: Ballantine, Del Rey, 1977])

Marion Zimmer Bradley became a best-selling author with her Arthurian fantasy *The Mists of Avalon* (1983). Among her many other novels are *The Sword of Aldones* (1962), *The Winds of Darkover* (1970), *The Spell Sword* (1974), *The Heritage of Hastur* (1975), *The Shattered Chain* (1976), *Sharra's Exile* (1981), and the historical fantasy *The Firebrand* (1987). Her Darkover novels are especially popular, and she has edited several anthologies of stories by other writers set in her world of Darkover; several writers of fantasy and science fiction began their careers by publishing stories in these books.

About her life as a writer, Marion Zimmer Bradley has written:

The secret of life is to do what you enjoy doing most, and to get someone to pay you enough so that you don't actually have to starve while you're doing it. People who want other things, money and status, baffle me. I write professionally because it's the only thing I can do well, and every other job I have had has either bored or frustrated me past tolerance; and since I write compulsively and would no matter what else I was doing, it's wonderful that I can get paid for it. (From *Twentieth-Century Science Fiction Writers*, Second Edition, edited by Curtis C. Smith [Chicago: St. James Press, 1986])

Zenna Henderson, who died in 1983, was an elementary-school teacher who lived and taught for most of her life in the American Southwest. During World War II, she taught Japanese-American children at the Japanese Relocation Camp in Sacaton, Arizona. She is best known for her stories about the benevolent aliens known as "The People," which have been collected in *Pilgrimage: The Book of the People* (1961) and *The People: No Different Flesh* (1966); her other collections are *The Anything Box* (1965) and *Holding Wonder* (1971).

In 1981, she made the following comment about her writing:

> When I was about twelve I began reading science fiction—Jules Verne, Haggard, and Edgar Rice Burroughs, and all the current magazines I could get hold of, but it wasn't until I had graduated from college that I began writing fantasy and science fiction. I have only a sketchy scientific background, so of necessity I write from a non-technical viewpoint. . . . Mottos I try to observe when I write: stories consist of unusual people in ordinary circumstances or ordinary people in unusual circumstances; write about what you know; don't let your subtleties become obscurities. (From *Twentieth-Century Science Fiction Writers,* edited by Curtis C. Smith [New York: St. Martin's Press, 1981])

Sonya Dorman Hess is both a poet and an accomplished writer of science fiction. Her stories have appeared in *Orbit, Redbook, The Magazine of Fantasy & Science Fiction, Galaxy, Interfaces,* and *Edges,* and she is also the author of a novel for young adults, *Planet Patrol* (1978). Her poetry has been published in her collections *Poems* (Ohio State University Press, 1970), *Stretching Fence* (Ohio State University Press, 1975), *A Paper Raincoat: Poems* (Puckerbrush Press, 1976), *The Far Traveler* (Juniper Press, 1980), *Palace of Earth* (Puckerbrush Press, 1984), and *Kingdom of Lost Waters* (Ahsahta/Boise State University Press, 1994). She lives in Taos, New Mexico.

Of her writing, Sonya Dorman Hess has said: "I like speculative fiction because I believe art and science should be lovers, not enemies or adversaries." (From the introduction to "Go, Go, Go, Said the Bird," in *Dangerous Visions,* edited by Harlan Ellison [New York: Doubleday, 1967])

Ursula K. Le Guin has become one of the most widely respected writers of science fiction. She has won the Nebula Award, the Hugo Award, the National Book Award, and many other honors. She is the author of the fantasy novels *A Wizard of Earthsea* (1968), *The Tombs of Atuan* (1971), *The Farthest Shore* (1972), and *Tehanu: The Last Book of Earthsea* (1990). Her science fiction novels include *The Left Hand of Darkness* (1969), *The Lathe of Heaven* (1971), *The Dispossessed* (1974), and *Always Coming Home* (1985). Among her other books are *Orsinian Tales* (1976), *Malafrena* (1979), *The Beginning Place* (1980), and *Searoad: The Chronicles of Klatsand* (1991).

Ursula Le Guin has said the following about science fiction writers she admires:

> They write science fiction, I imagine, because what they have to say is best said using the tools of science fiction, and the craftsman knows his tools. And still, they are novelists, because while using the great range of imagery available to science fiction, they say what it is they have to say through a character—not a mouthpiece, but a fully realized secondary creation. The character is primary. . . . The writers' interest is no longer really in the gadget, or the size of the universe, or the laws of robotics, or the destiny of social classes, or anything describable in quantitative, or mechanical, or objective terms. They are not interested in what things do, but in how things are. (From "Science Fiction and Mrs. Brown," in *Science Fiction at Large,* edited by Peter Nicholls [New York: Harper & Row, 1976])

Katherine MacLean began publishing science fiction in the late 1940s and won a Nebula Award in 1971 for her novella "The Missing Man." Much of her short fiction has appeared in *Astounding* (later *Analog*) magazine; her novels include *Cosmic Checkmate,* written with Charles V. De Vet (1962), *The Man in the Bird Cage* (1971), *Missing Man* (1975), and *Dark Wing,* written with Carl West (1979). Her short fiction has been collected in *The Diploids* (1962) and *The Trouble with You Earth People* (1980).

In an essay about possible problems in communicating with non-human intelligences, Katherine MacLean wrote:

> Who can communicate across differences of values? Writers, poets, singers, people who play with value-shifting for pleasure. Also the dangerous and logical cynics and traders from the areas of destroyed

ancient value systems, men freed of taboos, who can profit by playing middleman in contacts between harshly different societies. . . . Others who can shift value structures easily are women, assistants, lieutenants, any assistant to an executive whose job is to aid the boss in pursuit of his goals and still do some independent thinking. Pursuing the pattern, we see that any being who must travel a lifetime with another gets an evolutionary screening for ability to understand and aid the beings with whom she travels. (From "Alien Minds and Nonhuman Intelligences," in *The Craft of Science Fiction,* edited by Reginald Bretnor [New York: Harper & Row, 1976])

Anne McCaffrey was the first woman to win both Nebula and Hugo awards for her science fiction. She is best known for her extremely popular Pern series, which includes the novels *Dragonflight* (1968), *Dragonquest* (1971), *The White Dragon* (1978), and *Dragonsdawn* (1988). Other novels include *The Crystal Singer* (1982), *Killashandra* (1985), *Nerilka's Story* (1986), *The Rowan* (1990), and *Damia* (1992). Among her novels for younger readers are *Dragonsong* (1976), *Dragonsinger* (1977), and *Dragondrums* (1979). She lives in Ireland. Anne McCaffrey has said the following about her life:

The early lessons I learned, generally the hard way, in standing up for myself and my egocentricities, being proud of being "different," doing my own thing, gave me the strength of purpose to continue doing so in later life. You have to learn how not to conform, how to avoid labels. But it isn't easy! It's lonely until you realize that you have inner resources that those of the herd mentality cannot enjoy. That's where the mind learns the freedom to think science-fictiony things, and when early lessons of tenacity, pure bullheadedness, can make a difference. Most people prefer to be accepted. I learned not to be. (From "Retrospection," in *Women of Vision,* edited by Denise Du Pont [New York: St. Martin's Press, 1988])

Vonda N. McIntyre, who has a B.S. in biology and did graduate work in genetics, won a Nebula Award for "Of Mist, and Grass, and Sand," and Nebula and Hugo awards for her second novel, *Dreamsnake*

(1978). Her short fiction has appeared in *Orbit, Analog, The Magazine of Fantasy & Science Fiction,* and other magazines and anthologies. With Susan Janice Anderson, she edited an anthology of humanist science fiction by both men and women, *Aurora: Beyond Equality* (1976). Her other books include *The Exile Waiting* (1975), *Superluminal* (1983), *Barbary* (1984), *Starfarers* (1989), *Transition* (1991), *Metaphase* (1992), *Nautilus* (1994), and *Fireflood and Other Stories* (1979).

About science fiction, Vonda McIntyre has commented: "Science fiction is the only genre in which a writer can realistically explore societies that don't yet exist." (From a letter to Pamela Sargent, 1994)

Judith Merril has contributed to science fiction as a writer, as a critic and reviewer, and as an editor. From 1956 until 1967, she edited a critically acclaimed, and still widely admired, series of annual volumes of the best science fiction of the year. Among her novels are *Shadow on the Hearth* (1950), *The Tomorrow People* (1960), and *Gunner Cade* (1952) and *Outpost Mars* (1952), both written with C. M. Kornbluth under the pseudonym Cyril Judd. Her short-fiction collections include *Out of Bounds* (1960), *Daughters of Earth* (1968), and *The Best of Judith Merril* (1976).

Judith Merril has written the following about her writing and her life:

I grew up in the radical thirties. My mother had been a suffragette. It never occurred to me that the Bad Old Days of Double Standard had anything to do with *me.*

The first strong intimation, actually, was when the editors of the mystery, western, and sports "pulp" magazines, where I did my apprentice writing, demanded masculine pen names. But of course they were pulps, oriented to a masculine readership, and the whole thing was only an irritation: as soon as I turned to S-F, the problem disappeared.

At the end of World War II, the wonderful working-mothers' day-care centres all closed down, and from every side the news was shouted that Woman's Place was after all In The Home. . . .

There was a lot of pressure; one couldn't help wondering. Could it be true? I didn't think so; neither did my returning husband. We were thirties radicals, after all, so what if it was the forties. . . .

Ten years later, I had a growing "name" as a writer, a lot of good colleague/friends, and two divorces. Complicated. One worried, and kept trying to figure things out. (From *Survival Ship and Other Stories* by Judith Merril [Toronto: Kakabeka, 1974])

C. L. Moore, who died in 1987, was one of the first women writers to make her mark on science fiction. She published her first story in the magazine *Weird Tales* in 1933. Her fantasy adventure stories featuring a heroic woman, Jirel of Joiry, were also published during the '30s. In 1940, she married the science fiction writer Henry Kuttner, in collaboration with whom she wrote many works, among them *Fury* (1950), *No Boundaries* (1955), and *The Dark World* (1965). Collections published under their pseudonym Lewis Padgett are *A Gnome There Was* (1950), *Mutant* (1953), and *Line to Tomorrow* (1954). Her own books include *Judgment Night* (1952), *Doomsday Morning* (1957), and *The Best of C. L. Moore* (1975).

C. L. Moore once wrote about the genesis of her first published story, "Shambleau":

I lived in a large midwestern city and the depression of the 1930s was rampant over the land. So I was snatched from my sophomore year at the state university and crammed into a business school. . . . By incredible good fortune, before I'd finished the course, a job opening in a large bank loomed up and I leaped at it, unprepared but eager. . . .

Well, I was adequate, but typing was something I practiced in every spare moment. And this is where "Shambleau" began, halfway down a sheet of yellow paper otherwise filled up with boring quick-brown-foxes, alphabets, and things like "The White Knight is sliding down the poker . . ." to lighten the practice.

Midway down that yellow page I began fragments remembered from sophomore English at the university. All the choices were made at random . . . In the middle of this exercise a line from a poem . . . worked itself to the front and I discovered myself typing something about a "red, running figure." I looked at it awhile, my mind a perfect blank, and then shifted mental gears . . . swinging with idiot confidence into the first lines of the story which ended up as "Shambleau." (From "Afterword: Footnote to 'Shambleau' . . . and Others," in *The Best of C. L. Moore,* edited by Lester del Rey [New York: Ballantine, 1975])

Kit Reed, under the name Kit Craig, is the author of two recent suspense novels, *Gone* (1992) and *The Burned* (1993). She is completing
a third. She has received both a Guggenheim Fellowship and a five-
year grant from the Abraham Woursell Foundation for her writing. Her
non-science-fiction books include *Mother Isn't Dead, She's Only Sleeping* (1961), *At War as Children* (1964), *Cry of the Daughter* (1971),
Tiger Rag (1973), *The Ballad of T. Rantula* (1979), *Catholic Girls*
(1987), and *Thief of Lives: Stories* (1992). Among her volumes of
science fiction are the novels *Armed Camps* (1969), *Magic Time*
(1980), and *Little Sisters of the Apocalypse* (1994), and the short-
fiction collections *Other Stories, and The Attack of the Giant Baby*
(1981) and *The Revenge of the Senior Citizens* (1986).

Kit Reed has said about science fiction:

> I like science fiction's off-the-wall quality, and the suspension of
> disbelief, and the idea that anything can happen . . . but so much
> of science fiction is so *unreal*, it seems unimportant to me.
>
> I've seen too many people who have escaped into genre fiction
> as a way of avoiding any of the real things about living and writing.
> The minute you put two characters on a planet and get busy with
> the hardware and the scenery and all the rest of it, you have caught
> the interest of a certain kind of reader, when you wouldn't have
> caught his interest if your characters were living right here and
> now in a split-level, where you might have to look a little more
> closely into what their souls are like and what problems they might
> have. . . . I don't think books can tell you how to live, but on the
> other hand, I don't think they should tell you that you don't have
> to think about it. (From "Kit Reed," in *Dream Makers: Volume II:
> The Uncommon Men and Women Who Write Science Fiction*, by
> Charles Platt [New York: Berkley Books, 1983])

Joanna Russ published her first story in 1959; she soon became one
of the most innovative writers in the field and one of the first to draw
explicitly on feminist thought for inspiration. She has won the Nebula
and Hugo awards for her fiction and the Pilgrim Award for her science
fiction criticism. Among her books are *Picnic on Paradise* (1968), *And
Chaos Died* (1970), *The Female Man* (1975), *The Two of Them* (1978),
The Zanzibar Cat (1983), and *The Hidden Side of the Moon* (1987).
Her critical work *How to Suppress Women's Writing* (1983) has pro-

voked much discussion both inside science fiction and outside the genre.

Joanna Russ, in discussing the attention paid science fiction by academics, wrote:

> One can't get minority work into the canon by pretending it's about the same things or uses the same techniques as majority work. It probably isn't and doesn't. It may very well look like nothing ever before seen on earth. When science fiction first entered academia, the mistakes made about it by critics were grotesque. They continue to be, from time to time. This was due not only to a lack of scientific background—for example, some critics saw classic alien-background stories as nightmares, being unaware of the accuracy of the background and the delight in this as the story's point—but also to a lack of any knowledge of the field's history and conventions (including lack of the knowledge that it *had* a history and conventions). (From *How to Suppress Women's Writing* [Austin: University of Texas Press, 1983])

Margaret St. Clair began publishing science fiction during the '40s but became more widely known during the '50s; she also wrote under the name of Idris Seabright. Her stories have appeared in *The Magazine of Fantasy & Science Fiction* and other publications; some of her short fiction has been collected in *Change the Sky and Other Stories* (1974) and *The Best of Margaret St. Clair* (1985). Among her novels are *Agent of the Unknown* (1956), *The Green Queen* (1956), *Sign of the Labrys* (1963), *The Shadow People* (1969), and *The Dancers of Noyo* (1973).

About the possible role of science fiction, Margaret St. Clair had this to say:

> The historic task of science fiction is to develop a global consciousness.
>
> This is the task of our age: to rise above our petty jealousies and hatreds, to learn to use our admirable local loves and loyalties as the binding cement of a larger loyalty. We must learn to think of ourselves as the inhabitants and citizens of the third planet from the sun. . . .
>
> I have . . . disavowed pretensions to being a prophet or a seer,

and now I am talking like one. Yet there is a difference. It is one thing to point out goals for humanity—"tomorrow the stars"—and another to contribute to the realization of a fact: that we live on a fragile, destructible planet. (From: "Introduction: Thoughts from My Seventies," in *The Best of Margaret St. Clair*, edited by Martin H. Greenberg [Chicago: Academy Chicago, 1985])

Josephine Saxton, one of the many gifted British writers who began contributing to science fiction during the '60s, has published short fiction in *New Worlds, Orbit, New Dimensions,* and other magazines and anthologies. Her books include *The Heiros Gamos of Sam and An Smith* (1969), *Group Feast* (1971), *The Travails of Jane Saint* (1980), and *Queen of the States* (1986).

Josephine Saxton says about science fiction and her own writing:

The term "Science Fiction" may be taken to cover a broad spectrum of work, in my case an exploration of the subconscious mind, extrapolation from current scientific ideas, and stories arising from the premise "what if . . . ?" Later work arose from autobiographical memories and was therefore much nearer the surface. (From the author's vita, "Josephine Saxton. Brief publishing history," 1994)

James Tiptree, Jr., was the pseudonym of Alice Sheldon, who also wrote under the name of Raccoona Sheldon. She grew up in Africa and India, worked for the C.I.A., and later earned a Ph.D. in experimental psychology. Her writing was honored with Hugo and Nebula awards. Her novels and short story collections include *Warm Worlds and Otherwise* (1975), *Star Songs of an Old Primate* (1978), *Up the Walls of the World* (1978), *Brightness Falls from the Air* (1985), *Tales of the Quintana Roo* (1986), and *Crown of Stars* (1988). She died in 1987, taking her own life and that of her husband, Huntington Sheldon; he had Alzheimer's Disease and Tiptree's own health had grown more uncertain. The James Tiptree, Jr., Memorial Award, named in her honor, is given annually to a work of science fiction or fantasy that explores and expands gender roles.

She had this to say about the ways in which men and women write:

As to the question of whether there are male and female writing styles . . . I feel that by their sins shall ye know them, which is to say that there are separate styles of *bad* writing. Rebecca West has said that the sin of men is lunacy and the sin of women idiocy. She meant that men have the weakness of seeing everything in black and white, as though by moonlight, with all the colors and pains left out, like a shiny new machine. And "idiocy" derives from the original meaning of "idiot," a *private person*. Women can be over-obsessed by minutiae, by trivial concerns with no broad implications. . . . When women write badly, they fall away from the larger human concerns into too-private trivialisms. When men write badly, it is about some sublunar crackpot idea with no regard for its real human consequences—like their wars. (From "A Woman Writing SF and Fantasy," in *Women of Vision,* edited by Denise Du Pont [New York: St. Martin's Press, 1988])

Lisa Tuttle, born in Texas, has lived in the United Kingdom since 1980. She published her first science fiction story at the age of twenty and won the John W. Campbell Award for Best New Writer in 1974. She is the author of the novels *Windhaven,* written with George R. R. Martin (1981), *Familiar Spirit* (1983), *Gabriel* (1987), and *Lost Futures* (1992). Her short-story collections include *A Nest of Nightmares* (1986), *A Spaceship Built of Stone* (1987), and *Memories of the Body* (1992). She was also editor of *The Encyclopedia of Feminism* (1986).

Commenting on changes in science fiction's portrayal of women, Lisa Tuttle wrote:

Positive changes in the literature have been countered by a retrogressive movement in popular SF films, where women's roles are limited and male-determined. . . . The role played by Sigourney Weaver in *Alien* (1979) stands out as a notable exception. . . . She is just as human as the rest of the mixed-sex crew, and is menaced by the alien to the same degree and in the same way. . . . But in the sequel, *Aliens* (1986), the human/alien battle has become a heavily symbolic fight between two females. Weaver's character is lumbered with a stray child to make the final battle acceptable to even the most fearful of immature male viewers: this isn't a woman fighting a monster, but two mothers doing what comes naturally, battling to protect their children. (From "Women As Portrayed in Science Fiction," in *The Science Fiction Encyclopedia,* edited by John Clute and Peter Nicholls [New York: St. Martin's Press, 1993])

Joan D. Vinge won a Hugo Award in 1978 for her novelette "Eyes of Amber" and a second Hugo in 1981 for her novel *The Snow Queen* (1980). Two more novels, *World's End* (1984) and *The Summer Queen* (1991), are part of the Snow Queen sequence. Her other books include *The Heaven Chronicles* (1991), *Eyes of Amber and Other Stories* (1979), and *Phoenix in the Ashes* (1985). *Psion* (1982), *Catspaw* (1988), and *Dreamfall* (1995) are novels featuring her character Cat.

Joan Vinge, who has a degree in anthropology, had this to say about that subject and science fiction:

> "Broadening" is a word that I am generally reluctant to use, but it's the only one I know of that expresses the thing I find appealing about both science fiction and anthropology: they prove to me over and over again that the way I live life in twentieth-century America is not the only way there is; that people in other places and times on Earth (and probably off of it) have dealt with the universe and its perversities in very different ways. . . . A B.A. in anthropology is not generally a terribly useful degree . . . , but I have found it to be extremely useful in my writing. Not only did it teach me to look at human behavior from a fresh perspective, with a kind of parallax view, but it also gave me the ethnographer's structural tools for creating imaginary societies, for building worlds that I wanted to write about. (From "The Restless Urge to Write," in *Women of Vision*, edited by Denise Du Pont [New York: St. Martin's Press, 1988])

Kate Wilhelm, one of the most important writers of science fiction, is equally accomplished at suspense novels and fiction that often crosses genre boundaries. Her stories have appeared in *Redbook, Omni, Orbit, Asimov's Science Fiction,* and elsewhere; she won the Hugo Award for her novel *Where Late the Sweet Birds Sang* (1976) and three Nebula Awards for her short fiction. Her novels include *More Bitter than Death* (1963), *The Clewiston Test* (1976), *Fault Lines* (1977), *A Sense of Shadow* (1981), *Welcome, Chaos* (1983), *Crazy Time* (1988), and *Death Qualified* (1991).

In an interview, Kate Wilhelm spoke about her life before she began writing:

> I didn't believe people who told me I had talent and could write. I think it was something about the high school situation that just

made me not believe them; I don't know why. So I became a very unhappy housewife. I was a miserable person, I had migraine headaches, I had insomnia, I was not at all content. And I didn't know anything to do. I got busy on all kinds of school work, and . . . social things, volunteer work . . . and possibly I would have continued a life like that. . . . It's hard to say. I thought writers were gods; I thought they were very, very special people. And I knew I wasn't. (From "Kate Wilhelm and Damon Knight," in *Dream Makers: The Uncommon People Who Write Science Fiction,* by Charles Platt [New York: Berkley Books, 1980])

Chelsea Quinn Yarbro, a trained musician and composer, is known for her popular Saint-Germain series of historical fantasy novels with a sympathetic vampire as hero, but her earliest published work was science fiction. Her science fiction novels include *Time of the Fourth Horseman* (1976), *False Dawn* (1978), and *Hyacinths* (1983); novels in the Saint-Germain series include *Hotel Transylvania* (1978), *The Palace* (1978), *Blood Games* (1980), *Path of the Eclipse* (1981), *Tempting Fate* (1982), *Out of the House of Life* (1990), and *Darker Jewels* (1991).

About her writing, she has said:

I'm not a dogmatic writer. I don't write stories to do anything more than entertain my reader—and entertainment to me is not an offensive word. Because I am a feminist, I tend to tell stories about women, but how those women function is up to the character and the story. Quite often my characters, even sympathetic ones, do things that I would not do. But I feel that my job as a writer is to be true to them, because it is the story and the characters that are important, not me. . . .

Look: for a fiction writer, *any* fiction writer, his or her characters must be as real, or more real, than the people around them. And for that reason, they must have the rights to their own triumphs and dooms. (From *Frontiers: A Journal of Women Studies* [Boulder: Women Studies Program, University of Colorado, Number 3, Fall 1977])

Pamela Zoline was born in Chicago, attended Barnard College, and studied at the Slade School of Art in London, where she lived for many years. "The Heat Death of the Universe," her first published story, appeared in *New Worlds* in 1967 and immediately won critical praise; she also did illustrations for that magazine. In 1968, with John Sladek, she was editor of *Ronald Reagan: The Magazine of Poetry,* and she was named a PEN New Writer of the Year in 1985. Her short fiction has been collected in *The Heat Death of the Universe and Other Stories* (1988). She lives in Telluride, Colorado.

In one of her stories, Pamela Zoline offers the following cogent insight: "The stories we tell ourselves are whatever is necessary for going on." (From "Instructions for Exiting This Building in Case of Fire," in *The Heat Death of the Universe and Other Stories* by Pamela Zoline [Kingston, NY: McPherson Press, 1988])

About the Editor

Pamela Sargent sold her first science fiction story during her senior year at Binghamton University, where she earned a B.A. and M.A. in philosophy and also studied ancient history and Greek. Her novel *Venus of Dreams* (1986) was listed as one of the "100 Best Science Fiction Novels" by *Library Journal; Earthseed,* her first novel for younger readers, was named a 1983 Best Book for Young Adults by the American Library Association. Her other science fiction novels include *Cloned Lives* (1976), *The Sudden Star* (1979), *Watchstar* (1980), *The Golden Space* (1982), *The Shore of Women* (1986), and *Venus of Shadows* (1988); she has won a Nebula Award, a Locus Award, and has been a finalist for the Hugo Award. She also edited the anthologies *Bio-Futures* (1976), and, with Ian Watson, *Afterlives* (1986). Her most recent novel is *Ruler of the Sky* (1993), a historical novel about Genghis Khan, in which the Mongol conqueror's story is told largely from the points of view of women. She lives in upstate New York.

Recommended Reading

The following list is intended to direct readers to science fiction written by women. Books and stories were included on the list because of their historical interest, their literary merit, their popularity, their worth as entertainment, or their importance to and influence on the genre. I have tried to make this list representative of all kinds of science fiction and to include as wide a variety of works as possible, but the list is not meant to be comprehensive.

An attempt was made to limit this list to works of science fiction and to exclude fantasy, horror, prehistorical fiction, historical fantasy, and other related categories of fiction; but some writers resist classification, and often it's hard to know where to draw the line. Many of the writers on this list are equally accomplished at other kinds of writing (a few have only occasionally ventured into science fiction), and some writers often claimed by science fiction do not appear here. I have tried to be as inclusive as possible, but had the list grown to encompass works that are, in my judgment, only marginally related to science fiction, the list would have been the size of a book.

Any such list is subject to the prejudices of the person making it, but I have tried not to let my personal tastes interfere with listing as many different kinds of works as possible. Even so, it seems impossible to escape a system for noting especially important books and stories for readers unfamiliar with the genre. Those works that I feel deserve more attention are marked with one star. Important works that, in my opinion, belong in any basic library of science fiction by women are marked with two stars. No ideological yardstick was used to measure these works; although they are all by women, some do not reflect a feminist sensibility.

The following books and publications were of great help in compiling this list:

Anatomy of Wonder: Science Fiction, edited by Neil Barron. New York: R. R. Bowker, 1976.

Anatomy of Wonder: A Critical Guide to Science Fiction, edited by Neil Barron. 3rd ed. New York: R. R. Bowker, 1987.

The Encyclopedia of Science Fiction, edited by John Clute and Peter Nicholls. New York: St. Martin's Press, 1993.

Index to Science Fiction Anthologies and Collections, edited by William Contento. Boston: G. K. Hall, 1978.

Locus: The Newspaper of the Science Fiction Field, edited by Charles N. Brown, various issues. Oakland, Calif.: Locus Publications.

More Than 100 Women Science Fiction Writers: An Annotated Bibliography, edited by Sharon Yntema. Freedom, Calif.: Crossing Press, 1988.

Science Fiction Book Review Index, 1923–1973, edited by H. W. Hall. Detroit: Gale Research, 1975.

Science Fiction Book Review Index, 1974–1979, edited by H. W. Hall. Detroit: Gale Research, 1981.

Science Fiction and Fantasy Book Review Index, 1980–1984, edited by H. W. Hall. Detroit: Gale Research, 1985.

Science-Fiction: The Early Years. Everett F. Bleiler, with the assistance of Richard J. Bleiler. Kent, Ohio: Kent State University Press, 1990.

Twentieth-Century Science-Fiction Writers, edited by Curtis C. Smith. 2nd ed. Chicago: St. James Press, 1986.

Twentieth-Century Science-Fiction Writers, edited by Noelle Watson and Paul E. Schellinger et al. 3rd ed. Chicago: St. James Press, 1991.

I have listed only works published in English. Foreign-language science fiction in English translation is barely represented here for the following reasons. The genre has, throughout much of its history, been overwhelmingly dominated by English-speaking writers, and American science fiction publishers, with few exceptions, have not been that receptive to science fiction from other countries. Also, not many women in other lands write science fiction, although some do write what could be labeled fantastic literature. There are a few signs that the numbers of women writing science fiction in non-English-speaking nations may grow, especially in Russia and Ukraine, but at present little is available in English translation.

One of the difficulties in preserving science fiction's history is that so many science fiction books rapidly go out of print or are published in less durable paperback form; hardcovers are often printed only in small numbers. Today, the field has grown tremendously in size and diversity, but most books, both hardcover and paperback, seem to remain in print for increasingly brief periods of time. Publishers have also become even less receptive to quirky or highly original writing that doesn't seem to fit the market and do not often reprint older works of science fiction unless the author is extremely popular or still productive. A few specialty presses, happily, are reprinting some science fiction books in more enduring editions.

Preserving the genre's short fiction is a problem as well, since magazines and anthologies of new work rapidly disappear from newsstands and bookstores, and fewer trade publishers are willing to do collections of short fiction by individual authors, although some excellent small presses are publishing such collections. Many fine anthologies reprinting science fiction stories are available to interested readers, but most of these do not remain in print for as long as they merit.

This list includes novels, collections, anthologies, and short fiction. Some of the works listed were originally published for younger readers but are worthwhile reading for people of all ages. Novels are designated by [n], short fiction collections by [c], anthologies by [a], omnibuses by [o], and chapbooks by [ch]. Books for young adults are labeled [ya]. Titles of individual pieces of short fiction are in quotation marks; I have tried to avoid listing stories that can be found in story collections by their authors.

It is my hope that readers will find this list a useful took in seeking out some of these works, and that renewed interest in them may help to bring some of them back into print.

★Ashwell, Pauline. [Paul Ash, pseud.] "Unwillingly to School." *Astounding Science Fiction,* January 1958.

Bailey, Hilary. "The Fall of Frenchy Steiner." 1964. Reprinted in *SF 12,* edited by Judith Merril. New York: Delacorte, 1968.

———. "The Ramparts." *Universe 5,* edited by Terry Carr. New York: Random House, 1974.

Bennet, Margot. *The Long Way Back.* London: Bodley Head, 1954. [n]

Bisland, Elizabeth. "The Coming Subjugation of Man." *Belford's Magazine,* October 1889.

Boye, Karin. *Kallocain,* 1940, translated from the Swedish by Gustaf

Lannestock. Reprint, Madison, Wis.: University of Wisconsin Press, 1966. [n]

Brackett, Leigh. *The Sword of Rhiannon.* New York: Ace, 1953. [n]

★★———. *The Long Tomorrow.* New York: Doubleday, 1955. [n]

———. *The Halfling and Other Stories.* New York: Ace, 1973. [c]

★★———. *The Best of Leigh Brackett,* edited by Edmond Hamilton. New York: Ballantine/Del Rey, 1977. [c]

Braddon, M. E. "Good Lady Ducayne." *The Strand Magazine,* February 1896.

★Bradley, Marion Zimmer. *Darkover Landfall.* New York: DAW Books, 1972. [n]

———. *The Heritage of Hastur.* New York: DAW Books, 1975. [n]

★★———. *The Shattered Chain.* New York: DAW Books, 1976. [n]

Brown, Alice. *The Wind Between the Worlds.* New York: Macmillan, 1920. [n]

Brown, Rosel George. *A Handful of Time.* New York: Ballantine, 1963. [c]

———. *Sibyl Sue Blue.* New York: Doubleday, 1966. [n]

———. *The Waters of Centaurus.* New York: Doubleday, 1970. [n]

Bruere, Martha S. Bensley. *Mildred Carver.* New York: Macmillan, 1919. [n]

Bryant, Dorothy. *The Kin of Ata Are Waiting for You.* New York: Moon Books/Random House, 1976. [n]

★Burdekin, Katherine. [Murray Constantine, pseud.] *Swastika Night,* 1937. Reprint, New York: The Feminist Press at the City University of New York, 1986.

———. *Proud Man,* 1934. Reprint, New York: The Feminist Press at the City University of New York, 1993.

★Butler, Octavia E. *Patternmaster.* New York: Doubleday, 1976. [n]

★———. *Mind of My Mind.* New York: Doubleday, 1977. [n]

★———. *Survivor.* New York: Doubleday, 1978. [n]

Calisher, Hortense. *Journal from Ellipsia.* Boston: Little, Brown, 1965. [n]

★★Carter, Angela. *Heroes and Villains.* New York: Simon & Schuster, 1969. [n]

★———. *The War of Dreams.* (Published in Britain under the title of *The Infernal Desire Machines of Doctor Hoffman.*) New York: Harcourt Brace Jovanovich, 1974. [n]

★———. *The Passion of New Eve.* New York: Harcourt Brace Jovanovich, 1977. [n]

★★Charnas, Suzy McKee. *Walk to the End of the World.* New York: Ballantine, 1974. [n]

★★————. *Motherlines.* New York: Berkley Books, 1978. [n]

Cherryh, C. J. *Gate of Ivrel.* New York: DAW Books, 1976. [n]

————. *Well of Shiuan.* New York: DAW Books, 1978. [n]

Clayton, Jo. *Diadem from the Stars.* New York: DAW Books, 1977. [n]

Cliff, Catherine. "The Chain of Love." 1955. Translated from the French by Damon Knight. Reprinted in *13 French Science-Fiction Stories,* edited by Damon Knight. New York: Bantam, 1965.

★Clingerman, Mildred. *A Cupful of Space.* New York: Ballantine, 1961. [c]

Corelli, Marie. *A Romance of Two Worlds.* London: Bentley, 1886. Reprint, New York: Garland, 1976. [n]

————. *The Young Diana: An Experiment of the Future.* New York: Doran, 1918. [n]

Davis, Grania. "Young Love." *Orbit 13,* edited by Damon Knight. New York: Berkley Books, 1974.

————. "Last One In Is a Rotten Egg." *Cassandra Rising,* edited by Alice Laurance. New York: Doubleday, 1978.

de Ford, Miriam Allen. *Xenogenesis.* New York: Ballantine, 1969. [c]

————. *Elsewhere, Elsewhen, Elsehow.* New York: Walker, 1971. [c]

Delaire, Jean. *Around a Distant Star.* London: John Long, 1904. [n]

Dieudonne, Florence Carpenter. *Rondah; or Thirty-Three Years in a Star.* Philadelphia: T. B. Peterson, 1887. [n]

Dodd, Anna Bowman. *The Republic of the Future or Socialism a Reality.* New York: Cassell, 1887. [n]

★Dorman, Sonya. [Now Sonya Dorman Hess.] "Building Block." 1975. Reprinted in *The New Women of Wonder,* edited by Pamela Sargent. New York: Vintage Books, 1978.

★————. "Go, Go, Go, Said the Bird." *Dangerous Visions,* edited by Harlan Ellison. New York: Doubleday, 1967.

————. "Bye, Bye, Banana Bird." *The Magazine of Fantasy & Science Fiction,* December 1969.

————. *Planet Patrol.* New York: Coward-McCann & Geohegan, 1978. [n-ya]

★Eisenstein, Phyllis. "Attachment." 1974. Reprinted in *What Did Miss Darrington See?,* edited by Jessica Amanda Salmonson. New York: The Feminist Press at C.U.N.Y., 1989.

————. "Lost and Found." *Analog,* October 1978.

★★Elgin, Suzette Haden. "For the Sake of Grace." 1969. Reprinted in *The*

Norton Book of Science Fiction, edited by Ursula K. Le Guin and Brian Attebery. New York: Norton, 1993.

———. *Furthest.* New York: Ace, 1971.

———. *At the Seventh Level.* New York: DAW Books, 1972. [n]

★★Emshwiller, Carol. *Joy in Our Cause.* New York: Harper & Row, 1974. [c]

Engdahl, Sylvia Louise. *Enchantress from the Stars.* New York: Atheneum, 1970. [n-ya]

★Engh, M. J. *Arslan,* 1976. Reprint, New York: Arbor House, 1986. [n]

Ertz, Susan. *Woman Alive.* New York: Appleton-Century, 1936. [n]

Felice, Cynthia. *Godsfire.* New York: Pocket Books, 1978. [n]

Friedberg, Gertrude. *The Revolving Boy.* New York: Ballantine, 1966. [n]

Fuller, Alice W. "A Wife Manufactured to Order." *The Arena,* July 1895.

Gale, Zona. *Romance Island.* Indianapolis: Bobbs-Merrill, 1906. [n]

Gaskell, Jane. *The City.* New York: St. Martin's Press, 1966. [n]

———. *A Sweet, Sweet Summer.* New York: St. Martin's Press, 1972. [n]

———. *Atlan.* New York: St. Martin's Press, 1977. [n]

★★Gearhart, Sally Miller. *The Wanderground: Stories of the Hill Women.* Watertown, Mass.: Persephone Press, 1978. [n]

★★Gilman, Charlotte Perkins. *Herland.* 1915. New York: Pantheon, 1979. [n]

Gotlieb, Phyllis. *Sunburst.* Greenwich, Conn.: Fawcett, 1964. [n]

———. *O Master Caliban!* New York: Harper & Row, 1976. [n]

Gould, Lois. *A Sea-Change.* New York: Avon, 1977. [n]

———. "X: A Fabulous Child's Story." *Ms. Magazine,* December 1972.

Griffith, Mrs. Mary. *Three Hundred Years Hence.* 1836. Reprint, Boston: Gregg Press, 1975.

★Hamilton, Virginia. *Justice and Her Brothers.* New York: Greenwillow, 1978. [n-ya]

Harris, Clare Winger. "A Runaway World." *Weird Tales,* July 1926.

Hawkes, Jacquetta. *Providence Island.* New York: Random House, 1959. [n]

★★Henderson, Zenna. *Pilgrimage: The Book of the People.* New York: Doubleday, 1961. [c]

★———. *The Anything Box.* New York: Doubleday, 1965. [c]

★★———. *The People: No Different Flesh.* New York: Doubleday, 1966. [c]

★———. *Holding Wonder.* New York: Doubleday, 1971. [c]

Hess, Sonya Dorman. *See* Dorman, Sonya

Hoffman, Lee. *The Caves of Karst*. New York: Ballantine, 1969. [n]

———. "Soundless Evening." *Again, Dangerous Visions,* edited by Harlan Ellison. New York: Doubleday, 1972.

★Holland, Cecelia. *Floating Worlds*. New York: Knopf, 1976. [n]

Holly, Joan Hunter. "The Gift of Nothing." *And Walk Now Gently Through the Fire,* edited by Roger Elwood. Philadelphia: Chilton, 1973.

———. "Child." *Demon Kind,* edited by Roger Elwood. New York: Avon, 1973.

★★Jackson, Shirley. "The Lottery." 1948. Reprinted in *The Norton Anthology of Short Fiction,* edited by R. V. Cassill. New York: Norton, 1978.

———. "Bulletin." 1954. Reprinted in *The Best from Fantasy & Science Fiction 4,* edited by Anthony Boucher. New York: Dell, 1955.

★★———. "One Ordinary Day, with Peanuts." 1955. Reprinted in *SF: The Best of the Best,* edited by Judith Merril. New York: Delacorte, 1967.

Jaeger, Muriel. *The Question Mark*. London: Hogarth Press, 1926. [n]

Karl, Jean E. *The Turning Place: Stories of a Future Past*. New York: Dutton, 1976. [c-ya]

★Kavan, Anna. *Ice*. New York: Doubleday, 1970. [n]

★Kidd, Virginia, editor. *Millennial Women*. New York: Delacorte, 1978. [a]

Lane, Mary E. [Mary E. Bradley and Princess Vera Zarovitch, pseuds.] *Mizora: A Prophecy*. New York: G. W. Dillingham, 1890. [n]

Larionova, Olga. "The Useless Planet." 1967. Translated from the Russian by Mirra Ginsburg. Reprinted in *The Ultimate Threshold: A Collection of the Finest in Soviet Science Fiction,* edited by Mirra Ginsburg. New York: Holt, Rinehart & Winston, 1970.

Laurance, Alice, editor. *Cassandra Rising*. New York: Doubleday, 1978. [a]

Lee, Tanith. *The Birthgrave*. New York: DAW Books, 1975. [n]

★★———. *Don't Bite the Sun*. New York: DAW Books, 1976. [n]

★★———. *Drinking Sapphire Wine*. New York: DAW Books, 1977. [n]

★★Le Guin, Ursula K. *The Left Hand of Darkness*. New York: Ace, 1969. [n]

★★———. *The Lathe of Heaven*. New York: Scribner, 1971. [n]

★★———. "The Word for World Is Forest." *Again, Dangerous Visions,* edited by Harlan Ellison. New York: Doubleday, 1972.

★★———. *The Dispossessed*. New York: Harper & Row, 1974. [n]

★★————. *The Wind's Twelve Quarters*. New York: Harper & Row, 1975. [c]

★★L'Engle, Madeleine. *A Wrinkle in Time*. New York: Farrar Straus, 1962. [n-ya]

★★————. *A Wind in the Door*. New York: Farrar Straus, 1973. [n-ya]

★★————. *A Swiftly Tilting Planet*. New York: Farrar Straus, 1978. [n-ya]

★★Lessing, Doris. *Briefing for a Descent into Hell*. New York: Knopf, 1971. [n]

★★————. *The Memoirs of a Survivor*. New York: Knopf, 1975. [n]

Lichtenberg, Jacqueline. *House of Zeor*. New York: Doubleday, 1974. [n]

Lightner, A. M. *The Day of the Drones*. New York: Norton, 1969. [n-ya]

Lynn, Elizabeth A. *A Different Light*. New York: Berkley Books, 1978. [n]

McCaffrey, Anne. *Restoree*. New York: Ballantine, 1967. [n]

★★————. *Dragonflight*. New York: Ballantine, 1968. [n]

★★————. *The Ship Who Sang*. New York: Walker, 1969. [c]

★★————. *Dragonquest*. New York: Ballantine, 1971. [n]

————. *Get Off the Unicorn*. New York, Ballantine, Del Rey, 1977. [c]

————. *The White Dragon*. New York: Ballantine, Del Rey, 1978. [n]

McIntyre, Vonda N. *The Exile Waiting*. Greenwich, Conn.: Fawcett, 1975. [n]

★————, and Susan Janice Anderson, editors. *Aurora: Beyond Equality*. Greenwich, Conn.: Fawcett, 1976.

★★————. *Dreamsnake*. Boston: Houghton Mifflin, 1978. [n]

★★MacLean, Katherine. *The Diploids and Other Flights of Fancy*. New York: Avon, 1962. Reprint, Boston: Gregg Press, 1981. [c]

————. *The Man in the Bird Cage*. New York: Ace, 1971. [n]

★————. *Missing Man*. New York: Berkley Books, 1975. [n]

MacLeod, Sheila. *The Snow-White Soliloquies*. New York: Viking, 1970. [n]

————. *Xanthe and the Robots*. London: Bodley Head, 1977. [n]

————. *Circuit-Breaker*. London: Bodley Head, 1978. [n]

Mark, Jan. *The Ennead*. New York: Crowell, 1978. [n-ya]

★★May, Julian. "Dune Roller." 1951. Reprinted in *Alpha 7*, edited by Robert Silverberg. New York: Berkley Books, 1977.

★Merril, Judith. *Shadow on the Hearth*. New York: Doubleday, 1950. [n]

————. *The Tomorrow People*. New York: Pyramid, 1960. [n]

————. *Out of Bounds.* New York: Pyramid, 1960. [c]

★————. *Daughters of Earth.* New York: Doubleday, 1969. [c]

★★————. *Survival Ship and Other Stories.* Toronto: Kakabeka, 1974. [c]

★★————. *The Best of Judith Merril.* New York: Warner Books, 1976. [c]

★★Mitchison, Naomi. *Memoirs of a Spacewoman.* London: Gollancz, 1962. [n]

★★————. "Mary and Joe." 1962. Reprinted in *Nova 1,* edited by Harry Harrison. New York: Delacorte Press, 1970.

★————. "Miss Omega Raven." 1972. Reprinted in *Best Science Fiction of the Year 2,* edited by Terry Carr. New York: Ballantine, 1973.

————. "The Factory." *Nova 3,* edited by Harry Harrison. New York: Walker, 1973.

————. *Solution Three.* New York: Warner Books, 1975. [n]

Moore, C. L. *Judgment Night.* New York: Gnome Press, 1952. [n]

————. *Doomsday Morning.* New York: Doubleday, 1957. [n]

★————. *Jirel of Joiry.* New York: Paperback Library, 1969. [c]

★★————. *The Best of C. L. Moore,* edited by Lester del Rey. New York: Ballantine, 1975. [c]

★Moore, Raylyn. "A Different Drummer." 1971. Reprinted in *The Best from Fantasy & Science Fiction: 20,* edited by Edward L. Ferman. New York: Doubleday, 1973.

————. "Trigonometry." *Showcase,* edited by Roger Elwood. New York: Harper & Row, 1973.

————. "Fun Palace." *Orbit 17,* edited by Damon Knight. New York: Harper & Row, 1975.

Morris, Janet. *High Couch of Silistra.* New York: Bantam, 1977. [n]

Nesbit, Edith. [E. Bland, pseud.] "The Five Senses." *London Magazine,* December 1909.

————. "The Pavilion." *The Strand Magazine,* November 1915.

★★Norton, Andre. *Star Man's Son: 2250 A.D.* New York: Harcourt Brace, 1952. [n-ya]

★————. *Star Rangers.* New York: Harcourt Brace, 1953. [n-ya]

★————. *Star Guard.* New York: Harcourt Brace, 1955. [n-ya]

★————. *The Beast Master.* New York: Harcourt Brace, 1959. [n-ya]

————. *The Sioux Spaceman.* New York: Ace, 1960. [n-ya]

————. *Judgment on Janus.* New York: Harcourt Brace, 1963. [n-ya]

————. *Victory on Janus.* New York: Harcourt Brace, 1966. [n-ya]

★————. *The Book of Andre Norton,* edited by Roger Elwood. New York: DAW Books, 1975. [c]

★Obukhova, Lydia. *Daughter of Night*. Translated from the Russian by Mirra Ginsburg. New York: Macmillan, 1974. [n]

★Piercy, Marge. *Dance the Eagle to Sleep*. New York: Doubleday, 1970. [n]

★★——. *Woman on the Edge of Time*. New York: Knopf, 1976. [n]

★Piserchia, Doris. *Mister Justice*. New York: Ace, 1973. [n]

★——. *Star Rider*. New York: Bantam, 1974. [n]

——. "Quarantine." *Galaxy*, September 1973.

——. "Idio." *Orbit 13*, edited by Damon Knight. New York: Berkley Books, 1974.

★——. "Pale Hands." *Orbit 15*, edited by Damon Knight. New York: Harper & Row, 1974.

——. "A Typical Day." 1974. Reprinted in *Best SF: 1974*, edited by Harry Harrison and Brian W. Aldiss. Indianapolis: Bobbs-Merrill, 1975.

——. *A Billion Days of Earth*. New York: Bantam, 1976. [n]

★——. *Earthchild*. New York: DAW Books, 1977. [n]

★Rand, Ayn. *Anthem*. Los Angeles: Pamphleteers, Inc., 1946. [n]

——. *Atlas Shrugged*. New York: Random House, 1957. [n]

Randall, Florence Engel. *A Watcher in the Woods*. New York: Atheneum, 1976. [n-ya]

Randall, Marta. "A Scarab in the City of Time." *New Dimensions 5*, edited by Robert Silverberg. New York: Harper & Row, 1975.

★——. *Islands*. New York: Pyramid, 1976. Revised edition, New York: Pocket Books, 1980. [n]

——. *A City in the North*. New York: Warner Books, 1976. [n]

——. "Secret Rider." *New Dimensions 6*, edited by Robert Silverberg. New York: Harper & Row, 1976.

——. "The State of the Art on Alyssum." *New Dimensions 7*, edited by Robert Silverberg. New York: Harper & Row, 1977.

★——. *Journey*. New York: Pocket Books, 1978. [n]

★Reed, Kit. *Armed Camps*. New York: Dutton, 1970. [n]

★★——. *Mister da V. and Other Stories*. New York: Berkley Books, 1973. [c]

Robertson, Eileen Arbuthnot. *Three Came Unarmed*. New York: Garden City Publishing Co., 1929. [n]

Roger, Noelle. *The New Adam*. Translated from the French by P. C. Crowhurst. London: Stanley Paul, 1926. [n]

★Russ, Joanna. *Picnic on Paradise*. New York: Ace, 1968. [n]

★——. *And Chaos Died*. New York: Ace, 1970. [n]

★★————. *The Female Man.* New York: Bantam, 1975. [n]

★————. *We Who Are About To . . .* New York: Dell, 1977. [n]

★★————. *The Two of Them.* New York: Berkley Books, 1978. [n]

St. Clair, Margaret. [Idris Seabright, pseud.] *Agents of the Unknown.* New York: Ace, 1956. [n]

★————. *Three Worlds of Futurity.* New York: Ace, 1956. [c]

★————. *The Green Queen.* New York: Ace, 1956. [n]

★————. *The Games of Neith.* New York: Ace, 1960. [n]

★————. *Sign of the Labrys.* New York: Bantam, 1963. [n]

————. *Message from the Eocene.* New York: Ace, 1964. [n]

————. *The Dolphins of Altair.* New York: Dell, 1967. [n]

★★————. *Change the Sky and Other Stories.* New York: Ace, 1974. [c]

Sargent, Pamela, editor. *Women of Wonder.* New York: Vintage, 1975. [a]

————. *More Women of Wonder.* New York: Vintage, 1976. [a]

————. *The New Women of Wonder.* New York: Vintage, 1978. [a]

Saxton, Josephine. *The Hieros Gamos of Sam and An Smith.* New York: Doubleday, 1969. [n]

————. *Vector for Seven.* New York: Doubleday, 1970. [n]

★————. *Group Feast.* New York: Doubleday, 1971. [n]

★Scott, Jody. *Passing for Human.* New York: DAW Books, 1977. [n]

★★Shelley, Mary. *Frankenstein, or The Modern Prometheus.* 1818, revised 1831. Reprint, New York: Modern Library, 1984. [n]

★————. *The Last Man.* 1826. Reprint, Lincoln: University of Nebraska Press, 1965. [n]

————. *Tales and Stories by Mary Wollstonecraft Shelley.* 1891. Reprint, Boston: Gregg Press, 1975. [c]

★Shiras, Wilmar H. *Children of the Atom.* New York: Gnome Press, 1953. [n]

Silverberg, Robert, editor. *The Crystal Ship.* New York: Thomas Nelson, 1976. [a]

Smith, Evelyn E. "Tea Tray in the Sky." 1952. Reprinted in *Second Galaxy Reader of Science Fiction,* edited by H. L. Gold. New York: Crown, 1954.

————. "A Day in the Suburbs." 1960. Reprinted in *Sociology Through Science Fiction,* edited by John W. Milstead and Martin H. Greenberg. New York: St. Martin's Press, 1974.

————. "Softly While You're Sleeping." 1961. Reprinted in *The Best from Fantasy & Science Fiction,* edited by Robert P. Mills. New York: Doubleday, 1962.

————. *The Perfect Planet.* New York: Avalon, 1962. [n]

————. *Unpopular Planet*. New York: Dell, 1975. [n]

Stevens, Francis. "Friend Island." 1918. Reprinted in *Under the Moons of Mars: A History and Anthology of "The Scientific Romance" in the Munsey Magazines, 1912–1920*, edited by Sam Moskowitz. New York: Holt, Rinehart & Winston, 1970.

★————. *The Heads of Cerberus*. 1919. Reprint, New York: Carroll & Graf, 1984. [n]

Tillyard, Aelfrida. *Concrete: A Story of Two Hundred Years Hence*. London: Hutchinson, 1930. [n]

★★Tiptree, James, Jr. [Raccoona Sheldon, pseud.] *Ten Thousand Light-Years from Home*. New York: Ace, 1973. [c]

★★————. *Warm Worlds and Otherwise*. New York: Ballantine, 1975. [c]

★★————. *Up the Walls of the World*. New York: Berkley Books, 1978. [n]

★★————. *Star Songs of an Old Primate*. New York: Ballantine, Del Rey, 1978. [c]

★Van Scyoc, Sydney. "A Visit to Cleveland General." 1968. Reprinted in *World's Best Science Fiction 1969*, edited by Donald A. Wollheim and Terry Carr. New York: Ace, 1969.

————. "When Petals Fall." 1973. Reprinted in *Best SF: 1974*, edited by Harry Harrison and Brian W. Aldiss. Indianapolis: Bobbs-Merrill, 1975.

————. *Assignment: Nor'Dyren*. New York: Avon, 1973. [n]

————. "Deathsong." 1974. Reprinted in *1975 Annual World's Best SF*, edited by Donald A. Wollheim. New York: DAW Books, 1975.

★————. *Starmother*. New York: Berkley Books, 1976. [n]

————. *Cloudcry*. New York: Berkley Books, 1977. [n]

Vinge, Joan D. *Fireship*. New York: Dell, 1978. [c]

von Harbou, Thea. *Metropolis*. Translated from the German by an anonymous translator. London: Reader's Library, 1927. [n]

Webb, Jane. *The Mummy! A Tale of the Twenty-Second Century*, 1827. Reprint, London: Warne, 1872. [n]

Wilder, Cherry. *The Luck of Brin's Five*. New York: Atheneum, 1977. [n-ya]

Wilhelm, Kate. *The Mile-Long Spaceship*. New York: Berkley Books, 1963. [c]

★————. *The Downstairs Room*. New York: Doubleday, 1968. [c]

★★————. *The Infinity Box*. New York: Harper & Row, 1975. [c]

★★————. *The Clewiston Test*. New York: Farrar Straus, 1976. [n]

★★————. *Where Late the Sweet Birds Sang*. New York: Harper & Row, 1976. [n]

★★————. *Somerset Dreams and Other Fictions*. New York: Harper & Row, 1978. [c]

★Wittig, Monique. *Les Guérillères*. Translated from the French by David Le Vay. New York: Avon, Bard, 1971. [n]

Yarbro, Chelsea Quinn. *Time of the Fourth Horseman*. New York: Doubleday, 1976. [n]

————. *False Dawn*. New York: Doubleday, 1978. [n]

★————. *Cautionary Tales*. New York: Doubleday, 1978. [c]

Young, F. E. *The War of the Sexes*. London: John Long, 1905. [n]

Zhuravleva, Valentina. "Stone from the Stars." 1962. Translated from the Russian by R. Prokofieva. Reprinted in *More Soviet Science Fiction*. New York: Collier, 1962.

————. "The Astronaut." 1964. Translated from the Russian by Leonid Kolesnikov. Reprinted in *Russian Science Fiction*, edited by Robert Magidoff. New York: New York University Press, 1964.

————. "Hussy." Translated from the Russian by Arthur Shkarovsky. *Everything but Love*. Moscow: Mir Publishers, 1973.

PERMISSIONS ACKNOWLEDGMENTS

WITHDRAWN